The Year of the Red Door

A Fantasy
by
William Timothy Murray

"Whosoever discovers the Name of the King,
so shall he become King."

The Year of the Red Door

Volume 4

The Dreamwalker

William Timothy Murray

"Whosoever shall discover the Name of the King,

so shall he become King."

The Dreamwalker
Volume 4 of The Year of the Red Door

Second Edition

Copyright © 2017 by William Timothy Murray

All Rights Reserved

This book or any portion thereof may not be reproduced or used in any manner whatsoever without the express written permission of the publisher except for the use of brief quotations in a book review.

ISBN: 978-1-944320-38-6

This is a work of fiction
Names, characters, businesses, places, events and incidents
are either the products of the author's imagination
or used in a fictitious manner.
Any resemblance to actual persons, living or dead,
or actual events is purely coincidental.

For permissions, review copies, or other inquiries, write to:
Penflight Books
P.O. Box 857
125 Avery Street
Winterville, Georgia 30683-9998
USA
infodesk@penflightbooks.com

Be sure to visit:
www.TheYearOfTheRedDoor.com

pfbcsrev18/2

To
Philip and Stacy

Table of Contents

Preface ix
Maps xi

Prologue   A Lesson in Kindness 3

Part I
Chapter 1   The Falls of Tiandari 11
Chapter 2   Doubt's Offspring 16
Chapter 3   The Intruder 34
Chapter 4   The Pool of Desire 51
Chapter 5   Conner Faddus 56
Chapter 6   Prince Carbane's Ships 69
Chapter 7   General Vidican's Spy 82
Chapter 8   A Shortcut 90
Chapter 9   The Guest 108
Chapter 10   Company for Supper 127
Chapter 11   The Other Guests 143
Chapter 12   Enter Griferis 155
Chapter 13   Finn 166
Chapter 14   To Get to Boskland 178

Entr'acte   To Pay a Debt 189

Part II
Chapter 15   To Fail as a Friend 195
Chapter 16   Mirabella the Assassin 208
Chapter 17   A River of Memories 217
Chapter 18   Swyncraff's New Master 226
Chapter 19   A Return to Passdale 233
Chapter 20   A New Kingdom 252
Chapter 21   The First Battle of Tallinvale 269
Chapter 22   The Lady Shevalia 307
Chapter 23   The Duel 329
Chapter 24   The Second Battle of Tallinvale 341
Chapter 25   A Thing to Figure Out 361
Chapter 26   Miller's Pond 370
Chapter 27   Much to Do 392

Afterword 407

Preface

Welcome to *The Year of the Red Door*. For those of you who are curious, I invite you to visit the accompanying web site:

www.TheYearOfTheRedDoor.com

There you will find maps and other materials pertaining to the story and to the world in which the story takes place.

The road to publishing *The Year of the Red Door* has been an adventure, with the usual ups and downs and rough spots that any author may encounter. The bumps and jostles were considerably smoothed by the patient toil of my editors who were, I'm sure, often frustrated by a cantankerous and difficult client. Nonetheless, I have upon occasion made use of their advice, which was sometimes delivered via bold strokes, underlines, exclamation points, and a few rather cutting remarks handwritten across the pristine pages of my manuscripts. Therefore, any errors that you encounter are due entirely to my own negligence or else a puckish disregard of good advice.

For those of you who might be a bit put off by the scope and epic length of this story, I beg your indulgence and can only offer in my defense a paraphrase of Pascal (or Twain, depending on your preference):

I did not have time to write a short story,
so I wrote a long one instead.

The Author

x

Maps

A Note from the Cartographers

The geography and place names depicted on the following maps are generally accepted to be accurate as of the year of their preparation (869 Second Age). Distances are approximate, given the scales of the maps. However, these are only intended to give a general sense of the scale and relationship of the various regions and features. They are not intended for travel or navigation. Any mishap as a result from the use of these maps for such purposes of travel are the responsibility of the user, not the mapmakers.

For maps more suitable for travel within particular regions of the world, all interested parties are invited to inquire at our establishment.

Brannon & Gray Cartographers
No. 16, Miller's Pond Lane
Duinnor City

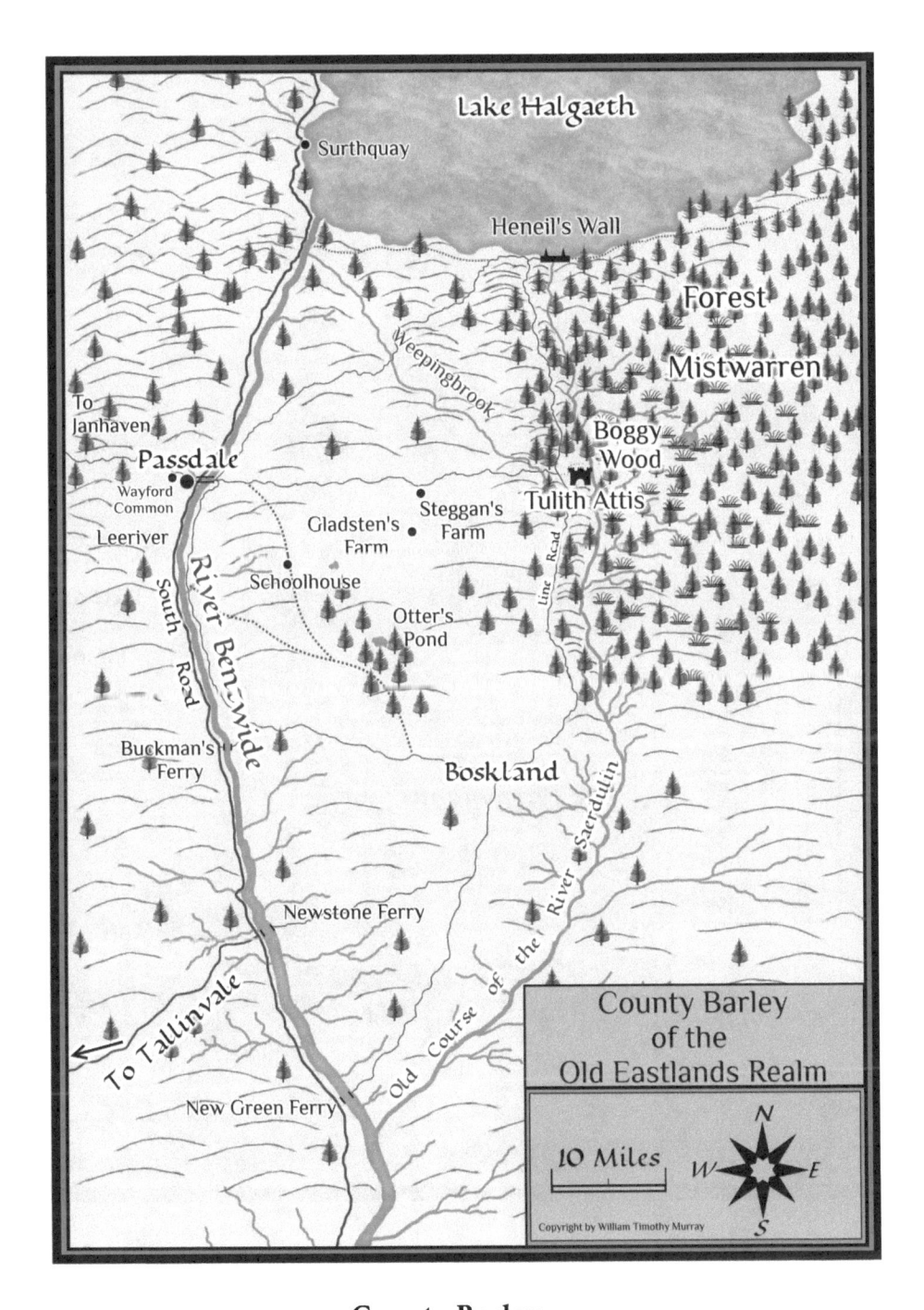

County Barley
Detailed maps can be found at:
www.TheYearOfTheRedDoor.com

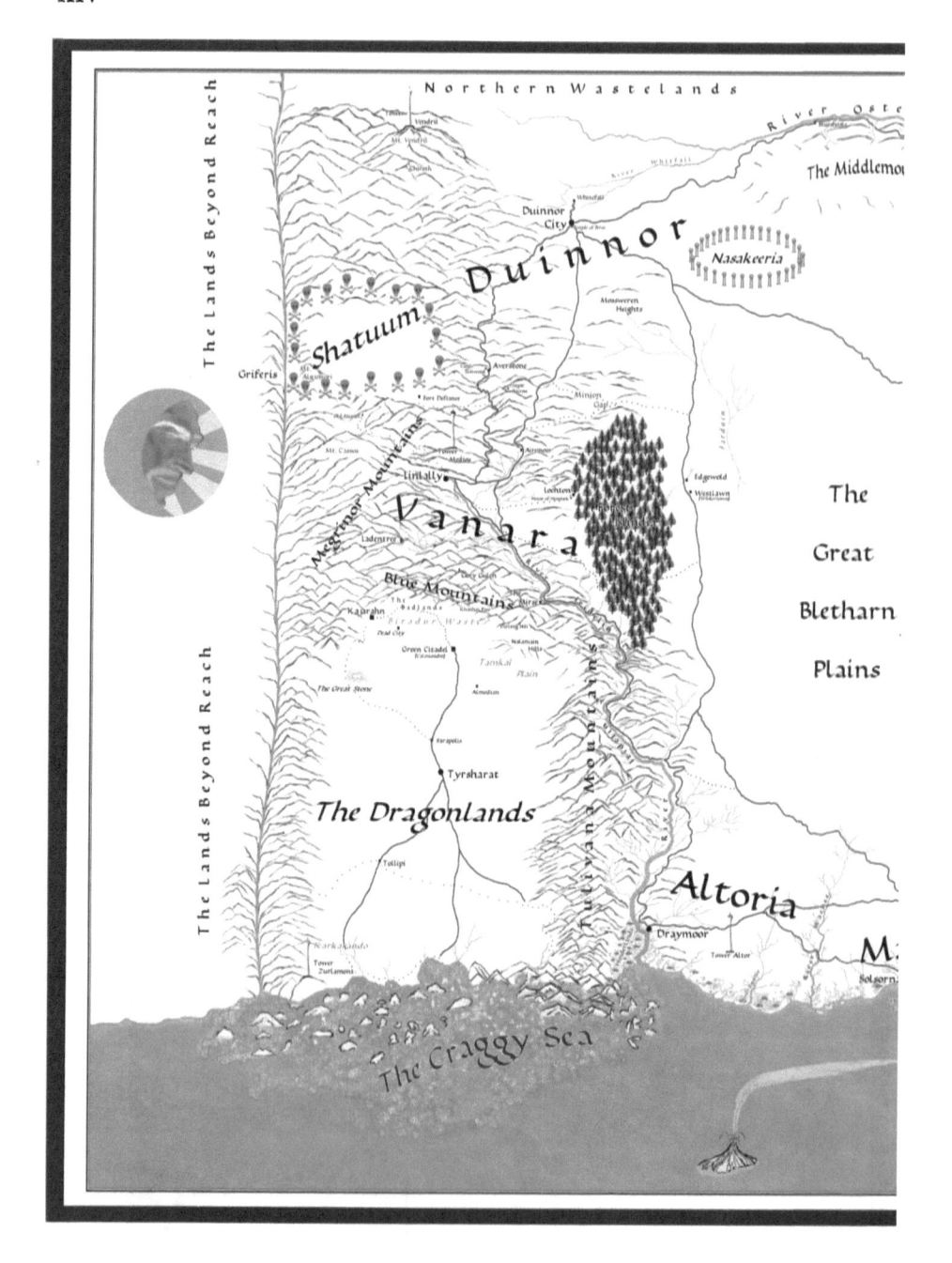

The Western World
Detailed maps can be found at:
www.TheYearOfTheRedDoor.com

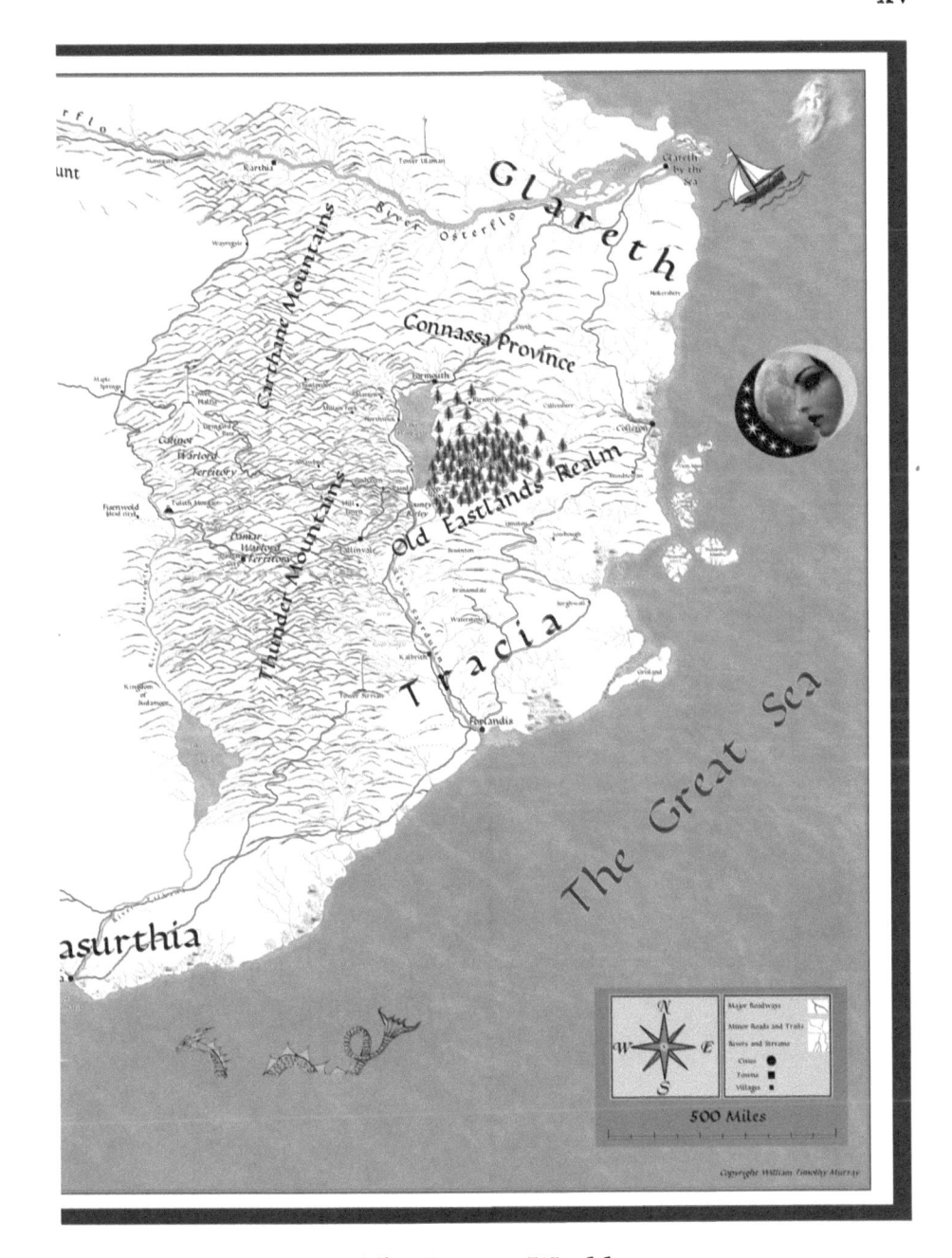

The Eastern World
Detailed maps can be found at:
www.TheYearOfTheRedDoor.com

Duinnor & Shatuum
Detailed maps can be found at:
www.TheYearOfTheRedDoor.com

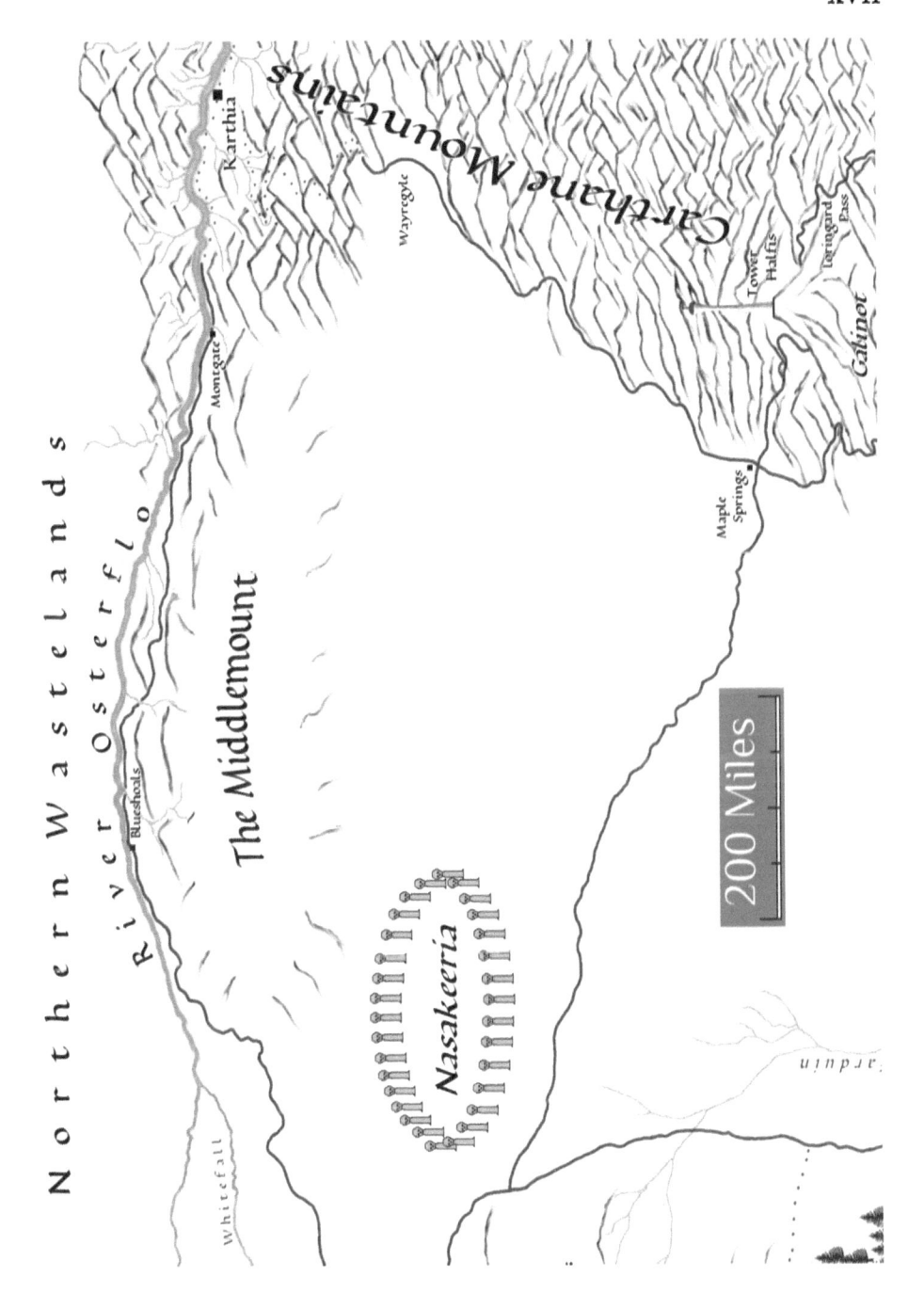

Middlemount & Nasakeeria
Detailed maps can be found at:
www.TheYearOfTheRedDoor.com

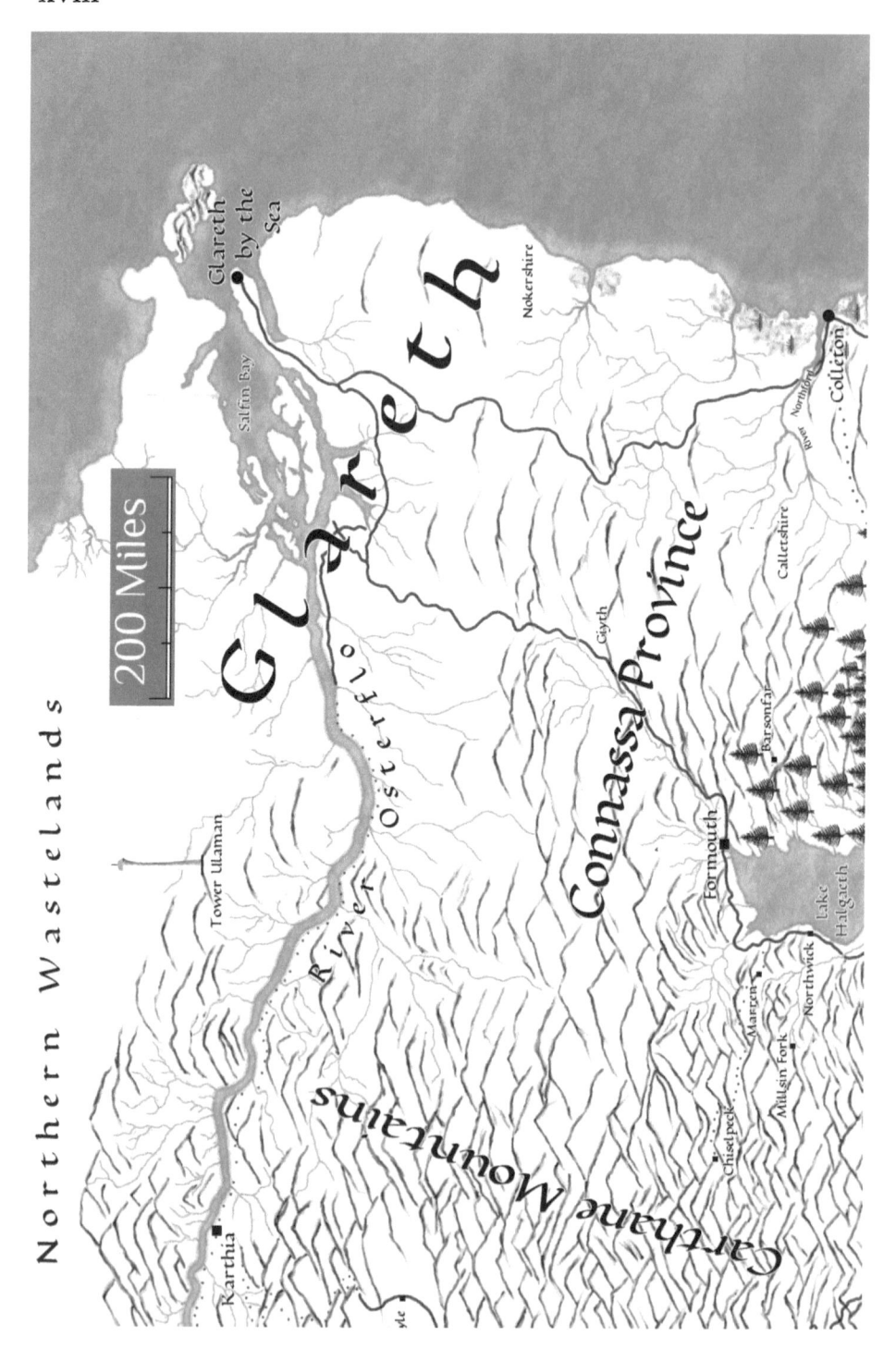

Glareth
Detailed maps can be found at:
www.TheYearOfTheRedDoor.com

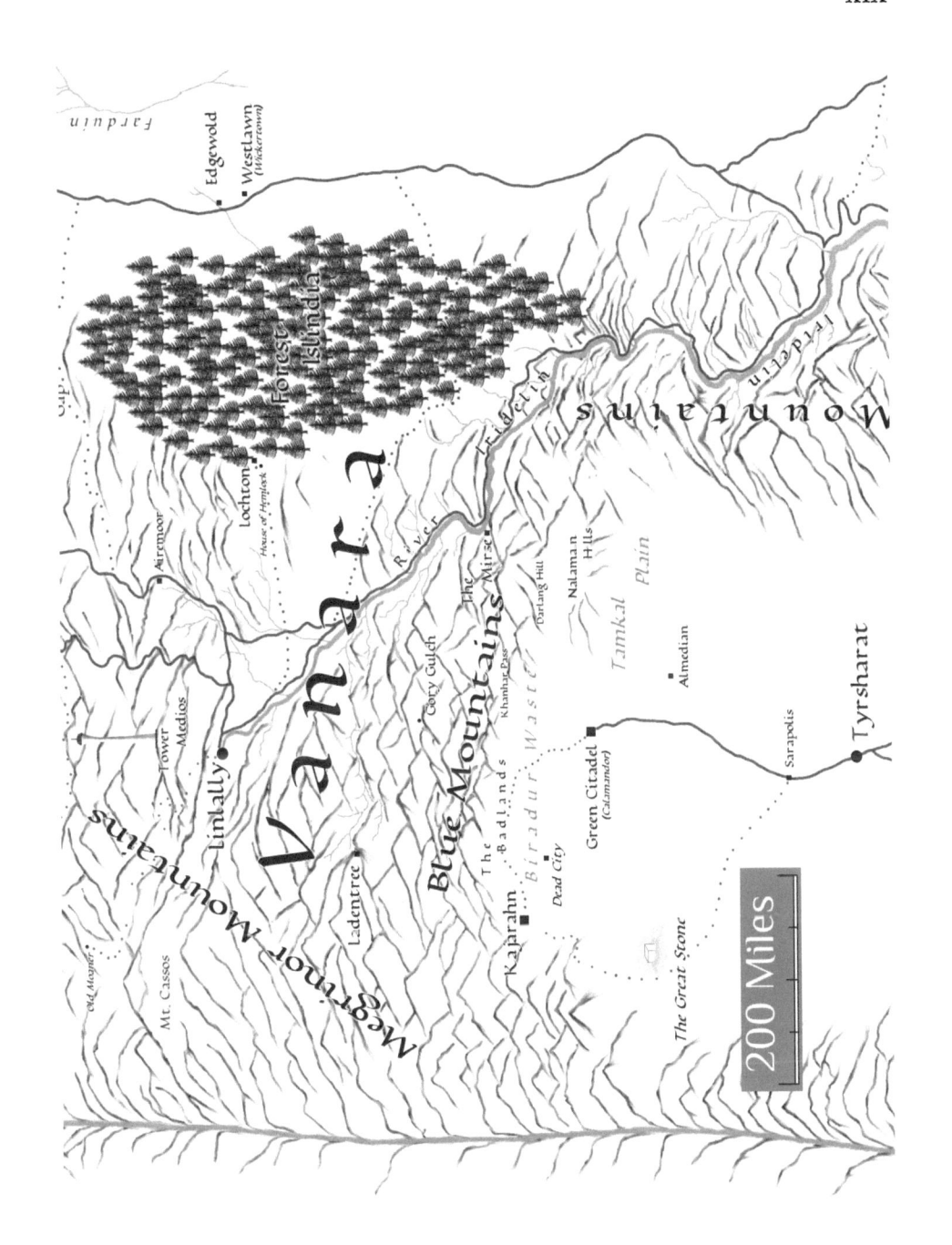

Vanara
Detailed maps can be found at:
www.TheYearOfTheRedDoor.com

The Great Plains of Bletharn
Detailed maps can be found at:
www.TheYearOfTheRedDoor.com

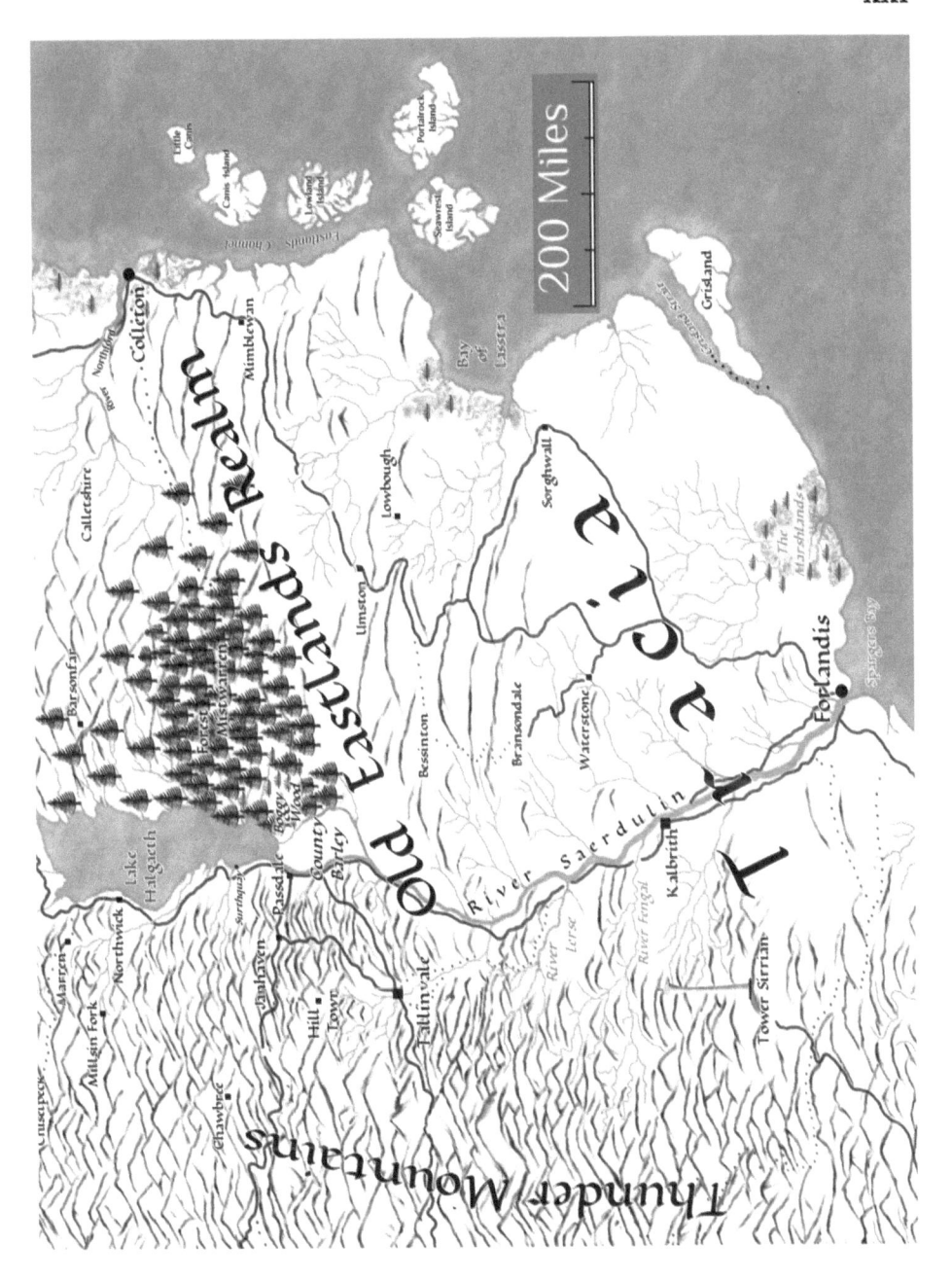

Tracia & the Old Eastlands Realm
Detailed maps can be found at:
www.TheYearOfTheRedDoor.com

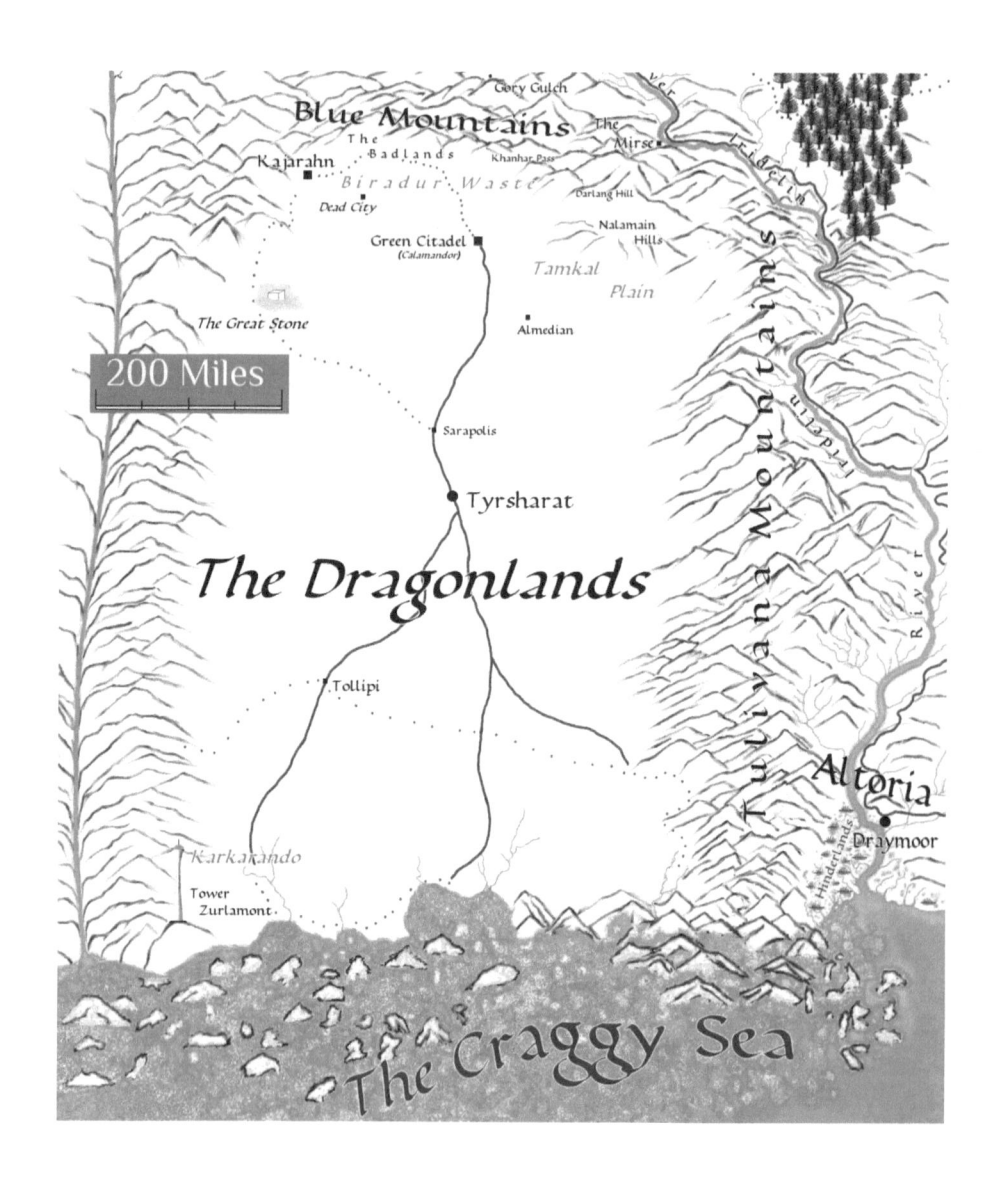

The Dragonlands
Detailed maps can be found at:
www.TheYearOfTheRedDoor.com

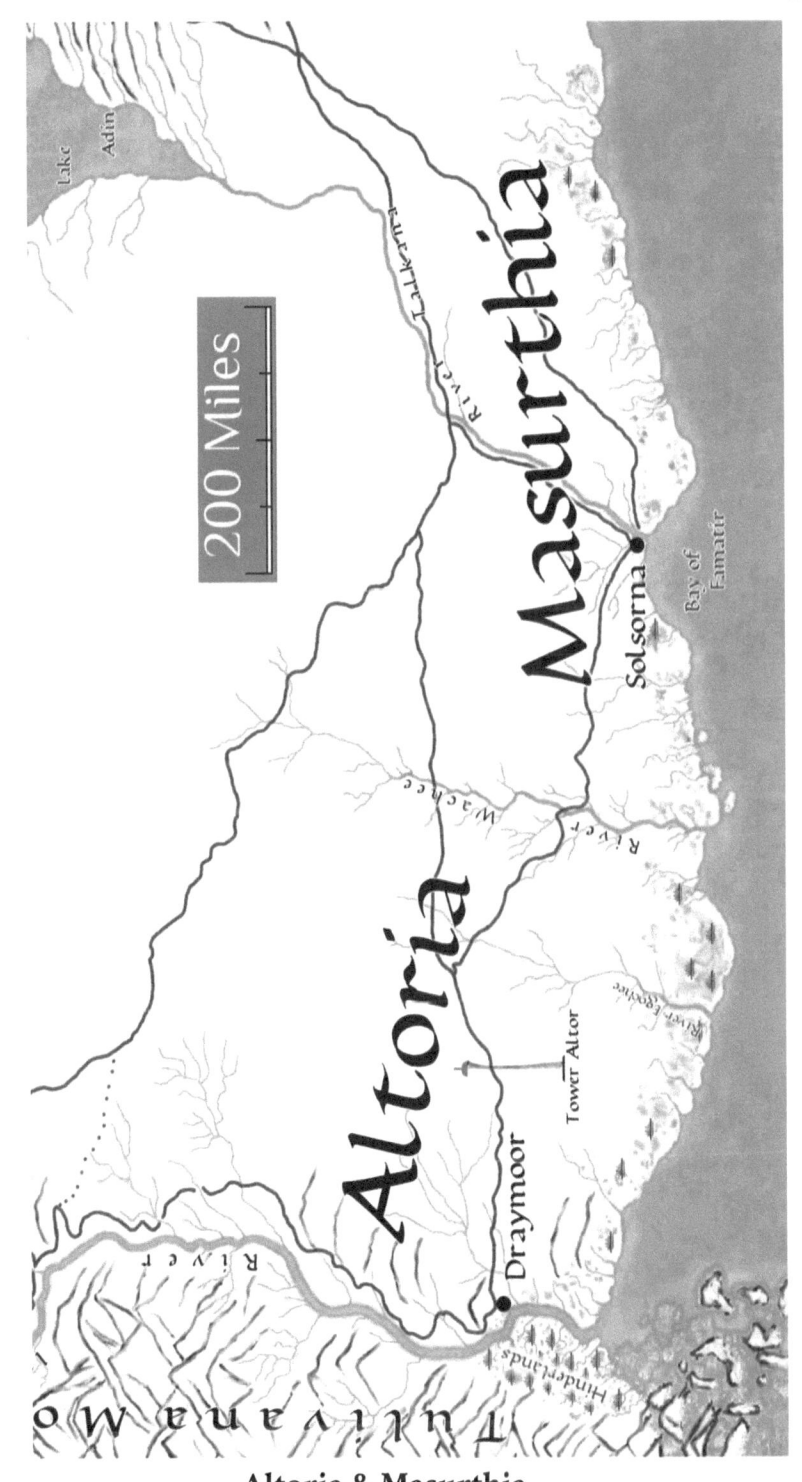

Altoria & Masurthia
Detailed maps can be found at:
www.TheYearOfTheRedDoor.com

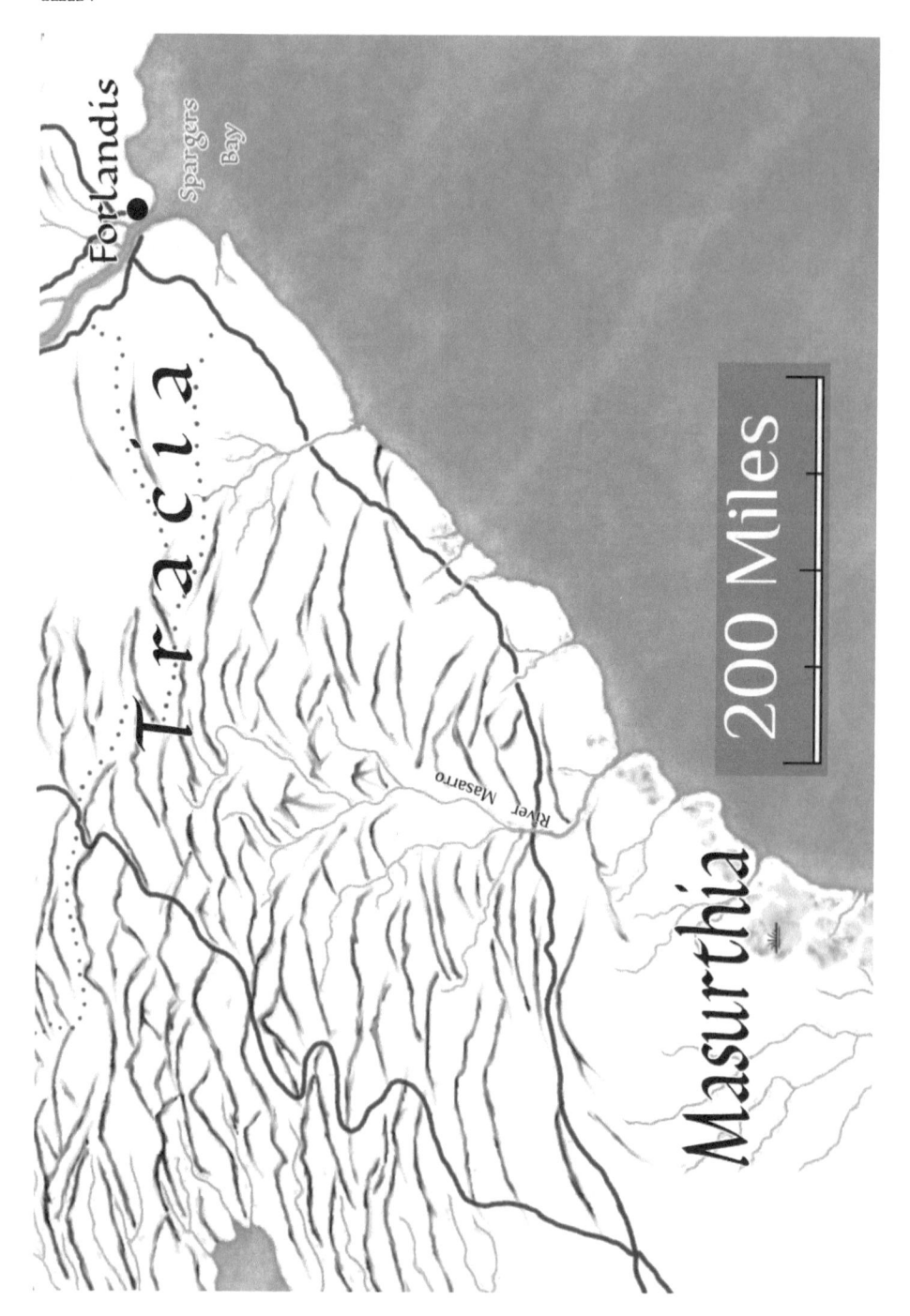

The Frontier between Tracia and Masurthia
Detailed maps can be found at:
www.TheYearOfTheRedDoor.com

The Dreamwalker

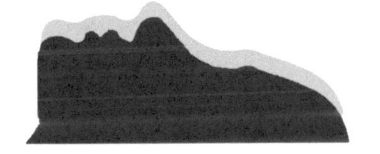

"Whosoever discovers the Name of the King,
so shall he become King."

Prologue

A Lesson in Kindness

It was a very nasty late autumn storm, many years ago. The wind blew chunks of ice from thickly coated branches as more sleet and freezing rain fell in noisy pellets. The roads were slippery and treacherous, and some of the paths were so cluttered with drooping and crackling brush and by fallen limbs that they were hardly passable. But it was along one of these that a bent figure struggled. He had a thin blanket pulled over his head and shoulders, a ragged affair made even less effective against the elements by the many strips he had torn from it. The strips were wrapped and tied around the remnants of his shoes, and a few more he had wrapped about his hands against the cold. With one hand he clutched the blanket at his chin while with his other he pushed away the obstacles before him. His face was speckled with flecks of ice, his beard well-coated. His breathing rasped in stark contrast to the ticking sound of the sleet, now mixed with the occasional flake of snow.

While pushing aside a thick bough full of crystalline needles, his footing slipped and he awkwardly fell, snapping the branch he sought to move and crushing the needles in a shower of miniscule shards. He remained motionless for a long while, panting away the jarring pain that hammered his joints.

"What is the point?" he cried out. Desperate tears formed around his bloodshot eyes. He wanted to weep, he wanted to surrender, he wanted to die. But weeping did not come, the means to surrender evaded him, and death was denied at least for the moment.

He struggled to his knees and managed to get his blanket back around his head. Slowly, he extricated himself from the broken bough and pulled himself to his feet. He pushed through the branches and continued along the twisty path. He did not know where it would take him. He could not guess how long he had been upon it. He could not remember being warm. And was it yesterday when he last ate, when he stumbled into a cache of walnuts? Or was it the day before? It was before the ice. He remembered that much. And he remembered smashing the hard shells with a rock, and how when his grip slipped the rock nearly crushed his fingers. Now they were covered with scabs. One had reopened when he fell, and he absently noted that it was bleeding again.

He pressed on. He did not really notice when the snow overtook the sleet. He did not notice when the path broadened, just as the hoary light of day began to dim. Nor did he notice when he emerged from the forest and passed between snowy fields. So intent on merely moving ahead, it was not until he fell once again and got back to his knees that he saw his surroundings. It was a shock to him. Where was the forest? Gone, and instead he was now in the open, on a trackless snow-covered road. And along the road just before him was a sight that filled him with fear.

Ahead, only a few hundred yards away, was a group of cottages to either side of the road, and beyond them was a small town or village. Smoke drifted from chimneys, but, thankfully, no one was in sight. The memory of the last town terrified him, and the stripes on his back still stung, as did those given him by the village before. He vaguely remembered fleeing around a small lake, eluding his pursuers in the wooded hills.

His heart quickened, his breath grated more violently, and his mind sharpened as he hunched lower lest he be seen. Twisting around, he assessed his situation like a stalked animal preparing to take flight. Behind him, far and away, was the dark misty line of the forest. To either side were broad open fields and no cover.

Turning, he looked again at the forest, nearly a mile back, he guessed. Perhaps he could make his retreat without being seen. He got to one foot, his other knee still on the ground, ready to make a run for it. Then he hesitated. Why would he want to go back that way? It would only take him back to those he had wronged, to those who had wronged him. To shame, to whips and taunts, and to worse.

"Oh take me away, I beg of you!" he hoarsely cried out to the sky, blinking away the snow that melted in his eyes. "Is this to be my punishment? To be cast out in such a manner?"

There was no answer, only the faint tick of snowflakes as they landed.

With strength enough for one last supreme effort, he put his head down and gathered his determination. He would make a dash through the village, through and on and on, until he came out of it and beyond it. Perhaps then he might find some desolate barn, some lonely shelter away from everyone where he could rest, where he could sleep.

He got to his feet. He was resolved to run through the town as quickly as he could. But after only a few steps, the best that he could manage was a terribly awkward shuffle, punctuated by clumsy strides like those of a frail old man, not someone who was only a short time ago in his prime. He passed the first few cottages and entered the town proper, his head down, glancing aside at the lampposts and shops to keep himself in the middle of the road. He felt as if the buildings pressed in against him, their windows like eyes upon him, driving him on. But his strength ebbed quickly, his ability to control his gait abandoned him, his legs now uncoordinated and wild. His knees jerked up and hammered down, though his feet barely raised a hair with each step. His strides became a grinding shuffle, sometimes a foot would drag, sometimes he would step on the loose rags around one shoe with his other. Clutching the blanket around his chin with both hands, his body crooked lower and lower into a precarious stoop, his leaning weight pulling him forward. His feet could not keep up, and he stumbled, falling flat onto his chest, unable to break his fall, his arms and hands fairly crushed.

As quickly as he could, but with agonizing slowness, he got back to one knee. Then he heard the door open. Terrified, he saw a man hurrying toward him with a stern expression as a woman stood in an open doorway behind him. He froze, knowing what was coming, instantly resigning himself to the repetition of his fate. The approaching man suddenly pulled off his long coat, revealing a muscular figure. The stricken traveler turned away, looking down at the snow that caked the rags around his shoe. Somehow, it was like a kind of lacework such that he had seen somewhere before. He closed his eyes, waiting for the blows to fall.

Suddenly he felt a weight upon him as something draped over his shoulders, something warm. Then he felt someone gripping his arms at the elbows. Raising his head, he saw the townsman's face only inches from his own.

"Come," the man said. "It is not fit to be out on such a raw day. Come inside where it is warm and dry. Here, permit me to help you up."

Confused and astonished, the traveler recoiled in fear.

"No, no. I'll not have you out here in the open. I insist that you come inside to the hearth."

Somehow the traveler allowed himself to be coaxed and lifted to his feet, now realizing that the man had draped his own coat around him. He was led to the cottage and inside, then guided to a chair beside a crackling fire.

"Here," said the woman as the man took away his coat. "Let me trade you that shawl for this."

He clutched his ragged covering defensively, but her warm hands loosened his grip, and she gently removed what had been his only shelter for so long and put a warm soft quilt over his shoulders. She pulled it around in front of him and guided his hands to hold it in place.

She moved off to her husband who was closing the door and now hanging his coat on a peg.

"I'll go and fetch a bowl of soup for our guest," she whispered. "Look at how the poor thing shakes!"

"Aye," nodded the husband. "It's a sorry circumstance, I'm sure, to be caught out like so. Run along and hurry back. I'll keep an eye on him."

As she went to the kitchen, he took a chair and sat across from the unexpected guest.

"It's an early winter coming, looks like," he said. All the while, the stranger had watched the man and his wife, his expression blank, but his eyes stark and glittering.

"Yes. A poor time for traveling, as it turns out. Though it was fair and warm enough only four days ago."

The stranger, saying nothing, simply gazed at the man.

"Hm. Well, soon enough it'll pass. Likely it'll be clear and fairly warm again, as it often happens, before the winter really and truly begins. No doubt you are anxious to be on your way? Perhaps you go to Duinnor? They say they have a new king, the sixth, I believe."

The stranger managed an almost imperceptible nod.

"Well, we'll have you back on your way soon."

The wife emerged bearing a tray with a steaming bowl that she put on a side table. Then, taking the bowl and a spoon, she looked at the still-quivering guest.

"Here," she said, putting the spoon down, "take this with both hands and sip right from the bowl. It'll help warm your fingers. It's not too hot."

Seeing the man's hesitation, she glanced at her husband.

"Go ahead. My wife makes the best soups and heartiest stews in town."

The wife put down the bowl, then adjusted the blanket around her guest to free his hands before offering the bowl again. Gaping at her face, he took the bowl into his shaking hands. He glanced around, not knowing where he was, and his expression seemed to soften, though he still shivered, and the firelight danced madly in the pools of his eyes.

"There. See? Just holding a warm bowl feels good, don't it now?" she said.

"Oh, don't hesitate on our account," put in her husband. "There's plenty where that came from, and we'll be joining you when you have your seconds. Meanwhile, I think I'll fetch my pipe."

"Did he say where he's from?" whispered his wife when she joined him at the cupboard.

"He hasn't said a word."

The man found his pipe and pouch, but lingered on the other side of the room as the guest sipped, gradually at first, then with increasing voracity until, very quickly, the bowl was emptied. When the wife took it from his hands, the guest stood uneasily and moved to the door.

"Oh! What's this? Wouldn't you like a bit more?" she asked.

"Where are you going? You can't go back out into all that!" her husband stated.

The guest turned to them and looked from one to the other.

He nodded, which was all the gratitude that he could express. Then he stooped to pick up his tattered blanket that had been left beside the doorway, but he lost his balance and fell against the door heavily. Rushing to him, the man and his wife helped him back to his feet.

"No, no. I do insist that you remain here for a while longer," said the man. "At least until you get your feet back under you."

"Oh," said the woman, putting her hand on the man's forehead. "He's burning up with fever!"

Meanwhile, the visitor was awkwardly clawing at the doorknob, but with no real coordination. Then he crumpled over, in spite of the hands trying to steady him, and he slumped to the floor.

"Oh, oh!"

"Dear, go fetch the neighbors," the man said. "We'll need help getting him upstairs and into bed."

• • •

The next many days were ones of delirium for the traveler. He was put into a bed, covered with blankets, and spoon fed. He vaguely sensed comings and goings. Hands pressed to his forehead. The worst of his fever passed quickly, although it came and went over another week. With help, he managed to stand and walk around the room, and he slowly gained back his strength. Then he had another bout of fever that put him back in bed for two days. During that time, he knew he was dying. He was certain of it because a man came in who was dressed in a fine black suit. Lying motionless with his eyes open, and surrounded by his hosts and a few others looking on seriously, he watched the man as he took a roll of string and measured from his head to his toes. Then he measured across his shoulders. It was for a box, he was sure, and he closed his eyes as the man measured again and again.

Two days later, when his fever at last departed for good, the guest opened his eyes and saw hanging at the wardrobe on the other side of the room an outfit of clothes, a nice wool coat, and, on the floor nearby, good walking boots.

• • •

Twelve days after he had arrived, the man put on the warm clothes that had been made for him, laced up his boots, and pulled on the shoulder bag full of provisions that had been prepared for him. Then he went downstairs, and gave the lady of the house a hug.

"We'll walk you to the edge of town, if you don't mind," said the lady's husband.

Their departing guest nodded.

Outside were gathered a few others of the town. The tailor, the cobbler, their wives, and some of their children. They all walked silently through the main street of town. It was a beautiful day, warmer than it had been for weeks, and the snow was fluffy and bright under the clear blue sky. There was a crisp note on the air, though, Sir Winter's whisper that he would soon come again and would stay until spring. They all felt it, even the guest who was a stranger to this region. But no one commented upon it, least of all the stranger, who had not said a word, and, they all felt certain, had no ability to speak. At the edge of town, the man who had been their guest stopped, then turned to them and shook hands with each, giving the women good hugs and deep soulful gazes.

"Well. Goodbye," said the man who had taken him in.

"Won't you stay until spring?" his wife asked again. "Soon we'll be having our Midwinter's feast, and it will be a fine affair that you'd be sure to enjoy."

For the first time, the stranger smiled, but he shook his head while doing so. Then he turned away but had walked only a few yards when he stopped and turned back to them.

"Other strangers will come and pass through your lands," he said softly. "Treat them with the same kindness and charity as you have treated me, and your lands shall prosper, your people shall thus be happy in their goodness, and the shelter the forest gives you shall be preserved. Verily, one shall someday come and, though he shall not be known to you, he shall become your King, and he shall remember you."

Astounded by his speech, and mystified by his words, the small gathering watched him depart northward. His gait was steady, his stride relaxed but swift. When he rounded a bend in the road and disappeared from view, they turned away, full of discussion as they went back to their shops and homes.

They did not see, and would not have understood if they had, that the stranger continued to smile as he hiked along. He no longer cared where the road took him. He now knew why he was sent this way. He had learned the sharp guilt of error, the cruel consequence of injustice, and the sting of abiding shame. But he had also learned that there were some people who cared not for such things, or, if they did, they had the heart to look beyond them. He had also learned that kindness and mercy were as important as justice and right. And far more powerful.

Imbued with a sense of resolve, the mystery of his existence permeated his thoughts. When he reached the top of a hill, he paused to look back at the far-off town. As he contemplated, a bluish light appeared behind him as a pinpoint, then it billowed and swirled. He felt the light's presence, its call. Suddenly, as if pulled by an invisible rope about his waist, he flew backwards into the glowing vapor. The next moment found him regaining his balance, standing in a wide circular room. There were many doors surrounding the place, doors that might lead to trial, perhaps to horror. But he stood and stared at the open door before him as it faded and disappeared from sight, replaced by the smooth gray stones of the wall.

Part I

Chapter 1

The Falls of Tiandari

Day 162
83 Days Remaining

Four days after Robby and Ullin made their desperate escape from the burning White Palace in Linlally, a large crowd gathered around the rim of the lake into which the five Falls of Tiandari poured. They stood well away from the spray of the cascade, and with their heads craned upward, they could see the top of the falls where the ornate flight deck jutted out from the walls that bordered Cupeldain's high and marvelous lake. They watched a lone figure who stood at its edge, a mere dot against the intense blue sky. Now and then, a smudge of smoke wafted across the scene above, as if in testament to the reason for the proceedings that were about to take place. Even over the incessant roar from the base of the falls, some thought they heard the duh-duh-DOOM, duh-duh-DOOM, duh-duh-DOOM of a slow-beaten cadence.

Long after the crowd had gathered, but not yet at the appointed hour, Lord Seafar sat at his desk in the Scribblers Room where he had been for most of the night and all of that morning. He had not eaten supper the night before, nor yet had any breakfast, and he refused assistance from the other officers of the special corps, choosing to work alone with True Ink and paper. For long periods he sat, pondering many points and questions, only to suddenly write out some line or other and watch it fade or remain. After careful and deliberate consideration, he would then write out another line and repeat the process. This went on all night, and the answers he received sometimes caused him to stand up and pace back and forth, sometimes hurrying back to pen and ink, bending over the table to jot another line. Once, he was so moved by anger that he kicked a chair across the room. The uncharacteristic outburst served only to shock the others in the room, busy at their own work which seemed all the more pressing since the attack.

Fortunately for the Scribblers, the fire had spared their secret working chambers, and though the damage was severe, only one wing of the Palace was completely lost, along with part of the rooftop landing for the flyers. Indeed, the entire south wing was destroyed, with its several stories that held the guest rooms and the dining halls and secondary kitchens. All that remained were the stone walls, and some of these had crumbled when the great timbers within collapsed. Gutted all the way down to the water's edge, there remained only a massive pile of charred rubble, jumbled beds and furniture, and great old timbers, many of which still crackled and smoldered. Besides the south wing, the adjacent west tower was also damaged, including part of the large flat deck of planks from where Robby and his rescuers had flown, now partially burned away so that no flyers could take off or alight there. The worst of it, though, were the many casualties, those killed and wounded by the fighting and the fire. Among the known dead were many of the Palace staff and thirty-seven members of the Gray Guard. This included the two young Scribblers who had given Robby their weather report from the Eastlands, killed before the alarm had sounded as they turned a corner, very likely laughing and joking as they came upon four of Faradan's men who were attempting to secure an escape route to the causeway. In the confusion, their bodies, hastily dragged into a nearby alcove by their killers, were not discovered until yesterday morning. Many others were still missing, including Henders and his assistant, Sonya, and they would likely not be found until the debris and wreckage of the fires could be excavated.

• • •

"Sir. It is almost time."

"Yes, thank you, Harrin," Seafar nodded, rising from his chair and carefully placing his notes into the stove. "Please have the staff, officers, and watch gather at the east palisades."

"Yes, sir."

He hastened to his quarters, where his man, Janson, was waiting with towel and basin, and Seafar methodically washed and shaved. Janson then helped Seafar change into a clean uniform to replace the blood- and soot-stained one he had worn for almost four days. He was helped on with his tunic jacket, his many ribbons already attached, his sword and harness, and then with his long gray cloak, tied back over his shoulders. Seafar then stood until Janson had circled him, inspecting his polished boots, belts, and the gold and silver of his medals before nodding.

"Very well, my lord," he said. "I think that will do."

"Thank you, Janson. I'll be back very shortly to change once more."

"Certainly, my lord."

Seafar walked out of his apartment to keep his appointment. Detachments of the Gray Guard, some in dress uniforms, others in battle gear, saluted as their general passed, then fell in behind him, all walking at a quick and purposeful pace. As they marched along the halls and down the stairs, and even through one of the galleries where some of the fighting had taken place, Seafar's mind ran from thought to thought. As horrific as the attack was, it had failed to accomplish its mission. His guests had made good their escape, the archives and the Scribblers Room were unscathed, and, thankfully, the Queen was far away in Glareth. Captain Faradan and three of his men had been captured, but all except Faradan had died from battle wounds in the interceding few days. Now, watched from above by those gathered at the east palisades, Lord Seafar and his company passed through the gates of the Palace and out onto the causeway. He could hear for the first time the field drums, their dreary toll floating across the lake from the flight deck overlooking the falls.

The True Ink had confirmed that Robby and his party were safe and were well on their way. And the ink revealed more than Faradan ever would, to be sure, but Seafar still had many questions that remained to be answered. The attack had been too carefully planned, and too expertly carried out, to have been hatched so quickly after Robby's arrival in Vanara. Seafar knew from his own sources that Faradan reported to Count Dialmor, who was missing. Seafar had questioned the man for hours on end, and Faradan remained amiable throughout it all, resigned to his fate, but he would say nothing but that he served his king. Now, since there was no point in delaying his duty in useless hope of revelations from Faradan, Seafar hoped that Queen Serith Ellyn, by using her own supply of True Ink, was apprised of the situation and would approve of the way this was being handled.

Arriving at the wall on the edge of the lake, Seafar marched up the stairs leading to the platform above. A few steps from the top, he paused, took a deep breath, cleared his throat, and quickly straightened his tunic before proceeding the last few steps up and onto the flight deck followed by his Chief of Staff and two adjutants who took their places near the drummers.

Atop the flight deck were twenty officers of the Gray Guard standing in a line at the north side of the platform. They snapped to attention as Seafar stepped forward. To Seafar's left, along the west side of the deck, were ten more officers, and behind them were many members of the Queen's Council, four or five lords and ladies of Vanara, Lord Faslor and his sister Coreth, as well as Ambassador Lord Tarlway of Glareth, and Ambassador Lord Arleman of Duinnor. Members of the Duinnor Kingsmen and Duinnor Regulars were not invited to attend this gathering, regardless of their rank and in spite of their protests, but no doubt they watched from below.

The drummers stationed to Seafar's right continued to beat in unison, the slow somber blows of their sticks underscoring the gravity of these proceedings, and the officer in charge stepped forward and raised his hand in salute. Seafar raised his and held it long. He doubted if any living mortal had ever witnessed this ancient ceremony, and doubted if any of the Elifaen present had, either. His hand swept down, the drums ceased their beat, and for a moment the only sound that followed was the gentle snap and rustle of the Queen's pennant that flew from a wing-topped mast behind the dignitaries.

"How are things, Commander Staysul?" Seafar asked.

"All present and correct, my lord."

"Very well. Read the order, if you please."

"Yes, my lord."

The officer reached into his ornate shoulder case and withdrew a scroll, broke the seal, turned to face the gathering, and read loudly:

"All present, bear witness! By order of Queen Serith Ellyn's Lord Chancellor and High Regent, it is declared that Titus Faradan of Duinnor has committed dishonorable assault upon the Queen's subjects and upon Her Majesty's property. He has insulted the people of Vanara by conspiring to commit acts of treason against Realm Law, and by conducting unwarranted and unprovoked acts of a warlike nature against Vanara. He has carried out these acts upon Her Majesty's loyal officers, upon Her Majesty's loyal subjects, and upon Her Majesty's honored guests. He has committed assault and murder within and upon the soil of Vanara, and he has committed other acts of tyranny against the Laws of this Realm and against its people. It is the conclusion of a right jury of this Realm that Titus Faradan is guilty of these acts. Further, it is found that, since a state of peace exists between Her Majesty's Realm and the Realm of Duinnor, these acts are indeed treasonous to that peace. It is therefore ordered, according to the Laws of this Realm, and by the power granted to the Queen of Vanara by her people, and to Her Chancellor and Regent, being Judge Advocate General, the Lord Seafar, and by the will of the people and the courts of Vanara, that the Queen's Justice is hereby to be carried out in accordance with the Ancient Laws and Customs of this land."

The officer put away the scroll, saluted Seafar again, and returned to stand with his men.

Seafar walked stiffly to Lord Arleman and stood close before him.

"Lord Ambassador."

"Lord Chancellor."

Seafar did not acknowledge or return Arleman's slight bow.

"I have received your protest. Do you have anything to add?"

"I beg you to put a halt to these proceedings until the King has made his wishes known pertaining to this unfortunate affair."

"Anything else?"

"Only that Vanara will answer to the King, if you continue."

"Vanara answers to her Queen, and the Queen to her people."

Lord Arleman shook his head regretfully. "Then be it upon your head."

Seafar turned away and walked across the deck to the far side where Faradan stood facing him, his hands shackled before him. Just behind him, on the very edge of the platform that jutted far out over the falls, rested a large oblong block of stone, nearly waist-high, stood up on its end. To the top of the block was spiked a chain that draped down the stone then up again along Faradan's back to an iron band around his neck. He looked at Seafar without emotion, drawing himself more stiffly to military attention.

"It is not too late," Seafar said in a soft tone so that none but the condemned man could hear. "If you will confess the details of your raid, how it was planned, and who was responsible for it, I have it within my power and authority to commute your sentence."

"Thank you, my lord, but no. I shall only say what I have said all along. I am my King's servant."

"I see. Then I must do my duty."

"Of course, my lord."

Seafar stepped to the side of Faradan and drew his sword. Faradan looked up at the sky and smiled, his hardened visage softened by the sunlight on his face. Seafar put the tip of his blade against the top of the stone and gave it a slight push. It immediately fell over the side of the precipice, pulling the chain.

"Long live the Ki...!"

Faradan was gone.

Chapter 2

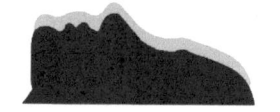

Doubt's Offspring

Odds were even that a person summoned by the Avatar would never be seen again. An ordinary summons was enough cause for alarm, especially when those commanded to come were not accustomed to it: The appearance of the Kingsmen at your step, the sound of pommel upon door, the steady tramp of a dozen guards surrounding you as they took you away at quickstep. When the Kingsmen alone were sent to fetch those summoned, it was often as a guard of honor, for the Lords of Duinnor loved the display of pomp. Sometimes the Kingsmen were sent as intimidation, for the Lords of Duinnor also loved to display their power, especially when it could be exerted over others.

Still, when only the Kingsmen came, the people they passed merely looked on and hardly paused in conversation or work. Children sported about before them, trying to bring a smile to the soldiers' austere faces, while adults stood aside out of respect. And, as soon as the Kingsmen had passed, they were forgotten, and the people in the streets of Duinnor went on with their mundane affairs.

But when the Avatar came, whether by night or by the broad light of day, the stir it caused in the streets was one of dread and fear. Both the high and the lowly shrank from its approach. Everyone moved quickly out of the way, parents pulled their children with them, and the weak-hearted felt faint as it silently floated along the avenues and streets. Making no sound, the Avatar had the effect of also hushing the usual street noise, becalming all activity before it and for some distance in its wake. People hurriedly crowded into shops or any door that would open to them. Blinds were pulled and shutters closed as conversation paused until goosebumps subsided. Workmen who could not release the loads they were hoisting, or drivers who could not drive away into some side alley, held tight their ropes and reins and averted their eyes until the Avatar had safely passed. Some whispered silent prayers that it would continue on its way, that it would not stop (Please, let it not stop!), but would keep going (Please, let it keep going!). Pigeons fluttered off well before its coming, and even the chipping sparrows ceased their titter. Cats and mongrels slinked away, cautiously glancing over their hunched shoulders.

Those who spent their days and nights as beggars outside the Palace walls made to each other a count of each time it emerged from the gates, saying, well after it had passed, when the noise of their market had resumed, "Twelve times, in as many weeks," or, "That's twenty-seven this year, so far."

A dreadful thing it was, therefore, to see it come and go, and even more dreadful to have it arrive at your door. And so it was that Beauchamp, like all animals who have in some way more sense than their masters, perked upright, his long ears straight up and twitching, poised with intense alertness. With one of his powerful hind legs, he released two hard thumps on the rug where but a moment before he had been napping. He then bounded two strides to his left, and thumped again, his posture now crouched in readiness. It was the third thump that finally got Raynor's attention.

"What is the matter, bunny-boy?" he asked, leaning sideways from his desk and looking over his spectacles at the rabbit. It was then that Raynor became aware of the dense silence of his apartment, and he slowly placed the quill he held back into the inkwell. Looking toward the open window, he placed a sheet of paper over the note he had been writing. As he rose from his chair, Beauchamp thumped again and darted behind a table. A hard bang landed on the building's front door, as if it had been hit with an iron-shod mallet. Raynor stepped out of his room onto the landing and looked down the stairs at the front entrance just in time to hear the next thud. The door jarred so violently under the blow that it shook on its hinges, and dust fell from the lintel above.

"Well," he said to Beauchamp, now sitting at the hem of his robe, "this is not entirely unexpected."

In response, Beauchamp thumped again, made a circle around Raynor, and stopped to thump yet another time.

"Now, now. Who knows what this may be about? Perhaps our appeals are being answered. So, before the landlady has our silver for damages, we may as well answer the door. Ha, ha! Did you hear what I said? 'Answer the door!' Get it? 'Answer the door?' Ah-ha-haw! Now, where's my big hat?"

Just a moment later, wearing an overcloak and a tall pointed hat that looked too big for his crown yet nevertheless rested well on his head, Raynor emerged from the front entrance of his apartment building and faced another door. It was tall, and, other than the fact that it hovered about a foot from the ground and was painted bright apple-red, it was in every manner of appearance an ordinary door that might lead to a bedroom or chamber. And though it had no doorframe, threshold, or lintel, it was equipped with plain iron hinges and an iron knob, all old and worn as if from years of use. Raynor was tempted to reach out and turn the knob, just to see what might happen, but as the thought came to him, the mysterious thing swung on its own and turned completely around, its backside no different than its front, and it began to move away. Raynor shrugged, adjusted his heavy hat with both hands, and followed.

"At least it is daylight," he said, "since it is usually far worse for those fetched at night."

• • •

In and around the land of Duinnor were many palaces and fine estates, both within the city and also scattered throughout the Realm, on the fertile plains and up into the hilly highlands nestled on the slopes of the western mountains. While some were more ancient, and others more pleasurable to behold, none were so vast or held so many secrets as Duinstone, the Palace of Kings, where resided the one King With No Name, King of all Kings and Sovereign Ultimate of all the Seven Realms. From the spires to the foundation, and all within its rosy hued marble walls, it reeked of power and authority. No one knew all of its secrets, and few desired to delve into its mysteries and its recesses. But many had acquaintance with some portion or other of its interior, either the Hall of Lords, from where the empire was administered, or the Hall of Warriors, wherein Kingsman generals made their headquarters. There were many bureaus and many rooms of clerkish work, many places of meeting, and many vaults and archives full of riches. It was a place wherefrom commerce was guided, laws were formed, and justice meted out. And there were places, dark and deep, where less savory business was conducted—punishment, imprisonment, and worse.

In its upper stories, lofty and removed from the more mundane duties required for governing, were other halls and chambers for more inscrutable activities. Astronomers had their observatories, apothecaries mixed their potions, and alchemists worked, all charged to perform their own secret experiments and to make their own arcane calculations. Surrounding these places, along the rim of the sprawling building, were many towers from where the agents of the King watched over the city and looked beyond its walls, their eyes intent to their spyglasses, their minds wary and suspicious, their hands writing down the things they saw. Higher still, above even those places, rose up the High Tower itself, made of cleverly laid blocks so that the uppermost portion was wider than its base. Within the interior of the turret was a winding staircase that emptied into a long foyer outside of the High Chamber, the abode of the Unknown King and his mysterious Avatar. One could only hope for, or have dread of, a summons to this place, to an interview within the High Chamber. For some who came here, it was the last place they would ever see sunlight, afterwards taken to the deepest places of the Palace, thereafter becoming lost and forgotten.

It was not the first time Raynor had been to the Palace. In fact, long ago, he himself had chambers there, overseeing the education of those selected to become Kingsmen. But that was very long ago, and by now nearly all of his former students had passed away of old age or had died in the many wars and conflicts that vexed the world. And, since his fall from favor those fifteen decades ago, this was not the first time he had been summoned back to the Palace. But it was the first time he had been taken upward instead of downward, and up and up the Avatar led, along with an armed escort of Kingsmen, winding around and around the marble staircase, on and on. At last they emerged into a long wide hallway, passed through guarded doors, and entered the High Chamber itself. There, waiting for him, was Lord Banis of the Elifaen House of Elmwood, one of the few Elifaen to ever hold a position of high rank in Duinnor. Yet he was the First Lord of the High Chamber, the highest minister to the King, as he had been these past two hundred years and more, the second most powerful person in the world. He stood to one side of the room, near an open window, with his back to the glowing curtain that stretched across the chamber, behind which the inscrutable King stood, his light emanating through the fabric. The Kingsmen escorts retreated as the Avatar floated across the floor to take a place on the opposite side of the room from Banis. The doors behind Raynor closed with a soft but firm bump.

It was an oddly pleasant chamber, the late afternoon sun shining through the tall window to warm the tile floor. Odd, because there was not a stick of furniture to be seen, nor was there a speck of adornment anywhere within the room, other than the simple green curtain that crossed all the way from one wall to the other. In striking contrast to the rest of the Palace, there were no statues here, no tapestries, no paintings or displays of weapons, nor were there any cases of treasure or any artifacts from Duinnor's long history. Yet the simple room seemed appropriate, for the glow behind the curtain, and the knowledge of who gave off the light, was awesome enough.

Adjusting his hat, Raynor turned his attention to Banis, a figure who appeared to be about thirty years old, but Raynor knew he was a hundred times that age at the very least. Lord Banis was dressed in a loose-fitting robe of the darkest red, gathered at the waist by a silver mesh of fine chain. His hands were held casually together before him, his fingers entwined, and his long silky brown hair draped smoothly downward and then flowed back up and over his shoulders. The resemblance to his daughter, Esildre, was remarkable, and he shared her beauty, too, in a gender-defying way. Yet his face was completely without expression, his amber eyes vaguely distracted by thought as he continued to gaze out through the window.

"Our King wishes me to put certain questions to you in his presence," Lord Banis said in a soft and delicate voice.

Raynor bowed low, holding onto his uncooperative hat as he did so.

"I am at the King's service, my lord."

"How many of your kind, the Melnari, are there in the world?"

"I do not know." Raynor cocked a shaggy eyebrow at the unexpected question. "But only a very few, surely."

"Please name all that you know, or have ever known of."

Raynor scratched his ear, and, adjusting his hat, he shrugged.

"Well. There was Ishtorgus, who, it is said, was lost in a maelstrom off the coast of Glareth. And, let's see, Barian the Counter, who traced the stars and delved into their mysteries. He was killed when struck by a burning rock that fell from the heavens. At least, that is what I heard. Then there was Tolimay the Angry, who had such an ill temper. He became so upset at a trick played upon him by a little boy that he exploded into a thousand bits. Hm. Messy, I'm sure, but I'm positive there must have been more to it than that. Um, then, oh, yes! Micharam, the forest poet who lived nearby to the land where Halethiris once was, and who, it is told, was chased down and beaten to death by an offended butterfly. Yes, a preposterous tale!"

"Is that all?" Banis asked.

"All? Let's see. Myself, of course, Ishtorgus, Barian, Micharam, Tolimay..."

"Do you not forget Collandoth?"

"Oh, him! Collandoth the Wanderer. How silly of me!"

"Our King wishes to know if you have forgotten any others?"

"Hm. I don't know...let me think. But if I have forgotten, how would I know?"

"Do you know the whereabouts of Collandoth?"

"Yes. He has taken up residence in the east, so I hear."

"In the east. Yes. A place called Tulith Attis. Do you know of that place?"

"Indeed, I do, as would anyone who knows something of the history of the Seven Realms."

"Then you know also how it fell."

"Yes. The defenders were betrayed to the powerful and overwhelming Dragonkind army that swept through the east in those days and besieged that place in fearful battle."

"So the story goes. And the famous trap laid by Heneil failed to prevent it."

"And the Bell was not rung to warn the embattled people," Raynor said.

"Ah," Banis said. Raynor perceived a shadow, perhaps that of a large bird, interrupt the sunlight that bathed Banis's face.

"But you know better, don't you Raynor?" Banis continued. "As all who have been keen to understand the mysterious events of this past summer. In fact, the Great Bell was rung, and with its three mighty tolls, it released the incantations laid upon it into the air and into the earth, setting off every bell, chime, and gong in this city."

"So that is what caused the alarm!"

"Do not play ignorant." Banis's tone changed instantly, though he still looked away from Raynor. "Your kind may hide your thoughts from the Throne, but there are other ways, less subtle ways, to obtain cooperation."

Banis let that sink in, then turned, frowning at Raynor, and gave a shrug. "We know that you received a visitor recently. From the east. And we are certain that you received some message from Collandoth, and our...agents tracked the returning messenger as far as Nasakeeria."

"Nasakeeria?" For the first time since the interview began, Raynor was concerned, and he stiffened slightly. If Certina had entered that land....

"That is so. Therefore, your reply to Collandoth, whatever it was, went no further than that place, for, as we all know, none ever emerge from there."

"I really don't know what you are talking about. Collandoth is an old colleague from my days at the Academy. And I did write to him using the King's Post. But that was quite a while ago. And none but my own feet have stepped across my threshold in many a month, save the charwoman of my apartment and perhaps a book buyer or two."

"Collandoth's messenger, as you well know, would just as easily come in through a window as a door. Let us forego pretenses and play-acting. We know of your collaboration with Collandoth and with Lord Seafar of Vanara."

"Seafar? I have never met the man."

Banis coolly ignored Raynor's statement, saying, "The wind of conspiracy softly blows through all of your affairs. Shall I tell you the note it plays? It is the music of treason, no less!"

"Treason," Raynor stated. "Conspiracy? You would speak to me of conspiracy. You, who have guided the unjust to play for you the song of corruption. You, who have cast down great and noble houses to advance your power over others. And you have done far worse!"

There was a disturbance behind the curtain as Raynor spoke, and a low hum filled the room.

"Treason?" Raynor went on. "From the mouth of he who has turned his back upon his own people and has turned the fabled justice of Duinnor against them?"

Banis crossed the room quickly and, without changing his mild expression, slapped the mystic so hard that Raynor's hat tumbled from his head and landed upright onto the floor a few feet away.

Raynor glared at Banis, a trickle of blood dripping down from one corner of his mouth. He glanced at his hat, and touched his cut lip. He looked at the spot of blood on his fingertip, then back at Banis, his glare turning to a smile. "Has it been so long since these chambers have heard truth?"

The hum changed tones, and Banis suddenly put his hands over his ears with a look of pain. Turning away from Raynor, he staggered a few steps toward the glowing curtain and fell to his knees. The curtain then was parted by a thread of bright-glowing amber. Now Banis covered his eyes, bowing low. But Raynor stood firm, did not bow, and did not avert his eyes as the King emerged from behind his veil like a ball of golden yarn, slowly spinning. The edges of this weird form seemed to waver and shimmer, as if great heat emitted from it, and Raynor squinted to maintain his gaze as the room grew brighter. But the air noticeably cooled. The Red Door remained as it was, passive, as if it was indeed the inanimate object it represented. The King floated forward, coming to stop just in front of the trembling Banis.

"I can speak in words for ordinary ears," came a male voice as if from a great distance. "To Lord Banis and all others of the world, I may speak to directly, if I wish, without the need of sound, so that only the one I speak to may hear my words, and only I may hear their reply. But you and your kind are different. Do you not fear me?"

"I do not."

"I believe you. And it is refreshing, I must say. If it is truly true. But, I dare say, you *do* have fears."

Raynor watched the spinning cloud of fibrous light move away from Banis and approach the window where a dark form now sat on the ledge. Shielding his eyes from the glare, Raynor saw that it was a black eagle.

"I, too, have my Familiars. And what I do not see for myself and through my servants, such as Banis, the eagles see for me."

"The black eagles of Secundur serve none but him," Raynor stated.

"Oh, I did not say they were loyal to me. You see, Secundur and I have a longstanding accord. We sometimes share resources, too. I lend him my servants, when it suits me to do so. And he lends his to me."

"The Dark One has no interest but his own gain."

"Do you think I am so foolish? But why should I do what others would do for me?"

"Any bargain made with him is foolhardy. He is intent upon your downfall."

"Oh? Then you and he have something in common."

"Your influence wanes while his grows. I need do nothing to play midwife to change. By your own actions, and those you choose as your servants, the Throne hastens things, and weakens with every passing day. Long have you been obsessed with the subjugation of Vanara, yet your grip weakens upon the other Realms. You have done nothing to stop the rebellion in the east, while the Dragon King marshals his armies to the south, preparing them to strike."

"Let them strike! Vanara is still strong and will take the edge from his threat, as Vanara has always done. Tracia will return to the fold, for its own sake, and order will be established once again in that land."

Raynor realized, of course, that there was much else at work here. The King did not merely want order, but something else, too: *His* order.

"In the early years of your rule," Raynor said, "you united the Realms under your justice, bringing peace and security. In those days, despots and warlords had no share in your bounty or protection. Thugs of every rank feared your law and the swift and sure hand of your justice. But all that changed. The King's Men were given great authority, and the Edicts of Vanara began taking the fruit of Vanaran lands and labor, and, eventually, began taking the land itself. Thus was Vanara made to reward your servants in Duinnor, in lease and in treasure. Vice and corruption found new houses among the mighty of the Realms and in the Courts of Duinnor. In your name, all manner of acts are perpetrated upon the meek and the disfavored. The Realms now vie amongst themselves, straining the union of your rule. Duinnor and its people have put themselves above all others, and they suffer by it. Shadows now creep back into the lands of the earth. The Dragonkind bide their days in preparation, and Shatuum sends forth its minions to probe and provoke. And the spirit of the Dark One himself has found ears among the highest of the lands, driving wedges into every crack he finds."

"It is all for the best," the King replied mildly. "Indeed, even Banis believes so. The world does change, and it is my duty, not yours, to guide that change. Or is that what the Melnari think to be their purpose?"

Raynor remained silent as the King floated nearer. The trembling Banis remained kneeling, as if unaware of the conversation.

"Certainly Ashlord has been no stranger to meddlesome change," the King went on. "And now, it seems, he seeks to usurp my rule and to install an upstart in my place. Yes. I have many agents. I need not gaze into your mind to know these things."

Raynor noted that he called Ashlord by the name given to him by Men. Might this be a clue to the King's identity?

"Even now he approaches the city," the King continued. "But why? Is he so audacious? Does he not know that none may take my throne save he who knows the Name? Do not be so shocked by my words, Raynor the Wise. None who seek my throne can take the direct path to it. This we all know, do we not? Surely Ashlord does. So I am puzzled, you see. The Bellringer is Ashlord's companion. But can the Bellringer be the Usurper? Why else does Ashlord bring him forth to me? Your colleague is a deep one. Or else he is imprudent."

"Your agents do you a disservice," Raynor countered. "Or perhaps they are not so astute as they lead you to believe. I will tell you, then, that it is for the preservation of Duinnor that my colleague comes. It is news he brings, and people to bear witness to his tidings. The rebellion in Tracia that is made little of here has now spilled its ambitions abroad. Indeed, they go to war against Duinnor by striking first the old Eastlands Realm."

"Glareth and Tracia have squabbled over the Eastlands ever since King Inrick died," stated the King. "Tracia is jealous of the regency of Glareth over those lands, and there is now greater animosity among the ruling rebels since Glareth sent aid to the ousted Prince. Glareth is not threatened by any Tracian foray, no matter how insulting it may be. I have left that dispute to my judges to sort out in their good time."

"King. Collandoth, the one you call Ashlord, comes to tell of this latest incident. And he suspects Tracia has designs on her neighbors in the south and west. She is emptying the Eastlands of food and forage to feed and supply a massive army now poised against Masurthia. And there is reason to believe that the Triumvirate of Tracia has made an alliance with the Sun King of the Dragonlands."

Squinting, Raynor watched the uncomfortable light from the King spin more intensely, in a manner that he could only interpret as agitation. Then, in spite of the brilliant light that made his eyes water, Raynor perceived a shape within it, the vague figure of a man. At that moment came a sudden pounding in Raynor's head, an attempt by some force to probe his mind, to merge thoughts, perhaps as he and Beauchamp did. Though painful, Raynor easily resisted the assault, and the sensation faded.

"You do not know whether to believe me," Raynor stated.

"There is more that you do not tell me. What of the Bellringer?"

"I do not know how the Great Bell was rung. Or why it was done. When Collandoth investigated, he found only a young man, a mere boy, who knew nothing of its import. Shortly afterwards, he wrote to me. I still have the letter, if you care to see it."

Raynor knew that the letter, sent by Ashlord two weeks after the Bell had rung, was read by the King's spies before it had ever arrived. Although carefully resealed, they had failed to rearrange its complex folds in the proper way. And, Raynor was sure, they had failed to detect the encoded message hidden within the plain words. Ashlord had written: "He comes." Raynor smiled inwardly.

"That is a kind offer," said the King, now hovering again in front of Lord Banis. "Perhaps you would share what news his messenger brought to you?"

"I have done so already. He relayed to me the events of the attack on the Eastlands, carried out by armies from Tracia, and that he and witnesses to those events were traveling in haste to Duinnor to spread the news."

"Is that all?"

"That is the gist of it. But, apparently, the Throne is not without its defenders, no matter that they are far away and forgotten by you. Lord Tallin proposes to engage the Redvest forces of Tracia, though he is profoundly outnumbered. Collandoth was brief, and he relayed only that Tallin makes a bid for time, believing he can stall the Redvest army throughout the winter, and thereby perhaps delay their spring offensive. He most certainly hopes to weaken them. Through Collandoth, Tallin sends his plea for aid."

"And why have you not come forward with this news before now?"

Raynor shrugged. "I informed General Kecker of the King's Men and also Lord Gateway. They have both refused to see me, and I have had no response to my several notes sent to them. Indeed, I assumed that was why I was summoned, and I expected to see one or both of those gentlemen here."

Raynor, who had seen many strange things in his time, could not help but notice how truly bizarre this scene was. A great black eagle, servant of Secundur, sat on the window ledge staring at him (Or was the bird's eye fixed upon his hat on the floor? A hat that had inched its way all but unnoticed into the corner of the room.). Lord Banis continued to cower on his knees, his eyes covered with his hands, and…was he trembling? The Avatar remained motionless a few yards away like a piece of building material, as if waiting for some workmen to come haul it away to a construction site. And here was the very King of Duinnor, shrouded in his mysterious cocoon of silken light, conversing with Raynor like, well, like anyone might do. Though Raynor remained outwardly calm, even cool, his mind raced, guarding each word, observing every nuance. Besides his concern for Collandoth, and all of the cautions that filled his heart, Raynor also felt a strong desire to know this King. Who was he? What was the secret of this force, this enveloping vision of light? He remembered, without allowing his mind to stray, when the Last King was replaced by this one.

• • •

At the time, Duinnor was already a mighty kingdom, exerting its influence through wealth and arms throughout the world, overseeing the defeat of the last invasion of the Dragonkind. It was the Fifth Unknown King who had sent troops to retake Tulith Attis and who thereafter made alliance with Vanara and Glareth, freed the Eastlands and Tracia of the Dragonkind, and secured the regions of Masurthia and Altoria. But within ten years, his reign was over, replaced by this present King after a fantastic battle in this very tower.

Like others who were brave enough to stand out of doors, Raynor watched from a hill nearby to where his present apartments were later built, and from there he saw the clouds roll and heard the thunder rumble about the Palace. The battle began three nights before the Spring Equinox and carried on until dawn. During the day there was peace, but the Palace was surrounded by a strange fog that no eye could penetrate. At sunset, the battle resumed in greater fury and again waned away at dawn when calm settled over the Palace, shrouded once again with fog. Then, at sunset on the third day, the clash resumed with even more terrifying ferocity, shaking the ground throughout the lands and blinding onlookers with its yellow flashes of lightning. At dawn it did not stop but continued even louder, and the sun rose red and angry through the smoky storm. The white smoke and billowing clouds, shot with lightning and rainbows, grew darker as the day progressed until they were black and blotted out the sun from the city. As he watched, Raynor could only imagine (but would later learn about) the panic and terror that the Lords and Ministers of the Realm were experiencing throughout the nights and days of the struggle.

And a struggle it was! For the King had no intention of yielding his throne. But when, upon the nearby mountain, the sandglass of the Oracle was turned, and the noontime gong of the Temple was struck with a loud bang, the noise of battle abruptly ceased. The black rolling clouds grew purple and then blood-red as they churned around the Palace. They quickly faded to pink and finally to white as they thinned and blew away to the east, and the sun once again lit the city. Who was the victor in that awesome battle? All who were within the Palace had long since fled from the place, and silence fell upon the city as people gathered in the streets and on the rooftops, watching and waiting for a sign.

Then came forth the Avatar in the shape of the year, the Year of the Quill, and it remained before the Palace gates, allowing no one in, save twelve monks of the Temple, sent by the Oracle, while all the Lords and Ministers of the Kingdom, and all the King's Men, and many of the people of the land gathered before the Palace. In some places of the city, there was much fear and panic. Fires broke out, and several shops and market places were looted as a great commotion of violence threatened to overtake the city. But a strange thing happened, and all the people, all but Raynor, stopped whatever they were doing, as if listening intently to something only they could hear. Raynor heard only the soft breeze, no matter how hard he tried to listen.

The gong of the distant Temple rang again, and the doors of the Palace were pushed open from within. First came two monks of the Temple swinging smoky censures. Behind came four more monks bearing on their shoulders a litter upon which lay the figure of a man robed in fine silks. His hands were crossed over his chest, his head adorned with a crown of gold and sapphire. His brown beard, streaked with gray, was carefully combed, and his long hair flowed around his shoulders. Two monks followed the litter, one bearing a scepter studded with jewels that flashed in the sun, and the other held in his outstretched hands the offering of a great sword wrapped with scarlet cloth so that his hands did not touch the blade or the hilt. Strangely, behind these two monks walked a young boy, barefooted and simply dressed, weeping as he followed the litter, his hands covering his face in inconsolable grief.

Behind the young boy, as if at a respectful distance, came the Avatar in the shape of a quill, floating silently along, followed by four more monks bearing an ornate sedan chair. Sitting upon the chair was a glowing form, vaguely in the shape of a man, though no eye could focus upon it to see what manner of man it was. It was the New King, appearing in the same inexplicable countenance as had the Old King during his reign. But the Old King was dead, and, mysteriously, everyone recognized the body as truly that of the Old King, whom they had never seen with their eyes until now at the time of his funeral.

As the procession emerged from the Palace, the people parted and knelt at its passing. Some wept while others trembled, and those who tried to gaze at the New King were struck dumb, and, if they gaped too long, they lost their senses and fell into a deep contemplative swoon from which they would never recover.

The solemn line continued through the streets of Duinnor. As the gong from the distant mountain temple rang out a doleful tone twice every passing minute, the procession made its way through the south gate of the great city. Slowly it crossed the plain, the people of Duinnor following behind, and then it turned to wind its way up Mount Onuma to the steps of the Temple of Beras overlooking the valley. There, at the base of the Temple, the New King descended from his chair, and as the body of the Old King was taken up the stairs to the Temple, he followed.

Inside the stone and glass sanctuary, the Old King was placed on an altar of carved hickory. The monks of the place filed into the great sanctuary. They chanted and lit candles while the priests and priestesses washed the Old King's body and anointed it with oil. They carefully bound his body in linen, taking from him his crown to be placed into the hands of the Oracle.

Meanwhile, on the front portico of the Temple, a lone acolyte pronounced, "The King is Dead!" The gong rang, and the people and all those within the Temple cried out, "Long live the King!" For two hours this was repeated, twice each minute. When the sun reached the forks of the distant snow-covered peaks of the west, the percussionist's soft mallet was replaced by hammers of iron, and with those he beat a rapid cadence upon the gong, loud and harsh, as the body of the Old King was taken up and conveyed outside. The New King and the Avatar remained within as the Old King was carried down the long stairs and along a side way to a place of tombs. There he was laid within a vault beside all the previous Kings of Duinnor. When his crypt was closed and the door of the tomb was put back into place, the banging of the gong ceased, as did all of the chanting, and a profound silence fell over the land as the shadows of the western peaks spread over Duinnor. Above the city, the four Stars of Duinnor shone brightly, then faded and disappeared. This filled the people with fear and wonder, and as night settled upon the land, they made fires at the base of Mount Onuma and all across the plain before that place, and they kept vigil all through the night. Raynor was among them, going around to hear what he could, and even going up to the Temple to watch, if he could, what was taking place there. But the path was blocked by armed monks, and he did not press them.

Those were the days before the King's Academy, and with Raynor were two companions in his tutelage. One was an Elifaen male who had just gone through the Scathing, still weak from his ordeal. The other was a boy of Glareth, and both had come to Raynor to be tutored before joining the ranks of the Kingsmen. Raynor asked them what they were feeling, and they both told him: A great void in their minds, one that had a sound, like the hum of a moth's wings. As they followed Raynor, he kept a close watch upon them, frequently asking what they felt, for their faces expressed confusion and bewilderment and, sometimes, fear.

"You do not feel it, Master?" asked the boy.

"No. I do not. I only sense it in you and in others who are hereabouts."

"Then you are blessed," said his Elifaen student. "For it bends our thoughts painfully as the string bends the bow, and it fills our hearts with perplexing feelings."

At the hour when dawn's eastern light began to show, the pipes of the Temple sounded a long, deep blast, and the gong rolled like thunder. The Oracle emerged from the Temple and stood on the portico as the echoes of the sound faded away.

"The King cometh!" he proclaimed loudly. "Make ready for the King!"

At this, all of the armies of Duinnor marshaled, and all of the Lords and Ministers and Judges of the land and all of the people made ready. As Sir Sun rose from his bed and stretched his bright arms across the land, banners and pennants and streamers of every design and hue were unfurled to the breeze, representing all of the Houses and Lords and Guilds of Duinnor, making the plain between the mountain and the city a tumult of color, while the people thronged to be nearby to the coming procession.

The Oracle cried out, "Behold! King of Kings, Lord High of Duinnor who reigns henceforth as Liege! Let the greatness of Duinnor be proclaimed throughout all of the lands of the earth, unto every corner, from the sea to the mountains. Duinnor the Mighty! Duinnor the Merciful! Duinnor the Bountiful! Duinnor the Just! Let it be thus as a sign to all people, that Duinnor thrives in the Heavens as upon the Earth! Receive your King!"

A brilliant flash of light appeared overhead, outshining the new sun. Five stars appeared, all in an arc high over the city, where before there had only been four. This sight brought forth cheers and clapping from the crowds which lasted many moments until the Temple pipes were blown once again and the mighty gong rang. The Oracle then cried out, lifting up his staff to those Five Stars, "All hail the King!"

Then the King himself came forth from the Temple, his robes and his figure shining so much like the sun that none could look upon him. The Oracle stepped aside, bowing, and then came the Avatar in the shape of a silver chalice, and it hovered beside the New King as a great and mighty roar of approval swelled upward from the plains and from all around. Together the two mysterious beings descended the steps as those gathered at the base of the Temple bowed down and averted their eyes. All but the Kingsmen did this, and one other person. The Kingsmen took up their places, shoulder to shoulder, lining both sides of the way, shields up and swords drawn, sternly facing the crowds with their backs to the

King's procession. The other who did not bow or turn away was a wizened old man with long white hair and matching beard. Walking barefoot, and dressed in a plain brown robe, he descended the long stairs of the Temple some distance behind the New King and the Avatar, his head up confidently. At the base of the stairs, the New King ascended his sedan chair and was lifted up by four monks. The three, the Avatar, the New King, and the old man, continued along the straight road to the city, going between the lines of Kingsmen who repeatedly cried out in unison, "Hail, King of Duinnor!" And this was loudly echoed by the crowds who also cheered and cried out, "Long live the King!"

As the King's procession moved toward the city, trumpets blared forth joyous calls, and all of the bells and gongs of the city rang his welcome.

• • •

"Perhaps my appearance is symbolic in a number of ways," the King was musing, "for I am surrounded by secrets and mysteries, deceptions and subterfuge. Some are of my own making. And some are imposed upon me by the fact of my existence. But the deceptions and secrets of others play against my will, and that I will not tolerate!"

"No, King," Lord Banis uttered. Raynor detected a sharp tone in the King's voice, a note that only one of Raynor's peculiar abilities might hear.

"But am I so different from the others who have gone before me? I shape and am shaped by time and by history. And though I must respond to the needs that arise, I also insist that my will, the will of the Throne, be done."

"The Throne of Duinnor is one thing, Sire," said Raynor, "and he who sits upon it yet another. The demands of one are not always the desires of the other. And the needs of one may sometimes overwhelm the needs of the other so that both are hindered."

Raynor, whose eyes were now keen upon the King, saw the form beneath the golden veil turn, and he perceived somewhat of a face looking at him.

"Whether I was ever a Man, or whether I was ever one of the Faerekind, or even some other creature, is of little consequence. I am no longer that which I was before, so long ago. Few who knew me then remain in this world. Who I was is forgotten to them. And the name by which they knew me was never written in any books. It is as if I never existed. But I did not take this mantle willingly, nor did I defeat the Old King with pleasure in my heart. I was called to the throne by those very powers which sought to preserve the Old King's reign. I became the fruit of his dread, just as he was brought to the throne by the actions of his predecessor. It is as all Kings of Duinnor have done since he that first sat upon the throne. Long ago it was, and many generations of men passed away under my reign before I saw the truth of my fate, that I am to go the same way as they did. And there," a filament of thread shot out toward the Avatar and then snapped back into the spinning glow, "there is my ever-present reminder, the image of an event. A loop of chain, pulling as effortlessly as a grain of sand that falls through an hourglass pulls upon the next grain, linking every other loop, every other grain, every other event to my fate. But I have grown wise. To others, the Avatar may be a sign of some threat to my rule, but to me it is a clue to my own preservation, if I but see it as such. Duinnor is great because I understand these things. Duinnor is greater than ever before because its King is greater than all others who went before. The world of Men will be greater, still, and shall have true dominion over all the earth under my rule. That, then, is my will. The will of Duinnor!"

Raynor felt the conflict that ate away at the King. In spite of his disguise, somewhere, there was a heart with passion and, thus, with feeling. "Oh, if only I had had this meeting centuries ago!" Raynor thought with sadness. "What might have been averted?"

"King," he spoke instead, "surely you recall much that others have forgotten. But have you not also been forgetful? Or did you never know life as people live it? Do those who surround you show only avarice and ambition? Do they only serve your power as an increase to their own? What of those who care not for the power that wealth or station may wield, but who use what wealth and power they have for the well-being of their families and neighbors? What of those who seek to alleviate pain and to relieve suffering? Is there not power at work within them? And by their ministries, do they not spread and increase a sort of wealth? And what of those whose work and effort bring good living to all, kith and kin alike? Others, too, who, by their longsuffering efforts, by their patience and faith, bring fair and just arbitration to those in need of it, and resolve deep matters without the resort of arms or cruelty. Do they not serve you, too? And better? They are many, oh King, with names great and famous and names unknown. And they struggle daily, here in this Realm of Duinnor and also abroad, for the honor of the Seven Realms. Does not Lord Tallin, whose House is of another land, defend your throne today as he and his sons did in the past? He pours out his wealth like water to put out the fires that threaten the throne. And Vanara, ancient and noble, chafing under the yoke of foreigners who abuse their honor and swindle them of their lands and the fruits thereof. Do they not still honor your law? Do they not still stand against the dreaded armies of the Dragonkind, with little aid or hope of aid, to defend your empire? What do these good and loyal subjects ask that is so much? Is fairness so heavy a thing that the might and power of Duinnor must strain for it? Is it so shadowed and vague that the Stars of Duinnor may not illuminate it? Let not the legendary justice of the Kings of Duinnor fade from memory! Let not those who care not for honor tarnish this worthy land! For what honor is there in power without justice? In authority without moderation? In strength without restraint? Where is honor when the loyal are stripped of dignity and their pleas for redress are ignored? I beg the King to look upon all of his people, the low and the high, and hear them. Judge yourself their deeds, not only their words. Let the King call forth the Congress of the Seven Realms, as was done in the days of yore, and let him preside over their petitions and to grant righteous justice unto all his subjects!"

"Your impertinence is boundless! That you should give me such a speech!"

Raynor judged rightly, for his risky lecture did not solicit anger from the King. Indeed, as he foresaw, the King was shaken, and his voice carried the intonation of mild shock, mixed with amusement, and a tiny bit of...doubt? Yes, and it was that doubt, the mightiest of all subtleties, that gave Raynor hope. For Doubt's dream, whether dark or light, is one filled with possibilities, and its offspring is Change. Too often was Doubt made the servant of shadow, but she was not loyal only to Secundur, Raynor knew, but served faithfully any who called her forth.

"Are all your kind so fervent?" the King went on. "Do all Melnari share your power of words? So convincing, full of such soft provocation! No wonder so many consider the Melnari dangerous, and consider them to be full of sorcery and guile."

Raynor did not respond and needed to say no more. Long after he was taken away to his fate, his words would continue to do their work. The King moved toward the curtain.

"But you are right. I do remember. I do remember life and those who were once my friends. Those who helped me come to this place and gave me their friendship and honor. I remember my mother's lips upon my cheek, and my father's hand in my own. I remember much from before. Like you, I do not sleep. I do not take food, nor do I drink. I do not see as I did before, nor do I feel as I once did. Those temptations do not exist for me, and no longer am I weak as others are. Yes, I remember. Your words do not provoke me, nor can any action you take threaten me. But I have heard enough. This interview is concluded. I leave you to Banis who has his own business with you."

Baffled and somewhat disappointed that the encounter was suddenly ended, Raynor bowed, and the King receded behind the green curtain. Lord Banis rose, and when he turned, Raynor saw that his face was red with embarrassment and insult. The doors of the chamber opened at the hand of the outside guards, and four of them lined the way as Raynor was motioned out. Lord Banis remained behind, and the doors shut again. The guards hurried Raynor along and into a side door, then down a different steep winding staircase than the one he had earlier ascended, one that became darker the deeper they went. The mystic knew where he was being taken, and when they came out of the stairs, he was nudged along a damp corridor, the sound of dripping water echoing from some vague source, the stench of waste and rot rising from the grimy floor. They passed many iron-shod doors, and, here and there, gaunt faces pressed against tiny barred windows to peer out at the passing group. They came to a wider torch-lit chamber filled with instruments of pain. Around this room, along the walls, men and women were chained, hanging limply from their cuffs, many bearing the obvious wounds of their abuse. Most of them raised their heads weakly, their faces completely blank, to watch Raynor's arrival. But a few, he saw, were already dead.

"This place is an outrage! An outrage against the honor of Duinnor!" he cried out loudly, glaring at the guards. The guards were stunned by his outburst, but the jailor gave Raynor a shove.

"Get on! An' shut up!"

Stumbling from the roughness of the shove, Raynor smiled, satisfied that his outburst had its intended effect.

"I shall not resist," he said gently, "and nor should you." The fire in the jailor's eyes subsided as he looked at Raynor, and his mouth opened as if to ask a question. The guards looked on, puzzled at why the jailor did not smash Raynor's head with his cudgel.

"Well, then," said the jailor, blinking as Raynor broke his gaze from him. "This way, if ye please."

Raynor was taken into another corridor, and then upward along a sloping incline to a dark passage where the guards picked up torches to light the way. The jailor took his ring of keys and opened a cell door. Raynor entered readily, turning to face the others.

"I've been told this ain't yer first visit," said the jailor gruffly, "so ye very likely recall how things work around here. Water and food once a day, if yer good. Ye clean yer own mess through the hole yonder. New straw twice a month, or when we get around to it. No talkin', no noise, no hummin', no whistlin', and no whimperin'. Ye get no writin' stuff, er books er anythin' of the sort. What ye have, ye have. No visitors 'cept Lord Banis, if he deigns. Enjoy yer stay!"

As the door was slammed and locked, the room went dark, and Raynor stood still, waiting for his eyes to grow accustomed to the deep gloom. There was not a window, unlike his previous accommodation here. Banis must have grown wiser to Raynor's communication skills. The room remained pitch black. He sighed and gave the jewel on his ring a little twist, and a soft blue glow appeared within it, growing brighter as he clenched his fist. When his ring gave enough light, he unclenched his hand and looked around. The ceiling was about as damp as the floor, only a few inches above his head. The room was not quite as wide as his outstretched arms, and, if he stretched out onto the floor, his feet would touch the door while his head bumped the far wall.

"Well. It's a good thing I left my hat behind!" he mused, smiling to himself. He closed his eyes as a slight worry crossed his mind. He had many worries; some were deep and powerful, having to do with unfolding history, and others were quite small, such as his concern not to get grime on his clothes. But the one that pierced his heart at that moment was quite personal. The kind of concern one would have for a dear friend, hoping he was safe and well, yet knowing he was, in point of fact, in very great danger.

Chapter 3

The Intruder

Ignorance is a necessary element of arrogance, and it is that element, so often voluntary in the conceited, and manifesting itself in ways great and small, that may cause the high to stumble and the mighty to be cast down. The arrogant, too preoccupied with weighty matters, will eventually fail to take notice of some small but vital thing, or, if they do observe it, may have no reaction to it. So it was that the King, once again behind his curtain, and Lord Banis, stinging from the King's rebuke as he left the High Chamber, both failed to take notice of Raynor's hat, sitting incongruously in the corner of the room, its peaked tip sagged over at an angle. As the light behind the curtain faded away with the King's retreat to some other recess of the tower, Lord Banis made his way downward to his awaiting guest. The black eagle remained, looked over its shoulder away toward the distant mountains, then turned its gaze again to the object across the room that he, keen-eyed, had been watching all the while. Now, left on its own, it leaned down from the ledge, stretching out its neck, and opened its beak to emit a snake-like hiss. As it was about to drop down into the room for a closer look, something made it flinch upright. The bird hopped around to face the other way. It flapped its powerful wings and took to the air with a quick glance over its shoulder, as if being shooed away. Rising up and up on ascending currents of air, the creature circled the tower twice, then bore away to the southwest on a long smooth glide toward the mountains as another dark bird gracefully circled over the tower and slowly descended.

The chamber was quiet, the curtain that divided it was dark, and the afternoon sun tossed a peaceful beam across the room. That was how things remained for many moments. Then, almost imperceptibly, the hat moved. A moment later, it moved again, and the front brim lifted from the floor just an inch before falling back down. The hat jumped up and down, moving along the floor a foot or so until a pink nose appeared under the brim, twitching rapidly. With a bit more effort, the creature had its eyes uncovered, its ears still pushed down by the brim, and it looked around. Beauchamp then raised himself up with all the power he could muster and sent the hat backwards off of his body. He darted away a foot or so and crouched as low as he could and still be on his toes, his eyes bulging with alarm, his nose twitching continuously, his ears raised and cocked forward. He took in every scent, scoured the place for any sound, and watched for the slightest threatening movement. Only the most sensitive nose would be offended by such a slight presence, but to Beauchamp the place still reeked of the black eagle, an awful perversion of what a bird should smell like, much worse than the little Certina, he noted to himself. But the odor faded rapidly as a fresh breeze puffed in, jostling the green curtain that divided the place. The odd door floating before him was disconcerting, at first. But it did not move. Beauchamp approached it and sniffed. It had no odor, which was even more disconcerting. His opinion was that things ought to have a smell. How was one to be a proper judge of a thing without a smell? He edged closer for a nibble, but just when he was about to do so, the door moved away an inch. Beauchamp flattened defensively. It was only a slight movement, barely enough to cause alarm. He stretched his neck out for another try. The door inched away once more. Sitting back on his haunches, he figured it did not want to be nibbled, which was also unusual for a thing. How was one to judge a thing unless it could be nibbled? This was most disconcerting, but there was nothing threatening about the door's slight movement away from the rabbit. Beauchamp decided it was not of interest.

More relaxed, he glanced around, then began to give himself a wash. Although Raynor was the most fastidious person he had ever met, the mystic was nowhere close to Beauchamp's most basic standards, and being cooped up in that old hat was simply intolerable, even if it had been necessary. Not that it was really old; the hat was actually fairly new, by Raynor's way of thinking, his previous one having been chewed to bits long ago. Still, a hat's a hat, full of the stuffy smell of silk-lined wool and hair tonic. How he then managed not to be killed when Banis struck Raynor was itself nothing short of a miracle, for he was a delicate thing. But Beauchamp had sense enough to smell danger, and he knew that often the best way to avoid harm was to be utterly still. After Beauchamp had nudged the hat into the corner, while Raynor distracted the King, the rabbit had done just that, remaining so still as to hardly even breathe. Not that he wished to breathe overly much inside the stuffy thing. Now that he was outside of it, and getting himself cleaned up, with fresh air flowing in through the window, he was beginning to feel much better. He washed his face with his paws, then tugged one then the other ear down to give each a good scrub, too, all the while keeping an eye on his surroundings. One could not be too cautious, after all.

Once his grooming was complete, he continued to gaze at the curtain before him, and he stretched out to lie flat, his legs out as far as they would spread fore and aft. The tile felt good, and he almost dozed, so peaceful was the room and so refreshing the cool floor. Eventually, his curiosity overcame him. He rose, stretched again with a broad yawn, and then hopped over to the curtain, his nails lightly clicking as he went. The breeze ruffled the curtain slightly, and Beauchamp gave it a sniff and a nudge. It was a thin light-green material, apparently of the same stuff that Raynor's house robe was made of. He nudged the hem, which just touched the floor, and gave it a little nibble. No, it was different stuff, much easier to shred. He gave it another nudge, low down, until he got his nose under it, and then he tossed it up. After only a couple of tries, crouching low, he head-tossed the curtain, and it at last fell across his back so that Beauchamp could see behind it. Right in front of him was the Throne of Duinnor.

Other than the King, and the previous kings of yore, Beauchamp's eyes were very likely the first from outside this tower to behold it for over six centuries. To Beauchamp it was just a chair, like any other, one of the odd objects that people used. That it was the Throne of Duinnor, seat of the mightiest ruler in all the lands, impressed him not at all, though he well knew what it was. He was anything but an arrogant or conceited creature, too humble to care much for such things, rather than too proud, even if it had been the finest, most jewel-bespeckled, silk-cushioned seat ever made.

Which it was not. It was a plain, straight-backed chair of wood, with slats for its seat, held together by pegs. Beauchamp raised up on his hind legs and the curtain slid from his back. He hopped closer to have a look at the dusty thing—no one had sat on it for quite a long time—then he crouched by one of its cobweb-draped legs and gnawed at it for a few moments. It was not even a very tasty chair, definitely not made of any kind of fruitwood, probably ash or oak, or some other particularly tough and unsatisfying grain. He sat back on his haunches. There was not much else to see. Another window to the left, an identical mate to the one on the other side of the curtain, but its stained glass was securely shut. The same cool tile and bare stone walls, the same high arched ceiling. A bit darker since the window was closed. But there were doors, one to the right and about halfway down the long room, another one all the way at the end, and one to the left, just beyond the window. That door was ajar, and through it a beam of sunlight etched a golden line across the floor. Hopping over to it, Beauchamp pushed through and emerged outside onto a balcony of stone. Even standing as high as he could muster, the banister was still too high for him to see over, but the sky above was very blue, he noted. The floor of the balcony was littered with years of grime, and so thick it was in the corners that several dandelions struggled to hoist their yellow blooms through a thin layer of snow. Beauchamp hopped over to them and neatly trimmed the stalks with pleasure, each in turn disappearing stem first, bloom last, into his mouth. As he munched, he thought about Raynor and worried over what had become of him, remembering his instructions.

"Do what you have so often done before," Raynor had said to him as they followed the Avatar through the streets. "Remain still and quiet. And, when you have the chance, take a look around."

From under the stuffy hat, Beauchamp gave a light oink.

"True enough," Raynor replied, adjusting Beauchamp as he clung to Raynor's scalp, "but we've been in danger before. And, if we become separated, do as you have always done before."

Beauchamp hated being separated from Raynor, and he could not help but worry whenever his companion went out without him. True, Raynor and Beauchamp had been separated before, many times, and the last time was for a very long while, indeed. Oh, how Raynor rejoiced when Beauchamp finally made it home after so, so long! But that separation was due to a long chain of unfortunate accidents and mishaps. This was different, Raynor had asked him to take a look around, and he intended to do just that. Still, Beauchamp was not happy about it, and he softly oinked again as he peered back inside the High Chamber, trying to push away his frets. He had a job to do, he thumped determinedly, and he would not let Raynor down.

Though everything appeared peaceful enough, one should always be careful in any unfamiliar place. He hopped to the center of the room and looked back at the open door at the far end. Suddenly there was a sound, and Beauchamp flattened into a long crouch, ready to spring away. A figure walked out of the open door and briskly moved down the room and to the door on the right. He opened it and went in. It was a man of about average height, fairly young, wearing common breeches and a loose-fitting blouse. Miraculously, he did not see the terrified Beauchamp, so intent he was on some book that he was reading. As soon as he disappeared into the room, Beauchamp made a dash for the wall, retreating against the curtain, and crouched again. The figure re-emerged, with more books under his arm, and pulled the door to before hurrying back to the far room.

Beauchamp remained where he was for many moments, his ears twisting in all directions to scoop in every sound, his eyes wide and bulging, and his little heart racing. At last he calmed, hearing only the slight brush of the curtain against the floor as the air from the open window jostled it softly. He soothed his panic even more by grooming his flank. He was perfectly inclined to carry out Raynor's wishes, being a naturally curious creature, and so he hopped to the side door, pausing every few feet to watch and listen. When he arrived, he found that the gray door was slightly ajar. He put his head to the crack and gave it a little nudge. It was heavy, so he bit it. He bit it again, taking off a tiny piece from its edge. Sitting upright, chewing, he thought that it was an entirely unsatisfying door, probably made of the same stuff as the old chair. But there was something different, too. It was not very much like wood at all, in fact. He sniffed, then licked the place he had just bitten, noting a layer of red revealed by the tiny gouge he had made. He gave the nick a nudge, and another gray fleck fell away revealing more red paint. It was exactly the color of the other door, the one that

Raynor called the Avatar. Beauchamp shrugged then batted the door with both front paws, coaxing it to open a little more. Just as he was about halfway through, he heard a sound behind him, and with renewed panic he charged into the room, darting this way and that, and then under a low cabinet just as the door swung fully open and the person walked in again. Shrinking against the back legs of the cabinet, he crouched, his nose wiggling and his eyes bugging in fear, watching the feet and pants of the man go right past him and then cross to the far side of the room.

Beauchamp could only see up to the man's shins, but he heard him shuffling some things about. In spite of his fear, the timid creature's nose twitched at a familiar and comforting aroma quite nearby. Glancing to the side, he saw the source of the smell: A book! Of all the objects of people, books were his favorite things. One of these objects had been dropped—an old one, the best kind—and it had somehow gotten kicked or shoved underneath the cabinet where, judging by the dust, it had remained undisturbed for years and years. It lay open, and a few pages were wedged against the low bottom of the cabinet. Unable to resist, Beauchamp slinked over to it and gave it a sniff and a rub with his chin. Stretching out his neck, he was just able to reach one of the pages, and he took a little nibble. It was quite palatable, he thought, and he took another and another bite. Very comforting, books were. Just the thing when one was nervous or worried, something about the refined and pressed fibers, perhaps, or the musty bouquet of deterioration. And old books, like this one, were indeed the very best. This one was not as good as *his* book, the one Raynor had given him. But it really was not half bad. Absorbed in his rapture, he did not notice the feet on the other side of the room when they turned around to face his way.

"What's that?" the person said.

Beauchamp froze, mid-munch, a shred of paper protruding from his mouth, his eyes bulging once more. The person approached, and Beauchamp tensed even more, ready to flee. He saw the man get down onto his knees. A hand reached under the cabinet and felt around. Fingers found the corner of the book and as it was dragged out, Beauchamp hurled himself against the back wall, cringing. The hand and the book disappeared from view.

"So that's where this got off to. I've been looking for this for ages! Uh, oh. What's this along the edge? Don't tell me we've got rats in the tower!"

He got to his feet, and Beauchamp watched him return to the other side of the room. After a few more moments, the man left the way he had come. Beauchamp immediately went to the edge of the cabinet and peered out. The door was wide open, tempting him to make a hasty exit. But he chided himself for not being careful and for letting his guard down. He quickly chewed the shred of paper, still dangling from his mouth. I must do my job, he reminded himself as he swallowed, and then find my way out of here. His nose twitched as he came fully out from under the cabinet, and the familiar aroma of books continued to comfort him. This place can't be all that bad, he concluded, looking around.

In fact, it was a library of sorts, with stacks of scrolls and books piled onto shelves and tables and chairs and scattered around on the floor, too. There was a stained glass window on the far side, and many oil lamps burning brightly. It was a large room, and Beauchamp took his time going about it, cautiously exploring between the rows of shelves, sniffing the furniture, and, just to get the flavor of the place, taking a nibble now and then from a table leg or a bookcase. But it was, in spite of the books, rather uninteresting to Beauchamp, and he eventually found his way back near to where he had seen the man standing. It was just a table, pushed against some shelves. He stood on his hind legs, trying to peer over it, but it was too tall, and even the scrolls that draped over its edge were out of reach of his mouth. He turned around and sat. The door was still wide open, and his ears detected no sound. He hopped to it and stopped, glancing back to his former hiding place under the cabinet. Going to the door, he looked around it and heard a scratching sound, so slight that only his own ears could have heard it, coming from the room farther on along. But it was distinct enough for Beauchamp to recognize as the scratching of a pen, a sound he often heard coming from Raynor as he sat at his desk. He crouched, glancing again toward his hiding place, hesitating before going through the door.

It was only then that he noticed how odd the cabinet was, the one he had hidden under. It was something like a cupboard, only much wider than it was tall. Above its base was a polished front of dark wood, and above that was a long glass case. Behind the glass were many glinting objects that immediately riveted Beauchamp's attention as he bolted upright on his hind legs.

The objects were round, about the size of large daisy blossoms, arranged in orderly lines. Like golden flowers, each had a center of some other color, some green like fresh parsley, some purple as violets. Some of them were blue like the sky, and others had centers like glittering red apples, while others were amber like golden honey, and others were white, like the clear crystals that hung from Raynor's lamps, shimmering in the light. These were curious things, indeed! And Beauchamp perked up at the sight of them, hopped a bit closer, and stood up, stretching his neck and stepping forward and backward on his hind legs to keep his balance. He could not count very well. Raynor had been trying to teach him, though Beauchamp always got muddled after six. But Raynor kept trying, anyway, and Beauchamp did, too. Now, he tried very hard to count. He fell down onto all fours and stood again. No, there were too many. He tried and tried, and lost himself in the effort as surely as if he was gnawing on his favorite book. It did not help that the green ones were such a delicious green, and his eyes kept going back to them as if they were inviting him to taste them. To nibble them would be impossible, of course, for he could never get to them. But each row had a green one, and there were plenty of them, if only he *could* get to them. The blue ones looked inviting, too, but the green ones were surely the most delectable. Suddenly he realized that he had counted the green ones without even thinking. There were five of them. Surely that was plenty, a stupendous number, quite a large quantity, nearly the greatest amount, as far as he was concerned, that there could possibly be.

Beauchamp's little mind fairly boggled at the trove! And there they were, just out of reach. His head spun with the desire to taste the green ones, and each one placed right between a blue one and a red one, which were looking better and better, too, although just as unreachable.

Wait!

He shook his head, fell to all fours, then bounced straight back up, twisting his body around as if full of electricity, shaking his head once more. He ran a tight circle, then raised up to look again. Yes! There were five of the blue ones and five of the red ones! A cornucopia of delight! In fact, as he stared with growing amazement, he saw just as many of the others as there were of the green ones. Unbelievable! His brain truly spun at the inconceivable number, his head dizzy with desire for them, and, after all the exertion of looking and counting and longing for a taste, he was fairly done in. Not knowing what to do, whether to bound or binky, he flopped over onto his side to rest.

Normally, he spent most of his daylight hours dozing. Night-time, too, since his preferred activity time was at the endings and the beginnings of each day. He was not accustomed to exertions such as this, at this time of day. To be so alert and ready to hide or flee at a moment's notice was exhausting, true. But, worse, it interrupted his daily routine. And Beauchamp reveled in habit. There was a time to eat, a time to explore, a time to play, to meditate, and to sleep. At the moment, by all that was right, he knew that he ought to be sleeping, stretched out beside Raynor's couch or balled up beneath his desk. And, before very long, it would be time for a nice meal of timothy hay and, if Raynor remembered, perhaps a raisin or two for dessert.

It was very quiet, but as Beauchamp drifted in thought, his eyes half-closed, his left ear turned toward the door. Eventually, the sound, only perceptible to that ear, filtered to his attention. Getting up, he stretched his body as long as it would stretch, gave a wide yawn, and hopped back to the open door. After a quick glance outside, he moved along the wall to the far corner, then on to the open door down the way. He sniffed the door frame, crouching, and stepped closer to peer inside.

It was a small room and was much like Raynor's bedchamber. There was no bed, but there were several tall wardrobes and, directly across from the door, a writing table. There the man sat, his back to Beauchamp, scratching away with pen and ink. The man paused, heaved a great sigh, and shook his head. Another figure appeared, the King, resplendent in his golden cocoon-like robes, so that Beauchamp, now squinting, could discern no features. The King approached the table, giving it additional illumination far greater than the oil lamp on the desk.

"Sire, my abilities are inadequate to the task. Surely there are others better trained, with greater knowledge than I."

"You have done well. Yes, there are others I could call that are more learned. But you can be trusted, and they cannot."

"Your loyal servants are countless, surely."

"Loyalty and trust are not the same. Even the loyal and the faithful may be tempted and bribed. Those who cannot be purchased may be deceived by their own hearts, and even the ones who are steady and without illusion may be too timid to speak to me. But you, like Raynor, are Melnari, and may speak frankly. You have no reason to lie or to deceive. And you have no fear of my power. Although I am older than you, I am not immortal as you are. I will tell you a secret about the Melnari that even the others of your kind do not know. There have been twelve of you. Ashlord, Raynor, and the other four that he named. Though they do not know it, I have deduced that the Melnari come into the world in pairs. They first appeared on the very first day of the Year of the Inkwell."

"Was that not the year that the First King of Duinnor came to the throne?"

"That is so. See? You do know history, somewhat at least. When the First King came, he was given the Avatar and a servant, as every King as been given since. It was a condition ordained by Beras, through His Oracle. But there are stipulations. The servant could never be physically touched by the King, lest the King should die. The servant would be immune to all the powers of the King. All of this I discovered when I became King. But I have learned more. You have a twin. Each Melnari does. This the Oracle did not explain to me, but I learned of it nonetheless.

"On the day you were brought forth to me, your brother was also brought forth, in some unknown place. Both of you came into being in the likeness of a Man. You came to me first as a youth in his prime, but, by day's end, you were a wizened old man. Your twin, I have come to believe, began as an old man and probably ended his first day as a youngster. Whereas you must remain in these chambers while I am King, lest you die, your twin is free to roam the wide world. Whereas you are bound by your Creator to serve only me, your twin may choose his own way, to serve or not, owing no allegiance but what he freely gives. And, as your twin slowly ages with the passing years, you grow younger. As he grows in confidence and in power and knowledge, you become less assured, less skillful. And more forgetful."

The youngster took it in, nodding as the King spoke. "I see. Yes. That makes sense to me, somewhat. Yes. It does. I once easily calculated the way of things. I remember that I did. But now I struggle. I once understood great affairs. But I fear they are now beyond me."

"When we first came here," the King went on, "I did not know these things. In the early years of our rule we did many wise and good things for Duinnor and for all the Realms. Your wisdom and patience were profound, and guided me in my judgments. Over time, things changed. I have become, through the years, wiser than I was before and, through your guidance, a better ruler. Although my body did not advance in age, I have changed."

"And what will become of me when…if…"

"When I lose the Throne?"

"Yes."

"When I am put into my tomb, you will take your place among the Stars of Duinnor."

"I see. And which is my twin?"

"Ashlord is your twin."

"Oh! Oh, my! And if something happens to him? To Ashlord?"

"Do not worry. Your lives are not connected in that manner. You do not feel his pain or suffering, nor does he sense your existence at all. I know that if he were destroyed, you would be unharmed. Except for the fact of your existence, bound with his own creation, you have nothing to do with him."

"Why do you tell me this?"

"Because I now see what has happened. I have watched you grow younger and younger. But at first I did not understand that as the years came off of your age, so, too, would your wisdom diminish. I began to trust more in those who Raynor claims are untrustworthy."

"But do you not see into their hearts so that nothing is hidden from you?"

"My powers wane as yours do. Yes, I may still speak into their hearts and even hear their thoughts. But, as with you, I understand less of what I see and hear. So great was my power in the past, and still remains, that I am still feared. But some suspect, perhaps even know, that I do not see as I once did, nor do I disturb their minds as I once did. And now all seek to deceive me."

"Why have you not told me before?"

"I have. But you are forgetful."

"Oh. And so, just when you need me the most, I am of least use to you."

"As King, perhaps. But there are many ways a person may serve another. Ways that may be more valuable than any servant can be to any king."

"How do you mean?"

"I mean that in all the centuries of my rule, having lost every friend that I ever knew before, I have come to have at least one who has been my faithful companion all along."

"Oh, sire! Surely that is the highest honor one may have."

Beauchamp, if nothing else, was a good listener. His ability to hear a gnat buzzing at twenty yards or even, on a still night, the faintest whoosh of a falling star, was quite natural for him, a sense even more acute than those other creatures whose form he took. But hearing and listening are not the same, for to listen is to add something, some effort to one's hearing so that something of what is heard is comprehended. Through his listening, he was able to spend hours with Raynor, understanding his companion's life. The subtle turn of page, the scratch of pen, the soft pace of the mystic's shoes across the floor spoke as much to Beauchamp as did words. Through these sounds, he perceived mood and inclination, and he anticipated actions. The language of the spoken word was Beauchamp's special gift. Like Certina, and all others of their kind, he heard all words in the First Tongue, regardless of the language or dialect of the speaker, and so he understood all. He could only speak to Raynor; at least, he had only ever been inclined to speak to Raynor. And when Certina had visited, the little bird's ability to converse with Raynor made Beauchamp quite put out. It did not help when Raynor, as gently as he could, suggested that to communicate with others was not so much a matter of ability than of will, and that Certina was certainly strong-willed.

Now, as he listened to the gentle exchange between King and servant, he felt an odd urge to join the conversation. As they spoke, he put his head down and rested his chin on the floor. They did not seem all that bad, he thought, once you just listened.

"And the Avatar? What becomes of it?"

Beauchamp heard a little chuckle, and from its tone he could tell that it accompanied a shrug.

"It will serve and torment the next King."

Beauchamp turned an eye across the room toward the green curtain. The window on the other side now threw a portion of its beam across the length of it, shining through a verdant glow. Suddenly, Beauchamp stood. Time to go! He scampered back through the curtains with his nails clicking on the tile as he went.

"What's that?" he heard the King say. The room lit up with the King's presence, and Beauchamp's own shadow shot out in front of him. The rabbit bounded straight for the curtain and dove under it to the other side. He did not notice, in his panic, the great black bird now sitting on the window ledge, taking a keen interest.

"Intruder!"

The doors were flung open and guards streamed in, their pikes at the ready, but Beauchamp shot between their legs.

"Stop that creature!"

The Kingsmen pounded the floor with their pikes in a confused effort to impale him, but Beauchamp zagged and zigged, and when the soldiers farther along drew their swords, he zipped out of the way. Blades rang on the floor sending sparks and stone splinters flying just behind him. He turned sharply, seeing a large doorway, and slid across the marble, his feet beating a cadence for purchase, the soldiers stumbling and tripping past him. It was the landing of a grand spiral stair that he darted for, but just as he got to it he saw more soldiers charging up. Spinning around, his ears flat, he circled around the feet of one soldier and flashed between the legs of another whose sword-tip jabbed the floor right beside him. Shouting and cursing, and hardly believing their own eyes, the soldiers careened into each other. But suddenly Beauchamp sensed another shape, a dark shadow more terrifying than the jabbing swords. Dodging a kick, the rabbit ran from right to left, oinking loudly, oblivious to the new cries of dismay coming from the soldiers. Then, the black shape covered him, talons clutched his body, and he heard the awful sweep of powerful wings as he was lifted up and carried through the air.

"Stop that bird!"

But it was too late, and the bird's wings too powerful. It flew through the window and out from the tower, flapping hard to carry its heavy load.

Beauchamp fainted.

• • •

Unaware of the tumult above, and oblivious to the pandemonium that Raynor's companion was spreading throughout the Palace, Lord Banis, having spent many minutes recovering his composure, now calmly stood in Raynor's cell. He had dismissed the jailor, who had placed a candle into a niche in the wall, but the guards remained just outside.

"The last time you were with us," Lord Banis was saying, his eyes dark upon Raynor who was standing but three feet away, "you had more spacious accommodations, I believe."

"What do you want, Banis?"

"I want to know where my daughter is."

"Esildre?"

"She was last seen traveling eastward with two of her kin."

"Your daughter goes wherever she wishes to go."

"You see, that's just it, isn't it? She has spent the better part of two hundred years avoiding travel. Isolating herself in her shadowed castle far up in the mountains, shunning visitors, capturing a few others, I hear it told, communicating with none outside her estate. Not even with her father."

"Perhaps she valued solitude during that time. And perhaps she no longer considers you her father."

"Do not provoke me. The King will not save you a second time."

Raynor smiled in the dim light, and Banis could see it was a smile without fear.

"Suddenly," Banis went on, "Esildre ends her seclusion and comes to Duinnor. And of all the places she could visit after so long an absence from the world, it was the Temple she went to. Where you met with her."

"She went there because she needed a safe place in Duinnor."

"And she could not find such a place in her own home?"

"Her home is not in Duinnor. And you well know that the safety she sought was that of others who might encounter her, not for herself. You, of all people, can hardly be unaware of her curse, since it came about by your effort to join your House with that of the Enemy."

"I do not know what you mean. Her liaison with Secundur, if that is who you mean, was of her own making. Their falling out from each other was likewise."

"Was it not you who coaxed her to go to Shatuum? When Islindia rejected Secundur, you thought to promote yourself by offering Esildre to him. For centuries you tried to convince her. And you almost did, and Secundur, too, coming to her by night with his attentions. Then the lands were attacked by the Dragonkind, and when Queen Serith Ellyn rallied the west, and she and the Fifth King sent their armies to Tulith Attis, Esildre and her brother Navis went with them. This angered Secundur. That she should choose duty to her Queen over his entreaties. And it was a serious blow to your designs. It was many years before you could once again resume your plans. By that time the current King had taken the throne, and you had grown powerful in Duinnor. All this I have learned from Esildre herself, and from others, and the rest is plain."

"I see that you were more than a tutor to her," Banis said with sarcasm. "But what you say is unimportant."

"Is it? Esildre now knows the true fate of her brother, your son. Yet she refuses to believe your role in her brother's murder. Yes, I said murder."

Banis stiffened, and Raynor could see his face redden. But Raynor did not give him a chance to recover.

"Navis was my pupil, too, as you know. And when Esildre at last took up with Secundur in the land of Shatuum, he was determined to go to her and bring her away from that place. I tried to dissuade him from his quest, knowing that only Esildre could set herself free, and that any effort by Navis would be fraught with danger and apt to fail. But he was hotheaded, determined, and strong-willed. And he was not without high connections. He pleaded with the Court for support to find his sister. The King's advisors argued against Navis, saying that any attempt would anger Secundur against Duinnor. But one advisor took the case before the King. That was you. And the King gave permission. A guide was found to lead Navis to the border, and five stalwart men were chosen by you to accompany him. When his party reached the deep forest gorge that divides the frontiers of Duinnor from the territories of Shatuum, they made camp and prepared for the next day's crossing of the gorge. That night, the men with Navis set upon him while he slept, killing him with their swords. They threw his body and all of his belongings over the cliff. Later that night, they tarried, making their plans so that they would tell the same story when they returned. One of the murderers, the guide hired to show them the way, gave drink to the others. When they were made drunk, he cut their throats so that only he remained. He alone returned, saying that the others had gone on into Shatuum but, having guided them as far as the border, Navis had released him to return."

Banis listened without further reaction as Raynor continued.

"Years later, the guide was rewarded with lucrative contracts to acquire property and wealth. He kept his secret well, and so did the advisor to the King, you, who had hired him and who rewarded the assassin. Both rose to have great power, and one, that is, you, eventually became First Lord of the High Chamber. That was when you began working against your former associate, convincing him that you would be immune to any blackmail on his part but holding over him proof that he was the murderer of your son. Thus, under threat of exposure, he was forced to do your bidding. I am sure you are wondering how I came to know all of this."

"You speculate wildly. I did encourage Navis, and supported him in his mission. All know that. The King was gracious enough to give his permission and even to equip those who went with Navis. But I miss my son as much as any, and I am the last person who—"

"There was a witness," Raynor said, cutting him off. "Unseen by any of the dastards. The witness did not relay what he had seen because he was simply unable to do so, and dared not do so until recently, when he told me all. Ironically, the witness did not know who these men were, or why the fearful act was committed. Why six men set upon one. Then, one of the six set upon the other five. Long ago, yes. But the witness still easily recalled the clothing Navis wore, the elm tree embossed on his breastplate, and the dark blue surcoat, rimmed with gold, his long fair hair, and his broad shoulders. Among those still living who knew Navis, who would not remember his favorite surcoat? And who would not recognize his House's emblem, embossed upon the breastplate that Queen Therona gave him in a previous age? Who else but Navis could it be?"

"I think you merely guess—"

"All these years, everyone assumed that the land of Shatuum had swallowed them up, that Secundur's minions had captured or done away with them. But it was you who directed the vile act. Who but you could parley the cooperation between Shatuum and Duinnor through the offering of Esildre? Who but you could have introduced the black eagles to the skies of Duinnor and the Tower of the King? Coming as they did, when Esildre entered Shatuum? Who but you could convince the King to use those eagles? And who directs those eagles hither and yon to spy upon the lands of the world? All your power would be threatened if Navis succeeded, great warrior that he was. That, you could not allow."

"You seem to know all."

"No. I cannot fathom why. Why murder your own son? Prostitute your own daughter? Why bring shadow-creatures into Duinnor? What gain do these unnatural acts yield? You know, of course, that Secundur sees all that they see, hears all that they hear. Why do you play helpmate to Secundur, knowing as you do his aim for the destruction of your own race? You *do* know that is what he intends, do you not?"

"You have proof of nothing. Where is my daughter? On what errand does she go east to fulfill? If you do not answer me here, civilly, I will obtain the answers in a much less amiable manner, I assure you."

"You forget, Banis. I said there was a witness."

"Then I suggest that you produce this witness at once and make your accusations openly for all the magistrates to hear."

"That has already been placed in motion, and, in due time, you will answer for your infamy. As we speak, your accomplice is being sought out, and he will be found. I am assured that he will be offered a lenient judgment in exchange for his testimony."

"Enough! You know not what you meddle in!"

A messenger from the tower arrived, waving aside the guards to interrupt the exchange.

"Lord Banis. Pardon the intrusion, my lord, but the King desires you to return to him immediately! There has been an incident in the Tower."

"Very well," Banis replied. Turning back to Raynor, he said, "We shall discuss these matters another time."

The jailor entered the cell, took the candle, then departed after Banis, slamming and locking the door as he went.

It would have pleased Raynor to no end had he known that his humble little Familiar, Beauchamp, was the cause of the uproar in the Tower. But it only occurred to Raynor as a passing thought, one that was overwhelmed by a sudden wave of worry for his furry friend. Pacing back and forth in the dark, he spent the next few hours trying to reassure himself that, for all his innocence, the little fellow was wise enough to get out of any trouble he got himself into. After all, no ordinary rabbit could possibly have survived those centuries in the desert, much less made the dangerous trek back home. In the end, Raynor gave in to a nervous chuckle, speculating on the mischief Beauchamp must have made. Then, out of the blue, it occurred to him that he had just done what he warned Esildre not to do; that is, confront Banis directly with his knowledge of the death of Navis. And he had all but told Banis that Esildre went to find Bailorg. He smiled and shrugged. If he died at the hands of Banis, it would matter very little. But Esildre was different. She still had work to do in the world. Letting her go to Glareth, from there to begin her search for Bailorg, was probably no more dangerous than if she remained in Duinnor. But that was before Ashlord's Familiar, the owl, made her appearance, before he learned that war was now in the eastern realms. What agents might Banis have in Glareth? And would Banis send the eagles to track Esildre so that those agents could lie in wait for her?

"Oh, I am such a fool!" he muttered, pacing back and forth in the dark.

• • •

Banis saw the King once more, who instructed him to locate the rabbit at all costs, sparing not man nor treasure. Still shaken from the instructions, uttered with a ferocity that he had never experienced from the King, and dismissed with such abruptness, Banis hastily issued orders for the city to be searched for any rabbits fitting the description given by the numerous soldiers party to the incident, commanding the inept tower guards to see to the search themselves. It was embarrassing, and the incredulous looks of the hardened soldiers gave lie to the ludicrous nature of the whole affair.

Frustrated at the distracting commands, Banis made his way home to his apartments in an exclusive district of Duinnor. There, he ordered his dinner plated, dismissed his servants, and gulped down half a bottle of wine in an attempt to regain his composure. Just as the wine began to have its effect, and he had seated himself at the table, a servant returned.

"My lord, pardon the intrusion."

"What is it?"

"A soldier is here to see you on urgent business, he says."

"Show him in."

Banis expected one of the Palace Kingsmen come to report success in locating the rabbit, but it was a swarthy man wearing the brown and red garb of a Duinnor Regular under his travel-stained cloak. Recognizing him, Banis put down his fork.

"What do you want?" Banis demanded as soon as the door was closed again behind the servant.

"My lord," the man said. "I have just returned from Vanara. Dialmor sends word that Faradan's Daggers are in place. Seafar rarely leaves the White Palace since the Queen is away, and so Dialmor waits for an opportune time to give the word. He believes he will wait until General Orkane's Twenty-Second Corps are nigh upon arrival, to take advantage of the confusion that Faradan's attack may provide."

"And did you deliver to him the Summons upon the Ribbon boy?"

"Yes, my lord. Dialmor understands that he is to act on his own judgment should he obtain knowledge of the boy's whereabouts."

"Very well," Banis said, trying to suppress a smile. He knew that Orkane had with him orders declaring that, in a Vanaran emergency, Kingsmen under General Portius were to be placed at Orkane's disposal. General Orkane was inexperienced, corrupt, and inept. Just the kind of leader required to add to the confusion. And General

Portius, too sympathetic to the Vanarans, would be outraged and insulted. With Seafar assassinated, it would be an easy matter to insist that Duinnor take over security of Linlally. That would require more Vanaran treasure, in particular, the Queen's Seven Bloodcoins. The Usurper was another matter entirely, and was nearing Duinnor City. But should he escape Duinnor, and flee to Linlally, Dialmor would be waiting for him.

Neither the messenger nor Banis could know that Dialmor ordered Faradan to act shortly after the messenger had departed for Duinnor. Nor could they know that Faradan's orders had been changed, that Seafar was not the target of the attack, or that the attack had already taken place and had failed, and that Faradan was now dead and Dialmor was fleeing into the Dragonlands. So, in his ignorance of the true state of affairs, and confident in Faradan and Dialmor, Banis was pleased.

"I wish to know nothing more about events there until there is official news from the Vanaran ambassador. Have the couriers that follow you report to you first. I will summon you for details sometime after news has broken. Do you understand me?"

"Yes, lord."

"Meanwhile, I have another matter for you to attend."

"Yes, my lord?"

"There will be a party of six arriving from the east. In that party will be one named Collandoth, called Ashlord by Men, a girl, three boys from the old Eastlands Realm, and a Kingsman. All but the Kingsman and Collandoth are countryfolk from the east. You'll know Collandoth by his long black hair and his staff, and he is tall and thin. You are to dispose of Collandoth and bring the others to me. But you must first take care of Collandoth. If the Kingsman with them offers resistance, you may dispose of him, too. But the others are not to be harmed too much. Especially not the boys. Do you understand?"

"Yes, my lord. And Collandoth is also called Ashlord? Those names seem familiar."

"That is correct, Ashlord or Collandoth. I expect he will attempt to contact a colleague of his, Raynor."

"Ah, I know of Raynor. An old bookseller."

"That is so. Raynor's place is being watched, though I doubt Collandoth will be foolish enough to go there. At any rate, find Collandoth. Kill him. Take the others to Northgate Prison, not to the Palace. Notify me as soon as it is done."

"Yes, my lord. Lord?"

"What?"

"The means of Collandoth's demise. Is it to be public?"

"No, you fool! I will not risk any questions or meddling by friends that he may have here. Do it discreetly and dispose of Collandoth's body so that it will not be found."

"And do you know when they may arrive in the city?"

"I do not. But I believe they will come very soon, perhaps within the week. I have prepared a writ for you. There, on that table. It will ensure cooperation should anyone question your actions."

Chapter 4

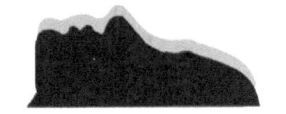

The Pool of Desire

Eldwin, of all his people, worried the most about their plan and the uncertainties of the future. It was a persistent, ever-present ache, nagging him even when it was not foremost in his mind. Although it did nothing to outwardly alter his gentle demeanor, he was aware of the change that his anxieties worked within him. When he was with others, working on the tree-lifts for the swine, or meeting with the other Elders, he caught himself edging toward ill temper, and he sometimes bit his tongue to stop a hurtful or sarcastic phrase. There were a few others, he detected, that also seemed to show signs of worry, but, like him, they spoke very carefully of it, striving to cast things in the best light. Soon, however, they would know for certain whether they would remain as they had for all these years and generations, or whether the fog that surrounded their existence would lift, allowing them to have some role in the outside world.

The more he thought about it, the less comfortable Eldwin became. In the weeks since the departure of Robby and his company, the Nowhereans had accomplished the construction of the tree lofts, according to the instructions given to them by Billy. Esildre and her strong great-nephews were a great help in the work, and they seemed to enjoy it. There had been only a few mishaps; the first hog they hoisted fell through its harness and was killed, and the water troughs were leaky and difficult to fill. But none of the Nowhereans had been hurt during the construction, thankfully, and hoisting the pigs, though difficult, went smoothly after they learned how to do it. It was all done, now, and a number of enclosures on the platforms were now occupied by their swine. It seemed such a ridiculous thing to do, but if it worked, and if Bailorg's curse was lifted....

"Can it be," Eldwin often wondered, "that such a thing as a curse can be lifted by such a decidedly unmagical act?"

He shook his head as the thought came to him again, now, as he stared through the iron bars at the Hoard's glittering contents. "The fact that we never thought of it before ain't a credit to our wits," he mused. "An' how on earth will we fare against all those on the outside who spend their days an' nights thinking up every manner of devious act?"

Lord Ullin's charge came back to mind, and Eldwin's shoulders slumped with the additional weight. How could they, half the size of grown Men, hope to render aid to Tallinvale? If what the visitors said was true, great battles were to be expected, and Eldwin's memory was still keen with the horrors he had witnessed as a young man at Tulith Attis. Even after all the years since, the things he saw there still invaded his dreams, waking him in a cold sweat.

"We must learn stealth," he said aloud. "An' we must watch without bein' seen, to judge how we should act."

"Talking to yerself's a sure sign of age," came Herbert's voice from behind. Eldwin turned and faced his fellow Elder.

"Just thinking aloud."

"Right. Well, when yer done with yer thinking, the Elders would appreciate yer presence," Herbert said gruffly. "There's a sow clearly expecting, an' so it's time for getting things ready. If there's anything to get ready for."

"When do we meet?"

"As soon as I get around to letting everyone know," Herbert complained, "seeing how I'm just a messenger, these days."

"I'll be along, directly," Eldwin sighed. Herbert shrugged and departed.

Their dislike for each other was growing apparent. Herbert was clearly jealous of Eldwin's increasing status among the Elders, and Eldwin was hard put to contain his impatience with Herbert's bluster and arrogance. Some of the Elders had even asked Eldwin if he would consider taking Herbert's place as Sheriff, but Eldwin made it clear that he did not want the position. Lately, he had become aware of growing friction between Herbert's supporters and the council as a whole. Added to that, and especially since the first really cold weather came, many of the people had become downcast, glum, and even sullen.

"Well, no wonder. We've been fairly happy up to now, haven't we?"

Eldwin continued his musings as he left the Hoard. He nodded to Millithorpe, still a fixture in the caves, and emerged into the windy afternoon air, a few flakes of snow swirling past. He put his fingers together to pop on down the path to town but hesitated, looking up at the rolling gray clouds that churned overhead. Pulling up his collar and shoving his hands into his coat pockets, he suddenly turned right and made off along the seldom used path that followed the base of the cliffs, thinking over the plan that he felt obliged to propose to the Elders. Even though the idea was his own, he did not like it. There were so many uncertainties, so many ways the people might react. Many had already expressed hopes of traveling beyond the boundaries of their land. Others had expressed concern for the safety of their homes should too many of the Elders leave to fulfill Ullin's charge.

Arriving at the pool at the base of the waterfall, Eldwin stepped up onto a rock and sat down, letting his legs dangle off the side since they were not long enough for his feet to get wet. The sound of the water was soothing, and he closed his eyes, going over his plan once again.

First, once they were sure that they could leave their lands, a group should scout the way east, moving as quickly as they could, using the maps that Robby gave him before departing. He and Millithorpe had already made several copies of each map, one set to be kept in Nowhere, and another set for each member of the scouting party, which he would lead himself. If Herbert protested, he would be reminded that, as Sheriff, his duty was to stay and protect the home lands. But, with luck, they could find their way to Tallinvale and have a look at the situation there. Only then could they learn what aid they might be able to render. Who knows, Eldwin thought, maybe they won't be needed at all.

Assuming they saw some way to help, and they could not do it with the few in the first group, they would come back for more of the Elders.

Esildre had not yet made her own plans known. She said she would wait until she knew what Eldwin and his people planned to do. Having her in Nowhere was a great comfort. Her experience in battle, the advice and training she gave in the use of bow and sword, and her silent but stern great-nephews all contributed to a sense of determination, in spite of everyone's misgivings about the future. But she had never been to Tallinvale, and Lord Ullin never shared much about the lay of the land or about Lord Tallin's defenses. No one, not even Esildre, knew what they should expect. Eldwin ached with longing to just live out his days in peace, making tables and chairs and such, and enjoying the company of his grandchildren, leaving such things as battles and war-making to others.

"Well, there's no use in thinking a thing to death," he said aloud. "We've just got to go to Tallinvale an' have a look, don't we?"

"I thought I might find you here," Esildre said from down the path behind him.

"Ah, Lady Esildre. Have ye come to fetch me to the meeting?"

"No."

She seemed hesitant, at first, as if unwilling to approach the place. But then she pulled her cloak about her and came to sit crosslegged on the rock beside Eldwin. They looked at the pool and the reflected gray sky rippling around the ice-frosted edges. For a little while, they said nothing as the nearby waterfall lulled their thoughts.

"What is on your mind, Eldwin? I have noticed that you have been less talkative these past few weeks. Do you worry about what will become of your people?"

"Yes, I do. I wish I could think of other things, but whenever I put me mind to them, I always come back to worries."

"I will help in every way that I can. I, too, have been concerned about Nowhere."

"It is as if, for all these generations, things have only been put off."

"What do you mean?"

"I mean we should have stood up to Bailorg before we ever left our first home. Every day that passed while we were with him was a day we should have stood up to him. Together, we might have overpowered him. Maybe we could have escaped. Maybe, without us, he would not have been able to steal the treasure. We should have tried. We should have, even if it meant getting hurt. Yer brother Navis spoke truly when he said we were a little people."

"Hm. Perhaps that was true, then. If so, then it is not true any longer, I think. None of us are strong all the time, if being strong means to do what is right. Of all people, I should know that. If you have been weak, then I have been weaker. If you have been cursed, then I have been damned."

Eldwin looked at Esildre. Her veil prevented him from seeing her eyes, but the downward turn of her lips hinted at her pain.

"Is that why ye wear the veil?" he asked. "Is it to hide the scars of yer curse? Everyone is afraid to ask."

"Scars? No. And, yes. It is not easy to explain. But it is for my own good, and for the good of others, that I wear the veil."

"How long have ye worn it?"

"Since I departed Duinnor to come east. Before then, I kept to myself."

"Is that why ye never married? Oh, pardon me for asking! It is none of me business, dear lady."

"Oh, no pardon is needed between friends," she said, almost laughing. "But I don't know the answer to your question. Even before my curse, I was never very interested in having a husband or a family. I think I was too wild and too lighthearted. But, well, things change."

"So there was never anyone who sparked love in ye?"

"No one," she said. "No, that is not true. I am not sure. There was one gentleman, well, he was a rogue, really. My thoughts are upon him very often. Every day, in fact. I miss his company, and I…"

Her words trailed off. Sometimes words were not needed between friends, and he looked at the pool before him.

"I dream about him, sometimes," she went on, tentatively. "Odd, the dreams one has. For my kind, they are almost always unpleasant, full of longing, full of terrible memories. But the dreams I have of him are different. I don't even know what he looks like! I never saw him because I was blind at the time I met him. I won't explain why I was blind. But he helped me to travel from my home to Duinnor which, owing to my blindness, took nearly a month. Along the way, he talked almost incessantly! But during the entire time we were together he never said or did anything that was unbecoming. Now, in the darkness of my sleep, I hear his voice. I would recognize it anywhere. When I wake, my heart is full of longing. And regret. Sometimes I wish I had remained in Duinnor, until at least I could see him when my sight was restored. Perhaps from a distance, without him knowing that I looked upon him. Anyway, when I dream of him, my dreams are pleasant. Warm."

As she spoke, the water's gurgle played counterpoint to her words, giving the place they shared a dreamlike quality, and Eldwin felt the feelings in her heart. He looked back at the rippling pool, saying nothing while the sound wrapped around them. He felt something for her, love perhaps, admiration, surely, but also a kind of pity, a wish that he was not so powerless to ease her sadness. But, he sighed inwardly, there was little he could do even about his own.

"Strange," Esildre thought, "that I should be speaking of Tyrin at this place, where my shame reasserted itself! What a bewitching place this is that makes me so vulnerable. Yet, its power turns as easily from darkness to light, from despair to hope. Or, if not hope, then to wishful thinking."

"This is a powerful place," she commented aloud, smiling.

"We call it the Pool of Desire," Eldwin nodded, "because when we come here, we think on things we wish for. Things pent-up inside."

"An apt name."

"Yes."

They both pondered the place a few moments longer, until their cares returned.

"Have you a plan? For when you go to the aid of Tallinvale?" she asked.

"I think so. It is simple, really. Scout the way. See what we may see. Do what we can, perhaps returning for help, if need be. Let things go from there."

"Hm. I will depart when you do," she stated. "I will go first to Janhaven, riding as fast as my buckmarl may go. I have letters to deliver. From Robby, Ullin, and Billy. Then I shall hie south to Tallinvale, too."

"Ye will not have the protection of speed that we Elders have. Perhaps it would be better to allow us to escort ye to Janhaven?"

"Perhaps. How many of you will be going to Tallinvale?"

"I had in mind no more than a dozen, at first. Give or take."

"Well, I think I'll take you up on your offer, if it will not be a burden or a danger. That may be the best stop for us all, before going on toward Tallinvale. Robby's people may have useful news."

"I thought of that. But if I understand the maps, it will be difficult to get to Janhaven from here without first going nearly all the way to Tallinvale. The next best way would take us northward, then east to Janhaven."

"I know. I have looked at the maps, too. You decide. I will go first to Tallinvale with you, or split from your expedition and go to Janhaven, then return to Tallinvale as soon as I can, according to your judgment."

"I have no experience at these things. I would rather ye be the judge."

"But you know your people," Esildre shrugged, standing. "And they trust you. No. I will do as you wish, and offer my advice where I may."

"If ye go to Tallinvale with us," Eldwin said as he stood, "then it should be ye who directs our aid. Ye've trained us well, but we will still need a capable captain."

"If you wish. But first let us get there."

Chapter 5

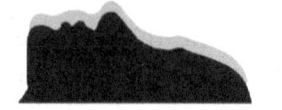

Conner Faddus

It was a dreary sleety day, after two previous days of freezing rain, that Mirabella spent at the Narrows. It was aptly named, for there the road from Janhaven to Passdale went through a pass where the long sharp ridge running north and south was broken by a cleft barely forty yards wide, made deeper by a thousand years of foot and wagon traffic. After a long climb from Passdale, the road rose sharply between ever-steepening banks of rock until, at the Narrows, it now was blocked by a set of logs laid so that anyone coming along the road had to zig and zag back and forth before coming between the newly erected stockade-like ramparts on either side which further choked the way. Atop and behind the walls of timber were platforms for the watches and for bowmen who commanded the passage below and between. There were also, on either side behind these walls, simple shelters made so that those not on duty could find some respite from the cold. For these past few days, like most days, there was not much activity, most likely due to the horrible weather, and the men Mirabella spent her duty with were happy to have such strong fortifications to hide behind, and grateful, too, for the words of encouragement she always had for them. Like all within the little army she commanded, she took her turns at various duties, whether watch or guard or scout or training, while still finding time to perform all of the other things required of a leader. But she was glad to serve, and after her two days at the Narrows were done, she climbed the ridge overlooking the place and spent another two days serving there, watching both day and night for intruders who might march up the road or sneak through their defenses. Now, just before dawn, her relief arrived in the person of Winterford, and when he got his wind back from the long climb, he gave her the news, such as he had.

"We turned back sixty riders along the road from Tallinvale yesterday mornin'," he told her. "They came up from the army surroundin' the place. Probably to test our defenses. We had word of them long afore they got within thirty miles of us, so none rode back. More fine horses, though."

"Good," she nodded. "We need as many horses as we can get."

"Passin' through Janhaven, I was told by the Capt'n that a feller was picked up some ways behind us here, sneakin' through the hills. Says he came lookin' for Sheila Pradkin."

"Sheila?"

"That's right. Wouldn't tell his name, or none of his business, though. So Makeig says to tell ye, if ye don't mind, to come right away to the stockade. The feller's being held there until ye decide what's to be done with him. Might as well tell ye, though, he's a Tracian feller."

• • •

Durlorn pointed Mirabella to a side room, outside of which Makeig was standing.

"Glad ye made it alright," Makeig said. "We got us a bit of a mystery man in here."

"Has he said any more about what he wants with Sheila?"

"Nope. An' I ain't pressed him none. Figured to wait on ye."

"Do you know him?"

"Nope to that, too. An' none of me people what have seen him recognize him."

"I heard you had a skirmish yesterday with Redvests coming up from Tallinvale. Were any of your people hurt?"

"Not a single one!"

"Good."

Makeig opened the door for Mirabella and followed her in, taking up a place to the side. Within, at the other side of the table, sat an older man, unkempt, obviously weary, and in rags and dirty shreds that were once fine clothes. He stood when Mirabella entered.

"I am told you came here seeking Sheila Pradkin," she said. "What business do you have with her?"

"That is between Miss Pradkin and myself," the man replied.

"I need not point out a certain hostility toward strangers that my people have. Especially Tracian strangers."

"That has been made exceedingly clear to me."

"We are wary of spies and agents sent against us."

"Naturally. And rightly so."

"Suspicion alone is enough for most, I dare say. And others hold it expedient to execute suspected spies even when there might be doubt."

"Ah. Yet I sense that you doubt that I am a spy."

"I do," Mirabella nodded. "But I am perfectly willing to be expedient."

"I take your meaning. I am no spy. I have given my oath to my master to do my duty and I will carry it out, or die trying, even though I am much delayed from it and my master is long dead. I must see the girl. Then, if I am to submit to the hangman, I shall do so clear of conscience. If you will not permit me to see her, I can only promise that I will struggle and squirm and cry out most dishonorably, fighting tooth and nail, and I shall make as much mockery of your justice as my old body and voice may inflict and endure. And shame be upon you!"

Mirabella glanced at Makeig, who stood leaning against the wall and met her look with a cocked brow.

"Is there no way you can tell us more?" she asked the man, taking a seat across the table from him. "At least tell us why Tracia would be interested in Miss Pradkin? Or how you came by her name and whereabouts?"

"Tracia is not the least bit interested in her. Only I. I arrived in Barley eight days ago. It has taken me that long to find her house, now occupied by Redvests, and then to make my way here, having learned that some of the people of Barley escaped the Redvests and made an encampment in these parts."

"You do not deny you are from Tracia."

"I do not."

"As it happens, we have other Tracians among us."

"I have recognized the accents of a few," he said, glancing at Makeig. "And I have heard that there is a place somewhere in this region where I may find some refuge among my own countrymen. I thought to try to find that place once my task with the girl was completed."

Mirabella sat back in her chair and crossed her arms. "I have no desire to hang an innocent man, or to antagonize our Tracian friends by doing so. Is there anyone who may vouch for you in these parts?"

He shook his head, "I doubt if there could be anyone. All who may have known me are likely dead. Or rotting in prison."

"Can you at least tell us the name of your dead master?"

The man shifted back and forth on his feet nervously, then made up his mind.

"Naming my master would be a certain death warrant in some parts, but I think I will tell you. And I will tell you proudly. Since childhood, I have lived in Weatherlee, in Tracia, and have served the House of Waterstone, and, though dead, the Lord Waterstone is my lord and master, whom I yet serve."

From the corner of her eye, Mirabella detected a movement on the part of Makeig, and she saw that he recognized the name.

"The House of Waterstone is a famous one," Mirabella stated.

"Aye. They were amongst the first Men that came on the Great Ships, so the family lore goes."

Makeig, silent until now, cleared his throat and stepped forward.

"Waterstone had many servants, I'm sure. But if I have me facts straight, Waterstone was among those loyal to the Prince afore the takeover."

A gleam came into the stranger's eye, and he even managed a wry smile, saying, "You are right on both points, fellow Tracian. He and his many servants were arrested and dungeoned at Brightpool twelve years ago, next spring."

"An' d'ye know the fate of his family?"

"Lady Waterstone died some years before her husband's arrest. Lord Waterstone died more recently. In prison."

"When did he die?"

"Five years ago."

"So how come ye to be on a task for him?"

"I was charged with my task before he was arrested."

"Why did you wait so long?" Mirabella asked.

"I was forced to wait, by my own circumstances. I carried out what parts of my task that I could before I, too, was imprisoned, seven years ago. But, last year, all of the prisons were emptied of all the able-bodied to work as slave labor for the army. Making roads, bridges, pulling wagons. A few of us managed to break our chains, and so I escaped six months ago. I eventually made my way here. As soon as I could."

Makeig pulled out a chair and shoved it at the stranger.

"Show yer marks."

An odd expression formed on the stranger's face. He frowned and scowled at Makeig, his eyes glaring with what could only be described as pride or defiance. He put his left foot, covered by rotting leather that was once a shoe, onto the seat of the chair and pulled up his pant-leg. He wore no stocking on that leg, and on his lower shin, just above his ankle, was a cuff of iron, wrapped and stuffed with bits of cloth.

"Remove the rags, if ye don't mind," Makeig ordered.

The stranger did so, and a few links of chain dangled from the ring on the cuff. Makeig took the rags to look at, then he bent to examine the man's leg. The scars were old and calloused underneath the loose iron. Makeig handed back the rags and nodded to Mirabella.

"A Brightpool anklet, indeed," he said. "An' worn for a long time, I'd say. No fresh blood or cuts. The man knows how to take care of a leg in irons."

The stranger carefully put the rags back around the cuff, wrapping the chain meticulously so it would not dangle or rattle, saying as he worked, "I have not had the means to remove this."

"There are too many mysteries about you," Mirabella said. "I ask again, is there no one who may vouch for you?"

"I doubt it. Though the girl, or even her uncle, Steggan Pradkin, might recognize me."

"Steggan has been dead for many months."

"Oh! And the girl? What of her? Is she safe?"

"I do not know. She departed with a party sent to Duinnor to carry word of our predicament. That was nearly three months ago."

"Then I must go after her! Wait. What of her things? The property. Steggan's property. Did it become hers upon his death? Did she bring anything away from there when the Redvests came? A smallish wooden box, perhaps? Rosewood. With brass hinges and locks?"

"She abandoned her uncle before he died. Eventually, she became a part of my own household. But she brought only what was on her back. As far as I know, there was nothing of value in Steggan's house when the property was disposed of. Everything there was carefully accounted for, I assure you."

Now the stranger became truly agitated, and he gripped the back of the chair for support, his face full of confusion as his eyes watered.

"This is too much!" He sat down heavily. "Too awful! Was there nothing that she retained?"

"What 'xactly are ye lookin' to find from her?" Makeig asked. "Out with it, man! What's yer business with her?"

"I can't. I can't!"

He propped his head in his hands, his elbows on the table, and shook his head as if he was sick. "But I suppose I must. You will not help me if I do not tell you. I must find her, you see? It is very important!"

"I don't think we can help you find her, one way or the other," Mirabella told him. "By now she is surely very far away."

"It doesn't matter how far away she is! I must find her. That is what I've sworn to do. That is what I must do!"

"Then tell us all," Makeig insisted. "If it's so almighty important, tell us! Or ye'll get no help whatsoever, an' likely little sympathy."

"I think I can assure you," Mirabella offered gently, "that you are safe among us." She looked at Makeig, who stepped back from the man and nodded to her as he pulled up a chair to sit, backwards, straddling his legs around it and crossing his arms over the back. "Forget what I said about spies," Mirabella went on. "And forgive our harsh treatment. But we are in a difficult and precarious position. I doubt if you can appreciate this, but we are in the midst of war, and our people are caught right up in the middle of it. We must be careful. We can't afford to be too trusting."

"Yes. Of course you cannot," the man looked back and forth from Makeig to Mirabella, then reached into his shirt and, undoing some straps around his chest, removed a leather sleeve. He placed it on the table and removed from it a thick folding of oiled parchment. Opening that, he removed two packets, one smaller than the other, both sealed with twine and a heavy wax emblem pressed through the knots.

"I am charged to deliver these to the girl," he said. "This is a letter from the girl's father, Lord Waterstone, explaining much, I assume, of how she came to be in Barley and why she was sent away."

He put his hand on the other packet. "These are the deeds and titles to all his lands, estates, and holdings, including a trust of gold and other assets put aside for her in Glareth. All prepared for her years ago."

Makeig pushed his hat back from his raised eyebrows while Mirabella, expressionless, nodded.

"My story is of no consequence," the man went on, "except so that you might understand further. My name, for what it's worth, is Conner Faddus, and I was Lord Waterstone's valet and often acted as seneschal of his eastern estate at Weatherlee. My lord foresaw the coming of these dark days and the eventual rise to power of those who now rule in my country. He secretly opposed them, and made preparations. Later, his opposition was more open. To safeguard his daughter, he instructed me to purchase the farm for Steggan and to convey it to him with a charge to safekeep Shevalia. Steggan is, or was, Lord Waterstone's illegitimate half-brother, unknown and given no consequence by any, friend or enemy. Such was my lord's plan, but he was hesitant to make it so, for his daughter was very young, and he was loath to be parted from her. In those days, plague followed plague, violence spread throughout the lands, and things grew rapidly worse. My own daughter, the same age as Shevalia and her playmate, died, and it was she who was placed in a grave made for Lord Waterstone's child. Do not think him cruel, it was at my own suggestion that the swap was made. I saw a way my own child could perhaps save her friend, even after death. So whilst Waterstone attended the funeral of my daughter, in guise as his own, I brought Shevalia to Steggan. Each year thereafter, I came to look upon her and to vouchsafe the box that was given to her as her property. There was little I could do to help the child. Waterstone was arrested, and I, myself, was a wanted man with bounty hunters upon my trail. Eventually, five years after his arrest, I was captured in Glareth by Tracian agents and taken back and placed in Brightpool prison. It was only then that I learned that all else of his household had been arrested and taken there, charged with treason. There was a public spectacle, a mockery of a trial. But Waterstone fell ill and died before they could hang him."

"Captain Makeig, would you step outside for a word with me?" Mirabella suddenly asked, rising from her seat. Makeig nodded and stood, glancing at their prisoner as they closed the door behind them.

"What're yer thoughts on the feller?" Makeig asked.

"I think he's telling the truth."

"An' the girl is who he says she is?"

"I believe so. It actually may explain some things."

"Ye know her well?"

"Not as well as I should," Mirabella lowered her eyes. "And because of my ignorance and neglect, she suffered needlessly."

"Hm. Well. Have ye a private word with him, then," Makeig said.

"I know you have much to do," Mirabella said. "Later, perhaps you might consider taking Mr. Faddus to Hill Town. Possibly someone there may know him. Or would you rather that I find a place for him here?"

"Oh, no. The poor feller's been through the mill, I'd say. He might find some comfort among his countrymen."

"That's what I was thinking. Good. Meanwhile, on your way to the armoury, would you send over the blacksmith with his tools?"

"It would be me great pleasure."

"Then I shall see you later today."

"Afore dark, certainly."

Makeig bowed and swaggered off just as Durlorn passed through the room. Mirabella waved and went over to him.

Meanwhile, Faddus sat nervously. He was exhausted by his long ordeal of many years and was further depressed by the news that Sheila was long gone and far away. As Mirabella and Makeig chatted outside the closed door, he wondered if he had it in him to continue his quest and to make the long trek to Duinnor to find the girl. He was still quite muddled over this dilemma when Mirabella returned. She brought with her a tray of food and drink and left the door ajar.

"Please eat," she said, putting the tray in front of him. She sat nearby in the chair Makeig had used. Faddus looked at the tray and then at her.

"I have already eaten," she said to him. "Please. Do eat."

"Thank you."

She watched, seeing his hands shake as he picked up a slice of bread and nibbled on it. He chewed and swallowed, then, the bread still poised near his mouth, he closed his eyes. After a moment, tears etched down his old year-lined face.

"Pardon me," he said. "Forgive me." His voice cracked. "I am most grateful. Truly, I am. I suppose I am in a rather wretched state, aren't I?"

Mirabella smiled and rose.

"I will let you eat in peace. But I will be back shortly, and we will talk some more."

She left and crossed through the great room and sat on the bench beside the fire. Seeing her, Durlorn came over and asked, "Should I look in on our guest for his needs?"

"No. I think we ought to let him be while he eats."

"Very well, ma'am."

"Do you know where Mrs. Bosk might be? I didn't see her at the infirmary earlier."

"Yes, ma'am. She took one of our wagons and a few lads to go with her down to the lumber yard."

"I see. Thank you."

"May I do anything for ye? A cup of tea, perhaps?"

"No, thank you."

Mirabella decided not to wait for Frizella Bosk to return, and to continue the interview with Faddus alone, once he had eaten. She mulled over everything Frizella had ever mentioned about Sheila, which was a fair amount. For years, the two women sent notes to each other to keep in touch and to share news and happenings of interest. That the two were such fast friends was something of an oddity to other folks, considering how different the two women were. Much was owed, certainly, to Frizella's straightforward, no-nonsense manner, her energy and patience. She had always been what people called an "old soul," wise beyond her years. Mirabella saw that aspect of Frizella back when they first met, and, somehow, Frizella found a kindred spirit in Mirabella. Though Elifaen, Mirabella was someone with a fair share of experience on her own soul. It was true that all Elifaen were by definition old souls, but as a people they did not start out that way. And Mirabella still had in her a spark, the same spark that her people sometimes envied in the Newcomers, a freshness that was renewed in each generation of Men. The spark had been dimmed by her grief over the death of her brothers, and the terrible things she saw during battle in the far-off Dragonlands nearly extinguished it. But it grew bright again when she met Robigor. And it was shortly after her encounter with her future husband that she met Frizella, who was all too happy to keep an eye on Robigor, who was friends with a certain Boskman that Frizella had her own eye on. For a year, Frizella managed to report to Mirabella regularly concerning Robigor's activities and successes in spite of all of the obstacles that Lord Tallin threw at the Barleyman as a cruel test. That spark was perhaps what Frizella and Mirabella shared, igniting the warm flame of their friendship. And, Mirabella, for her part, ironically saw in Frizella a sisterly figure, one seemingly older and wiser, in spite of being so much younger. That was the thing about Men, she thought. Their mortality was so certain, their lives so short and sharp, that they did not have time to grow up. So they remained children all their lives. And, perhaps, they retained some of the wisdom that only children may have.

Her thoughts were interrupted by the entrance of the blacksmith who came in with a clinking bag of tools. He stopped, looked around, then saw her.

"Ah! Mrs. Ribbon! I hear tell thar's a feller hereabouts needin' some jewelry removed."

Faddus was finishing his meal, wiping his mouth with his provided napkin. When Mirabella and the blacksmith entered, he stood.

"I thank you for the meal," he said. "And I apologize again for my moment of despair."

"You are welcome, and that is quite alright. This is our blacksmith, Mr. Clingdon, and I have asked him to take a look at your leg to see if he can free you of your shackle."

Clingdon examined the ring and the cuff, paying careful attention to the hinge and pin. He took from his bag a heavy iron block, like a small anvil.

"Rest the edge of the cuff right there," he instructed Faddus, and he helped him to position his foot. "Now grab the back of that chair to help ye keep balance."

Satisfied, Clingdon took out a cold chisel and a heavy iron hammer. He carefully placed the chisel against the hinge pin and looked up. "Do ye trust me?"

Faddus nodded tenuously.

"Take a deep breath, then, an' keep very still."

With one powerful stroke, the pin shattered under the blacksmith's blow and the cuff fell away.

"Thar ye go! I reckon that'll feel a sight better, eh?"

"Why, yes! Thank you!"

Faddus shook Clingdon's hand vigorously and beamed as he watched Clingdon bow to Mirabella, smiling and nodding to her, as he departed.

"I don't know how to thank you," Faddus said to Mirabella.

"Please sit. You can thank me by telling me the rest of the story. The important parts that you left out."

His smile vanished as he slowly sat, and he looked for a long time at Mirabella's expressionless face before speaking. He leaned back in the chair and began.

"Lord Waterstone's wealth was great. But the most valuable of all his treasures was something that came into his possession through his marriage, something that had been kept secret for almost twenty generations of Men. A secret kept and safeguarded since the fall of Tulith Attis and the time of Heneil. Something held in trust from that time onward. There was a solemn pact, a promise, to keep it hidden from the world, but to be ready to deliver it back to the person who entrusted it to a member of Lady Waterstone's family. However, that person remains hidden, or else has departed from the world, so the treasure I speak of remained in Tracia, for all these generations, whilst the family waited for it to be claimed."

"How could it be claimed if it was kept in secret?"

"I do not know the answer to that."

"What object could be so valuable?"

"I will soon tell you. When the girl, Shevalia, was brought into hiding, at the last moment Lord Waterstone directed me to deliver with her a small wooden case, fashioned of rosewood. Steggan was entrusted with the girl and with the wooden case. Each year I was to visit and to check on the well-being of the girl and the security of the case and its contents. I have, and still have, the only key to it. If the case became damaged in any way, or if the contents were meddled with, I would know by my examination of it. It was made clear to Steggan that the case, as well as the girl, were to be kept safe and together until they were both fetched from him. Otherwise, his life would be forfeit. It was, as it turned out, a very poor plan, made in haste. It became apparent to me very soon that Steggan was unreliable. But it was too late. I was a fugitive from Tracia, performing my annual visit as a bluff, hoping that Steggan had not heard of the fate of Waterstone, and seeking in the between time to acquire the means to free them from Steggan. Alas, I was arrested before that could happen."

Mirabella tried to remain patient, knowing that the man had to tell it in his own way, having already deduced what had been in the box and also what had happened to it and its contents. But she wanted confirmation, so she held back her questions. She could see that Faddus did not want to reveal things as he struggled against the oath he had given his master to keep the secret.

"When I escaped," he went on, "I first had to recover these documents that I had hidden in Glareth before my arrest. Then, well, I have told you the rest, except for what was in the box. Seven small items, part of an ancient legacy given by Aperion to the Elifaen. I suspect that you are Elifaen, and I believe you have heard of them. To the uninformed, they would look like marvelous coins, each with a jewel in its center, like the old coins once used in Vanara."

"One of diamond," Mirabella stated, "one of ruby, one each of amethyst, amber, sapphire, and topaz, and one of emerald."

Faddus nodded. "Have you seen them? Do you know where they are? The girl has them?"

"No. That is, yes. I have seen them. But I did not know what they were, at first. Though I later suspected."

Mirabella told Faddus about the strange Faere coins that Lally Starhart had passed along to Mr. Ribbon. She speculated that Steggan was the man who had given them to Mrs. Starhart for payment of letters her husband was to take from Steggan. But when Mirabella told Faddus that she sent the Bloodcoins with her son westward, Faddus stood and paced back and forth.

"I did not think the Seven would be safe if they remained here," she said. "As for the box you mentioned, an empty and broken rosewood box was found among the things at Steggan's house and auctioned off. I believe the local schoolmaster obtained it to use for his writing tools."

"It is a great and horrible shame!" Faddus said. "A tragic bungling of things from the very beginning. If I had not been so clumsy and dim-witted! I should have contrived some means to get the girl away sooner. I did try. After the last time I saw her. That was why I was in Glareth, trying to make a place for her there. But I only managed to get myself arrested."

Faddus held his hands up in a gesture of surrender and then placed them down on the packets of documents before him.

"What would be the best way to find Shevalia and your son?"

"I hope by now they are very far away, perhaps even in Duinnor," Mirabella said. "Any attempt to follow them would be impossible for the foreseeable future."

She went on to explain to him the condition of the mountain passes, the situation with the western warlords, and the impossibility of putting together any party to go searching for Robby and Sheila.

"I assure you that I am as distressed over all of this as a person can be," she concluded. "But we must manage the best we can until events reshape the way of things."

She rose from her chair, then sat back down. "I would like for you to tell me more about the girl's family. Her mother, in particular."

"I know more about her father's family. Her mother's name was Faeanna and had been a servant of the lesser House of Turnbuckle, one of the old houses of Men. Her family, it was said, was linked in some way to the Elifaen House of Elmwood. That was many generations ago by the reckoning of Men. When the House of Turnbuckle was dissolved, Faeanna came to the Waterstone estate as a lowly housemaid. She was very unusual. Though young, she was erudite and learned beyond her years. She was possessed of a charming wit and uncanny beauty that, coupled with her rather adventurous manner, completely won over the young lord's heart. It was a mild scandal, for it was understood that Lord Waterstone was intended to marry another lady as arranged by his parents before they died. That wedding was called off, Waterstone married Faeanna instead, and the two were very happy and the best pairing you could imagine. Shevalia was born a year after their wedding."

"Do you know anything of the Turnbuckles?" Mirabella asked.

"The name, I believe, stems from a Man who was one of the first to land on these shores. It is said the House of Turnbuckle refused to support the Pinewood Uprising and suffered because of it. I do not know how Faeanna came to be in service to the Turnbuckles, for she was not kin to them. Lord Waterstone told me, though, that Faeanna was somehow related to the ancient House of Elmwood, a name once famous, he said, in the Westlands, but one that had fallen into disrepute. I am only certain about what I saw with my own eyes. That is, the lord and his lady were as happy and loving as any who ever smiled upon one another. And their daughter was their greatest treasure."

"But you said that Lady Waterstone died. Was it the plague?"

"That is what many were led to believe, for she fell ill during that time. But I believe that she was poisoned by enemies of the family. In those days, while the Prince still ruled, many loyal Houses of Tracia were attacked in the most despicable ways, to lessen the influence of those who supported the Prince. It was suspected by some of our household that the poison was intended for Lord Waterstone himself, and that the job was bungled. One evening, when the Lord and Lady prepared to dine, he was suddenly called away to the city. She saw him off, then ate alone. But immediately after she dined, she fainted. She wasted away unconscious for nine days before she stopped breathing."

"Poisoned."

"Yes," Faddus nodded. "The wine decanter that she was served from was later found emptied of its contents. I was there. And there was the slight scent of foxdire from it."

"I know of that poison," Mirabella said, remembering that Frizella used it in some of her concoctions, and always warned against anyone taking it, especially if they were Elifaen.

"I thank you for your honesty," she told Faddus as she stood. "I believe Captain Makeig will make arrangements for you to stay with his people. He will answer your questions about our situation. I ask only that you do not share any of your news with anyone, not even Makeig, concerning the Seven. Those objects were hidden for good reason. If anyone comes to suspect that you have knowledge of their whereabouts, or even that they still exist, I'm afraid this land would be scoured clean of every living soul in search of them. You know what happened at Tulith Attis, when, it is said, the Dragonkind took those belonging to Heneil and Lyrium. Should our present enemies learn of those objects, and think that they are here in Janhaven, I do not doubt they would instantly turn their entire might against us."

"I quite understand, my lady."

"Good. Meanwhile, I wish I could help you more. But until my son and Sheila return, there is very little that may be done. Perhaps it is a good thing that the objects are with him, or else they might have already fallen into the wrong hands. I hope to talk with you later, if I may."

Faddus stood and bowed.

"Thank you for everything you have done for me."

"A Mr. Durlorn," she said with a smile, "is foreman of this building. I am sure you would be welcome at the hearth. Good day."

There was so much she needed to think about, but Mirabella had hardly stepped outside and back into the chilly afternoon when a rider tore into the yard.

"Word from our scouts!" he called to her. "Redvests're movin' through the north hills in force. They're tryin' to work around an' behind the Narrows. They'll make the ridge above by this afternoon."

"How many?" Mirabella hurried to nearby Anerath.

"We make at least three hunnerd of 'em."

"Get to the armoury and find Makeig! I'll muster the fighters and meet him in town."

• • •

In less than an hour, Mirabella led a group of fighters into the woods north of the Narrows while Makeig took another group through the Narrows to a point closer to Passdale than was comfortable, but from where they could see the high lookout place up on the ridge to the south. Winterford was up there, much to his frustration, for he had missed yesterday's fighting and would miss today's, too. But his duty was to watch for a signal from Mirabella, from a ridge a mile north of the road that passed through the Narrows. He was to then signal by smoke to Captain Makeig who would move up into the woods with his men.

It was a quickly laid but cruelly efficient trap. The four hundred Redvests, moving on foot from Passdale up through the foreign hills, made so much noise that they could be heard from a mile away. When they at last arrived at the base of the ridge they were to take, they stopped for nearly two hours to eat and rest. This gave Mirabella, a few hundred feet above them, time to put her archers in concealed emplacements already prepared weeks in advance, according to a plan drawn up by Ullin Saheed before he had departed. Piles of brush, hidden platforms in the trees, and rocky outcrops were occupied by fighters dressed in mottled brown and grayish-white cloaks, blending into the snowy wood. They had orders to wait until Billy Bosk's cousin, Parth Bosk, blew his hunting horn. With horn in hand, he crouched with Mirabella behind a well-situated blind commanding the slopes down to the unsuspecting Redvests below. Next to him was a bowman with oil-dripping rags tied to an arrow, and Mirabella held a firestick, ready to strike.

They waited and waited, until some began to think that maybe the Redvests prepared to make camp. But then came shouts from below, and the crowd of red began moving up the slopes as a great mob, not even bothering to have their weapons at the ready. They had sent their scouts ahead, and none had returned with any warning to halt. But the local fighters had allowed the scouts to pass right through their hidden lines, and when the scouts were well out of sight from their comrades, they were silently dispatched.

"Get ready," Mirabella whispered, kneeling with her hands ready to strike her match, watching the approach. By now, the noise of the climbing enemy was so great that it nearly drowned out the sound of a hundred creaking bows, straining to free their deadly missiles. When the first Redvests were within ten yards, she struck her firestick.

"Blow your horn, Parth," she said, putting fire to the arrow.

The horn blew, and hundreds of arrows flew downward while one flew up, clearing the trees, trailing a black line of smoke.

" 'Bout time!" Winterford said, putting a torch into a pile of green pine boughs.

A moment later, Makeig saw Winterford's signal, and waved his men into the woods. The Redvests who had the good sense to retreat from the slaughter ahead of them turned into Makeig's awaiting men. From two sides, the Redvests met with arrow and steel as Mirabella's fighters pressed the invaders into the advancing Thunder Mountain Band. As the woods and hills grew dim and the day came to an end, only a handful of Redvests managed to escape northward, becoming lost in the forest. And it would be several days before the last few Redvest survivors trickled into Passdale to report their misadventure to General Vidican.

Chapter 6

Prince Carbane's Ships

Ten days after being dumped into Lake Halgaeth, and narrowly escaping the fate that befell Falgo in the belly of the lake serpent, Mr. Ribbon stumbled into a village on the northeastern shores. Sick and shaking with hunger and cold, he spent the next four days going in and out of feverish delirium. The villagers were so alarmed by his ravings that they locked him inside a cottage, allowing no one to come or go from it but an old woman who was brave enough to tend to him. It was a great surprise to them when, on the day that Mr. Ribbon woke from his sickness, and tried to escape their caring hands to continue his journey, none other than Prince Danoss rode into their village. He saw the crowd gathered outside of a cottage as several villagers tried to push Mr. Ribbon back through a window out of which he endeavored to crawl.

"Do you keep lunatics, now?" laughed the Prince.

Seeing him dismount in all his finery with his falcon on his wrist, Mr. Ribbon knew at once that at last someone important had happened along.

"Save me from these people, I beg ye!" Mr. Ribbon cried out, gripping the shutters of the window and jamming one leg against the window frame to resist the villagers' insistent shoves. "I've got important business with the Prince, I tell ye! Unhand me, man!"

"The Prince, eh?" said Danoss. "By the look of you, you've had a bit too much of the vineyard."

"My lord," said one of the women, "he's sick an' ravin'!"

"The feller come into our village some days ago, my lord," said a man as he bowed, "sick an' pitiful-like, sos we took him in."

"An' he's been goin' on 'bout havin' business with ye, ever since comin' to."

"An' jabberin' 'bout Redvests an' the like, too!"

"Redvests? Tracians, you mean?" asked Danoss, coming up to Mr. Ribbon who was hanging half in and half out of the window. "What about them?"

"They invaded, that's what about 'em, sir. Now tell these folk to let me get on an' warn the Prince in Formouth, an' then onto his ruling father in Glareth!"

"Invaded where?"

"Passdale an' County Barley, that's whar! Let go of me, woman!"

"Climb out of there, and speak with me plainly," commanded Danoss. "I promise that the Prince will hear you."

"That *is* the Prince," whispered a boy to Mr. Ribbon as he fell out of the window and picked himself up.

"Steady there!" Danoss cried, grabbing Mr. Ribbon by the shoulder to help balance him. "I see you are still somewhat weak."

"Me lord, are ye the Prince Danoss?"

"I am."

Mr. Ribbon fell to his knees and fairly burst into tears, crying, "They came into Barley by night, burnin' an' pillagin'. Then, next day, they come into Passdale, an' we couldn't hold 'em off! Please, good Prince, send help!"

"Come, come, man! Get up from there," Danoss said, somewhat embarrassed and helping Mr. Ribbon to his feet. "Madam, is there some place where I may interview this gentleman?"

"Pardon, me lord? Enter what, me lord?"

"Chairs, perhaps?"

• • •

Soon the Prince had Mr. Ribbon's tale, and with Mr. Ribbon sharing his horse, he rode swiftly to his camp and his hunting party. From there, with a fresh horse and one for the Barleyman, the Prince and Mr. Ribbon rode on to Formouth, not resting or stopping for a day and a half until they arrived. The Prince ordered that Mr. Ribbon be given the best guest room in the castle, food, bath water, and clean clothes.

"Rest this afternoon and tonight," Danoss told him. "Tomorrow morning we ride for Glareth by the Sea."

And they did, with horses to spare and food and water enough so that they would have no need to stop at any village or inn, sleeping only when they required it, and resting and eating meager meals only when their mounts needed their own. It was a long journey, and it snowed and sleeted so that, after a week, they had to slow for the safety of their mounts, even though there were two weeks more ahead of them. Along the way, Mr. Ribbon told the Prince all he knew, which was not much, of the Redvests, their general, and the effort to move the people west to Janhaven. And Danoss told Mr. Ribbon how, on the day they arrived in Formouth, he ordered that all men in his province were to be mustered, equipped, and ready to march within a month.

"I can raise two thousand out of Connassa Province at the very least," he said. "But we will need more than that if a greater invasion is afoot."

On and on they rode, and when after another week, Mr. Ribbon saw the first spires in the distance, he rejoiced, thinking his journey was near the end. But it was only the first of many great and beautiful towns of Glareth, and they rode on through without stopping.

At last, toward the end of the third week of their travel, they reached Glareth by the Sea. Mr. Ribbon was amazed and bewildered by the vast stretch of buildings he saw, and the many boats and ships along the River Osterflo and out upon the Bay of Salfin. Everywhere, it seemed, was wealth and commerce, and he thought surely this land could field a great army. The people on the streets and avenues were finely dressed, and everywhere, on shop doors and hanging from the lampposts, were wreaths and ribbons and greenery. It seemed to Mr. Ribbon that the folks he saw were happy and full of mirth, but their mood did little to dispel his own forebodings or the worries he had about his family and the friends left behind those many weeks ago. Prince Danoss was greeted as they rode along, and he waved and answered them in return, wishing them joyful days.

On to the Palace they went, arriving on a day when the father of Danoss, Ruling Prince Carbane, held court with his honored guest, Serith Ellyn, Queen of Vanara. There were many people present, men in colorful cloaks and tunics, and ladies in long beautiful gowns and bespecked with glittering jewelry. It was a merry occasion, and most had wineglasses in their hands, or cups of punch. Bright sunlight flooded into the hall from high clear windows while musicians played lively tunes, and hearths crackled gold and warm. A dance had just come to an end, amid applause and laughter, when Prince Danoss and Mr. Ribbon entered. As the clapping subsided, and the two arrivals were seen, the people bowed and parted before them. Prince Carbane was sitting with his wife at the front of the hall in grand chairs, along with Queen Serith Ellyn also, and when he saw his son, Carbane rose and came to greet him.

"Joyous day, my son!"

"And to you, Father."

"I did not expect to see you again so soon after your last visit!" he said. "You honor our festivities with a surprise."

"You may not think so when you hear my news, sire," Danoss bowed. "Mother, my best wishes. Queen Serith Ellyn, I am again honored to see you."

"Likewise, Prince. What news do you bring?"

"Although I hate to dampen the merry spirit of this Midwinter's gathering," Danoss said to his father, "I must report that at last the despots who overthrew Tracia move against their neighbors. They have attacked the Eastlands, driving as far north as the southern shores of Lake Halgaeth, looting and pillaging."

A wave of muttering and dismay swept through the hall, and, with a gesture, the Queen sent Gaiyelneth to fetch Thurdun.

"This man has striven long to come with the news, but was beset with accident and adversity, and dogged by Redvest hunters. He is the right Mayor of Passdale, Robigor Ribbon, of the County Barley."

Mr. Ribbon bowed.

"When?" Carbane demanded.

"Just more than a month and a fortnight ago," answered Danoss. "By now, who can say what mischief they have done."

"Why have we not heard of this until now?"

"Me lord," Mr. Ribbon bowed again. "I came as quick as I could, an' would've been here sooner but that I was attacked an' driven off me course."

"And what of the other counties and towns? Calletshire and Colleton?"

"I know not, sire, of them places, or what goes on tharabouts. I only know me own land."

"Sire," Danoss interceded, "I am convinced of this man's integrity, and I do not doubt his tale. At Formouth, trade has been mysteriously disrupted with the south. With his news, we now know why. Therefore, before departing Formouth, I put my province on a war footing, and my soldiers gather as we speak."

"Lord Starshell," Carbane gestured and a man approached. "Please notify the ministers that I would like to meet with them tonight. Let us have Admiral Bargus and his staff be there, too. Inform the Admiralty that I will require all warships to be at the ready for orders. Send word to Prince Lantos. I believe he is at a gathering of his people in Riverton."

"Yes, Prince Carbane."

"Queen," Carbane then said, "please forgive this disruption. I am sure that you understand. As soon as I have met with my ministers, I shall endeavor to inform you about how things stand. Ah, Lord Thurdun! You most likely should join me. We go to convene a council of war."

"My people," Carbane then addressed the gathering, "there is ample food and drink for all, and let it not go to waste, I beg you. Those of you not required to be elsewhere, please remain for as long as you wish. I thank you once again for your good service to our realm, and I wish all of you and your families a happy Midwinter's. Please excuse me."

Carbane and Danoss began to walk away, but Mr. Ribbon stepped up.

"Sires," he said, bowing again, "what would ye have me do?"

"I beg your pardon, Mr. Ribbon!" Danoss said. "Please make yourself at home, enjoy something to eat, I beg you."

"I shall take charge of Mr. Ribbon for a time," said Queen Serith Ellyn. "I have a feeling we have much to talk about."

Carbane raised an eyebrow, then departed with his son and many of the ministers and officers of the Glareth army and navy who were in attendance, leaving Mr. Ribbon looking somewhat lost. The Queen approached him with Gaiyelneth at her side.

"Mr. Ribbon," said Gaiyelneth, "allow me to introduce you to Serith Ellyn, Queen of Vanara."

"I am honored," Mr. Ribbon bowed.

"I am honored," said the Queen, smiling, "and I shall tell you why if you would care to join me in my apartments."

"Of course, ma'am. I am at yer service."

The Queen and her retinue, save Thurdun who went with Carbane and the others, left the Hall, and Gaiyelneth followed behind the Queen with Mr. Ribbon beside her. In the corridor, members of her Gray Guard fell in behind them, and Mr. Ribbon felt quite out of his element.

"My name is Gaiyelneth," the girl beside him said. "I am the Queen's maidservant."

"I'm pleased to meet ye."

"And I am very pleased to meet you, sir."

"I can't imagine why. I don't bring happy news, surely."

"Maybe not. But you'll soon learn why."

Up stairs they went, along halls decorated with tapestries and paintings, between statues and suits of armor, and they at last came to a broad foyer, and then, crossing it, into a large parlor of sorts. But it was so lavishly outfitted, with fine divans and settees, richly upholstered chairs, and thick colorful carpets, that it seemed to Mr. Ribbon that they entered yet another palace. To one side of the room blazed a fireplace large enough to walk into, and on another side were dozens of glass windows overlooking the bay.

"Please, take a seat just here, Mr. Ribbon." The Queen gestured to a comfortable-looking chair nearby as she sat on the divan.

"That will be all, Garlan," said Gaiyelneth to one of the guards. "Perhaps you should send someone to find Captain Chanter, as I'm sure he would like to be with Lord Thurdun."

"Yes, me lady."

Gaiyelneth closed the door and sat in a chair across from Mr. Ribbon on the other side of the Queen.

"I have had the honor of making your son's acquaintance," said the Queen.

"Aye, ma'am. Robby told me about meetin' up with yer party. He had a fine time, too, he said."

"It was good to meet him. But I suppose those were happier days, were they not?"

"Yes, ma'am. They were at that."

"And do you know where Robby is now? And your wife? Mirabella, I believe is her name."

"I don't rightly know. I think, an' I hope, both are up around Janhaven. That's whar the folks whar tryin' to go to when I left, an' me wife was put in charge of gettin' 'em thar."

"Janhaven is not far from Passdale, if I recall."

"That is so, ma'am. Around ten or twelve leagues west."

"Are you concerned that the Redvests will go there?"

"Why, yes, ma'am. It's been an awful worry to me."

"Well. What if I told you that your son is now farther away from Janhaven than you are?"

"Why, I'd be mighty surprised. An' I'd wonder how it is that ye might know such a thing, though I'm sure the ways of queens an' lords are beyond me."

"I am not at liberty to say how I know," replied Serith Ellyn. "But I assure you that my source is true. I cannot say how Janhaven fares, but I will endeavor to learn as soon as I may."

"Well, I'm astonished," Mr. Ribbon said, looking from the Queen to the smiling Gaiyelneth. "An' I wonder how far away me son is, an' his whereabouts, an' why ye may bother to know about him, just to name a few things that I wonder at."

"In fact, Robby is in the outlands of Vanara."

"Vanara?"

"Yes. He has traveled west along with Ashlord, the Kingsman Ullin Saheed Tallin, and three other friends."

"But, but," Mr. Ribbon was floored, and fumbled for words.

"They go on very important business."

Mr. Ribbon closed his open mouth and blinked.

"I shock you with this news," said the Queen. "I do not mean to. Your son is unique. I immediately saw that when I met him. Tell me, sir, how much do you know about his adventures at Tulith Attis this past summer?"

"Why, um, well, that is to say, I know Robby had some trouble out thar," Mr. Ribbon said. "It was durin' the big storm, an' Robby got turned about, on the way to see Mr. Ashlord."

Mr. Ribbon continued, saying what he knew about Robby's adventure. Serith Ellyn listened intently, then told Mr. Ribbon that Robby rang the Great Bell, and Mr. Ribbon nodded, having already put it all together. She went on to relate her own adventure that took place the night the Bell rang, out on the plains, when the storm broke upon their camp. She explained how the uncanny ringing caused their camp to rise to a state of great alarm. As a result, those who tracked the Queen's party and sought to do them harm had turned away rather than risk an attack.

"That is why I am indebted to your son," she concluded.

"Well, I'm sure Robby only did what he had to do," Mr. Ribbon said.

"That is what he said to me. Now, tell me, Robby isn't his true name, is it?"

"Pardon me?"

"You and your wife had him named in the old way, did you not? By a dying relative?"

"It beats me, ma'am, how ye could know that, it bein' all done secret-like."

"Again, if I told you how I know, I would be saying too much," she replied. "There are some things, good man, that are best left unsaid, for the good of all. Saying them would promote too much hope, and too much fear."

Mr. Ribbon glanced at Gaiyelneth, who was no longer smiling. Like his son, he never cared too much for riddles and innuendo, and he shook his head.

"Queen," he said at last, "if Robby is in some great danger, I wish ye'd say so, plain an' simple-like."

"I know," she said, smiling. "Robby once complained to me, wishing that I would speak plainly to him, too. I cannot tell you overmuch because, for one, doing so would reveal secrets that I am sworn to protect. And, for another, I do not wish to give you false hope. Robby is safe. But his journey is a dangerous one, and it is not over. Although I know where he is, I cannot say why he goes the way he goes. I suspect, however, that he goes to Vanara to seek help."

"Why go thar, an' not to Duinnor?"

"He may go to Duinnor, if all goes well. Or he may not. I cannot guess which way he might turn next, or be turned by events yet unforeseen."

"Yer words do not lighten me heart," said Mr. Ribbon. "Indeed, I am more afraid now than ever. Can't ye tell me more? Do ye know when Robby might come back?"

"I do not know. But I promise you this: I shall tell you what I can, as soon as I learn more."

• • •

His interview with the Queen was interrupted by her brother, Thurdun, who was pleased to meet Robby's father. But he and the Queen had to go immediately to meet with Carbane, so Gaiyelneth took Mr. Ribbon to rooms that had been prepared for him, not far from the wing where the Queen had her apartments, rooms that were finer than any he had ever seen. After Gaiyelneth instructed the staff to bring food and other necessaries, she, too, departed, leaving Mr. Ribbon staring out of the window at the brooding sea. He was still there after dark, being one moment enthralled by the beauty of the vastness that stretched out to the edge of the world, and the next moment filled with a deep sense of loss and foreboding.

A maidservant knocked and entered, followed by a man carrying several parcels. While the maidservant lit the lamps and went to turn down the bed, the man put the parcels on the table and then turned to Mr. Ribbon to explain.

"My name is Shackle, sir. I am to wait upon you."

"Oh?"

"Yes, sir. I apologize for taking so long to come to you, but Prince Danoss sent a note informing us that you departed Formouth in haste, and that you have no baggage or belongings other than what you wear," he said. "I am only now returning from the shops in the city. Here are bedclothes, slippers, robes, and other garments. I hope they will do for tonight."

"Oh, me! Thank ye, Mr. Shackle."

"Not at all, sir. I have arranged for a tailor to come tomorrow after breakfast, to measure you for your other needs."

"Oh, I'm sure that I can manage just fine with what I've got for the short time I'll be here. Besides, I've no way of payin' for anythin'."

"If I may say so, sir, the clothes you wear were put together in haste and do not fit you as well as others would. And, sir, all is paid for already."

"Oh!" Mr. Ribbon picked at his jacket and glanced at the travel cloak he had tossed over the chair. Shackle went to pick it up to hang in the wardrobe. "Well, I reckon I ain't been much concerned over dress these past weeks."

"I'm sure things of greater concern have occupied you," said Shackle. "I myself have relatives in the Eastlands, near Mimblewan, and we are all very concerned by the news that you brought. I do hope both our families are safe."

"Me, too."

"If that will be all, sir?" asked the maid.

"That will be all, Sasha," said Shackle. "If there is anything that you require, Mr. Ribbon, simply pull on the bellrope, regardless of the hour. When you desire breakfast, give it a tug, and we shall attend. Otherwise, a servant will see to the fireplace during the night, so do not be alarmed at his coming or going."

"Thank ye, Mr. Shackle."

"Good night, Mr. Ribbon."

Suddenly the prospects of a good night's sleep in a warm bed overwhelmed Mr. Ribbon, and after changing into the nightshirt left for him, he went to bed. In spite of his worries, and owing to the exertions of his long journey, he was soon asleep.

• • •

The next day saw little in the way of what Mr. Ribbon would call action. He was asked to recount the events in County Barley, and over the next week he repeated his tale again and again, to ever-differing groups, and sometimes to the same group as he had before. The Queen and Prince Danoss assured him that things were moving along, and they begged him to be patient. The Queen also told him that his wife was safe, though it still baffled Mr. Ribbon how she might know. Gaiyelneth took Mr. Ribbon under her wing and constantly assured him that Prince Carbane was nothing if not meticulous, and that he was acting as swiftly as things allowed. But the days of the next week were, for Mr. Ribbon, full of worry and anxious waiting, and he continued to let it be known that he desired to return to Passdale as soon as was practical, suggesting that he should return alone.

"I would not advise that," Danoss told him. "The roads are treacherous with ice and snow, and it would take a large party and much effort to see you all the way home. And, besides that, the invaders may still occupy the land. I have sent trusted scouts to see what they may learn. I beg you, let us be patient. A hasty move could cost many lives. So please put the notion of returning out of your head for the time being. I assure you that I and my father are putting things together as quickly as can be done. I'll have you back in Passdale just as soon as it is possible."

Mr. Ribbon could not gainsay the argument. So he waited, keeping to his rooms, or in the court, or wherever he could be close at hand should some development take place.

On the sixteenth day since his arrival in Glareth, as the air grew ever colder, Gaiyelneth took Mr. Ribbon sightseeing. In fact, she had to insist that he come.

"You do nothing but pace and fret and worry," she said to him. "I promise that you won't miss anything important while we are away. In fact, my Queen orders me to take you out from the Palace for your own good, and I must obey my Queen! Besides, while there is little you can do here, there is much we can do in the city. And I think you'll like what I'll show you."

Reluctantly, Mr. Ribbon gave in. Since it was a cold day, and windy, a carriage awaited them, and they rode in style and comfort down from the craggy heights where the Palace was situated, and into Old Town, as the oldest part of Glareth by the Sea was known. They stopped at a tavern along the way for hot spiced tea laced with whiskey. Gaiyelneth talked almost incessantly, cheery and seemingly without a care, telling Mr. Ribbon, as if she had not already done so, about how, on the night she met his son beside Lake Halgaeth, she and Robby had danced until they fainted, "a little worse for drink, if you know what I mean."

Mr. Ribbon smiled amiably but was clearly distracted by his own thoughts. Passing on through Old Town and into the city proper, they came to a street lined with warehouses and workshops wherein was made everything from ropes and sails to harnesses and wagons, and from wrought iron lampposts to copper kettles. Mr. Ribbon could not but be interested in such things, and with the carriage following them, they walked along the busy sidewalk, peeking into windows and sometimes going into the shops to view how things were made. In one, Gaiyelneth noticed how Mr. Ribbon fingered a little oil lamp. He commented that he owned one just like it, and how Mirabella loved to read or do her knitting by its light. He sighed, and she guided him back outside and to the next shop, but he seemed even more distant and sad to her observant eye. After a few minutes spent watching weavers make rope using an ingenious loom, she took him back to the carriage, and they climbed inside.

"I know things are very difficult for you, Mr. Ribbon," she said as they gently bounced along. "It is not easy to be far from those you love and care for."

"No. It ain't."

She turned to look through the window, and Mr. Ribbon saw her lips crease downward.

"But," he ventured, "I ain't the only one far from home, am I? I imagine yer as homesick as I am."

"I may be. Who's to say if one person is more lonesome than another?"

"Not me. I'm sorry for ever thinkin' only of meself. It's hard not to, but that don't make it right. I'm guessin' thar's a beau waitin' for ye back in Vanara."

"I don't know."

"Ye don't know if thar's a beau? Or ye don't know if he waits for ye?"

She looked at Mr. Ribbon and smiled, a little blush coming to her cheeks that was not due to the cold.

"He is above my station," she said. "And he is much older, too."

"Hm. Well, I can tell ye that neither don't matter much, when it comes to it."

"You don't think so?"

"I know it ain't so. Me wife's nearly twice me own age, though she looks as though she could be me daughter."

For the first time, Gaiyelneth saw Mr. Ribbon chuckle.

"An' it were quite the scandal, I can tell ye, when I tricked Mirabella's old man into lettin' us marry. Ye met Ullin, I think, Mira's nephew. But do ye know much of the Tallins?"

"Only that it is an ancient and proud family. A Named House, and a Joined one. And Lord Tallin, Ullin's grandfather, is a powerful man."

"Indeed, an' mighty wealthy, too! But, the thing of it is, Lord Tallin's own daughter an' me fell in love, an' we married, in spite of all."

"You said you tricked Lord Tallin?"

"Oh, well, out-tricked him, is more like it. See, the feller tried to make things mighty hard on me, to make it whar I couldn't marry Mirabella. But I reckon the mighty lord didn't know just how much the lowly country boy loved his daughter. I found one way an' another to come around all the problems I faced durin' the year I was to wait. 'Course, I didn't know it was Lord Tallin his own self what put such problems before me. Didn't matter. All this is to say that if ye really love someone, an' they really love ye, too, ye can nearly always make it so as the two of ye can be together."

"Hm. Do you really think so?"

"I do, lass."

"Then I will tell you a secret," she grinned, reaching over and taking him by the hands, "but you mustn't tell anyone at all!"

"Oh, I give me word!"

"I keep a love letter with me all the time. From him. He wrote to me on the day we left Vanara, and put it into a little locket. See this?"

She tugged back her scarf, and pulled on a chain to reveal a tiny locket of gold. As she leaned close for him to see, she went on.

"See how small it is? It was delivered to me by my brother who told me it was from a secret admirer. I was so heartsick when we departed Vanara that I didn't even bother looking at it, and just threw it in with my things. Chanter pestered and pestered me, saying I should take another look at it. When I finally did, and he asked what I thought of it, my answer did not satisfy him. He kept after me to look at it more closely. I didn't do so until the night we arrived here in Glareth, when I once more unpacked it. It was only then that I noticed the tiny crest on the back of it. The crest belonging to the House of the man I adore and love!"

She held it out so that Mr. Ribbon could squint at the tiny engraving of a sailing ship on the back of the case.

"Well, I'll be!"

"That's not all! Look!"

She opened the locket and showed him the tiny inscription within.

"It says, 'Because I long to be near to your heart, if I cannot be within it.' What do you think of that?"

"I think it is most amorous!"

"I know!"

She put the locket away, and then took Mr. Ribbon's hand again.

"I do miss him! Just as you miss Mirabella. And I hope that we shall both be reunited with our loves as soon as may be possible."

"Me, too. Me, too!"

"Oh, and look! We are at our next destination."

The carriage stopped at a shop atop a bluff, and they entered. It was a tea shop, and Mr. Ribbon let his young escort show him the way to a line of tables in the back next to rows of windows that overlooked dockyards and wharves. She ordered coffee for him because she knew he preferred it and tea for herself. Meanwhile, Mr. Ribbon gazed at the many buildings between them and the docks, amazed at all of the boats and ships moving back and forth across the bay, their sails tight with wind.

"Those are Prince Carbane's docks," she told him as cups were set and their drinks poured. They heard the ringing of a little bell, and Mr. Ribbon looked at Gaiyelneth questioningly.

"Oh, we are just in time! Look, down there. See that building? Watch!"

Mr. Ribbon did so, not knowing what he should be seeing. The building in view appeared to be a large warehouse of some kind, right at the water's edge, with stacks of lumber behind it. He could only see the back of the structure, but there were workers coming and going, and many of them were hurrying toward the water at the far side of the building. As he watched, the hull of a ship emerged from inside the building, going down long skids into the water where it splashed and rolled before settling upright. Other patrons of the shop who also watched now broke into applause.

"Oh!" declared Mr. Ribbon. "Now that was somethin' to see!"

"Yes," Gaiyelneth said. "I thought you'd like that. And you'll like it even more when I tell you that it is to be a warship."

"Oh?"

"Yes. See those other buildings to either side. All eight of them, I am told, have launched a ship this week, and are already busy at the next ones. Prince Carbane intends to add twenty new ships to his fleet before another fortnight. He employs not only these workers, but those across the river, over there, see? And I am told that he has already purchased many smaller vessels, too. All this since you arrived."

"Really? Ye don't say!"

"I do say. Some of the work was already underway before, but your news has sped things up. Now they work day and night. I can tell you this much: Prince Carbane plans something big, though I do not know the details. Here, take this."

She took from her pocket a little spyglass and gave it to Mr. Ribbon.

"Is this a spyglass?" he asked, turning it over in his hands. "Ullin Saheed had one years ago, an' he showed me how to work it."

"Yes, I always bring it when I come here," she said.

Grinning, he peered through it, looking at the ship that had just been launched and was now being pulled by lines to a nearby dock.

"Look out there, toward the mouth of the bay. What do you see?"

Mr. Ribbon pointed it where she instructed, straining at the eyepiece. At last he saw many tiny points, like the trunks of tall thin trees without limbs, all jutting up from the glare of the water some miles toward the sea.

"Are those the masts of ships?"

"They are. On the day you arrived, Prince Carbane sent fast little sloops up and down the coast, summoning every ship and seaman. Now, over a hundred are readying, and more arrive every day. Do you want to know what I think?"

"I certainly do."

"I think there is a big war coming, or threatening to come. And I think the Tracians you brought word about prepare to make it come. But I think they don't intend coming north, for Glareth is far too powerful. I think they raid the Eastlands for the things they need elsewhere."

"Elsewhar?"

"Masurthia, their weak neighbor to their west. It is said that storms and drought have made Masurthia weak, and its people are unsettled concerning their new Ruling Prince, who is but a boy. They say that his regents do not understand how to make things better for their people, and that Duinnor cannot act to help them, either. So why should Tracia attack Glareth when Masurthia would be easy pickings? That's what I think."

"Hm. I don't reckon I know as much about things as do others," Mr. Ribbon said. "But I can't see how it would be much help to make ships to go where ships can't go. Into the Eastlands, that is."

Gaiyelneth leaned over the table and whispered.

"I think Prince Carbane means to come up behind them."

• • •

Gaiyelneth's efforts paid off, and for the first time since riding away from Passdale, Mr. Ribbon had some hope returned to him. If nothing else, it was a comfort to know that action was being taken. He also realized that the workings of the world were more complicated than those in little Passdale, and that great powers moved slowly, but they moved nonetheless. After all, it must have taken a long time for the Redvest leaders to plan their invasion of the Eastlands. It only stood to reason, he thought, that it would take some time to counter it.

That night, back in his rooms, he went over everything in his head, wishing he knew how Mirabella was doing and whether Robby was safe. It would not have been much comfort for him to know that Robby and Ullin had fled Vanara, and were only beginning an even more dangerous journey. Nor would it be much comfort to know that Mirabella had taken up arms as in the days before they were married, and this day and night risked her life to repulse an attack by Redvests upon the Narrows along the road to Janhaven.

But Mr. Ribbon was tired of being comfortable. Sitting on the side of his bed, he blew out the candle and thought again about the ships, wondering how the Prince would put them to use. Suddenly, out of nowhere, he remembered those moments while aboard the fishermen's boat, his hand on the tiller and the other on the mainsheet. For just that while, before the storm hit and in spite of his worries, he had been content. Now, sitting in the darkness, he remembered those feelings. And he felt remorse, as if he should not have had such feelings until those he cared most for were safe and sound, until they were all back in their homes going about their lives. That was the kind of contentment, he now thought, that really counted.

• • •

The following morning, as Mr. Ribbon was dressing, there was a knock on his door. When he opened it, he was surprised to see Prince Danoss standing there, smiling.

"At last we move!" Danoss said before Mr. Ribbon could even express a good morning. He walked into the room and looked around. "Pack your things if you wish to return to Passdale. We leave today."

"We do?"

"Yes. My father's plan is put to action and begins. He sends forth the first of his ships this morning, to be followed by more throughout the month. Meanwhile, a land army prepares to march. But you and I go to Formouth. By the time we arrive, my forces there will be marshaled. And our Lakemen with their boats will be ready to carry us swiftly south."

Chapter 7

General Vidican's Spy

By the time the fishing boat bearing Robby's father pushed out from Northwick and hoisted sail, the first Redvest army had entered the lands south of Tallinvale. Just as Lord Tallin predicted, the army moved first to take the line of keeps and outposts along the southern border of the valley, but the Redvests found them empty. Two days later, a force of nine thousand footmen, three thousand heavy infantry, and a cavalry of five hundred horses approached the once-rich terraces of the valley, some twenty miles south of Tallin City. The crops were all gone, the vines uprooted, the houses and barns demolished, their stones scattered, and what remained of the beams and planks of their construction were cold ashes. Realizing that the main road was too narrow to move swiftly northward, the Redvest general ordered his army split in two, one to continue north and east, and the other to swing around along the road that ran west of the city. Meanwhile, he sent his horsemen galloping ahead, seeking likely targets to harry. These were all mistakes.

Tallin's men were watching, and they were ready. Knowing the lay of the land, they poured southward between the two forces and kept themselves hidden as they waited for the Redvests to pass on either side. Once the long columns had passed, the Tallinvalers split their force in two, each one stealthily advancing from behind the separated columns of the invaders.

Meanwhile, so eager to reach Tallin City were the enemy horsemen that they failed to reconnoiter the hills. When thousands of arrows rained down on their unsuspecting comrades following miles behind on foot, a great panic set in. At this moment, Tallinvale footmen carved their way into the rear of the Redvests, and they sprang out from behind every tree and bush and up from every ditch and streamed on either side of the Redvests. Tallin had ordered that the engagement was to last only for a period of one hour, and no more, so by the time the enemy had recovered their wits and regrouped to face south, the attackers were melting away into the dusk, leaving a sea of lifeless Redvests behind.

Nearly fifteen miles apart, it was the following day before either of the Redvest columns learned the fate of the other. So devastating was the blow that the commanding general decided to halt any further advance until his forces could reunite. He also knew that this failure and the loss of nearly half of his men was his undoing, and dishonorable shame would fall upon his name. So, late the next afternoon, he sat in his tent and nervously wrote dispatches giving the full details of the engagement and to request reinforcements be sent from the south. When this was done, he wrote out his final order for his next in command, and, without a word, he fell upon his sword. Following his dead general's order, the next in command cut off the general's head and sent it along with the dispatches southward.

Meanwhile, the enemy cavalry pushed on in spite of their losses only to circle Tallin City impotently. Finding no fodder to speak of, no food, and no assailable enemy outside the formidable walls of the place, they returned southward, now riding into scores of traps, tricks, snares, and spear-lined pits that spared neither man nor horse. By the time the surviving riders came upon their once-proud army, now in shambles, they, too, were greatly diminished in numbers and just as dispirited. Two days later, the entire army was ordered to fall back to the line of keeps they had bypassed, to prepare those positions against further attack from Tallinvalers, and to await reinforcements.

This turn of events was better than Lord Tallin could have hoped for, and his people were thrilled by their early and easy victory. Now the abrupt Redvest retreat, done in such confusion and disarray, offered yet another chance to hurt the enemy, and Tallin quickly organized new sorties. In a single bold strike, three hundred horsemen, led by Lord Tallin himself, overran and decimated the enemy rearguard before they could form a defense, and they penetrated deep into the retreating columns with merciless effect. Stealthy bowmen poured into the wide gap that was punched through the Redvest lines. They spread out, separating into pairs, moving during the next few days from hiding place to cover, sniping ceaselessly and with unerring deadliness, until, out of arrows, they slowly filtered back to Tallin City.

Under this onslaught, the first army to invade Tallinvale collapsed. Only swift and cruel discipline prevented a complete rout, so fearful had the Redvests become of every bush and rock, and of every dusty cloud on their horizon. Infuriated, the Tracian High Command ordered four of its best generals to march immediately northward, with their combined armies of over seventy thousand men. This was exactly what Lord Tallin desired, and he was thrilled by the reports of his spies.

It gave him time, nearly a fortnight more, before the enemy could encroach in great force. That meant two weeks less food for the invaders, food that would be needed for winter. Two weeks longer that the enemy's ultimate plan would be delayed. And two more weeks to lay more traps for them, making every roadway and path a hazard, devised not only by Tallin and his people, but also by the people in and around Janhaven and their allies, the Hill Town folk, who also rejoiced at these early victories. So preparations continued, made all the more urgent by the sure knowledge that bloodshed had begun, and by the certainty that soon

Tallinvale would be cut off from those in Janhaven and Hill Town by the overwhelming might of a vast encircling army.

• • •

During this time, with no care to any of these events, Sir Winter strode south across the River Osterflo and into the high Carthanes, spreading his icy robes first upon those mountains, then setting his eye upon the Eastlands. He came slowly, at his ease, sending sleet and fog ahead and then cold, bone-jarring rain. Sir Wind then joined in, sending two of his children, Gust and Gale, through the Thunder Mountains and southeast across the old Eastlands Realm. Knowing that his message was delivered for Sir Winter, Wind recalled his offspring and they moved away to other parts. Winter, too, retreated for a while, permitting Sir Sun to shine brightly again through a calm and breathless sky onto the chilly blood-soaked lands.

• • •

In Passdale, General Vidican received word of his countrymen's advance by fast riders who plied up and down the road that ran along the Saerdulin and Bentwide Rivers. Heartened by the early reports of an unopposed advance, he made preparations to send more wagons south to meet them, loaded with much needed grain and food. But more than a week passed without further news, and when it came, it was shocking. Vidican was angered by the waste, the awful incompetence of his countrymen, and the implications for his tenuous occupation force, so far from any support. Weeks dragged by, made miserable by sleet, snow, and damp weather, and he fretted that Tallinvale would mount a northward strike against him. He prepared contingency plans for withdrawal, back the way they had come, swinging past Tulith Attis and on through the Boggy Wood. But, thankfully, his scouts reported no movements on the part of the Tallinvale defenders.

General Vidican's captive labor force, somehow learning the news, now worked all the more clumsily, and all the more slowly. They would soon be a liability, he knew, and sooner than he had expected. A few had even managed to escape, and had set fire to several wagons in the process. Normally, this would result in the execution of as many prisoners as had escaped, to discourage further attempts. But he needed labor as much as he needed wagons, and recalled more of his patrols to put their shoulders to the work of building more transport.

All of this was very distressing to Vidican, on top of worries that the mayor of the place had evidently escaped to Glareth. Until the main Redvest army arrived at Tallinvale, and could send relief, he faced the possibility of defending against Glarethians from the north while at the same time containing the Janhaven people to his west. Now there seemed to be a new threat mounting. Dispatches arrived stating that the last two trains of wagons that he had sent south never arrived. Bandits, it seemed, prowled the roads south of Barley. From then on, Vidican was forced to send a portion of his soldiers to guard the shipments. When he sent dispatches to his superiors requesting the return of his men, he received no answer. Instead, he received new instructions ordering him to load all remaining wagons with provisions as soon as possible, to destroy the town and all remaining structures, and to move south with all his force to ensure the delivery.

Holding his men in check was difficult enough, and only the stiffest punishments, swiftly carried out, prevented insubordination. If the men got wind of the prospect of moving out, there was little he could do to keep them from the prisoners, amongst which were more than a hundred women and girls. Already there had been incidents, and the bodies of two of his soldiers still hung from the porch of the sundries store where their acts had been committed. That summary punishment, and Vidican's firm assurances to the rest of the prisoners, was the only thing that prevented their all-out revolt.

Needless to say, none of this made Vidican happy. And those were two good fighters he had executed. His little army was spread thin, and grew thinner by the day. Two hundred men were lost within the first few days, in fiercer fighting than was expected, along with nearly all of their horses. Then, in an attempt to flush out the fighters protecting the Narrows that guarded the road to Janhaven, he sent three entire companies into the hills in a flanking maneuver. Of nearly four hundred men, barely a hundred, wounded and unnerved, managed to return; the rest had been cut to shreds in a series of ambushes and in fierce woodland combat. And he lost another fifty men with each shipment sent south. All that added to this miserable cold spell. His men were beginning to fall ill, and even though they were all quartered indoors, his laborers could hardly supply enough firewood for heat and cooking while at the same time keep at their work preparing materials for shipment. If this were not such a bountiful land, his army would be in dire straits, indeed. All the same, Vidican mused, at this rate of loss there would be precious few of his men left by spring to join the fighting at Tallinvale.

He put down his orders, leaned back in his chair, and gazed up at the well-trimmed beams of the room. If this Common House was any sign of the Eastlanders' wit and skill, it was no wonder things were so difficult. It was a strong building, with only a few adorning features, but airy, clean, and tidy. All signs of a meticulous and conscientious people. These were not at all the simple bumpkins he had expected to encounter.

"I warned you not to send those men into the hills."

Vidican turned to see Galatus, his advisor, standing at the doorway.

"Shut up," Vidican enunciated. "When I desire your advice, I shall ask for it."

"Then you had better begin asking," Galatus said, calmly walking over to the table. He poured himself a glass of wine, inhaled its bouquet with his mouth and nose, then sipped, admiring its flavor. He pushed some papers aside and sat across the table from Vidican. For a moment, he was content to enjoy the wine and the warmth from the nearby roaring fireplace. Taking another sip, he then picked up the bottle and examined the paper label glued to it.

"I have always said that you can judge a people by the wine they produce," he commented. "At least, certain aspects of their character. But it takes no wine taster to know these are a careful lot. They plan well in advance of their needs, and they lay in against unexpected chance. They are patient. They are confident in their crafts. They had their own school, right here in this county. And, judging by how thoroughly they record so much in writing, they are not entirely unlearned and illiterate. Do you know, this bottle is marked with not only the year of its vintage and the winery, but even with the name of the field from which these grapes were picked?"

Vidican closed his eyes while he exhaled wearily from his nose.

"Have you determined whether or not they were forewarned of our coming?" he asked.

"No," said Galatus. "That is, I do not believe they were. I know you find it implausible that you encountered two militias here, in a single county, when you did not come across as many on the entire trek northward through all the rest of this old realm. But I see no sign of any foreknowledge."

"Then why were they so well armed? So well managed and prepared? No, no! Do not repeat your opinion that the Kingsman was responsible. One man could hardly prompt these people to commit the men and treasury required."

"I do not know. But I sense no Kingsmen in Janhaven. Perhaps the one you saw was killed in battle. We know that Makeig's band of pirates and hill people assist those in Janhaven. Makeig was, in his day, a formidable sea captain before he ran from capture, known for his cunning. I am sure he and his followers are nearby. However, I believe there is another who holds the reins of power in Janhaven, and directs their actions. A woman. And she is Elifaen. My divinings tell me she is the key to their successes against you."

"Elifaen. Be that as it may," Vidican stated skeptically, "we hardly have the power to eliminate her since not even our scouts have made it into their encampment. It seems your usefulness lessens with each passing day. Perhaps your powers have diminished."

"My usefulness? Hardly. My powers? I assure you, they have not. If you had sent for me sooner, and if those damn soldiers had not stopped me at the frontier, I would have been able to provide more to you. Nearly a month wasted, while your lieutenants pressed you into rash actions. As it is, perhaps if you listen to me now, my powers would prove themselves to you, as I have done all these years since our association began."

"Do not remind me again how you saved me from obscurity. How I owe to you forewarnings of my enemies' intrigues within the courts of

Forlandis. Or how I would not be a general today if it were not for your soothsaying. I tire of such comments, and I will not tolerate any more of them. If you have something to say to me, some useful advice to offer, now is the time to do so. Our superiors grow impatient, and I do not blame them."

"Very well." Galatus took a gulp of wine. "There is a line of hills to the south and west of us. They are part of the ridge that separates us from the region of Janhaven. There is a shallow lake on the east side, not very large."

"What of it?"

"There is an old troll cave there. It is really a tunnel, cut clean through the ridge to the other side. A strong force of men could easily move through it, and come at Janhaven from the south."

"Why did you not tell me about the place before?"

"I only divined its existence last night."

"What else did you divine about it?"

"Only that it was once used by bandits. And that it is abandoned and unguarded."

"Is it on any of our maps?"

"I have not seen it marked. But I feel sure it is there."

Vidican stood and walked to the door. He looked back at Galatus for a long moment, then put his head through the door.

"Captain! Send one of your scouts to me."

Turning back to Galatus, Vidican said nothing, but his glare made the seer swallow hard. For his part, Vidican's doubts nagged at him, and he hated his association with Galatus. That his rise to power was due to this so-called diviner! Did his military prowess count for nothing? Were his connections in court and among the High Command of Tracia of no consequence? Galatus was not always correct in his advice, and he was secretive about his methods. Unlike other practitioners of the divination arts, this man did not throw bones, never offered sacrifices, or even took the time to make star charts. After nearly ten years, Galatus was still an enigma to Vidican. And Vidican mistrusted enigmas.

"Our scouts will find the place," Vidican stated. "And it will be as you say, unguarded and an easy passage to place our men behind the Janhaven fighters. If it is not, well, you can certainly divine your own fate, I'm sure."

• • •

The next afternoon, owing to the mysterious description given by Galatus, General Vidican's scouts found the place. They returned to confirm the location to the General, much to the soothsayer's relief. Indeed, the scouts reported that it was unguarded and was a quick route around and behind the Janhaven lines. Vidican sent another large party of elite heavily armed scouts to the place, pulling back many of those who watched the road between Passdale and the Narrows. This second party was to take and hold the troll cave, set watches at its far side, and then send a squad to find the best way from there to come at Janhaven from the south. That same day, the High General Mar Henith, who commanded the forces around Tallinvale, sent new dispatches reiterating the need to come with supplies, but added new orders for Vidican to take Janhaven at all costs and with haste, to capture and secure all of the food, stores, and materials found there, and to transport everything southward immediately. Apparently, Vidican surmised, his superiors did not have the force to send against Janhaven, or else they had already tried and failed. Either way, Vidican was determined not to disappoint, and he had already begun preparing his own troops.

With fewer than two thousand men left to him, he feverishly set to work reorganizing his small force. Two platoons would stay in Passdale. One would round up and guard all prisoners. The remaining men would make feints along the roadway at the Narrows, as if probing for an attack from that flank. Everyone else, every last soldier available, would push through the cave, up the trails blazed by his scouts, and be in position to strike Janhaven. It would take five days to prepare and another day to move the army into position. Even with his diminished force, Vidican was confident he would succeed.

Vexingly, Vidican's scouts still could not surmise the number of fighters that would be faced. Some said less than a dozen, while others reported more than six hundred. Survivors of the ill-fated attack on the Narrows claimed thousands of fighters had fought them back. It was galling to have such discrepancies, and Vidican pressed Galatus for answers, just as he pressed his scouts for more accurate numbers. But, with or without proper intelligence on the Janhaven fighting strength, Vidican was determined, as much by pride as by desperation, to move ahead with his plan. While he refined his plan, word was given for his troops to prepare to march and for battle. Weapons were honed, bows restrung, packs repaired, and rations prepared and distributed.

He stood at his map table, speaking to his field commanders, going over the plan again and again. After a long evening, they all seemed happy to get back to the business of fighting. In the corner of the room sat Galatus, with a book on his lap as a table for his glass of wine, quietly watching the proceedings with a look of contentment that irritated Vidican every time he glanced that way. After several hours of working through details, even Vidican's countenance started to shift toward weary satisfaction that all that could be planned was planned, and all that could be prepared was being prepared.

"You have five days more, then you must be ready to march on the morning six days from today. All are to carry full kit, as we will not be coming back to Passdale. I intend to lead the attack personally, and I will amply reward those of you who display the greatest valor. And, to assure our success," he added with a tone of sarcasm, "Mr. Galatus will be at my side throughout."

For the first time in years, Vidican saw on Galatus an expression of surprise and dismay. This made Vidican even more satisfied with the evening's work. He dismissed his captains and lieutenants one by one, to prepare their troops, until only one captain remained. Vidican walked him to the door, his hand on his shoulder as he spoke softly.

"Captain Pargolis, a word before you go."

"Yes, General?"

"I know that you are disappointed to be left behind, as it were. And that I chose Captain Toradatis to go with me as my second-in-command."

"I do not question your decision, sir. But I am disappointed to miss the fight."

"I know you are. But there will be plenty of fighting to go around in the next few weeks, I assure you. I leave you in charge here to see to an important task. The prisoners have no doubt observed our preparations. When the assault force moves out, tell your men to instill calm amongst them. Have the prisoners prepare the last of the wagons, filled with anything of value in Passdale. While they work to do this, perhaps let it be suggested that an advancing army of Glarethians are but a day or so away. Their hopes will make that plausible. Let it be known that we move to join our comrades in the south before the Glarethians arrive. Perhaps insinuate that they will soon be freed to fend for themselves, once their work for us is done. Say whatever you must to keep them calm and unsuspecting. But," Vidican paused at the doorway, lowering his voice further, "after we have departed, and as soon as practical, begin moving all of your men south with the remaining able-bodied men and women. Use them to pull whatever wagons you may not have teams for. Dispose of any who are not cooperative. I leave that to you, but they will be useful laborers at the siege, and I'm sure our superiors will be grateful to you for bringing as many as you can. Deal with the girls, the young, and the infirm however you wish. So long as none can escape to forewarn Janhaven. Burn or destroy everything you leave behind, houses, buildings, everything. Do you understand me?"

"Yes, General Vidican."

"Be delicate until all is ready for your departure. Then be ruthless."

"Yes, General. You may rely upon me."

"Good. I will see you again at Tallinvale in a fortnight, or less."

"Yes, General. Good hunting, sir!"

• • •

None in the meeting, not even Galatus, suspected that there was a spy amongst them. Without being seen or heard himself, this spy saw and heard everything within the room. When Vidican saluted and dismissed this last officer, the spy departed, too, as unseen when he left as he had been when he entered, determined to carry warning of the impending attack to Mirabella.

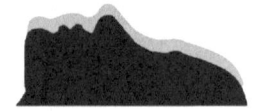

Chapter 8

A Shortcut

Day 165
80 Days Remaining

"When I was in the desert," Ullin said as he and his companions negotiated their way up an icy defile, "I longed to be in the snowy mountains."

His speech was stuttered, each crampon-fitted boot making sure of its grip, each jab of his trekking poles cracking and thudding. Conversation was difficult and seldom long; the effort needed was too great, the distraction too annoying, and the focus on each step too critical. Besides, between the whistle of the wind and the muffling covers around their faces and ears, it was often too hard to be heard unless one shouted, and such lung-effort was usually reserved for less idle words. But they had trudged all day with hardly a sentence shared between the men, each to his own mind, and each keen-eyed on his own steps and on the cliffs and peaks that surrounded them. It was but another day like the day before and the day before that. How many days had it been since they fled Linlally and its burning White Palace? Ullin interrupted his thoughts to ponder the question. Seven? No, this was the eighth day out.

By now, Ullin knew every stitch of Haskin's backpack, every seam and every binding, and he could tell by the bend of his hood which way the man was looking, whether down or up, or left or right. Likewise for all the others in line ahead of him, Robby, with Gullwing ahead of him, then, farther along, Tiller, Sterns, and Sergeant Hull. He could as easily identify each of them by the way they moved and stepped as by their faces. Ullin was sure that Buckwise, the man behind him, was just as familiar with his own pack and stance.

Eight grueling days of endless, perpetual cold. Commander Strake and the Sergeant both said they were making good progress, no more than three or four days to the outpost, a speck called Fort Defiance. Good progress, considering that a snowstorm on the third day out held them in camp for an entire day. Good progress, considering the avalanche that just missed them yesterday, falling not a hundred yards behind the last man and obliterating the pass they had just climbed through with crushing boulders and ice in a billowing cloud of snow. It was a narrow miss of only a few minutes, and though not a man was hurt, it filled them all with such terror that they gaped and stared for a long while, every knee quaking long after the last thunderous echo faded far away and the last fleck of the snow-cloud settled around them. A bad omen, someone commented, as it was not yet the season for avalanches.

Even in the shelters—crude rock structures with barely enough space for all of the men and their gear—it was bitterly cold. But at least the shelters were stocked with thick blankets and plenty of food. And each night, they huddled together, making repairs to their equipment, eating, and sleeping. Meals consisted mainly of a concoction called "snowbutter." It was, Ullin surmised, made of butter, lard, sugar, and nuts, and it was hardly more edible than jawrock. Standard issue to mountain troopers, snowbutter came in one-pound chunks that was certainly as hard as jawrock, at least until it was thawed. And each man was expected to eat at least two pounds of it every day, and two more at night. If it was not tasty, it at least staved off hunger for a few hours. Some of the men put their snowbutter into their cups of hot tea—the only form of hot food that was served. Ullin tried it, too, and found that the tea did soften the snowbutter enough to chew, but it made the tea taste more like leather. He did not complain. The troopers that escorted them knew their business, knew how to survive the cold, and Ullin knew that he could learn much from their example. Sleep came quickly after eating, and perhaps so many men crammed together under piles of blankets did more to keep the shelter warm than the tiny iron stove full of glowing coal. Then came morning, more snowbutter, more tea, and back out into the wind and ice.

Only eight days, Ullin mused, trying thrice before getting his foot planted firmly enough to put weight on it for the next step on the crusty ice. In spite of the slits he looked through, his eyes hurt with the glare, the sun reflecting harshly from the glittering ice and bouncing spitefully and without the least heat from the snowy slopes and crystal-sheeted cliffs. It was a good while after his comment and several hundred yards farther along before Ullin was answered.

"Well, we've all served in the desert," someone chuckled, "and had the same wish."

"Things have a way of turning about, don't they?" Buckwise said from behind Ullin.

"Tighten up!" called back the Sergeant while acknowledging with a wave that he understood the signal from the lead group on ahead. "We're coming up on the rough bit."

"The rough bit?" Robby muttered as he planted his trekking poles and then his right foot. Looking up, he saw that they were headed into a box canyon that cut in between two legs of the mountain. The two opposing sides rose sharply into sheer faces covered with icicles hundreds of feet long. "If one of those broke off and fell...," he thought darkly.

It hurt too much to look for very long, the glare was tremendous, and his pack prevented him from tilting his head back far enough to see the tops of those walls. As slow as they were going, he could see that his squad was gaining on members of the first squad who were using their ice axes and working their way up what appeared to be a frozen waterfall that stretched across the narrowing canyon. Following Sergeant Hull's lead, he and his team took out their own ice axes and secured the loops around their wrists. Robby had by now learned why plenty of rope stretched between them. Just a few days earlier, while trekking slowly across a broad ice sheet, he saw one of the men of the first squad fall. There was a yell, and the fallen man's mates dug in hard as he slid backwards, flailing to gain some purchase. The men ahead and behind threw themselves down, flinging their bodies against the ice and driving their crampons and their ice axes hard until the rope went taut, snapping the hapless man to an awkward and abrupt halt. It happened so fast, and Robby only chanced to be looking up to see it, but it made him all the more careful, seeing the risk each put the others in, the responsibility of all to save the one who fell, and seeing the effort it took them to pick themselves up and resume their course. Amazingly, as inexperienced as they were, neither he nor Ullin had fallen a single time, though there were plenty of slips and short slides, especially during the first few days. Owing to the quick response of their mates, and to the care and coaching they continually received, everyone in Robby's squad managed to stay on their feet.

As he tried over and over to plant his crampons into the rock-like ice, Robby only imagined the pain the men ahead must be enduring. Being half-numb from cold did not help, and only made every movement a jarring, aching thud in every joint and muscle.

"Only a bit farther to Ol' Moaner, boys," the Sergeant called.

Robby had no idea what he meant, but they inched on, now traversing a frozen stream, cracked and jagged, as if layers had ground together, heaving blocks up and atop others. They zigzagged, picking their way through the maze, sometimes jumping awkwardly in their gear over narrow crevasses. When, an hour later, they made it to the frozen falls, Robby saw that it was not as sharply inclined as it had appeared from a distance. Instead, it unevenly sloped upward as if shoals lay under the thick flow. They found, too, that the squad that went first, now on the top, had chiseled foot holds into the face of the sloping ice and were now suspending ropes to help the second squad along the harder part of the climb. In some stretches, they were able to go from foot to foot, but in other parts of the climb, they were forced onto their bellies, scrambling to drive their toes in, pulling against their ice axes with one hand while clinging to an anchored rope with the other. Their advance was very slow and got steeper near the top, the ice hard and clear, and Robby struggled to move up and forward. He slipped several times, but caught himself each time with his axe until his arm was burning with soreness from dangling too many times.

Then he slipped again. As he fell, the loop around his wrist tightened and held yet again, spinning him by his right arm around onto his back, his feet kicking with no purchase until one heel caught hold. He hung there for a moment, somewhat awkwardly, facing across the long vista, the way they had come.

"This is ridiculous!" he panted.

Sensing a nearby movement, he craned his head to his left. Just below, Gullwing was working his way closer to him.

"Just hang on a moment...UGH!"

The trooper steadily worked his toes and axes together, spider-like, grunting as he came, small chips of ice flying, some striking Robby's mask-covered face. He stopped a foot or so beside Robby, his head near Robby's waist.

"How're you doing, lad?"

"Fine. Just fine. You?"

"Not too bad. Still got your line snugged up good?"

Robby tested his line, tightened up by Sterns about ten yards above and ahead of him.

"Yes."

"Alright then. Sterns!"

"Aye?"

"Pass the word for a spare axe, would you?"

As the call went up and a spare was found to pass down, he explained.

"Now look," he said pleasantly as if he and Robby were leaning against a bar rather than a shelf of ice seventy feet up in the air. "We can't hang around here all day, can we?"

"No, sir. I'm very sorry."

"No, no. None of that. I'm just saying, when you get the axe, the first thing is to get it well strapped on. Right? Then, when you give me the signal, I'll cut you free of me. As soon as that's done, you go straight up, see? Straight up, not that way. Up. As fast as you can, using both axes and the very toe-tips of your crampons. Don't mind how much ice you chunk downward or churn up. We'll all be ready for that. Mind that you don't cut your lead rope because those up top will be pulling you up with that. Here we go."

From a hidden place over the top a new rope dangled downward with an ice axe on the end. Gullwing helped Robby slip a hand through the loop on the axe, and then he secured the rope to Robby.

"Right. All set. Straight up. Claw, claw, claw like fury itself. Got the idea?"

"I believe so."

"Can you do it?"

"I dunno. I think so."

"I think so, too. Now the hard part: getting you turned around. I'll help you with that, just hold tight a moment longer."

His own grip none-too-sure, Ullin watched from just a few yards below, and worried that Robby's arm and shoulder must be near to breaking from the way he was so twisted around. Putting his head down and away from the ice flying from Gullwing's clawing picks, he toed in firmly and prepared for the climber to fall on him. But the trooper managed to get himself up and beside Robby. He heard Gullwing's instructions but wondered if Robby had enough strength to make it. Then, after some nerve-racking dangling and twisting and shoving, Gullwing managed to get Robby turned back around facing into the ice and ready to go. They cut the line, and, with a couple of quick swings of his axes, Robby was off.

"Up! Up!" cried Gullwing

"That's it! Lay into it, mate!" cried the others, forgetting their station for the moment. Now, in spite of the chips that showered down, Ullin watched, astonished that Robby could move so quickly, rapidly working his left arm and right leg, then his opposite limbs, like an insect. Twenty feet up, the face truly did lean outward and Ullin caught his breath as Robby's legs swung away, unable to find a toehold. But Robby kept going, continuing to pummel and crack the ice with his picks alone. Almost immediately he was up and over and out of sight.

A cheer went up as Robby was pulled over the top, and many hands were soon hauling and pulling him along until, grasping a hand, he was pulled up to his feet. He grinned, panting and unable to speak for many moments, bent over with his hands on his knees, watching those who were behind him being helped over the top. Commander Strake gave Robby an encouraging shoulder slap, but all Robby could do in response was shake his head and utter, "Sorry!"

"You did as well as any and better than most," Strake stated, turning to watch the others come up. "This bit has always given us trouble. Someday maybe we'll figure out a better way up or around."

They were joined by the equally winded Ullin and others of Robby's squad, and slowly the group reassembled. They stood at the top of a frozen pool and at the base of the back of the canyon. An odd sound came on the breeze, a low hum, then faded away as the air shifted. Glancing at Ullin, who was trying to walk off his exertions, Robby was not sure if anyone else had heard it.

"All up and accounted for, Commander."

"Thank you, Sergeant. Good work, all of you. Let's bear onward a bit longer. Night comes swiftly!"

"Aye, sir!"

"Aye!"

Soon they were moving again along the frozen surface of a stream toward a looming wall shadowed by the arms of the mountain. Several times Robby thought he heard the same faint sound, tentative and low, but he could not decide where it came from. Indeed, it was difficult to tell where any sound came from as every noise of their movement bounced and echoed all around them. Still, the odd noise came and went until it was completely obscured by the crack and crash of axes ahead. Looking up, Robby saw they had reached the end of the canyon, and members of Strake's team were hacking away at a cave opening that was nearly covered over with thick sheets of ice. Oddly, and in spite of the noise of the men's work, the hum seem to grow louder and louder. Robby's group gathered around to watch the men work, and Robby noticed they were putting away their poles and axes.

"What is making that sound?" he asked.

Sergeant Hull looked up from his pack and grinned. "Why, that's Ol' Moaner!"

"Who?"

"Not who. What," Haskin said, nudging Robby and gesturing toward the troopers still hacking away. Just then a large stubborn sheet of ice gave way to their strokes and crashed downward and crumbled away, revealing a large cave entrance. At the same moment the hum grew in volume and the pitch lowered considerably.

"That's what we call this tunnel," the Sergeant explained. "Sometimes, you can hear her complaints from over a mile back. Kind of quiet, today."

"Rather," agreed one of the troopers.

"Sergeant!" Commander Strake trudged over.

"Sir!"

"We'll go in as usual," Strake explained.

"Very good, sir."

"We'll bivouac in the Blue Room."

"As you say, sir."

"Weapons!" Strake bellowed.

At Strake's command, those who had not already removed their outer mittens did so, and all made ready their arms, checking swords and daggers and making certain they were ready to draw.

"A precaution," Strake explained to Robby and Ullin. "We approach the borderlands. These caves and tunnels are a quick way through what would otherwise take three weeks of ropes and ice axes to go up and over. But not just for us. We've had a few encounters in the past. Nothing serious. But be at your wary. If there are any of Secundur's creatures within, our banging has given them ample notice of our arrival."

Ullin and Robby looked at each other, remembering the specimens Seafar showed to them, then each scrambled to put away their poles and axes and to loosen their swords.

Strake's team split up, just as he had ordered, and the entire group entered the cave. Lamps were lit and passed around. A strong breeze blew through from the far side of the chamber.

"Let's get unhitched," Haskin said to Ullin who was staring distractedly at the oddly painted figures that covered the walls. After he had untied his part of the rope and was free of it, he took a lamp and held it up high.

"What are those?" Robby asked, coming to stand next to Ullin. The grayish tan wall was smooth, and there were many white and blue and red symbols and pictures painted in what seemed a random order. Handprints, elongated and large, were next to leaping deer and rows of stick-figures, many holding jars. There were other figures engaged in what appeared to be wild dances. In another broad section of the wall was depicted, in similar primitive fashion, some kind of battle, with clusters of stick-men wielding swords and clubs against each other.

"Look there," Robby pointed to several figures above all the rest. Some of these had wings and were ascending a carved path into white clouds. Others, however, were falling, their wings detached from them, their arms flailing in despair.

"These caves are ancient," said Strake who appeared next to Ullin. "Lord Seafar has been here many times, to copy what you see and to study this place. He thinks it may have been one of the first dwelling places of the Elifaen after the Fall. But none of the living Firstborn remember this place, so Seafar says. In those days, he thinks, the land was not as it is today. Not so cold or barren. These may not be the last paintings you see, but we do not have time to examine them. We must keep moving for another three hours or so before we rest."

"As before!" Strake called out. "Single file. Every other man with a lamp. Tiller, you and Sterns take point and wait for us at the first fork. You know the routine."

"Yes, sir!"

The two turned away with their lamp and almost immediately disappeared around a corner into blackness.

"Very well. Let's go!"

• • •

The passages varied from very narrow with low ceilings, where the wind blew through furiously, to very wide and large so that all their lamps did little to illuminate the sides or ceiling. In many stretches the floor showed signs of work, carved steps in some places and in others a smoothed floor through coarse rocks and stalagmites. When they emerged from one narrow climbing passage, they came onto a landing of sorts. The wind died to a mere puff but the sound of running water was all around them. The troopers followed along a ledge, the void on their right growing wider and wider as the rumbling sound of gushing waters grew louder.

"Must be a river down there!" Robby exclaimed.

"Indeed," answered Buckwise, "as you'll soon see. Mind your step along here. Can be slippery."

Their shadows danced and floated along at the swinging lamplight, and Robby had to watch his way very carefully, though Gullwing tried to hold his lamp steady. Only now did Robby realize that he was much warmer than before, in spite of the cool draft and the damp air. He noticed, too, that the steps they now climbed were coated with water, not ice. They ascended, turning left around a broad bend, the noise of the water growing even louder until it was a thundering roar. They were all soon coated with a fine mist, stepping through puddles as they passed tiny streams that glistened down the walls to run across their path and over the nearby edge. Still they advanced, slowly, around yet another leftward turn up a series of stairs cut into the ledge until, by the swinging lamplight, Robby saw a bridge of stone jutting out above and to their right, disappearing into the far gloom. They continued to climb toward the structure, and Robby saw that it was not constructed or carved by hands but was a natural formation of rock made, he supposed, by the torrent of water that cut through underneath it. But the flow itself, though pounding as if from every direction, was still invisible. The bridge grew in size as they climbed, and only when they neared did Robby see that the top of it had, indeed, been carved somewhat by people to serve as a kind of avenue for crossing over it. The way across, between two stone banisters, was some twenty feet wide and was smoothly cut, rising slightly in the middle before descending away toward the other side. Still many yards away, Robby saw the lead group moving onto it, and soon Robby's group was out on the bridge, too, their lamps revealing nothing in the darkness surrounding them. Strake called a halt just as Robby and Ullin reached midpoint.

"White flares on the ready! Every other man from me. For our guests."

"Aye!"

"Aye, Commander!"

"Ready, sir!"

"Ready!"

Ullin and Robby looked back and forth trying to surmise what they were doing as the men pulled some devices from their packs and called out.

"Ready!"

"All ready, Commander."

"On my start."

Robby heard a scratch and saw a glow from near Strake, like a large firestick being lit. Suddenly a brilliant white light blazed out, held aloft by Strake's trekking pole, like the white flame that Ashlord used but obviously some kind of burning device. Quickly, another and another and another flare was set off and held up along the bridge, and as the light of each joined to the others, Robby's mouth fell open at the sight.

To the left of the bridge, some hundred feet away, was a shining wall of cascading water, almost as wide as the length of the bridge. It fell straight down from the ceiling, about fifty feet above them, and churned into a rumbling mist several hundred feet below where they stood. The water gleamed white as the remaining flares were lit, and there were so many gemstones and sparkling minerals that every rock glittered like beacons. Just as the light from the flares reached its most intense and then began to fade rapidly, the huge sheet of water took on a different aspect, more like that of wavering glass. Behind the liquid window hovered a face of gigantic proportions staring back at them.

"Oh!" Robby gasped.

"Look at that!" Ullin muttered.

The bright light of the flares faded and quickly darkness pushed from all around them, closing in from every direction until only the soft glow of their lamps barely held it at bay. After a few moments, Robby's eyes readjusted and they resumed their gloomy march.

"What was that face?" he asked as they exited the far side of the bridge.

"Ol' Moaner herself!" laughed Sterns.

"Seriously?"

"Naw," said Gullwing. "He don't know. Nobody knows. Ask Lord Seafar, next time you see him. He discovered it when he was no older than you. I'm sure he's got some notion or two on it."

"He's the only one who's ever touched it," added Haskin.

"Touched it?"

"Aye. He figured a way to climb over there. Spent a fortune of his own gold to do it. Brought in tons of flares and lamps, drove spikes into the walls to hold ropes and the like. Took him the better part of a year, with a bunch of men helping."

"Then," continued Gullwing, "so they say, when he finally got to it, he went behind the falls for a closer look."

"What did he find?"

"Never heard. Maybe ask Strake. He's closer to Seafar than any of the rest of us."

• • •

After crossing the bridge, they continued on, now steadily climbing. The passageway was narrower in some places than before, and they had to take their packs off to squeeze through a few parts. In other places, they passed through great underground chambers, some so high that the light of their lamps did not reveal the ceiling. In one immense cavern, they hiked through forests of stalagmites well over their heads. In another twisting portion of the way, Robby saw by the waving lamplight glittering colors in the rocks that made up the walls, blues, reds, and gold.

"Are these—?"

"Yep," answered Gullwing.

"Are they mined?"

"Oh, no. Not in the ordinary way. But, once in a while, the Queen sends a few of us to bring some stones back for her. If any get caught nicking some, well, a right fine example's made of 'em. Keep an eye to your way, there. This is a tricky stretch."

It was, cutting sharply upward and broadly turning leftwards for such a long distance that Robby realized they were in a spiraling ascent. Steps had been cut to help with the steepest sections, but for the most part it seemed a never-ending twisting slope. But it did end, at least the turning part, and the passage straightened somewhat even though it kept climbing until the walls broadened out, the ceiling disappeared, and they entered a large smoothly floored chamber.

"Finally!" Haskin uttered.

"Fall out!" Strake commanded. "Sergeant Hull!"

"Sir!"

"Make your details."

"Aye, sir! Buckwise, Sterns, take point ahead, first watch. Gullwing, Haskin, see to our charges, then pull coal for the stove. Tiller, you and Green take the rear watch. The rest of you get the lamps lit and help with the rations."

Robby and Ullin were taken to one side and helped off with their packs while the others got busy. Soon additional lamps were lit, and it became apparent that this was the Blue Room, so named for the marvelous bright blue sapphires that glittered all over its walls. On one side of the room trickled a stream, while on the other was a long set of shelves holding crates, blankets, tools, and supplies. There was even a little kitchen, complete with an iron stove, a cook table with pots and pans and plates stacked up, and a long table with folding chairs lined around it.

"We've been using this place to stay the night in for a long, long time," Haskin said to Ullin who, standing around with Robby, was feeling useless and fairly in the way. "Like the outposts we stayed in last night and the night before, we keep this place stocked and ready."

"It must take a lot of work to get all this stuff here," Robby commented.

"Yeah," agreed Gullwing, rummaging in a bin for coal. "Summers are pretty busy, since that's when we do most of the work maintaining and resupplying and so forth."

"Why don't you have a seat over yonder with Commander Strake," Hull suggested. "And we'll have a meal up in no time."

They did as he suggested, and Strake pulled out chairs for them, motioning for them to take a seat.

"How much farther is it to Fort Defiance?" Ullin asked.

"Another night in the caves," Strake said, sitting and passing a water flask to Ullin. "Then less than a day to Defiance. But tomorrow will be a real hike. The easy part's behind us."

"Oh!"

"Right," continued Strake, "and the thing of it is, the closer we get to the far side of these mountains, and toward the opening back outside, the more careful we'll need to be."

"Because of Shatuum?" Robby asked.

"Yes. When we come out, we'll be overlooking the southern borders of that place. The enemy knows that we have a way through, but has not yet discovered it. At least, we hope not. We've only had a few bad encounters in here, but they all ended well enough. It's really outside that things can get hairy. Actually, it may be a good thing that we move in winter. Our shadowy foes don't seem to care for the cold, and, for the most part, they keep off the slopes until well into springtime or after the snows melt. But the lord of that place is inscrutable. He and his minions are unpredictable, so vigilance and caution are essential."

Strake shifted in his chair uncomfortably, and leaned closer.

"I will tell you that I did open my orders and read them, night before last, as I was instructed. They are very disturbing, and I have not shared them with the men. I wanted to speak to you two first. Our previous stops found us too tired and cold and cramped for much discussion, but at last I have a chance to speak."

"And do they pertain to where we go?" Robby asked.

"They do," Strake nodded to Robby. "Lord Seafar knows of my education, and knew when he wrote the orders that I would understand them without too many questions. Commander Tallin, here, said something to me the night we escaped the burning Palace. Do you recall?"

"I told you that it is Robby, not I, who is important to this mission," Ullin replied.

"Right. My orders, as I now know, are to get you—the both of you—safely to Mount Algamori. That is where the place is that Elrasil the Hunter told King Parthais about. Upon the western side, overlooking the great chasm at the edge of the world, is a mysterious gate, the Gate of Griferis."

"That is where I must go," said Robby.

"Then I can only assume that you are the one legends have foretold," said Strake, frowning. "But, unless you have some way there that you wish to reveal to me, I don't see how we may safely accomplish our task."

Robby looked at Ullin, then shook his head.

"I know less than you do, Commander," he shrugged. "I assumed it would be dangerous to move through Shatuum. That's why I begged Lord Seafar to let us go alone. The last thing I want is to endanger anyone else."

"That speaks well of you. Hm. In that case, I should like to think things through a little longer and try to decide the best way to take. I would prefer that you refrain from saying anything to the men until we speak again. Many of them know as well as I do what is said to be on Algamori's western shoulder. Meanwhile, eat, and try to get some sleep. I daresay you'll be warmer tonight than you have been for days. If there is anything I or any of my men can do for you, just ask. We'll continue our discussion about our route tomorrow when we stop for the night."

• • •

In spite of their exhaustion, the room was full of talk. Gullwing explained to Ullin and Robby that the Blue Room was so called because of the sapphires that bespeckled the walls and that, on each return trip, they took some back with them to help finance their secret missions.

"It is but one of the ways our Queen keeps one step ahead of Duinnor," Strake stated, "and is able to pay the expenses of the Gray Guard and other activities."

Then the talk turned back to the adventures of Lord Seafar, as a young member of the Guard, and how he explored many of the caves and passageways. Robby was told again that no one knew who had carved the likeness they had seen, or who had made the paintings, but that he should ask Seafar when next they met.

Soon after eating, the day's toils caught up with them, and Strake ordered watches set while the others slept. Robby, in spite of the fatigues of the long cold marches, had not been idle in the dreamworld. Since his discovery about other dreamwalkers, the very night Faradan had led his attack on the Palace, Robby's understanding of the dreamworld increased by leaps and bounds. Not only did he now travel without the need to jump from dreamer to dreamer, but he also began to understand more about the creatures that inhabited the world he explored, the dreamdogs, as he thought of them, and the cindergnats, as well as the blue firefly-like insects that seemed to favor soothing dreams. It was good that he learned quickly about these things, and many more things besides, because he also needed the rest that could only come from true sleep and the mundane dreams it brought. So this night, as during the previous nights of his travels across ice and snow, he spent little time dreamwalking, going only to check again on Sheila and her company who were still on their way to Duinnor. Satisfied that they were safe, he returned to his sleeping body, and he slept as well as any of his companions.

• • •

The next day was not so long, but much more difficult. They constantly climbed, either through long winding and sloping passages, or up twisting stairs. Twice they stopped to refill lamps, taking a quick rest while this was done. Otherwise, they kept steadily on until cold air blew into their faces as they neared the far side of the mountain. They entered a wide opening where Strake called them to a halt and gave orders for Hull and two men to move ahead and reconnoiter the nearby exit. Hull soon reported back, saying it was already dark out, and Strake set watches and ordered the men to take their rations and prepare their blankets. Robby noted that this room, though not as large or well-equipped as the Blue Room, was also a storage place with very long odd-looking bundles stacked against the wall, tied up in canvas coverings. There were kegs of oil, too, and an assortment of crates that presumably held other supplies.

"In the morning," Strake told Robby and Ullin, "the three of us will step outside and take a look around before we leave. Meanwhile, have a bite and get some sleep. We'll need our rest for tomorrow."

• • •

Robby was particularly difficult to wake the next morning, owing to his sojourn far away to Passdale. He was determined to contact his mother and warn her about Vidican's spy, the dreamwalker he had discovered the night he and Ullin had fled the burning Palace in Linlally. Since then, each time he went to Janhaven to find his mother, she was either not yet asleep or had already begun her day, well before dawn. Meanwhile, he could at least keep a watchful eye on the Tracian general in Passdale. If the general kept making mistakes, there would not be much to worry about. But with his dreamwalker spy, even the most inept general could gain an advantage. And, as he discovered, Vidican was, indeed, making plans to move against Janhaven by sending his men through the old troll tunnels. Ullin at last convinced Robby to rise to the day, but Robby only did so with the determination to warn his mother at the very first opportunity.

"I'm sorry, Ullin," Robby sat up and rubbed his face. "I'm back to my old habits of sleeping very hard."

"I wish I could sleep as easily as you!"

"It isn't very restful, actually."

"Well, Sterns is cooking a bit of breakfast. So come along, then."

"Very well. If I must!"

When everyone had eaten and cleaned up their belongings, Strake took Robby and Ullin on ahead along the passageway to the exit. So bright was the daylight that poured in that it set them blinking. Strake held them back a few yards from the opening.

"Lord Seafar knows this mountain as well as any, and he knew why this route toward Fort Defiance was the way to go. But he never intended us to take you there. I know him well enough to know what he had in mind. But I'm afraid you won't like it. And neither will the men."

"What could be worse than going through Shatuum?" Ullin asked. "After what Seafar showed us, the creatures in the menagerie, well, frankly, I fear the worst."

"Right that you should. I can see only one chance to get you onto Algamori's slopes, but no one has ever had reason to try it. And, even if we make it to that mountain, I don't see how we may ever get back, though that may not be an issue."

"I trust your judgment, Commander," Robby said. "And if you say 'go this way,' that's the way we'll go. But, is it necessary that all your men come? Couldn't you describe the route to me and Ullin, and leave it to us to make it there on our own?"

"I don't think you have the skill to make it without us. And not all of us will join you. What I have in mind, surely what Lord Seafar had in mind, too, is a very daring and dangerous idea. But I think I had better show you something, first, so that you will understand. This way, if you please."

Strake led Robby and Ullin to the opening, where Hull crouched, sword out.

"All clear?" Strake asked Hull.

"All clear from Gullwing. Just watching for Haskin, sir. There he is! All clear, sir. Careful of the ice, sir."

"This way gentlemen," Strake motioned and they crouched at the mouth of the cave, then scurried out along a ledge. Robby could hardly believe what he saw. They were higher than any of the other peaks nearby. Most were snow-covered, but many of the lower ones were brown and gray, devoid of growth, and in the valleys between rolled dense and dirty-looking fog. Strake led on, then turned into the rock and began climbing up a steep series of step-like rocks. At last, nearly out of breath, the three came to the top of the peak, buffeted by a bitterly cold and hard wind. Strake motioned the other two to come close to him and he reached with one arm around Robby and clutched Ullin's sleeve to pull the two closer so that he could be heard over the howling wind.

"Shatuum!" he cried, waving with his other arm across the scene. "All of the peaks with snow are outside Secundur's realm. Those others, blighted, are his. We stand on the highest mount between here and the southern border of Shatuum. This side of the mountain is nearly impossible to scale, so we are fairly safe." Turning them, he pointed to the northeast direction. "There, see where the brown in the distance changes to green a bit farther on? It marks the edge of the forest, and just beyond is Fort Defiance. You saw the equipment in the room below? They are our wings. Our usual way is to fly down from here to Fort Defiance, landing a mile or so away from the outpost."

Strake turned them to face northwest, the wind biting their faces cruelly, then he pointed.

"There! Look there. See that mountain next over, that one? The one with the crooked top? Yes, that one. That is Mount Algamori. I reckon it is about half the distance from here as it is to our landing place near Fort Defiance. But our path would go over Shatuum. And I don't know where we'd land."

"What are you suggesting?" Ullin cried.

"From what I gather, you won't be happy with how we must get down from here," Strake told him. "We either fly down to Fort Defiance, then trek on foot through Shatuum, probably fighting the entire way through, with little food, no support, and no way of turning back. Or, we can make an attempt from here to Algamori."

"You mean fly there?"

"Yes. And that is what I believe Seafar meant by sending us with you, along this route, rather than the longer but less arduous way around to

Fort Defiance. And why he specified that every man amongst us be an expert flyer."

"Can it be done?" Robby asked.

"I don't know," Strake answered bluntly. "We have here a number of wings. Two of them are what we call Condors. They are large, designed to carry very heavy loads, supplies and such. Each is more than capable of carrying the weight of two men and their gear. They are not very nimble, but they can fly far. Haskin and Gullwing are our most experienced Condor men. If anyone can get you to Algamori, they can. Do you have a better idea? If you do, then now is the time to say so. I don't want to give my men much time to think about it."

"Won't we be seen by those within Shatuum?"

"I expect so. But we dare not fly you that way at night, over terrain we do not know, unable to see the destination. If we are lucky, we may land you near the top of the place, or else along its slopes. If we are not so lucky..."

Ullin had pulled away and was fishing around within his coat. He brought out his spyglass and asked Robby to lend a shoulder to rest it on. He looked for a long time toward Algamori.

"It is a fortress," he said, not taking his eye from the glass. "Even from here, I can see walls, keeps, and watchtowers all along Algamori's shoulder."

"Only on its south and eastern sides," said Strake. "We've studied the place for years with our own spyglasses."

Ullin handed Robby the glass and traded places so that he could prop the device on Ullin's shoulder and look.

"I see trails of smoke, I think. Black smoke."

"They burn coal in their furnaces," Strake explained. "Let us go back inside the cave and decide what to do."

On the way back, Strake recalled Gullwing and Haskin, and left Hull to keep watch by himself. When they were back inside with the rest of the men, Strake took Robby and Ullin aside.

"So what do you think?" he asked.

Ullin was shaking his head. "It seems to me that we don't have much choice, do we?"

"My thoughts exactly," agreed Robby. "But what are the chances of getting to Mount Algamori?"

"Fair, I'd say," Strake stated. "But much can go wrong. Who knows what the winds are like down there? We could get pushed off course."

"But we are just as apt to land right in the middle of one of Secundur's forts, aren't we? If that's the case, I'd rather go at night than be seen and have them waiting for us."

"Secundur's powers are greater at night," Strake countered. "As are those of his followers. And if we cannot see where we are going, we may not land on the right mountain at all."

"Can't we be guided by the stars?" Ullin asked.

"Well, yes. I suppose so."

"I have to agree with Robby, then. At least at night we may have some chance of being a surprise to them, if they see us at all, that is."

After a moment of thought, Strake nodded. "Very well, then. Let me put it to the men."

• • •

Strake did, and after some discussion, all was decided, and the men began their preparations. By late afternoon, as the sun set far off in the west, everything was arranged and ready. Two of the largest flying craft, the Condors, would take off for Mount Algamori. Robby and Ullin, wearing heavy backpacks full of the needed gear, would ride piggyback with Gullwing and Haskin. Commander Strake ordered the other six available craft made ready for a flight to Fort Defiance. Those men left behind were ordered to make their way back to Vanara.

Needless to say, Ullin was terrified at the prospect of taking to the air again, but he held his fear in check, the only indication of his nerves being his short, correct answers as he was harnessed up. Robby was nervous, too, but before he knew it, the sun was below the distant mountains, he was being strapped onto Gullwing's back, and it was too late to change his mind about things. Strake, Hull, and Buckwise took off in quick succession, bearing off toward the northeast. After a moment, Ullin and Haskin jogged heavily off the end of the cliff and disappeared over the side, with Gullwing and Robby following immediately behind them, bearing to the northwest.

Peering over Gullwing's shoulder, Robby could see Mount Algamori outlined against the still-glowing horizon. It was just as cold as their first flight, but Robby was too anxious to notice. He could feel their apparatus jostled by gusty winds, and Gullwing deftly banked and turned to be carried toward and not away from their target. But for the buffeting of their craft, and the sound of air whistling through its struts, it seemed to Robby that they hung motionless, the mountain before them hardly changing in aspect as they neared. Below were the fires of many furnaces, glowing dark orange through a sooty haze that hung low over Shatuum, and occasionally he caught an acrid whiff. Suddenly, from the corner of his eye, he caught a bright light dropping down in the distance like a falling star. Then, as it disappeared behind a hill, another and another one fell. They were flares, he realized, like the ones used on the underground bridge, and they were being dropped by Strake and his flying comrades many miles to the east. At first, he could not work out the purpose, then he understood with horror that they were creating a diversion, giving themselves away in an effort to make all eyes below look in that direction. Robby turned back to their destination, now suddenly looming large before them. It seemed to him that Gullwing was veering off too much to the left, and he was almost in a panic before he saw a shadow ahead of them that sharp-eyed Gullwing followed. It was Haskin and Ullin.

Faster than seemed possible, the mountain rose over them like a hulking shadow racing toward them. Ahead, nearly level with them, was a line of fires, apparently along a stretch of wall, and the cinder-laden smoke rose up and was then swept away to the right by the wind. Apparently Haskin had seen this, and knowing his art well, aimed upwind of these markers, a sign that a strong wind wrapped around the slope. As they flew over the south face of Algamori, Gullwing turned westward into the wind, and their craft bucked then pulled them upward. After a few moments, with the spars of the wing creaking under the strain, Gullwing banked right again, toward the darkness of the mountainside, pulling up hard. Robby heard the snap and crack of Ullin's apparatus somewhere above them, it seemed. Gullwing pulled up even harder, their wing being pushed by the tailwind, then a gust spun them over.

They hit very hard, striking an ice-sheeted cliff, snapping the frame of their craft as they started sliding downward. Gullwing released the controls and swung an ice axe against the rocks only to have it glance off. Now the weight of the crumpled wing pulled them down and skittered them sideways against the icy wall, like a sail flapping wildly, and it threatened to carry them into the black canyon below. Time and again, they struck the rocks, Gullwing swinging his axe madly. Miraculously, Robby got his dagger out and cut away the lines that attached them to the wing just as Gullwing's axe struck home. The pair crashed against the cliff face, dangling from Gullwing's axe, and chunks of ice tumbled down around them as their wing fluttered away and disappeared below.

"Easy! Easy!" Gullwing panted. "I've only got the one arm."

Robby stopped struggling and made each move as deliberate as he could, while trying to move quickly, too.

"Just be as quick as you can," Gullwing whimpered, trying to reach up with his left hand to take hold of the axe that the two hung by. "I think my right arm has come out of its socket."

"Almost there." Robby finally had his axe and got its thong around his wrist. After a few frustrating tries, he was able to drive it home. It was a good thing, too, that Strake insisted they wear crampons; with his axe holding he drove his toes into the ice, and finally got some of his weight off of his pilot. Gullwing hung limply, unable to move. Looking up, Robby could see nothing but ice glowing dimly in the starlight.

"Alright, alright," Gullwing panted. "That's better. Now, can you reach around me and get the loop of this axe hooked to my harness? My grip is getting loose. I'll pull up just a bit with my good arm."

Gullwing carefully pulled himself up, and after some fumbling, Robby found the cord on the axe and hooked it to Gullwing's harness. Gullwing eased his weight onto it until he was sure it would hold.

"Good, good. How're you doing?"

"I'm good, I think," Robby answered.

"A bit of a rough landing. Sorry about that."

"Could have been worse, I imagine."

"Oh, yeah? This seems pretty bad to me."

"I admit, I've been in better places."

Gullwing managed a weak laugh. "Me, too. Let's just rest a moment. Take stock. Still got your knife?"

"Right here."

"Good. Why don't you start cutting the straps that hold us together. I think that might take some strain off our axes."

Robby did as he was told. The wind was too stiff to hear any more sounds from their comrades, and he figured they were in just as much trouble.

"I think that's the last strap," Robby said. He managed to slip the knife away just as his axe-arm was becoming numb, and he grabbed its head with his other hand.

"Look here," Gullwing squeaked. "Do you remember the other day, back when I helped you up the ice sheet?"

"Yes."

"Remember how I got to you? And how you scrambled on up?"

"Yes. Like a spider you were."

"Right. So that's how you have to get up off this cliff face. Use both axes, one to a hand. But go slow. Get a really good purchase with one, test it, then get your toehold, then the other axe. Make sure every hold—axe and toe—is a good one before you pry loose with the other. Got it?"

"I believe so."

"Good, good. Now, seeing as I've only got one good arm, there's no way I can climb. When you get up there, head off for Griferis and don't look back."

"I've still got the rope coiled around me. I can go up a bit and pull you after me. Bit by bit, we'll make it."

"No. I don't think so. Besides the arm, I think I've got a cracked rib, too. It's freezing up here, and getting colder. I won't be any good to you all busted up like this. Look, do as I say and get going. I don't mean to order you around, but that's the size of it. You've got to get off this cliff before you freeze. Get on to Griferis. Don't let me and my mates die for nothing."

Robby swallowed hard, trying to see Gullwing's face. But it was too dark. He got his other axe loose and tied it around his wrist. After a few swings, he started climbing. A few yards up, he was beginning to get the hang of it and stopped to let his heart calm down a bit.

"Good. Keep going like that," Gullwing called up. "Just one last thing."

"What's that?"

"Be a good king."

Chapter 9

The Guest

Day 167
78 Days Remaining

The road northward from Vanara to Duinnor was ancient and well-made, having been maintained for centuries by the King's taxes and tributes. Where it ran through villages and towns, it was better kept, often with long stretches of paving stones or gravel to keep down the dust, culverts to direct water away, and bridges to accommodate the many wagons and carriages and coaches that rumbled from place to place. But in the country, or in poorer villages, the roadway was often no more than a dirt track, rutted and bumpy, and, especially this time of year with cold rain and snow, such stretches were filled with mud and potholes brimming with ice and water. Most of the traffic was of the pedestrian sort, farmers going along to their fields with their hoes and mattocks over their shoulders, herders driving their cattle, or tradesmen with their tools upon their backs, all going to or from their work. It was ever a busy road, and these short-distance travelers often shared the way with those who trekked from far and wide, coming from or going to Duinnor. As it is so often the case, the foot-travelers were sympathetic with the others they met and to the efforts of such journeys whether they were short or long.

It was along one of the short stretches between two close abiding villages that some midmorning groups of travelers went, negotiating around the boggiest portions or carefully stepping around long runs of ice not yet melted into puddles or crushed by heavy wheels. From the south there came an open carriage, jostling along at a fast pace, its horses nearly at a canter. Hearing its approach, the pedestrians parted to both sides and onto the banks along the road, seeking to give it room to pass. One small group, consisting of an old woman with a sack of potatoes on her back followed by several small children with lesser sacks of vegetables, came toward another small group of travelers with backpacks and shoulder bags. When the two groups met, there was a muddle as to which way to go, none wishing to walk through mud, just when the carriage also arrived from behind the travelers. The conveyance did not slow one bit. Indeed, the driver cracked his whip so that the horses would pull all the quicker through the slippery trace. At the last moment, the people on foot dashed for the sides of the road. The carriage splashed by, slinging mud and ice in its wake, and the two passengers, finely attired in velvet coats and fur-lined caps, were completely oblivious to the hapless people being pelted and splattered as they passed. The old woman seemed not to care, nor was she concerned that her children were filthier than ever. But one of the other travelers stood gaping after the carriage, plainly outraged.

"How rude!" yelled Sheila at the receding rig. Wringing dripping mud from her hands, she then shouted, even louder, "You ought to be ashamed!"

Billy, who was fairly covered from head to toe, looked at Sheila and cocked his head. "Yer lookin' a bit like yer old self, Miss Sheila!"

Ibin nodded. "Yeah, like, yeahlikethe, like, yeahyoulooklikeyoudidwhenwefirstmet, Sheila. Back, backwhenwewerelittle."

"Welcome to Duinnor," Ashlord said. Somehow, either by deftly moving to just the right spot, or by some other magic, he was not touched by a single speck of flying mud. "Let's move along. We'll ask at the next village just yonder for a place to clean up and eat."

They had hiked since before sunrise, so this was welcome news on all accounts. After parting company with Robby and Ullin, Ashlord had driven them almost without mercy, and they covered better than twenty miles almost every day. During the first three weeks on their way to Duinnor, they camped when they had to, villages and inns being few and distant from each other. But for the past week, owing to the frequency of towns along the way, they were able to stay at inns or purchase lodgings in stables or barns. At last, they could surmise that they were nearing the great city, for the frequency and size of the villages had increased from small hamlets to bustling towns, one nearly pushing against the next. In between were few fields, anymore, but more shops and smithies, workhouses, trading floors, and markets of all kinds selling and making and trading cloth, spices, tin and copperwares, vegetables and meats, furniture, and weapons.

A little while later, Ashlord turned his group into the yard of a busy inn, and for a couple of silver coins, the keeper gladly gave them the use of a bucket and some rags to wash with, pointing to the well. Here they cleaned their faces and daubed away the thickest of the mud from their clothes, as the cook brought them a tray of cheese and bread, putting it on the table at the side yard. As usual, Ashlord hurried them through the breakfast, and urged them to pick up their things to be on their way.

This village, as it turned out, almost ran right into the next, and from there on, for the rest of the day, they hardly passed an open space on either side of the road that was not occupied by some house or building. By the time noon came and went, the road was thick with the traffic of horses, wagons, and throngs of people, all coming and going in a great hurry, it seemed.

"Arewe, arewethereyet?" asked Ibin, amazed and alert and beaming at all who passed by.

"No," Ashlord repeated for the fifth time in so many days. "You will know Duinnor City when you see it."

"Oh."

"But we must be gettin' close," said Billy, gesturing upward at the five bright stars, visible even during daytime. They were steep enough upward, but not directly overhead.

"Do not point at the stars, Billy!" Ashlord said in a hushed tone.

"Is it bad luck to do so?" Sheila asked.

"For us it may be," Ashlord explained. "It is the mark of newcomers to point and gawk at them. These people are accustomed to the stars and take little notice of them. Let us not draw any more attention to ourselves than need be."

"Oops," said Billy, shrugging at Sheila.

"It is hard not to look at them," she said in reply. "Shining so beautifully, and in the broad daylight."

"Yes, I admit it is," Ashlord nodded. "But refrain from even that, if you can."

Just then, Certina darted past them, turning heads all around as she cut sharply to the left and shot skyward.

"Talk about attractin' attention," Billy muttered.

"We go left at the fork. Just ahead, there."

They approached the intersection, congested by many carts and wagons negotiating turns in every direction, and Billy could not help but notice that the signpost indicated Duinnor City was to the right, and only three leagues away.

"We take a side route to the city," Ashlord stated in answer to Billy, who was tugging his sleeve and gesturing in a careful fashion at the sign. "And we make a slight detour along the way."

"Oh?"

After weeks of traveling with Ashlord, his companions all knew that if he did not give a reason for something he said, then it was because he assumed they understood it, or assumed they accepted it, or else he was waiting to see who would be the first to ask for an explanation. They made their way between the carts and throngs, knowing by his tone that they should just accept what he said about the detour and keep up with him. Billy could sense this as easily as Ibin or Sheila, but that did not keep him from asking, anyway.

"So why the detour?"

"I need to see someone before we enter the city. I know you are all tired. But we'll soon have rest and good beds to sleep the night in. And, yes, Ibin, a wholesome meal, too. Let us keep up our pace, though."

Within an hour more of walking, traffic had become light enough for them to often walk abreast. The roadway they took passed through several more villages, and as they progressed these became more often separated by fields and gardens and pastures so that, to their unspoken relief, the way was less hectic and took on a more rural aspect once again. Bearing westward, with the five Stars of Duinnor above their right shoulders, they traveled through dales and up hills where the bounty and richness of the Duinnor soil was made apparent by the well-kept farmhouses and barns, orderly fences and hedgerows, and by the plentitude of cattle and swine and poultry they saw. Being a chilly day, the breeze struck them in cold gusts as they passed through open spaces. In the hollows, large patches of snow were common, protected from the sun's melting light by the shadows under dense stands of fir. They crossed many streams spilling white water over rocky courses, and stone bridges capable of supporting heavy wagons were fairly frequent. But farther along, as the road narrowed and became more like those in Barley, the bridges became mere plank decks and, even farther on, as the way narrowed to a broad path, they were no more than wide footbridges, where there were bridges at all. Eventually, they seldom saw other travelers, and the only noise to be heard was that of birds and the gush of wind through the woods.

"Look!" Ibin said as they topped a rise. Through the trees to the right, they saw a broad expanse of fields stretching out below them, and, away on the far side, the great city itself.

"It's huge!" Billy exclaimed.

"Come along," Ashlord said. "We'll soon have a better view."

It was difficult for his companions to keep an eye on the path and at the same time stare away through the trees, but they managed, glimpsing various portions of the city as they went. It was apparent to them that they were following the high rim of a wide valley, and that the city, its light-gray walls set with brass-colored gates, was no more than a mile or two away. On the flat plain below them, they could see the trace of roadways crisscrossing fields beside the red-tiled roofs of a few cottages. The path narrowed as it turned away and upward through a thick pine wood, but it was now paved with cut stones, the edges trimmed with moss. These became widely spaced steps as the path grew steeper and turned sharply one way and then the next as it climbed the side of a hill. Suddenly they came onto a tiled walkway that led through a sort of woodland garden and then onto a wide landing from which a gently sloping road descended away from them and led, straight as an arrow, across the valley to Duinnor City, just over a mile away. Ashlord stopped to let them take a long look. Behind the walls of the city, thin trails of smoke rose from countless chimneys, making a layered haze over the valley. From their vantage, they looked across the plain and down across the walls to the sprawling complex of towers, houses, buildings, parks, and streets within. Over all of these, in the middle of the city, was a pale rose-colored palace, splendid even at a distance, its grand tower rising higher than all of the rest by twice, at least. And, shining over all, lined across the sky over the city in a gentle arc, were the five Stars of Duinnor, mysterious, twinkling, blue-white lights.

"Aw, well, it ain't all that big," Billy uttered, even though his eyes were as wide with wonder as they could be. Sheila giggled and elbowed him.

"Alotof, a lotofpeople, ofpeoplelivethereIguess," said Ibin.

"Yes. Many," Ashlord nodded. "But most live outside the city proper. In the many towns and villages such as those we have seen already. Shall we continue onward?"

They nodded and moved toward the inclined way that led to the city.

"No, friends. We go this way."

They turned around and saw Ashlord pointing over his shoulder and upward. So full of amazement at the city, the three only now saw the stairs behind Ashlord. It was wide enough for six people to walk abreast, and it rose straight, high, and far, made of pale creamy marble with balusters and handrails of the same stone. They had to tilt their heads back to see the structure at the summit far above.

"Up thar?"

"Yes, Billy. To the top," Ashlord smiled, turning to lead the climb.

"Good grief!" Sheila uttered. "What is that place?"

"It is the Temple of Beras," Ashlord said. "Come along. It won't be so bad coming back down. And you will be well rested by then!"

Ibin glanced at Billy and Sheila, not understanding their hesitation, and strode up after Ashlord.

"Oh, well," Sheila said, starting up. Billy cinched up the shoulder straps of his pack and followed, muttering to himself.

It was not as steep as it looked, and the rise from one step to the next was an easy height. But it was a long climb, and in a few places ice coated the stone. The air grew cooler as they went higher, and its bite sharpened, though their exertions kept them warm enough. As they gained altitude, the structure above loomed larger and more interesting, though all they could really see was the massive front portico. It had the same general lines of the little Common House in Passdale, Billy noted, but was twice as high and wide, at least. But the Common House was built of wood and mortared stone, this was entirely of laid stone blocks, with no mortar. Its four round columns, each nearly as thick as a cottage, were ornately carved with all manner of glyphs and runes from bottom to top. And whereas the porch of the Common House, from where Ullin once announced his orders to the militiamen, was made of hewn timber, this one was faced with gold, glistening in the sun, and in the center, directly before them, were fashioned two very large eyes, each as big as a man was tall, made of the same gold material. What Billy at first thought to be a nose and eyebrows, he saw as he neared were the carved forms of a tree trunk and two separating branches, one branch over each eye. The eyes were closed, and Billy could not help a chuckle.

"The place is asleep!"

From below, he could only see the portico and not the whole temple. So high was the little mountain they climbed that only from a distance, and from the heights of Duinnor's highest towers, could the whole structure be seen. And it dwarfed the portico that Billy was now stepping under. The others were waiting for him, their packs on the marble floor.

"Whew!" he exclaimed, shaking his head. "Some climb, eh?"

"Look, Billy!" Ibin pointed, and, as Billy unslung his pack and turned, he saw Duinnor City, spread across the valley floor.

"Gar! What a sight!"

Now they could easily see into the city and take in its complexity of streets and avenues and its buildings and towers. Glass glinted, green copper roofs glowed, and what must have been very large pennants floated over towers and spires. The rosy palace, prominently centered, dominated the entire city with its many turrets and lofty spires and with its magnificent tower so high that it seemed to float. Billy had the sense that its top-most rooms must be fairly level with his own position, but it was too distant for him to tell whether or not another set of eyes gazed back from its windows.

"That is where the King resides," Ashlord stated. "May I have one of your coins, Billy?"

"Sure," Billy replied, shrugging and digging into his coat pocket to find his purse. "Gold or silver?"

"Have you any coppers?"

"Um...lemme see here. Sure do."

"That will be sufficient. It is only a customary token. Thank you."

Ashlord took the coin and walked toward the tall double doors set into the tree motif. They were at least twenty feet high and appeared to be made of the same white marble as the rest of the building, but framed with plates of heavy brass. On each door was carved the likeness of ivy with polished opals for tiny blooms, and scattered around the vines were hundreds of eight-pointed stars of inlaid gold. In the middle of each door was hung a large wreath of gold, and Ashlord lifted one of these from its hinge and let it fall with a single dull thud that sent cooing pigeons astir. After a long moment, one of the doors swung slowly and silently inward, then a middle-aged man stepped out. He was dark of complexion, with his head in a sky-blue turban and robes of the same color. His face was clean-shaven, and he smiled and bowed. Ashlord bowed, too, saying, "Sancti gal timala, Norwali," gesturing at his companions. "Jour calli te naswari."

The man bowed again slightly and replied, "Bonleave, bonleave. Tulith Beras, Teye aswar?"

"Jour nad Oest te Sollund."

"Then we will speak the Common Tongue," the man said, smiling and bowing again toward the three others. "Welcome, welcome, to the House of Beras."

"Thank you," replied Ibin returning the bow. Sheila and Billy bowed, too.

"Please enter. I will take you to our Master."

Ashlord gestured for his friends to come along, then Certina flitted by.

"Yes. I think you'd be happier outside, though I'm sure you'd be welcome."

"All are welcomed in this House. So long as, within here, our rules are followed," said the monk, bowing again.

"Of course," Ashlord replied. Then, to Certina, "Do not go far!"

As they entered, he said to the others, "Certina is most definitely not a vegetarian."

Billy looked at Sheila and said, "Veget…? I should say not! More along the lines of poultry, I reckon."

Sheila nodded at Billy, and Ibin shrugged.

"Certina would not appreciate that comment!" Ashlord responded with a glare.

"What'd I say?" Billy asked Sheila, whose turn it was to shake her head and shrug.

"Certina eats meat, which we shall not do during our stay here," explained Ashlord.

"We partake of flesh only during High Holy Day, once every year. And on other very rare occasions," the monk explained. "But on those days the Temple is closed to all but members of our Order."

"I see." Billy only half-heard what the man said, for as soon as they had entered, his attention was drawn to the interior sights of the place.

It was a single enormous room, very long and wide, lined with reddish polished columns every several paces reaching upward to the high arched spans that crisscrossed the vaulted ceilings. There were brilliant lamps, but not too many, so that the whole room was comfortably lit, and the scenes painted on the ceilings above glowed. Each vault had is own theme. One was of the night sky, painted dark blue and speckled with all the familiar stars. Another depicted a pastoral scene, trees and lakes and fields, with winged figures emerging from these places, flying toward the bright gold sun in the center. Some scenes were repeated but with different landscapes. And one showed a king, seated on a grand throne, robed in patterned green silk, Sir Sun and Lady Moon holding hands and shining together above his crown, and every manner of beast, as well as men and women, bowed before the sovereign.

Billy reckoned the room was as wide as Bosk Manor and that he could fit five of his former home end to end across the length of it, and stack two atop each other to reach the ceiling. The floor was laid with small green octagonal tiles connected with white diamond-shaped ones, giving the place a grassy look. As well as the lamps, there were tall blue-stained glass windows making brighter patches here and there. Along the walls beneath and between the windows were shelves holding thick white candles, their golden light illuminating murals of Faerekind and Men, and even animals, some with bejeweled eyes and teeth.

Ahead of them were scores of monks, kneeling in rows on little rugs with their hands held up, facing a large globe of gold balanced atop a pyramid of clear glass. The pyramid itself was uplifted from the floor by four figures, cast in gleaming silver. These figures knelt, one to each corner of the pyramid that rested on their outstretched hands. From their backs, curving up and forward, were feathered wings framing the angled edges of the glass structure. Within the glass pyramid was suspended another orb of gold, the same size as the one suspended above it.

At their guide's gesture, the group stopped just behind the rearmost rank of monks, and no one had to tell them to be quiet, such was the effect of the place upon them. They heard a voice from the distant far end, and it was then that they saw a man, robed as the others, standing in front of the mysterious sculpture, his hands raised upward like those who were kneeling. Though of average build, he only stood a quarter of the height of the pyramid behind him. He spoke more words, and the monks chanted a reply in soft unison that filled the spacious room with its hum. With the first syllable of their chant, Billy went rigid, as if he heard something that no one else did, and, inexplicably, his eyes watered and a lump came to his throat that he desperately tried to swallow. He felt, more than thought, of home, the sweetness of the life he had known before, his father and mother and sister, and the fields of Boskland.

There was only a slight echo when the monks concluded the short phrase and the one at the front spoke again, the distance making his voice seem small. Billy blinked back the mist in his eyes and gently cleared his throat, glancing at his friends. To him, they seemed rather unaffected. Sheila watched the proceedings with interest, Ibin was wide-eyed and smiling, and Ashlord had his head bowed respectfully. Realizing that another chant was coming, Billy steeled himself, but when the congregation repeated their line, his reaction was not as intense as before, though he felt a slight palpitation of the heart. By directing his entire attention at the gold ball that loomed over the presiding monk, Billy managed to gulp away a sob. The orb was not smooth all around, he saw, but had circles made into it, one smaller than the other, and as far as he could see, the one inside the glass pyramid was just the same as the one above. Then, with a shudder, he realized they were eyes, and as the chant passed, he had the distinct and uncomfortable feeling they were staring right at him.

The monks all rose together and began silently filing out of the room, going forward and bowing to the structure before exiting through a side doorway.

"The afternoon prayers are over," their guide explained. "We may now speak more freely."

Ashlord offered Billy's coin, saying, "A token of gratitude for shelter. One night, we desire to stay, if it pleases the Temple. And, if it pleases the Master, I wish to speak with your Guest."

The monk raised his eyebrows as he took the coin.

"We are all but guests," he replied, smiling, but eyeing Ashlord carefully.

"I seek the one who has abided here since shortly after the founding of the present dynasty of Unknown Duinnor Kings."

"You speak of he who was brought here to be mended, and who has remained here ever after," said the monk, "save once, many years ago when he roamed away, only to return. But he has not left us since then. His mending continues. And will continue until the breaking of the world, so it is said, or until his spirit departs from it. How you know of him is a mystery. None but the Chosen of the Oracle may know his history. To all others, he is only the Guest. None may see him except the Chosen, and none may call his name or speak of him to outsiders."

"I know that you are one of the Chosen, for only those of this Order are given the duty of Doorkeeper during prayers," answered Ashlord. "So I know that I may speak freely with you about this matter. Do not fret over my companions, either, for greater secrets than the things of this house have been entrusted to them, and they are faithful keepers of those things. I know of your guest by the word of Lord Tallin, who desires that I see him."

The monk considered Ashlord's words and nodded. "Then it is time."

"Yes. It is."

The monk's smile vanished, and for a moment it appeared that he was in deep contemplation. He blinked and smiled again as he gestured toward the front of the sanctuary.

"You may seek permission of the Master," he said

He led them forward, through the rows of prayer rugs. They were nearly under the great orb when the monk turned to the left and after a few paces stopped and bowed. It was only then that they saw the person to whom he bowed, slouched in a plain wooden chair near the corner of the room. There was a small brazier nearby, and his eyes were fixed upon the low flames that flickered up from it. He was dressed in a gray robe that had seen better days, and it was opened in a casual manner so that his bare chest was exposed somewhat as was the green loincloth that draped between his sprawled out legs. One arm dangled over the side of the chair and in his other hand he clutched a short walking stick. He was old. His face appeared wind- and sun-worn, covered with wrinkles that made patterns in the white stubble that coated his face and chin. His hair was white, matted, and clumped. He seemed as dirty as his clothing, smudged all over with dust and grime and soot. He was, in fact, a shocking sight compared to the neat, clean, and fine-looking monks they had seen, and compared to the splendor of the surroundings. A shiver of revulsion went up Sheila's spine. Billy's neck hairs stood on end. Ibin stared aghast and wondered how long it had been since the old man had bathed. The thought made him put his head down toward his own armpit and sniff, thinking how nice it would be to soak and scrub and soak some more. Ashlord, ahead of them by a few long paces, signed for them to wait. He approached alone to within a few yards of the person, went down on one knee, and laid his stick on the floor before him, bowing his head.

"Oracle of Beras," Ashlord said. "I have come."

The Oracle did not look toward Ashlord, but kept his gaze toward the flames as he spoke.

"Who is the Bringer of Doom?" he asked in a casual, almost distracted manner.

"All bringers of change, Master."

"True. It is the fabric of creation. For all things change, and so the passing away is the passing into. Such is doom."

Now the old man turned his head and looked toward Ashlord vacantly, as if not seeing him at all.

"Your coming was foretold to me. Indeed, I have waited for you since before you walked the Earth. Soon your time will come, in the remaking of the world, which this visit shall bring about. Though I know this from vision and divination, others also know, from their own arts. And so Collandoth the Watcher is himself watched. Those who would put off their doom by forestalling you only hasten the End of Days. The Time of Seeing is nigh upon us, the time for the Hidden One to be revealed, and the fulfillment of prophecy. I shall not gainsay the Will of Beras. You may see the one you seek here. But know this Collandoth: Long shall be the age that comes, and it shall not pass until the stars of heaven have left their course and returned again to their old homes in the turning of the Great Wheel. It will be an age of resurrection. That cannot be changed. The struggle that comes decides not the nature of the age, but the nature of those things to be resurrected."

"Master, do you see the outcome of the struggle that comes?"

"I see. But it is not for me to understand. I see darkness. I see death that is not death, and life that is not life. I see consuming fire that does not burn, and ice that flows like water. I see a desolation of souls. I see the King of Kings, who rules over the darkness and who gives life and death. And I see his many servants, terrible in their beauty, beautiful in the terror they bring. I see the Firstborn bowing down, many in shackles. I see awful demons who guard a New Throne. I see Men transformed into other creatures, and other creatures made into Men. All of this I see at the feet of the New King to come. But it is not for me to understand. Beras does not give me hope, nor does he take hope away."

He stood up from his chair, still looking past Ashlord. "Go. Do that which you came to do." Then, supporting himself with his stick, he went slowly to the brazier and put a hand into its bowl. Muttering, he daubed his face with ash.

Ashlord rose, picking up his staff, and bowed. When he approached his companions, the monk who waited with them said, "I shall take you to him."

Billy glanced back at the Oracle, who continued to pat himself with soot and ashes, embers sometimes falling from his hands or swirling about his clothing.

"Why do they let him do that?" Billy whispered to Sheila. "Don't they know he might hurt himself?"

Sheila gave Billy a scolding look for his quip, and immediately regretted her glare, seeing that his concern was genuine. She realized in that moment that she had of late often caught herself mistaking some remark of Billy's for a joke. Now, upon reflection, she knew that she should not be so dismissive. Something was at work in Billy. Something deeper than his lighthearted demeanor could contain. Of all people, she should be the last to scold anyone. After all, she knew firsthand the sting of cruel and thoughtless reprimand.

They passed out of the sanctuary and in single file followed the monk through what seemed a maze of corridors and halls and up and down stairs. Through open doorways Sheila saw rooms of books and scrolls and monks at their studies, reading and copying. They passed other rooms that seemed to be places to do chores. There was a workroom with a large kettle of hot water over which a monk labored with a large paddle, lifting out clothing and hanging the wash on lines to drip. There was a shop where stools were being repaired and where chairs were caned and crutches were being fashioned. All the while the monk spoke to them of their life, their vows of poverty, and the strict rules for silence during certain hours, of their daily prayer routines, their manner of dress, and their diet.

"In our workshops, we make crutches and other things to help the crippled and maimed to get about. And we tend to the sick among the poor and homeless, maintaining infirmaries in the city and in the surrounding countryside. We have a modest income from making and selling brooms and brushes, and we run a workshop in the city to employ those who are too weak for other kinds of work. Besides that, the King is our patron, and provides an annual gift for the maintenance of the Temple and the monastery. There are other donors who bless us with their gifts, too."

"An' do ye have many stayin' with ye?" asked Billy as they turned a corner.

"We have one hundred and forty-seven members of the Order who call this place home. Some are in the city or elsewhere at any given time. Besides that, there are two hundred or so acolytes who assist us. Most have their own homes, but a good number of those remain here at all times."

"Who else may stay here?" Sheila asked, thinking of the one Ashlord came to see. "Besides those of your order, I mean."

"Anyone may seek refuge here from the troubles of the outside world. We turn away no one. And they may stay as long as they care to abide by our rules and do not disrupt our tranquility. Very few stay for long. But there have been exceptions."

He pulled a door open and held it for them, and they entered an outside courtyard. Following along, they crossed it and descended a long flight of steps cut into the mountain's rock, descending onto a path that wound around the rim of the temple's foundations and then away southward through thick stands of camellias, their winter blooms a rich red against dense green leaves. The stone-paved path continued to turn and then, after just a few minutes of walking, the monk stopped.

"I ask that you wait here. I don't know how much you know of our guest," he said, "but a companion has joined him. His companion is, well, protective of our guest. And he is somewhat—how shall I say?—somewhat reserved. And somewhat lacking in manners, too. They might be reluctant to have visitors."

"If it may help," said Ashlord, nodding in understanding, "tell him I am recently arrived from Thunderfoot's land."

"Thunderfoot," the monk stated. "I will tell him. Please wait."

The monk left them and disappeared around the bend.

"Whois, whoisThunderfoot?" asked Ibin.

Ashlord sighed. "An old, old one. As old as these stones," he tapped his staff on a flagstone.

"Doesone, does, doesoneoftheFaerekindlivehere?" Ibin asked.

"Yes."

"It'sasecret, isn'tit?"

"Yes, Ibin. It is. Outside this monastery, only one other person knows this secret."

"That Thunderfoot feller," Billy stated. "Who is he? Another one of the Firstborn?"

"No. Thunderfoot is not one of the Firstborn. He lives in the Eastlands. In a manner of speaking, you might say that the one we are about to meet is Thunderfoot's father. And, if my suspicions are correct, we may also meet one of Thunderfoot's distant relatives."

"How long have you planned to come here?" asked Sheila.

"Since we left Tallinvale. When we began our journey, I thought I'd accompany Robby to Griferis, if possible. But it became evident to me that Ullin would make a better companion on that leg of Robby's quest. And since rejoining you at Westlawn, it has been my thought to come to Duinnor."

"Do y'think they've gotten to Griferis yet?" Billy asked.

Ashlord shook his head.

"I hope they have made Linlally by now," he said, "and have met with Lord Seafar, who rules Vanara in the Queen's absence. If things go as I hoped they would, Robby has made a deep impression on Seafar, bearing Swyncraff as he does. Seafar is a learned man, quick-thinking, and decisive. He will be a valuable ally to Robby and Ullin. And since Ullin and Robby will not linger any longer than they must, they will want to be on their way north and west as soon as possible. Seafar, if he is the man he ever was, will act to help them."

Ashlord did not care to mention any of the many things and situations that might arise to thwart Robby from his quest. But it would have surprised him to know how far along Robby and Ullin were, that this very day they were surveying the land of Shatuum from their mountaintop perch, and that they were preparing for a daring flight in order to reach Algamori.

Hearing someone approach, they turned, expecting the monk. He emerged from around the bend, smiling, but behind him was another person who stunned them by his appearance. He was taller than Ibin by a foot, broad-shouldered, his bare arms bulging with muscles. He wore a simple white toga, pulled over one otherwise bare shoulder, belted at the waist with brown leather and a silver buckle, and he was shod in thick sturdy sandals. On the belt hung a heavy short sword, his massive hand on its hilt. He was pale-skinned and had close-cropped sandy hair. His angular nose and thin lips exaggerated his broad stern face and hard square chin, and his green eyes cut at them like sharp emeralds in the sun. These things the group noticed immediately, and the combination of his appearance along with his stiff demeanor communicated that he considered them a threat. But what dismayed them the most was his skin. It was the color of cream, glistening as if oiled, with soft veins of silver-gray running all over his body and face. He seemed impervious to the chilly air, impervious to any threat they might offer, too, but altogether menacing.

"This is our guest's servant," the monk stated. "His name is Lythos."

"Howdoyoudo?" Ibin said with a weak smile and weaker bow.

"He will take you on from here," the monk told them. "I'll see to it that rooms are prepared for you, and I will send someone to fetch you when they are ready."

"Thank you," Ashlord bowed.

"This way," Lythos stated abruptly in a deep voice, and he turned to lead the way. Ashlord followed, then the others, walking fast to keep up with the long heavy strides of their new guide.

"Thar's no end to odd-lookin' fellers 'round this place," Billy whispered to Ibin, who nodded, neither taking their eyes from Lythos. The path descended a little more and then opened into a herb garden. They passed through it to a small cottage made entirely of stone, from the slate roof to the marble doors. These doors were set into a wall of granite so finely cut and dressed and laid that no mortar at all was used and even the joints were hard to see. Sheila, walking just behind Ashlord, was wary of Lythos but could hardly take her eyes from him. He seemed heavier than one should be, even for his size, and she could have sworn that some of the flagstones actually cracked under his tread. And there was something familiar about him, she thought, but she could not put her finger on what it was.

"Wait here," Lythos ordered as they neared the porch. He gave each of the group a cold look, then went to the door and pushed it open. He hesitated, looking back over his shoulder at Ashlord and Sheila. His face was blank, but a shiver went up Sheila's spine. Lythos turned away and entered the cottage, leaving the door ajar.

"He recollects us, I think," Ashlord said to Sheila softly. She could not tell whether he spoke to her or addressed Certina, who had just landed on his shoulder and was pushing at his earlobe with her beak. Before Sheila could ask, Lythos reappeared.

"My master will see only the one called Collandoth," he stated.

"I am Collandoth," said Ashlord. Lythos gestured for him to enter and when Ashlord disappeared inside, Lythos pulled the door closed and turned to the others who remained.

"I am instructed to offer you refreshment such as that which my master takes from the mountain. If you would come this way."

He went to the left but when he realized they were hesitant to follow, he turned back.

"You do not care for refreshment?"

Billy pushed past Sheila and stood bravely, looking nearly straight up at the man who turned his head down toward him. There was a peculiar blankness about his eyes, Billy noticed, the coldest, hardest green he had ever seen.

"Well." Billy cleared his throat. "It's only that we'd rather stay close by our friend, y'see?"

Lythos turned his head and gazed for a long moment at the door. It was as if he forgot that anyone was there at all. In the awkward silence, Billy glanced at Sheila and gave her a slight shrug, rolling his eyes.

"Friend," Lythos stated. He looked back at Billy. "I see."

"Yeah. So we'd rather just stay here."

Lythos nodded and gestured toward a low stone wall that bordered the garden. The movement was so sudden that Billy flinched.

"Sit. I will bring refreshment to you," Lythos stated. He spun around and stomped away. Except that he did not appear to stomp; his movements, though stiff, were strangely graceful. But his heavy footfalls were anything but soft as he disappeared around the corner of the cottage.

"Whew!" Billy exhaled, easing his pack off and slinging it down. "Don't he beat all!"

He made a pretense of dusting off the top of the low wall and then sat. Ibin followed and sat beside him, but Sheila hesitated.

"Howcomehelooks, howcomehelooksatyouso, Sheila?" Ibin asked, beating Billy to the question.

"I'm not sure."

She slowly unslung her pack and took a seat beside him.

"As if he knows ye from somewhars," Billy added.

"Yes. Most peculiar. And, the thing of it is, I feel I should recognize him. But I can't put my finger on how, or why, or where from. It's the strangest thing."

"Hm. Well, I for one can't say I've ever seen the likes."

"WhodoyoureckonAshlord'stalkingto?" Ibin asked. "Doyouthink., doyouthinkmaybeit'soneofhisownpeople?"

"What? Ye mean one of them Melnari fellers? Ye think it might be Raynor?"

"I don't think it is," Sheila shook her head. "The Melnari aren't the same as the Firstborn. And, anyway, remember what Ashlord told us, over and over. Should anything happen along the way, go to Crescent Avenue, in the city, and that's where we'd find Raynor. No. This is someone else Ashlord hasn't told us about."

Though it was still chilly, the spot they sat in was sunny and the light made the smooth dark marble warm. Ibin absently ran his fingers along the lighter lines that ran through the capstones. Billy watched him, noticing how big Ibin's hands were, and thought how the patterns his friend traced were similar to those of Lythos's skin.

"Stonesdon't, stonesdon'tbleed," Ibin said to himself.

Billy cocked his brow at the statement. Sheila looked startled and suddenly jumped to her feet.

"What's a matter?" Billy asked, standing.

Before she could answer, the sound of heavy footfalls came, and then Lythos appeared from around the corner. He carried a wide slab of rock like a tray, and stacked on it were several large cups, a large pitcher, and a bowl brimming with nuts. He put the tray down on top of the wall and handed each a cup. Sheila took hers with one hand and immediately grabbed it with both. Billy did the same.

"It's made of stone!" he exclaimed, running his fingers around its polished rim.

"Water," Lythos said, gesturing at the pitcher, made of the same material. Ibin stood and turned to lift it but only made it budge a little on the tray. Putting his cup down, he was about to try again with both hands when Lythos stopped him.

"I will pour for you."

He easily lifted the pitcher and poured into their cups. They were grateful for the cool drink, which they gulped down quickly in spite of the quantity the cups held. Lythos poured refills and then took up several walnuts. He rolled them between his palms, easily cracking the shells to bits. He turned aside and, holding his hands to his face, blew away the dust and chips, then offered the remaining meat.

While they ate, he repeated the process and soon had a pile of prepared nuts on the tray for them. Picking up a bit of white rock, he rubbed it between his finger and thumb, sprinkling the pile with the grains that fell away.

"Salt," he said.

All the while, Sheila studied Lythos thoughtfully, and her trepidation subsided.

"Thankyouforthenuts, thankyouforthenutsandwater," Ibin said.

"You are welcome."

While he served them, he often looked toward the cottage door and, just as often, at Sheila. His face, though stern in features, was not without expression, she noticed. He did not return Ibin's normally infectious smile, but neither did he frown. Billy and Ibin could not but notice how often he looked at Sheila. Once all the nuts were cracked and salted, he lifted the pitcher again ready to pour at the asking.

"I notice you have a scar on your forehead," Sheila said to him. Lythos lifted a hand and ran a finger across a small nick just above his left eye.

"Yes. It is from an arrow that struck me there."

"I am sorry."

"It does not hurt. And the arrow did not hurt when it struck me."

"No. I mean, I'm sorry that I did that."

Billy and Ibin stiffened, brows up, but said nothing. Billy's eyes darted back and forth between Lythos and Sheila, baffled.

"You were just trying to help your...your friend," Lythos stated, gazing at Sheila without any hint of expression. "It was good for your friend that you came when you did."

"Yes. It was," Sheila nodded, searching his eyes. "But you had already saved him. I know that, now. And I thank you for that."

"I would not have spared him. I thought I was doing my duty. I thought the wolves were only the start of the fight. But we were summoned too late."

"Yes, I know. But you saved my friend from the wolves that otherwise would have killed him."

"It was all for nothing. I am saddened by our failure."

"Then you know what happened there?"

"My master has told me."

"I see."

They continued to look at each other. Sheila's companions remained silent, understanding that they were witnessing something very deep and, to Lythos, very, very sad.

"What became of your comrades? Those who fought the wolves with you?"

"My memory is weak. It is vague. We left the fortress of Tulith Attis. We grew heavier with each step we took. The waters were high upon us, and we sank into the mud. Some of us were lost, disappearing into the soft ground. But the rest of us could not stop moving. Trees fell around us, and the sky cracked with jagged light, and the storm-drums of the sky beat loudly, but we kept on. Those of us who remained came upon a swollen stream. Rising out of the waters on its overflowing banks were women, frozen into their gestures of grief and mourning. There, some of my comrades recognized wives and lovers, and they sought to join them. But when they touched, they were joined together and turned into frozen stone. For a long while, perhaps a whole day, I looked upon them. No one mourned for me. I had no wife or lover, and no family. I wanted to stay with my companions, but I could not. A strange urge drove me onward. The many weeks that followed took me slowly west. But the world was strange to my eyes. There were towns where I remembered forest, orchards planted on hillsides where once I picked the wild blackberry. But the mountains remained the same. And the open plains beyond. Eventually, I arrived here, where my feet guided me. Here, I found the one who delved and cut the stone of which I was put into. It was the stone of my making that urged me to come to him, though it was not he who put me into the stone. But I had forgotten much of what was before, so my master explained things to me."

As he spoke, Sheila remembered the awful night when Robby came to Tulith Attis. She recalled the leaning stones that lined Weepingbrook and how Robby had almost succumbed to their enchantment. She remembered, too, when she first went to stay with Ashlord, how he took her to see the fortress and showed her the mysterious columns that stood about the place. And she remembered Robby's account of the soldiers who came out of those columns when the Great Bell rang and broke them open. And she certainly remembered the sight of them gathered around Robby, about to execute him.

"You were a soldier. I mean, before you were put into the stone."

"Yes. I was Captain of Heneil's household guard. We were sworn to protect his family. I and a company of my men volunteered to be put into the stone, made to slumber within by a conjurer, waiting to be summoned by the Great Bell. We were to surprise the enemy who would come by way of the river entrance, through the bell room. We knew it might be a long time that we would wait, but...."

Lythos stopped. After a moment, he said, "Your friend was wounded, I believe. Has he mended? Is he here? I would like to speak with him."

"Yes. He has mended. But he is far away."

"I see."

It had, by now, dawned on Billy what Lythos and Sheila were talking about and who, if not what, Lythos was. Robby had recounted the story often enough, and Sheila as well. With some prodding, Billy had even got

Ashlord to relate portions of the story, too, once or twice along the long way westward. And he had often been to Weepingbrook and had seen the strange leaning stones, having been told by his mother, in the sternest way, to stay away from there. Having lived under the shadow of Tulith Attis, frequently riding the Line Road, Billy always had a morbid interest in the place. Of a sudden, Eldwin's tale, describing somewhat of the carnage he had witnessed at Tulith Attis, struck Billy.

"Now," Lythos continued, "since I could not protect my old master, Heneil, then I seek to protect my new master."

Billy saw that Sheila was not ready to ask any more questions, her head bowed over her cup thoughtfully.

"Um," he turned to Lythos, "yer master...d'ye mind tellin' us his name?"

"My name is Alonair."

Standing with Ashlord in front of the open door of the cottage was a person of stocky build, about as tall as Sheila, but with arms and legs as thick as Ibin's, and as muscular as Lythos. His face was round, but hard like a field hand's, and his nose was thick and flat over thick lips. The close-cropped locks were curly and thick, the color of slate speckled with mossy green.

"Master," Lythos bowed. "I did not recognize the two at first. They look different, now. But they are the two I saw at Tulith Attis."

"Yes, I know," Alonair said, looking at Sheila. "Do not fret about it, Lythos. My dear," he bowed to Sheila and then, slightly to Ibin and Billy.

"These are my friends and travel companions, Billy, Ibin, and Sheila," Ashlord said.

"You are far from home," Alonair commented to them. "And Collandoth has related something of your travels and of the happenings in the world. He has much else to say to me, I'm sure. But I wanted to see for myself the one who so daringly assaulted Lythos and his men at Tulith Attis."

Sheila saw the wry smile on his face but still felt a pang of defensiveness.

"I have apologized already to Lythos," she said, "and explained that I was trying to protect my friend."

"Yes. So I have been told by Collandoth. And so I gathered from the tale Lythos gave me when he arrived here some months ago."

"Ah! Now I remember!" Billy suddenly blurted out.

"Oh? What do you remember, Boskman?" Alonair asked.

"Well, that...," Billy looked at Alonair and his grin suddenly turned to a look of bafflement, "...yer..." he hesitated, catching a look drilled at him by Ashlord. Billy glanced at Lythos, then, a bit helplessly, at Ibin and Sheila. Finally, he looked back at the expectant Alonair.

" 'Sixty cubits cut from rock, wide by long by high," the smiling Ibin quoted in a sing-song way. But the bit of poetry only provoked a somber stare from Alonair.

"Where did you hear that, Ibin?" Ashlord asked gently.

"From Robby. Robby, Robbytaughtit, taughtittomethedaybefore, thedaybeforewelefthimandUllin. Itsoundsbetterwhenyou, whenyousayitright. Initsown, itsownlanguage. 'Taha li al namis thet, kanan, denan, d'lami…"

"Speak not that cursed tongue here! How dare you, you crass imbecile!" Alonair, red-faced, commanded Ibin, holding up his hand and visibly shaking. But he quickly recovered his composure and said, "Forgive me. But I abhor the sound of the Dragon Speech."

Ibin was stunned, and Billy, burning suddenly with hurt and anger on behalf of his friend, stepped forward, his fists clinched.

"Who do you think you are?" Sheila said to Alonair, her tone harsh as she pushed in front of Billy. "We may be insignificant mortals to you, but long after the last of you and your kind are gone and forgotten, we'll still be here! The least you could do is show some courtesy to your betters!"

"Sheila!" Ashlord cried, stepping between her and Alonair. Lythos, in two quick strides, pushed Billy and Ibin aside and loomed behind Sheila.

"No one means offense to anyone!" Ashlord said to them all.

"Ye could've left," Sheila shouted in spite of Ashlord's effort. "Ye could've gone away with the others when Aperion took 'em, couldn't ye?"

Ashlord stared at her, shocked by the sheer anger in her tone, her language reverting to her old way of speech.

"Why didn't ye, then? I'll tell ye: ye wanted to make damn sure folks'd keep hatin' the Dragonkind, eh? An' thet them desert folk'd keep hatin' the rest of the world, too!"

"Sheila. For shame!" Ashlord scolded.

"No," Alonair looked at Ashlord and shrugged. "I'm sure she says only what many must think."

"Then why else do ye hide away? Ye started this mess. Why ain't ye tried to fix it?"

Sheila was trembling with anger, her face red and her finger jabbing at Alonair.

"Alonair alone is not to blame," Ashlord stated firmly and loudly.

"But it is true," the First One nodded, "that I do bear a great portion of blame for what has transpired."

"It was Secundur who goaded the ancient King Kalzar," Ashlord countered. "And he who has fostered discord and thwarted reconciliation among peoples."

"I hide here," Alonair said to Sheila, apparently unmoved by her anger and unconcerned by her aggressive manner, "because Secundur cannot come upon these sacred grounds and darken my mind as he once did. I stay here to wait."

"Wait? *Wait?* An' f'what?" Sheila shot back at him.

"For the day when I may keep my promise to the people of the desert lands."

Chapter 10

Company for Supper

Ullin and Haskin fared far better than Gullwing and Robby. Sir Wind took them up just at the last moment and bounced them right onto a large sloping ice-covered ledge so that they floated down onto their feet. They both exhaled with relief.

"Whew!" said Haskin.

But, ever capricious, Wind gusted hard, and before they could plant their axes, the nose of their craft wedged into a crack, filled with air, and lifted the two men up and flipped them, yelling in surprise and fear, over onto their backs atop the apparatus, with Haskin landing on top of Ullin, knocking the breath out of him. Haskin pulled on his release knots and they both rolled, still strapped together, off the upside down craft, and slid several yards toward the edge before Ullin's axe drove home. Fearing to move, they remained motionless then heard the crack and shatter of their companion's wing somewhere below. This served to invigorate the two men, who now feverishly undid the straps binding them together. Once free, they worked their way using their axes back to the flying apparatus.

"I'll take care of this," Haskin cried. "See if you can locate our comrades!"

Without hesitating, Ullin pulled off the heavy backpack he wore, stowed it securely against the rocks, then negotiated his way back toward the ledge. Planting his axe carefully, he got down onto his belly and dug in the toes of his crampons and eased his head over the edge. Lady Moon, now rising up over the southeast mountains, illuminated the ice and surrounding mountains with an eerie pale light. Glancing toward the east, he saw the edge of what appeared to be fortifications, far off and below, with garish orange fires dotting the dark lines of walls. Looking downward, and stretching out as far as he dared, fighting off yet another wave of dizziness, he could see nothing but a long sheer sheet of ice, broken here and there by rocky outcrops. He heard Haskin up behind him hammering metal against metal. A few moments later, the pilot was working his way to Ullin, using a rope to ease his way down the sloping ledge. He lay down next to Ullin.

"I don't want you to move an inch until you've got a good hold of this rope," Haskin instructed. "Here, wrap it around your free hand several times. Good. That'll have to do for now. Didn't realize this sloped down so steeply, or was so slippery. See anything?"

"No. Heard them, I thought. Sounded like they hit pretty hard. Listen!"

They heard Robby's axe cracking into ice as he climbed, a bit off to their right. Then, slowly, it seemed to grow closer.

"Let's see if we can move around this ledge and get over them with some ropes."

Haskin patiently helped Ullin retreat, and the two made it back to the top of the ledge with only a few scary slips. Ullin saw that Haskin had somehow disassembled the craft and folded it up into a long bundle. Panting from their effort, Haskin released the rope from the spike he had hammered into rock, then picked up a small heavy pack.

"How's the apparatus?" Ullin asked.

"Amazingly, it ain't busted. This whole thing is pretty amazing, though. The wing ain't meant to take so much buffeting, not with so much weight, the two of us and all the gear. It's a wonder it didn't just fold up and tear to shreds at the first updraft."

"Oh?"

Ullin was aghast, but Haskin did not notice his expression as he moved off along the ledge. Looking up, he pointed at the mountain above them.

"Looks like unless this ledge leads somewhere," he commented, "we've got a good climb ahead of us. But, first things first. Ready?"

"Yes. Lead the way."

"Right."

• • •

Robby never thought he could ache in so many places at once. His muscles burned, and his face was fairly numb from the cold, his breath beginning to freeze around his mouth. He kept on, doing just as Gullwing had instructed, planting first one toe, then an axe, then the other toe, and the other axe. Fortunately, it was not straight up, and the farther he climbed the more confident he grew that he would eventually reach the top. Still, it was slow going, and the backpack seemed to be getting heavier with every foot he climbed. Pausing, he looked down, and saw Gullwing, still hanging by his arm, only a hundred feet below.

"Oh!" he said, disappointed that all his effort had only gotten him a short distance. He fought a wave of fatigue and felt himself sinking into hopelessness. Muttering to himself, he continued a few more feet, then stopped, listening. The wind was now fierce, blowing grainy bits of ice down onto him. He heard it again. His name.

"Here!" he called upward. He choked, heard his name again, and cleared his throat. "Here!"

"Hang on!" he heard Ullin call down.

"We're going to drop a rope!" came Haskin's voice.

After a moment, he heard the sound of a rope snapping down to his right.

"Is it too far right or left?" Haskin called.

Robby strained to see the rope, but could not. Shifting his weight, he started his way toward it, but found that moving sideways seemed much more difficult than going straight up.

"Wait!" he cried. "I'm going to try to get to it!"

"We ain't goin' nowhere!"

After another several minutes, Robby could at last see the rope, but it was still far out of reach. Now, so anxious to get to it, he started making mistakes. First, his right foot lost its hold. Scrambling, he got his purchase with it just as the ice crumbled away from his left axe. He froze, panting, trying to force himself to calm down. Then, making doubly sure of every move, he continued.

"I'm at the rope!"

"Good. Are you still wearing your harness?" Haskin called.

"Yeah!"

"Great! Can you put the hook on the rope into your harness?"

"I think so. Let me pull it up some. Might take a bit of trying."

"No worries. Take your time. Let us know when you've got it hooked in."

Now Robby had to let go of one of his axes, and he really did not want to do that. Summoning his courage, he gently wiggled the one in his right hand until it was loose. Carefully lowering the axe to hang from its loop, he took Swyncraff from his waist and flung it out, uncoiling it toward the rope. Swyncraff touched the rope, then curled around it like a vine. Robby gave a tug and Swyncraff bent, bringing the rope to him. It was only then that he realized he could not let go of Swyncraff, much less pull up the rope with just one hand. So he made Swyncraff curl again, bringing the rope to his face. Robby bit into the rope, and held it tight in his teeth. Then he released Swyncraff to wrap around his waist while he took the rope in his now free hand, letting it fall out of his mouth as he pulled upward. He brought it to his mouth and bit again, letting it dangle from his teeth as he pulled up another length, spat it out, and chomped onto it again. Bit by bit, he worked the rope up until he felt the hook and immediately snapped it into the ring at the center of his harness where it ran across his chest. Then, he got his grip onto his axe and swung it hard into the ice to take the weight from his sore left arm.

"Got it! I'm hooked."

"Wonderful! Now. You're still going to have to help out. Just be sure not to cut the rope with your ice axes!"

"Right!"

"As soon as you feel us pulling, you go at it. We ain't gonna let you fall, so just go at it like there's no tomorrow!"

They pulled, and Robby clawed and climbed. In less than five minutes, he was up, rolling over onto his side, panting as Ullin and Haskin collapsed beside him. After a moment, and before Haskin had the breath to ask, Robby got to his knees, squirming to get the backpack off.

"We've got to go after Gullwing!"

"Right! Is he below?"

"Yes, but he's injured. Made me climb away. But I can't leave him!"

"What shape is he in?" Ullin asked.

"He says his arm is pulled out of the socket. He's dangling by it, unable to get to his other ice axe. He thinks he cracked a rib, too."

"How much farther down from where you picked up the rope?"

"A hundred feet, maybe? Maybe a little more."

"Hm. Do you still have that coil of rope about you?"

"I do."

"Then I suppose I ought to get going," Haskin stated, getting to his feet. "First, let's get your rope spliced into this one. I'll need you two to pay out the rope whilst I climb down."

In a few minutes, all was ready. The ropes were spliced, several anchor spikes were hammered into rock, and Robby and Ullin's ice axes were driven and set so that they could sit side-by-side with their feet against them, the rope going around their backs. Haskin was leaning backwards over the edge.

"Easy does it. Just let it out easy, and I'll take as much weight as I can with my axes. Now, just to go over it again. When I get to Gullwing, I'll get him secured onto the rope. Then I'll come on back and help you pull him up."

"Is there no way you can use the rope to come back up?" Ullin asked.

"No, I don't want to trust that you can hold the weight of the two of us, should he, being injured, be unable to keep an axe planted, and should I slip. I'll be fine. Done a lot of this kind of thing. See you later!"

And off he went. It took him only a short time to reach Gullwing, who was very surprised to see his fellow trooper. After a few jokes and just a little struggle, Haskin hooked the rope to Gullwing's harness, and began making his way back up. Robby and Ullin took the slack out of the rope but waited for Haskin to reappear before doing anything else. A little more than an hour after going down, Haskin was chopping his way over the ledge and back into view of Robby and Ullin. It was a few minutes longer before the climber was able to speak.

"Right, then! Getting awful bloody cold, so let's get my mate on his way. He's pretty banged up, but he's got one strong arm and both legs, so he can help some. Let's start pulling. Slow and steady."

Slow it was. As they worked, the eastern horizon grew pale red and purple while the wind increased. When Gullwing's face finally appeared over the ledge, it was a bright and blinding morning, though brief, for they had hardly caught their breath enough to congratulate each other when clouds rolled down from the north filling the biting air with blowing snow. Moving as quickly as they dared, and with a care to their injured friend, they got back to the place where the flying apparatus was stowed. Carefully spreading it to avoid damage, they made a bit of shelter against the rockface, and they crawled underneath and huddled together while they discussed their situation.

"How far do you think it is from here to Griferis?" Gullwing asked as Ullin gently placed his arm into an improvised sling.

"I have no idea," Robby said. "I don't rightly know where we are. The gate to Griferis is on the west-facing side of the mountain, but not at the top."

"Well, we're nowhere near the top, either," said Haskin. "I imagine we're maybe a bit over halfway up. Maybe higher up than that."

"At any rate," Ullin added, "we'll have to pick our way around and upwards."

"Well, I'm afraid I'm in no shape to be picking my way around in any direction," Gullwing stated. "I can't move my left arm at all, and I can't feel the fingers on my right hand, though I think I see them wiggling inside my glove."

"That's alright," said Haskin. "I'm not sure I can feel my toes."

"One thing is certain," Ullin said. "We can't stay here much longer."

"I agree."

"Didn't you say this flyer was still in good shape?" Ullin asked Haskin.

"Yeah, she's fine. Scuffed up some, but sound."

"Can you fly Gullwing to safety from here?"

"I don't know. And I don't know where safety might be. We started out a lot higher up. And we're surrounded by Shatuum."

"What if you went south and west from here," Robby suggested. "You might make the frontier at least."

"Maybe. It's only a few leagues off."

"We could get more distance if we cut between the peaks," Gullwing picked up. "But then, you'll be piloting, so I'm not so sure."

"I'm not the one who crashed into the side of a cliff!"

"Well, if it hadn't been for that foul gust, things might have been different."

"Still, you haven't flown the same rig twice, have you? It's a wonder they'll even let you take another one up."

"Gentlemen!" Ullin cut in. "Save that for another time."

"Just sayin'."

"But can it be done? Can you fly out and away?"

• • •

Whether they could or could not, they decided to make the attempt as soon as the snow eased up. But Haskin and Gullwing insisted on leaving all of the rope and more than half of the rations with Robby and Ullin. By noon, the snowfall had ceased, except that which blew down from the heights above, and Robby and Ullin set to work helping Haskin reassemble the flying apparatus. After getting Gullwing strapped to Haskin, Robby and Ullin then held the tips of the wings steady until the pilot nodded. Letting go, they watched him lumber down the short icy slope, hardly more than a quick walk, then over the side they went. Robby caught his breath. A moment later, they reappeared, speeding away south and west. Ullin took out his spyglass and watched as long as he could keep them in sight. Then, he turned back to Robby.

"I lost them behind that ridge yonder."

"Well. Let's hope they make it to safety. I suppose we had better get going ourselves. Let's see how far this ledge goes around the mountain."

• • •

Robby well knew that one could not learn all one should know about negotiating snow and ice and mountain ledges in such a short time, but he was now thankful for the long trek that had got them here. Lessons that were learned during that journey, with many helpers around, he would not soon forget. Ullin apparently felt the same way, and while neither spoke on the subject, they hoisted their packs, got their ice axes ready, and silently tied a length of rope between them. Ullin insisted on going first, and when the rope had no more slack, he planted his axes and crampons while Robby worked his way up. In this manner, first one then the other acting as an anchor, they inched westward along the ledge. It quickly became not much more than an icy outcrop barely shoulder-wide, gradually ascending until it became so steep that they had to wholly depend on their equipment. Still, they edged on all afternoon, and the ice gave way to rock as darkness began to settle once again on the mountain. Stopping at a relatively level spot, Ullin set his axes and feet, then nodded for Robby to come up. When he made the short stretch, Ullin pointed upward.

"Look there. I think we might be able to climb up from here."

It was a craggy slope, with rocks jutting out every few feet, much less steep, it appeared, than the way they had just come.

"Well, let's see how far we can get before it's too dark," Robby agreed.

The first fifty feet or so were the hardest, but from there on, they moved quickly, climbing from rock to rock without relying so much on their axes. Suddenly Ullin stopped and put his hand up. He put his finger across his lips and gestured for Robby to come up quietly.

"Do you smell that?" Ullin whispered.

"Smoke."

"We might have company."

"Can you tell where it's coming from?"

"No. The wind is so back and forth."

"Well, we had better be as quiet as we can. Maybe we'll find a decent place to shelter until morning. Pretty soon it'll be too dark to see friend or foe."

Ullin nodded. "I agree. Let's get rid of this rope. If I stumble into something, there's no point in them finding the both of us. Besides, it looks fairly easy going compared to what we've already done."

Robby coiled the rope as Ullin moved on up. When he had it wrapped over his shoulder, he followed. But after only a small distance, Ullin stopped again, peering over a rock. He gave Robby a hand, and they crouched, their faces close together.

"Take a look over there," he told Robby. Robby carefully stood and looked over the rock. The face of the mountain curved inward so that a wide bend was in deep shadow. There, not even ten yards away, a yellowish glow flickered against a boulder. Crouching back down, he shrugged.

"A fire?" he whispered.

"Must be a cave of some sort," Ullin said.

"Do we take a look, or go around?"

"Well, it looks as though our ledge ends there. I think I ought to go take a look. Unless you want to go back down the way we came and look for another way."

"No. I don't think I do. But it must be some of Secundur's creatures, don't you think?"

"Undoubtedly. But how many, and of what sort? We sure could use a place out of the wind. And they've got fire." Ullin was loosening the straps holding his sword in its scabbard as he spoke. He put one of his axes through his belt and gripped the other. "Wait here, keep low, and be watchful. I'll signal for you to come."

"I think we'd stand a better chance if we both went," Robby said, pulling out Swyncraff. "I'm right behind you."

"I don't guess there's any point in arguing."

"Let's go."

As stealthily as they could, they eased toward the light. It was the opening of a cave, twice as wide and a bit higher than Ullin was tall. The Kingsman crouched near the opening and leaned to look within. Its mouth was lined with ice that reflected light from deeper within. Still crouching, he stepped farther along to get a better look, and Robby followed close enough to touch him. They were both familiar enough with the sound of picks on rock to recognize the noise they now heard, echoing from somewhere farther in. Entering, the smell of the fire filled the air as smoke floated over their heads and out through the mouth of the cave, and the ceiling and upper portions of the walls were sooty from years of it. The passage before them descended, and they eased their way down to a bend. Incongruously, they heard someone humming and talking.

"Ah, dat's a good bit dat is! Hmm. Hm-hm-hm."

When they looked around the corner, what they saw surprised them even more. A tall man, as thin as a rail and dressed in ratty fur-lined leather, was striking the wall with a large pick, stopping after every few strokes to examine a chunk of rock before either tossing it over his shoulder or slipping it into a bag at his feet. Behind him was an iron brazier filled with burning coal, and hanging from a hook nearby was an oil lamp, its wick burning bright yellow.

"Oh, ha! Now, thar's a pretty bit of rock. Yes, siree!"

As the man resumed picking away at the rock, Ullin and Robby retreated a few steps.

"What do you think?" Ullin whispered.

"Looks like a miner."

"Here? In Shatuum, of all places?"

"Do you suppose he's by himself?"

"I guess there's only one way to find out," Ullin concluded. "I suppose we ought to introduce ourselves. I'll go first."

"You realize we're going to frighten him. And we can't let him go, or else he might bring others to find us."

Ullin stood and shrugged. "Then let us move quickly."

The man heard them coming, turned, and screamed as he raised his pick. Ullin grabbed his arm and tripped him, and Robby kicked away the pick. The man kept screaming, trying to crawl away, but Ullin had him by the feet.

"We mean you no harm!" Robby cried.

"Ayieeee! Ayieeee! Ayieeee!"

"Quiet! Do you want to bring all of Shatuum down on us?"

Now the man was kicking and squirming, while still screaming. Robby slung Swyncraff around his ankles and drew it tight, but he still thrashed about with his arms until Robby stepped on one wrist and Ullin knelt down on the other. Still the man screamed, taking a long breath, coughing, then another deep breath, his blue eyes wide with terror. Looking from Robby to Ullin, he paused, then started screaming again.

"Please, stop!"

"If you don't stop your screaming, I'll have to gag you. Robby, hand me that cord laying over there beside those tools."

A moment later, Ullin had gagged the man with the cord and tied his hands and feet. They sat him up and leaned him against the wall. But he still moaned and whimpered loudly and pitifully. Standing, Ullin pulled back his hood and stood near the brazier, pulling off his gloves to warm his hands at the fire. Shaking his head, Robby did the same, ignoring the man for a moment as feeling came back into his fingers.

"Look, sir, we apologize for giving you such a fright," Ullin was saying to the man. "But it couldn't be helped. We're freezing and tired and rather lost. There's no use in carrying on so, as we mean to do you no harm."

"We don't want to hurt you," added Robby. "But we don't aim to get captured. So if you promise to behave, we'll take the gag out of your mouth. We're just as surprised to see you as you are to see us, I'm sure. Well, nearly."

"If we meant to harm you, we'd have done so already."

The man looked from one to the other, tears running down into his gray beard. But he stopped his crying, and slowly nodded.

"So you understand us? You understand our speech?" Robby asked.

"Uh-huh," the man nodded.

"If I take the rope from your mouth, will you keep quiet?"

"Uh-huh."

Robby looked at Ullin, who nodded. After Robby got the gag out, the man swallowed hard, but did not scream.

"My name is Robby. What's your name?"

"Tarkin."

"Tarkin? Well, Mr. Tarkin, this is Ullin. Where are you from?"

"East. Back east," he said tentatively, looking wide-eyed back and forth from Robby to Ullin.

"Oh, whereabouts?"

"Millsin...Fork."

"Millsin Fork? Why I know of that place! Up around Northwick, I think. That's not far from where I'm from, Passdale."

"Passdale?"

"Yes. My family ran the sundries store there. We used to get flint from Millsin Fork. Striking flints."

"Flint. Aye, flint. We had lots of flint in Millsin Fork."

Tarkin stared at Robby, and his expression softened from fear to wonder.

"Passdale," he repeated. "Passdale."

"Down along the Bentwide. In County Barley."

"Aye, Passdale. I've been thar."

"You are probably wondering the same things about us that we are wondering about you," Ullin said. "What are we all doing here? Whether we are Secundur's followers."

"Secundur! Bah! I spit at him!" Tarkin really did spit, but on the wall next to him. "He'll not get me! No, no, no! Won't never find me! Else he would've, right? Right!"

"Now he's the brave one!" Robby said to Ullin. "Mr. Tarkin, before we cut you loose, you had better explain what you are doing here."

"Ye explain first!" he said indignantly. "This here mine belongs to me! An' ye ain't been invited. Who's to explain! Ye explain the meanin' of this here enterusion!"

"Well, seeing as how you're the one all tied up," Ullin pointed out, "maybe you should go first. How did you get here?"

"Hrumph!"

"Have it your way. We'll just be moving along, then."

"I was brung here! What d'ye think? I come all this way just to scratch rock? Are ye really from back east?"

"Yes. Who brought you here?"

"That thar fairy queen's who. Er else her folk."

"Queen Serith Ellyn?"

"That's what I said."

"I don't believe you," Robby shook his head. "I've met her. And she doesn't seem the sort to do such a thing."

"Well, ye better start believin'. She's in cahoots with Secundur, she is! I was a right fine soldier, fought in the desert lands an' everythin'. Got taken first by them lizards, who done killed all me mates but two. They packed me off to the Free City with a bunch of renegades an' sold us all to a feller thar. He done packed us up agin an' marched us right up through Vanara, right past Linlally, an' right into Shatuum. Shore couldn't a done it without her knowin' 'bout it, is what I say. An' the feller what brung us to Shatuum was one of her fellers, one of them fairy men, a real dandy! All fine-dressed an' dainty-wainty. Baylerd, er Baylard, Barlord, er…"

"Bailorg."

"Aye! That's the feller!"

"I assure you," Robby said, "he was not one of the Queen's men."

"Well, them Faerekind is all the same, if ye ask me!"

Robby looked at Ullin who was shaking his head.

"Seems that there's no end to Bailorg's mischief," Ullin said.

"Well, you'll be happy to know that Bailorg is dead," Robby said to Tarkin.

"Dead! Dead? Why dead's too good for him!" Tarkin turned his head, cleared his throat, and spat again.

"How did you escape from Secundur?"

"Why he let me go. An' the rest of me feller prisoners. Said it was a kind of race. Whoever got up this here mountain an' found the magic gate would win his freedom. An' I won! Leastways, if y'call bein' stuck up here a prize."

"Why did they do that?" Ullin asked. "Was it for sport?"

"Look here, fellers," Tarkin said. "I can tell ye ain't too knowin' 'bout these here parts. An' I don't mind sayin' I don't 'xactly trust ye, no offense. Them gobs an' critter's an' witches an' such got sneaky ways, an' I ain't a mind to let on more than that. I figger if ye mean to do me in, like ye said, ye'd have done it already. So, why keep me all trussed up? Eh? Purty soon the fire's gonna run out an' we'll be gettin' cold, for sure. I got a place up the hill a bit, an' I got some food, too, up thar. What d'ye say? Why don't ye cut the old man aloose?"

"Like you say," Robby replied. "Sneaky ways, and all. How do we know you're not going to run off and let Secundur know we're here?"

"Well, in the first place," Tarkin smiled wryly, "if ye think a body can just walk up t' ol' Shadowface an' say hello an' how d'ye do, ye don't know much. If I was to run off an' tell anybody, it'd be Throgallus, not Secundur. Since ye don't even know that much, I'd say ye don't know much at'all. An' in the second place, I don't reckon I'd get along too well with them stinky folk, havin' outwitted 'em all these years. No, I reckon yer purty well lost, an' purty lucky, too, gettin' up here through the legions down the mountain. Granted, sneakin' up this side is purty smart, being out of sight, generally, from them lookouts. Mebbe, I can trust ye, after all. Now, ye'll only trust me if I can prove me trust to ye, eh? An' I can't very well do that all tied up like this."

Ullin pulled out his dagger, threw it at Tarkin's feet where it neatly cut the cord between his ankles and embedded into the ground. Ullin walked over and picked up the dagger, and looked at the stunned old man.

"Just to let you know that my dagger sticks into whatever I throw it at," Ullin said. "So if you try to run, you had better be faster than it."

Ullin then cut the cord binding Tarkin's wrists, and the man slowly stood, squinting at Ullin.

"I believe yer the type what can take care of hisself, alright," he said. "Oh, I can't say how fine a thing it is to see reg'lar folk! After all these years! Oh, how fine ye look, too, oh, oh!"

Filled with emotion, Tarkin's eyes sparkled as he grinned, and he suddenly reached out and gave Robby a hug.

"Yep, yep! A fine young man! Kinda scrawny, mebbe," Tarkin said as Robby gently pushed him away. He went to Ullin as if to hug him, too. But Ullin stepped back cautiously, and raised his dagger.

"Oh, just a handshake, why don't ye?" Tarkin said. Ullin warily offered his free hand, and Tarkin took it, squeezing it firmly while gripping Ullin's bicep.

"Oh, yer a strong one, I can tell! Plenty of meat an' muscle thar. A soldier, I bet, fit an' fine!"

Ullin waved his dagger and Tarkin stepped back, apparently delighted as could be at the company.

"Who is Throgallus?" Robby asked.

"Why that's what they call their gen'ral, a big feller, who does the orderin' an' such. Big, fierce-lookin', an' nearly always in company with his slavedriver capt'ns, what are ruthless an' as cruel as any."

"So they have an army?" Ullin asked as he slipped his dagger away.

"An' how else do ye reckon they keep thar kind in check?" Tarkin shook his head. "A mighty ignorant pair, ye are! Of course they got an army. They've got walls all around these lands, an' keep watch so that none can come or go. Ever' once in a while, thar's a breakout. Once, when I went down to fetch up a shovel, I seen a great big fight break out among the workers at the forges, an' along come a thousand of their soldiers, with Throgallus at the head, an' they killed every last one of them smithy folk. They burned the carcasses. See, it's like this: they're all kept hungry. Time to time, it's too much for 'em, an' they kill one of their own, secret like, an' eats him up."

"Kept hungry?" Robby asked. "Why's that? Is there not food?"

"Food! They ain't got a stick of grain, nor cattle, er any manner of fish nor edible fowl in all of Shatuum! An' I thinks," Tarkin leaned in close and dropped to a sort of whisper, "it's all a-purpose of some kind. It's like them henchmen an' Throgallus knows that if them creatures eat, they won't be no good for somethin', though I ain't got any idear of what that somethin' might be. Lord help the lands surroundin' if they ever let loose from this place! Why they'd be like locusts, they would!"

Tarkin continued to gaze back and forth at them, grinning, then suddenly exclaimed, "Oh, what a fine pair ye are! So wunnerful that ye came along!"

"How many live in Shatuum?" asked Ullin.

"Oh, well that's a question, ain't it?" Tarkin scratched his beard. "More than I'd care to count. I've only ever been on this side of these lands, close by to me mountain, ye see. But I reckon I've seen thousands an' thousands, just along these slopes. No tellin' how many they got in all the rest of Shatuum."

Ullin and Robby looked at each other, not really knowing what to make of what Tarkin told them.

"Well, you said you have a place nearby?" Robby said.

"A hut I made," answered Tarkin. "Not much to it, but it's cozy an' dry. I warn't countin' on havin' company for supper, but I'll manage to fix ye up right nice."

"We have our own food," Ullin said. "You won't need to share yours."

"Maybe you should show us the way," Robby suggested.

"Yes, sir. Just let me get me bag."

"You can come back for it after we leave," Ullin said. "Not too sure I want you to have a bunch of rocks, just yet. And leave your tools, too."

"Yes, sir. Well, let me have me lantern, at least. Unless yer eyes don't need light."

"Go ahead. But go slow. No sudden movement."

"Yes, sir. This way, then. It'll be such a fine thing, havin' company for supper!"

Tarkin led the way along the cave, into a low passage, and they began climbing a rough-hewn stair.

"So why did they have the contest?" Robby asked. "Was it a game?"

"That's what I figgered. At least, at first I did. A mighty cruel one, too. Thar was twenty of us they let out. I was pretty poorly, health-wise, but some were worse than me, others in right good shape. They gave us one whole day head start. No food, no water, no nuthin'. Watch yer heads, a bit low right here. Anyways, by the end of the next day, I done seen six of me feller prisoners dead, done in by traps an' snares an' the like. All them feller's, some Dragonkind, were way ahead of me an' the rest of us. Then them gobs started catchin' up an' comin' up on us. To make a long story shorter, I was the only one what made it. By the time I got halfway up the mountain, they done give up an' quit chasin' me. Didn't know that, of course. I was so scared, I kept climbin' an' scratchin' an' clammerin' up. By the time I got it into me head I was safe from 'em, I was purty near dead from hunger an' thirst. Anyhow, somethin' 'bout the upper parts they don't take to. In all me years up here, I ain't never seen one of them critters nowhar near this high up. I think it's the gate what keeps 'em back."

"The gate?" Ullin looked back at Robby, close behind him.

"Yeah, the weird gate what's on the back side of this here mountain. Up a ways, purty nearby me hut. I've come to think mebbe it's the gate that's what they're afraid of. Sometimes gives off a most peculiar noise an' glow. Ye ain't never seen the likes of it, I'll bet!"

"Maybe you can show it to us," Ullin suggested.

"Mebbe."

"How long have you been up here?" Robby asked. "And where did you get all your things? Your tools and such?"

"Oh, I stole 'em all." Tarkin pointed at the opening ahead and began trudging up a steep incline to a snow-filled crack. "Some storm we had earlier. Thought I'd be stuck here a few days."

They stepped through to the outside. The wind had died down considerably, and the stars were shining brightly.

"But it seems to have cleared up right nice. This way. Watch yer step. Yep, I stole everythin'. Got plenty hungry after a day or so. So I snuck back down an' took some food an' back an' forth with other stuff. I don't like goin' down thar, but ain't no helpin' it, since nothing grows up here an' thar ain't no game to speak of. 'Cept down below. Thar's game lower down. Nearly got caught a time 'er two, I can tell ye! I got most everthin' I need, now. So I only go down for food, heh-heh. Do a bit of trappin', in a manner of sayin', down below. Elsewise, I only go down yonder when somethin' gets broke, like a tool, er such."

"I thought you said there wasn't any food down below."

"Well, the game I mean ain't proper food, now is it? Not like ham 'er taters 'er bread 'er puddin'."

"How long have you been here?"

"Well, I'm purty sure it's been thirty-seven years, give 'er take. Got real sick one year an' sorta lost track."

"Thirty-seven?"

"Give 'er take. But mebbe yer ready to tell me how ye came to be me guests? Was it another one of them contests?"

"Not exactly."

"What, then?"

"We got off course a bit," Robby explained. "And we found ourselves on the wrong side of things. We were lucky to find your cave, or your mine. What exactly do you mine for, anyway?"

"Why this!"

Tarkin suddenly reached for his pocket, Ullin reached for his dagger, and Robby reached for Swyncraff.

"Wait! Wait! I only mean to answer ye!"

"Then answer slowly," Ullin suggested.

"Right, right!" Tarkin eased his hand back out and held out a lump of rock. Ullin took it, and Tarkin held the lantern close as Robby peered over Ullin's shoulder. The rock gleamed with yellow flakes.

"Gold?" Robby asked.

"That's right! This here mountain's full of the stuff! When I leave here, it's gonna be a rich man what goes back home! Keep it! I got plenty. An' plenty more's to be had, too! Consider it a down payment on takin' me along with ye."

"Take you with us?" Ullin asked, handing the rock to Robby. "So you know a way out of Shatuum?"

"Why, no. I figgered with two young fellers like yerselves, armed an' capable, an' with me own way of gettin' by them stinky critters, we'd have no trouble gettin' clean away!"

Ullin did not know what to say, and neither did Robby. Tarkin held the lantern up higher to read their faces.

"Ye don't seem much keen on that notion," he said. "Figgered that'd be the way of it. Say, whar're ye fellers headed for, anyways, eh? An' why wouldn't ye wanna tell me? Don't trust me, eh? Hm. I wonder why!"

Tarkin swung the lantern at Ullin's head, but missed. Ducking away, Ullin swiped at Tarkin with his axe, but also missed. The lantern rolled off, extinguishing in the snow, and in the sudden darkness, Robby felt Ullin's hand clutch his arm, pulling him down in a crouch.

"Be still and quiet!"

They heard Tarkin crunching away quickly, then the sound stopped and was replaced by the noise of rummaging a few yards in the miner's direction, followed by a creaking sound and a sharp click.

"I know that sound," Ullin whispered, pulling Robby behind some rocks. "He's got a crossbow."

"Ahh, good laddies! Ye done saved me a trip downstairs. Was gonna do me trappin' tomorrow, but a fine table ye'll set!"

"What's he talking about?" Robby whispered.

"Ye can run all ye want," Tarkin said. "But I've got eyes like a cat. An' I know these rocks an' cracks like the back of me hand."

Robby was taking off his backpack and rummaging through it as quickly and as quietly as he could. They heard Tarkin coming back, softly crunching through the snow.

"I've got a flare," Robby whispered.

"What do you have in mind?" Ullin asked.

"I don't know. Blind him, maybe?"

"Right."

"Yum, yum, yum!" Tarkin was saying tunefully.

Robby moved off to the right, while Ullin moved to the left, out from behind their cover.

"I hear ye!"

"I don't care if you do!" called Robby. "You'll still have to come and get us!"

"Oh, I'm a comin'!"

Robby shook his head. The man was clearly deranged, and half deaf, too, if he did not realize how much noise he was making himself. Robby squeezed behind another rock, listening to Tarkin approach. When he judged the man was only a few yards away, he struck the flare on the rock, igniting it brilliantly, then tossed it over the rock at Tarkin and ducked as the man turned, squinted, and shot. The bolt glanced off the rock right beside Robby's head, and he heard the noise of a scuffle and a soft thud as something fell.

"You can come out now, Robby," Ullin said.

Robby peered over the rock and saw by the light of the fizzling flare that Ullin was standing over Tarkin's body. Ullin reached down and pulled his dagger out of Tarkin's back.

"Foolish man!" Ullin said, wiping the blade on Tarkin's collar.

Coming out, Robby stood next to Ullin.

"Thanks," he said. "I guess we should have kept him tied up."

"I guess so. I wonder how much of what he said was the truth," Ullin sheathed his dagger and looked around. "We just signaled anyone who might be watching, I mean."

"You're right. Sorry. I didn't think about that."

"It was a good plan. Don't be sorry. Especially since it worked. But I think I'll take this."

Ullin reached down and picked up the crossbow.

"And I think I'll take this." Robby picked up the lantern. "Do I dare light it?"

"Do you have any firesticks?"

"Yes, plenty."

"And I still have flares. So let's hold off on the lantern and see how well we can get on by starlight."

"Alright, then."

Robby stepped on the fizzling flare, extinguishing it, and they waited for their night vision to return.

"I wonder if he really had a real place around here," Ullin said, "or if he just lived in caves."

"I don't know about you, but I'm just about sick of caves."

"Me, too. But I'd take a cave over the cold wind."

"Why did he have a crossbow hidden away? Why not keep it with him?"

"He said he served in the desert. We would leave caches of weapons along our trails, just in case. I imagine he's done the same."

"Hm. Maybe so. Look, do you see a path?"

"No. I wish Lady Moon would finish her makeup and hurry her stride over the mountain."

"Me, too."

"Every night she arrives later than the night before," Ullin joked. "Just like a lady."

Suddenly, Robby thought of Sheila dancing in the moonlight on Passdale Green the night he met Thurdun. Now he knew that he might never see her again. Looking at Ullin, he wondered how often the Kingsman thought of Micerea in somewhat the same way.

"I don't relish the idea of stumbling around all this ice," Ullin said, breaking into Robby's thoughts. "But we can't stand here all night or we'll freeze. Let's move over to those rocks and huddle down until the Lady shows up."

This they did, pulling up their legs and putting their packs on top of them to help keep the air off, then they pulled down their balaclavas, snugged their caps, and drew down their hoods. Pretty soon, they were each to his own thoughts, and Robby's turned back to Sheila while Ullin thought of Micerea, as he did nearly all of the time, now. Since leaving Islindia, he had not once been bothered by visions of Esildre, and his mind was ever on the desert, and Micerea. This night, as he often did, he imagined what it would be like to go back and find her. He fancied they could go to the Free City again and live out their days without care. It was all just a dream, he knew. Like Robby, he also realized that he would never see Micerea again except, if sleep was kind, in his dreams. Closing his eyes, he remembered her aroma, the scent of desert sage and myrrh, and he recalled how she teased him for bathing so often, saying that he was surely a poor Northman for keeping so clean. He smiled at the fond memories. At least he had those.

"Looks like the Lady arrives at last," Robby said. Opening his eyes, Ullin saw the moon peeking over the edge of the mountain, quickly spreading her light.

"Let's give her time to find her stride," he said. "Let her get high so that we won't have so many shadows to worry us."

Robby scrunched back down and was soon asleep. He had business to attend to back in Janhaven, if he was not already too late, and he might just accomplish it before Ullin woke him. He needed to find his mother and warn her, but, though he found her easily enough, she was just waking and dressing to go to late night duty on the walls of the stockade. He followed her and waited, hoping that she would doze off as so many of her comrades at other parts of the wall did. Finally realizing that she was too conscientious for that, he was about to go look for Frizella and pass his warning to her when Ullin woke him.

Chapter 11

The Other Guests

About the same time that Ullin and Robby waited for sunset and for Commander Strake's order that would send them flying to Algamori, their friends sat with the monks in their dining hall to share the evening meal. It was a plain setting, nearby to the main kitchen of the monastery, and a vegetable soup was ladled into their wooden bowls. Billy and Ibin started right in, slurping in their usual manner, but Ashlord waited until all of the monks were seated and bowed their heads. Taking her cue from him, Sheila did likewise, while Billy's eyes darted back and forth, a dripping spoon halfway to his mouth. When the moment of silence was over, and everyone was eating, Ashlord picked up his spoon and began, too. Unsatisfied by the encounter with Alonair, Sheila had remained sullen for the rest of the afternoon, and she said little as they ate. Across from Ashlord sat the monk who had been their guide, and after a few sips of tea, he spoke.

"Did your interview go well?" he asked.

Ashlord nodded. "As well as could be expected, I suppose."

"And did he mention our other two guests?"

"No. Other guests?"

"Yes. They arrived not long ago. I think you will find them interesting. And I believe, somehow, that you may know one of them."

"Oh?"

"After we sup, I will take you to them. If you wish."

"Certainly. What are their names?"

"They never said."

Sheila listened and watched, noting Ashlord's look of surprise and, she thought, a mischievous glint in the eyes of the monk. He threw a glance her way, smiling.

"Ashlord," Billy spoke up from down the table, "when are we goin' to the city?"

"Soon, Billy. Perhaps tomorrow."

"We'regoing, we'regoingto, we'regoingtomeetyourfriend," Ibin stated.

"Yes. And to see others as well."

"Hm. We have noticed," said the monk, "that, over the past week or so, travelers are questioned as they enter the city. The Kingsmen ask after any who come from the east, particularly if they are in a group of six."

"Oh?"

"Yes. They look for five men, one a Kingsman, with a young lady in their company."

"Hm. Is that so?"

"Yes."

"Well, I'll be," said Billy as he glanced at Sheila.

"That cannot be good," Sheila said.

The monk picked up his bowl of soup and blew on it as Ashlord considered. Sheila and Billy said nothing more, but they could not but notice the looks and glances of interest from the other monks at the table.

"Tell me," Ashlord asked, "how often do your brethren go to the city?"

"We have several groups who go each day."

"Then, perhaps some of your fellows might act as guides for my friends and me. Going at different times with each?"

"That would be easy enough to arrange."

"Thank you."

Sheila still had many questions but was in no mood to ask, especially in front of the monks. She was beginning to regret her outburst at Alonair, not because she regretted anything she said, but because she had lost her temper so horribly. Now, sitting with the monks and sharing with them a peaceful meal, she felt the calming influence of her surroundings. Ashlord had not said anything about the incident since they left Alonair, but Billy, in a whisper on their way back from Alonair's place, had thanked her for standing up for Ibin. Still angry, she had only nodded to him. Now, she ate slowly, knowing that her temper, worn thin by the past months, had gotten the better of her. With Alonair, just as with Billy earlier that day, she had spoken before she thought.

After they ate, they were shown to the rooms where they would sleep, each to a humble cell along the same hallway. The one shown to Sheila was, in fact, the very same one that Esildre had occupied earlier that year, and the others were given rooms next door and across the hall. After assuring the monks that the rooms were more than adequate, and putting away their packs and things, the group was guided to a courtyard, somewhat like that seen before on the way to Alonair, but this one was on the southern side of the monastery grounds. It was a meditation garden, their guide explained, and several monks were sitting here and there beside a little stream or on the flagstones that paved the yard. Even though it was winter, there were blooms, yellow and orange, their colors enhanced by the low sun now sinking behind the mountains in the southwest. But, very strangely, a huge black bird sat on the south wall, his head hunched into his shoulders.

"There is one of them," the monk said.

"A buzzard?" Billy asked.

"Vulture," Ashlord said. Turning to the monk, he said, "I don't understand."

"It seems to serve our Guest in some fashion. Or have other business known only to itself," the monk explained. "It caused quite a stir when it first arrived. Many of my brethren and sisters thought it was one of Shatuum's black eagles. They hover over Duinnor constantly, these days. But, as you can see, it is not an eagle. It is a humble creature, doomed to its nature. Not a hunter of the living. And, six days ago, it brought another guest to us."

"Oh?" said Ashlord, looking around at the monks. "And who was that?"

"The little fellow, just over there, asleep in that beam of sunshine."

The monk motioned to their left at the eastern side of the garden, to an open area between camellias. There, stretched out with his chin down upon the stone, was a rabbit.

"Beauchamp?" Ashlord uttered. "Can it be you?"

Beauchamp raised his head and saw Ashlord. He got up, stretching and yawning, and hopped over to Ashlord, circling him twice.

"Oh, my!" Sheila said, grinning. "Ashlord, do you know this rabbit?"

"I do! I do!" he replied, and he crouched to pet Beauchamp on the head and to scratch the creature's brow. "The vulture brought him?"

"Yes," nodded the monk. "It was most bewildering. And I'm afraid the bird frightened the poor animal so terribly that it didn't eat for nearly a whole day. But it found its way into the herb garden, just over there, and has been making free with the parsley. And, you may be interested to know," the monk lowered his voice, "they arrived on the very same day that the Kingsmen of the city began scouring the streets, gardens, and byways for rabbits. No reason was given, but many creatures were captured and taken to the King's Palace. You may draw your own conclusions."

"If you are here," Ashlord nodded to the monk, but addressed Beauchamp, "then what has become of your master?"

At the question, Beauchamp became quite agitated. He oinked softly, thumped, hopped back and forth in an unsettled way, and returned to Ashlord. He nudged the toe of Ashlord's shoe with his head, and then bit at it.

"Do you have something to tell me?"

Ashlord knelt. Then, to the surprise of everyone, he got down on his hands and knees, and he put his face very close to Beauchamp's. The two remained frozen in that aspect for many moments. Ibin, grinning, tugged Billy's sleeve, but he said nothing while Billy turned his head to Sheila who put her finger to her lips. The monk merely looked on with a slightly amused expression. Suddenly, Beauchamp blinked, leaned forward, and licked Ashlord's nose. The mystic smiled, got to his knees, and petted the rabbit.

"You must be beside yourself with worry," he said. "I can only imagine. But be proud of yourself, and thankful to your savior." Ashlord glanced at the vulture that was observing the group from its perch many yards away. "I think you have done well, and Raynor would be very proud. I promise that I will do all that I can to reunite the two of you, as quickly as I may! But you must be patient."

Picking up his walking stick, Ashlord stood, went over to the vulture atop the wall, and looked up at the creature.

"And do you wish to impart anything?" he asked. "No? Then, I believe the one you wait upon has a task for you."

The bird spread its wings and gave several flaps, disappearing over the wall before reappearing, still flapping as it banked around the monastery toward the western side.

"May I speak with my friends privately?" Ashlord asked the monk.

"Certainly. Will this place do?"

"I do not wish to interrupt the meditations."

"An interruption is merely a change of flow," the monk said. He clapped his hands three times, and when the other monks look to him, he gestured to the garden gate. The other monks rose from their places, and without any sign of curiosity or annoyance they mildly filed out of the place. Their guide bowed, and retreated with them. After they were gone, and the garden door closed, Ashlord turned to his companions.

"Raynor has been taken prisoner by Lord Banis, and is probably within the dungeon of the King's Palace, if he is still alive," Ashlord told them. "Beauchamp is his Familiar. Somehow, the little fellow managed to get into the King's High Chamber, and saw and heard many remarkable things. He was chased from the place, but saved by the vulture, who took him up and flew him here for safety. I know! It is much to take in! How all this came to be is every bit a mystery to me, too."

"Didn't ye tell us that Raynor was the one who could help us tell folks in Duinnor about the Redvests?" asked Billy. "Are thar others what might be taken prisoner, too? Who else might give us a hand?"

"And what about Robby?" Sheila asked. "Does Raynor know about Robby? Will he tell?"

"Likely the King already knows about Robby," said Ashlord. "As for our task of warning Duinnor about the happenings in the east, Raynor already knows about the invasion. Through Certina, I sent word to him back when we left Tallinvale. I imagine Raynor has already stirred that pot, and has been telling his associates."

"Is that why he was taken?"

"I don't know. I doubt if that was the only reason, if it played a role at all in his arrest. But Raynor has been out of favor in Duinnor for years and years, ever agitating, in his way, for change and reform. And he has been arrested before. For sedition, if you can believe it. But, this time, I imagine they grow nervous about Robby."

"But how would they know?"

"I suspect the black eagles are behind it, somehow." Ashlord creased his brow in thought, and rubbed his chin, by now having a mix of gray and red whiskers. "When I met up with Robby and the Thunder Mountain Band in the troll cave, and examined Bailorg's body, I remember seeing signs of a large bird of prey within the place. The creature may have witnessed something there. Also, Certina was attacked by a black eagle on her way back to me from Duinnor. The black eagles are minions of Secundur, but have been seen over Duinnor, even at the Palace, for many years. That they are loaned to Duinnor does not bode well. But they must be behind the King's knowledge about Robby."

"Well, what should we do?" Billy shook his head. "I mean, do we or don't we try an' add our news to Raynor's? I still need to talk to the Court of Houses, don't I?"

"You have the right to do so, if it is convened," Ashlord said. "If you dare to try, I will help you gain a hearing. Meanwhile, I must also strive to learn Raynor's fate. Let us rest tonight, while I ponder our best course of action. We'll have breakfast with the monks, and make our arrangements to go to town, unless I come up with some other plan."

• • •

On another side of the mountain, Lythos knocked on Alonair's door and stepped in.

"My lord, the bird has returned."

Alonair looked up from the fireplace and stood from his chair.

"I will come outside to see him."

The vulture sat on the low stone wall just outside, and Alonair went and sat beside him.

"I must ask you to go on a long journey, and to go as swiftly as the air may carry you," he said to the bird. "I have put this off for too long, and I only hope that my stubborn disposition will not cost too many lives. Twice in one day to have the language of the sands uttered here! And now out of my own mouth! But here it is, and you must carry it true."

Alonair gave the bird its instructions, and he watched it take off into the night. Lythos stood nearby, saying nothing. Turning to him, Alonair shrugged.

"I sense that our time here may be coming to an end, old friend."

• • •

Later that night, Billy could not sleep. He was tired, but restless, and he tossed and turned ceaselessly until he flung his feet out of the cot and sat up in frustration. A dim light showed through the crack under the door, and he occasionally heard the soft shuffle of a barefooted monk go by. Getting up, he dressed and opened the door to peer outside. The hall was empty and quiet, and the doors to his companions' rooms were closed. He shoved his hands into his pockets and ambled down the hall. Pretty soon he was lost within the place, having passed in and out of the sanctuary several times, up and down stairs, through workshops where monks still labored at their trades, and in and out of various courtyards and gardens outside. He did not care that he did not know his way, and he thought it rather nice to wander around in a safe place for once. And he had a lot to think about. He knew that, as much as he liked telling stories and jokes, he was not prepared to speak before an august body such as the Court of Houses. During their journey, Ashlord tried his best to prepare him, lecturing him on the proper way to address lords and powerful people, how to act before them, etiquette of court behavior, what to say, and on and on and on, so that Billy became so confused and turned around about things that Ashlord finally threw up his hands.

"I will endeavor to find a smaller, less intimidating audience for you," Billy remembered Ashlord saying. "Perhaps we can find a way to ease you into things. Now, let's go over it again."

Now that the time was growing near, Billy wished that Robby was with them. Not that he could help much. It was just that as long as they were all together things never really seemed all that bleak.

"O' course," he thought, "things never seemed to rest on me shoulders 'til now, did they?"

Cutting through a lantern-lit garden, Billy absently followed a path downward, and before he knew it suddenly came upon Alonair's hut. A jolt of fear gripped him when he saw what he had mistaken for a tree suddenly turn and face him. It was Lythos, and Billy backed away, prepared to run.

"Do you wish to see my master again?" Lythos said. "He is within, beside his fireplace."

"Er, well, sir, I seemed to've lost me way," Billy stammered. "I took a wrong turn, ye see."

The door to the cottage opened, and yellow light flooded out. Alonair stood in the doorway, the fireplace blazing across the room behind him.

"Master Bosk, I believe?"

"Yes, sir. Sorry! I didn't mean to disturb. Kinda lost me way. I'll just be gettin' on back."

"I was about to have a tankard of beer," the Elifaen said. "Might you care to join me?"

Billy hesitated, then, realizing he was licking his lips, shook his head.

"Oh, naw. But that's mighty nice of ye."

"At least come in and take the chill off for a few moments."

Billy shrugged nervously and nodded. "Well, alright, then."

"It is a simple place," Alonair said, closing the door. "But it has been home for many years. Have a seat by the fire. I'll fetch the beer."

"I really can't stay," Billy stated.

"Not even for one cup? It is the only luxury that I allow myself. Brewed in a village not far from here. I do a bit of carving for the monks and they trade my things for this. Sit! Sit!"

"What about Lythos?"

"He doesn't drink."

"But ain't it gettin' cold?"

"He doesn't seem to mind the weather at all, cold or hot, rain or shine."

Billy reluctantly sat, accepted the tankard that Alonair handed him, and took a sip. It was quite good, lighter than ale but not too frothy. He took another sip as Alonair stood by the hearth and adjusted a log with an iron.

"You and your companions judge me too harshly, I think."

Billy shrugged.

"I'm not a great one so far as history an' such goes," he said.

Alonair nodded, putting down the iron and taking a drink from his tankard.

"I have done bad things, surely. And there was a time when I thought I was right in doing them."

"Well, we all make mistakes, don't we?"

"Yes, I'm sure everyone does. But my mistakes were those of pride and of spite. Your friend, the girl, she thinks I am a coward, and said as much. But I am not. I do not hide here out of fear that those who hate me and who blame me for the woes of the world may find me and kill me. Believe me, I sometimes think death would be sweet! But if I died, then I could never fulfill my promise. Yes, I made the challenge to Kalzar, and I knew the task was beyond him. But I made a promise, too, and trapped myself when I thought to spite him."

Alonair shook his head. "But I never guessed what would come to pass because of it. Though, even if I had known, I suppose I would have done it still. That is, the person I was then would have. Not me, who stands before you now. Things change. And if people live long enough, they, too, will change."

"So what brought ye here? To the Temple?"

"I only came recently, so to speak. A long time ago, surely, by your way of reckoning time. When I was Scathed by Aperion, I, like the rest of my kind who remained on earth, wandered for many, many years. Later, I tried to help Cupeldain, but did little good. I tried to help Heneil, too, but to no avail. And there were many who sought me out, to have their revenge upon me, or to enlist me in their cause. So I was always on the run. Along the way, I had my adventures. I have seen much. Not all bad. And not everyone who discovered my identity was filled with hatred. One of those, a Man, even saved my life once. I am mindful of him this night, and mindful of a promise to repay him, if I could. I keep my word, however long it takes."

"Is that why Ashlord came to see ye? Or was it about the Great Stone?"

"We spoke of both matters. Collandoth has a way with words, and he convinced me to hold to my promise to the man I spoke of sooner rather than later, and to repay him as I said I would. But Collandoth also spoke of the days to come, of opportunities that may arise for keeping other promises."

"Yeah, that Ashlord's a deep one for wantin' folks to do what's right."

Alonair nodded.

"An', like ye said," Billy went on, "folks do change, if given reason to, or the tools, or, like ye say, time to do it. I don't think they can rightly help it, 'cause it seems to me that the world changes an', well, we gotta live in the world, don't we?"

"Yes. The world does change," Alonair agreed. "And we, too. But it is so slow that it is hard to notice. Like melting snow on the fields, trickling away from underneath until, one day, it is all gone. I remember that I used to feel connected to the forest, for instance. But I no longer remember what it felt like. I remember speaking with Sir Oak and patiently listening, sometimes for sunset after sunset, as he creaked of the seasons and noted to me his days of warmth and of stretching for the sun. Of sleepy winter days, he spoke, too. But I do not remember the words, the sound of his language. I remember, too, laughing with Lady Brook. I do not remember what it was that made us laugh so. I still hear her, but it is as if her back is turned to me as she carries on with someone else that I cannot see, and I am not privy to their jokes and mirth or what she says or laughs at. Sometimes I think she laughs at me. And I sat for eons, ages ago, listening to the rocks of the mountain speak their slow words, hard and coarse, as they were gradually made smooth by wind and water. I still hear them, too, somewhat, and I better understand what they say than the other things of the earth. But I fear that soon I may not hear even those old friends. My hearing fails with age, you see."

He ran his hand across the smooth stones of the hearth as if trying to remember something about them, too, something faded from his ability to recall.

"I am not alone in this absentmindedness," he went on with a shrug, taking a full swallow from his tankard. "Many, if not most, of my kind have grown forgetful. It is a curse to us, you know. For in all other matters we have perfect memory from the beginning of our days, every event, every sunrise, distinguished clearly one from the other. Every taste and every moment of taste a world unto itself. Every pleasure, every pain."

Then his eyebrows went up in a moment of light.

"Children born of Elifaen mothers and fathers are Scathed in the womb, as you may know. But those born of mixed parents are not, and, until they are Scathed, at least while they are very young, they seem to have knowledge of those things that the rest of us have forgotten. It is uncanny, to be jealous of a child, I, who have the long chain of years upon me! But it is true that I am jealous. I presently have a granddaughter of only three years and a grandson of seven. You look surprised. Yes, I had a wife, once. And five children, now all gone but two. And they have children. I still have my means to learn about my children, though they have not seen me for over a thousand years and do not know where I live. Or even that I do live. But both of my daughters recently married Men of Vanara, and my grandchildren have not yet been Scathed. I am told that they are happy children, somewhat precocious, and have some special way of knowing the world that we, their elders, have forgotten. And I have noticed, too, that some Men, well into their years, seem to have a notion of those First Things, even though they were not here when the First Things were made, and their ears have never heard the Language of that Time Before Time. Some of the monks here are like that. They seem older than their years, to me, and yet younger than their days, like we Elifaen, but with some gaining of what we have lost."

Billy listened intently and politely and did not interrupt. He thought of his own mother, wise and earthy, and sipped his beer thoughtfully to her memory, wondering how she was getting along and what she might say about all that he and his companions had seen and been through.

"Your companion, the big one, is one of those, I think," Alonair went on. "But he is far different than most of the race of Men."

Billy shifted in his chair, his defenses going up slightly, as they always did when people spoke of Ibin behind his back. But he remained silent, respectful even, of the Ancient One.

"I sense you have a special connection to him, and saw how you stepped up for him this afternoon. I am sorry that I spoke harshly to him."

"Yep," Billy dismissed it with a wave. "Bygones. We're great friends, Ibin an' me. But it didn't all start out that way. Only, well, he saved me life one time, an' I ain't forgot it. A person can live his whole entire life an' not repay such a thing as that."

"Of course not."

"An' yer a purty glum feller, did ye know that?"

Alonair smiled and nodded. "My apologies, good sir! It is no way to entertain a guest, is it?"

"Aw, I didn't mean it that way. These here are glum times, though, ain't they?"

"I suppose they are."

"So, if ye don't mind me askin', how did ye think them Dragonfolk might move that ol' rock of yers?"

"Do you know," Alonair grinned, "you are the very first person ever to ask me that!"

"Well, thar ain't no accountin' for folks, but it seems a plain enough thing to wonder at."

"Well, at the time," Alonair sat in the other chair beside Billy, and waved his hand in the air, "it was a simple thing for my kind to do. Remember, that was before we lost our wings. I thought, at least I suppose I thought, that if the desert people ever became more like us, they'd learn how to speak with the stone and get it to move, just as we moved the stones of our cities, by merely coaxing them. Of course, I was wrong about that, as I was about so many things. But I was young at the time."

Billy giggled, "That's a good'un!"

Alonair looked askance at him, then laughed at what he had just said. This made Billy laugh harder. They each took their turns at their cups, nodding like old chums. Indeed, Alonair, in this light, seemed not that much older than Billy. And when Lythos looked in at the unusual sound of their mirth, and they turned in their chairs and saw his concerned face, Billy and Alonair fell into hysterics.

• • •

Hours later, and after having passed out at least twice for drink and lack of sleep, Billy staggered back to his cell. When he fumbled with the door, Sheila opened hers and stuck her head out into the hall.

"Hulloooo, Sheila!" Billy made a tilted bow, then fell against the wall. "An' how might ye be, thish fine ev'nin', eh?"

"Where have you been?"

"Whar? Gettin' drunk, 'at's whar. An' I been with a fine drinkin' feller, too, 'at's what."

"Shh! You'll wake everyone!"

Sheila took Billy by the arm and guided him into his room.

"Ye know, Sheila, I kin call ye Sheila, can't I? Of course I kin call ye Sheila. I done already done it. Ye know, Sheeeeila, that ol' Alonair feller ain't such a bad feller for such an ol' feller. Not that he's old. Not that he's young. Not that he's, that he's, well, I ain't rightly sure what he is, tell the truth of the matter. Any'ow, not a bad chap, once ye get to knows him."

"Billy Bosk! You are drunk!"

"I done said I was, didn't I? Er, did I? No, I said I was gettin' drunk, which ain't 'xactly the truth seein' how I was already gotten drunk. Or got drunk. Anyhows, I'm drunk. Er, elseways, a lotta beer got drunk. Imagine that! A drunk beer, all staggerin' 'round an' 'bout. That'd be a sight!"

"Sit down before you fall down!" she ordered, pushing him down onto his cot and sitting beside him to unbutton his coat.

"Too late! To-oo late! I done falled, felled, fell down, done I. Didn't I done? Twicsh. At leasht that I can recollect."

"It's not like you to wander off like that," Sheila said, pulling off Billy's coat and tossing it aside. "Much less take up with strangers."

"Shtrangers! Us're the shtrangers! An' gettin' shtranger ever' day, too! Ain't ye notished? An' 'sides, I reckon I needed a little walkie-walk, an' one way led off to another, an' then thar I was. An' Mr. Alonair was most hospitabubble-like."

Suddenly Billy's face grew serious and he leaned in close to Sheila.

"Sheila, Sheila, I been havin' the sshtranger, er, sshtrangestest dreams, lately. All 'bout Robby. Well, not 'bout Robby. Robby's in 'em. But it ain't

Robby! I mean, it is Robby. But it ain't. An' he keeps tryin' to tell me things."

"Go to sleep!" she ordered, wincing at his breath. "It's almost morning."

Sheila stood up, lifted Billy's legs onto the cot, then went to the door.

"Wait, wait!"

"What?"

Sheila stopped at the door, rolling her eyes, and turned back to Billy who was struggling to lean up on an elbow.

"What, Billy?"

"I'm sorry, Sheila."

"It's alright, Billy. Go to sleep."

"No, I mean, I mean I'm sorry things got so meshed up for ye."

"Billy—"

"No, I mean I should've done somethin'. I should've," Billy clinched a fist and swung at the air. "I should've done somethin' to ol' Shteggan, long time ago."

"It wasn't your place, Billy. Go to sleep."

"It dang well was me place! It dang well was! Only, only. It vexates me. Can't get it out of me head. I hate meself over it, an' a number of other things, asides that, too. Only, some folk I can't even appleogize to any more. Not that appleogizes're worth anything. Anyways, I'm sorry I been such a lout all these years. I should've been better. I should've done somethin'."

"Go to sleep, Billy."

Sheila left and closed the door. She had just returned to her cell, after her own spell of wandering the halls of the Temple, when she heard the sound of Billy coming along. Now, she leaned her head against the inside of her door, and began undoing the buttons of her blouse. A few months ago, Billy's words might have brought tears to her eyes. But tonight she, too, was in a mood, and it was not a sad one. After her outburst with Alonair, she felt empty, as if the last feelings she had were poured out, leaving her feeling rather numb.

"I wish you had, Billy. I do wish someone had," she whispered into the wood of the door, then turned around and went to her cot. She tossed off her blouse, pulled the blankets up over her, and blew out the candle, remem-bering, without pain, how the only person who helped her that awful night was a total stranger who did not even stay to see if she would be alright.

"Whoever he was, he just dumped me on Frizella's step and ran away," she said to the darkness. "Just like everyone does, it seems."

Only she did not mean everyone. She really only meant one person, the same person who tormented her own dreams as much as he seemed to be doing in Billy's. It was funny, she thought, since Ullin and Robby went their own way, she hardly thought about Ullin at all. But she thought about Robby constantly. If things went well, she might see Ullin again someday. But she knew that she would only see Robby again in her dreams. They were not unpleasant dreams, and if she could live in them always, and never wake up, that would be fine. She turned over, closed her eyes, and sighed.

"Oh, well," she thought. "I suppose the morning must come. Meanwhile, a dream is better than nothing."

Chapter 12

Enter Griferis

Day 168
77 Days Remaining

"Let's see if we can find our way, Robby."

Ullin stood, nudging Robby awake. Blinking, Robby stirred, shaking off a shiver, and tried to get his bearings. He had been dreamwalking, and he wanted to warn his mother about Vidican's dreamwalking spy. But she had not been sleeping, and he was beginning to wonder when she ever did. When Ullin woke him, he was about to go to Frizella instead, who was sleeping in a chair and dreaming of her husband.

"Yeah, sure," Robby said, getting to his feet. Lady Moon was high, and he slung on his pack and followed Ullin.

"It looks as though this is where Tarkin kept his weapon," Ullin said, pointing out an oilskin bundle under an outcrop. Picking it up, he shook out of it several bolts. Then, looking around, he pointed at a path lightly covered with snow that wound upwards.

"Looks as though it is this way."

They picked their way carefully, not trusting the path, and when Lady Moon playfully hid behind a racing cloud, they paused. When she emerged, lighting the way once again, Ullin put his hand out, halting Robby.

"What is it?"

Ullin pointed down. "Back up, very slowly."

Robby still did not see what Ullin was looking at, but he obeyed and stepped back as Ullin, crouching, backed up in front of him. Then, taking out his ice axe, Ullin knelt, looking to see that Robby was safely behind him a few feet, then tossed it to land a few inches from where they had paused. The pick snapped a thin cord, releasing a knot on a boulder that toppled onto the path with a ground-shaking thud.

Robby blinked.

"We were lucky we stopped where we did," Ullin said calmly, glancing up thankfully at the insignificant lone cloud.

"Uh-huh," Robby agreed. "I suppose we should be more careful."

"I think I'll light the lamp," Ullin said. "Might help some."

After a moment, Ullin had Tarkin's lamp lit, and he handed Robby the crossbow. Then Ullin proceeded to lead the way, holding the lamp low to the ground, looking for more snares. They squeezed around the boulder, and slowly inched along the path. Ullin found two more traps, one that made a many-pointed arm fly across the path, and another that caused the ground to give away, caving into a deep abyss. But, in spite of the lamp, Ullin missed one that was cleverly hidden under the snow. Robby stepped into it, a loop of rope that snared his right leg and dragged him away as the other end, tied to a rock, fell over a ledge and off a cliff. Ullin flung away the lamp and dove back at Robby, grabbing his wrist with both hands, and the two were dragged together first upward, over the ledge, then toward the edge of the cliff. Squirming and kicking, Ullin got his feet around and jammed his legs into the gravelly ground as Robby slung Swyncraff into a crack in the rocks. Their slide ceased, Robby's legs dangling over the drop-off, and neither dared move for several moments.

"How are you doing?" Ullin asked, not daring to ease his vise-like grip on Robby's wrist.

"Well," Robby said, "my leg's about to pull right out of the socket, but other than that, I'm just fine. How are you doing?"

Ullin tried not to laugh, shaking his head at their predicament.

"Do you think you can grab my harness?"

Ullin nodded, slowly adjusting his grip until he could release one hand to quickly take hold of Robby's chest straps, then the other hand.

"I don't think I can pull you up," Ullin said. "Just don't have my feet situated right."

"I don't care. Just don't let me slide. I need both my arms to get this thing off my leg."

Robby drew his knife.

"I don't understand how you are going to reach your ankle."

"Watch."

Robby got his dagger, then, to Ullin's amazement, he held it by the blade so that Swyncraff could wrap itself around the handle. Then, holding Swyncraff by the other end, and without even looking, Robby reached out to the rope on his leg. Swyncraff swiped, cutting the rope cleanly. The rock and rope fell away, crashing far below, and Ullin fell backwards, pulling Robby to safety.

"Oh, man!" Ullin uttered, patting Robby on the backpack.

"Oh, man, indeed!"

"Remind me to thank Thurdun and the Queen next time I see them!" Ullin said, getting up and helping Robby to his feet.

"I've lost count of how many times Swyncraff has saved my life," Robby nodded. "And you, too. Thanks!"

"All in a day's work, my friend!" Ullin laughed. "But next time, try not to make me laugh right in the middle of things."

"What did I say?"

"Never mind. Only, I think Billy's been a bad influence on you."

"Good ol' Billy. He'd certainly have a comment or two!"

Chuckling, they got their breath back and resumed picking their way along the path.

"How many traps do you think that old man set?" Robby asked.

"I don't know. I just wish I hadn't lost the lamp. And why did he set so many if he thought he was safe from Shatuum up here?"

"I hadn't thought of that. It does seem a bit much. And, by the way, I lost the crossbow, too."

After another hour, they had not encountered any more traps as they continued along the path, switching back and forth up the mountain, with the wind getting colder and colder the higher they went. Just when Robby was wondering if they could trust anything that Tarkin had told them, the path became less steep and they entered a broad flat shelf, bounded on one side by the mountain and, on the other side, by a southwestern view of the range. They stopped to gaze at the tremendous gorge that cut straight away from north to south. It was so wide that they could barely make out the sharp snow-capped mountains on its far side through the cloudy mists that rose out of the canyon.

"That must be the Crack at the End of the World," Ullin said. "I never thought I'd see it."

"Me, neither. I guess I thought it was just a legend," Robby said. "But if it is truly there, then Griferis must be real, too, and very close by."

They stood for several minutes in awe of the sight, until Ullin turned to continue on.

"Look!"

Following Ullin's gesture, Robby saw a small hut made entirely of stacked stones, just a few yards away.

"Oh!"

"Let's be careful. He may have the place rigged with more traps."

The door of the place, made of several layers of hides on a frame, swung inward at their push, but nothing happened. Lighting a flare, Ullin thrust his arm inside, then carefully stepped in, motioning Robby to wait. A few moments later, he was back, holding a lantern that he had lit with the flare.

"Looks safe enough, though foul-smelling," he said. "And there's a fireplace with lots of coal in a bin. And loads of other gear."

When they had the door closed against the wind, Robby looked around while Ullin prepared the fire. There were a lot of mining tools, crudely made picks and shovels, odd bits of metal, lamps, and ropes. And, nearby to a pile of clothing, furs, and blankets, was something that sent a chill up Robby's spine.

"Ullin."

"Yes? What is it?"

Robby gestured, and Ullin came to stand beside him to look. It was a large pile of bones.

"That's what the smell is!"

Ullin picked at the bones with the poker, and a couple of human skulls with bits of hair still on them rolled out of the pile.

"This I cannot abide!" Ullin said, flinging off his backpack. He pulled up some of the clothing to use as rags so that he would not foul his gloves, and he began piling the bones and half-eaten carcasses onto a nearby pelt to drag the hideous things outside. Robby followed suit, cringing at the sight. They dumped the bones over the side of the hill, and made several more trips, also tossing off bloody clothes, including odd capes and cloaks, and a pot full of stinking stew, pot and all. After an hour, they had the place fairly well cleared of the horrible mess, and had picked through the blankets and furs to find those that seemed the cleanest. Now exhausted, they sat down on the hearth, since there were no chairs or any furniture, and melted snow into the little tin cups from their kits. With hot water to drink, they took out their rations, snowbutter, and ate and drank.

"Not much of a meal," Robby said, "but I'm grateful for it."

"It beats jawrocks, any day."

"Jawrocks?"

"Kingsmen rations given to those in desert service. Terrible stuff. Hard to chew, hard to swallow. I have some in my pack, somewhere."

"You were in the desert a lot, weren't you?"

"A fair bit."

"You don't talk about it much."

"Not much to say about it. It is hot, dry, and dangerous."

Robby was about to tell Ullin about Micerea, about dreamwalking, but Ullin said, "I think as soon as it is light, we should look for the gate."

Robby nodded.

"Yes," he said. "I suppose there's no sense putting off. Do you mind if I try to get some sleep? You could probably use some, too."

"Of course I don't mind. I may rest some myself."

"And will you wake me at first light? If I don't wake you?"

"Certainly."

Ullin looked at Robby, noticing how mature he seemed compared to just a few months ago. He wished Robby would tell him his secrets, for certainly he had them. But he knew better than to press him. Secrets were best revealed in their own time, in the holder's own way, if possible. Good people keep them for good reasons, usually. And Ullin was convinced that Robby was a good person. If Robby succeeded, Ullin was sure he would be a good king, too. If he succeeded. If he survived Griferis. If he discovered the Name. If, if, if! This entire quest was nothing but one if after another. But they had gotten this far, hadn't they?

Robby stretched out on the floor, and pulled a few of the cleaner blankets over himself. He only needed a little nap, just long enough to get to Janhaven and warn his mother about Galatus. Fortunately, he fell asleep quickly, and flew eastward to find his mother. Fortunate it was, too, that she was finally asleep and not on duty somewhere or other. Robby quickly entered her dream, and, after some difficulty, he delivered his message, hoping that she would believe him, and not just pass it off as, well, as just a dream. But it was the first time he had visited her that way, so it was reasonable to expect that she would be skeptical.

Hardly had he completed his task than he felt wakefulness pulling at him. In fact, it was Ullin nudging him awake.

"You said to wake you at first light."

"Yes. Yes, thank you." Robby sat up and quickly got to his feet. "May as well go the rest of the way," he said. "I have a feeling that we are very close. In fact, I believe the gate is just up the hill and around the corner."

"What makes you say that?"

"Tarkin spoke of the sound that the gate made," he explained. "And I read about it. I don't think Tarkin would have approached near to the gate, so he must have heard it from here. At least I hope so."

"Right." Ullin stood, nodding, and pulled his gloves on. "Ready."

• • •

In fact, it took them several hours and a few false starts along trails that led to dead ends or around and back to the hut before they found the place where the gate stood. It was at the very edge of the immense canyon, standing on a flat shelf on the western face of Mount Algamori, several hundred feet below the summit of the mountain. But, in the time it took them to get there, the weather had changed. It grew increasingly windy and overcast with low clouds that blew around the mountain, and snow swirled thick and heavy through the air. When Robby and Ullin came around the rock face and saw the gate, obscured by the blizzard, they had to shout to each other over the gale.

"There it is!" Ullin pointed, holding his hood down against the wind.

"Let's have a look!"

"Be careful!"

It was a strange and marvelous structure, just as was described in the Last Book of Nimwill. Two upright pillars of white marble held an arch made of bright untarnished silver fashioned like leafy vines. At the highest point of the arch was a black oval disk, about a yard and a half wide, and on the silver ring that held the disk was a strange writing, somewhat like the writing in the First Tongue.

"Bridge of Rulers," Ullin read loudly. "Gateway of Worthy Kings."

Robby stepped up onto the flat marble landing under the gate, and then carefully stepped through it, peering down the other side. All he could see was flying snow and mist, as if he looked down into clouds. Going back through the arch and standing several yards away, he looked up at the inscription.

"Well," Ullin said. "Now what?"

"Now we wait," Robby said. "Maybe over by those rocks, and out of the wind!"

Moving off several yards and behind some boulders, Robby was about to crouch when Ullin tapped him.

"I think I see a little cave," he pointed, then walked to the place where the mountainside shot up vertically to its peak. At the base was, indeed, a small opening, and Ullin crawled in, with Robby following afterwards. It was close, but out of the wind, and much quieter. They huddled for a few more hours, not talking, each wondering what might happen next, if anything.

"Perhaps we ought to go back to the hut," Ullin suggested.

"No. I don't think we'll have to wait for very long. I don't want to leave until we have to, or when the sun sets. Not that we could tell through all these clouds."

A brilliant light flashed into the grotto, immediately followed by a clap of deafening thunder. They both jumped at the crash.

"I think that is my sign." Robby shouted, since the wind had suddenly become fierce. Crawling back out, he stood, looking around. Ullin came out and stood beside him when another bolt of lightning shot across the sky and the mountain shook with its thunder. The sky darkened with the storm and hard sleet clicked down, bouncing off the rocks and coating their hoods and shoulders while another sound began to crescendo as background to the storm's noise. Ullin pointed at the gate. The black disc at its apex was now glowing bluish-purple. A bolt of lightning struck it, yet no spark or flame was thrown from the disk as it lit up like a blue-white star. As bright as the strange star was, it was not hurtful to look at; in fact, it was hard not to stare at it, so beautiful it appeared. Filled with a strange and almost trance-like contemplation of the light, it was a moment or two before Ullin and Robby noticed the change around them.

The gate now rang with a steady tone, as if a large bell had been struck but did not fade, and no other sound could be heard, not a whisper of air moved, and there was suddenly no sleet at all. It was an eerie scene, the clouds like puffs of purple-gray cotton, veined with the frozen bolts of jagged lightning too bright to look at for more than a glance. They saw a long causeway going from the gate to a floating island far out over the canyon. And on that distant island was an extraordinary walled palace of bluish-white marble with balconies and rows of glass windows and many tall verdigris-topped towers. So distant was the palace at the end of the causeway that they barely even saw the gate from which emerged the tiny dot of a figure. They watched until they saw that it was a child, barely old enough to walk, waddling toward them. He held in his tiny hands two objects, and when he reached the landing, the child stopped and lifted a sandglass, then turned it over. He then struck it with the wand of wheat held in his other hand, and the sand began to fall from the top to the bottom of the glass. At this moment, the incessant ring of the gate changed in pitch. Ullin, staring at the child, felt the strong desire to run away as fast as he could, and he barely managed to control the urge.

"I must go," Robby said, overcoming his own fear and stepping toward the gate. Ullin followed just behind. When Robby hesitated at the threshold, Ullin put his hand on his cousin's shoulder.

"Robby!" he cried.

Robby turned and saw the concern in the Kingsman's face. Ullin, for his part, saw that Robby was not unafraid but was nonetheless determined.

"Well, then," he said. "How long will you be?"

Robby laughed nervously. "I hadn't thought of that. It may take me a long time, so I suppose you should make up your own mind on how long to wait. There is our food and some stores at the hut. It should last you a few days, I suppose. Don't save any on my account. I will return as soon as I can, but there's no use waiting for someone who may not come back at all. I suppose I have a lot to learn, so it may take months, or even years. You must follow your own heart. Here," Robby removed Swyncraff and straightened it to a rod. "Hang onto Swyncraff for me until I get back. I'm thinking I won't need it in there."

Ullin took Swyncraff and embraced Robby with a handshake.

"Then I shall wait for you."

Robby nodded. "If you wish. But do not wait long. Who knows when I'll be back? Or if I'll be back. You must find a way out of Shatuum whether I am with you or not. Thank you for getting me here. Now it's up to me, I suppose. Be careful. Farewell!"

Robby turned and stepped over the threshold and approached the child holding the hourglass. The little one looked up and gestured with his wand of wheat toward the palace. Ullin watched as Robby nodded and then began walking across the causeway toward the far off castle with the child following just behind. To Ullin, it all seemed too sudden, too dreamlike, and as Robby receded, a pang of sudden loneliness clutched Ullin's heart.

Then, with alarm, Ullin saw another figure emerge onto the bridge from the distant far side, a figure draped in dark cloaks and with a hood pulled low over his head. Ullin stepped forward with his hand on his hilt, but when his boot struck the threshold, fear paralyzed him. Not fear for Robby, but fear of upsetting things. As Robby and the mysterious person came together midway on the bridge, Ullin saw that they slowed for a brief moment, perhaps exchanging greetings, before continuing each on their own way. Whoever it was did not seem like a threat, but Ullin backed away cautiously, retreating into the cover of the rocks. From there, he could barely see Robby near the gates of the castle, just as the hooded figure reached the threshold of the archway. As Robby stepped through the far gates, and the newcomer passed through the near arch, sudden thunder hammered the peak, the wind blasted a howl, the storm resumed with a fury, and the clouds boiled and spilled around the bridge and the mysterious castle. Ullin instinctively crouched, pulling his cloak around himself against the pelting sleet, and he ducked behind the rocks. The figure hunched into the tempest, holding his hood down with his one hand as his cloak whipped and snapped in the gale, his other hand held out, letting the sleet bounce from his open palm. Ullin winced at the sleet that stung his face and watched the stranger who seemed to revel in the storm. But, with a final gust, the storm suddenly dissolved, the sleet ceased, and the peals of thunder echoed and rolled slowly away across the mountains. A strange reddish light glowed in the sky and Ullin stared in wonder as the setting sun broke through the parting clouds between the far western peaks. It was as if Sir Sun looked over his shoulder with one last glance before walking on, his head quickly receding behind the snowcaps, pulling his red cape behind until only his purple hem remained.

The causeway and the castle were gone.

• • •

Ullin shook himself and looked at the lone figure standing near the silent gate. The stranger's hood drooped over his face so that Ullin could only make out a dark full beard, streaked with gray. Cold air settled around them as they watched each other and as night gathered itself to fall, but for a long while neither man spoke or made any movement. Finally, holding Swyncraff loosely so as not to seem a threat, Ullin cautiously stepped out from the rocks and approached to within a few yards of the stranger.

"I cannot vouch for the safety of this place," Ullin stated.

The stranger nodded as he looked back over the great chasm. Ullin thought him to be distracted, perhaps still recovering from some ordeal in the place Robby had just entered. Seeing that the stranger was in no mind to leave right away, Ullin spoke again.

"We should at least get out of the open and out of the night air." He gestured toward the nearby rocks.

"Yes. I suppose we should."

The stranger walked past Ullin and the Kingsman followed, glancing back toward the gate and beyond to the open space where, just a few moments ago, had spanned a long bridge to a fabulous castle. He saw the stranger make for the crevice where he and Robby had taken refuge earlier.

"Here is a good place," Ullin called, pointing to the rocks where he had just hidden.

"This is a better shelter," said the stranger.

"Aye, but from here I may keep watch on the gate," Ullin said.

"Come sit with me for a while," the stranger replied.

Seeing that Ullin hesitated, he added, "Your friend will take longer than he realizes. Sit with me. Then, if you must, you may continue your watch."

"Why do you say that? How would you know?"

"Because I just came from there, did I not? Griferis is full of mysteries," the stranger said. There was something terribly sad about the man's voice, something heavy and weary. Ullin approached, the sky grew rapidly darker, and snow began to fall.

"No doubt you have many questions," the stranger said as they crouched into the cave and sat in the cramped and gloomy place, "and I will have few answers, I'm afraid. But perhaps by morning you will trust me better."

They sat in silence for a while, the dark fully enclosing their little grotto so that they could not see each other at all.

"I myself am full of wonder," the stranger said at last. "I can hardly believe I have left that place after all these years."

"Do you mean to become ruler of some land?" Ullin asked abruptly, hearing the anxious tremor in his own voice. The fact of the stranger's presence, newly emerged from Griferis, could only mean one thing: Their plans and hopes to make Robby the King of Duinnor might now be dashed. He swallowed, slipping his dagger silently from its sheath. "What throne do you seek?"

"The same one that your companion seeks, I am sure."

"How do you mean to take it?"

"The same way he does."

"And how is that?"

"Oh! He has not told you. Well, then. Nor shall I. The answer would fill you with dread. He knows that you would try to stop him."

"It is not he that I would stop."

"You would not mean to. But it is beyond your powers of belief, and you are already filled with doubts, and you are contemplating dark thoughts. Perhaps even murder."

Ullin's muscles tensed to spring. Even in the dark, by sound alone, his skill could bring his dagger's point home, and quickly.

"But I mean to see to it that your companion succeeds in his quest," the stranger calmly stated, either oblivious to Ullin's threat, or else with the greatest of nerve. "For, as strange as it may sound, that is the only way that I may succeed in mine."

"You speak riddles! And with the smooth and familiar accent of my kinfolk in faraway lands."

"I am a riddle. But I am too tired to resist you. I ask only that you abide with me until morning. Then, if murder is still in your heart, I will yield without struggle. Between now and that time, perhaps you will come to a better understanding of things. That, too, is my hope."

A nagging feeling began to grow inside Ullin, the notion that he should know this man. It was a very unusual accent, with strong hints of the Eastlands but without the drawl or sing-song manner that so many of that realm had. This stranger's voice was easy but more formal. And though Ullin could only make out the barest dark outline of his shape, there was nothing in the stranger's movement or attitude that gave Ullin the slightest hint of threat. The Kingsman's sense of danger, that peculiar sensation, the ability he had since childhood, had faltered several times in recent months and was now completely absent. Divided of mind and confused of heart, his grip on his dagger eased and his shoulders drooped as he slightly relaxed.

"It would be better if you convinced yourself," the stranger said, "than if I persuaded you of my intent."

"I am in no mood for twenty questions, or for any other game."

"Have it your way."

"What is your name?"

"I wish I could tell you, I truly do. But I do not know my name."

Ullin nodded in the darkness. This person's story must be much the same as Robby's, being named in the old way, by a dying elder. And, like Robby, the stranger must also be seeking Duinnor's throne. Ullin clenched his knife, and made ready to spring. Then, suddenly, he wanted to ask about that story. Was this man's quest, to come here and to endure Griferis, as fraught with mystery and danger as Robby's own tale? Did he, too, encounter and overcome as many difficulties and dangers on his way here? Ullin's thoughts and emotions raced, some contradicting others. Suddenly, he found himself feeling a great concern for Robby's plight within the secretive walls of Griferis and, at the same time, a strange but powerful sympathy for the man who had just escaped the place, the man now sitting in the dark grotto before him. Snowflakes occasionally blew in and invisibly touched Ullin's cheek or nose or landed on his hand, distracting a distant portion of his mind with the slight sensations of their melting. He was completely relaxed of body, now, and the dagger in his hand may as well have been a teacup or a quill or a blade of grass for all he minded it.

"Can you tell me," he said at last, "anything of your trials within Griferis? Or how long you were within that place?"

"Hm. How long? By my reckoning, it has been twenty-six, no, twenty-eight years since I entered that place."

"Twenty-eight years!" Ullin suddenly wondered how long it would take Robby. And, at the same time, he wondered about this man, and what events, twenty-eight years ago, may have conspired to stop him from coming here, and conspired to bring him here nonetheless.

"Yes, that long. I went in full of hope. Over time, that hope diminished until it was completely gone. Those were terrible years, and I'm afraid I nearly faltered. I don't know how I kept going, really. No. I do. I had help. Then, at last, when I had no hope at all left to me, when my only thought was to escape that place, only then was hope restored to me, and in greater measure than ever before I went in. Indeed, it was only when I passed back over the causeway, and saw your companion as he approached the castle, only then, when I saw the hope in his eyes, did I realize that I had been given a great source of hope all along, since the very first moment I arrived at Griferis. Though, to my shame, I never knew it. But within the passing glance of a complete stranger was the glorious miracle of hope given back to me. It is almost too much to bear!"

Ullin heard the stranger's voice crack and grow hoarse with emotion.

"As we sit, hope continues to dawn upon me, and the heavy tasks remaining for me to do seem somehow the easier to contemplate. All those things that I endured, and all that was endured by others for my sake, perhaps have not been endured in vain. That is now my hope."

He still speaks riddles, Ullin thought.

"Am I really here? Have I really come out of that place?" cried the stranger, stifling a sob. Then, after a moment, he said, "I am so happy to be out from there! I will try to tell you about it."

Ullin was baffled and alarmed for Robby's sake. That this man was so shaken, and so relieved to have come out of Griferis, moved Ullin deeply. His heart softened toward the stranger while, at the same time, his fears for Robby increased.

"Oh!" the stranger continued. "To speak of those things within Griferis is hard. I am perhaps too soon from it, and my memory too fresh and full, having just now emerged. And you are too distant from any experience that could be likened unto that place. I will share just a little of my story. How I came to Griferis, and how I came to be here sitting with you this night, I will not relate. That will be revealed to you on its own as you get to know me better. Where, then, to begin? Perhaps it would ease your mind to know that there is one person, at least, who will help your friend within those walls. He is trustworthy and gentle, and he will become a good friend to your companion who just entered Griferis. Your friend, during his time within Griferis, will meet many people and will be subjected to severe trials. He will know pain and suffering, love and companionship, prejudice and sympathy, betrayal, loyalty, temptation, seduction. In short, he will experience every manner of manipulation, done to him by those sent by the Judges to face him, and by the Judges themselves. He will be changed from the person who entered into a different person."

The stranger paused, but before Ullin could form another question, he continued.

"There is one within Griferis who is called Finn. I will tell you how he and I met, though I imagine our meeting was just the same as all who went before me. He will be the first person that your companion meets there, and the last he will see before the Judges of that place releases him from there."

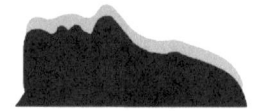

Chapter 13

Finn

Robby hesitated and looked back across the floating causeway toward the mountain and the arched gateway. Ullin was nowhere in sight, and the stranger he passed was just now reaching the other side. Though they did not speak as they passed each other, the looks they exchanged were deep, each sizing up the other. For his part, Robby thought that he must be a competitor, since the man was leaving Griferis, and that made him deeply uneasy. And there was something odd about the way the stranger stared at him, a bewildered look, as if disoriented. The way the man held his gaze to Robby was unsettling, too, so much so that chills ran down Robby's spine. He made note of the man's appearance, should he ever encounter him again. Dark blue woolen cloak, the hood pulled over his head. But Robby saw enough of his black graying beard, the weather-beaten face, and the hard, dark eyes, to remember him well.

Looking through the large doorway before him, he could see little but that there was a room with dim torches along its walls, and there appeared to be another large door at the far side. The gloom within was too dense for him to discern much else. He stepped through the doorway, and immediately a grinding sound came from behind him causing him to jump forward in alarm. Turning, he saw a stone door slide down, blocking his retreat. The child who had escorted him within was gone.

"Oh well," he said, his heart thumping. "I'm all in, now."

The torches along the walls flamed up brightly, giving more flickering yellow light to the place, and he looked ahead toward the door at the other side of the room.

It was a very tall door, three times Robby's height, made of bronze, with lines of writing cast into it, and it stood between two large stone figures, each carved into the likeness of a stern warrior, and each holding aloft a bright steel sword as if ready to strike the other. Unlike the crude figures that guarded the Iron Door of Tulith Attis, these two were done in much greater detail, like those in the bell room itself. And though the figures were of stone, their armor, clothing, sandals, and all of their accoutrements were very real. Robby cautiously approached, having the uncanny sense that they knew he was there. Staring up at them, looking from one to the other as he neared, something cracked under his feet. Looking down, he was shocked to see that he had stepped on a skeleton. Stepping back gingerly, he discovered that the floor was haphazardly littered with bones and skeletons, and each with its neck severed, its skull nearby. Rusted helmets, shields, and weapons lay all around the room, too, and the clothes of the dead, rotted and tattered by moth and time, were the faded colors of Vanara, Duinnor, Glareth, and Tracia. He even thought he saw a set of coppery light-armor of the sort worn by many of the Dragonkind.

Robby's skin crawled with a spasm of goosebumps, he felt lightheaded, his heart racing, and he wished he had not left Swyncraff behind. Getting a grip on himself, he picked his way carefully forward until he could read the writing on the door, the two sentinels looming over him, their eyes fixed upon each other. In the First Tongue, he read:

> *Confront the Truthsayer and the Liar.*
> *Each other alone, do they comprehend.*
> *With battle-locked eyes, they never tire.*
> *Thou must pass to enter in.*
>
> *None but the Truthsayer may open this door.*
> *None but the Liar may take thy head.*
> *Command one and live some more.*
> *Command one and then be dead.*
>
> *To one only may you ask*
> *A single question for the task.*
> *One yes or no to receive,*
> *A word of Truth or one to Deceive.*
> *But ask ye two, and here remain,*
> *Nor see the light of day again!*

"Oh, good grief!" Robby uttered, stepping up and giving the door a shove. Nothing happened. He pushed again, but it was solidly closed, and his ability was useless here. Frustrated too quickly, he almost asked what color were his eyes, but hesitated. He always thought of his eyes as brown, but what if the sentinel he asked thought they were walnut in color? Would that be a truthful answer? He glanced at the surrounding bones, realizing that they, too, must have asked some similar question, the answer to which they must have thought to be obvious.

"Each other alone, do they comprehend," he read again. He bit his tongue, for he almost asked aloud, "What does that mean?"

It must mean, he thought, that they only know about each other, and know only the nature of each other. But how does that help?

"One yes or no to receive."

Robby pondered for only a moment, then posed his question to the sentinel on the right.

"If I commanded him to open the door," Robby jabbed a finger at the other sentinel, "would you kill me?"

The head turned toward him, cracking as it did so, and the stony face took a breath.

"Yes," it said, soft and hoarse, almost as a whisper.

"Then if you are the Truthsayer, you would say no, for it would be he who would kill me, not you. But if you are the Liar, you would lie and say yes, but you would not kill me because you were not commanded. Therefore, you are the Liar."

Turning to the other sentinel, Robby said, "I command you to open this portal!"

Immediately, the sentinel lowered his sword as the startled Robby stumbled backwards. With much cracking of his limbs, the sentinel stepped in front of Robby, faced the door, and gave it a push, swinging it wide. The sentinel stepped back to his former place and raised his sword as before.

Robby entered the next room cautiously for it was completely dark within, only the light glowing through the doorway behind him lit the gray stone floor. The door slammed shut with a jarring ring, and immediately the room was illuminated by light streaming in from high arched windows. Outside, the storm had evidently passed, and night had turned to day, for he could see a blue sky.

Hearing footsteps, he saw a man approaching from the other side of the room. He appeared to be in his sixties or seventies, was thin and tall, with white hair and a clean-shaven face. He wore a trim black jacket, buttoned up to the neck, black woolen breeches down to the knees, white stockings, and polished black shoes with silver buckles. His bright blue eyes fixed Robby as he approached.

"Hello," Robby said as the man stopped and bowed smoothly.

"Good day, sir," the man said in an easy voice. "Allow me to introduce myself. My name is Finn. It is my duty to act as your servant and somewhat as your guide while you are here. I will provide you with food and drink and all of the accommodations that you may require. You are permitted to ask anything of me, though I may not be able to answer you or provide that which you might ask for."

"I see. Well, it is nice to meet you. I am called Robby." Robby offered his hand. Finn hesitated, then awkwardly took it, as if amused by the gesture, but he gave a firm shake.

"You may summon me at any time," Finn went on. "However, if you are being tried by the Judges, I cannot answer your call. The Judges, too, may send me to you of their own accord. Your first trial is over, and as a result you have truly entered Griferis. I come to you now, before your next trial begins, to introduce myself and to provide for your needs."

"Oh."

"Are you hungry?"

"No, sir. Thank you. But may I ask a question or two about this place?"

"Certainly, sir. As many as you wish to ask, though I may not be able to answer. I am not privy to much of what goes on here."

"I see. Well, what are the rules of coming to and going from this place?"

"I know that only one candidate may enter Griferis at a time. No other candidate is called or may enter until the previous has departed from this place. I know also that others are brought here as needed by the Judges, for the purpose of the trials. The manner of their coming and going is unknown to me, and their presence and reasons for being here will remain a mystery to me unless you tell me about them. If a candidate fails any trial, he leaves by being cast into the chasm below us. If a candidate passes all of the trials, he may then leave to take up his place in the world."

"How much time is given to each candidate? To undergo the trials?"

"Each according to his wits, his ability, and his progress. No two candidates are alike, and each trial is different. But however long as the candidate is here, all his needs are provided for, be it for days, for months, or for years."

"When a candidate passes all the trials, what does he gain from the ordeal? I mean, does he gain the power to become a ruler?"

"Not directly. A successful candidate shall be granted three boons."

"Boons? Wishes, you mean?"

"Yes, wishes, if you will."

"And may they be anything? Can you name some?"

"I am permitted to know that in the past, the three most common boons asked for have been the boon of health, so that life will be long. Another is the boon of wealth, so that great power may be exerted. Another is the boon of desire, that which one most longs for."

"And are there any limits upon them? May, for example, the boon of health make one immortal?"

"Unless that person meets with violence, he may live longer than the world itself. But health is not the same thing as safety."

"And does the treasure that comes with wealth have some end to it? Could it ever run out?"

"If asked for, it will be enough wealth to acquire whatever may be sold. But some things are without price."

"But what if a person desires the impossible? May even that be granted?"

"In time all things may be possible. But only one desire shall be granted and only once, if it be for good or ill."

Finn answered Robby's questions pleasantly enough, but without expression as Robby gazed back thoughtfully.

"Are you familiar with the proceedings of this place?" Robby asked.

"Somewhat, though the particulars of each trial are unknown to me."

"Have you been here long? And served many?"

"I do not know how long I have been here," said Finn. "But my guess is a fair long time because the stars in the heavens are different now than when I first came and my hair is white when once it was as black as yours. I have been the servant of many. You are the twenty-fourth I have waited upon."

"There was a man that I saw leaving just as I entered into this place. Can you tell me who he was? Did he successfully complete his trials?"

"I do not know," Finn said thoughtfully. "I am trying to remember. The last man that I recall serving never left here alive, I am sorry to say. Before that, I served a lady. This is truly a mystery to me, for I thought that I was the only servant here. Perhaps there are other servants, and perhaps I do not serve all who come here. Or perhaps the Judges have taken away my memory of him, as they have done of many things that I ought to remember, such as where I came from. Truly, I do not know who it was that you saw."

"Well, how much time do I have before the next trial?"

"That I cannot say. You may be called at any moment, or you may be given days to rest."

"I see," Robby said. "I have so many questions. And I don't know which are the most important to ask. Can you tell me the most important thing I should know about this place? Or about the trials I will face?"

"I am but a servant," Finn said, as if surprised by the question. "What I deem important may have little significance at all to you."

"That may be," Robby shrugged. "But I would still like to hear your answer."

Finn wrinkled his brow, turning aside his head in thought. "As far as I recall, no one has ever asked me that," he said. "Indeed, I am not sure what the answer may be. The most important thing? I have not witnessed any of the trials, not in my entire stay here. I have, of course, waited upon those who underwent them, as is my duty. The most important thing to tell you? Hm. Truly, I cannot say."

"Well, is there anything about this place that you can tell me that might be useful to me?"

"I really only know of those things having to do with my duties, sir."

"Very well," Robby sighed. "Then let us talk about that. How am I to summon you?"

"You need only call my name and I will come, if it is at a time when I am allowed. Not during a trial."

"And if I need water to drink. Or food?"

"I will be happy to provide those."

"And if I need to rest. To sleep?"

"All accommodations will be provided to suit you."

A soft chime rang, gently echoing throughout the hall.

"It is time for you to go," Finn said, gesturing to a door that materialized on the far side of the room.

"Oh. Already?"

"I must remain here until I am summoned. I hope that you fare well, Lord Robby."

"Thank you, Finn," Robby offered his hand again and Finn, smiling, took it. "But I am not a lord. I hope to see you again very soon."

The doors opened, and Finn watched Robby walk through them before they closed. Glancing at his hand, the one that Robby just shook, he smiled.

"Well, he is different."

• • •

It was a very large room, and near the far wall were seven thrones floating a yard or so from the floor. In those thrones sat four women with a man in the throne between each of them. Each was dressed in resplendent robes and wore a crown or an ornate headdress. Each held a staff, a scepter, or a rod of some kind. They watched Robby approach, remove his cap, and bow low before them.

"I am called Robby," he said.

"We are the Judges appointed to this place," they all said in unison. "You shall not see us again, unless you survive all your trials. If that is done, you shall come before us again, before the way of your departure is opened to you. You shall then be granted three boons as reward for success."

To Robby, they seemed very different from each other. One woman was very dark-skinned, almost black, and one of the men was of a reddish-brown complexion. Another man was as pale as moonlight, almost blue, with long gray hair. The third man was not as pale, but with a long thin wisp of a white mustache, drooping down to an equally thin white beard. One of the other women was ghostly pale, too, but with the looks of a Dragonkind woman, and another was red-cheeked and rather large. The last was unlike any of the rest, for they all appeared ancient in every way, from their wrinkled faces, to their gray or white hair. But the last one, the one sitting on the throne at the far left, seemed no older than Robby, but, he surmised, she could be Elifaen and as old as any of the rest.

They seemed to wait for him to have a good look at them before proceeding.

"Now that you have seen us, you know that we exist," they said as one. "Know this as well: Every trial do we watch. We see all. We hear all. Nothing is hidden from us during trial. But we have no eyes or ears for when you rest. However, we do watch Finn, your servant, for his safety. The time between your trials belongs to you, and we shall not intrude in any way by watching, or by listening, or by making any inquiries concerning you. During the interludes, your needs will be met. When the chime rings, you are summoned. Whether or not you wish to do so, you shall come."

"I see," Robby nodded. "Might you—"

"We do not answer questions. The time of your next trial is at hand."

The light through the windows dimmed quickly, then returned, but the Judges were gone. On the wall behind where they had sat, was an arched opening, evidently leading to the next chamber. Anxious to get on with things and to return to Ullin as soon as he could, he strode through and entered a wide circular room lit by a single large chandelier hanging from the center of a high vaulted ceiling. Around its perimeter were eight figures, fashioned of dark gray metal and in the likeness of strange Faere-like creatures. Each stood before a large, tall, dome-topped jar of glass, and each figure held out a hand, palm up. In the other hand of each of these figures was held a hammer, poised high as if ready to strike the glass. Across the top of each jar were figures of writing, etched into the glass, and within each jar was a different object. Something inside one of the jars nearest to Robby gave off a light, and he approached it first. Inside, suspended in mid-air, was a small oil lamp of silver. Robby read the etched inscription.

Knowledge.

In the next jar was suspended a marvelous sword of brilliant steel with a hilt of ivory and a pommel of knotted gold chain.

Power.

At the next jar he saw a small plant, the sapling of an acorn growing out of a small clump of earth, floating, as were the other objects, incongruously within.

Hope.

Then he came to the next jar and saw a skein of white cloth. Approaching closer, with his nose near to the glass, he saw that it was made of intricate lace.

Patience.

In the next was a hand mirror, mounted in plain wood.

Vision.

The next jar he came to as he circled the room was labeled "Wisdom," and it held a small leather-bound book. He came to another jar that held within it a small box, its lid opened to reveal a collection of gemstones and coins.

Wealth.

In the last jar, he saw a beautiful little girl in a blue dress, her blond hair done up in a fancy arrangement atop her head, and brass-buckled shoes on her feet. And though her brown eyes were unblinking, and she was as motionless as stone, the blush of her cheeks showed life in her. Strange, too, that in her arms she held a small gray and white rabbit that gazed up at her face with its dark blue eyes.

Companionship.

In the center of the room, he noticed a small pillar of polished stone, about waist high. Going to it, he saw on top of it a single gold coin. He picked it up—it was heavy—and he read the inscription.

"For what you most desire," it said. Turning it over, he saw a different inscription, "For what you most need."

Looking at the iron figures with their palms out and their hammers lifted, he pondered the coin's inscriptions.

He turned the coin over and over in his hand.

"Needs and desires. Different sides of the same coin. I suppose I am to place this coin into the hand of one of these...guardians. And," he turned, looking at the walls of the room, "there seems to be no way out, no window or anything. Even the way I entered has vanished!"

Indeed, the walls of the chamber were smooth and unbroken by any window or doorway. Robby walked around the room, more closely examining the place where he entered and all of the rest of the wall. He could not see or feel with his hand any crack or seam or sign of any door.

"Smooth as glass!"

Turning back around, he shook his head, "It seems I am forever getting trapped in places. Very well, if that's the way of it, I shall play this game. I must pick. If only I knew the purpose!"

At that moment, there rang a chime somewhere in the room, and a cracking sound came from above him. Looking up, he saw flecks of stone dropping from high upon the wall, as if an invisible chisel chipped away, revealing an inscription.

> *One gold coin there is to take,*
> *A vital choice must thee make,*
> *Else no door shall open thee,*
> *Trapped within forever be.*

"Well," he sighed, "unless there is some other coin hidden here, I don't see how I could do otherwise but take just the one."

And so he began thinking over his choices, noting how each, in turn, had its appeal.

"I certainly need knowledge," he said, standing before the silver lamp. "Like how to get out of here, for one thing. Then again, with the sword of Power, perhaps I could break open the other jars and obtain their contents."

His eyes turned to the girl, "And set you free."

Then he rapped on the jar before him, but it was so thick and heavy that it made barely a sound.

"Or maybe the glass would break the sword!"

Looking around at the other choices, he continued to muse.

"If only I could talk this over with Ashlord, or Sheila. Or even you!" He found himself again at the jar that contained the girl and her rabbit.

The longer he looked at them, the lonelier he felt. "If you didn't know what to do, perhaps your rabbit would. As things are, I certainly don't have much of that!" He shot a glance at the little sapling of Hope. "And there may be some more coins in the treasure box of Wealth to open all of these jars. And perhaps enough left over to purchase the means of protection, if I may ever get out of here. But, with my luck, this coin may be the only one that works."

He went around the room again, coming back to where he started.

"Is there something I'm missing?"

After a few more steps he found himself gazing at the mirror of Vision. "Perhaps some clue? And even if I chose the right one to somehow open a passage out of here, what might come later? I might need that sword or that lamp. I need to make a wise choice. A wise choice! That's it!"

Robby rushed over to the guardian beside the jar of Wisdom and almost put the coin into its hand, but drew back.

"But it is such a small book," he observed. "How can such a small thing contain all the wisdom that I need? The wisdom to help me survive this place? And to do what I must do if I ever get out of here."

Doubts began to grow within him.

"I bet that any one of these choices opens a door out of here. This is all about which one I choose. Or perhaps each one opens a different door, leading to some different place."

He wandered around the room until at last he sat down on the top of the stone pedestal. From there, he turned himself slowly, looking at each jar and rubbing the coin absently with his thumb.

"I wonder if those who came before me had this test? None of the jars are broken, none are empty. Maybe it is different for each person, like Finn said. Or maybe the jars are repaired and the contents replaced. Oh, this is getting me nowhere! I should just make a choice, any choice, and see what happens!"

He jumped to his feet and walked briskly around the room, once, then twice, and on the third round, he stopped, his heart pounding with frustration and annoyance. He stood before the lace and there was something about it that seemed different to him, a pattern he had not seen before, along one fold. It was hard to make out since the material was so white, but by pressing his nose against the glass he was able to distinguish the outline of a little tree. As he looked, more of the pattern revealed itself and the tree seemed to grow limbs, heavy with leaf. In another fold of the cloth, still hanging motionless within the jar, he thought he saw the outline of a hand mirror, much like the one in the other jar. Then, stepping around the jar to see more of the cloth from the other side, he perceived the intricately patterned outline of a hand placed inside another hand.

Then he understood, standing straight, and a smile crossed his face. With patience, all of the other things might be acquired. Wealth cannot buy it, power cannot force it. Companionship can only test it, and is worthless without it. Vision cannot be understood without it, knowledge cannot formulate it, and wisdom cannot exist in its absence.

Robby placed the coin into the guardian's hand and its metal fingers closed around it. Then, more gently than Robby expected, the iron creature's hand moved the hammer backwards then lightly struck the jar one time. Under the blow, the glass rang a clear note that hung in the air. All of the other jars answered with different softer harmonics, a soothing chorus that filled Robby with wonder. The soft tones faded into silence more profound than before, and Robby noticed that an arched doorway had appeared in the wall and was open to him. Reluctantly, and disappointed that the glass did not break and that he had nothing to show for his effort, he looked again at the girl and her rabbit as he moved toward the opening.

"Goodbye," he said. "Perhaps someday I, or someone worthier to the task, will find a way to release you. I am sorry."

He stepped through the passage and into another large hall with high vaulted ceilings. Near the tops of the walls were windows that streamed bright light from a deep blue sky that somehow comforted him. Glancing behind, he was surprised to see that the room he had just left was now completely empty. Gone were the tall jars and their contents, along with the hammer-wielding guardians as well as the little pedestal where he found the coin. The chandelier that hung above grew dimmer and the room darkened completely.

Turning his attention back to the large room before him, he stepped farther within and looked about cautiously. It was circular and of the same smooth gray marble as the previous room, but there were many doorways lined all around it. He counted fifty of them. But there was nothing else unusual about the place, no inscriptions over the doorways, no statues or decoration of any kind. The only thing in common with the previous room was another pedestal in the middle of the room. This one supported a sandglass mounted in a turning cage. Going to it, he saw that around the brass turning cage was writing, in the same odd script that was written the other inscriptions he had seen, the writing of the First Tongue.

> *These, the Doors of Time, await.*
> *Turn the glass to make a gate.*
> *The sand slips by, as does thy turn.*
> *The last grain falls, thou must return.*

"I suppose that means that the doorways only stay open until the sand runs out. But where might they lead to?" Robby asked aloud. "Some other place in Griferis, probably."

As he contemplated the inscription, he heard sounds, distant-seeming and muddled. Looking around, he realized they were coming from the doorways. He looked more carefully at them. None were closed, and all had strange material hanging just inches beyond, a shiny fabric. When he approached one, he saw that the view to where it led was blurred by this fabric, like a sheet of flowing water falling silently without splash or gurgle from an unseen source and flowing to an unseen destination. But he did hear, coming from the other side of the cascade, the distant noise of many voices. Some of the voices sounded angry, and there was also the sound of an object being struck. He could just make out movement, too vague and blurred to be discerned. When he put his hand carefully into the sheet of water, he was amazed to see that the liquid flowed around it, and he felt nothing at all, not coolness or warmth or any sensation of wetness. When he withdrew his hand, it was just as dry as before.

All of the doorways were similar, but with various levels of light showing through and with characteristically different sounds. Through one, he heard sounds of birds and wind blowing through treetops and saw a golden yellow light that reminded him very much of Barley on a late summer day. Through another much darker doorway, glowing red in places but otherwise black, he heard the faint ring of steel against steel, and cries of what Robby could only guess was some great struggle. A dull gray light came through the next one, sometimes flashing blue-white, and Robby could hear the distant thunder of a storm and the gusty rush of air and shush of rain. The next doorway showed only steady white light, not too bright, but he could distinguish no movement or sound. On he went, from doorway to doorway, until he came all the way around. And this last one was completely black, no hint of light at all came through it, nor did any sound whatsoever.

There was no obvious way out. And now he saw that the doorway through which he had entered was gone, replaced by smooth marble.

"Well, alright," Robby then commented, his voice echoing back from the cold walls. "But where might one of these doorways lead me? Yet another room, and another silly riddle, I suppose."

Then he heard again the cracking sound from above, and saw again an inscription being revealed:

> *One change only may thee make,*
> *One door only may thee take,*
> *Then closed forever will it be,*
> *Ere another opens thee.*
> *Decide before the moment dies,*
> *And what is left is naught but sighs.*

"Another riddle. I hate riddles! I didn't think Griferis was going to be like this at all."

Exasperated, he shoved his hands into his coat pockets. After a few moments, he heaved a heavy, frustrated sigh. "I suppose I should just bear up and do my best to get on with it. There's no point in being impatient now, after all that everyone has done to get me here!"

He slowly circled the room, looking at each doorway in turn. At one, though it appeared dark beyond the door, he thought he heard birds singing. From another came no sound whatsoever, and a third seemed to ring with the sound of battle. He thought he heard voices from another. On around the room he went, having no clue where any might lead him. He stood for a long time beside the sandglass, trying to figure how to make a good choice. Then, realizing the effort was futile, he abruptly turned the sandglass over in its gimbal, and walked through the doorway straight in front of him.

Chapter 14

To Get to Boskland

Who else could have endured his vicious attack? When Steggan burst into the cottage and found Sheila attempting to gather her things, she saw the rage in his drunken eyes. For a moment, she was frozen in fear, on her knees beside her cot, her arms still reaching for the small bundle of spare clothes tucked underneath. From that moment, and for each of the next moments, a long chain that would stretch into days, her memory would be a blurred tangle of pain, terror, and shock. She would remember his lurch toward her and her own dash for the open door. But suddenly there was another man standing in the doorway. In that eyeblink of hesitation, she saw the stranger's cold fair face, a hint of bemused surprise in his eyes as she stumbled right at him, and a slight smile across his thin lips. Steggan grabbed her, jerking her around and violently throwing her sideways across the room. By the time she crashed over the table and upside down against the far wall, Steggan was upon her, the mass of his arms around her waist like a vise, lifting her like a sack of apples and flinging her back across the room and against the hearth. Stunned, her head spinning, she screamed and kicked as he came at her again. She had no chance to wonder why the stranger did nothing. She was only dimly aware of his disinterested pose, standing just inside the door and off to one side, his arms crossed. Her blows and scratches, and her kicks and bites did little but incite worse in return from Steggan's fists and elbows as he tore at her clothes, punching her in the stomach and slinging her back down, throwing himself onto her. She was in no state to notice that his roaring curses and her howling cries were now matched by a storm that broke around the cottage like a vile chorus that filled the surrounding farmland. Steggan slugged her, stunning her nearly unconscious.

When he was finished with her and rolled away, she squirmed aside, trying to get to her feet while struggling with her breeches. The stranger, with the same bemused expression as before, stepped farther aside as she veered dizzily toward him and then fell across the threshold, desperately scratching her way out, out into the dark, into the rain, away, away. She sensed Steggan coming again, but she did not look back as she staggered up and into the rain-soaked night. She heard the heavy stomp of his tripping feet and the new curses he spat as she stumbled and fell, trying to make it to the barn.

"Ye don't get away that easy!" Steggan yelled, holding his breeches up, careening toward the door to pursue her. The stranger mildly raised his hand and slammed the door in the drunk's face, bringing him to a sudden and confused halt. Steggan's face rapidly changed from surprise to fear as the stranger's stick curled itself about his neck.

"You have had your fun," said the stranger smoothly.

• • •

As the stranger took up his business with Steggan, Sheila staggered toward the barn. She fell but kept on through the puddles, as much on her hands and knees as on her feet, until she at last stumbled inside and to the back stall, then dug rapidly through the straw for her knife. Gripping it defensively in front of her, she slumped against the wall, ready to kill any creature that appeared. Fear, anger, and pain, terrible pain, pounded her in churning waves, shaped the tenor of her sobs, and shook her so violently that she could hardly hold the knife.

"Oh, no!" she moaned, choking as she bent double, holding her belly and throwing up. Wiping her bloody mouth with her sleeve, she stood straight, stiff as a board, and leaned back against the wall again, her eyes flashing animal-like with the cracking lightning, pain wrenching upward through her. She dropped the knife and doubled over again.

"No, no, no!" she sobbed, struggling to recover her wits, to regain control over her body. She clutched for the knife, then suddenly scrambled for her other things, flung straw away to get at her bow and her small pack, and she dragged them out from the hiding place.

She could not think, at the moment, of any other goal but the barn door, and when she had made it that far, to cross the muddy yard was her only desire. Then, once she had crossed the yard, she staggered on toward the path, the rain soaking her through. Now, at the path, to follow along the edge of the bean field was all she wanted, going her way by years of memory in her feet rather than by any light in the pitch of the storm. At last, at the far side of the field, into the wood and away she fled. How many times she had already tripped and fallen just to get that far, less than a long arrow-shot, she had no care. Just to keep moving was everything, everything in the world. There was nothing else but the next tree, then to the next stone, then to tumble down the hill and through the stream, pausing only when her lungs could not manage their work and the stabbing jolts of agony within her gut cut off her breath, stopping only when her head spun so badly that she could hardly tell which way her feet should go, falling into bracken, against trees. She cried and screamed herself back onto her feet, and then to the next tree trunk to grab hold of, the next thorny brush to push through.

"Keep movin'!" she commanded herself as the thunder roared and the rain fell like waterfalls, the lightning more of a blinding hindrance than a guide. Her body knew the way, though she could not see a thing. But her body did not want to go. It wanted to keep her here, lying in the blood-filled puddle, to keep her here so that perhaps the pain would take her deeper into that other darkness where peace might be.

"No, no!"

She stumbled back to her feet, holding her belly with one arm and dragging her things with the other. Through her pain, she saw a light, and she realized that she had somehow made it to the neighbor's farmhouse. She stumbled onto the porch and banged on the door, slumping down to her knees as she knocked, crying out for help. She heard dogs barking from within.

"Who goes?" came a woman's gruff voice.

"Sheila! I'm...Sheila Pradkin from down the way!"

"What d'ye want?" This time it was a man's harsh voice, and the door cracked open.

Sheila groaned. Her plea stuck in her throat.

"We want nuthin' to do with yer troubles er antics, ye wretched girl! Begone, hear me? Afore I set me dogs on ye!"

"Please, Mr. Gladsten, sir! I'm hurt!"

The door slammed, but the dogs continued to bark, covering her sobs with their yelps as the man angrily tried to quiet them by his kicks and curses. Somehow, Sheila managed to get to her feet, and she shuffled away, sobbing.

Hours dragged, unreasonably stretched by the overwhelming detail of every inch of pain she crossed, by the unyielding particulars of every spasm of ground she felt. Her pain, her fear, her confusion and desperation merged with the physicality of the land, and all were obstacles to her, all became her enemy. In her agony, she was angry and impatient with each little root that tripped her, every rock that loosened and slid from under her feet, and angry at herself each time she fell, crying out in pain until she had little voice left. Sometimes she whimpered out one name—someone she wished would save her. Sometimes she sobbed another name—someone she thought might help her. And sometimes not even a name, addressing an apologetic moan to someone else who sensed, she was sure, every bout and spasm, every setback and stumble, and every hurt she suffered.

Was it hours? Or was it days or weeks or months or years that passed? And how many rain-drenched stone-bruised miles was it that slowly bled into leagues? She was beyond knowing such things.

Covered by new cuts and bruises sustained in her flight, she could no longer keep to her feet but for a few steps at a time. And, some long while later, not at all. She let go of her things and crawled. Forever she crawled, under fallen logs for lack of strength to go over or around them, through thickets of brush, along tiny runs where only the hares traveled, and along paths that flowed now with shallow runoff from the sudden showers. Slower and slower she went, and less clear became her goal, more meaningless her struggle. At last, she came to the edge of the wood. Looking up through the briars that she parted with her arm, she could see across the broad fields of Boskland. On a far hill obscured by mist and rain was the dim yellow light of the kitchen window. Almost there, less than a mile to go, she completely collapsed, her eyes still turned toward the distant light. She knew, with a clarity that fell upon her soul like a hammer, that she would not make it.

And now it was that her deepest, softest sobs came, filled with every regret and every sorrow of her lonesomeness, a life at odds with the world, all joined moment by moment into a relentless march through her heart. She was helpless against this last onslaught. Not closing her eyes, lying curled on her side with her knees up like a child, one arm pinned underneath her, she still reached out awkwardly with her other arm to weigh down the thorny weeds so that she could see that precious light. It was a terribly uncomfortable position, but she had no strength to turn over or to pull her arm out from beneath her.

She continually thought of the one person she longed to see more than any other, miles and miles away in the other direction, the one person she was now most ashamed to be seen by, but the one person she most wanted to honor, who never left her mind even for a moment, not during the worst of her ordeal. Yes, the one person who, no matter what, would still love her. A sob caught in her throat and she gulped. That she would never feel his touch again or see the kindness of his eyes was now her greatest regret. And with that regret came a terrible fear, greater than the pain of her wounds: fear that his eyes, carried within her, would never open to the world. That fear produced a final wave of desperate strength. Moaning, she rolled over, clutching the clumps of weeds to pull herself an inch closer to that tiny light.

"Frizella!" she screamed.

Her shrill voice cut through the misty air only to be swallowed by the night with not so much as an echo. As if responding to her cry, Lady Moon peeked aghast from behind her thin fan, and parted the clouds timidly to look, bathing Sheila with her cold powerless light. But Sheila did not notice. All seeing and all feeling left her as she spun into a bottomless dark. Nor did she notice the weirdly lit figure standing but a few yards away. Sheila was beyond hearing the forlorn song being sung in a voice that would fill any mortal with cringing terror. She could not see the banshee's approach or the arms reaching down to take her. She was not witness to the interloper who sprang forward and waved death's creature back with his frantic words and gestures. When she did regain some portion of her senses, she felt a strange sensation of motion, and a brief but peaceful indifference to her pain. For that short moment, when she neared the sea-surface of her blackness, she heard only the heavy tread of feet and the deep panting of whoever it was that cradled her and carried her. Words were being spoken to her. Words from an impossible voice. Then, after more lost blackness, she was roused by the sensation of being gently placed down, and she vaguely heard hard pounding on a door. A hand softly brushed her soaked hair from her face. The rain came again, and there was more pounding. And then, after a moment of silence, Frizella's distressed voice filtered into her awareness. Sheila burst into tears as the strong woman lifted her up into her arms.

• • •

As soon as Robby walked through the mysterious portal, there was a blinding flash and a crash of ear-stunning thunder. Now accustomed to the tranquility of Griferis, he recoiled. He thought the light and sound might have been due to his passing through the door, but when a distant bolt ran long and jagged across a parting cloud, he saw that he was in a dripping night-time wood. Disoriented, his eyes adjusting slowly, he stood still, listening to the receding rumble and the shushing breeze that gently rocked the trees overhead, sending a cascade of water clattering down all around. Through the canopy filtered a dim light as the crescent moon peeped briefly through a crack in the clouds. He heard another sound, fairly nearby, a cry, terrible in its pain, so stark and forlorn that he instantly spun around to face the way it came. He heard the name that was called, and a spasm of goosebumps ran up his neck and crawled down his arms. His throat caught his heart as he momentarily stopped breathing, then Robby shot through the wood toward the sound, pushing and flinging away wet branches and stumbling through the dark. He burst out of the trees, tripped and fell at the edge of an open field. Picking himself up, he quickly looked around. The clouds thinned, and the moon behind them revealed instantly where he was. But all was quiet. The breeze died, and he strained his eyes and ears across the fields and in every direction until he heard a faint, whimpering sob. Only a few yards away, in a bank of thick briars, was a dark shape. An arm raised weakly, reaching for the light off in the distance, and fell. He had only taken two long strides toward Sheila when a faint glow nearby grew into the form of a hideous woman, illuminated by pale-gray light. He stopped in his tracks. The creature's hair, long and black, was heavy with rain, the dripping gauze she wore ragged and torn. From her large red mouth, full of sharp crooked teeth, an uncanny voice grated out into the night as she reached down to the fallen figure with long spindly arms, arms with too many joints, like an insect.

"You can't have her!" he shouted, crashing through the brush and waving his arms. The apparition flinched, then stood upright and turned its eyes upon him.

"Begone!" he cried out.

The light altered somewhat, and the creature no longer appeared hideous, now transformed into a lovely spirit, fair of figure and face, her hair still black, but shining with reflected light, and her raiment floated as if in a gentle breeze. But her expression was stern.

"Ye speak the First Tongue," she sang, almost to herself. "I do not come for thee, but for her, and the one she carries."

"No! Get away!"

The banshee backed away compliantly as Robby sprang to Sheila and lifted her out of the briars.

"Ye cannot keep me from him," she sang, "for he has already heard the sweetness of my song."

"Leave us!" he cried, grunting to pick Sheila up. He cradled her close, struggled to his feet, and started out for Bosk Hall.

"We shall meet again, when comes thine own turn to hear my song."

He ran, holding Sheila carefully and firmly, with a strength he did not know he had. He ran, as fast as he could go, through the field and across the gentle slope toward the back of the manor house where a yellow light glowed from the kitchen window. Sheila moaned and, with tears streaming down his face, he slowed, trying not to jostle her so much. Panting and grunting with every uneven footfall, he finally stumbled to his knees. But he did not drop her. He got back to his feet, and he continued.

"I'm sorry, I'm sorry! Sheila! Sheila! Uhff! I'm taking you to Frizella. You are going to be fine. She'll save the baby, too! I know she will. Hold on, my love! Hold on! Frizella will know what to do. Oh, I'm so weak! And witless! Forgive me my love, oh forgive me! For leaving you with that terrible man! For not taking you away! Oh, dear! Oh, dear! Help!"

His voice broke, he had not the breath to speak loudly, and his cry for help was cut off by a bang of thunder, his words flying away on the cold wet wind. His knees cracked, his back and arms throbbed and burned with every jogging step. He held her as gently as he could, jogging on and on, out of the field, along the path, and over the footbridge at the edge of the manor grounds. His lungs were bursting for air, and his heart pounded nearly out of his chest, but he at last staggered into the yard and to the kitchen door. Kneeling as carefully as he could on the step, he eased Sheila down onto the landing, and, still cradling her, he freed one hand and pounded on the door.

"Just hold on, Sheila," he said. Then he banged again on the door.

"Dammit! Somebody answer!"

As he shouted, he felt a powerful and firm force grip his entire body, tugging him away. He fought to hold onto her, but his arms lost all strength, and Sheila settled down onto the landing.

"No! No-no! Wait!"

Robby was flung backwards through the portal, and sent sliding on his back across the marble floor. He scrambled back to the place where the door had been and beat his fists against the pitiless stone that was now in its place.

"No! I have to go back!" he cried, his voice echoing from the walls. He continued to protest as he beat the wall until he gave in to sobs, slipping to his knees, his head down, his hands against the wall.

• • •

That was where Finn found him. He knelt down to put a blanket around Robby's shoulders, but Robby pushed him away.

"Now, now, my lord," Finn said, putting the blanket back over Robby. "This trial is over. No doubt it was unpleasant. But come away. Let us get you out of those wet things."

A few moments later, Robby was led into a small simply appointed bedchamber. Robby said nothing, as if in a trance, and Finn, too, was silent as he gently undressed Robby, blotted his cuts, and put him into a fine nightshirt. He took Robby to the bed, eased him down into it, and pulled the sheets and blankets up around him. Finn picked up the wet clothes and reached to turn down the lamp, glancing at his charge who was lying still, staring up at the ceiling, tears running down from the corners of his open eyes to soak his pillow.

Finn turned down the lamp and quietly left the room. He knew nothing of what Robby had done or witnessed. Finn's only way to judge those he looked after was in the way their experiences marked them. He had waited upon many candidates during his time in Griferis; each came and went, and then the next came and went, too. They had subjected him to all manner of rants and curses, and to every variety of resentment as proxy for the cruel trials imposed by Griferis. He had even been cuffed more than once. But the Judges brooked no threats to his life, and more than one candidate had suddenly disappeared after making credible attempts to kill Finn. That much, at least, the Judges did for Finn. He knew he was safe, though little else could he say about the place, least of all why he was here or why he had been made to serve in this manner. It was his duty, that was all, and Finn did it without complaint, no matter how severely those in his care tested him.

Turning to close the door behind him, he looked again at Robby, wondering how one so young could endure this place. He pulled the door closed.

"But I hope he does."

• • •

Robby tried to dream, but could hardly even manage sleep. He lay on the bed while his heart bobbed up on crests of anger and sank into troughs of sadness. He sometimes cursed. Sometimes, he wept. He wanted to sleep, to dream, to find Sheila and talk to her, to tell her how sorry he was. But mostly he just wanted to see her. He tossed and turned, his emotions continuing back and forth from rage to grief for hours. Several times, he got out of bed, pacing. Once, he fumbled for his clothes, determined to leave Griferis immediately, whatever the cost. The only thing that stopped him was the numbness that comes of exhaustion and fatigue. For hours, he sat in a chair and stared at the low flame of the lamp. At last, he went over to the window and looked out. It was dark, and there were no stars to be seen through the frosted glass. Returning to the chair, he sat again, wishing he could sleep, but knowing he could not.

He was still sitting there when Finn knocked on the door and looked in.

"Sir," he said, "you should try to sleep."

Robby looked at him with blank bloodshot eyes.

"Well, let me at least set a plate for you. Then, we'll see."

Robby watched Finn leave and almost immediately return, pushing a serving cart. Finn set a plate on a nearby table, along with utensils and a napkin, and took a covered dish from the cart and put it on the table along with a decanter.

"Here is some whiskey," Finn said. "If you take meat, there is bacon here. Some eggs, too. Cheese and breakfast rolls."

In spite of his foul mood, Robby's stomach growled, and he stood. Finn pulled a chair out for him, and when Robby sat, Finn poured a jigger of whiskey, then took the lid from the covered dish, its aromatic steam rolling up pleasantly.

"I think a bite or two would do you good, sir," Finn said. "Then perhaps you will be able to find a bit of sleep."

"Perhaps," said Robby. "Thank you."

"Not at all, my lord."

"Robby. Just call me Robby."

"As you wish, sir."

Robby nibbled at a slice of bacon, chasing it with the whiskey.

Finn bowed and left the room, closing the door gently. Between long pauses, during which he absently stared at his plate without even seeing it, Robby did eat. And though it took him a very long time, he ate all that was provided. Shoving the plate back, he folded his arms on the table and put his head down. Later, when he realized that he had dozed off, he got up, took off his clothes, and went back to bed. Soon he was asleep. When the chimes woke him some long while later, he could not remember whether he had dreamed or not.

Getting up, he quickly dressed, splashed water into his face from the wash basin, glanced at himself in the mirror, and shook his head.

"I hope at least that Mother heeded my message about Galatus," he said to himself. "I must get back there as soon as I can! It seems forever since Ullin and I were in the caves on our way here. I hope he is safe, too."

The chimes were soft and insistent, so he hurried to the door, but he hesitated, looking through the high window at the morning sky. Going over to it, he looked out. He saw only blue above, and motionless clouds everywhere else, stretching out to a distant horizon without even a peak jutting through them. He wondered what would happen if he went back to bed and tried to sleep.

"I really need to get back to Mother and make sure she understood. And I really want to see Sheila. I wonder if the Judges would leave me alone long enough to do that? Probably not. Or else missing a trial might be the same as failing."

Making up his mind, he went back to the door, wondering what to make of yesterday's trials. It all seemed very unfair, he mused as he stepped out into a dark hallway. Cautiously, he walked a few steps more, and the place gradually filled with light, as if curtains were being drawn back from high windows. He was back in the circular room. It was just as it was before, with the sandglass sitting in its gimbal. Except one door was missing, the one he had first chosen. Glancing behind him, he was not surprised to see that the door to his bedroom was gone, too.

Entr'acte

Entr'acte

To Pay a Debt

Two riders emerged from the forest, one upon a horse and the other on a buckmarl, and they reined to a halt atop a windy bluff overlooking the long valley that opened before them and widened across the far distance. Meadows and pastures spread out for nearly a mile before coming to a place where a rocky promontory rose up, and upon its low summit they could see the ancient structure that was the House of Tallin, built, some said, from the timbers of the city-ships that first brought Men to the world.

"This is where I shall build my city," said the Man to his Elifaen companion. "And I shall have it well-fortified against the Dragonkind, should they ever come back this way. I mean to bring my family out of Vanara to live here, and I will not have the travesty of Tulith Attis repeated upon my soil."

"So this is the valley granted to your family as reward for your forebear's valor at that place."

"It is. And I call upon you to pay the debt you owe me by helping me construct its defenses."

"What do you have in mind that I may do?"

"It must remain a secret, between the two of us."

"I readily agree, for I have no wish for my existence to be known, or my whereabouts guessed."

"Good. You have it in your power to command the trolls that you created and that plague these hills and nearby mountains."

"I do, though they are crude works, and I do not wish them to be known as examples of my skill. And besides, they have their king, now, and obey him."

"I know. You must chain him and bind him so that he cannot interfere. As for the crudeness of your creations, they are a harsh race, indeed, lacking in civility and wit. But they are strong, and have not the needs or weaknesses that other races have. And, should the worst come, perhaps they may serve a purpose you never intended, and earn their honor by doing so. Until then, they will cease to plague the mountains as they presently do. Will you chain Thunderfoot? And then command the others?"

"I shall, since you have saved my life, and discovered my existence, too. Tell me what you wish for them to do."

"This is where they must gather, and build for me the things I wish, places beneath the ground and places above, places to stand firm on their own, and places that they must support with their strength until they are commanded to do otherwise."

"I sense a dark purpose."

"Nay, it is a way to defend this place. See my manor in the distance?"

"Yes. I see it."

"I shall have them blow hot stone to glass, and of that to build walls of my design all around that place. Within, they should pour the excavated rock and stone and earth, and they should pound it down so that it will be a level and solid place. On the far side is a sharp slope, such that no army may easily assail. Likewise, it is to the east and west. But here, upon the north side, the city walls will be the weakest, and is where the greatest defense is thus needed. Yet I seek to bring my family from Vanara, since the death of my father and the loss of my wife's lands by means of the Duinnor Edicts. Here my family will be safe, and any who are invited to come here to live and to work. This valley can be a fertile and prosperous region for farming, for trade, and for crafts of every kind needed by a small city, protected by uncracking walls, and by the other defenses I envision. With your people, that is, with the troll-kind, it is possible to do this thing, is it not?"

"It is, though a mighty task."

"Then, Ancient One, I desire that you make it so."

"It is a great thing you ask."

"No more than you have done before. And much less for the burden you have placed on the world."

"You do not care for me, though you saved my life."

"You arouse neither my affection nor my disdain, sir."

The two riders looked at each other for a long moment.

"Then I shall put a condition on it," said the Elifaen to the Man. "It is this: by the word that I alone may give shall those who serve you for a time respond when your defense is needed, a word that I shall retain to myself alone until that time of need. You must send for it. And I may judge if the time is right."

"That is not a reasonable thing. For the time may be too short from when the need is perceived to when I may acquire the word at such a distance from here to your western abode."

"It must be so, and a way will be found."

"You speak as if I have no choice, and that your life is not owed to me."

"Every debt has its limit. This is mine."

"Very well. I beg you to begin immediately," the Man said. He reached to his saddle and drew forth a long leather tube and handed it to the Elifaen. "Here are the plans and instructions that you are to follow. I shall oversee the work, and I must approve it. But if the plans are followed, I shall not make alterations or changes that you do not also approve."

The Elifaen took out the plans and examined them.

"It shall be done within a year from this day," said the Elifaen, putting the plans away. "I advise you to remove all of your kind from this region. I shall forge strong chains, and with them I shall chain Thunderfoot in his lair. And, within a fortnight, the trolls will come out of the Thunder Mountains to this place."

"Then I ride to warn the people to evacuate the valley," said the Man. He spurred down the hill and across the valley floor, going first to his manor to give word to the servants and workers there. Then, riding hard throughout the valley, he spread the word that trolls were coming, and that everyone was to leave at once for Glareth by the Sea.

In those days, very few people lived in the valley, only a few farmers besides those employed by the Tallin estate. So it was without much difficulty that they were convinced to leave, for they suffered from the raids of the trolls, and lived also in nagging fear that the Dragonkind might again break out from the desert lands and spread destruction across the eastern realms of the world as they did in the days of yore.

"You will all go in one great caravan to Glareth. Your stay there will be at my expense, for one year or longer," he told his people. "And when we return, we shall no longer be vexed by the trolls, and our homes will be safer and more prosperous than ever before."

They followed the Man's instructions, and, within a week, everyone was prepared with their wagons of belongings, their trade tools, and their livestock, and they moved eastward toward the old roads that led north to Glareth. Within another week, they were already far away, moving along the shore of Lake Halgaeth just as the first snows of winter drifted out of the sky.

Soon after the inhabitants of the valley were gone, on a moonless night laid with new snow, the trolls came out of the mountains and trudged in a line southward. The stamp of their feet echoed throughout the hills like thunder and shook snow from the green boughs of fir and from the bare limbs of the sleeping oaks. At their head rode the Elifaen upon his buckmarl, bearing the plans given to him. When morning came, they were gathered at the valley, and the Elifaen went from one troll to the next, giving his instructions. By the time the day was done, they were already well started upon their work. A week later, after seeing his people as far as Lake Halgaeth to the north, the Man returned to survey the work. He was very satisfied with what he saw, for already stone furnaces dotted the land, heating the many kilns that were made. Blocks of dripping glass were being poured and laid, making the walls of the city, and a great excavation was under way, too.

All throughout the year the trolls ceaselessly labored without rest or sleep or refreshment. During this work, the Elifaen went about from troll to troll, and he whispered to them in their own crude tongue, giving to them the instructions they were to follow when they heard the special word. He did this while the Man slept so that he would not know.

Indeed, it was one year to the day from when the Elifaen agreed to the bargain until his task was completed. Upon the same bluff as they had done before, he and the Man who had charged him with the task looked again across the valley. Now the land immediately below them was flat and level, crisscrossed with canals full of water. Farther away stood new walls that enclosed a very large area around the old Tallin Manor. And all of the trolls were gone from sight.

"I am pleased with the work," said the Man. "And I hope that I shall never need the word required to complete your debt to me."

"I also hope that you never need to send for it," said the Elifaen. "Now, I must depart. And I beg that you never say my name, or utter any hint of our pact."

"You can rest easy on that score. I bid you adieu! I must now bring my own workers to this place and take up my part of the labor. Adieu!"

"Adieu! And may the Dragonkind never dare assault you in this place, lest they are utterly destroyed!"

Part II

Chapter 15

To Fail as a Friend

Day 169
76 Days Remaining

As dawn drew closer, Ullin's concern over Robby increased. Hours earlier, the stranger had concluded his tale, revealing to Ullin only two of his adventures inside of Griferis. They were unpleasant stories. In one, the man told how he was forced by the Judges to sit himself in judgment over two men accused of separate murders. In each case, the evidence given by witnesses was overwhelming and clear. What made matters worse, in each case the victims' kin swore revenge for the acts should the accused be found innocent. The stranger related to Ullin how he tried to explain that he was no judge and that it was none of his business to decide these matters. But the people he was sent before seemed deaf to his pleas, and they were raucous in their insistence that he make his decision. And so, reluctantly, he did. In one case, the evidence given clearly exonerated the accused. In the other case, there was no doubt as to the man's guilt, and he even proclaimed as much before everyone present. So he was more than happy to find the first one innocent of all charges. And the other, he was sad to relate to Ullin, he sentenced to death according to the rules given to him. Only afterwards did he learn that the guilty man was falsely accused, and the witnesses were paid for their testimony so that the accused man's property could be cheaply acquired by those greedy for his lands.

"But why did he confess?" Ullin asked.

"After the man was executed, a letter was discovered hidden in the cell where he had been imprisoned," the stranger told Ullin. "It was, in essence, a threat against his family, ordering the man to confess and go to the gallows willingly, or else his family would be attacked and burned out of their home."

"Oh, my stars! And the other man, the innocent one? Was he actually guilty of the crime."

"Oh, no. He was also as innocent as could be. But I failed to ascertain the reason the man was even charged with the crime. If I had done so, I may have learned that a longstanding feud existed between his kin and those of his accusers. And, if I had learned that in time, I may have had it within my power to punish or jail the leaders of the conspiracy. Alas, knowing nothing, I did nothing. In the weeks that followed the man's release from prison, he was murdered, along with many of his kin. Fighting erupted all throughout the lands as clans aligned themselves with one another. Chaos and bloodshed reigned."

"That's terrible!"

"Yes. And all because I failed."

"But the Judges of Griferis must have thought you ruled correctly, for they let you leave the place."

"Ah, that. I don't think they really cared one way or the other about how I ruled."

"What do you mean?"

"I mean that perhaps they wanted only to see what I would do after learning of my mistakes, which is to say, whether I would repeat those errors in subsequent tests."

"And did you?"

"I don't really know. I never was tested again like that. But it did make me a cautious person, wary of the word given against others. And I will always remember the faces of those men."

Ullin thought about this tale, wondering what horrible situations Robby must now be facing.

"So, it was never a test of strength, was it? Or a test of valor, or courage."

"It depends on how you mean it. Of prowess in combat? Not really, although I saw my share of fighting. I was made to serve aboard a warship for four years, and we battled both the enemy and the sea. Once I fought aboard ship during a battle off the coast of Tracia. It was a furious fight, and they outnumbered us, swinging across on ropes, and swarming over the side. Our ship was on fire, and it sank beneath us as we fought. A year later, I was aboard another ship. A gale blew us into the Craggy Sea and we were shipwrecked. I watched all my shipmates slowly die of heat and thirst, and there was nothing I could do to help them. I, alone, survived. I was picked up by an Altorian fishing vessel that was also blown off course and only happened to see my signal. I don't know if I survived because I was strong. Stronger men died, but I did not. I think I was just lucky."

"Is everything in Griferis so terrible?"

"Oh, no. I was shown wondrous things. Beautiful things. And things that I hardly know how to describe, so mysterious they were. But I am not sure those things were worth all the rest. I'm not sure I'll ever know."

The stranger grew more reluctant to speak as the night wore on, and he finally fell silent while Ullin considered the man's tales. Outside, the wind still blew in fits, tossing stray snowflakes, and a semblance of light filtered through the clouds behind which Lady Moon made her nightly walk. Ullin, his own eyes drooping, drifted in and out of perplexing dreams, each one inconclusive, like his fitful sleep, interrupted by a spike of anxiety that snapped his train of thought and dissipated any meaning the dreams may have held.

Each time he awoke in this manner, he was startled by the presence of the stranger, who was apparently sleeping, his head tilted aside and covered by his hood. One time, so disoriented was Ullin upon waking, that he actually reached out to take the shoulder of the stranger, saying, "It's time to go, Robby." Then, realizing his mistake, he recoiled just before touching the stranger, chiding himself as the memory of Robby's absence and the reality of the stranger's presence slammed back into his awareness. Angry at himself for the mistaken gesture, Ullin pulled his coat tighter around him and shook his head, thinking, "This is no place to be so muddled!"

For a while he watched the sky grow slowly pale, but in spite of himself, he soon drifted off again.

But the stranger, who was never asleep at all, was interrupted from his own distant thoughts by Ullin's sudden outburst. He did not react to it. He watched the shadow that was Ullin's form shift uncomfortably, and he briefly wondered how the Kingsman might spin his own tale. The stranger soon retreated back into his own thoughts about his recent departure from Griferis, about the loss of nearly thirty years of his life, and about the boy he saw entering the place. His thoughts went back to the morning, and he remembered his last words with Finn. Sighing inwardly, he wondered if he would ever see Finn again.

• • •

"Finn, how old was I when I first came here?"

Finn looked over at his guest who had been washing from the basin but was now gazing into the mirror as the water ran down his face.

"I never asked your age," Finn replied, putting down the breakfast tray and pouring coffee into a cup. "And you never told me, I don't think."

"Hm. Well, can you say how long I have been here?"

"Well, let's see. That is a question, isn't it?"

"Could you venture a guess?"

"Well, I'd say, judging by your beard and the gray of your temples, and reckoning into it all the days I have brought meals to you...hm. Perhaps you have been here nearly twenty-eight years, give or take?"

Finn's guest nodded. "That would make me around forty-nine years old." He turned and smiled, "And you haven't aged a day."

"Ah, but I have, sir. It just doesn't show, perhaps." Finn smiled as his guest nodded again.

"I will miss you, sir," Finn said. "I will not forget you. Of all those I have waited upon, you are the one I am most proud to have served."

"You have been a good friend to me." The guest reached out and shook Finn's hand. "But for you, I surely would have gone mad and would have been utterly lost."

"That is kind of you to say, sir. But I doubt whether it is so. You have a strength from within that sustains you. I wish...I wish I could come with you, sir."

"Me, too. But you may have others to take care of, now, and I rely on you to do that just as you have taken care of me."

"Of course. I do not forget. And I assure you that I shall do my duty."

"Where are you going?"

They turned to a young girl standing in the doorway. She wore a simple blue dress and apron, brass-buckled black shoes, and a blue ribbon in her shoulder-length blond hair. In her arms, with its head tucked away under her ear, was a gray and white rabbit. She looked to be around fourteen or fifteen, though none could know her true age.

"Ah. Celia. I must go away for a time."

"Why?"

"I have errands to run. But I'll be back later."

"When?"

"I'm not really sure. That is up to others, not up to me."

"What others?"

"The Judges, for example."

"The Judges. I would surely like to meet them someday. Will you be back in time for tea?"

The guest glanced at Finn, who looked sympathetic but said nothing.

"If not, Finn will have tea with you. Won't you, Finn?"

"It would be my honor."

"And perhaps the two of you could enjoy a game of cards, as well," the guest suggested.

"That would be enjoyable," said Finn with a bow toward Celia.

"Very well," she said. "Do you hear that, Boxer? We shall have tea and play cards with Finn, today," she said to the rabbit. Then, in a whisper, "Perhaps we shall even let him win."

Boxer champed with pleasure.

"Run along, my dear," Finn said to her kindly, "and see what new blooms grace the gardens this morning."

"I shall do so. But don't be late, Finn!"

"I shall be prompt."

The girl smiled and disappeared down the hall.

Looking at the empty doorway, the guest said, "She has become like a daughter to me. Isn't that strange?"

"Not really. I confess a certain attachment myself. But, sir, to give her hope of your return?"

"Hope is never false. But I don't think she will miss me. You know how she is. I must go."

"Good luck, sir."

The guest went to the door and then turned back.

"If I do not come back, and others come here," he said, "would you tell them about me and ask if they have any knowledge of me? That way, you may at least learn what became of me. I would like for you to know."

"Then I shall ask."

∙ ∙ ∙

When the guest stood before the Judges, in the vast circular hall that contained only the seven Judges in their chairs and no other thing besides the guest himself, he said to them, "I am ready."

"Yes, you are."

"You have fulfilled and surpassed all tests put to you."

"And you have demonstrated the qualities needed to rule."

"You have borne the responsibility…"

"…exercised wisdom…"

"…carried out justice…"

"…and discerned truth."

"And so you must now leave this place."

"But you shall be granted three boons."

"Hm. May I ask anything at all?"

"Three, but only three."

"Not one…"

"…not two…"

"…only three."

"No more, and no less."

"To be fulfilled after you depart this place."

"And the doors are closed to you."

"Just as I thought. Very well. First, I wish to learn all that there is to know about Griferis."

The Judges looked at each other, and whispered heatedly for many minutes. Abruptly, they turned back to him.

"There is within this place a secret library wherein are all of the chronicles of Griferis, how it came to be, who we are who sit in judgment, who sent us to be here, those who have come to this place, and those who have departed from here."

"I see. Yet you do not tell me how I may find the library. I anticipated as much. And so, as my second boon, I also demand that Griferis in its entirety, and in no way diminished in its power or quality, as well as the summit, and the mountain whereupon the gate is, to be given over to me as my palace and as my estate, as the place from which I may exercise all those prerogatives that any ruler may wish for: to come and to go, to guard and protect, to invite or expel any person who I may wish to come or go, to have all powers over this place, to open any door, to go into any room or place, to summon and to dissolve the causeway leading here, and to alter these properties in any way whatsoever that may please me, and to leave to whosoever I select to be my successor."

Again the judges were filled with consternation, but soon turned back to face him.

"Griferis shall be yours. What is your final boon?"

"Since my coming here, you have endeavored to trick and to fool me by every devious means. I do not judge you, the Judges of this place, for surely you also only follow rules. Indeed, I have learned much, and the trials and sufferings that I have been subjected to have made me wiser than your reckoning of me. But well do I know that you have agreed to my first two boons only because you know that I must leave. 'To be fulfilled when you depart this place' is what you have said. I now demand as my last boon that which you have reserved as the trump to my first two boons: That never will the doors to this place be closed to me and, as proof, that I be fetched back to this place by Finn and any servants he may so choose, so that the first two boons may be fulfilled."

At this, the Judges stood from their thrones, grinning and clapping.

"You have chosen wisely!"

"And you have released us from service."

"Nevermore shall we need sit in cruel judgment."

"Nevermore shall we need mete out cruel punishment."

"And no longer need we be separated from our own people."

"For as you may learn, we are the prisoners of Griferis, not you."

"Made to spend our years waiting for the One who shall claim this place from us."

"Now, at last, do we speak with our own hearts."

"Go quickly, so that we may also leave this place."

"Go quickly, so that we may rejoin our loved ones, far away!"

"This place shall be yours!"

"Be at peace!"

"Rule wisely!"

"And may you meet with prosperity and success!"

• • •

For how long Ullin slept, he could not tell, but he awoke with a slow uncomfortable stretch of his neck, then with a violent start: The stranger was gone. No sooner than he saw this than he was scrambling up and out of the cave, gripping Swyncraff at the ready. It was overcast but the day's bright light effused the new snow so that there seemed to be no shadows. Ullin blinked but did not need to follow the tracks; the stranger was standing beside the gate many paces away with his back to Ullin. His hood had fallen back, and his hair, long and black and wavy, was streaked with gray, and was tousled by the breeze. Sensing Ullin's approach, he turned. For the first time, the Kingsman could see the stranger's face, his beard graying like his hair, neatly trimmed under cold-reddened cheeks. He was smiling, and he looked at Ullin with dark eyes that had an open and familiar aspect, and the eyes grinned as much as the stranger's mouth did.

"You've slept most of the day. But it is time we left this place, don't you think?"

Ullin stepped closer, studying the man's face with growing disbelief.

"You still don't believe your own ears or your own eyes," the stranger said. "Ah! My dear Swyncraff!"

As soon as its name was called, the object writhed in Ullin's hand so that he dropped it in surprise and dismay. When Swyncraff hit the ground, it flexed like a bow and sprang several yards through the air and into the stranger's waiting hand, then easily coiled like a rope over his shoulder.

"Can it be you?" Ullin asked in amazement, his knees trembling so violently that he crouched. "Or are you yet another trick of my head?"

"I can be none other, cousin. I am no trick."

Ullin stared, blinking.

"Surely Griferis is a place of terrible wonder!" he said at last in a horrified tone. "And hard, for you bear the marks not only of age but also of strife."

"Aye. I do. And it is a wondrous place, but not all terrible. Full of strife, perhaps."

"Robby!" Ullin slowly approached, his face contorted with sadness and horror, his eyes stinging, "What has happened to you?"

"Come, come! Don't be too happy!" Robby grinned. "Do I look so awful? You certainly don't."

Ullin shook his head and finally smiled, then slowly grinned, too, and took Robby's hand and shook it with both of his. They hugged, patting each other on the back.

"I thought all was lost," Robby said, still hugging Ullin, "and that I had gone mad. Until I saw you. But I wanted to wait until the light of day, to be sure of things. I'm sorry!"

"No, no! Don't be sorry!"

"I wanted to wait until the light of daytime to really get a good look at you, to get a sense of you. You have no idea how often I have been tricked and fooled and disappointed these many years."

Ullin gripped Robby by the biceps—strong arms, he noted—and looked at his cousin.

"It is I who am sorry," he said. "I had no inkling that you would suffer so!"

"It is done. And I am cold! I suppose that miner's hut is still there?"

"Yes! Let's go! Oh! I almost forgot! Do you have the Name?"

"The Name? Oh, no, Ullin. Griferis cannot provide the Name. I think I know how to get it, though. But, dear Ullin, when I have it, I think you will never see me again."

"What?"

"That's the way it has to be. Let's get to that hut, shall we?"

With joy exceeding, Ullin led the way quickly, his arm in Robby's.

"I think you are taller," said Ullin, laughing. "And you seem very fit."

"In spite of my age, you mean?"

Before too long they arrived at the hut, and Ullin immediately set to work rekindling the fire.

"The stories you told me," Ullin said as he carefully placed a pile of coal onto the fire, "would hardly be believable if you didn't bear the evidence of them on your countenance."

Settling down onto a pile of blankets, Robby stretched out and pulled his shoulder bag close by, rummaging around within it. He found his little pad of paper used to take orders for the store, and the pencil he always carried with it. Gazing at them, his hands trembled, and he carefully opened it to see on the first page, in his father's neat hand, written, "Ribbon's Sundries." Below that was a list of various items available at the store, and even the latest prices for them. At the bottom was written the date, "9/18/870 S.A., being within the Year of the Red Door."

Robby stared at the writing, running his fingers across the ink as if to touch the moment of his father's penning and, through it, his father.

"I can hardly believe it all took place in such a short while," Ullin went on, shaking his head and grinning enthusiastically over his shoulder at Robby. "Could you tell me more about the place? About the other things that you did there?"

Robby put the things back into his shoulder bag, and as he did so, he found the item that he looked for.

"I don't really have the heart, right now, Ullin," he replied. "I'm quite tired. Perhaps another time."

"Forgive me. I'm sure you need rest."

It was when Ullin stirred more coal into the fire, turning his back to the room, that Robby unplugged the stopper from the vial he had obtained in Vanara and drank the contents quickly. It was sweet and powerfully sour, and his face puckered. He had just regained his composure when Ullin put down the poker and turned back to him.

"There! That should keep us from freezing. At least for a while," Ullin said, smiling. "Are you hungry?"

"No, thanks." Robby felt his stomach churn, and he belched a little burp behind his hand. Ullin looked sideways, sniffing. But if he noticed the odor of foxdire, he did not place it for what it was. He rubbed his arms vigorously.

"Goodness! I can't seem to get rid of these shiverbumps!"

"Perhaps you should wrap up in some of those blankets."

"I'm too restless!" Ullin replied, standing up. "I cannot get over how much you are changed from just a few hours ago! Twenty-eight years! All in the blink of an eye!"

"Yes. Well, that was somewhat unexpected, eh?"

"I'll say!"

Ullin tried not to stare at Robby, who now looked strangely like a cross between Mr. Ribbon and Lord Tallin, which, of course, he was.

Smiling, he turned away to face the fire. Robby stretched out on his back and closed his eyes. The fresh coals were cracking, and he felt his face warmed. Or perhaps it was the foxdire. He could definitely feel drowsiness coming over him.

"Ullin, you have been a faithful companion to me," he said. "But I'm afraid I will soon strain you terribly."

"What do you mean?"

"I mean that an important task remains, one that I wish I could avoid, but," Robby shrugged. "I can see no other way out."

"Have you not been tried enough by this terrible place? What more is there that you can do?"

"Well, one thing more, certainly. I must obtain the Name, you know. And to do so, I must go to that place where all mortals are bound for. I don't look forward to it. No one that I know of has ever come back from that place. Except perhaps as an apparition."

"If I take your meaning, and I think I do, how? How can you pass from this world to the next with any hope of returning?"

"Hope? Perhaps that is too much to ask for. But you forget," Robby smiled wryly, "that no lock may hinder me, and no gate may resist my touch. Well, almost none. I have but to find the gate and pass through, and back through again to return."

Ullin stared at Robby, slowly shaking his head.

"What you are saying is...is madness!"

"There is no other way, cousin."

"But, still, even if you could do it, why? Who would you look for? How can you know who named the King? And, even if you found that person in the land of the dead, why should he tell you the Name?"

"I already know who it is I must find, Ullin. And I know he will give me the Name that I seek. Indeed, he waits for me now, and has waited, and will continue to wait for me. Until the end of time, if need be. You see, Ullin, it isn't really about the Name itself. It's about getting the Name. Although I am still baffled by how getting the Name will help. But first things first, I suppose."

Ullin paced back and forth, trying to find words to counter Robby's idea.

"I must do this if I am to become King. That is the only reason. Every sinew, every fiber of my being cries out against the thing. I dread it more than anything I ever faced in Griferis. But it is the only hint of hope that I have. All the many years within Griferis prepared me for this, not by trial or judgment, but by my incessant thinking on this very problem. I see no other way. And while some tiny part of me moves that way, to do this thing, it is powerful enough to drag the rest of me along. Frankly, Ullin, I am terrified."

Robby pulled his blanket under his head for a pillow and closed his eyes.

"Let me sleep for a time," he said. "I am very tired. We'll talk later, perhaps."

Ullin nodded, looking down at Robby.

"Certainly," he said in a defeated tone. "I'll just step out for a smoke before turning in myself."

"Alright, then," came Robby's faint voice.

Ullin went to the door, glancing back at Robby before pushing the door open and stepping out, carefully shoving it back into place behind him. The air felt good to Ullin, even though it was icy cold. He took out his pipe, but, having forgotten to bring an ember, put it back into his pocket and stepped out into the snow, his footfalls soft and muffled by the powder. By now, Sir Sun had departed with the day, and Lady Moon was rising between two narrow peaks, and even though part of her face was hidden behind her fan, she still shone brightly among the stars. As he stared at her, his thoughts full of despair at what Robby seemed utterly determined to try, her smile seemed to him somewhat wry, as if amused. Only a few moments ago, Ullin was happy, utterly thrilled that Robby was back. In awe of the change Griferis had wrought upon his once young cousin, but overjoyed at Robby's return. Now, his heart drooped like wet sails becalmed.

"If only Collandoth was here," he thought. "If Robby has some shadow over his heart that is drawing him toward this end, then perhaps Collandoth would know how to break the spell. It should have been he, not I, who came with Robby. What am I to do?"

He stepped farther out from the hut, looking back at it.

"In spite of what he says, he must be determined not to be King. It is too much for him. Maybe his pride, or perhaps his concern for the feelings of others poses his intent in this manner, to make me think him a better man than I might otherwise think."

Ullin paced nervously, his body shivering, longing to go back in. But his anxiety kept him pacing until he figured out what to do. Several times he went back to the door, and he even put his hand out to push it open, but some turn of thought, some hesitant hope of a solution distracted him, and he trudged back out into the snow.

"That is it, then," he mused. "It must be. He is trapped by this expectation, not of his own, but those of us who grasp at him. We shove our own hopes upon him, holding him up to an impossible standard. He is but a man! The world is cruel, and we are heartless! Why should we sacrifice our friend, our kin, to this reckless end?"

Determined to go back in and wake Robby, to tell him not to fret, that they would find another way out of this mess, Ullin's hand again reached for the door. But once more he paused and then turned away.

"What choice has he, really? Would not Duinnor's throne be an exile from all that is dear to him? That a man would rather die than be imprisoned is not so hard to understand. Yet, surely he sees that, even so, even from such a prison as that, he could still do, he *would* do great works! The truest part of him would show through, would remain free. He has not lost heart. That is it. The greatness of what he would become is like a flood, pulling him under, overwhelming him. And what has he to hang onto? All that is left to him is here. I, myself, am left to him. All others are so far away, too far away, and, for him, years and years have passed since he has seen them. Only I am here with him on this mountain. Only I am left. A feckless companion, drowned by the tide of my own gloom, walking through my days as a man whose life has left him, but who still hobbles along, crutched by honor and duty and pride, but with no joy in any step I take. No! No! No! I'll not let duty lure me again away from those I love as it has done before! He need not become King if he does not desire it, and I will not stand sentinel to his design to do away with himself!"

Ullin jogged back to the door, determined to wake Robby, to tell him that they could leave this place, that they could go away, perhaps back to Greenfar, or maybe even to the faraway Free City of Kajarahn, to live out their days under new names, and the world be damned!

For a third time his hand reached out for the door, but then, suddenly, an odd sound grated through the still air just as he touched it. The bumps and shivers on the back of his neck and running up and down his arms on the inside of his coat were not at all due to the cold. The sound grew louder as he turned away from the door and drew his dagger. It was a long, plaintive syllable, then a shrill discordant note like iron swords dragged across a stone floor, making Ullin's skin crawl all the more. He carefully inched to the corner of the hut and peered around, staring at what he saw.

As pale as the snow, a figure wrapped in gauze stood not a dozen feet away. The play of moonlight gave it a ghastly look, its arms outstretched toward the hut. Shaking with terror, he first thought it to be a witch, for certainly it was not Mortal or Faere. Its face was difficult to see, and it shimmered in the moonlight, as if shifting in and out of the world, from side to side, up and down, back and forth, like a mirage in the wavering heat of the desert. Its dark hair, the shape of its body, and something about the moan were all distinctly feminine.

But it was the voice, even more than the creature's appearance, that filled Ullin with horror and clutching fear. It was not the fear of threat that he felt, nor any fear of harm that might be directed at him. It was deep, black dread calling and scratching from its mouth, dread that spoke of the hereafter, not of the grave, but that which lay beyond. It was not Ullin's body that was touched by the sound, but the very core of his being, as if a void in existence itself was opened. It was at the encroaching brink of this void that Ullin's body at last instinctually reacted by recoiling and breaking the trance that had nearly overwhelmed him, jerking him back and away from the sight.

"Banshee!" he cried, dropping his dagger, covering his ears with both hands, and closing his eyes tight. His body filled with the electricity of terror, and his legs stiffened, pushing him back against the wall of the hut. Almost instantly, he felt something come very close by, like a swift, looming mountain, its silent mass overpowering all other sensations. As suddenly as it flew by, it passed, and all was silent. Ullin opened his eyes.

"She has come for Robby!"

Stumbling back to the door, he shoved it open and dove within, sliding to his knees, clutching at Robby, shaking him.

"Wake up! Wake! No, no! Wake up, Robby!"

But Robby was gone.

Ullin lifted his cousin into his arms, and the sound that he had heard before was now hoarsely echoed from his own throat as he groaned. Robby's arm flopped over, and out of his hand fell a tiny crystal vial, emptied of its contents. Ullin stared at it for a long time, then picked it up and lifted it to his nose and smelled the sour-sweet aroma of endless sleep. He put down the vial and gently lowered Robby as his eyes welled with tears. Ullin remained kneeling, slumped back onto his heels, and felt his heart breaking and breaking and breaking, pulled apart from the inside out.

In his heart, Deep Anger, full of resentment and shame, stood to one side and accusingly said, "You call yourself a Kingsman! You call yourself a friend!" Sad Empathy stood to the other side of his heart, understanding Robby's torture and his desire for release, mourning the tragedy and in awe of its power. And, between these two, stood dear struggling Confusion, listening to both, feeling the full weight of every accusation and acting as fertile ground for every regret.

It was too much. Holding his head with both hands against the bursting conflict within, Ullin cried out in a long anguished moan, rocking back and forth. He pounded the floor with his fists and sprang to his feet shouting with a cracking voice, "You fool! You blind fool! You should have paid more attention!"

This was not like battle, when the enemy was too swift upon a comrade, or when too many arrows flew too fast. This was not like some accident that causes one to fall into a river and drown, or like being thrown from a horse. This was coming all along. This was obvious all along! New, hot tears fell across Ullin's shame-red cheeks as he remembered every sign, every word, every nuance of warning from the moment they left Janhaven until now. No wonder Robby was so withdrawn during their journey, so filled with fatigue, so melancholy. No wonder Robby laughed less and less at Billy's jokes the farther they came west, and grew more distant from even Sheila as the miles went by.

"You understood all along how hopeless your fate was," Ullin said, looking down at Robby's pale cheeks. "And I turned a blind eye."

He sat down and slumped against the hearth, open-eyed and without sobs, letting his tears run silent courses down into his beard. Slowly, the flames receded into glowing embers and, later, the embers fell into ash as the stone hearth gave up the last of its heat, and still Ullin stared at Robby's lifeless body. Weariness slowly crept over the Kingsman, and his head eventually drooped. He closed his eyes and, at last, he slept.

Chapter 16

Mirabella the Assassin

Day 171
74 Days Remaining

Mirabella slowly raised her head from her prone position, leaves and twigs clinging to the hood that was pulled low over her brow. For the better part of a day, she had carefully worked her way through the forest well north of the road from Passdale to Janhaven, then back east and southward toward the town, stopping often to look for enemy sentries or patrols. In their red cloaks they were easy to spot from a long way off, but she trusted that their scouts and crack soldiers did not dress so unfittingly for stealth. Within two miles of Passdale, she saw the first one, not even thirty yards away, sitting with his back to her behind a moss-covered log, his bow across his knees and his quiver beside him. He was looking the other way as he drank from a waterskin, keeping watch over a stretch of the road. Crouching, she eased herself over to the base of an old poplar. Keeping her eyes on the Tracian, she then knelt and carefully crawled under a blackberry thicket. Eventually, the scout would be relieved by another, or else he would give up his watch and report to his commanders. And Mirabella knew, too, that others of his kind were likely scattered around the wood. The fitful wind gusted through the trees, rattling leaves and brush, and giving her the cover she needed to settle down in the dry leaves.

She did not have long to wait. In less than an hour, as the sunbeams angled low through the woods, footsteps crunched. Looking up, she saw that the sentry had also heard and had an arrow notched, looking toward the left. The crunching stopped. The scout got to his knees and lifted his bow, pulling back on the string as he made a long bird-like whistle. From the unseen approach, an answering whistle came.

Soon the approaching scout came into view, and the first one lowered his weapon as his comrade joined him, crouching behind the log. They spoke in low tones, and Mirabella could not hear their words. When the first got up and began moving away toward town, she used the sound of his passage to crawl out from under the briars. Notching an arrow, she watched the receding scout until he disappeared down the hill. Satisfied that he was out of sight and earshot, she quickly drew back her arrow and sent it flying into the skull of the newly arrived sentry.

Moving quickly to follow the first scout, intent upon where she put each foot, she was bemused at her own cold-bloodedness. But she had resolved to do what she came to do that very morning, when she first woke up, after a night full of strange dreams.

• • •

Without telling anyone of her intentions, she ate a quick breakfast and crossed the yard of the stockade slinging her quiver over her shoulder as she made her way to the infirmary. As foretold to her, Frizella was there instead of at her hut, putting the final touches on the special uniforms they needed. All was in a rush, since Mirabella's scouts had confirmed a great deal of Redvest activity around the old troll cave; and it appeared that Vidican planned to put his army through the cave and come out south behind Janhaven. Mirabella herself had spent a day tracking his scouts, watching their movements around the cave and the ridge that it passed through, and it was plain what Vidican intended. Seeing the opportunity to strike a crushing counterblow, she ordered that Vidican's scouts around the caves and south of Janhaven were not to be molested; it was imperative that Vidican suspect nothing. Meanwhile, the call went out from Janhaven for every fighter to muster, whether man or woman or brave youngster. Then, under Winterford's direction, they moved carefully into hidden positions around the cave's east and west openings, taking great care to move only in small groups and to remain well-hidden. After the bulk of Vidican's forces had moved out from Barley, and had passed through the caves, Mirabella's people would attack. And, meanwhile, that would give a detachment of her fighters an opportunity to rescue the prisoners in Passdale.

But it all depended on surprise. Vidican must not learn about the countermoves against him, or else the Redvests would be certain to gain the advantage.

• • •

Now, as she came within sight of the oblivious Tracian, and followed him at a safe distance toward Passdale, she went over again, as she had done already so many times this day, the strange dream that prompted this solitary foray into enemy-held territory.

She had dreamt that she was minding the store, putting away new glass jars filled with blinking fireflies while Robby and her husband worked at the ledgers.

"That's a lot of lightnin' bugs, Mira," she heard Robigor say.

Glancing at her husband, she smiled. He was looking over his spectacles at her. Beside him sat Robby, bent over his own ledger, scratching away furiously with his quill.

"And that's just what I have been looking for!"

Turning, she saw a tall man in a black tunic removing his hat as he entered the store. He turned to close the door behind him, but for some odd reason the door bell did not jangle.

"May I help you?"

"Hello! Yes. I see you have the very latest in fireflies," the man said, coming over and taking one of the jars from her. He held it up to his nose, peering at the creatures within that were now swarming frantically against the glass.

"Perhaps I will take a few jars. How much are they?"

"Well, I'm not sure," she said amiably. "Honey, how much are the fireflies?"

"Oh," said her husband, not bothering to look up. "Ask Ullin. I reckon he knows more about 'em."

"I think sixpence a jar would be fine, Mother," Robby said, glancing up as he turned a page. He ducked back down and dipped his pen to continue writing.

"That seems a bit steep," said the man, his pale eyes nearly a match to his gray hair. "Perhaps you might throw in a few other things?"

"It is a lot to pay for something that anyone may catch," Mirabella agreed. "But it is the jar that is the expense, you see."

"Yes, of course it is."

"What else may I get for you, today?"

"Well, perhaps you can give me the number of fighters that are with you in Janhaven?"

"Fighters?"

"Yes. How many fighters are there in Janhaven?"

"Five thousand, four hundred and seventy-two!" Robby said triumphantly. "Isn't that right, Daddy?"

"Well, let me see, son."

Mirabella looked over to see Robby pass the ledger to his father.

"That looks about right. But it don't include the Galinots that'll be comin' in, now does it?"

"Why no, sir. I'm sorry. Should I add them, too?"

"Might as well make it a correct reckonin'."

"There you have it, sir," Mirabella said. "Now. How many jars did you say?"

The man squinted at the two men working away at the ledgers, and he frowned.

"That number hardly seems credible," he said to her.

"It does, doesn't it? I imagine they've got their sums wrong, though it has never happened before."

"What do you suppose a more correct number might be?"

"Twelve thousand, six hundred, and thirty-five!" shouted Robby.

"Let me see," said Mr. Ribbon. "Why don't ye help yer mother with them jars."

"Yes, sir."

Robby hurried over and picked up a jar to shelve, but he fumbled and dropped it onto the floor where it shattered, setting free all the fireflies.

"Whoa!" he shouted. "Catch 'em before they get out the door! Excuse me, mister."

Laughing, Mirabella and Robby jumped and twisted, snatching after the insects as they floated around the store.

"Well," said the customer, putting his hat back on. "Perhaps I'll come back later."

"Very well!" Mirabella called after him. Robby hurried over to close the door behind the man, and peered out to watch him evaporate in the darkness outside. Robby then turned to his mother, and when she saw the serious expression on his face, she thought he looked careworn and tired beyond his years.

"What's the matter, honey?"

"Mother," he said to her urgently. "You must kill that man. Find the Redvest general, General Vidican, and you'll find him. Then kill him. If you don't, he will discover all your secrets and tell his general."

"How can he be so dangerous?"

"This was not the first time you have seen him, is it?"

"No, he has been coming to the store for the past few days."

"The store is gone, Mother. You are dreaming. And he has been in your dreams. His name is Galatus. He is a spy. And he has the means to learn what you are doing in Janhaven, and to look upon all of your plans and preparations."

"But how can that be?"

"The same way that I now speak with you," Robby stated. "He's just not as good at this as I am."

"At what?"

"At visiting your dreams."

"At *what?*"

"I don't have time to explain it all. Look, there you are. Sleeping."

Mirabella felt that she was being tugged away with Robby as he spoke, then the store shifted, blurred, and vanished, replaced by the room where Furaman let her stay. It was the same room that Durlorn, the building foreman, had lent to Robby when he was in Janhaven. Robby now motioned at the cot where Mirabella slumbered. She was astonished when she saw herself.

"The man," Robby went on, his voice growing more strident, "Galatus, he doesn't know how to dreamwalk very well, even though he thinks he does. He can only spy on dreamers and their dreams, not on the wakeful. But his skill is good enough to bring terrible harm to you and those in Janhaven. If you or any of our people have dreams about your plans to counterattack Vidican, or to go after our people who are prisoners in Passdale, Galatus, the spy, could easily learn about them."

"I don't think I understand."

"Mother, listen to me. Just now, he tried to get you to tell how many fighters you have. That's the kind of thing he does. It's like eavesdropping. And whatever he learns, he tells his Redvest general, General Vidican."

"How can this be?" she asked, her eyes drawn back toward the cot.

"You have to trust me. And I don't have much time with you. Someday, I hope to have the power to take care of the likes of Galatus. But by then it will be too late. I think killing him is the only way to stop him."

"But—"

"General Vidican thinks him to be a powerful sorcerer or soothsayer. He goes nowhere and does nothing without Galatus being nearby. Find Vidican and you will find Galatus. They are both quartered in the Common House, if that helps."

"But if he is always with the Redvest general, he will be surrounded by guards and the like."

"I know. I'm sorry, Mother, but you have to think of some way to get to him. You must try. But you must do it quickly. This very day, if you can. My time is nearly up. Mother, listen to me! I know your fighters prepare to meet Vidican's army as they come through the troll caves. That is good, and so far neither Vidican nor his scouts suspect anything amiss. But I'm afraid Galatus will discover all your plans very soon. Perhaps this very night. If he does, Vidican will bring his entire army at you from another direction while your fighters face the wrong way."

Mirabella shook her head slowly.

"Robby, I don't understand this. I thought you were far away."

"I am, Mother! I am at this moment on Mount Algamori. Ullin and I just arrived here, and I will soon enter Griferis. But I am a dreamwalker, Mother. Just like Galatus is. And I've been trying for days to get back to you—in dreams, that is—to warn you about Galatus."

"But—"

"You must believe me! And, Mother, because you will have doubts when you awake, I tell you this as a sign: Frizella spent the night at the infirmary with Mrs. Painmoor who has once again lived up to her name."

"Robby! I don't understand." Mirabella felt herself breathing hard, and the vision of her son grew dim as she stirred toward wakefulness.

"By the way," Robby said, "Daddy made it to Glareth by the Sea. He is safe, but he had a dangerous and difficult journey. Now he is on his way back to you, having aroused the Glarethians to action, and he is bringing help with him. But it will be another fortnight, at the very least, before they arrive in Barley. Tell no one that I have spoken with you or what it is that you go to do, else Galatus may be forewarned! Find him as soon as you can. Kill him! My time is up! I will try to talk to you again if I can. I love you! Be careful!"

Robby faded altogether, and Mirabella woke up instantly. Indeed, she found Frizella at the infirmary across the yard. The Bosk woman was very unhappy to hear that Mirabella might not be leading the men against Vidican.

"I may only be gone for a day or two, if I go," she explained.

"But whar to?" Frizella demanded.

"I can't tell you that. And I don't know when I'll have to go or if I'll be back in time. Makeig is sending Winterford along soon, and I must go up into the hills with him. I'll tell him to prepare to act without me, but I want you to tell him the same."

"He ain't gonna be happy 'bout that! Makeig, neither! An' I don't have a lot of patience this mornin', what with Mrs. Painmoor's antics keepin' me up all night tryin' to convince her the difference 'tween indigestion an' consumption, an' us tryin' to get them Redvest things ready. What's so important that can't wait 'til after things settle down? No! Wait. I don't want to know what ye've got in mind to do. Do I?"

"No. But I'll see you before I leave. If I leave. I'm undecided, still."

Frizella just shook her head as Mirabella left the room.

As the day progressed the dream continued to nag her. There were countless details to take care of if they were to succeed in their plans and defy Vidican's army. And the preparations for Makeig's special task were almost done. Her day was filled with riding here and there, up into the hills with Winterford to watch Vidican's scouts, to guide fighters secretly to the places where they were to hide, and back to Janhaven to help urge the people to leave their homes and come to the stockade. All day, though, the dream worried her, and it vexed her that it had such power to distract her from her duties. When at last she turned in for the night, knowing she sorely needed her rest for the days ahead, she tossed and turned until at last she did sleep. And there was Galatus, once again.

This time, he showed up in Tallinvale, as she dreamed of roaming about her gardens there. He dogged her steps, and finally came up to her and asked, "Mirabella Tallin, how many men, truly, are at the Narrows now? There can hardly be room enough for them behind the fortifications, can there?"

She woke instantly. Flinging off her covers, she threw on her clothes and went to see Frizella, who was already at work before dawn, making bandages in anticipation of the inevitable wounded.

"I suppose yer here to tell me yer goin' off on yer errand?" she said before Mirabella could speak.

"Yes." Mirabella smiled and nodded. "I've wasted a day, and put much at risk. So I am leaving right away. If I don't come back soon, don't waste time or effort looking for me. Take care of things here, and see to it that Winterford leads the men. Makeig is to do as we planned. I'll be back as soon as I can."

"Now, just hold on, dearie! Put what at risk?"

"Don't dearie me, Frizzy. I have to go! And you should get some sleep."

Though she intended to go on foot, she took Anerath by the reins, without his saddle, and led him outside the stockade. At the crossroads, where the road from Janhaven led east toward Passdale, she halted.

"You've been a good friend," she said to him, removing his bridle. "Now, though I'm sure you'd do anything I ask of you, I set you free to make your own way. Go! Go back home, if you wish. I know you can find your way. Give your back to those you wish to, and may Beras look after you."

Anerath looked at Mirabella, and nudged her on the cheek. Smiling, she nodded. "Go, now. And be a good friend to another."

He turned and cantered off a few yards, then turned his head and looked back at her. He whinnied, reared up, and galloped away along the west-leading road. Mirabella entered the woods and tossed the bridle away.

• • •

Still unaware that he was being followed, the Redvest scout jogged down the wooded hill behind the Common House and into the broad back yard where Ullin had once drilled his militia. At the side yard, the bell tower stood, and beside it a makeshift corral kept horses at the ready. One, a black stallion, Mirabella recognized as General Vidican's, having seen the general astride him across the Bentwide while meeting with her husband just before the assault on Passdale. Since his horse was not saddled, she surmised that he had probably made the place his quarters, as Robby had indicated. On the back stoop of the Common House were posted two sentries, and there were several more, some patrolling around the yard and others near the horses. Their presence further convinced her that Vidican was within the Common House. She was not sure that was a good thing. Only a true military man would forego the comforts of a real bedroom in one of the houses nearby, which spoke to Vidican's character and, likely, his intentions not to allow spoils or comfort to distract him from his duty. Bad for Barley and Passdale. But if Vidican was there, then Galatus must be there, too.

Taking this in, she moved carefully along the edge of the wood overlooking the yard until she could see a portion of the front of the Common House where more sentries were posted. She saw no way of stealing past the guards and into the Common House, so she continued down the hill a few yards, keeping low behind the brush between the trees, until she could see both the front and the back yards of the place. She thought she might steal into the corral, past the bell tower, and sneak into the Common House. But now she saw too many guards around the horses. Soon it would be dark. Perhaps some chance would present itself. Settling down inside a thick covering of wisteria, she decided to wait and watch. If no chance came by morning, she determined, she would have to make her own opportunity.

Throughout the night, she watched the Common House. Large parties of soldiers came and went, and rank after rank marched west along the road. She knew that they were not moving to the Narrows, but would turn off toward Wayford Common. As she watched the intermittent traffic, she came to believe that they would likely assemble and camp at the Common overnight, since there was an old trail nearby that led southwest through the hills and passed close to the troll caves. Likely, they would march at dawn. That meant she had little time to locate Galatus. Or perhaps he would not be joining Vidican's men. Either way, she needed an opportunity to get inside the Common House, but she failed to see one all night long.

Her chance did not come until daybreak. Several soldiers began the business of putting saddles and bridles on the horses, including Vidican's stallion. Seeing this, Mirabella moved quickly, notching an arrow as she edged down the slope and closer. And as luck would have it, Vidican was impatient to begin the day. Mirabella saw him come out of the Common House, trailed by several of his captains, all in full battle attire. With them was a plainly dressed man in a black tunic wearing a broad-rimmed hat. It was Galatus.

With practiced stealth, Mirabella closed the distance, advancing a little more downhill until she found a good spot overlooking her quarry as the Redvests noisily talked and laughed while Vidican's horse was led out of the corral. Galatus stood next to Vidican, looking unhappy. She took a deep breath, held it, and aimed. She heard something crack, and felt a burning stab run through her thigh. Stifling a scream, she rolled over as another arrow grazed her shoulder and glanced off the tree beside her. Turning, she saw her attacker, a scout barely visible in the predawn light, quickly closing in on her, crouching to move under low branches as he whipped another arrow from his quiver and notched it. She aimed and shot, and their arrows flew past each other, both finding their marks. The scout careened sideways, lost his balance, and crashed face down into a bank of snow. Still, Mirabella did not scream. Notching another arrow, she turned to the Common House, drew back on the string, and let it go. It passed almost entirely through the neck of Galatus and deep into Vidican's forearm, pinning the two together as Galatus fell against his general. On the verge of fainting, she spat blood from her mouth, quickly drew another arrow and finished Vidican with it. Satisfied that this was as much damage as she could do to the enemy, she smiled painfully and tried to stand, but she staggered backwards against the tree trunk, lost her balance, then slid down into a sitting position with her back against the tree. Putting her bow across her lap, she looked absently at the arrow in her thigh, then at the one in her chest.

Time grew thick, and its flow labored like sap. All sound abated but the long ringing toll in her ears, and her vision narrowed as darkness pushed in from all sides. A thousand thoughts pressed through her head as it tilted heavily downward, then they, too, halted. She struggled to remember something, anything at all, perplexed at her muddled state. Ironically, it was not her wounds that hurt the most, but the throbbing burn of the scars that ran down her back. Then, very quickly, all pain faded.

Sir Sun, climbing the stairs of morning, shot a narrow ray of glowing yellow through the dense canopy to scatter off the golden wedding band on Mirabella's finger. She stared at the fiery glint, unable to move her head or to close her eyes, even when she could see it no more. A moment later, a single tear fell on her ring, as if to extinguish the flame that glittered there, and the light faded. Sir Sun turned his attention elsewhere into the day that broadened before his stride.

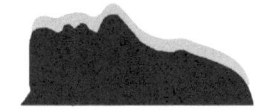

Chapter 17
A River of Memories

Robby hoped that he was not making a terrible mistake. He felt his heart speed up and slow down, there was an odd ringing in his ears, and he had to remind himself to breathe. He felt sleep coming, but it was not the usual sensation of drowsiness. This was much deeper, blacker, and irresistible. It was as if some creature covered him with thick blankets. A spasm of fear shot through him. Trying to open his eyes, he was barely able to squint before they shut with an awful finality. His heart thumped, paused, then thumped once more. A long moment came when he wondered if it would beat again.

"So this, then, is death," he thought.

Another spasm of panic gripped him and, suddenly, he was standing up, blinking down at his body. He leaned over, looking at himself curiously, and the pallor of his skin frightened him. A powerful urge gripped him to return, to wake up, to not give up his life in this way, and he even reached down to wake himself. His body took a deep, gasping breath, and Robby recoiled.

"No," he said to himself. "I must go through with this. As far as I can go, anyway."

He turned his attention briefly to his surroundings, seeing through the walls that Ullin was still outside. He then heard what he hoped he would hear. Turning his attention to the snowbank some few yards away, he saw her. Her form was hideous, and her song grated like metal scraping against stone. But he had heard it twice before, and he no longer feared her or her song. She saw him and her song instantly became less loathsome and her appearance less onerous. Hardly noticing the panic that Ullin was now in, flying into the hut and trying to wake him up, he approached to within two or three yards of the banshee. She was, in fact, the most beautiful creature he had ever laid eyes on, and her song was sweet and lovely. She turned and beckoned him to follow, still singing.

A portal appeared, outlined in white light, and through the gate was nothing but the blackest darkness. The banshee turned, standing before the portal, and ceased her song. She gazed at him with wonder in her eyes.

"Who are you?" Robby asked. "And what is this place?"

"What place? This is the gate which is called Death by thy people," she replied. "I? I am Caparrashee, Shee of thy blood and that of thy fathers, come to bring thee to the gate which leads to the life that is after life, to fetch thee as I have done all those of thy blood who have gone before thee. But whereof art thou? What manner of creature art thou? Dead thou art, but not gone from life? Alive thou art, but without the breath of the living? Have I been deceived? Unless thou art dead, the afterlife will not open to thee. And unless thou art living, I cannot send thee back."

"Do you not recognize me? Twice before, we have met. The first time when I was a babe. The second time was some while back. It was you who said we would meet again."

There was a distant hum as the apparition studied Robby.

"Thy countenance hast changed. Thou dost not wear the body of the living, nor of the dead, yet I do see thee, now, dimly as though a vapor. What manner of creature hast thou become that thou hast the power to trick me to bring thee here?"

"I am a dreamwalker, come to you in the spirit of death's dream, to enter into this place, and to find one of my forebears who has gone in before me."

"These gates are sealed to thee and to any but the dead. I cannot open them, nor may I shut them. I am appointed to accompany the dead of thy father's bloodline until I am no longer required, when they have joined with the spirits of thine ancestors, or have found their own way."

"That is all I require of you. To show me to the one who was known in life as Balfast Ribbon, whom you brought forth from life to this place twenty-one years ago, by the reckoning of the living."

"Here there are no names, for all are known by whosoever they art and not by what name they were called in life. Still I am perplexed. Thou hast the aura of Aperion's people about thee, yet thou hast not been Scathed, nor have the wings of the Unscathed."

"But I have the touch that will unbind the locks upon that portal."

"Such a thing is not permitted!"

"I do not come to release any who are kept here."

"This is no prison. Those within may depart from this place whenever they desire. It is life that is a prison. These locks bar only those still shackled to life, for within this place no shackles are known, no chain binds, and no passage is obstructed."

"Then stand aside, and I will enter to fulfill my quest and find the one I seek. Afterwards, I shall depart from this place and return again only when I am called by you."

She moved aside, and Robby approached the gate. But he turned to her and asked, "What do you usually say to those you bring here?"

"There is no need of words unless asked for. Then I answer them."

"The song that you sing. Is it your own?"

"No. It is given to me by thine ancestors, as thou mayst soon learn. I am thy Shee and the Shee of thy people. I am made of their memories, and I sing them."

"At first, your song frightened me, and I was repelled by its tone in my ears and by the way it charged my heart with anxiety. But then, as you took up new verses, I no longer felt that way, and the sound of your voice did not hurt my ears. At last, I felt comfort from your lyrics and was strongly attracted by the sweetness of your voice."

"It is the way of my kind and the form of all the songs of the Shee. We sing first of pain and of suffering. This is to repulse the spirit from these gates and to strengthen the resolve to stay within the body if the body possesses the strength to keep the spirit. Many times we may begin our tune during one's life, but often the spirit is not ready or the body regains its hold upon it, and our presence is not required. But if we remain singing, then we sing of the ordinary things of the life of those who passed before and sing no more of pain or torment. This is to remove the fear from the spirit so that, if willing, it may linger in the body until the body weakens its grip. At last, we sing of those sweet things of life, of the warmth of love and friendship, of the gifts of life and the boundless nature of existence. This is to reassure the spirit that its suffering is not lasting and that the familiar prison of the body is just so."

"Your words were not in the First Tongue, and I did not understand you as I do now," Robby said. "Yet they did affect me in the way you describe."

"We do not sing words. Our lyrics art made of the things themselves, and not of the symbols that the living uses for things."

"That is a mysterious thing to say." As curious as Robby was, he knew he had little time, perhaps only a few hours. "Will you be my guide?"

"I am obliged to guide to this place any that I summon, then to shew them to this entrance. But, be warned: Once thou enter, thou mayst never wish to leave by the way thou came."

"By the way I came? Do you mean back into life?"

"If that is what thou sayest. Or back into prison, as it surely is. And why should thy prison, thy body in life, call thee back? How can it, if it be dead, as all bodies that release their spirits must be."

Robby understood what she meant, but smiled at his trick. She did not understand his ability, and that was what he counted on. The urge to move on, to go through the gate, was powerful, and the power of it had little to do with why he came, but was mighty of itself. It pulled him and filled him with excitement and anticipation, irrationally, unreasonably tugging with a joyous gravity, the most natural force he had ever felt. How, indeed, could he want anything other than to go through it? The yearning made him understand something more of what the banshee had said, like someone standing at the edge of freedom.

"Is there any other way out?"

"There is every other way out. But only this gate leads to where thou came from."

"Have any others done this before me? That is, come before you as I have done?"

"None of thy blood."

"What of those not of my blood?"

Caparrashee thought about the question. She closed her eyes and sang in her wordless way a short melody, raising her hand for Robby to wait. What she sang was the question itself. She concluded her brief song and tilted her head to listen to a voice coming from within the gate, joined by many other voices, singing in reply, each giving a short, lyrical refrain. When the voices faded, she lowered her hand and opened her eyes.

"Yes. There have been others, but very few. And the mystery of how they came and went remains a puzzle to my sisters."

Robby nodded, turned back to the door, and reached out for it, but he hesitated once more.

"Then this is heaven?"

"There art many words in the tongues of the living that may describe this place. Yes, then. It is part of heaven. But, no. It is not heaven as thou mayst been taught. Perhaps it shall be to thee as a crossroad. Perhaps thou mayst know it as a courtyard, or even a workshop. Whatsoever thou bethink it now will not be the same as after thou pass through the gate. And I cannot say or even guess what it mayst be like to thee, for I perceive things differently."

"Well, then," Robby said, sending what he thought might be his last glimpse toward the light of his body, which was already being moved out of the hut by Finn while Ullin slept. "It is time to find out."

He touched the gate and it sent a shock through his whole being. For an eternal moment, his ears were filled with silence, his eyes could see nothing, he felt nothing, no sensation whatsoever. He lost all thought, all knowledge of his surroundings, and any notion of what was himself and what was not himself. All was colorless, notionless, motionless, silent, and dark.

• • •

In a gentle rush, it all came back. Though his eyes were closed, he sensed the light come, white and tangible, flowing around and past him, gently pushing and tugging, as if he stood shoulder high in the midst of a broad shallow river that stretched from eternity to eternity. The sensation eased, and the white encompassing river receded. His thoughts were fresh, and he knew he was where he needed to be. He sensed birds tittering and singing in the distance, and he heard a breeze softly rustling green leaves. He felt the moving air on his beard and the invigorating warmth of the sun on his face, and he opened his eyes and smiled, not surprised in the least at what he saw.

Perfect peace is not perfect stillness. It is not perfect contentment. Nor is it perfect understanding or perfect acceptance. It does not come with the perfect knowledge of any thing, or with perfect resolve about any thing. Perfect peace may only occur when all these things—stillness, contentment, resolve, knowledge, understanding, and acceptance—all happen and are in just the right balance and blend, each striking their notes upon the right pitch with the right strength, to form the perfect chord of wisdom. Robby now understood this and knew that the chord he now felt would shift and turn, emphasizing each note as required, one greater or lesser than another, as the song of this place unfolded. But the chord would remain.

He opened his eyes and looked straight at Sir Sun, gazing without fear at his face, and it did not burn or hurt him in the least as he watched his mighty fires and colossal flames shoot up over the infernal churning of his golden skin. And he appreciated it.

Robby smiled and looked around. Sensing where he should go, he started off down a path through the fields of this Barley. He walked for about a mile along the path, crossing over one of the higher hills. In some places he could see the Bentwide down through the trees off to his left. There were no buildings across the river, and no need of them. For though the fields he passed were neatly planted, the green stalks nearly to his knees, there was no sign of cottages and no activity where one might otherwise expect to see it. Robby did not expect to see such things, and he was not at all surprised by the absence of toilers. There were more trees in this Barley, and the woods were thicker and greener in places where, he remembered, farmsteads sat and roads were cut. But none of these trees had ever known such intrusions, and as he followed the curving path down toward the Bentwide, the air was full of the vibrant and woody scent of growth. Birds cared not for his passage, and rabbits, pulling tender shoots and chewing their delicious greens, watched him mildly and without the least alarm. Robby did not expect them to be afraid, and when they did scamper away, it was with playful binkies and delightful sprints and turnabouts, to show him they were happy and full of joy.

He knew who it was that he was to meet here, and though he did not know how he would recognize him, he knew that he would. As the path turned downward sharply through the trees, it forked. There he stopped, seeing a boy farther down on the left-hand path. This he did not expect, although the surprise was pleasant. The boy looked to be about ten or twelve, wearing simple breeches tied with a rope. The sleeves of his blouse were rolled up above his elbows, and he sat crosslegged on a rock that jutted out into the broad river. A fishing pole was in his hands, and the line from it was gently tugged by the cork at the end as it floated downstream. He had his suntanned face tilted back, his eyes closed at the sun, and his curly black hair was softly tousled by the breeze.

Robby looked on down the path, which now seemed to urge him to follow it on, and then back at the boy. He felt an equal urge to go join the fellow's company. He sensed, too, the faraway press of time, which was meaningless here, but then he realized that it did not matter which path he took. All paths here, he understood, rang with the same chord. Only the notes were differently played.

So he went down the left-hand path. Coming to the bank, Robby gingerly stepped out onto a rock a few yards upstream of the boy and sat down. He remembered the many times he had fished with Sheila, sometimes so content that he let the line stay long after his bait had been stolen by a hook-wise fish. He did not wish to disturb the boy's contentment. So he waited.

"I only ever caught one fish here," said the boy, turning his head to smile at Robby. "An' it whar a big'un, an' a battle royale! Pulled me clean off this rock an' nearly drowned me, thrashin' an' circlin' 'round, gettin' me line all tangled an' wrapped 'round me legs. But I pulled an' pulled. An' he pulled back, takin' me way on down yonderways, a-fightin' all the way, too. A wonder the line didn't break 'er tear off me hands."

"Well," he said, shifting his position to give the pole a little jiggle. "It went on an' on 'til I swallered purty near half the river, it seemed. But at last I got him by the gills. I reckon he was just about as tuckered out as me when I started in to'ard the bank. That was way down thar, near the bend yonder. So when I gets up to whar the water's at me waist, an' I cough me air back into meself, I seen what a jumbo he was, indeed! An' he looked at me an' said, as clear as day, 'If ye let me go, I'll give ye a wish.' "

The boy nodded at Robby, and kept nodding as he continued, "An' I said back to him, 'What could I wish for, 'cept a fine supper, which now I have?' An' he says back, 'I know Men love gold, in rings an' in coin, an' in all manner of form. If ye lemme go,' says he, 'I'll grant ye as much as yer weight of it.' So I says, 'What would I do with all that gold? What could I want that I don't already have comin' to me?' An' he says back to me, 'I know Men crave power over others, to make 'em do thar biddin' an' be held in esteem.' "

The boy pulled up his line, dangling an empty hook. Grasping it to the pole, he stood and hopped over to Robby to sit next to him, talking as he approached.

" 'An' if ye lemme go,' says the fish, 'I'll see to it ye become a mighty lord.' So I says to him, 'I already got the power I need over me own self. What business is it of mine to make others do for me what I kin do for meself? An' what would I want done that I can't do by me own self?' An' without battin' an eyelid, he says, 'I know Men love dry land, to make their fields an' homes on. If ye lemme go, I'll grant to ye vast acres.' An' I says back, 'me daddy's already got ye beat on that one. What's his is mine, an' that's as much as I'll ever want 'er need.' Now, by this time, I'd got right up near the bank an' was gettin' me grip to sling the great fish up thar. But he says, 'What, then, may I grant thee, so that ye'll let go of me so I can continue on me long course to the sea?' Well, I'm not a rash feller, so I stopped what I was doin' an' thought on it for a long while. I gave it good thought, but not easing me grip one little bit while thinkin' on the question. So, then I says to him, 'Well, thar's one thing I'm a hankerin' to do.' 'Tell me,' he says, 'an' that will be yer boon.' So I told him what it whar, an' he says, 'Ye shall do it. Let go of me, an' it shall be fulfilled.' So I did. An' off he went."

The boy gestured downstream. Robby could hear the swirl and gurgle of the water as the great creature receded.

"Many, many years later, me wish was fulfilled, though not in the manner I might've expected."

Robby was enjoying every aspect of the tale, the setting, the teller, and the familiar way the boy spoke, everything about it. Even though he knew exactly what the boy was going to say, he let it come, grinning with happiness.

"So," the boy went on, "when years went on by, an' as the end of me time approached, I remembered the fish an' its promise, an' I got suspicious that the ol' feller had tricked me for its life. But what I told that fish was that I had a wish to see the King all for meself, an' mebbe have a little chat, just him an' me, for just a little spell. An', as the song what beckoned me here got sweeter an' sweeter, 'at's just what happened. The King came to see me, 'an I had me a little private chat with him, 'an it whar the King's own eyes that I last beheld, afore me own closed an' I came away with the banshee."

The boy smiled at Robby and nodded. "An' that's why I've been awaitin'. An' it ain't a bad place to wait. Don't even seem like yesterday that I got here. But!" He slapped his knee and rose to his feet, and Robby stood with him. "I reckon I best be movin' on. Got things to do, ye know."

"I suppose I should be going, too."

"Yep. I expect ye got a great deal of business."

"Yes, sir. I do, indeed."

"If ye can pass it along, if or when ye ever see me grandson, tell him what a fine man he turned out to be, an' what a fine boy he raised. Tell him how proud of him I always was an' still am. An' tell 'im his mum an' his pop, are proud, too. Might help him to know."

"I will if I can."

"Well, then. Be strong, an' do right."

"Yes, sir. I will try my best."

"I know ye will. An' since yer resolved to do so, I'll say yer name out loud, an' give ye what ye came for an' more, I think. Are ye ready?"

"As ready as I will ever be."

• • •

So it was told to him. His own true name. That was not all, not just the word. As the sound of it echoed in his mind, it was as if a new gate was opened. Not just the name flowed in, but so much more besides. In fact, nearly everything. Robby did not expect this, could not suspect it could be like this. He immediately understood that it could be no other way.

In came all of the moments of his great-grandfather's life, and simultaneously came all of the moments of his grandparents, who died shortly after Robigor, Robby's father, was born. And came as well his own mother's life and his father's, too, and every person whose blood ran through his veins, and every thought and every dream and every feeling each of them ever had. He, through his ancestors, was now asking Lord Tallin for the hand of his daughter, Mirabella, and was also hearing through Lord Tallin's ears those words. Robby was with his great-grandfather as he plowed the fields of Barley, as he watched his own children die of fever, as he took up his son's son to raise, as he showed his grandson how to harness a mule, and how to plane a board smooth. Robby was with them both when the baby was given and taken to be named, hearing the call of the banshee in the storm outside the cottage. He was with Mirabella at the moment of her Scathing, with her in battle, and with her as she cradled her dying brother. He was with Mirabella's great-grandmother as she fell from the sky, her wings stricken from her. With his Mortal ancestors, watching their lands sink into the sea, laboring to keep their great ships afloat. And when their descendants first stepped ashore in this new world, Robby was with them, too. And he was with his Elifaen ancestors, hiding in the seaside forest, watching these Newcomers struggle to walk on unshifting ground. Robby, in the memory of one forebear, pushed aside a leafy branch, and he was filled with wonder and trepidation at the strange folk and their ships. And he was, at the same time, brimming with hope and caution as he took his first ever steps out from the surf and onto terra firma.

Thus, a mighty river was opened on every side from the moment of his birth backwards into time, each person's experiences stepping up from every direction, mother and father, to uncles and aunts, and distant cousins unknown until now. Through each of them, and all at once, like the universe within a droplet of water, and in the steady voice of a vast flood, they each and all came and sang their lives to him. There was no longer any difference between he and they. He, barefooted, moved along an ice-covered rope to free a whipping sail high over churning waters. He felt the soil, pressing it in his hands to judge if planting time was here. His feelings were hurt by unkind words. His heart sank at the sight of a broken sword in his hand, just when it was needed the most. He felt fear and joy in a thousand ways, and the peace of true love, too. He came into birth and went into death, violently and with awe, defiantly and with joy, weakly and with pride, and a thousand other ways. He was humiliated and gratified, resolved and unsure, and filled with all of the moments of wonder and delight a person could know.

• • •

"Well, thar ye have it," said the boy to Robby. "Good to see ye! An', of course, I'll be seein' ye again!"

"Until then." Robby grinned so as not to cry.

Then, as if the universe heaved a mighty sigh, it all began to fade. Pain returned to his chest as a hammer struck his heart. The river of memories flooded away, and Robby fought against it, his spirit desperately grasping at the receding tide. His heart hammered again, like a gavel's signal. Life called him back. Crying out, he gasped for air and sat up.

Finn was there, holding his shoulders, but Robby was momentarily too weak to say anything as Finn lowered Robby back onto the pillows. With his eyes open, Robby smiled and wept at the same time. At the foot of his bed was Caparrashee. Finn was not frightened of her, though her appearance to him was hideous and world-bending. To his ears her chirping was raspy and horrible, but to Robby she sang sweetly of admiration and of honor. Bowing to Robby, she let the light from the window pass through her, and through her song, too, as she and her voice faded from the room.

"Welcome home to Griferis, my lord," said Finn. "Rest easy, and all will be provided to you."

"Yes," Robby said through his tears. "A fine palace we shall make of it, too."

"Yes, my lord."

"And, Finn, won't you tell Celia that I'll soon wish to have a hand of cards with her?"

"Certainly. She will be pleased, I'm sure."

"And, Finn, you and I have a lot to discuss."

"I look forward to it, my lord."

"Philawain. My right name is Philawain."

"Yes, Lord Philawain."

"No. Just Philawain. I was named after one of my ancient forebears."

"Yes, sir."

"But first, I need to take care of some business, long put off. That is to say, I need to sleep!"

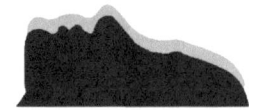

Chapter 18

Swyncraff's New Master

Ullin, exhausted by despair, was still asleep, slumped against the wall beside the hearth. At first, it was a deep sleep, with no dreams, no anxieties, and no grief. Eventually, a dream slowly formed and took on its substance, one that was stranger than any he had ever known before, even though it was in many ways quite ordinary.

In this dream, Ullin went about the final preparations for a long journey. It was a mundane task to him, having done it so many times, but one in which he took great pride and comfort. Spirited Anerath waited patiently, hardly able to contain his excitement, ready to get out of the stables and upon the open road. Ullin checked the cinches, straps, and harnesses of the saddle, retying his saddlebags, and stroking the good horse on his neck and patting him on his shoulders. It was a bright morning with yellow light streaming in from the high windows of the stables, with the smell of horseflesh, oats, saddle leather, and hay in the air. There was the usual hubbub of talk and noise, as other Post Riders came and went, making their preparations for their routes just as Ullin and Anerath did. Elsewhere nearby, other horses were being groomed, or were being led to or back from the farrier. Ullin was calm and did what he had to do with practiced attention. Everything was as it should be, and he was happy that it was so. It was almost a normal, ordinary morning.

What was out of the ordinary, what was strange and uncanny, was that Ullin knew he was dreaming. He did not mind. And he knew other things, besides. He knew that Robby's death was a tragic catastrophe. That when he awoke from this dream, he must somehow face that disaster. Now alone, Ullin knew that he could hardly expect to find his way out of Shatuum alive, and he did not really think there was much point in trying. And he knew that he was being watched by someone standing very nearby, someone who had not yet spoken, and who did not try to attract his attention, as if to let him have these moments of simple peace. Ullin continued his preparations. Sleep would pass soon enough. There was no need for haste. He sighed, giving Anerath another affectionate pat.

"He is handsome," Ullin stated. "Don't you think?"

"Yes," she replied. "I have long thought so."

He accepted what she said, knowing that she had never seen the horse before—there was no way she could have—but somehow knowing, too, that she spoke truthfully, as she always did.

"It has been a long time since I have seen you, even in my dreams."

"Yes. The last time our dreams touched was the morning you reached Passdale. The day Robby set out for Tulith Attis. He woke you from our dream, stumbling over your legs as you slept on the front porch of his family's store."

Ullin nodded, buckling up the flap on a saddlebag. He paused, then he turned to her, standing not two yards away. She was dressed in the same garb as when they had first met, far away in the deserts of the south. He was pleased that no one in the stables gave her much notice and passed by the Dragonkind woman as if she was a common sight.

"Why do you come to me now?" he heard himself asking. "Now, at the time of my greatest shame? To gloat over my failures? To take your spite for my infidelity?"

"No, no, Ullin Saheed. That is not why. You could not have resisted Esildre's curse any more than I could have. The shadow that she is cursed with took hold of you, according to its nature. I know that, now. I have looked upon her dreams, and I have seen her torment as I have seen her longing to be free of it. You have no need of forgiveness, nor should you be ashamed before me. I have more need of your forgiveness than you have of mine. I should have known your heart better. It is the source of the shadow that is to be hated. Secundur. I am sorry that I ignored you for so long, and stayed away from your heart and from your dreams. I know now how lonely you are. And I should have known that you longed for my company more than any other's. I was careless and foolish. Then, when you were with Esildre, I became angry. I was wrong, and I am sorry."

Her words gripped his heart.

"You were certainly justified," he began, but his heart thumped suddenly into his throat as he held onto the saddle with one hand and clutched Anerath's mane with the other, looking at Micerea through a suddenly blurry vision. "But now all is lost. Our quest is ended. Robby is dead! I failed him! Just as I failed you!"

"No, you have not failed! Robby's first quest has ended, but yours has just begun. I see this, now. I, too, was misled by my own desires, by my own misunderstanding of Robby. But he has done what was necessary for him to do, and he wishes for you to have patience and also some hope."

Micerea stepped closer to Ullin, speaking earnestly to him. She put her hand up on his, and his grip of Anerath's mane eased somewhat at her touch.

"He desires that you go to Nasakeeria and be his representative to those who live there."

"How can you know that? How do you know what he desires?"

"Because I have told her so."

Ullin straightened and looked over the saddle and saw Robby standing on the other side of Anerath, stroking the horse's neck with one hand whilst offering him an apple with the other. Robby smiled at Ullin, making Ullin's heart pound the more furiously, now, tears welling up in his eyes as he felt Micerea's hand clutch his even more firmly. While Anerath crunched on the apple, Ullin struggled to find his voice.

"My madness takes a new turn!" he croaked. "I know that I dream, and that this vision is not real. Do I need comfort so desperately that I conjure this vision from my soul? Who else that I have lost will now come to me? Even my faithful steed is here! Where is my father? Where is my uncle?"

With her other hand, Micerea took hold of Ullin's arm, smiling and shaking her head, saying, "No, no, my love! Let it be what it is for you, a comfort, the beginning of healing. This is no dream of idleness, no dream of fever or madness. We are here, truly, Robby and I, with you now. All else may be an illusion, but we are not. Can you not feel that what I say is true? Dear, dear Ullin!"

Ullin buried his head in Micerea's shoulder and wept. It seemed a long time, but it was not, for hardly a snowflake had fallen from the time Ullin had fallen asleep until now. Robby walked around Anerath and took Ullin's hand and put it on his chest.

"Do you feel? My heart still beats. Trust in faith, and listen: I haven't much time. There is much that I have kept from you, from everyone. I did so for my own protection and to protect others. The world is on the brink, and things are far worse than you imagine. Secundur gathers together a force the likes of which the world has never known. Witches, demons, goblins, all united under his rule. You remember what Seafar showed us. There are others, even more terrible, and in great numbers. Soon they will no longer be contained within Shatuum. Secundur has discovered the secret of breeding them. And he has groomed a mighty general to lead them. Already Secundur probes, and, as he ever has, he works his dark intrigues to prepare the way. Soon the world will be torn asunder by war, and at its height Secundur will release his servants to foment a chaos that will overwhelm all people, all things. The fate of Barley and Tallinvale are but trifles, and are only his opening moves, made by those who do not even know how they are used."

There was something in the way Robby spoke to Ullin that aroused the Kingsman's respect and attention. There was authority. Certainty. A kind of power. He could not but listen. He could not but strive to heed.

"Hear me, Ullin Saheed! There are places that even Secundur cannot go. Things that he cannot delve. Things beyond his comprehension or imagining. Remember Greenfar? And the little ones of Nowhere? Remember the place where you were shown water by the rabbit? In the middle of an arid desert? Recall, too, the peace granted to you by the visions of Islindia. It is from those places and out of such things that his downfall will come. Others will play their part, too. It will not be easy. Much will be lost. Many will die. And the world must be remade."

In spite of the dire words, Ullin felt peaceful. Looking around, taking in the busy stable, then looking long and deeply into Micerea's eyes, he nodded.

"I may be mad, but why should I care?" he said. "Robby, what is all this about going to Nasakeeria?"

"When you wake," Robby instructed, "go back to the gate upon the summit, the gate of Griferis. Take as much rope and coal as you can carry, and the tools and gear that you may need for ice and snow. But, most importantly, take my vest. Sewn within it are things of great power. If possible, wear it so that it will not be lost. When you get to the great chasm, look down and you will see a way out of Shatuum. Follow the way north. Go first to the Temple of Beras. Be there before the first day of spring. I will tell you what to do after you arrive. Micerea will help you and will give you my instructions if I cannot do so. As a sign of trust, so that you know this to be real, I give you Swyncraff, to be yours and to serve you. Reach out to Swyncraff, call his name, and he will spring to you."

Robby wiped his hands together to rub off the juice from the apple, and Anerath shook his head in thanks.

"Do you understand?"

"Yes. To the chasm. I will see the way. Take your vest. Call to Swyncraff. Go to the Temple of Beras."

"Good. It will be dangerous. Be careful. I'll leave you two, now. But we shall see each other again!"

Ullin watched Robby walk through the doors of the stable and disappear out of sight. Blinking, he turned back to Micerea, smiling as she stroked Anerath's neck.

"You will soon wake," she said. "I know you don't yet trust all of this, but you will very soon. Robby has shown me so much, and has explained many things to me. Now it is my turn to share some of those things with you. But first, tell me, would Anerath object to carrying two?"

Now the dream really began, and when Ullin rode out of the stable with Micerea astride behind him with her arms around him, the door magically led not into the streets of Duinnor, but out across the northern plains, so beautiful in the spring with new grass and wildflowers. They rode until they came to a stream and dismounted, holding hands as they walked along its banks while Anerath danced in the water. Ullin and Micerea laughed at his antics. They kissed.

• • •

Ullin reluctantly woke under a pile of blankets. Sitting up, he did not remember having bundled up. The fire had burned to only a few glowing coals, and as he rubbed the sleep from his eyes and blinked in the dim light, he sighed, then turned his head to look at Robby. But Robby was gone. Flinging off the blankets and leaping to his feet, he stared at the place where he had last seen Robby's body. There, neatly laid out beside his backpack, was Robby's vest. Staring at the spot where Robby died, he was filled with panic, thinking perhaps that Robby's body had been stolen by creatures of Secundur. Ullin grabbed up one of the ice axes and looked at the door.

"But why would they not kill me?" he asked aloud. "Or take me as a captive?"

Icy tracks led back and forth from the doorway to where Robby's body had been. Rushing outside, he trained his eyes upon the snow and clearly saw the tracks of one person leading to the cottage door, and two sets of tracks trailing off. He slowly followed, seeing that the two pairs of footprints were very close together, side by side. Ullin wondered at that as he continued on until he saw a scuffing in the snow. He paused, and his brow furrowed as he examined the markings. The signs were clear: One of the people had stumbled and fallen to his knees, and the other had stopped to help. Looking up, he now understood that the tracks led toward Griferis, and he began to understand the meaning of things. Abruptly, he turned and hurried back to the cottage.

Once inside, he rummaged in his coat pocket for a firestick, and he drew out the tin, along with a scrap of paper that fluttered to the floor. Ullin saw it, but turned his attention to relighting the fire, putting some twigs under the lit firestick and then a few lumps of coal. Once the fire was going, and throwing its light across the room, he turned back to better examine things. The place where Robby had lain was just as it was before, neatly arranged. It was as if Robby had just risen from a night's sleep, and had prepared his things for the day's journey, just as always. And someone had come to help Robby return to Griferis.

"What was the name? Finn?"

A flash of hope shot through him at the thought. Then he saw Swyncraff leaning against the far wall, and, when he remembered the strange dream, he held out his hand.

"Swyncraff."

The thing flexed and flew through the air at Ullin. He flinched, but he caught it at arm's length, and froze in that position, looking askance at the magical rod. Then he broke into a grin, relaxing.

"I am Ullin," he said, looking at Swyncraff. "And I am very pleased to make your acquaintance!"

Laughing, he shook his head, almost delirious with joy.

"Unbelievable!"

Then he saw the scrap of paper at his feet, and he picked it up and uncrumpled it. It was the much crushed and often handled little scroll he had received at the Feast of Solstice. Tucking Swyncraff under his arm, he carefully opened it. The words were still there:

Out of unfounded grief, a longed-for reunion shall come.

Ullin stared at the writing as a heavy tear dropped from his eye onto his hand. But he was smiling. In fact, he was filled with a strange and inexplicable joy.

• • •

Within the hour, Ullin had donned Robby's vest beneath his blouse, and he had gathered all that he thought he could carry into a single backpack, including many pounds of coal. He carefully dressed for the cold, and struck out with several coils of rope over his shoulder. When he got to the gate, he gazed for a long time at the castle floating very far out over the chasm. No causeway connected it to land and, with no clouds or mists swirling, he saw that the castle rested on nothing whatsoever, no peak, no mountain jutting up from the depths of the chasm, nothing at all.

Working up his nerve, he carefully stepped closer to the precipitous drop, and looked down. After a moment, he edged closer.

"Oh, good grief, Robby!"

It was a sheer drop, and vertigo made him step back quickly, shaking his head.

"Robby, Robby, Robby!"

In spite of the cold, a nervous sweat broke out on his brow as he forced himself to the precipice once more to take another look, gazing straight down. He saw it, about a hundred feet below, a ledge or outcrop of some kind. Going back to the gate, he got out the ropes, tied an end securely around one of the uprights, and went back to the edge, getting down on his belly for a safer look, holding onto the rope for extra security. Yes, definitely a ledge. And it seemed to go northward as far as he could safely discern. Tossing the rope over, he watched it unravel. Good, it went beyond the ledge, so there was plenty. Pulling it up, he untied it, then passed it around the upright again, and tied together the two bitter ends. He looped it around his backpack and lowered it, lying on his belly to pay out the line. When the pack landed on the ledge, there were still several yards of rope left. Before he gave himself time to back out, he gripped the double line with both hands and crawled backwards over the side, descending as quickly as he could, never looking down. Before he realized it, his feet were on the ledge.

Still gripping the rope tightly, he sat down with his back against the cliff, panting. The mysterious castle that was Griferis was now somewhat above him, but as he looked at it, while his heart resumed a less excited beat, he could still not see anything supporting the place. As for the ledge on which he sat, it seemed sturdy and wide enough; the edge was another two yards beyond his sprawled out legs.

"How did Robby discover this?" he mused, slowly getting up. He untied the knot and pulled one of the ropes so that the other went up. Soon the rope was cascading downward in loops and curls and Ullin ducked his head to let it drape all over him. As he worked to neatly coil the rope and to tie it onto his pack, he kept looking northward along the seemingly precarious way he was instructed to follow.

"I wonder how far this ledge goes, and to where?"

A few minutes later, he had his backpack on, and with Swyncraff around his waist and an ice axe in each hand, he began his trek northward, a deadly drop to his left, and an unscalable wall on his right. It was no place to be caught in a storm, he knew. Or to encounter anyone coming the other way. Surely, Robby and Micerea had a plan for him, knew the risks and dangers, and felt he was up to the challenge. And so Ullin felt a new confidence, akin to joy, as he had not felt for years. In only a few hours, things had gone from crushing despair to mystical hope. As he picked his way along, thinking of Micerea and Robby, and the dream he had, he smiled.

"Come what may," he said aloud, "I will not let them down again."

Chapter 19

A Return to Passdale

"What d'ye mean, she ain't here?" Makeig bellowed.

"I mean she set out yesterday mornin' an' ain't come back," Frizella said. "She only told me to say that all're to carry on without her, just as was planned."

"Well, that's just dandy! An' who is to lead the men against the Redvests comin' up the old troll caves, eh? It's bad enough we told them Redvest agents Lord Tallin sent on that we'd be joinin' the Redvests in Tallinvale. When they smoke our broken word, they'll send a force for sure! I'm thinkin' we'd better put off goin' to Passdale, to help take care of Vidican's men once an' for all!"

"We do no such thing, puttin' off!" Frizella held her ground, and the others in the room—her nephews, Furaman, Winterford, and a crowd of other men—looked on, not daring to interrupt. Many in the room wore the red outfits of their enemy, ready to go on their special task but for this argument. It was disconcerting to many to see each other so dressed, but not nearly as strange to see as Makeig's appearance, clean-shaven, with his hair closely-cropped in military fashion. And it was somewhat uncanny that he was now wearing a Redvest general's outfit, complete with a blue-sashed sword in place of his usual cutlass, holding an ornate helmet under his arm that had been stolen for this purpose from those bivouacked around Tallinvale. Many of his men stared at him, for this reason, if not for any other. And they were amazed at the Bosk woman's stubbornness and her pluck, getting right up under the towering man's face.

"Now's the time, then," she went on, her face angry-red, "an' the opportunity ain't likely to get any better. All the horses are outfitted, the men done up in thar uniforms, an' ready to go! If them Passdale Redvests get wind of the counter'tack, they'll likely do terrible harm to our kin. Now, ye promised Mirabella right here in front of all, day 'fore yesterday. An' we done our part. What say ye? Are ye one to count on, or not?"

"Yer a hard woman, Frizella Bosk." Makeig shook his head, frowning. "Course I can be counted on, an' don't ye be sayin' such doubtful things to me face again, or I might forget yer a lady. Only it's me duty to ask, an' me duty to act. But the question still stands: Who's to lead the attack against Vidican's men?"

"I shall do it, Capt'n," said Winterford, stepping up. "It's one thing to lead an attack, straightforward ye may say, than to go trampsing into Passdale. An' I ain't no officer, nor could pass as one, sir. But ye got a fair chance to bully them Redvests the right way, with the frame to match yer bluster, sir, if ye don't mind me sayin' so. We can't let these folks down, not after all they've done to get ready. 'Sides, me an' Lady Mirabella spent the better part of a week last month, working it all out in case they found them caves, an' she put it to me to stand ready to lead in her place, if she should fall to the enemy in battle. An' now that it's down to it, the plannin' she did'll pay off, for certain."

"I'm glad ye say so, Winter," Frizella said, smiling at him. "Yer just who Mira told me to suggest."

"Ye realize the stakes, don't ye?" Makeig asked Winterford.

"Ain't a man amongst us what don't, Capt'n. So if they'll follow, I'll lead."

"I'll follow," said Lantin Rose.

"Me, too," said Drayworth, taking a lacey handkerchief from his sleeve and dabbing his nose. "And I'd be most joyful to do so."

"Aye, and me. Winterford knows them hills best of any!" called another man from the other side of the room.

"An' he done got all the signals arranged, too, ain't he?" put in another.

Makeig was already nodding, and putting his hand out to Winterford.

"Very well," he said. "It's settled. Then let us beat to quarters!"

"Aye-aye!"

"Aye!"

Amid a chorus of cheers, the men quickly pushed out into the stockade yard, most wearing Redvest uniforms, armor, and surcoats meticulously mended and repaired, taken from the dead that littered the hills and byways. Forty horses awaited these disguised men, who were mostly Passdalers, along with a few of the Hill Town folk who had knowledge of the ways of the Redvest army. Having trained for this action for over a month, Makeig was sure of the abilities of the men, at least as far as looking and riding somewhat like proper soldiers. But he still had doubts about their fighting skills, though those were much improved over the last couple of weeks of skirmishes and small battles. They did best behind bows and cover. Riding bold-faced into Passdale might be another matter, and close-quarters work would almost certainly be required.

As they mounted and formed their ranks, the rest of the men hurried off along the south road with Winterford to join the two thousand men, combined from Janhaven, Hill Town, and the Passdale refugees, who were already in place to meet Vidican's army as they came through the troll cave where the Thunder Mountain Band had first met Robby. It was the perfect choke-point, and many, including Makeig and Mirabella, could hardly believe Vidican would attempt such a foolish expedition. But if the way seemed clear, who could pass up such an easy route, one that would take Vidican around and behind Janhaven? It had been Winterford and Makeig's duty, over the past few days, to let Vidican's scouts through, giving them nothing unusual to report. That was not easy, for at the same time, they secretly moved small groups of men, one group at a time, into positions that would not be discovered. But it seemed to have worked. They only had to kill one wayward scout who ventured too close to Janhaven. Now there was word that all of the Redvests who watched the Narrows had been pulled away, after they made some mischief with the Passdale men who manned that post. Having attacked in a halfhearted fashion, and doing little damage, the Redvests obviously intended to divert more Janhaven forces to defend the road. Again, in case scouts continued to watch the Narrows, Makeig made a big show of men to be seen pouring into that pass, and increased the number of campfires and noise around the post, only to stealthily pull the same men back through unwatched ways, to change clothes and repeat the performance again and again. Boskman scouts filtered in around the Narrows, to watch those of the Redvests, and it was confirmed that word was carried back by them concerning the great increase in numbers at the Narrows. The few men actually remaining at the Narrows kept up the ruse, getting little sleep as they constantly lit and put out campfires, banged pots and pans, and made other signs and noises as if they were preparing for Vidican. So, fooled by all these methods and many others, the Redvests confidently moved toward the troll caves, completely convinced that they were unexpected, unseen, and would be unopposed. Indeed, all was made as ready as Mirabella and her people could make it be. And once the bulk of Vidican's Redvests were engaged in battle around the caves, it would be an ideal chance to attempt a rescue of the prisoners held in Passdale.

 Still, a thousand things could go wrong, and this is what worried Makeig as he led his squadron of riders toward the Narrows. Vidican could change his mind and turn back to Passdale. Vidican could have arranged for his attack to be coordinated with forces coming up from the siege of Tallinvale. Or a foolish move on the part of any one of the thousands of men hiding in the woods and hills could give it all away. Not to mention a keen-eyed Redvest in Passdale who might spot Makeig's ruse. Makeig scratched his neck, uncomfortable in the itchy red woolen cloak.

 After Makeig and his riders departed, the word went out to everyone in the region of Janhaven who would not be participating in the attacks to gather at the stockade. Secrecy was key, and while nearly all the men had long since gone to their posts one way or the other, it did not take much prodding to get the women and children into the stockade. Within only a few minutes, every able-bodied woman that could shoot a bow, along with many of the elderly men, lined the platforms high up on the log walls. They, along with all of the others crowded within the fort, now awaited the outcome of the day's fateful events.

• • •

None of those who now moved against Vidican's army, or those riding toward Passdale, could possibly know the confusion and chaos that Mirabella's deadly arrows had ignited among the Redvests. Her body was quickly found and dragged to the Common House yard where she was stripped of all clothing and hung by her feet from the bell tower. After a brief and heated discussion among the officers, Captain Toradatis took charge in Vidican's place, and declared that the General's death changed nothing concerning their plan of attack. Toradatis had the bodies of Vidican and Galatus brought to Wayford Common where the army was already gathered. There, a funeral pyre was prepared, which took another hour, and Vidican and Galatus were laid upon it. The pyre was lit, and while it burned, Toradatis mounted his horse, explaining loudly the situation to the men and the need to make up their lost time. He gave a short but rousing speech, assuring the men of victory, and then led them off at a quick march toward the caves. Captain Pargolis, who was now to be in charge of Passdale and its prisoners, watched the last of the army disappear down the road before turning his own horse back toward the Common House.

The first thing that Pargolis did was to give orders that all of the remaining prisoners were to be gathered at the Common House yard. The prisoners had already heard of the death of Vidican, but when they saw Mirabella's body and her unmistakable flowing red hair, many wept, and some, including Mrs. Greardon, fell to their knees in grief before the bell tower.

"I am not as hard as you may think," Pargolis announced to them. "I see some of you recognize the murderer. I tell you that her fate was just. I am a soldier, but not without heart. You may take down the body, if you wish. I give you two hours, until sunset, to bury her according to your rites. Two hours, only! Then we have work to do before we, too, must depart."

Immediately, several prisoners ran to the tower and took hold of the ropes to gently lower Mirabella's body.

"Captain," one of the prisoners spoke up. "Captain, I beg yer pardon, if ye please, sir!"

Pargolis turned back and saw a stocky young man pushing his way through the prisoners.

"Let him through," Pargolis ordered. "Your name is Geever, I think."

"Yessir, Geever, of Boskland."

"What is it?"

"Sir, our way is to wash the dead, sir. With soap an' water, an' to put them in swaddlin' afore burial."

"If you can do it quickly, then proceed."

"Sir, I beg ye. The women must do it. It is unkind for the men to help in this, er, in the case of a lady, sir. An' she must be laid out proper. It takes more 'an a couple hours, sir."

Pargolis shook his head, glancing at those who crowded around Mirabella's body, taking off their own tattered coats and cloaks to cover her for decency's sake.

"We don't have all day," Pargolis stated. Then, knowing he must keep them in check for a while longer, he relented. "How long will it take? And what will you need?"

One of the women at the edge of the crowd called out, "Water, soap, wash rags, an' clean cloth!"

"An' a place to do her proper!"

"Very well!" Pargolis shouted. "You men, bring the body within. Select four of your women to help, and two more to bring water. Soldier! Fetch soap and strip Galatus's bed linens."

Frustrated, Pargolis turned back to Geever. "You must bury her here. I will not abide a procession to your burial place, wherever that may be. There are shovels over there, so you may as well start digging. All must be done by sunset! Done or not, at sunset you will be ordered away to your work."

Mirabella's body was brought inside and laid on the same table at which Vidican had so often studied maps while Galatus drank his wine. Geever came to the door and delivered some buckets of water and a bar of soap before departing. Mrs. Greardon, Mrs. Garvin, Mrs. Clingdon, and Billy Bosk's sister, Raenelle, took charge of Mirabella's body, weeping as they gently washed their friend. Pargolis looked on from the doorway until he was satisfied they had no other intent than to do their duty, and then he closed the door and stationed a guard outside. The women continued their washing, taking their time to clean Mirabella's wounds, to wash her hair, and to close her eyes. As they worked, their tears washed tracks across their grime-covered cheeks, and Mrs. Garvin broke down into sobs. Raenelle took the kindly woman into her arms. The tears of the Bosk girl were hot and as full of anger as of sadness. She had never been talkative, and said nothing now. Separated from her retreating family, she had been captured a few nights after Boskland burned. Since then, she had acquired something of the Bosk character that she had before lacked, and, along with Mrs. Greardon, she had been the most stalwart of the captured women, enduring the conditions of forced labor as well as several rude attacks on the part of the Redvests. When a knock came at the door, she turned. It was Geever who put his head in.

"I got the linens, Rae," he said.

Raenelle went to take them from him.

"We'll need scissors," she said, wiping her face, "or a knife to cut the linen."

"I'll see what I can do."

A short while later, Pargolis himself came to the door and handed Raenelle a small dull dirk.

"I'll want that back when you're done," he said.

"Yes, sir," she nodded, and closed the door.

Pargolis turned and strode down the hall, grinning at one of his men. "I'll have my way with her again, before the night's done. I'll take some of the feistiness out of her before you have her."

Inside, Raenelle knelt at the fireplace and rubbed the dirk's blade against the hearthstones to sharpen it. When she was satisfied that it would do, she handed it to Mrs. Greardon to begin cutting long strips from the linen. Raenelle took the strips, and with the other women she carefully began binding Mirabella, beginning with her feet and legs.

While the women did this, Pargolis went to look at Geever and the other men who were busy digging a grave in the back yard of the Common House. He was about to order a halt to the activity, deeming the grave deep enough, when a trooper came running.

"Captain! Riders approach from up the road. They're Tracian!"

"What?"

"Yes, sir. A whole squadron. None of ours, either!"

Running around to the front of the Common House, Pargolis arrived just in time to see a company of mounted Redvest soldiers approaching at a canter. Leading them was no less than a general. Quickly straightening his tunic, and glancing around for his missing helmet, left inside, he strode out to meet the newcomers.

"Captain," the general said as he dismounted and returned the salute. "Where is General Vidican?"

"Gone, er, dead, General, General…?"

"Keel, General Keel. Dead ye say?"

"Yes, General Keel. Murdered this morning!"

"Murdered?"

"Yes, General. He was—"

"Then who's in charge here? Speak up, man!"

"I am, sir."

"Oh? What's yer name, soldier?"

"Pargolis, sir."

"Well, Pargolis, where are all the men? Still cowerin' in Passdale, I suppose?"

"No, sir. I mean, we have a few there, sir."

"A few? Where are the rest? I am to take charge of Vidican's force an' take them to Tallinvale. Well, speak up, man! An' what're all these people doin' here, millin' about?"

"Sir, General, sir, I mean, they are prisoners, sir. The army has gone to attack Janhaven, sir. Just a few hours ago."

"What the blazes are ye talkin' about? We took Janhaven early this very morn! An' we saw no army on the road here!"

"Up through the hills, sir. They went to go up behind Janhaven, and take it that way, in a surprise attack, General Keel, sir."

"Surprise attack? They'll be mighty surprised, alright! Well, ain't this a situation!"

General Keel, towering over Pargolis, put his hands on his hips and strode past, looking over the astonished Redvests, and the equally surprised prisoners, all gawking. Spinning around, he faced Pargolis again.

"Well, don't just stand there, Captain! Have all yer men mustered, every last one of 'em!"

"Yes, General Keel. All of them? I mean, the men in Passdale, too, sir?"

"Didn't I say all? Get on with it!"

Pargolis shouted at a nearby trooper, who immediately mounted and rode toward town. Turning to his men, Pargolis shouted, "Form for review!"

The Redvests stirred themselves and began lining up in two rows, hastily dusting themselves off and straightening their tunics as they did so.

"General, would you care for refreshment? There is wine inside. While we wait for the others to arrive."

"Hm. Can't say it would go amiss. Are these all of the prisoners? I was led to believe that many more were taken."

"Over five hundred were taken when we took the county, General Keel," Pargolis explained. "But several died of wounds, and a few others escaped. We have already sent nearly two hundred south with our supply wagons. These are all that are left. That is, except four who are inside, sir."

"Inside?"

"Yes, sir. And three others are over there, digging a grave, General."

"For Vidican?"

"No, sir. For the woman who murdered General Vidican. She was one of their people, and I thought to keep the prisoners calm by letting them bury her."

"Woman, did ye say?"

"Yes, sir. I let the prisoners, that is to say, I permitted some of the womenfolk to wash the woman's body and prepare her for burial."

"She was killed?"

"Yes, sir. As I said, I sought to keep the peace by allowing them this indulgence, sir."

"Take me to them! Ye have a lot to learn, soldier. Are we to so kindly treat the enemy who resists us? Who murders our soldiers? Lead the way, Captain."

The rest of Makeig's men dismounted, and while some held the reins of the horses, the others were directed by the two Blaney brothers, who acted as officers, to line up in two groups. One of the brothers looked over at the real Redvests, now relaxing somewhat after the General and Pargolis moved off.

"Who said you were at ease?" Markum Blaney bellowed as he marched up to them, getting right into their faces. "Have you no respect for your superiors? Stand as if you were soldiers and not an idle mob! Line up straight! This ain't no chow line!"

Most of the Redvests obeyed readily, and the others reluctantly.

"That's better. Stay that way! You there! Coming along there! Get in line with your mates! Smartly! Smartly!"

This was shouted at those who were now coming up the road from Passdale with confused and bewildered looks, and at two more that came running from inside the Common House to take their places.

"You there, soldier!"

"Yes, sir?"

"How many's left of you? Can you count, son?"

"Yes, sir! I mean, there's forty-eight of us, sir. Not countin' the Capt'n, sir."

"Forty-eight here? Or forty-eight all told?"

"Er, sir, forty-eight all told, and, and, now here comes the last of us," the stuttering soldier managed to say as one of his comrades hurried up to join them.

"Very well, then. Very well!"

Markum Blaney moved back and stood beside his brother, and they both crossed their arms and glared at the Tracians. Every few moments, though, one or the other brother walked stiffly up and down their two lines, eyeing each soldier contemptuously.

Inside, Pargolis explained about the attack on Vidican to the newly arrived general. As he did so, Pargolis thought Keel's reaction was somewhat strange, as his story appeared to make the general pale and nervous-seeming. When they arrived at the door, Pargolis entered, still looking at Makeig.

"Here they are, sir," Pargolis said. As he turned to face the room, Raenelle was standing in front of him. With one powerful sweep of her arm, she sliced open the Redvest's throat, then turned on Makeig. He caught her hand just shy of his face, but missed the kick to his groin.

"Oo! Wait! Put that down, missy! I ain't yer enemy!"

Still Raenelle kicked and scratched, and now the other women came over, one wielding a chair, and the other two with fireplace pokers. Seeing them come at him, with his hands full of the girl, he shouted the only thing he could think of.

"Mirabella! Sweet Mirabella!"

Raenelle went limp onto the floor, astounded at the outburst, but her eyes were full of rage, and the other women froze, their weapons held at the ready.

"How do you know her?" Mrs. Greardon demanded.

"She's been me cohort an' commander these past many weeks, now," Makeig stated, his hand up. "An' tell me that ain't her, please, ma'am!"

"It is."

"No, no, no. Oh, dear heavens, it can't be!"

Raenelle, on her knees, glared up at Makeig. "Who are you?"

"Captain Martin Makeig, of Hill Town, lately of Janhaven," Makeig replied, pushing through to the table and looking down on Mirabella's face, not yet wrapped in linen. "Ah, no, no. This is a blow, a foul blow!"

He shook his head slowly, removed his helmet, and knelt beside the table. Putting a hand on Mirabella's forehead, he stroked her hair.

"I've lost many a mate, at sea, in battle, an' elsewhar," he said to her. "But never a braver, more beautiful one than thee, dear lady, as fierce in battle as ye are lovely to look upon. Nor one what cared more for others, as if they was yer kin. Oh, oh!"

The women, astonished at this display, hardly knew what to think. Mrs. Greardon took Raenelle by the hand and lifted her up, pulling her away from the pool of blood that now ran across the floor.

Makeig stood and walked to the door.

"Ladies," he said as he went, "please remain here until I return. It is for yer safety. Take that man's sword, too, just in case."

He turned back at the door, his eyes a watery blaze.

"An' don't heed any noises or cries ye may hear," he said. He pulled the door closed and strode down the hall, ramming his Redvest helmet back onto his head.

When he emerged, he immediately gestured to the Blaney brothers to come to him.

"See to the prisoners," he said to them. "Put plenty of men between 'em an' our Redvest comrades, here."

"First squad! On the double, form a line."

"Second squad, to me!"

Makeig's men, nervously waiting their moment, split into two groups. One group left the horses and ran behind the unsuspecting Redvests, while the other moved to stand in front of the ranks, still standing neatly in two rows.

"Move back, if ye will," said one of the disguised Passdale men to the prisoners. "Please, move on back, thar."

Geever, who was now sitting on the ground against a leg of the bell tower, recognized one of his fellow Boskmen in Redvest garb, leapt up, and pushed others aside to speak to Terrent.

"No, no!" Terrent winked. "Back up thar!"

One of the Redvests in line turned at the drawling voice, his forehead wrinkled.

"Helan," he whispered to the one next to him. "That ain't no accent heard outside of these parts!"

"An' see them saddles? Them lance cups? But do ye see any lances? Or any such garb?"

By now, the newly arrived force was in front and behind the gathered invaders, close enough to touch. Makeig stood in the middle of the front rank of his men. Satisfied that all was ready, he drew his sword.

In less time than it takes an upturned bottle to empty its wine, forty-eight men lay dead on the ground. During that short span, the prisoners screamed, recoiling from the vicious sight. Then, in the aftermath, while their rescuers pulled off their red garments and used them to wipe their swords, tossing the enemy attire onto the bodies that littered the ground in neat rows, Geever and many others shouted for joy and embraced their fellows and their rescuers.

Makeig, meanwhile, walked back to the steps of the stoop. Instead of going back inside, he suddenly turned and sat down. After a moment, he threw the Redvest blade onto the ground and put his head into his hands.

"Oh, dear lady. What brung ye to this end? Why, why?"

• • •

It was long after dark, and the battle in the hills was already engaged, when a rider came at a gallop along the road from the Narrows, pulling the reins of another riderless horse. He rode swiftly through Janhaven to the stockade, and called up to those who watched his approach.

"I come from Passdale!" Terrent shouted loudly. "Our people are safe! We count three hunnerd and some odd! I need to see Lady Bosk! Frizella!"

Amid shouts and cheers, the gate was flung open, and Terrent rode in, meeting Frizella as she came across the yard.

"Good news!" she said, giving Terrent a hug.

"Yes, ma'am. But Makeig wants ye to ride back with me to Passdale. Right away. I brung this horse for ye. Capt'n says right away, ma'am."

"Certainly! Are there wounded? Let me fetch me bag."

"No, ma'am. No wounded," Terrent lightly gripped her arm and lowered his voice. "It's Lady Mirabella, ma'am."

Frizella stared at him for a brief moment, then nodded. By now, they were being crowded with celebrants wanting more news, but Terrent shook his head as he helped Frizella mount.

"More news'll come real soon," he told them. "But the rest of ye must keep to the plan. Let us out, then close them gates tight until ye hear from Winterford an' our men at the caves. Are ye settled, me lady? Can ye ride?"

"Thar's only one rightful lady in these parts, which I think ye know, Terrent."

"Yes, ma'am. If ye say so, ma'am."

• • •

Hours later, by the time Frizella arrived at the Common House, Makeig and the others had explained the situation to the newly freed prisoners, telling them about the battle that now raged in the hills, and the larger situation, with Tracia and the Dragonkind arrayed against the world, with Tallinvale under siege. Many were looking forward to their first good night of sleep in many months, and some even in their own homes, or what was left of their homes after the looting and trashing done by the Redvests. But most remained at the Common House, anxious to set off for Janhaven and reunite with their kin. In spite of the cold, they were gathered outside under the front portico as Makeig urged them to stay in Passdale, at least until morning.

"If our boys don't stop the Redvests up in them hills," he told them, "or if the enemy breaks through, the Janhaven folk'll be comin' down the road to us. If they don't have warnin' or time, they'll make a defense at Furaman's stockade. Either way, we need to stay here until we get word. I gave me promise to protect ye right here, in case the Redvests turn about an' retreat this far. Which I doubt they'll be able to do. But this was Lady Mirabella's plan, an' I aim to stick to it!"

"What if they do come back?"

"Our scouts an' riders'll bring us word well afore any Redvests get here, an' we'll go north, as best an' as fast as we may go. So stand ready, one way or t'other."

At last, he saw Frizella riding up with Terrent, and most went to greet her as she came up the steps. But they sensed her sadness, and knew well the reason for it, and they allowed her to pass, reaching out to touch her kindly as she went up the steps where Makeig waited. He led her inside without a word and down the crowded hall, through more of her kin and friends who lingered around a door. He opened it and let her pass within, then closed it. After a moment, he went back outside. Since no one pressed him to talk further, he picked up a blanket from a pile and threw it over his shoulders then walked down the steps and along the road toward Passdale just as new snow began to fall.

Inside, lamps had been brought in and arranged about the room, and a fire made in the hearth. The body of Pargolis had been removed and flung onto the pile of the Redvest dead, his blood mopped away. As Frizella entered, the several women who were sitting within stood to face her. She stopped just inside the door, her eyes upon the table where Mirabella lay. She swallowed several times in an effort to preserve her composure, her eyes welling. Suddenly her daughter hurried to her, and they both burst into tears as they embraced.

"Oh, Mother!"

"Me love, me precious love!"

• • •

Word spread quickly back to Janhaven about the freeing of the prisoners, and the people of Passdale who were within the stockade were hardly able to contain their joy. It was tempered by the knowledge that so many of their menfolk and able women were now fighting in the hills south of Janhaven, and by the sad news of Mirabella's death.

"It seems that the good comes with the bad," Mr. Broadweed said to Mrs. Starhart.

"I just don't know," sniffed Mrs. Starhart. "Such awful days. Awful, awful!"

The two watched together from the walkway over the stockade's gate, along with many others. Already they had word from runners that the Barley coalition was fighting to take the heights above the caves, and that the Redvests were exiting the west side. On the far side, Winterford's force had to wait until all of the Redvests were within the cave before launching an attack upon their rear. But, according to the runner, a large portion of the Redvest army had exited before Furaman's fighters on that side of the ridge saw the signal from Winterford that the last of the army had entered the cave. It almost came too late, and Furaman's men, carefully falling back before the army, were now springing from their hiding places, surrounding the enemy on three sides, and pressing them inward and back into the crowded caves by volleys of arrows, and by lighting fires in the woods. Coming into the far side of the troll tunnel wearing the heaviest battle armor they could equip themselves with, Winterford and his Hill Town folk led five hundred fighters against the retreating Redvests, bottling them up inside and cutting them down in vicious close-quarters fighting.

Now, even from this distance, some twenty miles north, Broadweed saw the glow of those fires upon the overcast sky and knew that the battle had begun in earnest. And he knew, from having attended the planning for this battle, that all depended on getting the Redvests bottled up inside the caves before they could break out through Furaman's men. That meant that the heights above would have to be taken, so as to command the cave openings with bows and boulders, to let no Redvest out and none but their own fighters into the caves. Of course, Broadweed could not say if all went according to plan.

"There are the fires," he said to Mrs. Starhart. "You best get down and away."

"But what about the folks in Passdale?" she asked, moving to the ladder.

"They'll stay until they get word from us or from others."

On all four corners of the crowded stockade were log watchtowers, and from one of these a horn was blown by a man who also saw the evidence of the fires. This summoned all not already on the walls to come quickly with bow and quiver, and for the fires that boiled water to be stoked. Mr. Broadweed picked up his bow and checked his supply of arrows. Mr. Durlorn, who commanded the stockade in the absence of anyone more qualified, came along and stood with Broadweed.

"How long do you think it would take the Redvests to get here," Broadweed asked, "if they break through, that is."

"Not long. If they have horses, only an hour or so. Our men will outpace them, though, to forewarn us."

They both watched the sky southward while others joined them and took up their bows. In the yard behind them, the many kettles on tripods were being brought again to a boil by women who added wood to the fires underneath, and pots and pans and buckets were already stacked nearby not only for dowsing attackers with hot water, but also for the fires that might break out.

"I wish we could shore up them gates," said someone down the way.

"What? An' not let our boys in if they come along?" answered someone else.

Just then a rider came tearing along from the opposite direction, reining up before the gates.

"Durlorn!" the rider shouted up.

"Aye? What's the matter?"

"Three riders approach from the old west road!"

"West road?"

"That's right. Do we challenge or let 'em on through?"

"Soldiers?"

"Not sure. They ride buckmarls."

"Ye don't say! Let 'em through, by all means!"

"Aye!"

The rider reined around and galloped off into the darkness as Durlorn scratched his head.

"Buckmarls are only ridden by the western Elifaen," said Broadweed.

"I know."

"Any idea as to who they may be?"

"None."

They waited, a bit more nervously, while the red glow off to their right grew somewhat brighter. They looked from there to the other direction, along the road from town, and back, each wondering if there was anything else to be done but wait. On the right side, an old man made his way carefully along the narrow walkway toward them, and got close to Durlorn before speaking.

"Don't mean to cause undo alarm," he said to Durlorn as Broadweed listened in, "but we up on my side keep thinkin' we see some odd light or motion over in the trees across the way from us."

Durlorn and Broadweed looked to their left, each leaning over the wall a bit. Broadweed thought he saw a dim glow, but it faded before he could be sure.

"Don't see anything," said Durlorn. "Pass the word for all to keep a sharp eye."

"Riders!" came a call from the tower. "I mark three."

Leaning out again, they saw the three riders coming along at an easy pace. The men and women along the walls put arrows to string and held their weapons at the ready.

"Let's have some light, shall we?" Durlorn called. Torches were lit along the wall, revealing more about the strangers that now approached the gate of the stockade. Two had long blond hair, dressed alike in western tunics, and the other was a woman, in light armor. All had swords at their shoulders and bows and quivers hanging from their saddles. The woman wore an odd looking headdress that hung down over her eyes.

"State yer business!" Durlorn called down.

"Our business is with Mirabella Ribbon," responded the woman.

"An' what might that business be?"

"Are you Furaman?"

"No, I am one of his men, in charge of this gate."

"I was told to ask for Mirabella Ribbon at Furaman's stockade. Is this the place?"

"Aye, it is."

"Then I have a letter for her. I have a letter for Frizella Bosk, if she is also here. And I wish to speak with them both."

"We are presently very reluctant to permit anyone in," Durlorn said. "Perhaps ye might say who it was who sent the letters."

"Robby Ribbon, of Passdale, and Billy Bosk, of Boskland."

"Oh, my," said Broadweed.

Durlorn was already climbing down the nearby ladder, calling out for the door of the gate to be unbarred. He took a lantern on his way through, and Broadweed saw him approach the riders, holding up the light to shine in their faces.

"Where are ye bound for?" Durlorn asked.

"Here," Esildre answered. "Besides bringing letters, we come to give what aid we can against the invaders."

"Oh?"

"Perhaps you would bring Mirabella Ribbon. I believe she will vouch for us. Or the Bosk woman."

"They ain't neither of 'em available, just now."

"They are not here?"

"No, er. No, ma'am, they ain't."

"Where are they? I must speak with Mirabella Ribbon. Who is in charge here?"

"Why I am, miss. An' I'm a bit nervous standin' around out here. So if ye would turn over yer weapons an' such, I'll let ye inside where we can talk more civil-like."

Esildre hesitated, glancing up at the walls now teeming with bow-wielding people. She reached up and loosened the buckles on her harness and slid it around so that she could hand her sword to Durlorn. Her companions did likewise, then they handed over their bows to him.

"Open up! Let 'em in!" Durlorn called, and the gate was swung open. Inside, Esildre dismounted and looked around.

"It appears that you prepare for an attack."

"Just bein' prudent, is all," Durlorn replied.

"Will you send for the ladies, now? Or Mr. Furaman."

"I cannot do that. They are all miles away, ye see. An'," Durlorn hesitated then shrugged, "well, one is dead. Mrs. Ribbon, to be sure. Killed by Redvests."

"Oh, no!"

"Yes, miss. Why don't ye tell me how ye come by them letters, an' how ye mean to help us."

Esildre faced Durlorn, but owing to her veil, he could not see her eyes. She slowly shook her head.

"I am deeply sorry to hear about Robby's mother," she said. "What about Billy's mother?"

"She's safe, as far as I know. She went to Passdale a few hours ago, upon news that her friend, our friend, was killed."

"Passdale? I thought the town was occupied by Tracian Redvests."

"It was. Until this night. It's been taken back by force."

"And the red sky? That is not from Passdale, is it?"

"No, ma'am. Another battle rages there, against the main army of the Redvests in these parts, seekin' to come up behind us, as it were."

"Then we should go join the fighting," Esildre said, reaching out. "And avenge Robby's mother! Our weapons, if you will."

"Now, hold on a bit!" Durlorn backed away, clutching his armful of their weapons. "I ain't so sure ye can be trusted, pardon me for sayin'. Anyways, the battle is already afoot, an' ye wouldn't know friend from foe in the dark. 'Sides, ain't much just the three of ye could do, I reckon."

"Not three!" Esildre turned and made a gesture toward the open gates. Suddenly she and her companions were surrounded by mild explosions of bubbly bluish light, and before Durlorn could react, there stood twelve small figures, all armed with bows and swords.

"What's this? Where did ye come from?"

"You see," said Esildre, "I brought others with me to fight."

"What? Children?"

"We are not children!" Millithorpe stepped up, punching the bridge of his spectacles to push them back up his nose. "We are grown men and women."

"And we have been well trained to shoot and parry," said another little person.

"An' we have given our promise, an' we aim to do our part," said Eldwin.

"Oh?" Durlorn was taken aback, to say the least, as were the many onlookers. Mr. Broadweed had already come down from his perch and was at the edge of the group.

"Where do you come from? Vanara?" Broadweed asked. "Or were you sent by our friends who journeyed to Duinnor?"

"We come from the west," said Esildre, "but can say no more."

"No, there's one thing more, an' one thing only, that we may say," said Eldwin. "We serve the King."

"Well, I'll be!"

"So," said Esildre, "will you direct us to the fight?"

"No, no!" said Broadweed. "I beg you to stay with us. At least until we may tell you about our circumstance. Or until we receive word from those who fight. It won't take very long, one way or the other."

"Close the gate!" Durlorn ordered. "Everyone back at yer posts! Get on with ye! No, Mr. Broadweed, wait. Why don't ye take our guests inside an' tell 'em what news ye can."

Turning to Esildre, and eyeing the little people, Durlorn shook his head and gave back the weapons he held. "I'm afraid we've got little to offer in the way of victuals. But if we get good news, we'll be startin' up the kitchens an' all."

Esildre's great-nephews bowed their heads in thanks, and Broadweed gestured them to the great room of Furaman's warehouse. Inside were many women and children, making ready salves and bandages and splints. They were astonished by the crowd that entered, and Broadweed asked them to leave. One little boy, tall for his age, hesitated at the door, looking Millithorpe up and down before scurrying off with his mother.

"We can speak freely here," Mr. Broadweed said. "Please sit, or make yourself warm by the fire. I would like to ask you, first, what you can tell me about our friends. Were they all safe and well when you saw them?"

"Yes," said Eldwin. "They were."

"And you saw them all? Robby, Billy, Sheila, Ibin, Ashlord, and Ullin Saheed?"

"Yes, we did," answered Esildre.

"Will you tell me how you met with them?"

"We cannot say much," Esildre answered, glancing at the Nowhere folk. "Only that we met them back in the autumn. They were still on their way west, and far from reaching their destination. They came to trust us, and told us about why they traveled. They told us about the Redvests, Passdale and Barley, about the people who came here, and about Tallinvale, where we ultimately intend to go. Robby and Ullin Saheed, the Kingsman, asked us to come to your aid, and to the aid of Tallinvale, should the opportunity arise for us to do so. Our circumstance only just recently permitted us to come, and we came as quickly as we could."

"There aren't many of you. Tell me, and I don't mean to be rude or disrespectful," Broadweed looked at Eldwin, "but are you pixie-people?"

"No, we are not," Eldwin said. "Ye wonder at how we appeared so suddenly, out of nowhere."

"Out of nowhere!" someone giggled. "That's a good one!"

"Why, yes. We have heard tales, and who hasn't? About little folk who snap their fingers."

"An' who rob passers-by?"

"Er, well, yes."

"We are not those people," Millithorpe stated bluntly.

"But, owing to promises to our own people, an' to others," Eldwin took up, "we can say little more about where we come from, who we are, an' how we came to be here. Except, yes, we have the ability to move very quickly."

"I see. Well. First, my name is Gustan Broadweed. Until a few months ago, I was schoolmaster of Barley. Robby, Billy, and Ibin were all my pupils. I also knew Sheila, though not as well as I should have. Ashlord and Ullin Saheed are more recent acquaintances of mine."

"I am Eldwin," Eldwin said, offering his hand. Soon all were greeting and shaking Broadweed's hand, or bowing to him.

"I am Esildre, and these are my grand-nephews, Kranneg and Tulleg. What can you tell us about Robby's mother? The man outside said she was killed by the Tracian invaders."

"Ah, yes. It is very sad, and quite a shock to us all. But there is very little that I can say about it. We only learned about her death this very night. That is why Billy's mother rushed away to Passdale. No one here yet knows the circumstance, but she was not part of the mission to retake Passdale. I don't know what happened to her. I can only say that never was there a more courageous woman! And as kind as she was strong! Oh, my! Forgive me! She was a great friend to all of Passdale and Barley! If it were not for her, many of our people would be dead or captured long ago. Poor Mrs. Bosk! They were close friends. Mrs. Bosk is another strong lady, but I don't know how she can hold up to this blow! I think I shall take a seat, if you don't mind."

"And Mirabella's husband? Is there any word of him?"

"No, I'm afraid not. Not in all this time. We don't know if he ever made it to Glareth by the Sea."

"Then tell us first, and quickly if you can, of the Redvests and about the battle to the south."

Broadweed did so. He explained how it all came about, and about the Hill Town people who joined their ranks, though many of them were Tracians, and how their plan to free Passdale was to take advantage of the absence of the army. Owing to his school teacher practice at explaining things, and not one to overly burden any subject, he gave them a good lesson on their efforts, the troll caves, and Mirabella's carefully laid plan of battle. After only a few questions, he reached the end of his lecture.

"What of Tallinvale?" asked Eldwin. "If we cannot help hereabouts, we must go there."

"I don't see how you can," Broadweed said, and he told them about the various expeditions from Tallinvale that the enemy had sent. "And, the last we heard, from scouts that managed to get there and back, was that a tremendous army surrounds Tallin City. Our latest report, about two weeks old, put the enemy at around sixty or seventy thousand. And more seemed to be arriving, along with prisoners, slaves, and other people brought to serve the army."

Eldwin looked at Millithorpe, whose brow was wrinkled in some mental calculation.

"That is a great number, Eldwin. More than can be imagined, almost."

"Nonetheless," Eldwin said. "I feel I must go an' see for meself."

"Why?" asked one of his people. "What can we do against that many?"

"That is what I must go to see. Mr. Broadweed, we have maps, an' they say that the road just outside yer place here goes south all the way to Tallinvale. Is that so?"

"Yes, it does. Almost thirty leagues, would be my guess."

"Then I shall go. I'll follow the road, going as quickly as I can, an' be back just as quickly. After I have a look around."

"Eldwin," Esildre shook her head, "I don't think that is wise. All by yourself?"

"It is the safest way, don't ye think? No one else to look after, no one to drag along. An' I can cover the distance in a very short while."

Esildre, from her long acquaintance with Eldwin, knew there was no dissuading him, so they all walked with him to the gate, and he was wished good luck as he popped away and out of sight. The door of the gate was being closed once more when another Janhaven rider came galloping up.

"Two more riders come!" he called out. "And I mark one a Kingsman! They came down off the Hill Town path."

Thinking this could only be Ullin Saheed, and concerned that he should be coming this way, Esildre stayed nearby with her great-nephews. Soon the two riders came along, at a fast pace.

"Who goes!" came a shout from atop the wall.

"Sally Bodwin, of Hill Town," came a girl's voice.

"Captain Bartow of the King's Fourth!" called up the Kingsman who rode alongside of her. "We come at quick pace and hard ride to give news and to get news. Let us in! Our horses are worn out, and we need water, too!"

The gates were once again shoved open, and the two riders came in.

"Where do you come from?" Esildre asked immediately.

"From Hill Town," Bartow said, dismounting. "Give the girl some water and let her walk off her stiffness. She has guided me fast and faithfully through the mountains since before sunset to reach here."

"Is the Fourth in Hill Town?"

"I should say not," Bartow said, accepting a cup of water while Sally was given hers. After gulping it down, he continued. "I was dispatched to locate Janhaven and to receive news concerning the situation here and in

Passdale and Barley. The Hill Town folk gave me the gist, but my general will wish me to have it firsthand. So the battle that Miss Bodwin told me of is joined?"

"Aye," said Durlorn, "see yon red sky?"

"I do. And have seen it for miles."

"Where is the Fourth, then?" Esildre asked.

"We took Damar City yesterday, and utterly destroyed Cartu's fortress. I left my comrades there yesterday noontime, ordered to come here to scout news. So news I must have, then I must hie back the way I came, as fast as I can go. Is Passdale taken back?"

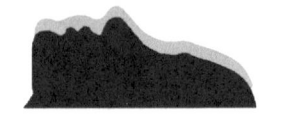

Chapter 20

A New Kingdom

"I killed my mother, Finn. I sent her to her death."

An hour had passed in silence since Robby uttered those words to Finn. They sat across from each other, at a table in the glass-enclosed sunroom, their plates untouched, the tea in their cups long cold. Nearby, Celia went from blossom to blossom, carefully making her selections and snipping them off to put into the basket hanging from her arm. Never far from her, Boxer followed patiently. Robby, expressionless and turned sideways in his chair, watched the rabbit. But Finn could see that his eyes were not really upon Boxer; they were distant, even when they moved to follow the creature.

"Sir," Finn said at last, "perhaps we should go for a walk."

"No, Finn. That's alright. I was just thinking how foolish I am. How careless. I was thinking of my father, and…"

Robby stopped, slowly stood, and placed his napkin on the table.

"Thank you, Finn. I think I'll go for that walk by myself."

Finn stood, not knowing what to say.

"We'll talk later," Robby said as he walked to the door. "Perhaps in the library sometime this afternoon."

"Certainly, sir."

Celia came over and plopped down in Robby's chair, putting her basket on the table.

"Finn, why is Robby so quiet this morning?" she asked, pushing Robby's plate aside and putting a bunch of flowers in its place. "He hardly said a word to me, and his smile was quite sad. Is Robby sad?"

"Yes, Celia. He is."

"Why?"

"He received some very sad news."

"Oh? What news?"

"His mother has died."

"Oh, that is sad. I shall make a posy for him. Did Robby love his mother?"

"Of course he did, child. What a question!"

"Well, I don't love my mother. How could I? I have never had one to love, have I?"

"I'm not sure how to answer that. Everyone has had a mother."

"Well, then, Finn, did my mother leave me here?"

Finn gazed at Celia, puzzled by these questions. In all the years since Robby freed her from the glass jar, she had never once said or asked anything so serious or deep.

"I am an orphan, aren't I?"

"I can't even guess how you know such words," Finn said. "And the mystery of your presence here is just that. I do not know if your mother left you here, or if someone else did. But I'm sure that if your mother did leave you here, it was because she loved you very much and wanted you to be safe and taken care of."

"Hm. I suppose you must be right. But, Finn, I think I do miss my mother, and my father, and my sisters and brothers, too, if ever I had any. You see, sometimes I think Boxer is the only friend I have. Don't misunderstand me; you and Robby are great friends to me. But you two are, well, so concerned with other things all the time. But Boxer cares only for me. I can't remember a time when we weren't together. He is always nearby. It seems to me that he takes the place of so much else. I do love him so! But, Finn, I don't think it is right, somehow. It is, I don't know, *off*."

"Off?"

She took a roll of green ribbon from her basket and began tying the flowers together and snipping off errant stems.

"Why, yes. Off. I mean, it's just the four of us here. And lately, since Robby left and came back, that is, I've felt different. It is as if I'm slowly waking up from a very long dream."

"I know the feeling, child. I have felt somewhat the same way."

"Finn, do you know how you came to be here?"

"No, Celia. That, too, is a mystery."

"Hm. Look! Do you think Robby will like these? I hope he does. I don't want him to be sad."

She held up the posy.

"Yes. The flowers are lovely. I think he will like your arrangement of them."

"Good!"

• • •

Indeed, many things had suddenly changed in Griferis. For one, days and nights here were like those elsewhere in the world, and time no longer stood still or moved back upon itself. Winter, hard upon the mountains surrounding Griferis, came here, too. Outside, snow had fallen on and off ever since Robby had returned. The Judges were gone, as well as all of the mysterious portals through which Robby was made to go during his many trials. But every remaining door and passage was open to Finn and Robby. It was a vast structure, with many towers and levels, each with its own places to explore, and around the entire palace was a high wall topped with ramparts befitting a fortress.

On the day Robby returned to Griferis, Finn first assured himself that he was recovering from his ordeal, from the foxdire dose he had taken. Then, while Robby continued to pass in and out of a mildly delirious sleep, he set about exploring Griferis. Finn quickly found that the place had an enormous wine cellar, full of casks, kegs, and bottles from every region of the world, wine, beer, ale, whiskey, and sweet liquors, including an entire keg of Fetch, from the Barley region. He also found a coal room, with small elevators like dumb waiters for pulling up loads of the fuel to various places above. There was fuel for lamps, tools and supplies of every description, including soaps and perfumes, barrels of cooking oil, sacks of salt, and crates of spices. The pantry was fully stocked, and the three kitchens gleamed with copper pots and pans, and had all the tools and utensils needed to cook for an army. There were five large gardens under glass, with vegetables growing in two, fruits in another, and shrubs and flowers in the other two. And there were three outside gardens, including one of nearly ten acres that was wooded with oaks and firs, among many other kinds of trees and shrubs.

For all that day and half of the next, Finn delved into the place, while Robby slept. On the afternoon of the second day, Robby woke and got up. After a bite to eat, Robby insisted that Finn show him around, and they speculated together on the marvels of Griferis. Then, late that afternoon, Robby set off on his own to see what else could be found as Finn went to make an inventory of the stocks and supplies already discovered.

At first, Robby found it rather eerie to walk the long halls, and to look into empty rooms. But he soon got accustomed to the peace, and his excitement and curiosity about the place overcame his lingering weakness. When he found the library, he was astonished. It occupied an entire floor of one wing, filled with shelves of books and scrolls, with rolling ladders to reach the highest volumes, and a balcony of alcoves along three walls with lamps and tables beside windows of clear glass. After some searching, he found an index of sorts that described the items within the library and listed the location of each and every book and scroll.

Robby also located several halls of bedrooms, two additional smaller and cozier libraries, a large sitting room, akin to the one in Tallin Hall, that opened to one of the gardens, and another smaller sitting room that adjoined the glassed-in flower garden. Although every room was richly appointed in fine leather, lavish drapes and carpets, and furniture of every description, there were no paintings, no portraits, statues, or mementos of any kind. Nor were there signs of any of the previous occupants or visitors.

Among the oddest discoveries were several rooms up in the highest tower containing mysterious devices and instruments. These seemed to be workrooms of some sort, but Robby could not surmise what kind of work might be done within. The tables held glass instruments, akin to

Ullin's spyglass, along with measuring tools, scales, and various other strange-looking things, some made of brass or other metals, and others made of wood or glass. Climbing an iron ladder located in one of these rooms, Robby opened a panel in the ceiling and emerged onto a high platform atop the tower. It was covered with a dome of glass, which he discovered could be opened by turning a crank. But what amazed him the most, in the center of the platform, was a large tube of brass, some fifteen feet long, held up by a tall complicated apparatus akin to a tilted wheel. Robby almost immediately realized that it was a huge spyglass. He spent the next hours trying to understand how it operated, turning various wheels and knobs and cranks to move it back and forth and up and down. When he peered through the small end of it, he saw nothing but fuzzy spots of blue light. He experimented with turning a knob on its side, and suddenly a distant mountaintop came into sharp focus. He could even see how the wind blew a thin curling wisp of snow from its peak. After another hour, he learned to turn the spyglass so that it pointed in any direction that he wished, and he spent a great deal of time looking past the shoulder of Algamori into Shatuum.

• • •

That night, weary and still suffering from the aftereffects of the foxdire he had taken, Robby tried again to locate his mother, but failed to find her. Thinking that she must be somewhere in the hills among the fighters who were moving to counter the Redvests, he turned his attention to other places, to see what he could learn about the events in other parts of the world. Ashlord, Billy, Ibin, and Sheila were safe at the Temple in Duinnor. Ullin had found the first of many caves within which to shelter along the way north, and he was asleep beneath his meager blankets. Micerea watched over him, and she was just entering Ullin's dreams to give him some company and some guidance for the next day of travel. Not wishing to intrude, Robby left them to each other without making his presence known.

He realized that he must soon resume his work in the world, but he was still filled with the strange and powerful memories of a thousand of his forebears and their histories, though he knew what he remembered was only a fraction of what had been revealed to him. And he had a thousand questions about the world that needed answers, about Secundur and his fierce creatures, about the King of Duinnor wrapped in his garb of golden threads, about Alonair, and Nasakeeria, and about the Familiars of Ashlord and the other Melnari. He even returned to Greenfar, to look upon those kind people, and then he ventured into Islindia's forest. He found the sad lady asleep on a bed of moss, her wings wrapped around her against the cold. She was weeping, and her tears ran down her sleeping face and dripped onto the moss, blooming into glittering amber flowers before melting away. When she dreamed, it was of the past, of the day her lover was murdered by Secundur. When she sank into despair, Robby stepped in.

"The past is hard," he said, taking her by the hand. "But you have it within your power to dream of anything you wish."

"Do I know you?" she asked, alarmed. Then she saw him more clearly. "Can it be you?"

"Yes, it is I. I have come out of Griferis, and I have entered back into it. I now make it the first of my many domains. You know this is a dream."

"Yes. What else is left to me?"

"Yet, I tell you that this is not like other dreams. And it is not a hopeless dream. I am not produced by your despair, but come to give you hope. Just as you gave me and my companions solace and safety, much needed, I now seek to return the favor."

"How? What might you give that would bring healing, that would recover what I have lost? I do not wish to sound ungrateful to your gesture, nor do I mean to be bitter, but I have no hope left to be dashed, and bitter sadness surrounds my soul."

"You do have hope. You gave it to Ullin Saheed. You spoke encouragement to my companions. Sadness is not all that is left to you. Please sleep well and soundly," Robby said. "Tomorrow, roam your forest, as you always do. But look upon the different places within as they may someday be, not as they once were. Look upon your forest as it might once again thrive, if not restored to its former glory, then at least healed of its painful blight, so that old seeds, long dormant, may sprout and flourish. Use your memories to imagine not the past, but a tomorrow of joy and rebirth. Speak to your father, King of the Wood, not of the angry past, but of the kind shelter that he provides to the good creatures that need such a place. Just as your uncle does for the people of Greenfar. Look upon those people. Speak with your uncle. Tell your father to partake of his joy and his hope. Let your uncle's fellowship be a tonic to you both."

As Robby spoke, Islindia looked at him in wonder.

"You ask much. I do not know if I have the ability to do such things, to dream of the future. And I do not think my father will listen to me."

"Try," Robby said. "And if, on the morrow, you try but a little, then try but a little more on the day after. And henceforth, try again each day and each night to see the good and to imagine the beautiful and the possible. Will you do that?"

"I will," she said, nodding. "I have never heard words such as these."

"Do not forget this dream. Remember how we have conversed in this manner. I will come back to you, and we will talk again about these things and about other things, too."

• • •

When Robby himself woke, he was still very tired, and he still felt somewhat groggy from the foxdire. But he was anxious to spend another day exploring Griferis, and once he got going, after breakfasting with Finn and Celia, his vigor seemed to return.

"Just one more day of rest and of looking about the place," he told Finn. "Before I have to really think about getting to work."

Which was just what Robby did, going again to find those places he had already explored, finding new routes to them, and spending a great deal of time in the libraries. He at last found a book concerning Griferis, including drawings of the layout of the palace as well as descriptions of the contents and purpose of each room. He also found within it instructions for conjuring the causeway, and making it go away, and for doing other things that he had not imagined. Taking the book, he walked the entire perimeter of Griferis, along its high walls, crunching for what seemed miles through the ice and snow upon the ramparts, until nighttime came. On his way back to his room, he ran into Finn who told him that supper was ready. So Robby dined with Finn and Celia before a blazing hearth, all as cheerful as could be, and they even played a hand of cards afterwards. When Celia could not stop yawning, Finn insisted that she go to bed. After she left, Robby, too, felt overwhelmed by fatigue. He excused himself, promising Finn that they would begin a meaningful discussion about their future in Griferis the following morning over breakfast. Finn bowed, and said his good-nights, too.

• • •

At first, Robby tossed and turned with so many things flying through his mind, but before long he settled down and fell asleep, and he dreamwalked back to Passdale.

Noticing the crowd around the Common House, he quickly surmised that Makeig's mission had been successful, for the former prisoners now roamed freely about the place. But he was baffled as to why they were still awake at such a late hour, not long before dawn. He saw Frizella ride up with Terrent and dismount. She was met with somber expressions, and Robby followed her and Makeig inside.

• • •

Robby was late coming to breakfast, and Finn had to knock several times before he had the nerve to enter. He found Robby sitting, dressed, at his table, and Finn reminded him that breakfast was ready whenever he pleased. Finn immediately sensed that something was terribly wrong, but asked nothing. Later, at the breakfast table, Robby made his shocking statements, saying that he had killed his mother. While Finn was still inwardly reeling from that, Celia made her remarks, and Finn thought them to be disturbing in their own way, too.

So Finn sat for a long time at the table, not knowing quite what to do before deciding that he should make himself busy. After he washed the dishes, leaving food on the sideboard should Robby return, he then continued his inventory, using a ledger found among the supplies, until it was time to look for Robby in the library.

"My lord?" he called out.

"Up here, Finn."

Looking up, Finn saw Robby at the banister above, with several volumes in his arms.

"You know," Robby said as he walked to the stairs, "there are more books and scrolls here than one could read in a lifetime, I think. Histories, books of art, music, poetry, alchemy, books on plants and animals, potions and concoctions, medicine, magic, astrology, you name it! There are even books on cooking, on making glass, how to make wine and beer, how to build things. Just about anything you'd care to learn, you could learn from this library."

Robby came down the stairs and gestured to a table where he dumped the stack of books.

"Have a seat, Finn."

"This is a most amazing place, truly," Finn said tentatively. He watched Robby carefully, trying to discern his state of mind.

"I know that you are concerned about me, Finn," Robby said. "I appreciate it. I will be fine. I had quite a shock, and I must come to grips with my mother's death. But, to do her honor, I must not forget why I am here. I have a lot to tell you, a lot of questions to answer, surely, for you must wonder at me! How, for instance, could I know about my mother?"

"I did wonder, my lord."

"I wish you would just call me Robby, since that is what you have always known me as. My real name may be Philawain, but I can't seem to think of myself as that."

"May I suggest, sir, that you think of yourself as Lord Philawain, King of Griferis, or just King Philawain?"

"I am giving it thought, Finn. But I'm not yet decided on it. Meanwhile, please call me Robby."

"Yes, sir."

"You know, for the life of me I can't understand why those who came before me did not ask for the same boons that I did. To have Griferis as their own, that is."

"Perhaps their hearts were set on other places?"

"Hm. Probably. Well, now. Finn, it seems obvious that the two of us cannot hope to look after Griferis on our own."

"Yes, that has occurred to me."

"So we must acquire a staff of people, as all the great houses have, trained and capable in all the ways of housekeeping and running an estate."

"Surely, sir. It seems necessary."

"Also, we shall eventually need things that are not available here."

"Most likely. Did you have any certain things in mind?"

"Well, I've looked high and low, and unless I've missed something, there's not a single weapon in the entire place. Not a dagger, sword, spear, or slingshot. Perhaps such things may never be needed. I hope not, anyway. But it seems odd for a place to have defensive walls, heavy doors, arrow slits and the like, but no weapons."

"Yes, since you put it that way, it does seem odd."

"So, in addition to the estate staff, that is, the household staff and those needed to keep the grounds, we will also need armorers and people to bear arms should ever Griferis need to be defended. Also, we'll need skilled craftsmen to make repairs that might be required. To replace broken windows, or roof tiles, or other things. Carpenters, masons, and so forth. Oh, and also, to have some account of what we do here, I'll need a scribe. A court scribe, I suppose it would be called. Someone who is able to write well and quickly, and who is able to keep orderly annals and such."

"Yes. Hm. It seems quite a lot of people would be needed."

"Well, some could do double duty, perhaps. When not needed for one thing, they could do another. But, yes, any way you cut it, a large number of people."

"But, as you have told me before, Griferis is cut off from the world. The nearest landfall, so to speak, is surrounded by Shatuum, a dangerous region. How are we to find those we need and convince them to brave so many dangers to come here? And how may we reward those who may come into service here?"

"Good questions, Finn. Well, I think I may as well tell you something that I kept secret from you all these many years we've been together, during my trials, that is. I have the ability to find those who are skilled and may be trustworthy, and who may wish for a place to live and work. And I can do so easily without really leaving our little kingdom. Only I don't have the time. There are other things that I must see to, things that urgently need my attention."

"Pardon me, but I'm not sure I quite understand, my lord. Does your method have anything to do with the sad news you imparted this morning?"

"Yes, it does, Finn. As I said, I am sure that I can take care of finding those we need, but I propose that you be in charge of that. At least for awhile. You see, I am a dreamwalker. And I think I may be able to teach you how to be one, too."

"Sir? You are a what, sir?"

"A dreamwalker. Tonight, when you go to sleep and dream, I will show you what I mean," Robby said as he stood. "The difficult part will be getting our staff safely here."

Finn stared after Robby, slowly rising from his chair as Robby went back to the stairs.

"Dreamwalker?" he said weakly. "What is a dreamwalker?"

"You'll see," Robby called back. He hesitated on the stairs. "Oh, and about those who will be our little army. As soon as I can, I intend to put into action a plan to make them as unnecessary as I can. But it may take many years to accomplish. I'll tell you more about that later on."

"You seemed to be quite resolved, sir," Finn called up to Robby, who was now walking briskly back above him along the balcony. Robby picked up another stack of books to bring down.

"Yes, Finn. I am resolved. And I've had years to ponder what I might do, given the chance. But I never thought I'd have such a place as this to do it from. It changes some things but not other things that I must do. It makes some things harder, but other things may be easier."

"Yes, sir."

"Oh, and Finn," Robby stopped and looked down at him. "Celia needs a governess, I think. And perhaps playmates that are her own age. Be thinking about that. And, one other thing, Finn. You and I must meet each day, whenever possible, to discuss things and so that I can share more with you about my plans, and about what is happening in the world outside. We won't have time to do so while in our dreams."

"No, sir. I mean, yes, my lord."

Finn watched Robby come down the stairs and back to the table, dropping the books down heavily.

"I have a lot of things to study!" he said.

"Is there anything I might do to help you, sir?"

"Not that I can think of. Perhaps you could see if this library holds anything that might concern running a manor or estate, or such. Oh!" Robby turned to Finn with an embarrassed look. "I hate to ask you this, but can you read?"

Finn nodded. "Yes, in the Common Tongues of Men. And somewhat in the older languages of the Faerekind. I have a notion, sir, that I was once a learned man. But my memories are vague. My lord, perhaps I could be your scribe?"

"Thank you for offering, but, to be frank, you are too important for that. I will need your help with other things. You said your memories are vague. But you do have memories?"

"Yes, my lord. Until you returned to Griferis, and during all my years here, I only had memories of this place. But for the past few days, I have been surprised at sudden recollections."

"Oh? Like what?"

"Like, for instance, a cottage. People—perhaps kinfolk of mine, I do not know—going about their chores. And, yesterday, in the pantry, while I was looking over a store of spices, I suddenly remembered walking down the market streets of Glareth by the Sea, with the aroma of baked pies and roasted nuts wafting from the stalls. There was snow in the air."

Robby pulled out a chair and sat, nodding. Finn shook himself from the memory and saw Robby's wrinkled brow.

"Sir, did I say something amiss?"

"Oh," Robby replied in a faraway tone, "no. You reminded me about my father, and..." His voice trailed off, then he looked at Finn and gulped, "It is a good thing he and I are so far away from each other. I don't think I could ever face him again."

"I'm sure he would be happy to see you."

"How could I do such a thing, Finn? I sent my mother off on a dangerous errand. And now she's dead. How could I have been so foolish?"

"I don't know how to answer you, sir. It was before you came here, surely?"

"Yes. The night before I came here."

"Well, you were a young man, then. I'm sure you only did what you thought was right. Even when you first came here, I noticed how careful you tried to be about all of your decisions. Having grown older, and perhaps wiser, would you do it differently if the problem faced you today?"

"I don't know. I want to think so. But I don't know."

"Well, sir, I don't know how your mother's death came about, or how you could even know of it, much less how you could be to blame for it. And, even if I knew those things, I would not be your judge."

"Hm."

"Your memories must surely be sweet and cruel, all at the same time. And, if I may be so bold, sir, I have often wondered if I really want my memories to return to me."

"What do you mean?"

"I mean, I must have done something terrible to have been sent here."

"Why do you say that?"

Finn shrugged. "Why else would my memories be taken from me?"

"Perhaps they were taken as a gift, to make your stay here tolerable, so that you would not pine away for missed loved ones. Or so that you would not try so hard to escape this place, or be hurt while trying to escape."

"Those are reasonable suggestions. Perhaps you are right. But I have no one to mourn for, nor anyone to mourn for me, as far as I know. You do. Perhaps that is not such a bad thing, however it may have come about. Now, sir, if you would excuse me, I think I shall do as you have suggested and have a look at this library's catalog of books."

"Yes. Thank you, Finn. Go right ahead."

A little while later, Finn looked up from the book he was delving into and stepped over to the balcony to look down at Robby. He still sat at the table before his stack of books, his hands in his lap, staring blankly across the room.

• • •

That night, in a dark mood, Robby went to Shatuum to look upon the place more carefully. What he saw was truly horrendous. The land appeared to be a great armed camp, for everywhere surrounding the dark realm there were walls and keeps garrisoned by what he could only describe as goblins and bogles and other strange and terrible beings like those in Seafar's menagerie. Though Robby could not tell where they came from, they numbered in the thousands, and he marveled that there were so many. They fought and argued constantly, and when one was killed, or severely wounded, those around would fly into a frenzy of feeding, often leading to more dead. At first, Robby took heart from this behavior, for surely any land so filled with violence upon itself could hardly be a threat to its neighbors. But then he witnessed one such fight among hundreds of these beings, and it was suddenly and brutally put down by the appearance of another band of soldiers very unlike those who squabbled. They came riding armored horses, and were tall in their saddles, dressed from head to foot in heavy black armor. When they appeared, most of the squabbling goblins and bogles shrank away, while those who were too distracted to notice kept fighting and eating one another. The riders rode into the crowd, wielding long whips that, when they were cracked, exploded those they struck into writhing snapping showers of red hot cinders. After only a few of these strokes, the riot subsided.

Then rode up yet another figure more terrible than any of the rest. He was bigger than any of the other riders, and his armor was banded in crimson, as was his black, horned helmet. His black horse snorted smoke from its glowing nostrils, and from its helmeted head also protruded two horns like those of a bull. When the rider dismounted, all those in his presence cowered, bowing away, and he strode silently into the crowd. Robby saw him turn this way and that, then point. From the crowd came a cringing creature, a thin, long-nosed soldier stooped under the weight of his crude armor plate. When he came before the awful warrior, he fell to his knees. The warrior put his hand about the creature's throat and lifted him up, high off his feet, and squeezed until the head dangled backwards from a pulpy neck, then he hurled the body far, right over the walls of the place and out of sight.

"Thus is the punishment for any who disobey Lord Secundur's law!" a voice bellowed from beneath the helm. "You will have your meat in due time. Until then, you do not eat, lest you die. You do not sleep, lest you die. You do only the bidding of your masters, lest you die."

"What say you to your leader?" cried one of the other grim riders.

"Hail, Throgallus!" came the chorus.

By now hundreds of other soldiers had come along the surrounding ramparts and along the tops of the keeps and surrounding battlements. They, too, rejoined the others below, and raised their crude maces and swords in salute.

"Well do you say!" cried Throgallus to the overlooking crowds. "Now witness the fate of those who risk my displeasure!"

He mounted his horse and rode away while his black-armored captains strode into the crowd with their whips cracking, killing scores before the others scattered.

Robby followed Throgallus into the mountain roads of Shatuum, through a myriad of strongholds, and up to a black tower set into the eastern slopes of Algamori. Inside were no lamps or torches, but Throgallus knew his way. Up winding stairs he went, and Robby, needing no light, for his dreamwalking eyes saw all, followed. But he was filled with fear, dread gripped his heart, and he fought the urge to flee. After a long climb, Throgallus entered a large empty chamber. In a far corner was an indistinct form huddling under a few tattered blankets. As Throgallus stood in the center of the room, Robby approached and looked at the sleeping person, seeing him to be a Dragonkind. As the sleeper tossed and turned, Robby saw that he wore robes very similar in style to those of the scribe who read to him under Micerea's direction. Turning, Robby saw Throgallus kneel and remove his helmet, revealing a pale face, and long white hair tied behind his head. Then, though there was no light in the room, Robby perceived that the place grew even darker, if that was possible, and he felt a chill run through his very soul. Around Throgallus, a thin shadow circled restlessly, then hovered nearby.

"You are troubled, my general," spoke a soft, soothing voice.

"The armies grow increasingly unruly and agitated, my lord," said Throgallus. "They sense, without knowing the cause, that we are threatened, and they turn their teeth too readily upon one another."

"You think we should proceed, do you not? That the time has come to leave Shatuum?"

"That is in my heart, sire."

"Do not fear Griferis, Throgallus. The one who is there cannot leave that place lest he cross over into our lands. And only by passing through our lands may he go to Duinnor. And so, the present Unknown King shall be the last, in spite of the legends. Soon enough, our legions will be free of Shatuum, and your captains shall spread destruction upon the lands of those who have defied me. Meanwhile, my birds still look upon the unfolding of our plan. We shall let Men and Dragon and Elifaen set upon one another for a time, for it is pleasing to me that they should weaken each other by war, and do much of our work for us. Soon war's offspring shall cover the lands of the earth, famine and disease and ruination, as it almost did when you first came to me. Forget not Tulith Attis. You failed your King, but by doing so, you served me, even before you came to me. You saw to the destruction of that place, and soon, a thousand such places of slaughter shall cover all the earth."

"Sire, I do not forget. But the objects that the Fifth Unknown King sought, the present King continues to collect. Serith Ellyn was not taken, nor her Seven. And the other Seven are still hidden from us. Lord Banis failed to obtain the Seven of Vanara, just as I failed to obtain those at Tulith Attis. But do you not fear that the King now has all of the Forty-Nine save those in Serith Ellyn's keeping?"

"Why should I fear that? Those Seven held at Tulith Attis are lost. But even if Duinnor's King had forty-two, which he does not, Serith Ellyn is far away with hers and cannot return soon enough. And why would she give them over to the King in Duinnor whom she despises? No, the Elifaen will not be called away. They shall remain to be our spoils. It is Men that we must first destroy, and the Dragonkind with them, for those races grow too numerous, and I have not forgotten their ancient spite against me."

These words Secundur spoke easily, in a tone of comfort that was difficult for Robby to resist. He felt within that voice a call to sympathy for Secundur's cause, a coaxing reason that should not be questioned.

"And Griferis, my lord? Before they died the Vanarans we captured said that four flew to Algamori upon the wings of their devices. And our sentries report seeing two Gray Guard fly away southward from Algamori."

"If it would make you feel better, send your guard to the place, unto the Gate of Griferis."

"But, lord, they cannot approach it, for the power of the gate weakens them. Even your eagles cannot fly over the place, so disquieting is the aura around it."

"Send your guard, anyway. And let them hurry back from the place. I am sure they will report pleasing news. Meanwhile, go to your consorts and make yourself at ease with them. I know they will do all within their power to please you."

Throgallus did not respond, and the shadow circled him again.

"They cease to give you comfort? Their powers no longer give you pleasure?"

"I have not been with them for a long time, my lord. Other matters seem more pressing, day by day."

"Go to them," said the voice. "By the time you arrive at their brothel, I will have spoken to them, and they shall be most gratified to receive you. Afterwards, decide yourself whether you must investigate Griferis."

"Yes, my lord."

Suddenly, Robby saw a bright bubble appear around the Dragonkind's sleeping form, and then out of it stepped the scribe, gazing straight at Robby who reacted by backing away.

"Do not go, I beg you!" cried the scribe. "Oh, please, wait!"

Robby hesitated, looking at Throgallus, who was arising to depart.

"They cannot see or hear us, I assure you! Please, stay!"

"Who are you? And what do you want from me?" Robby demanded.

"My name is Herzees. Like you, I am a dreamwalker. I am a prisoner here, brought from the desert lands of the south many years ago. Secundur keeps me here to guard against other dreamwalkers."

"And what do you do when you see other dreamwalkers come?"

"I have done nothing, for you are the first that I have seen."

"Well, what are you supposed to do?"

"I am supposed to learn where the dreamwalker sleeps, and warn Secundur, so that his assassins may be sent to that place."

"And why do you serve the one who enslaves you?"

"I do not! I tell Secundur, honestly, that I have seen no dreamwalkers spying upon him. I beg him to let me die. Six times I have tried to escape, and six times I was brought back, each time lashed for my attempt. After the last time, he told me that if I tried again then his agents in the Dragonlands would kill my family."

"Have you gone to see your family? Does Secundur have the means to carry out his threat from so far away? Or does he bluff?"

Herzees hesitated, then said, "I cannot go to them, or else I would. There is some magic in these mountains, or perhaps this tower, that prevents me from dreamwalking beyond these lands. The only dreams I find in Shatuum are those of Throgallus, and his dreams do not touch any others. But I must go from dream to dream in order to travel, as you must know since you must travel the same way. You must be very close at hand, or within Shatuum itself, since you are here."

"No, I am not within Shatuum. And, to answer you, few, if any, sleep within Shatuum, much less dream. It seems Secundur and his followers do not need sleep. As for myself, I have no trouble dreamwalking anywhere I please. I don't see how what you say can be so. How can you follow a dreamwalker, and find where he sleeps, if you cannot go far?"

"It is because my body is here, within this tower. Secundur says that I am to discover where the dreamwalker sleeps by engaging in conversation. If the dreamwalker will not say, I am to tell Secundur. Then he will make a way to find the place where the dreamwalker sleeps. But I think Secundur's fears are not warranted, for there are surely only a very few dreamwalkers. I have only ever known two others. One is dead, and I cannot say what became of the other one. They were students of mine, years ago."

"What is the name of the one who lives?"

"Micerea is her name, though I do not know if she lives."

"Hm. I must go. I will not tell you my name. Make your report to Secundur, if you must. Let him try to find me. But you will not be able to follow me, if what you say is true."

"No, please! Stay and talk! I have no news of my homeland, or anywhere else, save through listening to these two."

"I cannot stay."

Robby moved to depart, then turned back.

"Tell me," he asked Herzees, "does Secundur ever go from this tower to other parts of Shatuum?"

"I have never known him to go from here. This windowless place is his abode."

"And does he have a body, like others do?"

"I have never seen it. I can see nothing here, save his shadow as I dreamwalk. I do not even know if my eyes still see, as I have been in this chamber for so long."

"And where do his followers come from?"

"He breeds them from prisoners that are brought to him, and from other creatures that come from hidden places to serve him. He has sorcerers and witches, and, until recently, a great demon lived deep beneath Shatuum. But he was destroyed, somehow. I only know because I overhead Throgallus and Secundur discuss it. Secundur was very angry."

"Sorcerers and witches, too, you said. Do any of them leave this place?"

"All yearn to leave Shatuum," Herzees answered. "Sometimes, a few break away. As the demon did. A sorcerer did, too, a year or more ago. One called Bunar, a conjurer of plants and vines and the like."

"I see," Robby said. "And Throgallus? Is he a sorcerer?"

"Oh, no. It was he who built most of the fortifications hereabouts, I think. I know very little about him, but he has been here a very long time. He carries himself like a great lord, as if he had been one at some time. He is Elifaen, I think, and perhaps even one of the Firstborn of that race. Though I have never seen his scars."

"Very well, then. I must go. But I may return to see you. Tell Secundur about me, if that is what you must do. I go."

• • •

Robby went immediately back to Griferis. He awoke full of fear and dread at what he had seen in Shatuum. Glancing at the window, he saw that it was still night. Suddenly restless, and with his mind fairly reeling from his observations, he jumped up and got dressed. Taking a lamp, he went quickly to the library. By the time he arrived, he knew that he had much to learn and to figure out concerning Shatuum and Secundur, and he hoped that the books would help him. He also knew there were several other problems to work out, too. There was Duinnor, the reason he came west in the first place. Next, there was the situation in the east, and the great battle that was this very moment taking place around Tallinvale. So many things that, he knew, he would have to let play out for a while longer. Then, among many of these things, there was the Nimbus Illuminas, the Forty-Nine Keys, seven of which Ullin now carried toward Duinnor.

"Oh, why didn't I give them to Sheila or Ashlord?" he muttered as he lit a few lamps. "Poor Ullin! Struggling along so courageously! But by the time he gets to Duinnor, it may be too late!"

For a moment, he was tempted to go back to bed, to dreamwalk again and look for Ullin. But, in the middle of that consideration, hesitating before the library catalog, he realized that what he really wanted to do was to see Sheila.

"But I am now old enough to be her father!" he said, striking a table with his hand and sitting down heavily in a nearby chair. "This is too much!"

He looked at the window glass next to the alcove where he sat, staring not through it at the starry sky, but at his own reflection. Bearded, his hair thinner and straightened by age and streaked with gray, nearly all of his curly locks gone, his face sun-darkened from his last sea-bound trial before the Judges declared him ready to depart. He looked at his hands, callused and hard, the hands of a seaman accustomed to pulling ropes and sail. Though he was strong, he was old, his body covered with scars, and his bones ached where they never mended properly. He longed to look upon her, to speak with her, but he abhorred his appearance, and knew that she would, too. This was why he had not yet gone to see Sheila, not even to look at her, much less to visit her dreams. Robby's heart was still too much broken by his years of trial, and now by the shame and grief of Mirabella's death. And he knew it would never be the same.

If he saw Sheila, he thought, whatever was left of his soul would wither. But he longed to see her, to see that she was safe, true, but just to see her. He suddenly thought of Eldwin's locket, and the one just like it that his father showed to him the day all these troubles began, the day he went to Tulith Attis for Ullin. And Ullin had a locket, too.

"But I have nothing," Robby concluded. "Not a likeness of her to look upon, or even a strand of her hair. Nothing. Just to look at her, just to see her face once again. Would that be so terrible?"

He sat for a little longer, distracted by his longing for Sheila, until he concluded once again that, yes, it would be too terrible, too sweet, to endure. Shaking his head, he felt again how Ullin must have felt for all those years, separated from Micerea, with little hope of ever seeing her again. No family to speak of, no friends to keep him company, and nothing but duty and honor to sustain him. No wonder Ullin seemed so happy when he visited that day. He could have ridden on through Passdale, on to deliver the letters to Ashlord. But Robby understood now, remembering how he lifted and twirled Mirabella about in joyful reunion. Ullin could not pass up the chance for a visit, no matter how brief. The Ribbons were all Ullin had in the whole world.

And now even that was destroyed. Mirabella was dead.

"Oh, Ullin, I'm sorry!" Robby cried out, bursting into tears. "Oh, Daddy! What have I done? Oh, Mother, Mother!"

Sobbing into his hands, and pulling his hair, Robby's anguish and grief came full and without respite, and he wailed, lonely and miserable, for a long time. He did not notice the man standing at the door watching him from the other side of the library, nor the tracks of tears that ran down his face, too. Finn hesitated, then turned away and quietly closed the door.

Chapter 21

The First Battle of Tallinvale

Day 172
73 Days Remaining

The Redvest armies of Tracia were joined with those of the Damar warlord, and Tallinvale was surrounded. But it was not how Tallin or others of his war council imagined it would be. After the early victories against the invaders, and after a long lull, the enemy came swiftly and in great force, establishing posts and camps throughout the hills around the valley. They did not immediately come out onto the valley floor in force, though during the daytime their patrols around the edges of the vale were numerous. At night, however, their campfires dotted the hills, and night after night, week after week, the number of these yellow flickering points increased. By the second week of Firstmonth, the hills were ablaze, and the campfires outlined the rise and dip of the ridges. With every passing day, smoke from the fires grew thicker, drifting over the valley, making the clear winter sky hazy, and sometimes the smoke sank down upon the town, an inescapable sign of the army that was gathering.

Throughout the coldest days of Firstmonth, the fires burned and the forest thinned as more fuel was cut. But other reasons drove axe into bark, and the Tallinvale skirmishers who rode out daily to probe and provoke the enemy reported the sound of hammering, thudding, and ringing anvils. They reported, too, that the hills were densely fortified all around the valley, with well concealed platforms from which their generals could overlook the valley and the defenses of the city. None of the roads were open for coming or going from other parts, but Lord Tallin's spies stole out at night and returned before dawn to report the progress of the enemy's work.

It was clear, therefore, to every defender of Tallinvale that preparations were being made for a massive assault. From the walls of the city, they could see the work of the besiegers taking shape. At the base of the north hills massive towers on great wheels rose up, sheathed in the red shields of the invaders. Almost as large as the towers, six trebuchets were assembled, also on wheels, with long thick arms and with counterweights nearly as big as cottages. With their spyglasses, Tallin and his captains could also see wagons coming and going, bringing stones for the trebuchets to hurl and loads of timber for laying bridges across the canals. Slowly, meticulously, the Redvest leaders directed the building of these machines, the amassing of supplies and material, and the disposition of their troops. That they did not waste their efforts on useless assaults or forays against the walls of Tallin City spoke to the patience of their general.

But the people of Tallinvale were not idle, either. Within a month after the departure of Robby and his companions, the population of the city had swollen to more than ninety thousand souls. It was crowded not only with people, but also with grain, cattle, and food, with every scrap of iron to be found, mountains of lumber, stone, and firewood, and every imaginable item that could be brought from houses and farms throughout the land to within the city walls. Barracks were built for the thousands of families, and foundries and workshops sprang up making tools and weapons. Food was carefully rationed and medicines stockpiled. Hospitals were prepared, and people received training in the cleansing and mending of wounds and broken bones. Stores of water for putting out fires were deployed with buckets and pumps, too, and more water filled every jug and cistern, every spare barrel and keg for drinking and cooking. Every open space was used for training fields, including the grounds surrounding Tallin Hall, and the Hall itself prepared for wounded, serving also as both school and nursery for the young and as headquarters for those who planned and guided the defense of the city.

All of this, and a thousand other things, were done with very little discord. As usual, Lord Tallin was everywhere, supervising and seeing for himself the progress made, solving problems and disputes, advising, and even, with his sleeves rolled up, joining in to work alongside his people. For their part, they grew to love and trust him more than ever, so fair and generous he was with treasure and encouragement. To many, he seemed not so dark and hard as they once thought, for his energetic smile and his congenial tone had replaced sternness and brooding. And the people took their example from him, not only his commanders and long-time soldiers, but also shopkeepers-turned-watchmen and bumpkins from far fields who were now trained as metalsmiths, archers, and skirmishers. But to some few, this change in him was disconcerting, and none was more unsettled by this new aspect of Lord Tallin than his old friend, Dargul, who most likely knew him better than any man alive. On the afternoon that Makeig and his disguised men rode to the rescue of the Passdale prisoners, Tallin and Dargul sat across from one another at their table in their meeting chamber, having just finished reviewing the day's business.

"Your vitality has ever been a poultice for your heart," Dargul said to Tallin. "But it has never been applied with such zeal or optimism. I fear it is a mask, and I understand it, since so many look to you, and you would not have them take pessimism from your example. So it is not the mask, itself, that I fear, but rather some aspect behind the mask, darker than I can fathom."

"A mask?" Tallin responded. "Hm. Perhaps you are right, good friend. But if I wear a mask, I assure you that it is turned inward, for these last months I have had moments when I hardly seem to know my own self. It is not that I seem a stranger to myself, now, but rather that, for so many years, since Kahryna died until recently, I was a stranger. Now, when perspective comes to me, I look back and ask, 'Who was that? Who was that who occupied my body for all those years? That stern, angry man? Who was it who tried and tested my own family, to the point of rejecting my own children, my own daughter! Surely that man was not I!' Yet, I have his memories. I remember the long and fruitless journeys of his mind through the dark lands of his heart, through doubt, through ever-clutching grief. I remember his days and his nights. The motions he went through. Actions without passion other than anger and bitterness. Yes. I remember all too well the burden of time, the press of the sun through each day's sky, and the pull of each star from the falling to the lifting of every night. But what was time to me then but an empty house!"

Tallin put down the document he had been studying and looked at his counselor.

"Yet, duty has some sustaining power, Dargul, and I kept myself busy all those years with managing our affairs, with your loyal and able help. You did not know me very well before. That is, before my sons died and my wife wasted away into death. You did not know my pride and my joy, what love from day to eternal day surrounded me when these halls were filled with the laughter and drama of children and with music and gay celebrations!"

Tallin paused and nearly smirked.

"I now find that I have it all," he said. "My memories are alive to me. The window of passion that closed upon me when Kahryna died has been reopened, and I feel again the fresh joy of those happy days of life. I think now, if I had only managed to pry that window open years ago, what joy I could have shared with my people! I have all of the regrets I ever had, truly. And now even more, since I could have lavished the wellspring of that joy, that love, upon my family and friends. What rejoicing, what celebrations I could have sponsored! What great works I could have done!"

"It is good, perhaps," Dargul ventured, "that your recovery was delayed. Without the treasury laid up unspent during all that time, we would hardly have the means to carry out our defense."

"That may be so," Tallin nodded, "and so perhaps there is some fortunate consequence. It is an odd thing, how some good may come in spite of bad behavior. And how, I suppose, evil may come to those who are good."

"Yes. Odd, indeed, that it is sometimes the way of things."

"But all the treasure in the world and the most valiant actions of tomorrow cannot repay my neglect."

"Sir. You have not neglected Tallinvale, if that is what you mean. The valley and its people have prospered as never before these last years. Your guidance and rule have always been diligent. Because of you, we are strong and healthy. Because of your care and tireless exertions, we have held off the Damar and protected not only our own lands but those of the east and northeast from their expansion. Your years of diplomacy and the strength of our southern borders held Tracia at a distance. Little do I see to criticize. My only wish is that some way could be found out of this siege without bloodshed. Or worse."

"Yes, I regret, too, that I could not finagle some way around this siege," Tallin nodded. "As for the rest, it was my family that I neglected. But at least I still have Mirabella, and, should Providence provide, and she and I come through all of this, I shall redouble my efforts to be the good father that I should have been all along, the good grandfather I should have been to Robby and Ullin. This morning, since just after sunrise, I have been filled with thoughts of my beautiful daughter, and, I must say, I look forward to better days with her. That alone is enough to make me fight all the harder!"

There was a knock at the door, and one of many aides appeared.

"Another delegation approaches, my lord. This is the one you have expected. They carry the standard of a general of high rank. Several of his officers come with him."

"Ah. At last." Tallin rose. He and the aide walked quickly down the hallway, and Dargul followed. "Is the way made ready?"

"Aye, my lord," answered the aide. "The troops have been silently called and are taking their positions, and all the people are following the orders you have given."

"Very well. How many in the party?"

"Four Redvest officers, Cartu, and an escort of six riders."

"All of rank?"

"It appears so. Even the escort seems to be made up of commanders."

"Good. Let them enter and make their way to the Hall just as we have planned."

• • •

The North Gate was opened, and the Redvest delegation was permitted to enter Tallin City. This visit was expected, and Lord Tallin had carefully planned their reception. When the enemy horsemen emerged through the gate, they entered an orderly sea of soldiers, rank upon rank, to each side of the road, the pennants of their companies snapping in the wind, each shield joined to the next like walls, lances upright or swords drawn. Over the heads of these soldiers, the riders saw even more soldiers of Tallinvale lining the walls and parapets, their drawn swords flashing and the horsehair plumes of their helmets waving in the breeze. The way through the city was made narrow by the Tallinvale soldiers, and the riders were forced into a single line, each trying to keep his eyes sternly ahead. As they progressed, the way opened before them and closed behind with easy precision. Meanwhile, all of the blacksmiths and their helpers manned the anvils and beat them with iron hammers, all of the greater and lesser anvils ringing ceaselessly. The citizens and refugees in the city who were not within the ranks of soldiers remained unseen behind the thicket of lances and pennants. But these people beat pots and pans, and they shouted "Tallinvale! Tallinvale!" and rang bells and clapped their hands. The raucous din filled the city with a mighty noise that could be heard by the Redvest ranks far outside its walls, making many of the invaders uneasy.

As the visitors went along, they could not see the source of the sound, nor could they rightly judge the numbers within the city. By the time they reached the outer grounds of Tallin Hall, they were so utterly unnerved that it was only with the utmost effort that they stared straight ahead, jaws set and backs rigid, their hands tightly gripping the reins of their warhorses to keep them in control.

When they arrived at the doors of Tallin Hall, the spectacle did not abate, and while their escorts held the horses, the four generals and the warlord, Cartu, were met by Commander General Brennig and a group of his aides. Up the steps and through the doors the delegation was led, flanked by members of the household guard. The visitors removed their helmets and held them under their arms, but they were not made to put aside their weapons as they were ushered into the great hall.

There awaited all of the ranking men and women of Tallinvale, the city councilors and the mayors of surrounding villages, lairds of nearby estates and their captains, the leaders of the trading guilds, and the high-ranking staff of the household, including Windard. This reception was silent, and as the delegation passed through the banner-hung arches, the fireplaces blazing and the braziers bright with flame, the doors behind them were closed with a loud thud, and all of the noise that accompanied the delegation and echoed through out the city ceased completely. Now they heard only the sound of their own footfalls on the marble floor as they were led through the gathering toward the dais at the far end. There stood Lord Tallin, dressed for war. To his right was Dargul, and behind him were all of the commanders of the gates and walls, including Captain Weylan of the North Gate.

Brennig stopped and bowed to Tallin, then saluted, announcing the names of the visitors, much to the surprise of the Redvests.

"My Lord Tallin," Brennig said, "here come before you Pragon Mar Henith, Commanding General of the Sixth Army and of the combined forces of the Triumvirate that invade our valley. With him, my Lord

Tallin, come General Borkal, Second Army, Thirty-Third Division, General Menslay, First Army, Eleventh Division, and General Tireath, Third Army, Seventy-Third and Ninety-First Divisions. Also here is General Cartu, the warlord of the Damar rabble who is ally to the Redvest trespassers and pillagers."

Mar Henith dipped his head slightly to Tallin and spoke.

"Lord Tallin. So you know who we are, and you have marked well our battle pennants. You also know your situation. This city cannot withstand our assault. I personally bring to you this our last entreaty. Spare your people! Give yourselves over to Tracia. Swear oaths of alliance and avert bloodshed and destruction."

"You know our answer," Tallin shot back without hesitation. "Our oaths have already been given to Duinnor. Just as yours once was."

"Duinnor does not value loyalty. Indeed, such loyalty is ill-placed. Your King treats you as he treats Vanara, as a neglected land, used to buffer itself from its enemies. A source of wealth, unearned. A target of abuse, unwarranted. Now Duinnor has a new enemy. Our aim is nothing less than to remake the world and to re-establish the trade and rights that Duinnor has cut off from us, to take back those lands unjustly stolen from us generations ago, and to have returned to us the treasure and wealth of our people, removed by an age of tribute to Duinnor. What good were our oaths to Duinnor? Our sons were taken from us to useless wars in the west. Our treasure was taken while our people starved. Did Duinnor help us build our roads? Repair our bridges? Did ever the King send aid or succor when plague struck us? Food when there was famine in our lands? What did Tracia ever receive of Duinnor? Insult! What did Tracia hear from its pleas? Silence! What did Duinnor teach us? To be loyal to the unfaithful is folly! That is why we cast out Duinnor's puppet. That is why we now march!"

"What did Tracia ever do for the Seven Realms?" retorted Tallin. "Was it the fault of Duinnor that the Tracian people had industry only at the end of your whips? Was it the fault of Duinnor that your people would not heed the advice of its own wise ones? That, instead of laying aside some of each harvest, you consumed your seed and sold your grain for silver and jewels? Was it the fault of Duinnor that, when the land dried up, there was little to eat? That, when the floods came, your ill-tended farms washed away? Oh, but I forget myself! You tossed out the rightful Prince, who lavished all his wealth to forestall disaster and was criticized for it. You imprisoned and slew as many of the wise men as you could, those who spoke of folly and warned of reckoning. You severed civil communications, and punished free and honest discourse. You returned good will with thievery, raiding parties, and brazen fraud against your neighbors to the north and to the west. Why do you think Duinnor is cool toward you? And you complain! You should be thankful that Duinnor did not send its armies against you when your mobs burned your cities, when your leaders burned your books and scrolls, and when your prisons lost their capacity to hold those who had no means of bribing your bosses."

"But now," Tallin went on, "now that you have struck outside your lands, as invaders and marauders, Duinnor's wrath is only a matter of time. And it is time that Tallinvale gives to Duinnor. We do not seek to annihilate you. But we shall not ourselves be annihilated! Tallinvale will bleed with Tracian blood. This valley will be as a whirlpool, drawing you inward to the slaughter, not only your blood, but also your treasure and your time. Every day that you are in this valley is a day that you do not march against our neighbors. It is a day you do not spread your poison. Every day you spend here is another day you disappoint your allies. And another day that Duinnor draws closer. Every man who falls before us is one less to strike against the King. While your numbers thin, the hills, the mountains, and the plains grow thick with loyal steel. We will hold you here. Your food diminishes, while our stores are still full. Your men grow sick and weak, drinking waters fouled by their own filth. But we are healthy and strong. Your men grow restless, far from their families. But our families are here beside us, and we will protect them. Who protects your families while you are away? Did you know, General Borkal, that your son and all his family, his wife and children, were arrested two weeks ago and taken to Brightpool Prison not far from your estate?"

Dargul stepped forward and handed the rattled soldier a parchment.

"And General Menslay, why is it that your estates were recently confiscated by your government? You did not know? Yes. I'm afraid your wife and children are gone from there. I do not know where they were taken. General Tireath, your wife mourns the loss of her sons, neither more than ten years old, taken three weeks ago to serve on the ships of your navy. My knowledge of you and of your families is extensive, indeed. And, Cartu, you who call yourself a lord. The farmers of your hills revolt, rising up against your walled town to seek grain or other food taken from them so that they may feed what remains of their families. You do not care? How is it that I, a loyal subject of faraway Duinnor, a foreigner to your lands, may know that which you do not? Because it is within my power to know, through my resources, and through the mighty resources of my people. I will attack you wherever and however I may. With words, with deeds, with arrow, and with sword. You shall be made to hurt until you are dead or until you are gone from these lands."

"A most impressive speech, Lord Tallin!" said Mar Henith. "Your men finely arrayed. Your agents doing their worst. Your forgers busy!" Mar Henith snatched the document from General Borkal. He glanced at it and then let it fall to the floor. "No doubt your people think themselves prepared. But Duinnor will not come. Glareth has not the strength of arms to protect herself, much less come to your aid. No one rises up to help you. Spare your city and your people! If you submit to our Tracian law, you will be treated fairly. This one afternoon I give you. Until the setting sun."

"One afternoon?" Tallin replied, smiling. "You shall have your answer in one moment, for these gathered here are the true leaders of our people, not I."

Tallin stepped down from the dais and held his arms out. "What say you! Do we forfeit our freedom?"

A resounding "No!" boomed through the room.

"Do we give ourselves over to the care of Tracia?"

"Never!"

"Would you have Tracia set the price for your crops or your goods? Would you send your children to fight alongside the Dragonkind, as these here do? Would you join with these Redvests and tear apart the Seven Realms? Throw down your King as they have their Prince?"

As he queried the people, Tallin walked among them, and they all responded heartily, filling the room with their defiant answers, growing in volume and in fervor with every question he put to them. Tallin smiled again, and let the noise continue as he came back to face Mar Henith, holding up his hand to quell the cries.

"So there," Tallin said.

"You may think that you are strong and secure," said Mar Henith, "but how firm will you be when arrows fly? We know your strength and have taken care to measure it well. We know your defenses, the thickness of your walls, the height of your gates. We know of your coffers of oil and your intention to flood the canals with fire. We know about the bridges, made to fall when you wish. Do you think us so unprepared or ill-equipped? You have seen us fill your canals. You have watched the construction of our war machines. You have until sunset this day to reconsider!"

Tallin turned to the guard, saying, "Return these men to the gate."

Quickly the Redvests were marched out to their awaiting escorts. But as they rode away and back through the city, the armies of Tallinvale had dispersed and disappeared along with all of the crowds. Only an eerie silence met the Redvests, accented by the snap and flutter of banners. Besides the company who marched before them and behind them, no living soul did they see, not along the streets, nor in the yards they passed, nor in the windows or on the fortified walls. Intentionally, they were led along a more circuitous route, and as they went, the more unnerving the emptiness of the city became, until at last they arrived before the North Gate. Standing atop and looking down upon them as they approached was Lord Tallin and Commander Brennig, his arms crossed. Then, Tallin held up his hand for the delegation to halt.

"One last word to you, Mar Henith," he said. "The battle you bring upon this valley will be a disaster for the ambitions of your masters and will lead to the ruin of Tracia. If you survive this battle, you will not survive their wrath, even if Tallinvale falls. Even if Duinnor does not come. Your name is already written in the Book of Fate, and it has been sealed."

"Look to your own fate, Kingsman!" Mar Henith cried back, and he and his men spurred their mounts through the gate and away back toward their own lines. Tallin watched, satisfied that they had been shaken by their visit. Below and around him, people were emerging from their houses and from the buildings, up from the vast underground passageways, and out from the nooks and crannies. He held up his hand, watching the riders go back to their lines. When they passed over the nearest bridge, Tallin swept down his hand. Below the wall behind him, Weylan made a gesture with his fist, and, a few yards away, a man brought down a large mallet against a wooden stop. When it was knocked free, a large iron hammer swung and banged against an iron rod jutting from the wall. Behind the riders, the bridge collapsed into the canal, upsetting their horses. Reining his horse around, Mar Henith watched the dust settle before calmly resuming his canter. Bridge after bridge tumbled behind them, and even the ones beyond the Redvest lines on up the road. Then, in quick succession, all of the stone bridges across the westward canals fell, leaving only those beyond the east gate standing. But, as the fields there were now flooded, it was an inviting causeway that the enemy knew better than to cross.

"Now that was impressive," Brennig nodded, swinging his spyglass from one place to the next. "They all appear to be down."

"Good. Let them trust their own bridges henceforth," Tallin replied as soldiers took up their positions and posts along the walls and gates. "Send word to all the people that everything was well done. Tell them to remember their place and their duty. If our walls are breached, the battle will be fought amongst them. Seal the gates! Have every position doubled. Call the War Council to the East Armoury, all of the rank of captain or higher to be in attendance."

Orders went forth, drums beat, and trumpets called. Quickly, the walls and towers were fully manned, all drawbridges raised, every portcullis lowered, and the gates closed. Against the interior of each gate, new walls of heavy timber and stone were put in place, buttressing them against rams. As the engineers strove to complete their work, Tallin gathered the chief officers of his armies into the large armoury near to the northeast side of the town.

"Let me repeat," he told them. "At first, their attack will come at all sides of us. They have tried to drain the mire from the east and west fields, just as they have tried to drain our canals, but our weirs are strong and our springs are steady, and they have wasted men and supplies on their futile efforts to make dry ground. To the west, they will not be able to assault our walls, due to the mire of the flooded fields, and will soon give up, but they may try to reach us with large trebuchets. To the east, the fields are likewise flooded, but the Redvests may attempt to come in heavy armor across the causeway, tempted by the bridges that we left standing. Let us hope they do not learn too quickly that it is a death road, with no cover from our missiles, and too narrow to move in mass. As for the south, the rise up to the base of our walls is steep and rocky, and they have not built ramps or roads to bring up engines. However, since there is no moat, they will doubtless send thousands against those walls with ladders and grapples, but it is only to distract us. Their main assault will come against the north wall since those fields are broad, dry, and level. While they continue to bridge and dam the canals, they will attempt to assault the north wall with ladders and grapples, and that is where they will mass their archers and smaller ballistas."

Tallin looked at his men, nodding at the firm determination in their eyes. He continued.

"You have all seen the sea of men pouring into our fields. Indeed, it is a mighty army. We have all watched them build their towers, their massive trebuchets, and their other engines. Truly, they are feats of workmanship built by expert craftsmen. We must defend our walls and, at the same time, draw their engines to within range of our own. This will be difficult. At first, their trebuchets will outrange us. But we also know that their wood is green whilst our trebuchets are made of good cured timber and strong-forged iron and steel. Their machines will bend and crack and lose their range, and they will be forced to move them closer and closer to us. They know this, and they have made only a few ranging shots so as not to wear and weaken their greenwood or their soft-forged iron. Once the battle truly begins, however, they will not spare their machines. We must endure their barrage. It is imperative that we entice them to advance, and we must do so as quickly as we can. They know where our oil stores are and will aim to set fires and to sweep away our own batteries. So we must be patient. We must endure much from them. And we must refrain from showing the true accuracy and range of our own trebuchets. If they believe they have the advantage of us, they will move their engines closer to bombard our city, thinking to make a quick end to their siege. But our fire brigades are well trained, well equipped, and standing ready. And when the enemy is within range of our machines, we will give him a lesson in ferocity that he will not recover from."

Tallin's commanders grimly smiled at this, clearly in agreement with his plan.

"They have already dammed most of the streams feeding our canals, but they do not know about the underground waterways that will continue to feed them. General Mar Henith does not understand this, and surely he scolds his engineers for not being able to drain the canals and our flooded fields. They do not know all of our secrets, in spite of his claim.

Battle of Tallinvale

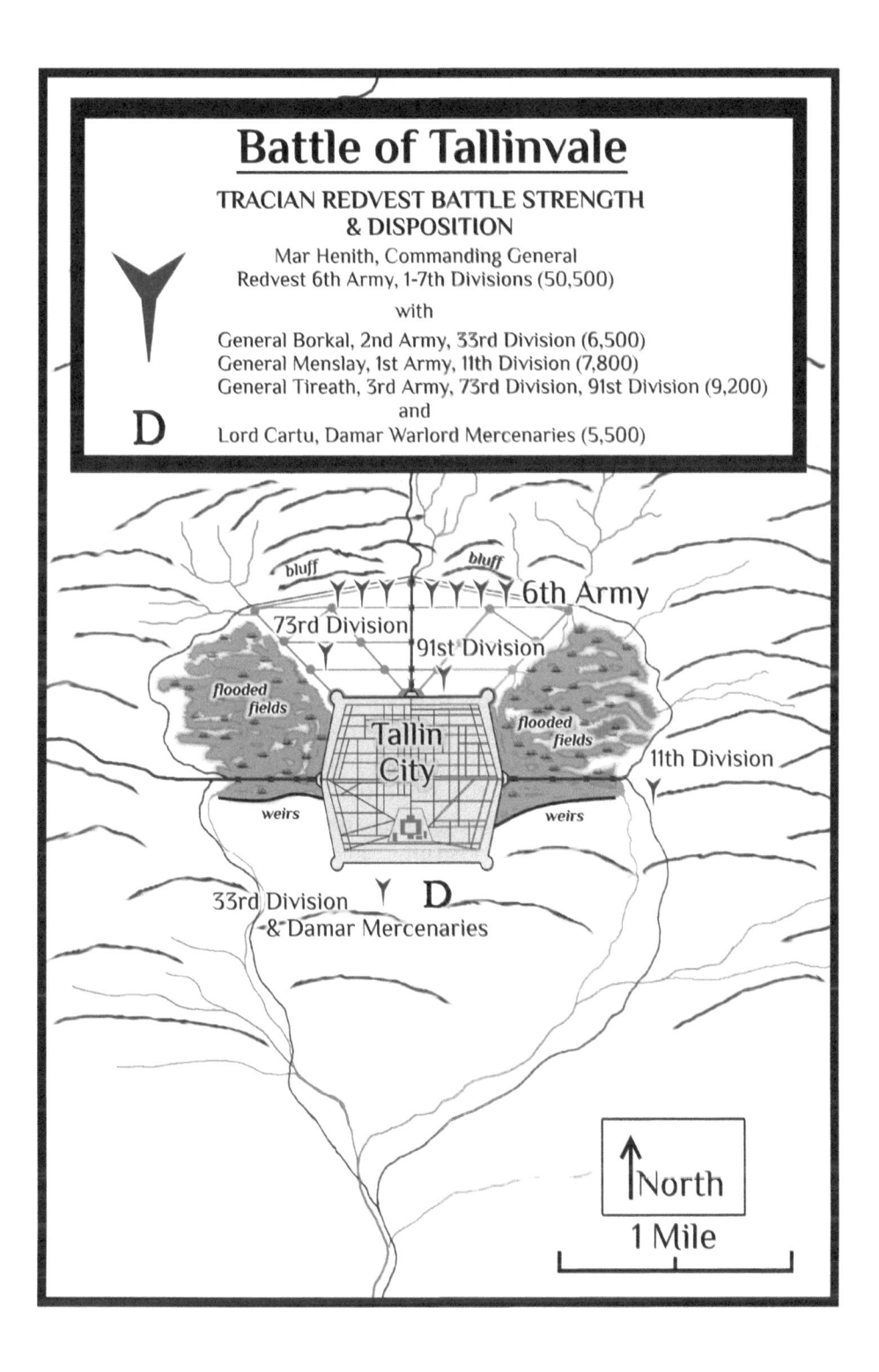

TRACIAN REDVEST BATTLE STRENGTH & DISPOSITION

Mar Henith, Commanding General
Redvest 6th Army, 1-7th Divisions (50,500)

with

General Borkal, 2nd Army, 33rd Division (6,500)
General Menslay, 1st Army, 11th Division (7,800)
General Tireath, 3rd Army, 73rd Division, 91st Division (9,200)
and
Lord Cartu, Damar Warlord Mercenaries (5,500)

bluff — *bluff* — 6th Army
73rd Division — 91st Division
flooded fields — *flooded fields*
Tallin City
11th Division
weirs — *weirs*
33rd Division & Damar Mercenaries

↑ North
1 Mile

"Now. We were given until sundown. It means that the enemy can wait no longer. His food and material are in short supply. He is cold, and he grows weak from hunger. He has obliterated our forest, and he forages farther and farther for firewood and material, but he has not yet managed to take Janhaven and its stores. All this is to our advantage. As careful as he is, Mar Henith will take risks, and he will make mistakes. We will watch for these and make him regret he ever saw our valley. If we fight well and prudently, we may deal them such a blow to make them stagger. If we are fortunate, they will not recover. Our aim is simple: Survive to fight, fight to survive. If we do this, their army will collapse. I believe Mar Henith will seek victory by sunrise, and, to that end, he will throw all that he has against us tonight. So! They already occupy the land beyond the third canal line. Let us draw the bulk of the enemy to within the second line of canals, as close to our walls as we can bring them. That stretch we have marked well, and we shall make it a death ground for any who tread there. So let them win it! We must be convincing, or else they will be tentative and hesitant. They will make us pay a heavy price, but we shall take the last measure from them."

• • •

The Redvest General-in-Chief stood on the exact spot overlooking Tallinvale, the valley, and the city, where Robby and his party had stood only a few months earlier. If they had seen at that time what Mar Henith now surveyed, they would have surely turned back in an instant. The plains below, and all the fields that surrounded the city, were now ringed with a red-cloaked army and their engines of destruction. As that ring thickened with more troops and equipment, it began forming itself into ordered ranks. By now, the siege towers were completed, their parts forged and fashioned throughout the winter and meticulously assembled in their approach positions. Each of them, sheathed with overlapping shields, stood over five stories high, some twenty feet higher than Tallin's northern wall. They were crammed with archers and crack assault teams, and each was armed with small catapults designed to rain missiles and jars of fiery oil upon the defenders once they were close enough. As well, each tower was served by over a thousand men, engineers and laborers whose task it was to propel each tower forward on its wheels by means of winches, springs, teams of horses, and other contrivances. Ahead of each would go fast soldiers and wagons of gravel and stones, to clear a path for the machines and to build their own bridges over the canals. Besides those there were thousands of others who would man the mighty trebuchets, the likes of which had never been tried in battle. In repose, they stood nearly as tall as the towers and were made on huge wheels so that they, too, could creep forward, hurling deadly boulders and flaming balls the size of horses. With them were scores of thousands of men, archers, pikemen, and footmen who would come with ladders and grapples to scale the ramparts, to set fire to the gates, to undermine the walls, and to storm the city.

All was ready.

General Mar Henith had always known that it would come to this. For weeks, he had refused to order the rash and futile attacks suggested by his advisors, impatient men who had no stomach for the privations of winter warfare; but such attacks would be like gnats stinging a bull for all the damage they could do. Instead, for the past month and a half, he had ordered and supervised the construction of his massive machines. Now they were completed, just as rations were being cut once again, and it was time for his decisive assault. To wait another week would risk the collapse of his army.

The sun settled into the western hills, glinting sharply off sheets of unmelted snow and yet-untrampled ice on the valley floor, and Mar Henith was pleased with what he saw. He smiled as his aide tied his battle cloaks over his armor. By this time tomorrow, he mused, the city, or what was left of it, would be occupied.. And he would be free to march his men back to the south to rejoin the bulk of the Tracian forces poised for the westward invasions.

"Good enough!" he said to the aide, and then he walked briskly to his waiting horse. He put on his battle helmet and rode with six of his captains down the hill to the nearest tower. There they dismounted, entered the rear opening, and quickly climbed the hundreds of rungs to the topmost floor. Even from this distance, Mar Henith was high enough to overlook the northern walls and see into the city itself. Bending over a spyglass on a tripod, he quickly swept the nearby fields, watching his men mass before him, and the last of the missiles being hauled by wagons and stacked at the trebuchets. He stepped away from the spyglass, and he looked out from the broad window-like opening before him, grasping the sill and leaning out to look all around. Then he gazed westward at the last pink clouds as they turned purple.

"Very well, gentlemen," he said. "Let it begin."

• • •

As the sun's final rays disappeared behind the mountains away to the west, Lord Tallin, Commander Brennig, and Captain Weylan watched from atop the North Gate. Before them, and to their left, some six hundred yards away, the first Redvest divisions began crossing the outer canals, pouring over hundreds of footbridges and into the middle broadland where the lesser ditches and streams were no obstacle for them. The Redvests set to work filling those with dirt and rubble to make way for their towers while others began assembling bridgeworks that they intended to lay across the canals ahead. More soldiers came crowding over the inner canals to gain the fields near at hand, spreading out into lines that formed into phalanxes a mere hundred yards from the walls. From their vantage, Tallin and the others could see similar movements on the east and west flanks of the city, but in lesser numbers indicating mere diversionary moves. Messengers came and went, bringing details of those movements as well as descriptions of the activities outside the south walls where the steepness of the land as it rose to the walls made that side virtually unassailable.

"They do not know the reach of our missiles," Tallin observed. "Let them gather and crowd."

The horde grew as a seemingly inexhaustible supply of men came over the far ridges, through the devastated woods, and flowed down into the valley. Many of the defenders who watched from the walls were filled with awe and fear. By the time the first stars of the evening were showing at their brightest, and the noise of the metal-clad besiegers grew to its mightiest, all was prepared. In the night-darkened fields before the defenders, dots of yellow-orange light glowed then suddenly rose up and flew through the air, trailing sparks as they came toward the city.

"Cover!" cried Brennig as all defenders scurried into casemates, ducked behind parapets, and threw up their shields. The six streaking fireballs came, each over two yards in diameter. Some struck the parapets, others exploded against the outer wall, but most cleared the walls and fell into the open yards behind the defenders, setting off fires along the edge of town.

Tallin, who had not budged from his post, now went quickly to a man bent over a transit mounted on the parapet.

"Can we reach them?"

"With the heavy ballistas throwing small light missiles. But just barely. They are too distant for our trebuchets to have effect."

Tallin turned away thoughtfully, looking over the town. People were scurrying about, but with organized purpose, putting out the fires before they spread. Only one outlying building was destroyed, a shed where tools were stored. So far, the town itself was unscathed.

"They are at the limit of their range," he announced. He chided himself for not anticipating this turn, so early in the battle, and he struggled with his decision while his men waited and the Redvests worked to reload their machines. It was during this pause that the great towers began inching forward, careful to keep clear of their comrades' trebuchets. Tallin glanced at them and then back at the town. From the base of the walls to the first rows of shops and houses was a span of nearly one hundred yards, more in some places and much less in other parts of the city. The open area was part of the defenses and Tallin never permitted any homes or buildings of commerce to be erected within those grounds, keeping it clear for the movement of troops and engines and for the positioning of archers and the staging of sorties. But now a grim choice faced him, and he made it swiftly, just as the second volley of fireballs arced through the sky. Like before, some fell short and others bounced off the top of the walls, but most landed with an explosion of flame against the nearest buildings.

"Commander Brennig, give the order for all outer houses and buildings to be abandoned. Tell the people to move quickly toward the central squares of the city. Move all troops and war materials that are above ground to as close to the walls as possible."

"Yes, my lord."

Brennig gave the order to one of his aides and followed Tallin as he walked along the inner edge of the wall, looking at his troops and engines massed below.

"We shall give them a volley by ballista and trebuchet, flaming bolt and fire stones. Trebuchets first, Batteries One and Three. Make the target fifty yards short. Match ballistas to the trebuchets. Short by fifty yards. Make as if we shoot for their trebuchets. Understood? It will not be a waste of missiles if it works."

As they spoke, they moved to cover, ducking behind the parapets as enemy fireballs struck again, bouncing and exploding along the ramparts, setting men and machines afire and filling the air with smoke, shooting flames, and screams.

"Quickly! We must take their aim from the walls and make them move closer to strike the town!"

Brennig sprang into action, barking orders, passing them along to Weylan and the other captains, and making them understand the tactic. It was a gamble. Tallin knew that if the Redvest trebuchets came closer, their strikes could destroy the entire city with fire. But at their present distance, they could bombard the walls and destroy the men and equipment needed for defense. Tallin gambled that his counterpart, Mar Henith, wanted a swift and decisive end to this battle, and that he would think a devastating blow to the city would force capitulation.

Word spread quickly, and the men behind the walls scrambled to load and set their machines. Each team was directed from atop the wall by a spotter and a signalman who gave directions of aim and distance to target. The crews of the machines responded immediately to each signal, turning their devices and straining at the pawling gears to tension the heavy springs of coiled rope. They knew their machines intimately, and, though they could not see their targets, word went about that they were shooting short of the mark. Some grumbled, not understanding the ploy, but all obeyed and were soon awaiting their next command.

"Battery One! Battery Three!" bellowed Brennig. "Trebuchets, loose!"

The long arms of the trebuchets swung upward gracefully, flinging their flaming payloads over the walls. Dozens of streaking arcs cut the sky and fell toward the crowds of Redvest soldiers who marched toward the walls. They now sought to scatter, holding their shields over their heads. For many it was futile, their lines smashed by the crushing fireballs that made awful carnage amongst them. But none of Tallin's missiles came close to the enemy's trebuchets.

"Ballistas! Loose!"

Now the faster, iron tipped missiles flew, each the length of a man's height, swathed with fiery cloth. They, too, struck short of the enemy machines and, in spite of the death and destruction wreaked on the exposed men who went ahead of their trebuchets, a taunting chorus of jeers went up from the enemy ranks. When Tallin and Brennig heard this, they were grimly pleased. To the Redvest observers, the intended targets were clearly apparent, and the aim of the Tallinvale defenders true, but their machines seemed too weak to reach the required distance. The chorus of insults increased as their own batteries answered Tallinvale with fire and stone.

"Again," Tallin ordered through the hail of missiles. "Have one or two decrease the range and go wide of the mark. Let us appear muddled and ill-equipped."

The incoming salvo of missiles was followed by a volley of arrows and bolts, shot from the nearest ranks of Redvests. Many upon the wall were struck down, and some who manned the small ballistas were killed or wounded. Others immediately filled the gaps.

"Light Batteries, all! Spikefists!" Brennig ordered.

Around the wall, smaller trebuchets and ballistas sent hundreds of the steel-spiked glass balls raining down on the Redvest ranks, shattering with awful effectiveness, opening wide holes in their lines.

"Have our archers mass against those bowmen, Commander," Tallin said in a calm tone in spite of the noise.

The night had been transformed into nightmare, a hellish place full of pitch-smoke and fire, the clank and thud of iron and wood, the swoosh of missiles and hiss of arrows, the cries of men, the determined giving their orders, and the dying giving their last voice to the night. But the front machines of the attackers did not immediately return fire. Instead, they again moved forward as did the siege towers. Every few yards of advance, the enemy machines launched a missile, a ranging probe to test the ability of the defenders to respond, while those high up in the advancing towers watched the results and gave their reports. By now, Tallin's men knew what gambit they played, and they found new ways to appear ineffectual. They shot tip-less bolts from their ballistas that flew erratically, cloth-wrapped stones that would barely stay alight, and fiery baskets that flew apart harmlessly as they streaked through the air. With every round that came over the walls at them, the enemy masses grew more confident and worked harder to draw closer their machines, and the massing ranks of soldiers hunched down in close formations to wait for their machines to catch up, overlapping their shields and appearing like hundreds of huge reddish turtles.

Meanwhile, the evacuation of the edge of town continued, with the expected confusion and despair on the part of the homeowners and shopkeepers. Few men could be spared from the fire brigades or from the walls, so most of the moving work was done by women, children, and elderly folk. But they had been forewarned of this possibility weeks earlier and were prepared. They were well aware that if some of the outermost buildings were set afire, the flames could spread to adjoining structures and eventually reach the safer places in the city center. For that reason, winches and ropes and stacks of axes and sledgehammers had been assembled in various places, ready to pull down any building that threatened others.

"My lord," a runner called, coming up the stairs to Tallin. "Commander Luard's compliments, sir. Ladders are being brought against the southern walls. And there appears to be some mining activity as well. Enemy arrows continually come thick, small missiles from ballistas, too. Our casualties are low, and we make ready to repel their assault."

"Very well. Give Commander Luard my compliments. Tell him to carry on with all means. I send reinforcements to him forthwith."

The runner rushed away, and Tallin turned to Brennig.

"Our south walls will soon be tested," he said. "Every fifth, Commander."

Brennig immediately spun around and shouted, "Every fifth!"

Two lieutenants sprang forward, going in opposite directions left and right along the wall, tapping men as they counted and ordered "South defenses!" with every fifth tap. The air was thick with missiles of all kinds, bolts, stones, arrows, some flaming, others glinting strangely by the many fires that now burned. One man on down the line was struck and flung away by a large bolt, and the next man automatically turned to take his place with those chosen to go south.

"Light Batteries! Fifty yards!" cried Weylan. "Sustain with flame and spikefists! Loose at will! Archers to the parapet with shields."

Tallin and Brennig both stood with spyglasses and examined as best they could in the mixed light the progress of the nearest tower as it slowly approached its new-made bridge. They also calmly swept the scene before them, studying how the Redvests moved their troops and equipment, formed their men, and held their shields, mentally noting which groups seemed to be the most orderly and which seemed to have trouble or moved awkwardly. The two observed with practiced skill as arrows hissed past them, and they did not waste a single moment of their exposure. It had been many years since Tallin faced such a battle, but through his precise and never-forgetting mind, he had lost none of his skills of leadership or any of his composure in the face of the enemy. Brennig followed his lord's model, being less tried but not without experience, and the two of them, with Weylan and other officers that the two had carefully groomed and cultured, served as examples to the others who defended the place.

"Ready the Medium Batteries at one hundred yards. Flamestones and spikefists following, by pairs," Tallin said, still looking through his glass. "Normal sustained rate of volley."

"Aye, Lord Tallin!"

"Archers to bear upon the confusion."

"Aye, sir." Brennig turned and called to the drummers. "Beat again to Medium Batteries! One hundred! By pairs, flamestones, spikefists. Sustained at signal! Archers at the ready!"

Immediately, two nearby battle drummers beat a cadence, picked up by drummers farther away, and, upon hearing the loud din, captains listened and took their orders from the signals, soon confirmed by young boys acting as runners.

Tallin turned and watched for a moment as his ballista teams up and down the wall and below all cranked and elevated their machines. Touching Brennig on the shoulder, he pointed to the nearest tower, still creaking forward, then down steeply at the infantry who were now laying bridges over the moat directly below.

"Make ready our oil. Use it just as we discussed. I go to the south. The North Wall is yours."

Brennig watched Tallin stride away, the soldiers he passed putting up their shields to protect him against missiles. Turning back, an arrow whistled inches from Brennig's nose guard and another glanced off his right spaulder. Putting his spyglass on the parapet, he brought the nearest tower into focus, now only a few yards from the first broad bridge across the canals.

"Make ready the oil, Number Seven!"

The drummers beat a different thumping cadence as he swung his glass slowly across, first to the left and then to the right. Two other towers were near to the bridges, but not so close as the one directly ahead. He could make out teams of workers scrambling over the bridges, shoring them up with long timbers.

"If we do the oil now," Weylan said, standing beside him, "the others will be warned off. And, besides, Number Seven is old stuff, barely more than pitch. Who knows if it will flow out, much less burn?"

"It is all a-purpose, Captain. If we don't use oil, they'll wonder why," answered Brennig, still peering through his spyglass. "Prepare to fire the moat. Number Seven, only."

By now, the smaller ballistas and trebuchets were launching their payloads in pairs, with firepots going over the wall first. As each blazing missile crashed into the advancing phalanxes, it was quickly followed by clusters of spikefists. The explosions of fire forced gaps in the Redvest shields, and the spikefist poured into these openings, exploding their glass and steel razors into the unprotected flanks before they could reform, spraying the attackers with blinding shards and splinters. The cries of agony that reached the walls filled the Tallinvale defenders with grim understanding, even as they suffered from the relentless weapons of the

Redvests. Yet more and more of the enemy flowed forward to take the place of the thousands that fell. To those defending the walls, it was like trying to stay the incoming tide of a furious sea.

"Is there no end to 'em?" Brennig heard a man nearby say.

He took his eye from the glass to look at the havoc close by when a fireball the size of a barrel came hissing just over his head from right to left skipping and crashing along the length of the parapet, crushing and maiming with its weight and fire, flinging scores of broken and burning men and mangled chunks of war machines flying, effectively wiping out nearly all of the defenders along that portion of the wall in one swipe. After the initial shock of it passed, Brennig spun around and looked eastward for the source. Although masked by darkness and smoke, he saw the trebuchet, unused until now. It was well within striking range of the town, so close, in fact, that it might even overreach the town with its powerful arm.

"How did we miss that one?" he shouted, bringing up his glass for a better look. "And how the blazes did they get that machine so close?"

"Clear away that wreckage!" Weylan bellowed, picking himself up, brushing smoking cinders from his sleeve, and ripping away a burning section of his surcoat. He pointed at a group of reserves standing in shock on the ground down below. "You men! Up here on the double!"

"Trebuchets East!" Brennig shouted to the drummers and then to the spotters. "They mean to rake us! Hurry! Battery Twelve, shoot when ready! Captain Weylan, send someone over there and find out why our spotters didn't report that trebuchet! And why the hell Battery Twelve hasn't eliminated it!"

"Aye, sir!"

The orders went out by shout and drum, and the large trebuchets and ballistas defending the northeast of Tallin City groaned and creaked as men turned and cranked and elevated them.

• • •

Tallin's mount reared as he pulled hard his reins to look back at the North Wall, now a half-mile distant, and saw the aftermath of the devastating strike. He almost went back, his anxious horse twisting and turning in the avenue. Then he heard the drums that told him that Brennig, or someone competent, was still in command, and he resumed his gallop southward. All the way, his path was cleared before him through the crowded streets as people carrying all manner of things saw him coming and cheered as he galloped by. Taking a shortcut through the grounds of his estate, where many of the wounded were being brought, he reached the southern walls just as enemy ladders were craned up. Dismounting, he ran up the stairs, his sword drawn, and entered the fray as Redvests and drab-garbed Damar poured over the top. Lord Tallin saw, after watching but a few encounters between his men and the enemy, that this assault was no real effort. Looking up and down the wall through the fighting, he saw that his men were having an easy time of it, allowing the enemy to gain the wall at purposeful salients only to be slaughtered between the Tallinvale formations that rushed in from either side. Tallin worked his way to the wall's commander and reached him as the wave of attackers reeled and were cast from the wall. Already, grappling hooks were being used by the defenders to latch onto the ladders, and they were being hauled upward and over the wall, terrifying those that were still trying to climb, shaking loose many others to crash down onto their comrades. As the ladders were drawn up and away from those that would use them, the Tallinvale commander shouted his orders.

"Strip them of weapons and cast the bodies over! Archers!"

While his order was quickly and gruesomely seen to, and as archers did their work on the retreating force, Tallin touched the commander's arm.

"They are fodder, Commander Luard," Tallin said, toeing a fallen Damar. "Redvest dregs and Damar mercenaries. They mean to sap our north walls with these useless attacks. Nonetheless, all the men we can spare are coming."

"Lord Tallin! We have more than enough for this rabble. We will let them climb if they've the stomach for it, and cut them down as just now," Luard replied.

"Good," Tallin nodded, now shouting over the cheers of the defenders as they threw the hundreds of bodies onto the wounded and retreating attackers. "They will come again and again until they, or we, are drained."

"My only hope is that they do not give up trying, my lord," answered Luard smartly.

They both grimly acknowledged that the more of the enemy who died here without purpose or gain would be that many fewer who could mass against the lower and weaker northern walls.

"Very well, then. Carry on!"

Tallin turned away, and another rain of arrows fell as he strode back to the stairs. Though shields were thrown up for his protection, one arrow rang off his backplate and another glanced off his cheekguard, shot under the cuff of his gauntlet, cut into the back of his right wrist and hand, and sent a searing jolt all the way up his arm.

"My lord!" cried a soldier, still holding up his shield. Tallin continued on down the stairs, aided by two other soldiers, one holding his arm while the other tried to remove the glove without causing further pain. Arrows continued to crack and ping against their armor as they descended.

"Just off with it!" cried Tallin impatiently. He stifled another cry as it was removed. Blood splashed out from the wound where the arrow point protruded, half buried into the back of his hand.

"Bind it!" he ordered as he tugged the arrow out, just when a surgeon's aide arrived with a lamp. Tallin was guided to a shielded area at the base of the wall where the young aide took several things from his shoulder bag, handing the lamp to a soldier.

"Just a moment, Lord Tallin. Sit there, put your arm on that table. I want to at least put a few stitches in that, else you'll bleed to death. Hold that lamp steady! You two there! Come here! Grip his arm, hold it fast against the table!"

Greatly perturbed by the inconvenience of the wound, and wincing with pain, Tallin acquiesced, saying, "I think you are a bit impertinent."

Some whiskey from a flask was drizzled on the wound, and Tallin cried out at the fire that shot up his arm as he kicked and nearly stood out of his chair.

"Be still! Hold him. Hold him, you oafs!" barked the youngster.

A needle and thread was quickly produced, and, before Tallin got back his voice, the aide was drawing together loop after loop through Tallin's flesh. On the wall above, steel and iron clanged and thudded among shouts and yelling and other noise. A few bodies fell from above and landed nearby, but the aide was not distracted by any of these things. Still grimacing, but fascinated by the boy's work, Tallin stared as his skin was sewn together.

"You are the tailor's son, Bart," Tallin finally managed to say.

"Aye, that is my name," replied the boy as he deftly snipped the thread with a knife and then produced a roll of bandages. "I do not recall you ever coming into our shop."

"I never have. I was at your naming this very day, twelve years ago. I have not seen you since."

"Your memory is remarkable," the boy said, hesitating only for a moment at the surprise. "And you never forget a face? Even though I was a baby at that time!"

"I never forget. It is not always a curse. That was a good day. Are you quite finished with me?"

"Almost," Bart said, putting a final turn of a bandage about the hand and wrist. "Try not to use this hand. Have the dressing checked twice each day for festering. Here," he handed the patient his gauntlet, "I doubt if it will fit over the binding. Excuse me, there are others I must attend to."

Before Tallin could say anything more, the youngster scrambled over a dead soldier who had fallen from above and bent over another who was still moving. Tallin tried to put on his glove, then tossed it away. He looked at the faces of the fallen at his feet, silently speaking their full names, a habit formed as a young soldier on battlefields forgotten by history, but not by him.

• • •

"Dammit! Don't just pick at it!" Brennig bellowed at the crew of the trebuchet. "Destroy that infernal thing before it kills us all!"

After the muddled orders, he himself ran the length of the wall to the eastern corner, and was berating the spotters and crew of Battery Twelve, situated at the northeast corner of the town.

"Commander! The towers are turning," called a runner, still approaching. Brennig ran back toward the North Gate, dodging men upon the ramparts as he went, eyeing the huge trebuchets that inched closer and closer. Before he got halfway back to the North Gate, he saw Weylan coming at a crouched run through a storm of arrows that glanced and clanked and cracked all around him.

"They're laying down their heavy bridges," Weylan called to Brennig. "Look yonder, at the wagons!"

Brennig took the spyglass that Weylan held out, put it on the wall, and, taking a moment to catch his breath, looked through it. Wagons and scores of men were coming alongside the siege towers, and Brennig watched by the yellow light of the wagoneers' torches as they maneuvered in front of each tower and carefully backed up to the canals to dump their payloads of stone, gravel, and soil. As soon as an emptied wagon was out of the way, another took its place, quickly filling the canal.

"At this rate, they'll have them bridged within the hour," Brennig stated. Swinging his spyglass back and forth to look at the other enemy teams at each tower, he tried to judge the speed of their work. "They bring Tower Four first. Probably to test us. The others move more slowly. This will be dicey!"

"Do we let it reach our walls?" Weylan asked. "And hope that they will bring the others on in? All the oil from Number Seven is in the moat, sir. And, sir, spotters report all of the enemy's trebuchets are coming just within effective range. The closest two are on the outer marker."

"I see them. Why are they not using them? Might they be out of missiles so soon?"

"I doubt that, sir."

"They are up to something," Brennig said, still peering through his glass. A glare to his right caught his eye. Turning to look back the way he had come, he saw a fireball soaring up from the vexing enemy trebuchet on the east. But it was off by too wide a margin to rake the wall again, and arched too high up. He watched with horror as the fireball struck his own opposing trebuchet, just as its arm swung a fiery payload upward. The two fireballs collided, exploding in a loud hissing crackle, engulfing the men and machines of Battery Twelve and sending a thick spray of oily fire upward all around. At the last moment, Brennig and Weylan dove under shields as burning chunks rained and splattered down on them. Jumping back to his feet, Brennig grabbed the spyglass, but it was shattered. Flinging it away, he pulled Weylan to his feet, brushing burning debris from Weylan's leg.

"You men! Get those fires out! And clear away the wreckage. Captain Weylan, get a team of horses over to Number Six Battery and haul their trebuchet to take the place of Battery Twelve. If you can't get rid of that blasted Redvest machine, we'll have to send out a sortie in force."

"Aye sir!"

Weylan scrambled off, and Brennig jogged on to the North Gate, turning his attention back to the closest trebuchets before him, wondering why they remained idle.

"Soldier," Brennig turned aside to an aide who stepped up to take Weylan's place, "fire the moat."

"Yes, Commander!"

A torch was dropped over the wall, and a rush of orange flames whooshed out from it in both directions. Peering through an arrow slit, Brennig was satisfied that it was enough to discourage all but the most zealous attackers, but not enough to stop the encroaching towers or trebuchets. He heard one of them groan and thump as its arm swung aloft. Looking, he could see no missile flung from it. Puzzled, he heard the other one do the same. Turning to the city, he scanned the rooftops, looking for any sign of a striking projectile, but saw none.

"What the devil are they up to?" he muttered, running over to a metal box and flinging it open. Pulling out another spyglass, he ran back to take a closer look. Again, the trebuchets waved their long arms, but no flaming missile issued from them, nor any boulders. As far as Brennig could see, no missile of any kind crashed into the town. The Redvests acted quickly, resetting each trebuchet with unmatched speed. Again and again, they flung up their huge arms, but to no apparent purpose.

"Beat to Five!" he shouted. "Destroy those machines, NOW! Let them have everything that can reach!"

In a rush, Brennig's comrades cranked, adjusted, and loaded their machines, and each captain held up his arm, giving the ready. In less than a minute, Brennig gave the order, and they all let loose with fireball, spikefist, boulder, and bolt, arcing swiftly in an eerie cascade over the walls at the two mysterious trebuchets. Brennig watched the Redvest crews running in vain, but one hurled a last shot before it flew apart in flaming timbers as the Tallinvaler's missiles hit. Over the cheers that went up from the wall, Brennig heard a strange cry, like a scream, passing high overhead. Turning his head to follow the sound, he saw the dark shape of a man collide against the side of a building in a splash of blood.

"Captain, you have the wall!"

"Aye, sir!"

Jogging down the steps, Brennig ran to the place where he saw the body fall, and pulled up when he found it.

"What the...?"

The man was dressed in a tight-fitting black tunic and breeches. In addition to a short narrow scabbard, he wore an odd-looking pack on his back, with straps across his chest and shoulders something like a harness.

"Soldier! Bring that torch!"

By the light that came, Brennig turned the body over to get to the pack. It was bound with cords, and when he cut them away and reached in, all he found was a large black cloth, light of weight and affixed with dozens of cords to the shoulder straps of the dead man.

"What is that, sir?" asked the soldier holding the torch.

"I don't know," Brennig said, still holding the cloth. He looked upward, absently noticing that the sky had become overcast and now glowed a sickly orange. Shaking himself, he shoved the cloth at the soldier and ran back to the wall.

• • •

The enemy trebuchets that were destroyed had done their job. High over the town, one of the last payloads floated down under a black canopy. Dangling from it by many cords, a man in dark garb descended onto a rooftop as the billowing cloth drooped down around him. He quickly gathered up the cloth, crouching as he worked. He squirmed out of his harness, and then hid the apparatus under a chimney. He ran to the edge of the roof and jumped to a lower adjoining roof, then, gripping the eaves, hung over the side to drop down into a narrow alley. He produced a short rapier-like sword, trotted to the corner of the alley, and, staying within the darkest shadows along the way, he disappeared down the next street.

• • •

When Brennig returned to the North Gate, his attention was fully on the towers and the other four remaining trebuchets that were being pulled and pushed over the earthen bridges laid with heavy planks. Immediately below, thousands more Redvests had once again made it to the moat and were struggling to erect footbridges to span it where only some of the fiery oil had reached. He grudgingly admired the work of the Redvest engineers. Their heavy war machines rolled easily over the quickly constructed bridges, and their wagons, dumping their loads under constant fire from Tallinvale's ballistas, effectively plugged up the canals so that very few obstacles remained before the besiegers. The light footbridges being brought forward were sturdy and easily handled. And Brennig could see that they were now constructing heavy rolling shelters, covered with shields and planks, large enough for their wagons to be protected as they moved against the next canal and then, ultimately, to the moat. Tallinvale archers were making all this work exceedingly dangerous, but not deadly enough.

"Hills and mountains," he said to himself, wondering at the vast amount of labor required to excavate and move so much fill.

He looked eastward. By now, Weylan's men were teaming horses to drag one of their trebuchets all the way across to the other side, to face the enemy's own outside of the eastern corner of the north wall. It had not stopped throwing fireballs, but now it lobbed them at the town rather than the walls. Already, several buildings were in flames, spewing cinders and smoke high into the air. Brennig watched as yet another fireball crashed through a roof and slammed into the side of the building next to it. It looked as though that one machine all by itself might defeat them.

• • •

High up in the rearmost siege tower, General Mar Henith and his aides watched the battle unfold. Using his own powerful spyglass, he scanned the walls of Tallin City as often as he studied the movements of his men and machines.

"General, the canals are bridged," said an aide, seeing through his own spyglass a signal from a more forward position. "The wagons are moving forward to the next one."

"Signal the towers and trebuchets Three through Six to advance. Trebuchets One and Two are to continue their mission."

"Yes, sir."

Just then a storm of fire and missiles arced over the walls and converged on the two trebuchets just mentioned. Henith needed no spyglass to see the destruction that rained upon them, and he shook his head in displeasure.

"They can indeed reach our machines," he stated. Turning his glass to the easternmost machine, the one that had been carefully brought up as close as possible, its men having worked in the dark to assemble and move it into place before they were spotted. It now threw blast after blast upon the town.

"Signal, sir. Trebuchets One and Two are destroyed completely. They cannot be repaired."

"How many of our shadow men got off?"

"A dozen, sir."

"Only a dozen." Henith straightened and looked back toward the North Gate. "Then, at best, only six survived their trip. Let us hope that will be enough. Signal Lord Cartu and General Borkal to throw all their force against the southern walls. Order all engines forward. Have Fifth and Ninth Battalions brought up as well. They are to mass against the north walls. Signal General Menslay to move against the East Gate immediately."

"Sir, what about their oil? Surely they have not used it all."

"I mean to provoke them to use what they have. Anyway, it is inferior, as you can see; it burns low and is easily put out. Lord Tallin evidently could learn a thing or two from our countrymen about pressing olives."

• • •

When Lord Tallin rejoined Brennig, Captain Weylan was just returning from his work moving the trebuchet across from the western to the eastern side, and which was now engaging the enemy machine that fired upon the city.

"Lord Tallin," Brennig reported, "the east Redvest trebuchet still harasses us and drops fire upon the town. So far we have not been able to reach it."

"Yes, I see."

"You are hurt, my lord!"

"It is nothing. What else?"

"Sir, the towers are but two hundred yards out, and closing. We have knocked out two of their large trebuchets, but the others are within three hundred yards, and are beginning to set up. Already they have knocked out five of our ballistas, and six of our trebuchets. Two more are damaged. We have but five trebuchets left, all told, and four heavy ballistas. Ladders are now against the walls, as you can see, though we repel the climbers with ease. We poured oil from Number Seven, and fired the moat. Their archers mark us well, though, and we have lost at least three hundred men in the last half-hour. We have brought up all of our reserves. All told, we have but seven thousand left on the north walls. Sir, when shall we use the good oil?"

"Begin pouring it right away, into channel six, Commander."

Brennig hesitated, looking quickly out at the horde.

"Sir, pardon me. My lord, if we pour all into channel six, we will have none for the moat or the near canals."

"Commander Brennig, all into channel six."

"Very well, my lord. But it will take almost an hour to pour."

"Then see to it immediately."

"Yes, sir!"

Brennig turned to go down the stairs just when a great black bird landed on the parapet beside him. A nearby soldier raised his bow, but Tallin put out his hand, stopping him.

"No, wait."

"Shoo-wee!" Weylan crinkled his nose.

Tallin smiled at the bird. "You can't help it, can you, old friend?"

Brennig cocked a brow, and the other men nearby stared in disbelief as Tallin held out his left arm. The vulture spread its wings halfway, walked to the edge of the stone, and hopped onto Tallin's arm.

"What news do you bring, eh?"

The creature bobbed its grotesque head, turning an eye at Tallin, then as Tallin held out his bandaged hand, it dropped a pebble into his palm. Tallin nodded, looking at the smooth bit of marble.

"Well done, well done," he said. "And do you have anything to say to me?"

"Ba-a baacar," the bird screeched hoarsely. "Ba-a baacar."

"A Dragon bird!" Brennig uttered, instinctively stepping away. "I know that language."

"No, he is not," Tallin said, "though that is the language of the word. Tell the one who sent you," he addressed the bird, "that his debt is paid.

That you have delivered the word to me, and I shall now strive to deliver it to those who sleep."

Tallin raised his arm, and with several powerful sweeps of its wings, the vulture flew off over the city, climbing into the orange sky.

"Commander Brennig, another order for you," Tallin said, smiling.

"Yes, my lord?"

"Do you know the odd device that is nearby to the oil tanks? The solid iron bar with the funnel atop it?"

"Yes, my lord. Who has not wondered at its purpose?"

"When the oil is emptied into channel six, return here with it. And hurry!"

"Yes, my lord."

• • •

Mar Henith was pleased at the progress of his attack. Fires from the city licked the sky, his men were already scaling the north walls, and several of his towers were almost close enough to rain their missiles down upon the defenders. His bowmen continuously shot bolt and arrow upward from close below the walls, and their armored shelters protected the wagons of fill that had nearly clogged the remaining canal, while more men were already at work filling the moat with earth and stone. It was only a matter of an hour, two at most, before his towers could roll over the moat and pour out their soldiers upon the walls themselves, overwhelming the defenders in the crush of their numbers.

"We shall move forward, now," he said to an aide. "At haste to catch up to the others. I would like to step out upon the north wall myself."

"Yes, General," the aide responded. He then called out orders that were passed down through the structure and would bring forward those men and horses waiting below to pull the general's tower forward.

"Runner from the south wall, sir. They continue their efforts, but their mines have hit solid rock. Lord Cartu puts forward more ladders, and Borkal brings up his bowmen."

"Good, good. Please acknowledge with my compliments."

• • •

Eldwin carefully made his way through the leftover scrub and stumps that were once the thick forest so carefully minded by generations of Tallinvale wardens. Seeking to avoid the camps and the throngs of the Redvest army and its followers, he popped quickly from cover to cover, going in short jumps of only a few yards at a time. He knew that the evidence of his movement could be seen as a remnant of soft dissipating light at the beginning and ending of each jump, so he made every effort to watch carefully before he did so. It was tedious, but he was patient and more than once his care paid off, allowing him to bypass sentries and those that watched the rear flanks of the army. He first noticed the bloody red glow against the southern sky miles away, and as he neared the valley, the stars were blotted out by an overcast sky made eerie with the glowing smoke that hung in the air. Now, as he neared the bluff directly behind the tower in which Mar Henith directed his troops, he could clearly hear the sounds of battle, the groan and creak of the great trebuchets, the dull clang of metal, and the shouts, yells, and screams that merged into one continuous chorus of a hundred thousand men. When at last he broke out onto the bluff, he lost his footing and stumbled as what he saw filled him with horror.

The terrible pink and red of the low overcast sky stretched like a ghastly canopy. Fires were everywhere across the land, the calls of the wounded and dying filled the air as thick as the smoke and biting odor of pitch. Long curving swaths of flames swept across the sky toward the city, trailing sparks as they flew. There were sudden streaks of fiery light as the defenders poured flaming oil down the sides of the walls, amid thunderous explosions as boulders hit the city. More missiles flew out from the burning city to crush and maim the attackers, scattering them like bowling pins. High red-sheathed towers crept across the awful landscape, as burning arches of arrows reached out from them and disappeared behind the walls of the city.

Falling upon one knee, and grabbing a root to keep from tumbling down the hill, Eldwin stared across the valley, paralyzed. His sharp eyes, even in the weird light, saw bodies thrown screaming through the air, and discerned detached arms and heads flying as missiles from the city struck into the throngs of pressing soldiers, sending out cloud-like bursts of red. Up and down the length of the city walls, men tumbled down one after another, as if some invisible hand swept them off as casually as crumbs from a table. In his eyes, the red cloaks and tunics of the Tracians became confused with the coppery armor of the Dragonkind, the gore-streaked walls with those of Tulith Attis, and the vast scene of destruction the very same as that to which the despised Bailorg had brought him all those years ago, until he knew not what time or place he had come to. It was all one and the same. And now, just as then, he was unable to fathom the hatred that could bring about such an expanse of carnage.

Gaping, his eyes burning with smoke and sorrow, he remained in that awkward position, unable to let go of the root that he clung to, unable to look away from the nightmare before him. Perhaps it was only moments, but in those moments thousands died before him. What brought him slowly out of his trance was the growing awareness of a faint light, blinking dimly across the field of attackers, on and off, from the left toward the right. Jerking to attention, he saw the light again. He immediately snapped his fingers and shot across the valley floor, dodging men and machines, sometimes stumbling when he popped to his next location, steadily nearer to the light. All around him, men were sweeping forward, across the footbridges and newly made earth and stone crossways that spanned the canals. He went with them, following the blinking light closer and closer to the city, around the mountainous machines, among the fires and through the spray of missiles, going on only because it took him closer to that fuzzy, blinking light. At last, he managed to pop close enough to see Herbert suddenly appear in front of a Redvest soldier and thrust a short sword up into the man. Laughing, Herbert snapped his fingers to pop over to another man, laying wounded on the ground. Herbert swung his sword against the neck of the prone figure, then, before Eldwin could catch up to him, he popped off again at a man who carried a comrade in his arms, dispatching them both with cruel jabs of his sword. Eldwin shouted, but Herbert could not hear him over the confusion and noise. Snapping his fingers, Eldwin popped right into Herbert just as he materialized near a trebuchet.

"Herbert! What are ye doing?"

"Eldwin! Oh, Eldwin, it is too easy!"

"What's the matter with ye?"

Herbert's eyes were wide and crazed, his mouth grinning, his once beautiful blue velvet coat now black with glistening blood.

"Just pop an' poke!" Herbert laughed. "Pop an' slash! Slash an' cut an' pop!"

"Stop it! Stop it!"

"Stop? That's why we're here, ain't it?"

"Yer not supposed to be here! Yer supposed to be guarding our people back home!"

Eldwin grabbed Herbert by the collar and swung him around violently. But Herbert only laughed all the harder.

"What? An' let ye have all the fun? Get out of me way!"

Dodging an onrushing soldier wielding an axe, Eldwin stumbled and fell backwards as Herbert, laughing hysterically, popped away and then behind the confused Tracian, running him through with his sword.

"See? Pop an' poke. Come along. I'll show ye how!"

As Herbert stooped down to help Eldwin up, a lance ran through his back and out his shoulder, its point barely missing Eldwin's face. Herbert, his eyes wide and blood pouring out of his mouth and nose, dropped his sword across Eldwin's chest as he was lifted up. The soldier flung the lance and Herbert aside and drew his sword.

"What have we? Some kinda pixie-folk what come to pester us?"

The Redvest raised his sword over the frozen Eldwin but was struck by a missile that took off his head before impaling four other men. Eldwin screamed, grabbed up Herbert's sword and hacked at the headless body that had fallen beside him. At the last moment, he became aware of a half-dozen other Redvests rushing at him, and he snapped his fingers only to come right into the path of another charging soldier. Out of desperate reflex, he raised Herbert's sword and caught the surprised man under the arm, just where a gap in his armor allowed the blade to go deep. Pulling hard, he freed the sword as the man fell, and snapped his fingers to pop away. But no matter where he aimed to wind up, he found himself facing scores of soldiers. Yelling with terror, stabbing and kicking and snapping his fingers to pop away, again and again he was faced by a seemingly endless crowd of Redvests, all towering over him with their lances and swords and shields and armor. Each time, seeing Eldwin's bloodied sword, they swung at him or charged him. Time and again, Eldwin jabbed and swung, seeking only to get away from the place, until at last he popped beside Mar Henith's tower and quickly crawled underneath it. On his hands and knees, he scrambled from side to side, looking for a likely place to pop off to. Just as he was putting his fingers together, the tower lurched and its four massive wheels began turning. Spinning around, he saw the feet of thousands of men as they strained on their harnesses to pull the heavy structure forward to the city.

• • •

It took three men to carry the iron device, one of them Brennig himself. They climbed the stairs up the wall and to the place over the North Gate where Lord Tallin waited. Arrows dinged and snapped off their armor as they put the thing down and caught their breath.

"Commander, see this hole, here in the stonework?" Tallin pointed down where he stood. "Help me drop the long end of the rod into the hole."

Together, Tallin, Brennig and Weylan lifted the heavy object, an iron rod as thick as a man's arm, about six feet long with a funnel cast onto one end of it. When they got the rod over the hole, they tilted it upward.

"Let it drop!" cried Tallin, and they did so. It slid down the hole about five feet, ringing loudly as it bounced twice. Then, mystifying the onlookers, Lord Tallin got to his knees and put his face into the funnel. He looked up at Brennig.

"The oil?"

"The last of it runs now into channel six, my lord. All tanks. Over sixty thousand gallons. But sir, where does it go? And what is this contrivance?"

"You shall soon see, my friend! Bowman! I will have your bow and a flaming arrow in but a moment or two!"

"Yes, Lord Tallin!"

Tallin put his head back to the funnel and spoke, "Baa bacar." Again, more loudly, he cried, "Baa bacar!"

These words, in the ancient Dragon tongue spoken in the time of Kalzar, mean "Now rest!" These were the words withheld from Lord Tallin when Alonair ordered the trolls to build the secret vaults that spanned beneath the fertile fields north of the city. Now Tallin said the words, and said them loudly. The sound of his voice, and those words, passed through the iron bar and into the stone of the gate. It went down through the walls of the city, and into the foundations, then out through the rock that was deep beneath the fields now covered with the might of the Redvest army. This was Tallin's great secret. This is why he had labored so secretly and so long before bringing his family east. Never did he think that he would use those words against any but the Dragonkind.

Beneath the once fertile fields north of Tallin City, fields now obliterated by war, the sound of Tallin's voice passed through rock and into carefully laid stone. It was a small and insignificant sound compared to the din aboveground, compared to the rumble and thunder that passed into the earth from the rolling wheels of the war machines and the tromp of the pressing army. Nonetheless, Lord Tallin's words were heard, ringing through the underground chambers that Alonair had so meticulously constructed long ago. The secret words were heard and obeyed. Over a thousand sets of massive arms, each pair holding aloft a great stone lintel, relaxed. Thus, each lintel fell.

• • •

Eldwin finally managed to scramble unseen from under the rear side of Mar Henith's tower, now creaking steadily toward the city walls. He quickly looked at the northern bluff and snapped his fingers. Twice more he popped, until he was atop the bluff behind a pile of brush. Diving into the cover, he sat in a daze, shaking with fright. As he tried to stifle his fear, he felt a dull rumble course through the earth. Pushing aside some of the limbs, he looked across the field toward the city as the ground trembled violently. Near the city walls, a trebuchet suddenly tilted. One and then another of the towers crashed as the ground sank away beneath them. All across the battlefield, the earth was falling into itself, and geysers of water shot up where the great machines fell. From the city's North Gate, the ground gave way, spreading outward across the valley, dropping a dozen feet or more. Men and horses disappeared amid desperate screams, siege towers toppled, coming apart as they fell, and trebuchets flew to pieces as they tumbled over. Eldwin backed away as the edge of the growing hole neared. But the quaking stopped. The ground ceased to fall away only a few dozen yards from where Eldwin watched, and a weird silence spread over the valley. This lasted only for a moment and was followed by an eerie chorus of moans.

It was as if a vast underground cavern had collapsed. Where a moment before a great army advanced against the city, there was now nothing but a churning lake. Awestruck, Eldwin unsteadily got to his feet. The tiny dot of a fiery arrow then arched high up and out from the city. He watched it, mystified, as it descended into the water. An inferno exploded where the arrow fell, and fierce blue and orange flames rushed quickly in all directions across the lake until it was a vast brazier-like cauldron, lighting the night with its awful blaze.

• • •

Lord Tallin handed the bow back to the stunned archer and turned away. Brennig stared aghast at the inferno, putting his hand over his eyes against the glare and leaning back from the intense heat. All who manned the walls gaped at the sight, and for a long while no one cheered.

"Second to the east," Tallin ordered. "Third to the fire brigades. Fourth to the south. Let Weylan have the wall, while you and I go to Luard."

Shaking himself, Brennig turned and looked at the city, dotted with fires. It began to dawn on the men that the battle was suddenly and awfully won, and the first tentative cheers went up. Brennig barked out his orders.

"Every second man to the East Wall, third to the fire brigades, and fourth to the South Wall! Captain Weylan, you have the wall."

• • •

Not every tower fell completely over into the inferno. The one that General Mar Henith occupied, at the rearmost of the burning lake, sank several yards nearly straight down, then tilted precariously forward, but it did not fall. All of Mar Henith's aides were spilled out of it, but he barely managed to hang on, clinging to its side. As it filled with acrid smoke, he sought some way out from the burning hulk. When the tremendous cave-in happened, creating a vast crater into the underground lake over which the fields were constructed, the unburned oil from the city moats gushed rapidly into the waters that churned with struggling men. But the tower from which Mar Henith directed his ill-fated troops was situated near to the northern rim of the lake, and now, as he crawled out through the roof, his remaining men who were safely ashore, saw him. Loyal to the end, they quickly began to construct an improvised bridge to span the flames to his disabled tower. Seeing him emerge and stand atop the slanting tower, they called to him to hold on. Standing with his legs apart, one foot on the roof and one on the back wall of the unsteady wreck, he saw them as he tried to wipe the soot and smoke from his stinging eyes. He faced south, toward the city, and looked upon his decimated forces, hearing their death cries, their calls for help, and the whoosh and crack of the burning engines. As he watched, the men who sought to reach him continued to work, pulling logs and planking from their encampments, pouring wagonloads of dirt down the bank into the steaming water. All the while, Mar Henith gazed, stunned and bewildered, watching men scrambling up the protruding remains of his trebuchets as they tried to outrace the flames behind them, many falling to their deaths. Then, sooner than one might suppose, the cries diminished, the calls for help faded, and all that he heard was the crackle of burning timber, and the distant crunch of disintegrating towers. Though he could not see through the thick smoke, he fancied for a moment that he could hear the remnants of his great army still fighting somewhere far away to the east and south. But he had no illusions concerning their prospects.

Turning around carefully, he looked over the flames at those seeking to rescue him, just now getting close enough to throw the last long logs out to reach the base of his burning structure. But the fire was all over the crippled tower, and it was too intense for them to safely approach. He raised a hand and held it in a casual wave, a signal for his men to halt their efforts. Their captain saw him, standing behind the flames and smoke, and he raised his own hand in return. The tower cracked and shifted, sending Mar Henith plummeting from it. Then, in a great groan, the structure fell upon him in a burning heap.

• • •

On the eastern flank, a different story was playing out. Redvest General Menslay realized the futility of moving his troops across the elevated roadway to assail the East Gate. The roadway was too narrow and one of the bridges was collapsed. On either side of the roadway, the fields that Tallin had flooded, and that the Redvests had labored to drain, were still a hopeless bog. After several costly attempts to cross the long straight approach, General Menslay pulled his men back to the heights beyond. He was preparing to redirect his force to join Lord Cartu and General Borkal in the south when the fiery catastrophe swept away the bulk of the army moving against the north walls. At first he watched in shock, as did his terror-stricken battalions. Then, feeling the heat of the inferno even from this distance, he quickly began scanning with his spyglass for Mar Henith's tower.

"Send a runner to inquire after General Mar Henith," he instructed his aide. "If he has survived, tell him that we swing around to join the southern assault. If he has not, then order all surviving men and material to come at once."

Then, shaking himself, he gave the order to march, and sent runners to Lord Cartu and Borkal to expect his force within the half-hour. Emboldened by this news, but not understanding what had taken place, Cartu and Borkal redoubled their efforts, bringing small ballistas and trebuchets to bear, lobbing boulders and missiles high up to reach over the steep slopes and come nearly straight down upon the defenders. When Menslay arrived, Cartu and Borkal met him, and he quickly related what he had seen at the north battlefield.

"Until General Mar Henith arrives, I am taking charge of the attack," he stated.

"On what authority?" the warlord Cartu demanded. "Has your general survived?"

"That remains to be seen. Regardless, I am next senior to General Mar Henith, and only he may countermand my orders. If you wish to withdraw your men, then do so. Borkal? What about you?"

"I stand with you, sir."

"Then recall your men to regroup. This is no longer a diversion. We still have over fifteen thousand men, and with them I mean to take this city. Where is your command post?"

"Just yonder, about a furlong down the hill."

"Let us go. Summon all senior field officers, and company captains. Have your engineers at the ready."

• • •

Lord Tallin, now back where he had been wounded, stood upon the southern wall directly behind the grounds of his estate and watched with Commanders Brennig and Luard as the enemy pulled back.

"Do they retreat?" Luard asked.

"Hand me that spyglass," Brennig ordered a spotter. Putting it on the wall, he examined the ranks of men as they melted away into the gloom. Although the sun was trying to gain the sky, it was an overcast morning, and a mixture of thin mist and smoke hovered over the fields. "I can only see about a hundred yards or so."

"Their ballistas still pester us," Tallin said. He flexed his injured hand, looking down at it. His fingers all still worked properly, but he had lost all sensation below the elbow which throbbed viciously. "They regroup to weigh their options, most likely. Send word to the west and east walls, every third man. Listen!"

Brennig stood straight, and Luard cocked his head.

"Quiet on the wall!" he shouted. A distant bumping could just be heard, in the distance directly in front of their position.

"Wagons?" Brennig asked.

"And equipment," Luard added. "But it don't sound like it's gettin' any farther away."

"They are building something," Tallin nodded. "Engines, perhaps."

"It's nearly two hundred yards to the nearest flat ground," Luard said. "They'd have to be buildin' a mighty trebuchet, indeed, to reach this far and this high up. An' they'll starve afore they get it done."

"Unless they expect reinforcements," Brennig suggested.

"No. I don't think they can expect reinforcements or fresh supplies anytime soon. It is something else they do. And until there's better light, or they reveal themselves, we won't know. Commanders, make the rotation of your men, an hour to eat, followed by one to rest. Luard, go with the first rotation. I go to see the wounded."

• • •

When Tallin came through the stable yard, striding toward the back entrance of his home, he had to dodge and weave to avoid the carts and wagons that continuously came and went, bringing wounded soldiers and injured townspeople to the Hall. Ducking inside, he came through the pantry hallway, and made his way by side passages. Although properly greeted by the crowds of nurses and physicians and orderlies, no one paused in their work or asked after the battle outside the Hall. When he emerged from a side door into the grand foyer, he hardly recognized the place. Everywhere were cots and tables, men and women moaning and crying in pain, blood running across the beautiful floor, and just beside him, a handcart filled with mangled limbs. The odor of foxdire was so strong that he wondered that everyone was not a-slumber, though he never heard of its aroma doing what swallowing the stuff did. Carefully picking his way through to the double doors that opened into the great hall, he found a similar scene as in the foyer, wounded soldiers everywhere, on the floor and on tables, blood spattered physicians and aides shouting orders as they worked amid the constant groaning and wailing. There were women and boys rushing around with baskets of bandages, carrying lamps and buckets of water, and taking away gruesome pails of limbs and gore. Spotting Dargul, who was delivering a basket of bandages to a far table, he made his way to him.

"Lord Tallin," Dargul took Tallin's arm, "you are wounded."

"A scratch. What is the situation here?"

"All I know is that we have accepted over twenty-six hundred wounded here at the Hall tonight. About half come with very serious wounds and burns. The rest we move outside as soon as we can. I've counted nine hundred dead. But you should ask the ladies at the door who receive the wounded for an accurate count. Our physicians wear themselves out. Tasdon, over there, gave up trying to direct things at the other infirmaries in the town, as he has been needed here. When last I spoke with him, he said the other infirmaries were filled, too. And more places are needed. I'm afraid we are overwhelmed."

"And the supplies?"

"We are nearly out of foxdire, and now save it for the worst off, those that need amputations. We use strong liquors for the others. We run short on bandages, and our salve for burns is almost gone."

"Have Windard take up the linens from all of the bedrooms and any like materials from the dining rooms. And also curtains and anything else that will serve. Spare nothing. Send someone to my rooms and bring down all of the liquor and spirits there."

"Yes, my lord," Dargul motioned at a passing aide. "Take a look at Lord Tallin's hand."

"No, go on with your duties. I did not come here for that."

"Sorry, my lord. But until I'm informed otherwise, in here I answer to Physician Tasdon, and he'd want me to look at you. It is your own order, sir."

"Very well," Tallin replied, somewhat frustrated, "then do it quickly."

As the aide unwrapped Tallin's right hand, Dargul moved to his left side and leaned close.

"Dare I ask how the battle fares?"

"Our enemy is all but defeated," Tallin replied. "The north fields have been fired, and Mar Henith's army there is destroyed. Many thousands to the south still work away at us. They seem to be building some mischief-making apparatus out of our view. All has gone as well as we could have hoped, I think. Daylight will tell, but it comes weak and foggy."

"Lord," interrupted the aide, "whoever did this stitching knew his business, and the swelling is not too serious."

"You can commend Bart, the aide who did the work."

"I would, my lord, but he was killed an hour or so ago. Let me apply this salve and rebind the wrapping. Does it hurt much?"

"It hurts not at all, Tom. In fact, it feels like it is asleep. He was quite young, Bart was."

"Yes, my lord. I knew him well. You say it does not hurt? Might not be a good thing. Let us hope it starts to hurt soon."

"If you say so. I'll not keep you, Dargul."

"Very well, my lord. Look, there comes Weylan, I believe. I shall look for you later, then."

Tallin turned to look toward the front doors.

"Hold still one moment longer, my lord," ordered the aide.

"You medical types are most curt!"

"Comes with the duty, my lord."

"Lord Tallin!" Weylan called out from across a litter that passed between them. "Fires are being set in the town."

"What do you mean?"

"My lord, some one goes about setting fires." Weylan finally managed to come up to Tallin just as the aide finished his work and hurried off. "At least two men were seen setting two separate fires, and one of them was killed in a fight with the townspeople. He wore our colors on the outside, but some other garb underneath. As if he hastily threw on the tunic of a fallen one. The other man who was seen wore black, from head to toe."

"Infiltrators! How the devil did they get in?"

Together they hurried outside where, on the front portico, they could see at least six separate fires blazing in different parts of town.

"How are things at the north walls, then?" Tallin asked.

"Quiet. I've already ordered all but a few to go fight the fires."

"Good man. That blaze yonder appears very close to our west storehouse."

"It *is* our west storehouse, my lord. Many are trying to empty it at their peril."

Tallin shook his head, knowing that it held grain and other food that would be sorely needed in the weeks to come.

"Set strong guards at every other storehouse and at every well. At least six men per door, and twenty at every approach. Only men that you personally know and can vouch for. No one without my personal authority, or that of Dargul or your own, is to pass. I mean no one! I'll issue an edict as soon as I can find something to write it on. Go!"

Weylan ran down the steps to his horse as Tallin turned back inside and hurried to the lady who oversaw the receiving of the wounded. He demanded paper and ink, and, as hastily as he could with his left hand, he wrote out four copies of the orders that he had just given to Weylan. Taking them, he hurried out and ran quickly around the mansion, through the stable yard, and then to the aide station near the south wall. There he ordered the aides to begin copying his edict, giving over two that he had already written. Taking his signet ring from his left hand, he pressed wax over his signature on the other two. Within a few minutes, two dozen copies were made, signed and sealed, and were being carried swiftly throughout town, to officers, soldiers, and the leaders of the townspeople. That done, Tallin went back to the top of the wall where Commander Brennig still watched the fog-blanketed southern fields.

"What word?"

"My lord, Weylan reported fires—"

"I saw him. The situation is in hand, I hope. We have infiltrators."

"So it seems, sir. We still cannot see what the enemy is up to, but there is a mighty sound of work going on. We distinctly heard chains, and mallets, too."

Tallin knew that the enemy, though defeated in the north, was still potent just beyond the misty veil before them. The Tallinvale soldiers along the wall watched pensively, squinting and passing what spyglasses they had from one to the other. Every word was spoken in whispers so that they could better try to decipher the sounds that came from the enemy ranks. Here and there, soldiers moved quietly along the wall, doling out water from buckets for the men to drink. Tallin, seeing all this, was satisfied that no one relaxed their vigilance, and that everyone remained at the ready for what might come. One of the water-bearers came to offer a sip, holding out a ladle to Tallin.

"Thank you, soldier," Tallin said. Lifting the ladle with his good hand, he eyed the man as he drank. He gave the ladle to Brennig. "Where are you from, son?"

"Up around Bluepine, my lord."

"Hm. I don't think we've met before."

"No, my lord. My name's Ralf. Ralf Napson."

"Napson. Napson."

Brennig took another ladle full, and as he drank, a loud clanking noise came from the fog. Lord Tallin turned to look out over the wall. Brennig, turning with him, picked up his spyglass with one hand and with the other held the ladle out for the soldier to take away. Impatient that it was not immediately taken, he turned to toss it back into the bucket.

"What the…!"

Brennig leapt at the man, who was now lunging with a short narrow-bladed sword at Tallin's exposed neck. The tip glanced off of Brennig's arm guard and found its way sideways under his breastplate, stopping as it passed through his body and hit his backplate. Tallin turned in time to see Brennig slump to his knees as the soldier withdrew his sword. The attacker lunged again at Tallin who threw up his hand to catch the tip of the blade with his bandaged palm, the force of the lunge driving it all the way through down to the hilt as Tallin leaned sideways, the blade barely missing his face. Surprised at Tallin's calm, the attacker froze as Tallin tightened the fingers of his impaled hand around the hilt.

"Lucky for me," Tallin said coldly, "I can't feel a thing in that hand. Unlucky for you!"

Wrenching the sword from the attacker, and using his good hand, he quickly drove it under the man's chin, knocking off his helmet as it came through the top of his skull. Jerking it back out, Tallin carefully drew the blade out of his right hand and tossed the sword down onto the dead man.

"Commander!" Tallin stooped over Brennig, who was still on his knees, his head down.

"I think I'm done for, my lord."

"Aide! Surgeon's aide! Hold on, Brennig. Let's get this armor off and see the damage. Get a litter up here!"

As Tallin knelt and carefully worked to remove Brennig's armor, others rushed to help, and four soldiers charged up the stairs with a litter.

"Um. Ouch," Brennig managed to say. "Ouch, ouch."

"Try to lie down on this litter." Tallin gently coaxed and eased Brennig over to sit on the litter as blood gushed from the wound in his right side. An aide was there, cutting away Brennig's coverlet and shirt. "I'm sorry, Brennig. I must be getting slow, or else I would have guessed what he was about. There are no Napsons in all of Tallinvale."

"Looks like it missed the heart," the aide said, staunching the wounds, "an' passed out his back. Easy does it, fellers! Don't jostle him so! This'll have to hold 'til we get him downstairs. Come along, then, lift him up an' quickly. Quickly! Come along, come along!"

Tallin followed to the steps and watched as Brennig was taken down to the place where he himself was earlier treated by the young Bart. The noise from outside the walls recommenced, and Tallin returned to his post. As he was about to lean over Brennig's spyglass, another aide appeared.

"Lord Tallin, let me see to your hand."

"What's that you say?"

Gesturing at Tallin's hand, the aide reached into his shoulder bag and took out a roll of bandages. Tallin held up his hand and saw that it was pouring blood.

"Oh, that."

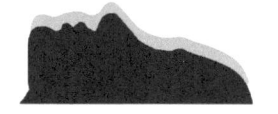

Chapter 22

The Lady Shevalia

It would be several days after Ashlord met with Beauchamp before he and his companions would leave the Temple, the delay owing to Ashlord's insistence that he first make a few inquiries. It was only prudent to wait until he had further news, he told his companions, given the report he had received from Beauchamp. It was just as well, too, since Billy nursed a terrible hangover for nearly an entire day, swearing that he would never again try to out-drink an elf. So, for five days longer, Sheila, Ibin, Billy, and Ashlord remained as guests of the Temple. During this time, they tried to stay busy and patient. Ibin made himself useful in the kitchens, and Billy began his tutoring with Ashlord, who instructed the Boskman on the history and political systems of Duinnor. This was no easy task, but Ashlord was incredibly patient. The rapscallious Billy seemed impervious to the trances that Ashlord tried, such as those he had used with Sheila at Tulith Attis. Still, Ashlord persevered by reciting to Billy over and over the basic important points about Duinnor and its workings. As he did so, Ashlord gained a new respect for the old schoolmaster, Mr. Broadweed, for resisting the temptation to use brute force to drive home his lessons into the wandering workings of Billy's intellect. For it was a powerful temptation, indeed.

Meanwhile, Sheila toured the Temple, exploring nearly every inch of the place. She spent one day with a monk who gathered herbs for the Temple's apothecary, and she helped him grind leaves and prepare a few unctions. Once, nervously, she even revisited Alonair, and under the watchful eye of Lythos, she apologized for her previous outburst. The Elifaen laughed it off, saying that she would have to try harder to match the anger and ire that he probably deserved. This made her feel all the more awkward, and she made haste to leave him, but not before he gave her a sack to take back to the monks.

"Something for the children of the city that the monks serve," Alonair said.

"Oh?" Sheila asked. Alonair opened the sack and showed her the many marbles within.

"They are just a little something that I have a knack for making. For the monks."

"Oh. For the monks?"

"Of course. They delight in giving toys and the like to children."

"Of course."

The four finally departed the following day, and the monks of the Temple managed to get their guests into the city, one by one, and without any great effort. Lying was unnecessary since the guards at the gates were looking for six travelers coming together, and cared little for the monks, acolytes, helpers, and unfortunates that accompanied them into the city. Ibin entered with a yoke of baskets full of food across his shoulders, and Billy entered with a separate group of monks who gave him crutches to walk upon. The guards did not question them, just as, earlier that morning, they did not pay much attention to the mumbling old beggar with the fancy walking stick who was carefully guided by a goodly monk. And they did not bother to search the cart full of blankets and bedding destined for one of the relief houses, but beneath the linens was hidden the nearly suffocating Sheila. In this manner, each was guided or taken to a district of the city where the monks had one of their infirmaries, and where they were all reunited. Certina was not concerned over any such disguise, having the best one of all.

"So," said Ashlord to his friends, "here we are. I've already made some arrangements by messenger, and we should get right to it because we have a busy day before us. After a few errands, we'll look to our lodgings. I have in mind a place not far from here, very close to Raynor's place."

"Won't that be dangerous?" asked Sheila. "Won't his place be watched?"

"I think it will be. Watched, that is," Ashlord said. "But it may be wise to keep an eye on Raynor's rooms should he return. Our coming and going would be less suspicious if we take lodging close by, rather than if we traverse the city to and fro. If you are ready?"

"I just wish I had me sword," Billy commented. "Feel kinda naked without it."

"Me, too," added Sheila.

"Now, that would make us appear suspicious, don't you think?" Ashlord said, going to the door and holding it open for them. "Let's just be thankful that we have not needed our weapons since leaving Edgewold. But, if it will make you feel better, rapiers are all the fashion in Duinnor, and I'm sure we can find something that will suit you. And we may as well try not to look out of place."

"So ye ain't glanced at a looking-glass, lately, have ye?" quipped Billy.

"Be nice," Sheila grinned.

"Yeah, benice," Ibin enjoined.

"I know," Ashlord chuckled. "There's not much I can do about certain aspects of my appearance. But if any descriptions of me have been passed around, they won't do anyone much good, will they?"

Much to Ibin's delight, and to the surprise of Sheila and Billy, Ashlord took them first to a tavern along a busy street.

"Why do we stop here?" Sheila asked.

"Let us have a table, first," Ashlord replied.

They entered and found a table next to the large many-paned window that faced the street. A waiter came and gave them each a menu while another man poured glasses of water for them. All this was something of a puzzle to Ashlord's companions.

"What's this?" Sheila asked, looking at the menu while Billy leaned over to look closely at his glass of water, turning it around and around.

"It is a drinking glass, Billy," Ashlord informed him. "And this is a list of dishes that you may request. Don't worry. I'll pay. Can you read it, Sheila?"

"I can make out the letters and some of the words," she said. "But I don't know what they mean. What is a salmon?"

"Salmon? It is a fish."

"Whatis, whatis, whatisalemonade?"

"It is a tart drink. It is also sweet. You would like it," Ashlord told Ibin. "I'll make our request for us. I promise you will be pleased."

The waiter returned, and Ashlord ordered a meal for each of them. When the waiter departed with their order, Ashlord explained why he had brought them here.

"This is a good place to see the people as they come and go. Look there, see that lady, Sheila? She dresses in a similar fashion as some of the ladies you may have seen at Tallin City. And there, Billy, look at that young gentleman. Yes, that one, but don't point, it is nearly always rude to point. But see his jacket and breeches? It is good that you have some idea how people here dress before we go to the clothier."

Peering through the window, Billy shook his head.

"These folk sure are pretty to look at," he said. "But I don't care how well ye dress me up, all I gotta do is open me mouth an' folk will know right off I ain't from around these parts."

"That doesn't matter," Ashlord shrugged. "Many of those people are not from Duinnor, either. Some, I can tell, are from as far away as Glareth, and others are from Masurthia, I'm sure. I can tell by the waiter's accent that he is from Altoria, originally, although, I observe, he has lived here for many years. No, the point is to look as if you are comfortable here, and that you are confident. To dress in good clothes will be less conspicuous for our purposes than to dress more plainly. Those who may watch for us will most likely be expecting an ill-dressed, travel-weary group, not attired in the styles of this city."

"I see many beautiful ladies," Sheila said, looking past Billy at the street. "And clothes to match their beauty. But I hardly think I could walk in such gowns or finery. Look at that hat, would you? Surely that is a high lady."

"Yes, I see her. Perhaps she is. See the many styles of dress? Look there. That is a lady from Vanara, surely."

Walking just past the window was a tall young woman with a fairly masculine green wool jacket with epaulets. She wore breeches tucked into high brown boots, and her long blond hair was tucked up behind her head into a flat-topped cap with a short bill. Over her shoulder was a sword.

"Now that's more to my liking," Sheila said.

"Mine, too," gawked Billy.

"I am not surprised," smiled Ashlord. " I can tell you that her attire marks her as from Vanara, and I'd wager she is Elifaen."

They continued to watch, sipping their coffees and commenting on what they saw. When their meal came, they had something new to gape at.

"Pancakes!" Billy cried. "I ain't had pancakes in I don't know how long!"

"Andeggs, eggs, too!" cried Ibin, though he had eggs that very morning before leaving the Temple.

"And what's this? Melon slices? How can that be, in the middle of winter?"

"One of the wonders of Duinnor is its winter glass-houses not far from the city. They are situated on hot springs that keep them warm, and inside they grow fruits that would normally be found only in the southernmost realms," explained Ashlord, grinning at their delight.

Billy was already slathering his pancakes with butter and syrup, and by the time he began eating, Ibin was nearly halfway through his stack, grabbing up the syrup decanter to coat the remainder on his plate.

Ashlord let them eat, amid many expressions of gratitude, and satisfied himself with coffee and his pipe, leaning back with his free arm slung over his chair in a most relaxed manner.

"Where's Certina?" Sheila asked between bites.

"Oh, I imagine she's off depleting the city of its mice."

"Oh!"

"You may as well know," Ashlord said to her, "that you are most astonishingly beautiful."

Sheila was taken aback, and she nearly dropped her coffee cup.

"Why, thank you for saying so, Ashlord," she said with suspicion.

"I say so for a reason. It is no good to hide your beauty here in the city. It would attract more attention than if you flaunted it, though I do not say you should do that, either. No, what I have in mind for you is a rather elegant look, befitting your beauty, whilst still being as practical for you as can be."

"What, what, whataboutme, Ashlord?" Ibin asked.

"I am sure we will find something appropriate for you, too, Ibin."

• • •

Shortly after noontime, Ashlord had the boys fitted out with their new clothes, Billy in brown corduroy breeches, jacket, and vest, with polished black boots. He even had a matching cap that had no bill but did have a small orange feather nearly the color of his hair. Ibin took a little longer, owing to his height and the girth of his shoulders. He was soon dressed in a dark gray wool coat, long to his knees, over black leather pants and boots. He liked his hat best of all, a round-brimmed affair of wool with a blue plume.

"Ye look nearly like Capt'n Makeig, Ibin!" Billy said.

"Andyoulooklike, youlook, youlook like oneofhis, oneofhis men, Billy!"

Ashlord had exchanged his travel-worn clothes, borrowed from a kind soul near Edgewold, for a modest blouse and waistcoat and a new long wool coat. They emerged onto the street, with Billy fairly strutting about, and Ashlord went into the women's shop next door to see how Sheila was getting along. When, after a long wait, Sheila came outside, Billy gaped.

"Is it all that bad?" Sheila asked.

"What? No, by no means, no! Ashlord was right, Sheila," he stammered. "An' that's puttin' it mildly, too!"

"Sheila, youlook, Sheila youlooklike, likeaprincess!" Ibin grinned.

Indeed, she did. She wore a long cream-colored coat, with cuffs and collars of fluffy light gray fur, and a matching hat rimmed likewise. And her hair was brushed and combed so that the breeze tugged it around her red cheeks, her eyebrows were lined and her eyes shadowed and she was made up most elegantly. Around her neck, and puffed out under her chin was a white scarf bordered with gold embroidery.

"Are you sure those boots fit properly?" Ashlord asked as he came out of the shop.

"Nothing that a little walking won't break in," she said, looking down at her high suede boots.

"Here," Ashlord said, "this is also for you. It is called a muff, and it is to keep your hands warm," he explained. "Ladies here do not go around with their hands in their pockets. It matches your coat."

"But I have these fine leather gloves," she said, holding up her hands.

"Still," Ashlord insisted. "You should have both."

"Thank you," she smiled, taking the muff and slipping it on. "Thank you for all of this!"

"Yeah, Ashlord, all this must've cost a fortune!" Billy said, admiring his reflection in the shop's window.

"It's nothing," Ashlord smiled. "Now, we should see to a few more things, just around the corner, yonder, though I hope they won't be needed."

They followed Ashlord down the street to a busy avenue, then turned along it until they came to another shop. Through the window, they saw various weapons, swords and rapiers and such, and they went in.

"May I help you?" asked a clerk coming around a table of daggers.

"Yes, I would like to make a gift to my friends, here," Ashlord said. "I have in mind something sturdy and well-balanced for the lady. A stiletto or dagger that is not too plain. Something nice, befitting her station."

"Ah, yes. And nothing else would do but the finest blade," the clerk said as he bowed low to Sheila, who dipped her head in return. "If you would care to look at our collection just over here, my lady?"

The clerk took them to a leather-topped table near the back where there were very elegant daggers, dirks, and knives, many with jeweled grips and pommels.

"Please," gestured the clerk, "feel free to examine any and all. Here, perhaps this one," he picked up a short dirk and sheath and showed her the diamond-crusted blade. "This style is quite the fashion this year."

Sheila sniffed and picked up a knife with a long narrow blade. It had a dark walnut grip and a pommel of polished silver set with a circle of green stones.

"Ah, that one we acquired from a Vanaran trader. He said it was made in the Free City of Kajarahn, in the desert. The Dragonkind make fine blades, of strong steel, too. Though most are not so elegant as that one. And see how the grip is carved with those desert designs?"

"While she looks," Ashlord interrupted, "I'd like to acquire new blades and accoutrements for my gentlemen. I was thinking perhaps for them something more utilitarian, but not without quality. For the big fellow, a sabre may be more along the lines, and for the other gentleman, a light but strong dueling blade."

"Why, certainly. Right this way, gentlemen, if you will."

Within the hour, they had their weapons. Sheila fancied the dagger from the Dragonlands, with a shoulder harness for the scabbard to wear under her coat, and she also found a smaller knife to tuck in her boot. Billy and Ibin were finely equipped, too. And when they stepped outside, Ashlord called them together.

"Now, my friends, a little play-acting is in order," he told them. "Billy and Ibin, I would like for you two to act as though you are Sheila's bodyguards. Try not to grin or smile too much, but don't be too stern. If we go to another shop or door, one of you must enter first, look around the place as if making sure it is safe, then gesture to Sheila and me to enter while the other one of you should remain outside until called for. Does that make sense? I shall play the role of Sheila's guardian and tutor. Sheila, try to let me do all of the speaking. If asked, we come from the south, which we did. If people think we come from Vanara, that is fine. If pressed, you may say that your estate is somewhat south and east of here. You do have an estate, Sheila, since Mr. Ribbon saw to it that you received the old farmhouse in Barley. That should be enough to account for your accent. Say as little as possible, do not look impressed, and if we must greet anyone directly, offer your hand, backside up, like this, for them to take. When they do so, curtsey, but only slightly. Or dip your head instead, like this. When around others, act as if you are not really interested in anything."

"Why all the actin'?" Billy asked. "If we give our names, we'll be made."

"Generally, you should not give your names. You should refer to Sheila as the Lady Shevalia. Our enemies look for coarse rubes from the east, not a beautiful lady and her escorts. Are we clear?"

Sheila was looking askance at Ashlord during all this, while Ibin was going from grin to frown to grin.

"Ibin, Ibin!" Ashlord shook his head. "Let Billy be the stern one, if you must. Ah, here is our conveyance!"

A horse-drawn carriage pulled up, and a man standing on the footboard on the back of the vehicle jumped down as soon as it stopped before the group. He then pulled a step down and held the door open.

"My lord, my lady," he said as he bowed.

"Billy, take a peek inside, and nod to us if it is empty," Ashlord whispered.

Billy strode forward, his hand on his new hilt, stuck his head into the passenger compartment, looked this way and that, then strode back, and nodded in an exaggerated manner.

"My lady," Ashlord said, offering his hand. She entered, and Ashlord followed. Ibin moved to enter, but Ashlord put his hand up. "You should ride on the footboard, if you don't mind. And, Billy, you should ride up top, next to the driver."

"Oh, Idon't, Idon'tmindAsh—"

Ashlord held his hand to his lips, shushing Ibin who, wide-eyed, backed out. Billy had already climbed up to sit next to the driver, so Ibin stepped up onto the footboard, making the carriage noticeably sag, and he mimicked the way the footman held on.

The driver clucked and shook the reins and soon they were off, Ashlord sitting comfortably across from Sheila.

"We may talk freely in here," he said to her.

"I've never been in a carriage before," Sheila said. "On our way here, as we neared Duinnor, I often wondered at the people who passed in them, and what it might be like to ride in one. Who does this one belong to?"

"It is one that is for hire," Ashlord explained. "When I arrived this morning, I sent a messenger to have one made ready for us and to meet us at the armourer. Otherwise, it would have been a long walk to Raynor's district, well on the east side of the city."

"You must be quite wealthy, then. This carriage, the breakfast, these clothes and weapons."

"Well, I am not without my own resources. After all, I have had centuries to acquire what I need and to lay aside funds for occasions such as this. I have sizable accounts in every realm."

"How do you earn your money?"

"Various ways throughout the years. I was a demon hunter for a while, a long time ago, and I was richly rewarded for that service. I sold potions and concoctions, acted as a guide for various expeditions. And I've been well rewarded for my services to Vanara and Glareth. I've had many occupations. But I have little need for wealth, other than a prudent amount laid by."

"A demon hunter? Demons like Valkose?"

"No, not like Valkose. I had never before faced any such as he. He was a Great Demon from the Time Before Time, created when dragons plagued the earth. No, the creatures I hunted were gnats compared to him. But dangerous gnats."

"Oh. Well, I thank you once again. You certainly have been my benefactor in more ways than one. Tell me, how are we to go about getting Billy heard by those who may act and do something about Barley?"

"It will take some doing." Ashlord shrugged. "If he is to speak before the high and mighty, I should continue to prepare him. He has learned from our talks along the road and at the Temple. He is not without some intelligence. But I would like to have more time with him. Those who may be our allies will want to hear his news about the east directly from him, as it was his homeland. He is from an Honored House, and that will give him some standing. If I can, I'll keep him to the gist of things without wandering all over the place in his story, as he is fond of doing. I hope that, between his news and my own account of things, the powerful will be stirred to action."

"Will you teach Billy in the same manner that you taught me? With trances and repetition and lessons?"

"Ah, well. He seems immune to my techniques." Ashlord sighed and shook his head. "I must say that he is a challenge. His mind tends to wander. I shall continue trying, though, so he and I will need some quiet time together. I would have preferred to stay at the Temple, but the longer we waited to come into the city, the more likely we would be caught by Kingsmen at the gates. Coming on as we did, I hope that you and the boys will have a chance to better understand the nature of Duinnor, various aspects of the city and the people here, and so forth."

"Well, Billy is anxious to have help sent back to Barley," Sheila said, looking at a fountain that was crusted with ice as they passed around a square. "I don't know how patient he can be."

"It is true that we must notify certain trusted people right away," Ashlord nodded. "It is urgent. Teracue has already sent his messages, and surely they got through. Our duty is to add authenticity to his reports, so that they are not taken as rumors. But we must be careful of the summons that Banis put on us, the one Teracue warned us about. So we must prepare a safe way for Billy to make his case."

"I was at Passdale, too, you know. Perhaps I could help by telling what I saw."

"You will play your part, certainly, but along different lines. We must allow certain things to play out, so to speak. No, although you would do an admirable job of relating those events, it is the Boskman's duty to do so, and I will help him. It may take time to put things into place, too."

Sheila nodded. "And Robby? Do you have any notion how far along he and Ullin might be?"

"I can only speculate that they are by now on their way to Griferis, and perhaps they are even close to their destination," Ashlord said, wishing that he could lay his hands on but a drop of True Ink. Although he was not one to make little of dire threats and nagging worries, he did not wish to say anything to discourage his companions from hope. Keeping his own worries to himself, he went on, "We must remain hopeful and confident in Ullin and Robby. And, should Robby successfully enter into Griferis and come out of it again, it may be a long time before we know. Meanwhile, we should keep to our role in things, doing what we should do here. Oh, look. There is Hanton Hall, wherein is a vast and fine collection of art and artifacts from all over the world. It is a place that I think you would enjoy visiting, for it contains many beautiful and wondrous things."

They rode along, and Ashlord pointed out certain features of the city, such as the Castle Frosmare, an ancient ruin now surrounded by trade buildings. He told her that it was amongst the first structures in Duinnor, built in the First Age during the early days of the Kingdom. They passed open parks with spraying fountains covered with dripping icicles, and over bridges that spanned other roadways below. They went up busy boulevards where they crept along, the footman going ahead to clear the way through throngs of pedestrians and carts and other carriages.

"Look there." Ashlord pointed to a broad walled structure that spanned several blocks of the city. Along the outside of it were scores of Kingsmen coming and going, and many others besides.

"That is the King's Academy, where Ullin trained and furthered his education. It is a vast school, not only for military arts, but also for many other disciplines. There is a hospital and school where physicians are trained, and an alchemist school where the art of making inks and dyes is taught along with other things: such as how spirits are distilled, oils are refined, and how grease is made like that used on the wheels of this carriage. Another school instructs students on the building of roads and bridges, mapmaking, and such. Those are but a few of the many schools within. I myself taught there for a short while."

"Oh, what did you teach? History lessons?"

"No, I taught the art of reading the stars for navigation. And I also taught courses on the Dragonlands. I enjoyed it, but not as much as my time teaching in Vanara, at the Queen's Academy there."

"My! You have done quite a lot in your lifetime!"

"Well, it is because I have been around for so long, and have the learning to share, and a variety of talents and experiences."

"There is something I've always wanted to ask you about." Sheila sat back on the cushioned seat and looked at Ashlord.

"You can ask anything you wish."

"Well, it is rumored, or was rumored by some in Barley, that you were once a king yourself. A conjurer-king, some said. And that man, Toolant, he said as much, too. After a manner."

Ashlord chuckled and shook his head.

"I was made king, once, of a very small realm in the northwestern deserts of the Dragonlands. That was when I was a youngster, and did not know much. Yes, I helped defend a small city against an army led by a rebellious Dragonkind general. During the campaign, the prince of the city was killed and all his family, too. Eventually, under my leadership, we defeated the general, and as a reward, and to keep me on as their leader, the people made me king. I agreed only so that I could negotiate trade terms with the Dragon King, who was grateful that we defeated his rebellious general, and with Queen Serith Ellyn who was grateful that our city prevented the rebel from turning north with his troops and attacking her lands."

"What happened? I mean, why didn't you stay there as king?"

"Well, I accomplished what I set out to do, and the city became a prosperous place, a free city where, according to treaty, all could come and go as they wished. It did not last. I was restless, and I abdicated to a council made up of the city elders and went on my way. Four years later, the region became infested with witches, and the city's population was decimated by them. I lost many friends. Nearly all of my friends, in fact. It was a bad time. That was when I became a demon hunter. I and eight others traveled far and wide, hunting down witches and sorcerers and demons throughout Vanara and even the Dragonlands."

"And the city? Was it completely lost?"

"Oh, no. People repopulated it, and it was renamed. Your dagger comes from there, the Free City of Kajarahn. But it is not the place it once was."

"And you said that the demons you hunted were not like Valkose."

"Valkose was a mighty demon, indeed, but a relic of the truly ancient world. Those that I and my colleagues sought out were lesser creatures, though formidable in their way. My purpose was to learn where they came from, but I never did. The Nine Banes, as my troop was called, encountered sixteen of them, and countless of their whores, but none that we succeeded in capturing. They fought like, well, like demons. They were bloodsuckers, all. Their witches, too. I suspect, though, that Secundur was behind the outbreak."

"And that is what you fear will happen again?"

"What I fear is much worse. But enough of that. We arrive at our destination!"

They came to a stop before a tall house, built very snug to its neighbors with only the narrowest of alleys between. The footman opened the carriage door and held Sheila's hand as she stepped out. Ibin jumped down from the footboard, upsetting the carriage enough so that Billy, who was climbing down, nearly lost his balance and fell. Ashlord instructed the driver to wait before bringing in the baggage, then joined his companions at the front door. After a quick glance and smile at them, he knocked, and it was quickly answered by a thin elderly woman.

"Yes?"

"Miss Tarrier?"

"Yes?"

"I was told that you might have apartments available, suitable for a lady and her escorts."

"Yes, I believe I can accommodate you. Come in, come in!"

They were led into a narrow foyer beside a staircase that went up one side of it. There was a parlor off to the left, and on down the way they could see the doors opened to a great room.

"We are just arrived in the city," Ashlord was saying, "coming from the south. You may call me Mr. Sootking, and this is my charge, the Lady Shevalia."

"How do you do, Mr. Sootking?" Tarrier curtseyed properly, and Sheila returned the gesture convincingly. "I am pleased to make your acquaintance, Lady Shevalia. You all may call me Miss Tarrier."

"Pleased, Miss Tarrier."

"And these are our escorts," Ashlord gestured towards Billy and Ibin, who bowed more flamboyantly than Ashlord thought appropriate. "We would like them close by, if at all possible. The rooms must be suitable for us and well-kept."

"Oh, they are! I assure you. There is a single room available upstairs, on the next floor. There is also a suite, but it is rented, though the man hasn't been here for a long while. Still, his rent's paid for all year, and I ain't about to put his things out premature-like. There's a large suite on the entire third floor. Four bedrooms, a parlor, a study, and a bath. I have my apartments down here, not caring to climb stairs any more than I must due to my age. Would you be wanting service and meals, too?"

"Yes."

"Pardon me for asking, but many what inquire ain't got the silver. I can see it is a fine company you are. Still—"

"Well, I hate to make my ward climb all those steps every day," Ashlord said. Sheila almost spoke that she did not mind, but Ashlord anticipated her, saying, "No, do not protest on my behalf! I am not as frail as all that," he said. "I still have plenty of vigor in me! No, no, I worry more for your constitution, my lady. Perhaps we should take a turn up the stairs and see for ourselves how strenuous it is?"

"Very well," Sheila said going to the stairs. She paused, waiting for Ashlord.

"I'll be right up, my lady," he said. She shrugged and began the ascent as he turned back to Miss Tarrier. "I do not wish to put too fine a point on it," he said, "but we have been assured that this is a respectable establishment. Are there any other lodgers at the moment?"

"Oh, my, no. I mean, not besides Mr. Raynor, who ain't here at all, and ain't been for weeks." She reduced her voice to a whisper. "I heard he was needed at the Palace, if you know what I mean."

"Hm. A disreputable fellow?"

"Oh, no! Not at all! A right kind and courteous man. My only complaint was with them friends of his, his hired men who stayed here a while back. Why they was rogues ever single one! Gentlemanly rogues, but partial to drinking and carrying on all hours, coming and going. Ate like horses, too, and messy as only men can be messy!"

"Oh, my! Perhaps this is not the place for us!"

"Oh, they all cleared out long back! 'Sides, they were really quite sweet, once you got to know 'em. Particularly one of them, bless his heart! Say? Did you say 'Lady Shevalia?' I know that name! An unusual name, it is, and I'm sure of it, now. She's the self-same young lady what broke the heart of the gentleman I just spoke of."

She went back to a whisper once again, leaning close to look up at Ashlord.

"She's the lady what Tyrin brought up from Vanara, ain't she? Oh, he got so drunk over her, like I'd never seen him do! All mopey and torn up. But I finally got it out of him, knowing that there's one thing, and one thing only, that'll make such a man behave so."

Ashlord shook his head, but Miss Tarrier continued.

" 'What's her name?' I asked him. Oh, why do menfolk have to act all surprised when you ask the obvious question? Anyways, he told me her name, and all about her. How pretty she was, and how kind and funny she was with jokes and such. Oh, he was smitten! Described her hair, and her smile, and nearly broke down right at my kitchen table. A great lady, he kept saying. I told him he should charge after her, if he cared half so much as his drinking indicated. But he'd have nothing of it, saying she was off limits, whatever that means. I kept after him, an' poured tea into him to sober him up some. Well, no sooner than he left out of here to go see her, all the city bells started ringing, that very night. Ever' single bell! Even the servant bells and them at the bedsides. What a commotion and stir! I nearly had an apoplectical breakdown, I did!"

"Woman," Ashlord said, "I have not the slightest notion of what you are talking about. When the bells of Duinnor rang, Lady Shevalia was in my presence, and we were hundreds of leagues away from here."

"You don't say?"

"I do. It must be some other lady you refer to, or else you mistake the name. The only other Shevalia I have ever heard of died tragically in the First Age."

"Oh? Hm. I could have sworn that was it. Oh, well! My mistake, I suppose," Miss Tarrier said with a skeptical expression. "I apologize for going on about it."

"As to the rooms. If the lady finds them suitable, we should like our meals there, although we shall be coming and going as our business in the city dictates."

"Of course, of course. I prefer that you take your meals downstairs, just down the hall there, in the dining room. And, not to be delicate, I do require references."

Ashlord now leaned down and looked at her, taking a slip of paper from his vest.

"As you can see, we have impeccable references."

"Oooh. I see. So you do, sir."

"Very well!" Ashlord snatched back the clothier's receipt that Miss Tarrier was blinking at. As he put it back into his vest pocket, she shook herself awake. "I shall go up, now, to have a look."

Upstairs, Ashlord found Sheila sitting in the parlor, her hands still in her muff, her head turned away, absently looking through the window on the other side of the room. He went about, peering into each room and closet, looking out from every window, and when he returned, she was standing, waiting for him. Billy and Ibin were also standing nearby, somewhat awkwardly.

"Well, my lady," Ashlord smiled, "how do you like these rooms?"

"They are very nice."

"But?"

"I just don't think this is going to work," she said. "I would be afraid to go out, should we need to, not knowing how to act or what to say. I'm sure I will give us away. I am no lady."

"Miss Tarrier thinks that you are," Ashlord replied, "and so do the driver and the footman. That's a start. Appearances go far in this world, whether they should or not. And, besides, you should think of yourself as a lady. Or as becoming one, at least. That, for you, would be a start. And, I daresay, you would make a finer lady than many of those who are called such!"

Billy and Ibin were both nodding. Going to the window, Ashlord pushed it open. Certina immediately flew in, circled the chandelier, and landed on his shoulder.

"And here's my other lady!" he declared. "Now. Billy, please go down and tell Miss Tarrier that these rooms will do. Give her these, on our account."

He handed Billy six gold coins.

"Then go to the carriage and ask the footman and driver to bring up our baggage."

"What baggage?"

"Our baggage. Tied to the roof of the carriage. Or didn't you notice?"

"Why, yes, I noticed. It's ours?"

"We'd look pretty silly if we traveled all this way from wherever with no baggage, wouldn't we? Get along!"

Billy shrugged and departed, and Ashlord turned to Ibin.

"Dear fellow, until we understand better the comings and goings of this house, I must ask you to remain standing, to the side of the room over there, whenever anyone besides ourselves is here. Otherwise, you may sit in that chair, over there. It is so that you will look more like a guard. Which I ask that you be, actually."

"Overherelikethis?"

"Yes, just like that. Standing there like that will remind any visitors we may have that they are watched."

"Yes,Ashlord. Ican, Ican, Imean,I'llwatchoverSheila!"

"Good! Thank you, sir."

"Youarewelcome."

Sheila shook her head, obviously unconvinced. There was a knock at the door, and a maid entered with a coal bucket, and she went about the business of lighting a fire in the parlor hearth as the baggage was brought up.

"Put that case in the far side room, just down the hall, please," Ashlord instructed. He shook his head at Billy who was about to help. "The black case goes into the room adjoining it. Yes, this bag goes into the center room, two doors down, just there. All of the others go into Lady Shevalia's room, to the other side, there."

When all of the bags were distributed according to Ashlord's instructions, he gave the driver and the footman each a silver coin and thanked them.

"We shall send for the carriage by messenger when we need it. Good day!"

They bowed and departed, and pulled the door closed behind them.

"All this is a pretty fancy act!" Billy said, swinging his rapier around so that he could sit in a wing-back chair. "All them empty bags an' such!"

"Who said they were empty?" Ashlord shot back. "I'm sure if you'd care to look, that you would each find something interesting. Ibin, your room is down the hall on the right. Billy, your room is next to his. Go look."

The boys hurried off. Soon the sound of Ibin's mandolin was gracing the air, while Billy found that his bag contained his spare travel clothes, left in the monastery, along with his other meager but comforting items, including the sewing kit that his mother had given him.

"I realize that unpacking bags is a task normally given to the lady's maid," Ashlord said to Sheila. "And I am somewhat remiss on that account, for not providing one to you. Meanwhile, perhaps you should look to the task yourself."

Sheila stood hesitantly, looking at Ashlord with suspicion.

"Go ahead. I'll be right there, should you have any questions. I think you know which room is yours."

Sheila went to her room, and there she found a trunk and four smaller cases. The maid had already been in to light the fireplace, and so Sheila took off her hat, gloves, and coat, put them with her muff in a nearby chair, and stooped to open the trunk.

A little while later, Ashlord knocked and entered. Sheila was sitting on the floor, her open luggage surrounding her, and she was holding a nightgown in her lap. The trunk held many things that a lady would need, including slippers, a nightcap, a shawl, a variety of gowns and sashes, belts, purses, and the like, and the other cases held combs, brushes, soaps and perfumes, hand mirrors, eyeliner, makeup, and many of the more personal things required for a lady's toilette. She looked up at Ashlord, her eyes filled with a mixture of wonder and excitement.

"I don't understand. Where did all these things come from? How did you manage to obtain them?"

"I have a trusted lady friend in town," Ashlord said, grinning. "I merely gave her your measurements and asked that she provide the essentials for a lady of your complexion and hair who had the misfortune of having many of her things misplaced during her journey here. I sent a message to her on the day before yesterday, asking that she prepare them in haste and send them on to the livery, to be delivered with the carriage that I would hire."

"My measurements?"

"I have a keen eye, and rarely miss in any calculation based on observation."

"Oh. And are these really for me?"

"They are yours. I hope they are adequate. At least until you may find items more to your liking."

"Adequate?"

Sheila leapt up and threw her arms around Ashlord, kissing him on both cheeks, and hugging him again.

"Thank you! Thank you!"

"Come, come! Let's not get carried away. It was the least I could do. Besides, I can't have the Lady Shevalia go a single night without the essentials, now can I?"

"You amaze me!"

"Oh," Ashlord fumbled in his coat pocket, "I would truly be remiss if I forgot this."

He held out a small book, the very same one that Mr. Broadweed had given her on the day they departed Janhaven.

"Oh, Ashlord," she said, taking it with both hands. "Thank you."

"Perhaps, later, you might share something of what is within that book with the rest of us," Ashlord suggested. "If you wouldn't mind."

"Oh, I would be thrilled!"

"Then I shall call upon you after a while."

• • •

As Sheila put away her things, she sat for a long time at the dressing table, fingering the vial of lip rouge that was in her hand, looking at herself in the mirror. She wondered at the image there.

"Is that me?" she mused. "It is, I swear. But, then, who am I? Was it only a few months ago that I went to gather my things, to steal off to Ashlord's? Only to be caught by Steggan. Or was it years and years ago? Was it only a few months ago that I returned to Passdale, to stay with the Ribbons, and to have for the first time ever a pretty dress? Was it so long before then that I was a child? When Ullin left those things for me in the river? When I first looked at my image as I do now, in that little handglass he gave me? Or," she stared at the mirror, momentarily transfixed by what she thought was another face there, like her own, but different. "Or, could that be my mother's face that I see? Whoever she was."

She twisted the cap from the vial of rouge, and she held it to her nose briefly. Then she closed it and picked up the bottle of perfume that was with the other things. She held it up to the firelight to see how the crystal glass sparkled and the yellow liquid within glowed. She caught a glint from the mirror and looked back at herself.

Reaching up, she touched the choker around her neck, seeing in the mirror how, when she turned a certain way, the purple amethyst glittered and the tiny yellow gems that surrounded it twinkled. The lady at the clothier had commented on it, saying that it was most unusual and fine. It was the first time anyone ever made mention of it, other than Robby. It was around her neck at Passdale, when the Redvests attacked, and still there when they rode away from Janhaven. It was there when they met Lyrium, and when they came upon the Nowhere people, and even during the awful battle against the Wickermen. The only time she had ever removed it, in fact, was when she washed in the river the night after the battle. There, in the privacy of her bathing blind, she washed her body, the gore from her hair, and finally, meticulously, she cleaned the choker. Then she put it back on, her proud symbol of Robby's love.

Shaking her head, she put down the perfume bottle and began the work of arranging the items, the purpose of a few of the objects a complete mystery to her. Opening a drawer, she found it empty and put in some of her new belongings. When she opened another drawer, she was surprised to find a man's comb of well-worn steel. She put it on the table, noticing how worn the table surface was, ink stains here and there, and she wondered at the many tenants these rooms must have had over the years. Reaching for a box of powders, she upset a jar of hair quills, and one fell onto the floor behind the table. Leaning over to reach under the table for it, she saw a wad of crumpled paper on the floor, wedged between the table leg and the wall. Getting out of her chair, she picked up the wad, and she immediately saw that there was writing on it. She put the errant quill away, unraveled the paper carefully, and held it near the lamp. It was a letter, and she was immediately taken aback, beginning with the first word she read.

> Shevalia,
>
> What's the point? I know very well there's no purpose in writing, yet I write, anyway. I was determined, earlier this evening, at the insistence of my heart and my landlady's advice, to call for my horse and to ride back to the Temple this very night. I had it in my mind to see you again, to beg a little bit of time with you in spite of the late hour. I don't know what I wanted to say. I don't think I wanted to say anything, really. I only wanted to be with you again. To see your smile again. Or perhaps, if I dared, to take your hand in mine, as I did on a few occasions during our journey together.
>
> You would be amused, I'm sure, at my visit. And you would be polite and kind and correct and patient. And I know that I would once more go away from the Temple without you, and that was what I feared the most, for it was hard enough to leave you today. I don't think I could bear to leave you again.
>
> Silly man! What would a fine lady as yourself find in a rogue such as I, a shiftless no-account without position, name, or wealth, without a grain of land to put a home upon, or to share with another, and without prospects for any of those things required by a lady.
>
> I may be many things, and lacking in many things, but I am not without wit, and I am not blind to how the world works. It is funny, is it not? That I, with my eyes, see only that which cannot be. And that you, without the use of sight, have looked upon me with a fair smile and with a knowing kindness upon your expression.
>
> Yet, what sweet torture it would be to sit with you for only a few moments! So off to the livery I went, rousing up the stableboy, saddling my horse with haste, and galloping away through the sleeping city. Alas, the bells that rang throughout the town only served to spur me on all the faster, as if they rang in gladness and anticipation of my destination. When I came upon the south gate, and I saw in

the distance the lights of the Temple upon the far mount, I urged my horse all the more. But the gates were closing as I arrived, and I was turned away.

As I said. What is the use? I am now returned to my rooms, having paced the city gates all night long, keeping watch, as all the soldiers of Duinnor do. Yet, whereas they watch for the enemy who surely approaches, my eyes were ever upon the Temple mount. The soldiers will not let me out. I fear the worst, and as the sun rises, I am being called, as is every able-bodied man, conscripted to serve until the crisis abates, or the enemy comes. By noon I must report, though this is not my home, and these are not my people. I use this chance to write. And, with luck, I shall see you soon and offer you my protection, which is all that I...

The letter abruptly ended. Sheila, amazed, read it again and again, wondering who had written it and who the other Shevalia could be. There was a knock at the door, and she swung around, holding the letter behind her back.
"Yes?"
"It is Ashlord. May I enter?"
"Yes."
Ashlord came in and left the door open to the hall. "Are you still getting settled in?"
"Yes. Putting things away. Arranging things. And so forth."
"I see. Well, I have just been speaking with our landlady, Miss Tarrier. She asked me when your maid would come, and where she would stay."
"Maid?"
"Why, yes. Your lady's maid."
"Oh?"
"Yes. I am aware that you know little about such things." Ashlord went over to the fireplace and held his hands out to warm. Sheila turned and quickly tossed the paper onto the dressing table, then turned back, keeping her hands behind her as before. "But, any lady of consequence must have one."
"Must they? Am I of consequence?"
"Of course you are."
"Why, I mean, what does a lady's maid do?"
"Why, she looks after the lady's needs. She waits upon the lady, helping with dress, with bathing, with the lady's toilette, and so forth. She sees to all those things that a lady is not trained to do. She makes the lady's needs known to the other staff, and generally serves as a sort of go-between."
"Oh. It seems a lot of bother for things I may do myself."

"Ah, but you cannot." Ashlord turned around, his eyes darting at and away from the dressing table. "Think of it as part of our disguise. Regardless, I informed Miss Tarrier that we hoped a suitable maid might be found for you here in the city, and thought to look to that business on the morrow. She informed me in return that her niece, who already lives in this house, has only recently lost her employment as a maid in a great house here in town, and has lost her prospects, therefore, of someday becoming a lady's maid. Miss Tarrier went on to suggest that, should we be willing to give an inexperienced girl a chance, we would not be expected to pay the usual rate. I informed Miss Tarrier that I would consult with you on the matter straight away. And here I am."

"But is that really necessary?" Sheila was suddenly gripped with anxiety over the prospect. "I mean, won't that be dangerous? She's sure to see right through me! And she'll talk to others, surely, about what a fake I am."

Ashlord chuckled. "You are not a fake, my dear! A bit rough around the edges, surely, but that will soon be remedied, I think. Why don't we ask for an interview? You won't have to say a word, if you do not wish to. I'll do all of the talking, if that suits you. If we don't at least see the girl, Miss Tarrier may take it amiss."

"Oh, Ashlord!" Sheila shook her head and sat down. "I can just hear Billy. Ye gotta maid? Ain't ye got the sense to comb ye own hair?"

"Give Billy some credit. His sister had a lady's maid. As did his mother, back years ago. Though Billy was probably too young to remember. Anyway, did you not ever talk to Mirabella about her days in Tallinvale?"

"No. Did she have one, too?"

"She did. So. Shall I ask Miss Tarrier to bring up her niece before the evening is too far gone? Or would you prefer to wait until the morning?"

"Go ahead, then. Let's get this over with!"

"Very well." Ashlord went over to the bed and picked up a shawl and put it across Sheila's shoulders. "I'll ask them to the parlor room."

A few minutes later, Sheila waited nervously in the parlor. Billy and Ibin were playing a hand of cards at a side table, having been instructed on what to do by Ashlord, and Sheila suspected their snickering was somehow directed at her. Ashlord entered, and held the door for a girl who followed him in. She appeared to be Sheila's own age or perhaps a bit younger, with a pale complexion, black hair neatly tied up in a ribbon, dark brown eyes, and wearing a servant's dress and apron.

"May I present the Lady Shevalia," Ashlord said. The girl curtseyed low, and Sheila responded with an awkward pause then gave a slight bow of the chin, staring at the girl with such intensity, bordering upon terror it seemed to Ashlord, that it was mistaken as anger by the girl. "Lady Shevalia, this is Miss Tarrier's niece, Reysa."

Billy and Ibin immediately stood and faced the girl.

"And these are Lady Shevalia's trusted escorts, who have faithfully seen us along our travels. Misters Bosk and Brinnin."

Both men bowed smartly, and she curtseyed to them, too, before turning back to face Sheila. The boys remained standing until Ashlord gestured for Sheila to sit. Once she had done so, putting her hands in her lap, Billy and Ibin sat, too, resuming their game of cards, though Billy cared more to watch the girl than the cards in his hand. Ashlord, glancing at Sheila, proceeded to address Reysa.

"Your aunt tells me that you have experience as a maid, but that you recently lost your employment. You left on good terms, I presume? And have references?"

"Oh, yes, my lord. It was with Lady and Lord Dassath, and I only left because they removed to Glareth, which is their homeland. I was in their service for three years. They gave me a fine letter of reference."

"You may address me as Mr. Sootking, my dear," Ashlord said as he took the note that she removed from her apron pocket and handed to him. "I see here that you were a house maid?"

"Yes, sir, Mr. Sootking, sir. But I waited upon Lady Dassath for nearly a month, last year, on account of her regular lady's maid being indisposed."

"I see. Perhaps, just to be clear, you could say what duties you performed for Lady Dassath?"

"Yes, sir. I laid out her morning clothes, helped her with her dressing, and toilette. I arranged her hair, which was most long and fine. During the day, while she was often out, I arranged for her evening gowns, laying out things appropriate for the occasion, and helping her dress and so forth. And, in the late evening, I helped with her nightgowns and night things. I did other tasks, too, as was needed, sir."

"And was it to your liking, then? To be available at all hours, day and night?"

"Yes, sir. It suited me just fine, sir."

"Hm."

Ashlord looked at Sheila with a questioning expression, as if it was Sheila's turn to speak. But Sheila only raised her brow with a slight shake of her head in response to him.

"Ahem. Well," Ashlord went on. "I have never met the Dassaths, though I have heard of them. I think you'll find Lady Shevalia quite different. She is young, as you can see, and she is new to Duinnor. She is also a very private person, having come here on matters that are not the concern of others. She is the sole heiress to an estate somewhat remote from here, and will undoubtedly require an experienced lady's maid. That is to say, the customs of households are quite different here in Duinnor, and it would be the duties of her maid to assist Lady Shevalia in the way of accommodating those differences with a minimum of inconvenience. Therefore," Ashlord sniffed and frowned, "I'm afraid a more experienced maid is what we are looking for. I am sure that you understand. Please thank your aunt for presenting you for our consideration."

Reysa curtseyed again, saying, "Thank you, sir. Thank you, my lady."

As Reysa turned to go, Sheila stood, giving Ashlord a look of surprise at his dismissive tone toward Reysa.

"Wait," she said. Ashlord looked at her with a tilted head and a challenging look that made Sheila hesitate. She chose her words carefully, and spoke slowly and deliberately.

"Miss Reysa," she said. "Forgive Mr. Sootking, but he is at times overly protective of me. He seeks to present me to Duinnor as a refined and elegant lady. He should know better."

Billy looked up from his losing hand with concern.

"However," Sheila went on, "I will tell you, frankly, that I am a fish out of water. I was an unruly child, an only child, and preferred the fields and woods of my estate to the table or parlor. I neglected my lessons, I was mean and rude to my playmates, and more than once I acted more as a boy than as a girl should. As a result, I am the least prepared to be a lady of any who may have that title. Only recently have my duties been pressed upon me," she shot a glance at Ashlord, "not without some resentment on my part. I will not bore you with the story. You seem like the kind of girl who could find a better position. If you are willing to overlook my shortcomings as a lady, I shall overlook your lack of experience. Doing so, perhaps we may help each other. Please tell your aunt that I would be happy to have you as my maid. I would like for you to start this very night, if that is acceptable to you."

Reysa hesitated, glancing at Ashlord, who was now smiling. She then curtseyed.

"I would be happy to begin tonight, my lady. What would you have me do first?"

"Perhaps you should inform your aunt first," said Ashlord. "Then, unless you must fulfill any duties to her, you could look in on Lady Shevalia in an hour or so."

"Yes, sir. Thank you, sir. Thank you, my lady."

The girl departed, and Ashlord grinned. Sheila, looking at him, made as if to strike him.

"You old scoundrel! You were rude on purpose!"

Ashlord laughed, his eyes twinkling with delight.

"Oh! Sometimes you are insufferable!"

"Oh?" Ashlord responded. "Perhaps. But, I must say, you spoke rather well, considering all. And I am proud of you for speaking as you did."

"Well," Billy said from across the room, "all I gots to say is that she's mighty cute!"

"Iwin!" said Ibin, throwing his cards down. "Iwin, Iwinagain!"

"Oh, Billy!" Sheila cried, plopping down onto the settee. "It will be nice to have another girl about, to give me some relief from all of you!"

"Indeed," said Billy.

"Now, Lady Shevalia," said Ashlord, rubbing his hands together in a satisfied way. "I believe you promised us a reading?"

"Yes, Mr. *Sootking!*"

Chapter 23

The Duel

While a cold fog continued to blanket Tallinvale, adding its obscuring mists to the smoky and smoldering remains of the night's battle, and while Sheila and her friends prepared to leave the Temple and go to Duinnor City, where they would soon enjoy the niceties to be had there, the day broke frigid and clear over the lofty mountains that lined the edge of the world along the far western borders of Shatuum. The sky was a deep blue, such as only winter skies seem to be, and the air was so thin and biting that great trails of Ullin's breath followed him. Though he had only departed from his night's bivouac an hour or so earlier, at the first hint of dawn, already the balaclava around his mouth was caked with ice, as were the lashes of his cold-reddened eyes. But he made good distance, at a fair pace, owing to the flat ledge that he traveled. Not in the past four days, since he began his precarious hike, had he encountered the least rise or fall in the grade; the ledge ran as straight and true as the cleft that it followed, as if struck by its architect's straightedge. Ahead and behind Ullin, the walls of the Crack in the World converged against the distance, varying in detail only by the mountains that it cut through, by the changing light and shadow, and by the everchanging clouds that sometimes swirled up from far below. Only once, two days earlier, had he any real trouble when he encountered a fall of snow and ice that had tumbled from above, forcing him to pick his way very carefully for several miles.

So he kept on, hugging the wall, only occasionally daring to step close enough to the edge to look down out of curiosity at the rumbling noise that rose up from the stark canyon. When he did so, all he could see was a sheer drop ending in what appeared to be clouds far below. Indeed, he was filled with wonder at the place, treacherous though his path seemed, and the mystery of how it could run so straight, curving neither toward the east or west. He marked his passage by observing the changing shapes of the blue and white mountains that scratched the heavens on the far side of the chasm. As for his own side of the Crack in the World, he could not judge if his ledge was a hundred feet from the top, or a thousand, so little could he discern by looking up. Without much in the way of perspective, he figured he must have gone at least ten leagues each day. Once, hearing a deep rumble, he looked directly across the chasm at a mighty avalanche sliding down from a distant mountainside, pouring its flood of boulders and snow over the edge into the cloudy abyss. He instinctively backed against the side of his ledge, but when a large chunk of rock teetered and fell, it was many moments before he heard its crack. This told him that the span from one side to the other was truly great, perhaps more than a league. The avalanche subsided, and the quiet solitude of the stark landscape pressed in, with only the breeze whispering around his hood. Taking out his spyglass, he peered across the void. But he saw no trees or structures or anything at all to give him an idea of the scale of the mountains or the true distance from his side of the canyon to the other.

He kept going. He did not try to count footsteps or mark the hour of the day from the angle of light. He gave up trying to judge his progress by this or that mountain for, whenever he looked up toward his reference point, it seemed he had made hardly any advance at all compared to it. Eventually the angle of the light betrayed the passing of time, and the frozen scenery across the void changed slowly as the miles went by.

From the moment each day started, Ullin began looking ahead to the day's end, his thoughts ever upon the prospect of sleep. This day, by the time the shadows of the western mountains crossed his path, the wind had picked up, biting most cruelly, and he began looking for the place he had been told to stay this night.

Indeed, he was sustained by his hope of nightfall, for the chance to rest and have a bite of food, surely, but mostly by the anticipation of Micerea's nightly visit. She would report on the way ahead, whether anything new lay before him, or if tomorrow's journey would be less monotonous than today's. And they would share sweet company. Last night, before leaving him, she told him that a furlong or so before he reached a grotto, he would come across a seam of coal. She instructed him to gather and carry as much as he could for tonight's fire and for tomorrow night as well. He smiled, watching his footsteps, thinking of her, remembering how she carried him within her dream to the south to enjoy some warmth.

"You still have a long march before you," she told him. "You have left behind the long shoulders of Algamori, where you started, but it is another week, at the very least, before you are out from under the shadow of Shatuum's mountains. Above you, the edge of this strange canyon is rimmed with overlooking walls, keeps, and watchtowers, and Secundur's followers ceaselessly patrol them, though the sentries are few and thinly spread out. So you must be alert at every moment. While you are awake, I may look upon you, but I cannot come to you until you sleep and dream, and so I cannot warn you of any danger that I may see."

"I will be careful," he said to her, tossing her long hair over her bare shoulder.

"The creatures of Secundur are hideous and without mercy," she insisted. "And I'm not sure what good Swyncraff may be against them."

"I am not afraid. Not any more."

"I am. More than ever."

"Don't be, my love."

Long after she left, he continued to dream of her. And now, long into his daily hike, he dreamed of her with his eyes open. What else was there to do?

He saw a black smudge ahead, and before long he was negotiating a section of the ledge strewn with chunks of coal, some almost as big as his backpack. After he made it through, he stopped and soon had his pack full, and his arms, too. It was longer than a furlong, he thought, and he was beginning to wish he had not gathered so much fuel when at last he came to a cleft in the wall. It was not much in the way of shelter, as he saw when he crouched and then crept into it. It had a narrow opening, but was wider inside, and he was surprised at how well it kept out the wind.

By the time it was dark, he had a small fire made, leaving the bulk of the coal safely outside on the ledge. Using the small tin cup that was part of his kit, he carefully melted snow for hot water, dropping a few chunks of jawrock into it to thaw as the water heated, crunching on some snowbutter as he waited. It was tricky. He did not have a cooking stand, but he managed without spilling too much, and he set his mittens on fire only once. He drank the water and fished out the thawed jawrock and ate. He chuckled, remembering the expression on Micerea's face all those years ago in the desert when she attempted to eat some of the dense chewy stuff. While he chewed and chewed, he added more coal to the burning pile, and heated more water.

"Horrible!" he managed to say with difficulty since it tended to stick to the roof of the mouth.

In spite of the meager fare, he was soon either satisfied or too weary to eat any more, so he piled on more coal, pulled his blankets around him, settled against his backpack, and closed his eyes. Outside, the wind whispered past the opening of his cave. Inside, the coal cracked and snapped. It was not long before he was asleep.

• • •

Though she dearly desired to visit with Ullin, Micerea did not want to disturb him right away, knowing that he needed his rest. Better that he get a few hours of good sleep, she thought as she watched him. Using the skills that Robby had recently taught her, she was now able to dreamwalk without recourse to other people's dreams, enabling her to come directly to Ullin, or go anywhere she desired without jumping from sleeper to sleeper. Now she floated up from Ullin's place of rest to view those fortifications directly above him.

It was a broad battlement, wide enough for a wagon to traverse, and it stretched north and south, with a few torches at far intervals and only a few lookouts here and there. Not wishing to look upon Shatuum again, she withdrew back to her lands and went to her own bed. She needed true sleep, too, and the past days of watching over Ullin were spent apparently sleeping, much to the dismay of her less indolent friends. But in spite of appearances she had been busy, dreamwalking beside Ullin as he walked in earnest. Each day was as long as it was monotonous until he found his nightly camp. Then, while he slept, she would visit with him and scout ahead along the path he would take the next day. But she was now very tired, having had little true sleep of her own. So she allowed herself to doze for a while, knowing that before dawn she would be briefly roused by the noise of the changing guard outside her desert home. Then she would turn over, go back to sleep, and dreamwalk back to Ullin. Thus she slept peacefully and deeply until the time came for the guards to give their stations to those who would keep watch until after dawn. In the courtyard below her window, they exchanged their greetings and pushed open and then closed the squeaky gate, arousing Micerea. Smiling, she turned over and went back to sleep and dreamwalked. She returned to Ullin, who was still asleep, and then went once again to look at the place that overhung Ullin's ledge.

Now she saw several wraith-like creatures, tall and bent over, dressed in shaggy furs and bearing long spears. They were shuffling up and down the battlement, first going one way for some distance, then turning around, slowly returning back to where they had started from. It was an odd behavior, she thought, for they did not pace like sentries do. Rather, they went tentatively, their heads down, or sometimes peering out into the blackness across the Crack in the World. Curious and suspicious, and zealously protective of Ullin, she drew closer to the pair, close enough to see their dog-like faces. They lifted up their heads and sniffed. Micerea instinctively recoiled, thinking they had somehow detected her. But it was not her; it was something else they scented. The two creatures went to the parapet, sniffing constantly, shaking in their furs, and dropping their spears to go back and forth rapidly, sniffing and whimpering, sometimes dropping down on all fours before jumping back up to lean out over the wall. They began to howl and bark words in a dreadful language. Micerea was jolted by the realization that they could smell Ullin's fire, and perhaps his scent.

Rushing back to him, she saw that he had roused and was adding even more coal, stoking the fire higher.

"Oh, no!" she cried. "Why aren't you asleep? Go to sleep so that I can warn you! Go to sleep, Ullin! No, no, what am I saying? Don't sleep. Don't. Listen, listen! Hear the creatures howl?"

She was relieved when she saw him peer outside, but her heart sank when he resumed his place within, staring at the flames.

"No, no! It isn't the wind! Oh, no!"

Rushing back upward, she saw more sentries gathering above, peering over the edge. A rider approached along the top of the wall, one of the captains of Secundur, cracking his whip to make the others move out of his way. Back down to Ullin Micerea fled, and she found him asleep, now, and just beginning to dream. Not bothering to create any dreamscape for them to share, she simply put her face very close to his and shouted.

"Fly! Awake and run! Run, Ullin!"

"What are you going on about, dear?"

"Shatuum is called out for you! You must run for your life!"

"What?"

Desperate, she closed her eyes and conjured the image of the dogwraiths above, and she presented it to him, right in his face, and she growled.

"Aiii!" Ullin cried. But instead of waking, he was suddenly engaged in a terrible battle somewhere in the far off desert, set upon by Dragonkind as he ran, turned and slashed, then ran again.

"No, no! Wake up!"

She withdrew upward to see the dark captain push aside the two sniffing and howling wraiths so that he could have his own look over the wall. After but a moment, he strode quickly to a torch some distance away, and came back with it. Leaning out, he dropped it, and all watched as it hit the ledge, several hundred yards below them, and bounce off to fall out of sight. And, now, another captain was riding up to join him.

Micerea flew away to Griferis, reaching the fabulous palace in an instant, looking for Robby. But when she found him, she saw that instead of sleeping, he was studying some books at a table in his bedchamber.

"No, no!"

Impetuously, she reached out and slapped him, but of course her hand only passed right through him and his book. He turned a page and continued reading. In a panic, realizing that she would have to figure this out on her own, she rushed back to Ullin, who was still in the throes of his nightmare, tossing and turning under his blankets. She entered his dream, dressed in her armor, and drew her sword. As he turned to dash across the face of a windswept dune thudding with falling arrows, she stood in his way.

"If you don't wake up, I'm going to kill you!"

"Micerea!"

She raised her sword. "Wake up! And run for your life!"

Confused and astonished, he shook his head as he slid to a halt before her and slipped on the shifting sand.

"What do you mean?"

"This is a dream, Ullin. Your dream. But while you sleep, Secundur's creatures close in on you!"

"Secundur? Here?"

"No, you stupid man!"

With that, she charged him. He woke up, and opened his eyes just in time to see that his blanket was on fire.

"Oh, good grief!" he uttered, tossing off the blanket, bumping his head as he did so, and snuffing it out quickly. "What was that all about? Oh, damn! There goes the fire."

He leaned over, coughing at the smoke that had filled the cave, and blew on the coals to try to rekindle his fire. But there was not enough fuel, so he crawled outside to fetch more. Above, Lady Moon had just cleared the eastern rim of the divide, and was now slowly walking across the sky toward the western peaks, setting their snow-draped shoulders aglow. Ullin looked up at the mountains in wonder at the light, just as another torch fell from above. It bounced, as he flinched backward and away, then it landed on his pile of coal.

"Oh, oh!" he cried, and scrambled back inside for his backpack and ice axes. "Now, I understand!"

He quickly rolled his burnt blanket back up and tied it to his pack, noting the queer feeling running up and down his body, setting his hairs on end.

"Indeed, I get the message!"

Back outside, he charged off, slinging the pack on as he went, keeping as close to the inside of the ledge as he could. He heard a sound and, turning to look back, he saw another torch tumble down past his cave, then several more in quick succession. He broke into a jog, but after only a couple of sliding steps on the icy ledge he thought better of such haste and slowed to a very quick walk. He was thankful that he had been too tired to remove his crampons the night before, and he now adjusted his stride to use them more effectively. Looking straight up, he saw yellow flickering points dotting the top of the heights far above.

"If they have ropes, I'm done for," he muttered, and he redoubled his pace.

He raced as fast as he dared northward. Micerea, watching, was now all too aware of the limitations of dreamwalking, maddeningly frustrated that she could not tell Ullin what was taking place above him. She flew continually back and forth, from Ullin to the scene above him, to Robby to see if he yet slept, then back to Ullin. By the time the sunrise approached, there was a crowd of wraiths, goblins, and bogles on the walls, looking down. Lady Moon chose to duck behind the western peaks, spreading shadows over Ullin, which was all that saved him from being spotted. Still the creatures tossed their torches down, but luckily far behind him.

Finally, Robby was asleep.

"Robby! Shatuum is called out for Ullin!"

"What? Let's go!"

In an instant, the two dreamwalkers arrived, and Robby saw for himself what was afoot.

"What can we do?" Micerea pleaded.

"I don't know!" he answered. Though asleep, he felt his face redden with anger at the thought that he may have sent yet another member of his family on a mortal mission. "I don't know what to do. I have no skill to distract those creatures. They don't sleep, for this very reason, I think. I think Secundur fears dreamwalkers. We must find some other way. Let's go to Fort Defiance. Perhaps we can convince the post there to mount an attack."

"But that is on the other side of Shatuum, leagues and leagues away. What good would that do?"

Already, Robby was at Fort Defiance, but a quick survey showed him that at most there were only a few dozen men there. Robby saw Sergeant Hull, asleep in the bunkroom, dreaming of a warm sunlit vineyard. The tough soldier was going about inspecting grapes as big as his fist, and cutting one or two to taste.

"Hello, Sergeant."

"Why, hello, Master Ribbon! My! You're much older than I remember. How do you like my grapes?"

"I like them fine, but I must ask you something."

"What's that?"

"Are there any horns or trumpets or bells or such at Fort Defiance?"

"Every patrol has a ram's horn trumpet to carry along."

"How many? How many trumpets do you have, that is?"

"Plenty enough for our patrols, and for answering from the fort."

"How many, though?"

"Well, I don't reckon I know. A dozen at the ready, maybe. A few more laid by and ready to put mouthpieces in."

"Good. I must tell you something very important. Only I can't prove it."

"What's that? Would you like a taste? It's mighty sweet!"

"No, thanks. Listen. As soon as you wake up, get all the trumpets, and pass them out. Send patrols north and south along the borders of Shatuum, blowing and calling, as if there's a great army on the march."

"And what's the point in all that? We ain't very many of us, you know. Besides, I've got work here to do."

"Just do it! Commander Ullin's life may depend on it! Make your best noise, and then have your men get back to the fort, prepared to defend it. As soon as you wake up! I'm going, now, to tell the others who sleep."

And that is what Robby did, going to each man he found to be dreaming, interrupting their dreams to make his request, and to insist that they heed it. Micerea nervously came and went, but he instructed her not to show herself, since the sight of a Dragonkind would probably upset the Gray Guard. At last, he had visited all the sleeping complement of men, and he revisited some for emphasis.

"Well," he said to Micerea as they returned to the Crack in the World, "that's all I can do, I think. But if they make enough noise, and in the right way, maybe Secundur will think something big is up. And maybe they'll turn their attention eastward."

"But it could be hours before we know if they heed you."

"I know. We'll have to wait and see."

• • •

By now, morning was fully arrived, and owing to the angle of the sunlight Ullin was still in the shadows of the cliff as he hurried along. Already he was miles away, and had eased his pace, settling into a steady stride that he would be able to sustain all day long. He could not suspect that, far from where he was, on the other side of Shatuum, a small force of men fanned out north and south from Fort Defiance, dividing into smaller groups along a five mile stretch of Shatuum's eastern border. When they came to the places they had agreed upon, they began to blow their horns, calling and answering with such vehemence that the mountains took up their noise and repeated it over and again, echoing into Shatuum. Within moments of the sound, refrains of other horns joined the mountain air, horns of Shatuum sounding the alarm up and down the eastern walls.

The sound was too far away to be heard by those who sought to trace Ullin's path below. And it was better than an hour before Shatuum's alarm, spread on blaring horns and thundering drums, reached its western walls. The drums and horns signaled that all were to go with haste to the east. A great Vanaran army had somehow gathered and was marshaling for attack. Throgallus rode forth at the head of his captains, and with them thronged thousands of wraiths and bogles, goblins and witches, and other foul creatures. Furnaces were stoked to heat iron missiles, pitch and oil were brought to the parapets, and all of Shatuum's machinery of war was made ready, all of its soldiers at their posts, watching and ready for the assault. Throgallus strode along the eastern walls, counting his horde, making note that all his captains were at their posts, cracking their whips to bring order to Secundur's hungry and unruly legions. Again, Throgallus counted his captains.

All were there but one. The captain at the western wall had remained, in spite of the urgent signals, and he rode northward along the top of the wall upon his cinder-eyed warhorse. He dismounted and stood upon the very edge of the parapet, his coiled whip in hand. Looking down, he searched the ledge far below, as a ruddy glow kindled brighter through the eyeslits of his helmet. After a moment, he remounted his steed and rode farther north, stopping frequently to repeat his search over and again. At last, some ten miles from where he began, he saw a figure dressed in the white gear of the Vanarans stumbling along the snowy ledge, no more than a hundred feet down. The captain stepped from his perch.

• • •

Ullin stumbled again, and he fell headlong into a pile of snow. As he crawled out of it, he saw the captain descend like a stone, crashing onto the ledge some forty yards ahead. The dark knight's armor clanged and sparked against itself as he landed on his feet and fell heavily to one knee. Astonished, Ullin's skin crawled as he saw the figure stand to his full height, some two feet taller than the Kingsman. The being was fully covered in dull black armor with a red hourglass painted on his breastplate. A black helmet enclosed the head, and its eyeslits glowed from within with a bloody red light. The black-armored captain unsheathed a sword with a blade the color of hot iron and unfurled his crackling whip.

Ullin's training and experience took hold, pushing away the panic that threatened to paralyze. He scrambled out of his pack, and struggled to pull off his coat to free himself for battle before Shatuum's captain reached him. Already Ullin's opponent approached, his iron shoes sizzling on the icy ledge, sending up clouds of steam with each heavy step. Ullin touched Swyncraff, and it unwrapped from around his waist into a straight rod, and with his other hand Ullin pulled his short sword. Then, there being nothing else to do, he pushed himself up onto his feet and charged. The captain, surprised at the sudden onslaught, hesitated, then he slung his whip out, cracking like thunder, striking the cliff just as Ullin ducked under its fall, sending a shower of molten spray behind the Kingsman. Ullin parried the sword strike with his own, then kicked the captain's knee with the sole of his cramponed boot and struck with Swyncraff such a blow against the captain's armored side that it showered blue sparks and rang like a desert gong. The crampon hung in the captain's knee hinge, and Ullin twisted on his other foot as the captain again brought around his whip, hissing through the cold air. Ullin flung Swyncraff spinning upward, end over end, and it sliced through the whip, scattering it into crackling cinders and sending a flaming orange bolt into the captain's gauntlet. Groaning, the knight released the ash that was the whip's handle and twisted to chop downward with his sword just as Ullin's crampon freed itself. Ullin rolled aside, and the ruddy blade struck hot cinders from the rocky ledge. Now behind the captain, Ullin whirled around, spinning on his foot, and kicked the creature behind his knee with his heel, felling him to his knees in a clanging crash of armor and sparks. Steam billowed up around the captain as Ullin struck a blow to the back of his helmet and reached for Swyncraff, now resting in a bank of snow. Swyncraff sprang to his hand as the captain twisted and leaned around, slicing the air with his sword at arm's length. The blade's tip caught Ullin's blouse and burned through it, cutting open the vest underneath and instantly cauterizing the wound that seared across Ullin's side. A sharp burning sensation jolted through Ullin's body, knocking him down sideways as a round object flew out of his ripped vest, twirling through the air, ringing like a tossed coin. Both combatants saw the flashing coin, momentarily mesmerized by the sound. Ullin suddenly lunged to catch it, but he only tapped it away. It flew over the kneeling captain's shoulder, bounced from a rock, and rolled several yards away, coming to rest at the very edge of the precipice. When the creature, still on his knees, turned toward it, Ullin sprang again, crashing his body against his opponent's hot armor, giving the captain another blow with the pommel of his sword, and the two flipped over, sending Ullin sliding head first on his belly toward the teetering object. He flung away his sword, grabbed the coin, desperately trying to stop his slide, then went over the edge and disappeared.

The captain of Shatuum slowly got to his feet and went to look. There, he saw Ullin dangling at the end of Swyncraff which had hooked one end onto the edge, its other end coiled firmly around Ullin's wrist. The captain crouched, meaning to pull Ullin and the treasure up by Swyncraff, but blue-white sparks arced out of Swyncraff at the vile touch. Recoiling, and dropping his sword to clutch his hand, the creature staggered out of sight. Ullin dared not move, having no notion of Swyncraff's strength. The captain reappeared, standing over him, and he spoke.

"Come up," he said in the Ancient Tongue, "and give to me the strange coin. In exchange, I will let thee live."

"This?" Ullin croaked, holding the coin out over the void, showing its amber jewel to the captain, ready to drop it rather than let it be taken. At that moment, Sir Sun ambled over the mountaintops and glanced down. His rays struck the coin and rejoiced upon it so much that the brilliance of the coin's luster and the fire of its jewel could not be contained. Golden beams shot from it and caught the captain of Shatuum full upon the eyeslits of his helmet.

"Ah, release!" cried the captain loudly, throwing his arms out and turning to the sky as bright yellow light streaked out from every crack in his armor, from the eyeslits of his helmet, and from every chink in every hinge and plate. Then, as suddenly as it had appeared, the light faded, and the armor fell in on itself, empty, clanging upon the ledge.

• • •

"There," Robby said to Micerea once Ullin managed to climb back onto the ledge. "He has done it. And the coins he carries have shown somewhat of their power. But that was a close call. As soon as you can, go to him, help him, if you can, to nurse that wound and get some rest."

"But won't they come back?" Micerea asked. "To look for their captain?"

"Most likely. But the same ruse may not work a second time," Robby replied. "And I fear Shatuum may now pour out upon those in Fort

Defiance and slaughter them all unless I can think of some ploy to save them. And I wish Ullin had longer legs!"

"He is wearing himself out," Micerea said pleadingly. "And now he is hurt. Isn't there anything we can do to speed his journey?"

"If you have any ideas, please share them!" Robby fired back impatiently. "Meanwhile, let me think! See, he puts himself together. He is made of strong stuff!"

Ullin was at the moment painfully putting on his coat and other apparel, somewhat gingerly due to his wound. Before buttoning up, he checked the vest, making sure of the other six, and tucked the amber coin into an inside pocket. Once dressed, he pulled on his backpack, keeping his little sword and Swyncraff at the ready, picked up his ice axes, and staggered off, leaving behind the pile of black armor, already frosting over.

Micerea was relieved to see him on the move again, but she was not happy, still terribly frightened by the incident. She wanted to press Robby on it but bit her tongue, knowing that he was just as upset.

"Look," Robby said to her, "the next time you need me, and I am not asleep, fetch Finn. I am instructing him how to dreamwalk. He is very clumsy, just as I once was, but he learns quickly. Give him your message, then frighten him to awake. He sleeps lightly and rouses easily, I have found. Have him come to me and tell me that you need me."

"What if neither of you are sleeping?"

"I'm working on that. But I can't put everything in place so quickly," Robby countered. Then, trying to control his own anger, he softened his tone. "I am sorry that Ullin is in this fix. But he is loyal, and I must use him. I don't like it, but that's the way it is. I will use anyone I must, now. If that sounds cruel and heartless, so be it. I don't have the time nor the inclination to explain everything. But you know that there is more at stake than our own lives or comfort. I trust you, just as I trust Ullin. I ask only that you trust me, too, though I can't promise you anything in return. Not success, not even survival. Ullin has made my cause his own. You must decide whether or not to follow his example. Already, thousands have died for our cause in Ullin's homeland, and I'll not dishonor their effort by shirking my duty. So, Micerea, you must be all in, or all out. If not for me, or for our cause, then for Ullin's sake."

Although the words sounded hard and cruel, Robby said them in such a gentle tone that Micerea felt mildly rebuked and somewhat small. She nodded, knowing that she and Ullin were committed to a greater cause, and had been before they ever met. And now that cause was bearing fruit. As she considered Robby's words, she sensed that he asserted himself without a trace of the timidity of only a few weeks earlier. Indeed, she now looked to Robby for aid and for guidance, rather than the other way around. He was now the teacher and she the naïve student.

"You speak as if you are already King," she blurted out. Robby turned back to her with a fierce look, then smiled.

"I am Philawain, Lord and King of Griferis," he said. "Fear me."

And, suddenly, for a moment, she did. He continued to smile and she relaxed. As he turned to go back to the floating castle, a shiver crawled up her spine.

Chapter 24

The Second Battle of Tallinvale

Day 173
72 Days Remaining

The fog that obscured the southern view from the south wall of Tallin City thickened as the day progressed and hid the object being constructed by the enemy forces. With several men beside him, Lord Tallin stood at the south wall and watched. Behind them, the townfolk and soldiers not required at the walls had by now put out all of the fires started within their city, but beyond the town on the northern fields, several orange glows marked where the Redvest war engines still burned. Tallin Hall did not escape damage, as another infiltrator ran from window to window, tossing in bottles of flaming oil, and it would have been worse had it not been for Windard. Coming around a corner bearing a tray that he intended to take to Lord Tallin, he saw the perpetrator striving to light another bomb with an uncooperative firestick. Windard carefully put his tray down on the ground, picked up the silver teapot, and approached the oblivious arsonist who was still struggling with the firestick. With one swipe of the teapot, he ended the Tracian's career. He then poured the tea onto the flaming bomb, frowned at the dent in the pot, and returned to the kitchen for another, leaving the firefighters to their work.

A little later on the south wall, when Tallin saw him climbing the stairs with his tray, he smiled at the housekeeper.

"Thank you, Windard."

"Not at all, my lord."

"How are things in the house? Is room being found for our patients?"

"Yes, my lord. I'm afraid there has been a fire in the east wing."

"Oh?"

"Yes, but the damage is confined to one or two garden rooms."

"I see. And the cause?"

"An unfortunate gentleman set them. He was dealt with. I took it upon myself to prepare a light repast for you, my lord. It is just here under the cozy."

"Thank you."

As Tallin took the bread and cheese, Windard looked southward for a moment as he poured tea, but saw nothing other than mist and fog. Chewing, Tallin looked from Windard toward the source of the continuing noise, the ringing and thudding of many hammers and mallets pounding dully through the murk.

"I'm afraid our company is cooking up something new," Tallin said.

"I am sure it will avail them nothing at all, my lord. Dargul sends his regards, and asks that I relate to you his wish that you find some rest."

"Tell him that I shall do so at the first opportunity."

"Very well, my lord. And should I send up one of the physicians to look to your wounds?"

"No, that is quite alright, Windard. There is a pesky aide that comes by every few moments, it seems. I still have use of my left arm, and hope not to need the other any time soon. Is there any news concerning Commander Brennig?"

"He is still unconscious, my lord. Tasdon saw to him personally, but does not hold much hope for his recovery, I am sorry to say."

Tallin shook his head as Windard refreshed his tea. Commander Luard came up the stairs just then, returning from his own bit of rest, and Tallin gestured to the leftover food on the tray.

"No, thank you, my lord."

"How are the men, Commander?"

"Thanks to Windard and all the others, they are well fed and now resting. They will report within the hour."

"Very good. Have the rotations continue until we are back at full strength. Thank you, Windard. That was thoughtful of you."

"Not at all, my lord. Is there anything else that you may require?"

"Not unless you have some way of penetrating this blasted fog."

"Alas, I do not, my lord."

Windard took the tray and departed as Luard picked up his spyglass.

"Any new developments out there?" he asked, sweeping the gray scene.

"Two hours ago, just after you retired," Tallin answered, "a report came from the eastern wall that winches were heard. Most likely the enemy has recovered the remains of the trebuchet on that side. I'm guessing they make use of its parts for some new machine. I've asked for Captains Newcomb and Landings to come, along with Captain Hemmings."

"A sortie, my lord?"

"That depends on what Hemmings says to my proposal. Ah, here they come!"

Three soldiers climbed the stairs and gave their salutes.

"Gentlemen," Tallin said, "we need eyes to penetrate our enemy's lines and to return with a report on what they are about out there. Captain Hemmings, what are the conditions along the east and west roads and at the bridges?"

"On the east road, the near bridge is intact, as is the far one, but the middle bridge was knocked down by an errant missile, my lord. I got a good look in last night's glare. The middle bridge is gone, for sure, though. As for the west, I cannot say about the far bridges, but suspect they are down since we had no trouble with Redvests at the western walls."

"My thinking, too. Can you put together a plan to repair the east bridge? It must be done rapidly and with surprise."

"I have already begun working on that, my lord," Captain Hemmings said, "thinking that we'd need a way to put sorties out. And, seeing Newcomb and Landings, here, I assume that the bridge would need to be sturdy enough for their riders."

"Exactly."

"Then, I think it can be done. I've got rolling stock already teamed, and spans are being made as we speak. We construct them with wheels so that they can be driven out. I'll lay them with fulcrumed pivots, so that they can be swung sideways over the canal. The wagons will come behind with planks for laying on the spans. Once we get to the bridgehead, we will quickly lay it all out and peg it down. It won't be wide, but will support the weight of many horses at once."

"Very good, very good! Your schooling in Glareth was worth your time away from us!"

"I hope so, my lord!"

"Captain Newcomb, can you assemble a reconnaissance in force? You will have to penetrate the flanks of the enemy and drive to the center, where they do their work. I guess it is about three hundred to five hundred yards out from here. But it is hard to tell."

Newcomb rubbed his chin, just beginning to show a youthful beard, and he nodded.

"I would need at least two hundred," he said. "But I'd like to have twice that many."

"Landings, how many skirmishers can you field?"

"With a couple of hours notice, three hundred pair, my lord?"

Tallin turned back to look once more at the mist, considering his options. He could wait and see what the Redvests were up to, revealed when they put the product of their labor to use, or he could risk hundreds of men for a bit of information.

"Very well," he said, turning back to the three. "Recruit as many as you need to complete your preparations, Captain Hemmings. Notify me when you are ready."

"Yes, my lord!"

As Hemmings hurried off, Tallin pointed out at the gloom.

"Out there is a machine meant to do us no good," he said. "I want it destroyed, if at all possible. Short of that, I at least want to know what it is so that we may prepare against it. We have at least three hours of light left to us, and this fog may work to our advantage. Let us assume we have destroyed only two-thirds of the enemy. That leaves roughly twenty thousand out there. Most likely they are well positioned against any sorties we might put out. But you know the terrain. I ask much. I want your riders to strike hard and strike deep. Find your way to their machine, do what damage you may, and return. If you see a way to destroy it, then do so. Captain Landings, your skirmishers are to be deployed to assist the return of our horsemen. Work out some method of coordinating so that word is immediately sent back to us on what you find."

"My lord, if I may suggest?"

"Yes, Newcomb?"

"Perhaps the long way might be the shortest," the captain said. "That is to say, if the army in the north is destroyed, perhaps we may ride the long way 'round, and come at their western flanks. We can send a separate force along the way they may expect, around to the east, as a diversion."

"Yes. Very well. Make it so. You may have your four hundred horses, if there are that many worthy mounts available. Go make your preparations, and send your aide to report when all is ready."

As soon as the captains departed, Luard held up his hand and barked, "Quiet on the wall!"

All obeyed, and every eye turned back to the south. The noise of construction had suddenly ceased. A slight breeze puffed across the battlement, teasing the moist banners over their heads, and the fog lifted somewhat, revealing a vague dark shape in the distance. Immediately, Tallin and Luard and all others who had spyglasses raised them and focused on the object.

"What do you see, my lord?"

"A squarish structure. You?"

"The same. I thought I saw wheels on it, higher than the thing itself."

"Yes. Odd."

The breeze died, the fog settled, and their glimpse came to an end.

"What manner of machine may be shaped like that?" Luard asked. "A box with wheels?"

"I do not know. From what I glimpsed, it does not seem tall enough to come halfway up our walls, even on level ground," Tallin replied. "I do not recall anything like it."

Their discussion was ended when a fireball came out of the mist and flew over their heads, followed by a rain of arrows. The fireball was wide of the mark and bounced harmlessly across the open space behind them, but the arrows struck down many defenders who did not duck in time. Then, out of the fog came two long columns of Redvests, each in tight formation, their shields held high.

"Prepare for ladders!" Luard shouted. "Archers!"

Already, Tallinvale arrows were glancing from the overlapping red shields, having little discouraging effect upon the Redvests, and Tallin studied their movements carefully. About fifty feet apart, the two formations came straight up the hill, holding their space from each other even when they encountered rough and rocky ground. Then, about thirty yards from the wall, they stopped and massed, still holding their shields high so that the men beneath them were protected.

"What are they playing at?" Tallin muttered.

Then came odd sounds, ringing and chopping, from beneath the shields.

"Luard, throw something heavy upon them!" Tallin said.

"They are too close for our ballistas, my lord. And too far out to toss anything heavy by hand."

Tallin glanced down the wall. Already, men were at work lifting their ballistas, trying to get them situated to shoot down at such a steep angle.

"Sir!" called a soldier, running up to Luard, "Ballista Four can reach, but only by shooting low along the length of our wall. And they can't see for the fog what they aim for."

"Then mark it off as you return, and allow for angle. Do your best!"

"Yes, sir!" the aide handed Luard a line from a spool, and he ran off westward unreeling it as he went.

"It will be a difficult shot, my lord," Luard said, clutching the line in one hand while ducking another rain of arrows. "We may ought to move away."

Almost as soon as they heard the thump, a long iron tipped missile came hurling out of the fog from their right, passing just over the wall, struck short of the closest Redvest column, then bounced up and flipped harmlessly into the space between the two.

"Mark plus twenty! Pass it down!"

Luard's correction was quickly called down the line to the far ballista. Meanwhile, the enemy hurled another fireball that followed the first without harm or damage to the Tallinvale defenders.

"They do not bother to spot their missiles," Tallin observed just as another of his own came flying toward them. Luard instinctively ducked, but it was off the wall at the correct angle to crash into the left column, sending shields and men flying into the air. The Redvests quickly reformed and continued their mysterious work.

"Continue! Pass it down!"

"Ladders!" called someone down the wall. Several more columns were emerging from the fog, quickly approaching with long ladders.

"Here they come again, lads!" someone else called.

"Make ready to repel ladders!" Luard barked at the drummers who immediately issued their staccato commands. As the Redvests massed at the walls, preparing to hoist their ladders, they were followed by hundreds of archers who pelted the defenders in an effort to suppress Tallin's own who answered from below and behind Lord Tallin. Soon, thousands of men were rushing from their meals and rest, pouring up the stairs to join Tallin and Luard. Immediately, the enemy faltered under the withering sleet of arrows, first taking out the attacking archers, then spraying down upon those striving to position the ladders.

"All this is to divert us from the first two columns!" Tallin shouted over the din.

Even over the sound of fighting, the noise of the Redvests working under their cover of shields continued to be heard. The assailants, working to put their ladders up, were all but decimated by the defenders before even a single ladder could be set, owing to the throngs of Tallinvale archers that had come from the northern walls. Suddenly, an aide was tugging at Tallin's sleeve.

"My lord!"

Turning, Tallin saw a youngster wearing a helmet too big for him.

"My lord! Captain Hemmings gives his compliments and says all is ready."

"Very well. Hurry back and tell him to await my command."

As the boy ran off, Weylan trudged up the stairs.

"Captain Weylan, news?"

"Yes, my lord. We move the largest trebuchets. They approach the Hall. Where would you like them situated?"

"Very good, Weylan! Very good! Have one placed directly behind us, just there. The other one is to be placed in the stable yards behind the Hall."

"But, my lord, sir, it will barely clear the wall at that distance."

"We may need it to drop missiles very close to us. How long before they are ready?"

"A half-hour, at least."

"My lord, they are placing pilings," called Luard.

Looking down, they saw the two columns slowly shift as they planted two thick, iron-shod posts into the ground, each a half-yard in diameter. Arrows struck down scores in each column before it was done, and the posts dropped into the holes prepared for them so that only a yard or two protruded. Quickly they reformed their shields and surrounded the pilings, continuing their secret work. Behind the first columns, two more approached, and the rattle of the chains they dragged was clearly heard. Indeed, after only a few minutes, the enemy workers began to retreat, trailing behind from both pilings great chains made of links that were nearly as big as a fist.

"Well that gives us some clue," said Tallin.

"They mean to haul up their structure, whatever it is," nodded Luard.

"Yes, Tracian engineers are among the best," Tallin commented, "and they'll do it, too."

"Perhaps it is a shield or covering so that they can mine our walls," Luard suggested.

"Perhaps. But I don't think so. They must know by now that we stand on solid rock. It would take them weeks just to get a few yards."

Now, as the day neared its end, and the last of the Redvests disappeared back into the fog, another aide appeared.

"My lord, Captains Newcomb and Landings send their compliments. All is prepared, and they await your order."

"They shall have it directly," Tallin replied, turning to look toward the roadways leading around the grounds of his estate where the trebuchets that Weylan brought were creeping along, pulled by teams of oxen and pushed by scores of men. "Have Captain Weylan, who sees to the trebuchets, come to me at once."

Below, outside the walls, the two long chains that merged into the darkening fog were drawn taut by unseen windlasses, as the Redvests began advancing their structure up the incline toward the walls.

"My lord, you wished to see me?" Weylan asked when he arrived a few minutes later.

"The trebuchets?"

"They are coming along in good order. Another half-hour, I'm afraid."

"Good. I have another assignment for you. You'll take men from here to the East Gate. There you will find Captain Hemmings, who means to repair the middle bridge along the east road. We send out sorties under Captains Newcomb and Landings. Your task is to assist Hemmings in placing the bridge, and once the horsemen and skirmishers are across, to hold the bridges and approaches for their return. It may be a long job, darkness falls, and you will be outside the safety of our walls."

"I understand, my lord."

"Luard, give Weylan every sixth for the East Gate."

• • •

As men peeled away from the south wall and hurried off with Captain Weylan, Tallin walked eastward along the wall, greeting his defenders, calling many by name as he went. When he reached the corner, he turned and continued along the less crowded east wall, picking up his stride until he arrived at a place where he could watch the defensive buttresses being cleared from the East Gate as quietly as the workers could do it. In the yard behind the gate were a thousand men under the command of Captain Weylan, along with several hundred more assigned to Hemmings and his engineers. Behind them, standing beside their horses, were Newcomb's riders. Directly beneath Tallin, gathered along the interior of the wall, were Landings' skirmishers in their drab tan and green garb, making good use of their wait by honing their knives and arrow tips to razor edges.

The gate buttresses came down, lights were dowsed in the nearby area, the gates swung open, and the portcullis was quietly raised. Out trotted Weylan and his men toward the destroyed bridge. They disappeared quickly into the foggy darkness. Behind them went Hemmings' wagons, pulled by Hemmings and his workers, rolling out softly on rag-wrapped wheels. Tallin watched, but his eyes were unable to follow them into the darkness, much less see through the persistent fog. Crossing his arms, he paced back and forth with uncharacteristic nervousness. He was sure that by now the Redvests were massing their troops around the structure or machine or whatever it was they had made. The enemy was probably gathered too thick for Newcomb's riders to penetrate, Tallin speculated, and he was gripped with a sudden desire to recall his men before it was too late. No, he decided, Newcomb and Landings were capable and clear-thinking soldiers. If Newcomb saw that his horsemen could not destroy the enemy weapon, he would not waste men trying. Tallin only hoped that Newcomb would retreat before they were trapped inside an enclosing throng of Redvest steel. As for Landings, perhaps sending his men out was foolish, too. But if direct assault failed, perhaps Landings with his crack stealthy fighters could do something.

Turning, he gazed across the town toward the south wall. The center of the wall, where Luard now commanded, was almost blocked from view by the spires of Tallin Hall. Tallin watched as another fireball rose into the sky. It crossed over the wall and fell precariously near his greenhouse. Evidently, the Redvests had moved their small trebuchets closer. The moments stretched out. Tallin continued to pace, continued to have doubts, and he fought the urge to call a halt to the mission. At any moment, enemy scouts would report on the activity at the bridge, and would summon forces to counter the move. Perhaps Hemmings had overstated his ability. Or maybe some stubborn wreckage had to be cleared away. But then Tallin saw the rest of Weylan's men pouring through the gate, a sign that the bridge was up. He knew that Weylan would place his men all along the roadway and would form defensive lines beyond the far bridge. A signal was received by Newcomb's horsemen, and they quickly mounted and rode out, followed by Landings' skirmishers with their bows and quivers, trotting out and filtering into the darkness. The gate was then closed.

Tallin heaved a sigh and turned to go back to Luard at the south wall. As he did so, the trebuchet behind Luard hurled the first fiery missile out toward the Redvests. Tallin watched it arc and then land in a burst of flames that set the mists aglow and briefly illuminated the hulking mass that crept closer and closer every moment. Tallin walked deliberately, but not fast, to show his people his confidence in them. He repeated his encouragements, saying how proud of them he was and what an honor it was to live in Tallinvale with such men. He smiled and shook hands with many of the soldiers, effectively hiding his misgivings and doubts.

"Thank you for your brave service," he said to one old gentleman.

"Stand easy," he told the men as he walked along. A young man, lately a cobbler, but now wielding bowstring instead of shoestring, saluted Lord Tallin as he came by. Tallin stopped and offered his hand.

"You do me great honor, sir," Tallin said to him.

"It is my honor," said the lad. "I shall remember these days to my children, and proudly tell the tale of your leadership, Lord Tallin!"

"It would be a short tale, but for your courage and determination," Tallin replied, gesturing to everyone nearby. Then, as he continued on, he said to everyone within earshot, "These are the days when little Tallinvale tilts the world! By men and women, brave and true! You have given fair notice to the Redvest and any else who may come. And notice they have taken from you, in steel and in courage!"

Saying this, Tallin arrived at the corner of the wall and turned to face inward as the defenders along the walls and those down below looked to him in admiration and pride. He removed his helmet, and raised it high in salute to them.

"Hail, Gallantry! Hail, Valor! Hail, Tallinvale!"

"Tallinvale! Tallinvale!" came the raucous cheer up and down the walls, picked up and echoed in a tremendous chorus of voices from all over the city. Men beat their shields, drummers spontaneously beat their drums, and the noise continued as Tallin put his helmet back on his head and strode on, his heart bursting with pride while at the same time melting with humility. Such a noise and tumult it was that many of the Redvests paused in wonder.

• • •

"How long before it gets to us?" Tallin asked Luard as soon as he returned to the center of the south wall. Another flaming missile flew up from behind them, cutting over at the invaders. It was right on the mark, and would have hit the structure if it had been fifty feet closer.

"It gets steeper for them as they near," Luard answered, his head behind his spyglass. "But I think by dawn it will be upon us. Maybe sooner. It appears, if I ain't mistaken, they go ahead of it, working the ground. Perhaps smoothing the way."

"What about their other machines?" Tallin asked as he picked up his own glass.

"They don't much pester us. I think they move them closer, too. Or have taken them elsewhere."

"Very well. Send off every tenth, but only the strongest, to the east armoury immediately along with four officers. Tell them to quickly dress for line battle and await at the East Gate. Hurry."

• • •

The Redvest General Menslay was no fool. He knew that his survival depended on success. And he was as meticulous as Mar Henith in his thinking. But when the inferno swept away the bulk of their army, along with Mar Henith and most of the senior staff, he knew immediately that he would have to act swiftly and decisively, even if it meant taking great risks. He also knew that Lord Tallin was a worthy opponent not to be underestimated. When he took command of the remaining armies, Menslay spent one hour consulting with the commanders, learning the numbers, disposition, and condition of all men, weapons, supplies, and other material. He spent another hour busily sending and receiving runners who gathered for him additional information and news. Thus he learned the state of things along the western side where a battalion was deployed to block egress from the city, and the condition of survivors and material along the devastated northern side where the bulk of his comrades had been destroyed. Then, without hesitation, he made up his mind and issued his orders. He sent fast riders south to summon reinforcements, but he would not postpone his own plan of attack. He did not tolerate debate or reluctance, and made it clear that any who did not obey were to be summarily executed on the spot. He still had over fifteen thousand men at his disposal, more than enough to do the job. So he split them into four divisions. The first was to be entirely devoted to the construction of their engine. The second division was to defend the workers and harass the defenders along the southern wall. The third and fourth divisions would be his insurance, and would take up defensive positions on their east and west flanks, with special attention to the east. If Tallin ordered a sortie, it would come from the east wall, and it would come in force. He hoped Tallin cared too much for his men to send them out, preferring to shelter behind the walls that served them so well. If not, Menslay would have his men ready.

So when word came that a large force was moving out along the east road from the city, Menslay was almost pleased. Then, on the heels of that news came the sound of hundreds of horsemen, breaking through the lines and riding down upon the Redvests who labored to move their great machine toward the southern wall.

"Signal, pivot east," Menslay ordered. Redvest drummers sent the order, and at the sound, the prepared Redvests wheeled into the onslaught. As planned, Redvest archers and pikemen cut the riders down long before they came within five hundred yards of the center. From his makeshift tower, Menslay heard the Tallinvale riders crumble between the jaws of his trap. He smiled when he heard the screams of Tallinvale men and horses. Just when he felt sure the horsemen would be completely wiped out, arrows zipped in from both sides of the Redvest lines, and the horsemen rode through. Then, to everyone's surprise, the alarm came from the west flank, where another squadron of horsemen attacked. Sensibly, the Redvest officers let them through, and closed behind them on both sides. In spite of the arrows that Tallin's hidden skirmishers shot, the horsemen were quickly trapped within a vise of Redvests, and hardly one in four escaped.

On the eastern side of the city, after the hidden Redvest division had let the horsemen and skirmishers through, they unleashed a furious attack upon Weylan's men who held the road. Small ballistas ranged from higher ground, and archers who hid waist-deep in the muck and mire to either side of the roadway loosed their deadly arrows. At the same time, a heavily armored formation of Redvests marched straight down the road into the Tallinvale fighters. Weylan's men, struck from three sides at once, were soon forced back. When their shields met against those of the Redvests, the crunch echoed back to the eastern wall. Three bridges lay between them and the city, along a narrow raised roadbed, and as they fell back, Menslay's archers moved with them, continuing their deadly sniping. Keen to his duty, Weylan ordered a runner back to report, but the man was cut down by arrows before he got twenty yards. Still he fought on, slowly giving ground, his men dropping around him like wheat before the scythe, as more men came running up to join him. Another runner he ordered away, and he, too, was killed. Finally, they came to the middle bridge, where Hemmings, comprehending the situation, had driven his wagons across his makeshift bridge and onward to Weylan, turning them over as barricades on three sides.

"We cannot hold this bridge this far out," Weylan cried, ducking under the cover of one of the wagons as arrows thumped and glanced around him. "We are too far for our own archers to reach!"

"Then we must leave Newcomb and Landings to their wits," Hemmings yelled back from across the way where he, too, huddled behind an overturned wagon.

• • •

As Weylan gave the order to fall back, Lord Tallin was at the East Gate, watching the next sortie depart. Below him poured out two lines of men bearing large shields and wearing heavy armor, going quickly but keeping close together, shield to shield, to make a channel between them for the retreating force. Behind Tallin, a trebuchet was set up and ready, its long arm in firing position, and its crew awaiting their orders. Leaning over the wall, Tallin watched as the first of Weylan's men came under the portcullis, many of them helping wounded comrades. But he saw none of Newcomb's horsemen, with or without their mounts. The line of Tallinvale shields folded in behind the last of the retreating men, and all were back through the gate. Looking to the inside, Tallin searched through the survivors and at last saw Weylan emerging from the gateway, among the last to return. He was carrying Hemmings who had three arrows in him. The portcullis rattled down and the heavy ironclad gates thudded closed.

"Captain Weylan! If you please!" Tallin called down.

Weylan passed Hemmings along to another man, and hurried up the stairs.

"My lord, my men fought bravely and hard, and followed my orders to retreat! I alone am responsible for yielding our post!"

"Then the enemy had nothing to do with it?" Tallin replied, putting his hand on Weylan's shoulder. "I am responsible, not you. A foolish gamble. Did all of Newcomb's force make it away? And Landings', too?"

"You are most gracious, my lord. Yes, they all got through into the night, but I fear the enemy allowed it, anticipating us."

"Quite. I share your fear. And now we know a bit more about the make of the man we face. Unless Mar Henith survived and is still in charge. Regardless, Newcomb and Landings will do their best, just as you have done. Oh, you are wounded!"

Weylan, with a confused expression, only then noticed the blood dripping from his beard and running down his breastplate. Reaching up, he felt his face.

"Oh. I'm afraid I've bit my lip open, my lord."

"Then go see to your men. Have them stand ready with Captain Green, if needed. Captain Green!" Tallin turned from Weylan and addressed the man who oversaw the gate's defense, "I put you in charge of the trebuchet. Put fire into the fields around the roadway, enough to light up any enemy movements and to cause consternation. Let the bridge remain unless there is an assault, then destroy it. If there is any good sign of our horsemen along the road, sally enough men to save them. You have the wall!"

• • •

By the time Tallin returned to the center of the south wall, the air had turned decidedly colder, and he felt the occasional snowflake on his cheek as he approached Luard. As he was about to speak, the trebuchet behind their position tossed a fireball high over their heads and down against the structure that still crept closer. The missile struck the side, coating it with fire that soon dripped away and faded. But in that moment, they could clearly see that the machine had the appearance of a large square box.

"I wish we could get the dimensions of that infernal thing!" commented Tallin. "It seems to be well sheathed against our flames."

"We've also tried heavier shot, my lord. It only bounces off," said Luard.

"Let them overshoot it," suggested Tallin, "and we shall see what that reveals."

The order went down, and the next fireball arced through the sky and dropped directly behind the object. They heard yelling and screaming and the apparatus lurched to a halt.

"Well!" commented Luard.

Soon a runner came to give a report from on down the wall.

"The last fireball revealed masses of Redvests gathering behind the object that they move," the runner told Luard.

"Could you tell what the thing is meant to do?" asked Luard.

"No, Commander. It appears to be much longer than it is high, and it is tilted, with the low end toward us. And it has great big wheels on the front of it and smaller wheels on the back end, which is somewhat raised, as if on tall wagons."

"How big are the wheels, Anders? And how long is it?" Tallin asked the boy.

"Well, sir, my lord, sir, I reckon the front wheels are maybe twenty or thirty feet. On the front end of what looks like a long box. And it seems to be maybe seventy-five or a hunnerd foot long, my lord. But, like I said, it's all tilted way up at the back end, up on some kind of scaffold or carriage on wheels."

"Hm. Very well. Thank you."

By now the apparatus was less than a hundred yards away and had resumed its approach, beginning the steep ascent up the slope before the wall. And, now, the defenders were once again pestered by arrows.

"They must have scavenged the leftovers of all of their northern machines to build it," commented Tallin as he and Luard crouched behind the parapet.

"But what is it to do? Is it meant to be a platform? Or perhaps some covering so that they can mine our walls?"

Tallin shook his head. When the rain of arrows passed, he cautiously stood, and looked through the arrow slit. An arrow came nearly straight down and shattered at Tallin's feet.

"My lord!" cried Luard. "That was close!"

"But it is pointless," said Tallin, reaching down to pick up the broken shaft.

"Not if it kills our leader!"

"That's not what I mean. The arrow has no point. Look, here, at this tied to it."

Indeed the arrow had a blunted tip, and tied around the shaft was a slip of paper.

"It is our fletching," said Tallin, unraveling the note and taking it into the light of a torch just down the stairs. It was a drawing, done carefully but in haste. It depicted the Redvest machine from the side, a long narrow box with two large wheels at the front. It was just as Anders described, and the rear end was shown to be up on some kind of rolling scaffold. It also showed what appeared to be hastily sketched windlasses and pulleys that were being used to winch it along, evidently by the great chains that were earlier installed by the enemy. Near one side was a little stick-man, giving the relative dimensions of the moving structure. Finally, scrawled in the margin were the words, "horsemen gone. cannot destroy it."

"One of Landings' men must have gotten close enough to have a good look at it," said Luard. Tallin handed the drawing to him and went back up to his post, wondering how many of the skirmishers were still out there.

"Horsemen gone," he muttered, just as an enemy fireball flew high into the air and came down just outside the wall.

"They are ranging our wall!" shouted a nearby soldier. "Get ready!"

Another fireball came from a second enemy device some fifty yards west. It angled high and then straight down onto the top of the wall, spewing fire and men in every direction. As men scrambled to recover from the blast, another rain of arrows fell down into them.

"Shall we answer their trebuchets with ours, my lord?"

"No. Throw everything at their machine. Have the Hall evacuated into the tunnels. Every third man to cover below the wall. Stand ready to repel their assault. Signal for all available archers to mass below."

The drums beat the signal, and runners went to the Hall where Dargul had already prevailed upon the physicians to move everyone below ground. Within a half-hour, the ground behind the south wall was crowded with archers from every other wall. As dawn approached, winter returned. Snow fell thick on attacker and defender alike as the Redvests and Damar mercenaries pulled and pushed and winched their machine closer and closer. The heave-ho cadence of the enemy was as loud as the creaking wheels of their burden, a strange counterpoint to the cries of the dying and wounded, the hiss of arrows and thump and whoosh of ballistas and trebuchets. A constant barrage of missiles, fireballs, and clusters of spikefists passed out and over the wall and down onto the contraption, but it slowed not at all. The enemy repeatedly sent men to threaten with ladders, only to be driven back by Tallin's archers. When an hour had passed, day was full, gray, and misty with snow and smoke. And, for the first time, the defenders saw what was arrayed against them.

From east to west, lines of Redvests and Damar soldiers stretched. In the center came the device, serviced by thousands of men, a tilted box covered with a thick scale of shields, like some red reptile, creaking and thudding on its two giant spike-treaded wheels. And now the Tallinvale defenders saw how, as it was propelled along, huge sets of pawls engaged each wheel so that it could not roll backwards down the steep approach to the wall. The two wide lines of the enemy kept apace behind the contraption, coming slowly, step by step, to maintain their distance. When it halted, the mysterious apparatus was only some fifty feet out from the wall, the top of it thirty feet below the defenders. Still the fireballs came down upon it, and still they had no effect. Thick lines of Redvests ran up alongside of the thing, their shields held high against the constant patter of arrows meant to stop them. But rather than seeking to free it so as to move it closer, the enemy soldiers began spiking its wheels into the ground. They piled up rocks around the wheels, too, so as to block them from moving, and chopped away chunks to make the wheels sink somewhat.

"Arrows loose!" cried Luard.

A gust of arrows rose and fell into the Redvests at their work, but more came to replace those who were struck down. Meanwhile, Tallin, with his eye to a spyglass, was gazing far out beyond the lines of advancing Redvests. Snow and smoke obscured the view, and flakes specked his lens. Enemy arrows shot by, and still he looked, his heart sinking at what he saw. There, at least two hundred yards behind the rearmost enemy lines, another line was forming, dark and vague in the foggy snow, appearing and disappearing as the mists shifted back and forth. But, clearly, the formation was approaching to join the ranks of the enemy. If he had the distance right, and the span of the vague line, it was at least three thousand more soldiers that came, besides the thousands already faced. It was probably the vanguard of a much greater force.

"They sent for reinforcements, after all. And so my plan has worked," he muttered, putting away his glass.

Turning away, he looked over the town as the rear end of the long apparatus began to slowly rise up. The throngs of Redvests that had been working at the wheels retreated to help those at the rear. Hauling on dozens of ropes and chains, the Redvests pulled and winched to crane the rear of the thing upward, using its large front wheels as a fulcrum, and they shoved forward the rear carriage beneath the long structure as a great pawl to prop it up as it lifted. Slowly it rose up, higher and higher, looming behind Tallin as he stared at his city. The lines of Redvests funneled to mass directly behind their machine, and a terrible onslaught of fireballs and missiles and arrows descended upon the wall and into the crowds of Tallinvale archers below. The remainder of the enemy now rushed the wall at various places to set their ladders and climb up.

Tallin, as if impervious to harm, slowly turned and watched the carnage among his men up and down the wall, and looked down into the ranks of his archers, falling in droves to the blast of enemy arrows. He seemed almost hypnotized by disbelief at the murderous doom that now befell his people, after victory seemed so certain. A bolt ripped through his cloak, and another glanced off the back of his helmet, and in spite of the blow he continued to gape. As a man ran up the stairs next to him, Tallin suddenly grabbed him by the arm.

"Tell the people to abandon the town!" he cried. "Send to Weylan and Green. Have them flee by the East Gate according to plan. Weylan will know what to do!"

"But, my lord!"

"Go!" Tallin pushed the man back down the stairs. "Go! Everyone is to make for Glareth!"

Tallin turned and looked up at the rising tower, unaware that the man he had just sent off was struck down only yards away.

"I wasted a whole day," Tallin muttered, "when I could have sent away thousands."

Staring up at the looming structure, now hoisted to its full height, Tallin watched it teeter, and for a moment he hoped it would fall back on itself. Instead, it slowly swayed, then descended toward him. Luard grabbed Tallin and pulled him away just as the massive thing came crashing down on top of the wall in a shattering of timbers and chains.

For a moment, all of the defenders were shocked and baffled, but before they could shake themselves out of their stunned silence, Redvests began streaming out of the shielded ramp and up their many ladders, pouring over the walls before the stunned defenders could react.

As havoc broke all around him, Tallin picked himself up and glanced out at the fog-shrouded line of approaching Tracian reinforcements, ghostly and ominous in the mist.

"So this is the end of us," he said, reaching for his sword.

• • •

Just over a hundred yards to the south, the dark line of men advanced. They could hear the turmoil at the walls in front of them, the clash of steel and the cry of battle, and through the snowy haze they could see their enemy. In their center rode a horseman, and to his left were three riders upon buckmarls.

"Give the signal," said Teracue, and a bowman shot a flaring arrow into the sky. Dismounting and taking his shield from his bearer, Teracue then nodded to Esildre and her kin, and he raised his sword to his soldiers.

"Advance!"

Ahead of them, eerie lights flashed and bubbled, quickly outpacing the Kingsmen as they came up behind the Redvests.

• • •

No one could get a shot at Lord Tallin. He and Luard, along with the thousand other men who crowded the wall behind him, were pushed back by the crush of Redvests pouring over the wall, coming through the tunnel-like ramp and over its roof. Such was the intensity of killing that the enemy had to shove the dead over the edge to continue their advance. Already Tallin could see Redvests charging down the stairs and into the grounds below, being met by pockets of his archers and footmen. More Redvests and Damar mercenaries scrambled up ladders and came over the top of the wall into the flanks of the Tallinvale fighters. With his numb and nearly useless right arm, Tallin clumsily swung a mace that he picked up while with his left he unerringly lunged and chopped with his heavy battle sword. Atop the ramp, Redvest archers marked him, and shot arrow after arrow down at him, felling Luard, then Captain Green. Suddenly, Weylan appeared at his side, furious and vicious. The enemy momentum eased, and Tallin saw General Menslay standing beside his bowmen atop the ramp, pointing directly at him. Then, strangely, a fuzzy light appeared next to Menslay. From the uncanny spray of light emerged a child. Tallin saw it plunge a small sword upward into the Redvest general, but had to turn his attention to more Redvests who were pressing down on him.

The fight continued, all the more furiously, every man caught in a frenzy of killing and dying. Cartu was soon upon the wall, surrounded by his hired executioners, stepping over the dead and pushing toward Lord

Tallin. Turning aside a pike thrust, and smashing a Redvest with his mace, Tallin did not notice the confusion outside the walls where Newcomb's surviving horsemen rode back and forth, cutting down those Redvests not yet at the walls. Nor did Tallin or many with him notice the gold-trimmed surcoats of dark green that slammed into the rear lines of the enemy, or the three beautiful warriors, like something out of legend, who strode confidently up along the top of the ramp, slicing away those before them who still thronged to the assault. And, amid the noise and desperation of a thousand confrontations, there was a single fighter, plainly dressed in tunic and breeches and riding boots, deftly conducting brief duel after duel with sword and main gauche, in spite of the two arrows in his back. He moved with skill, dispatching one after another of the enemy, ducking and spinning, sometimes kicking, sometimes using his pommel, until he, too, made it to the ramp and began his climb.

Esildre pointed her sword at Cartu, now within a few yards of Lord Tallin, and her two great-nephews hacked their way to come up behind the warlord. She turned the other way, leaping down from the ramp onto the wall right in the middle of a cluster of Redvests, dispatching them all with cool efficiency. Around her, lights flashed and little people appeared, doing their bit to push with her into the invaders with daggers and short swords.

The fellow with the arrows in his back emerged atop of the ramp at the wall, with Teracue and his Kingsmen not far behind. But he suddenly felt winded and shaky, keenly aware of the burning pains in his back. He weakly threw up his sword to parry a Redvest, then stumbled to his knees. He dropped the main gauche and tried to use both hands on his sword. But it was suddenly too heavy to swing, and was knocked out of his hands.

"Aw, heck!" he cried.

On the wall below and to his left, Esildre heard those words and instantly recognized the voice. She twisted around to see him falter, and she felt time momentarily retard, snowflakes slowed their swirling descent, and the sound of battle was far away. Confused and in disbelief that he was here, she saw the arrows in his back, and the Redvest who now moved to finish him.

"Tyrin!" she screamed, pulling a dagger and sending it up into the face of the Redvest. Spinning, she cut away the enemy around her, kicked another in the head, and jumped back to the ramp, scrambling to get to the top with her sword in her teeth as an arrow pierced her calf, another bounced off her backplate, and a third glanced from her shoulder guard. She slipped, clinging with her hands, then continued up, jabbing at the legs of another Redvest as she came over the edge. Another soldier charged her with a battleaxe just as she pulled herself over the top, but he met with Millithorpe who bashed his foot with a hammer and then chopped off his hand with a cleaver.

"Tyrin!" she cried again, as another arrow passed nearly all the way through his shoulder. He slumped, head down, and fell sideways, and she rolled over to him, getting to her knees in time to swipe away another attacker. Turning, she dispatched a Damar mercenary, and another arrow transfixed her forearm before she finally made it to the fallen rogue.

"Tyrin, Tyrin," she said, pulling him over onto his side as Kingsmen hurried past them and leapt onto the parapets to take up the fight. Tyrin opened his eyes and looked at her blankly, then with a quizzical expression.

"I reckon I might know you," he said.

"It is I, Esildre, I mean Shevalia!"

She jerked off her veil in order to see him better.

"Well, don't this beat all!" he smiled. "You can see!"

"Is that all you have to say?" she quipped. "Oh, my dear Tyrin! Look at you!"

"I only have eyes for you," he said so weakly that she could barely hear him over the noise around them.

"And I for you," she replied, and kissed him on the lips. Then, amid the turmoil and blood and terrible suffering around them, their eyes truly met. He smiled as her face lit up, as if some shadow fled away from her.

"You do have the loveliest amber eyes. The kind a man might fall in love with."

"Listen to you! Here, of all places!"

"Aw, it don't matter. But it's good to see you, anyway. Can't really imagine a better way to go out. I'd have a vision of you, anyhow. Whether you were here or not. Oooh! Kinda tired, all of a sudden."

"Oh, no, you don't!"

Heedless of her own wounds, she examined Tyrin as he passed out. The two arrows in his back were not deep, but his shirt and breeches were dripping with blood from his wounds. The arrow through his shoulder was shattered, though, and bits of the point were missing.

"I am going to take care of you, Tyrin. Just hold on."

Looking around for someone to help her with him, Esildre saw the townspeople rushing through the streets, wielding swords, axes, shovels, mallets, and scythes. They overwhelmed the Redvests and pushed them back into the regrouped defenders. Nearer at hand, she saw the warlord's head fly off from Lord Tallin's sword, as her two great-nephews dealt with the other mercenaries around him. Realizing that the battle was all but over, she broke off the arrow in her arm, for it was in her way, and then cut away a fallen soldier's blouse and began to staunch Tyrin's wounds.

• • •

A little while later, Lord Tallin stood with General Teracue, overlooking the aftermath of battle. The wounded were being seen to, the dead were soon to be carried off, and the many fires that had sprung up were now being put out. The two stood for a few minutes saying nothing, then Tallin turned to Teracue.

"Let me shake your hand once more, good Kingsman!" he said, taking Teracue's hand. "Your journey is unbelievable, and your arrival timely! Over three hundred leagues in less than forty days! Across the plains without forage, then through the mountains. And you sacked Damar City along the way. Surely none else but the Four of the Fourth could do such a thing."

"I only wish I could have brought more men," Teracue replied. "But I had to leave a fair number in Edgewold to keep order."

"And those who came with you? The little people, the Elifaen, and others? You picked them up along the way?"

"Not exactly. One man came this way before we did, having heard from your grandsons about the fight brewing here. A mercenary who fought with us, so to speak, back west. We picked him up just inside the Thunder Mountains. He was engaged with a company of Damar when my scouts came upon him. By all accounts, though outnumbered six to one, he had things well in hand. Upon learning where we were bound for, he tagged along. As for the others—Lady Esildre and her kin, and the little pixies, or whatever they are—they came to us last night, very late, having heard of us from one of my captains who went to Janhaven to reconnoiter the situation."

"Oh. And what is the situation at Janhaven? We have been out of touch with them for more than a week."

"Well, hm. By all accounts, the Redvests out of Passdale have been soundly trounced in a forest battle that took place night before last. The prisoners in Passdale were freed. But, my lord, you have had no word at all from them?"

"No, not for, oh, ten days at least."

"Oh," Teracue suddenly looked quite uncomfortable. "My lord, I do not know how to tell you…"

"Tell me what? What is it, man?"

"Your daughter, Lady Mirabella. She is dead."

Tallin paled, staring at Teracue.

"I am very sorry to give you the news."

Tallin turned to face out over the wall.

"When?"

"On the day before yesterday, I believe. I am afraid I have no details. You may wish to speak with Lady Esildre. It was she who told me."

Tallin cleared his throat, his shoulders sagged, and with his good hand, he gripped the parapet.

"Lord Tallin!" Weylan came up, and dipped his head to General Teracue, "I have the preliminaries."

Teracue shook his head at Weylan, but Tallin turned around, blinking, and said, "Yes, Captain?"

"The town is in good order, considering," Weylan reported. "First count puts us at nine hundred newly dead, over two thousand wounded. We have taken eight hundred of the enemy as prisoners within the town, many wounded. And we have counted, so far, twenty-nine hundred enemy dead, eleven hundred wounded and captured upon the walls or hereabouts, to be added to the Kingsmen's count beyond. The remnants continue to surrender. I am sorry to tell you that Commander Brennig didn't make it, sir. Captain Green and Commander Luard are also dead, my lord. Newcomb, too. Landings looks to his men, then comes to report shortly. My lord, trolls are on the north fields. They mull about, but do not attack."

"I don't think they will bother us," said Tallin distantly. "Let them be."

"Yes, my lord. How shall we disposition the men?"

Tallin blinked. "Men?"

Weylan saw that Tallin was not himself and hesitated.

"General Teracue," Tallin said at last, "would you advise Captain Weylan, and coordinate with your officers? I think I will take a turn along the walls."

"Certainly, Lord Tallin."

Weylan watched Tallin walk away eastward along the wall, stepping over the dead as he went. His fighters greeted him with weary joy, and they noted the tears streaming down his face as he kindly smiled back, nodded at their compliments, and shook their hands. He seldom replied, though, as he went along the victorious ranks, and when he did, it was with a soft, cracking voice.

Chapter 25

A Thing to Figure Out

Ullin fell against the ice-sheeted cliff and collapsed to his knees, gasping for air. The place where he fought the captain of Shatuum was a day and a night behind him, and he went as fast as he could, without sleep, to get away from the overhanging shadows of Secundur's realm. Now, as noon approached, he realized he was pushing ahead too hard. His side burned terribly from the wound, and he needed to see to it as much as he needed sleep and something to eat. But each time he found a place that he thought might be suitable, some crack or cleft that offered a bit of shelter, he decided against it, fearing that he was still in danger. He knew, too, that Micerea could not contact him if he did not sleep, and so he could not know for certain how far along he was.

Groaning with pain, he slipped off his pack and began the task of opening it. His hands were numb with cold, as were his feet and face, and even little efforts seemed more difficult than they should be. At last he had the flap unfastened and looked within. Only a few lumps of coal. In his haste to flee, he had failed to put any more fuel into the pack. Disappointed over the lapse, he continued to rummage. He found some bars of jawrock, but they were as hard as steel. Dragging the pack onto his lap, Ullin leaned back against the icy cliff and pulled out Robby's kit. Carefully removing his mittens, he opened it to look for the salve within. He found it, but the effort of opening the little tin was too much for his stinging fingers. He put the tin away, shoved everything back into the pack, and began the arduous task of fastening down the flap. Sighing, he pulled his mittens back on and closed his eyes, readying himself for the next effort. He turned over onto his hands and knees, and then painfully got to his feet. A rush of dizziness momentarily blinded him, and he put a hand against the rockface to steady himself. When the wave had passed, he staggered off, and had gone nearly a furlong before he realized that he had forgotten his pack. He stopped, shoulders drooping and head down as he fought away gripping despair. He turned around and trudged back. Once he had the pack on, he looked around to be sure he did not leave something else behind, then he resumed his march.

"Cold will make one crazy just as will heat," he muttered to himself, thinking once again about his many desert missions. He thought of Micerea, and lost himself within the prospects of sleep and the hope of seeing her. He absently saw a loose rock and stepped on it, anyway. His foot slipped, and the stumble jarred him back from distraction. He mentally shook himself, redoubled his efforts to pay attention to his surroundings, and sharpened his determination not to pass by any suitable place to shelter.

It was a long time before he found a place, and owing to the deepening shadows of evening, and due to his fatigue, he nearly missed it. The shelter, such as it was, was a tumble of boulders that had fallen from above, and when he crawled around them, he found that some had landed in such a way as to form a small alcove of sorts against the cliff wall. It was too low to sit up in, but there was room to stretch out, leaving space for a fire. And so, he enthusiastically settled in, arranging his pack to somewhat block the wind. He pulled a few rocks together into a tiny circle and put his remaining lumps of coal in the center of it. Then, lying on his uninjured side, he carefully prepared his other things, put ice into his tin cup, got out his jawrocks, and readied his firesticks. All this seemed to take forever, but when at last the fire was lit, he spooned around it as close as he dared, waiting for the ice in his cup to melt and the jawrocks to thaw. He drank it down, long before it was very warm, and added more to melt. By now the jawrocks had warmed enough to chew, and he ate with relief, if not with relish.

Soon he had swallowed enough water to satiate his thirst, and eaten enough to allay the worst of his hunger pangs, so he set to work undoing his coat, his tunic, and his blouse to reach in with a finger of salve. It was very cold stuff, barely warm enough to spread, and his wound stung and burned to the touch. Grimacing, he worked as quickly as he could, unable to see very much of what he was doing or the state of his wound. By now, the fire was all but gone out, his fuel used up. After getting his clothing back on, he wrapped himself with his blanket, putting some of the warm rocks from his fire ring under the blanket with him, and he put his head down on his pack and immediately fell asleep.

Whether he dreamed at all, he could not say, but when he woke, it was daylight. Worried that Micerea had not come to him, and thinking that something was amiss, he hurriedly put his things together, carved a chunk of jawrock to put in his mouth, and crawled out of his shelter to begin his day's walk. It had snowed in the night, or else drifts blew down from the mountains above him, for the ledge was coated as far as he could see with a fresh layer several inches deep. He sighed, worried about Micerea, and set off. She would have a good reason for not coming, he told himself, but he could not help being disappointed. For some reason, one night without seeing her, after all those years, was nearly unbearable. Trudging along, with nothing but his own voice to hear, aloud or in his head, and nothing but the ever-present void beside him and the overlooming mountains above, he began to have doubts about his chances. It was surely too far to go to Duinnor. Too far, even, to get away from Shatuum. If it were summer, if ever there was summer here, it might be different. If he had ample food, it might be different.

"What was Robby thinking, sending me this way? Could he not see that it was too much? Too dangerous? Why didn't Robby let me come into Griferis, if, as Micerea said, that is where he is? And why, why didn't Micerea visit me last night?"

Around and around his thoughts went, and back again they came. And he realized what he was doing—repeating his thoughts with no new conclusions, no new insights—and he tried to break away from such thinking, telling himself that Robby and Micerea had their reasons. After all, he thought, their extraordinary abilities must be matched by extraordinary concerns. Surely they looked upon other events, and other people in need, besides himself.

For a while this served to bolster him and to drive away his doubts. But the wear of his trudging increased with each mile, and after a long spell of concentrating only on putting one foot ahead of the other, he again began to question his mission. The objects in his vest were truly remarkable. Although he had only seen the one, he knew even before the captain cut him open that he carried seven of them; he could feel each of them inside the vest. The capacity to destroy the dark warrior was testament to some awful power they held. But why, then, would Robby want them taken to Duinnor? If they were so powerful, surely that was the last place they should go. Slipping his mitten off and putting his hand into his pocket, he made sure that the one that had come loose was still there. Relieved, he put his mitten on and kept going.

The sky grew suddenly overcast. An hour later, Ullin was marching against the wind through a blinding snowstorm. Drifts soon piled up on the ledge, and Ullin stepped very carefully in fear of going too near the edge. He used Swyncraff as a walking stick to probe the drifts that he waded through, with his other hand over his eyes to keep out the blowing snow. Finally, he had to stop. The effort was too much. Buffeted by the wind, even standing was a challenge. He huddled against the cliff face. Knowing that he could not go on, he struggled out of his pack, pulled out his blanket, and pulled it over his head, covering himself as well as he could against the storm.

The wind howled and snow piled up. Shivering ceaselessly, Ullin lost all sensation of time or place, too weary even to look inside the pack for food. Drifting in and out of consciousness, he was sometimes startled by the noise of the storm that sounded like the moaning of ghosts.

"Begone!" he cried out in delirious anger. Later, giving himself over to the incessant howl, he whimpered, "Go ahead and take me, then!"

• • •

It was only a single night. But, to Ullin, it was an eternity of fretful cold, filled with spiteful and fiendish noise. Floating back and forth out of slumber, Ullin exhausted himself further with fitful sleep until even the storm, with all its power, could not keep him awake. If he dreamed at all, he dreamed of stillness and of quiet. But, very slowly, Ullin returned to some semblance of wakefulness. As he came back, he gradually noticed a strange sensation of being pushed down. Startled by the weight upon him, he stirred, struggling to get out from under his heavy snow-covered blanket. Throwing off the blanket, he blinked at the sudden light.

There was not a cloud in the sky, nor even a breeze. So profound was the heavy silence, he could have heard a whisper from the far mountains, should someone there say something.

"Hullo, there!"

Turning stiffly, Ullin saw Ayreltide standing on the ledge beside him. He knew that he was hallucinating, and his disappointment at his condition would have crushed him, but for the fact that he was beyond caring.

"Why, hello, Ayreltide. What brought you here?"

"Ha! That's a good one! My wings, of course. Really!"

"Of course."

"Fine day! Been awhile since I've been in these parts. Odd sort of place, though. Not much to my liking."

"Mine, either."

"Well, then, why hang about, eh?"

"I don't know. It's a nice view."

"Oh, what a jolly fellow you are! But come along, I don't have all day, you know."

Ullin smiled at his pathetic delusion, blinking away tears that threatened to freeze around his eyes.

"I'll make it easy for you, sir."

Ullin watched Ayreltide get down on his hind legs in the snow, then down on his forelegs.

"There! Hop on, and we'll be off."

Ullin only blinked.

"Come along!" said Ayreltide. "I've only today, as my Lady's dream is for today only, and when it is done, so am I! At least that's what she told me to tell you. I don't really understand it, since I don't recall ever being, well, *not*. Not that I would recall, that is, seeing how there wouldn't be a me to recall such a thing. If you know what I mean, that is. So, climb up."

"I don't think I have the strength."

"Just give it a try, dear fellow. I know you can. First, just get up onto your feet. That would be a start."

Ullin, humoring the vision, and needing to be on his way, slowly started putting his things together, stuffing the frozen blanket back into the pack, then slinging it on. He tried to stand, but his stiff knees did not work properly, and he fell over onto his wounded side.

"Ooof!" he said, wincing.

"That's it. Try again," urged Ayreltide. "You don't want my wings to freeze, do you?"

"Can't have that," Ullin said, using Swyncraff as a crutch to pull himself up. Wobbly, he staggered, but remained standing.

"Very good, very good. Now just come this way. Hey, where are you going?"

In fact, Ullin was lumbering off the wrong way, but then turned around northward, facing the red horse, and trudged back. Just as he was passing by, he tripped and fell hard, landing beside the beast. The fall knocked the wind out of him, and it took him several moments to recover. Pulling off his mitten, he checked again that the strange coin was still where he had put it. Then he reached out to get up, and he touched something warm. Still on his belly, he turned his head and saw that his hand rested on Ayreltide's bent foreleg.

"Oh," he sighed, not realizing that illusions could be so real as to mimic warmth itself. "I am lost."

"Well, not exactly. Just in an odd predicament, I'd say. Just try to get atop of me."

Ullin looked at Ayreltide, the vapor coming from the horse's nostrils, and the big eyes looking back at him.

"Very well."

Eventually, Ullin was on Ayreltide's back and he threw Swyncraff around the horse's neck, wrapping it around each of his wrists for safety.

"Good, good. Now, let us fly away from this place, as far as my wings may carry us."

Ullin closed his eyes, and he put his head into Ayreltide's mane as the creature stepped from the ledge and began to soar. As smooth as glass was the ride, and though the air gushing by was frigid, after a few moments Ullin dared to look about. They were climbing out of the canyon, and to his right he saw a long line of walls at the top of the cliff. Higher still they went, until he could look down into Shatuum for miles and miles. It was a gray misty place, full of dark blotches, as if fire-scorched. He could see no snow or ice in that land, and instead of snowcaps, the mountains within its interior were covered with keeps and towers made of black or gray stone. There was not a single sprig of green, not a single fir or pine, nor any shrub whatsoever.

Keeping over the canyon, Ayreltide swiftly flew northward, his powerful wings gracefully beating the air. Then, after a long time of silence, Ullin spoke.

"I thought I was dreaming."

"Oh, you are awake. Well, yes and no, I suppose. I mean, aren't we all? No, I suppose not. But anyway, Queen Islindia gives her regards, and tells me to say to you that what you bear for your friend is priceless beyond price, and has the power to change the world."

"She does? How does she know? How is it that she sent you, or even knew where I was?"

"Oh, I don't pretend to understand her or her ways. I have my own concerns, you know. But she assured me that she wouldn't need me today. And she asked very nicely that I come. What else could I do? I'm not like my cousin, Shartide, who's given to fussing and arguing and complaining. No, no. I do as I am asked, and I'm glad to do so!"

"Well, thank you very much for being willing."

"Think nothing of it."

"So you don't know how Islindia knew where I was?"

"Nope! She didn't say. She just said that I was to fly west to the end of the world, look for the man who visited recently, the one I served as his mount, and fly him north and east, in the direction of Duinnor. She also said that I was not to fly over Shatuum. She said I was to go slow and easy, as you might be too weak to hold on."

"I see."

"Now, I don't know, exactly, where this Duinnor place is, but I expect if I fly northeast you'll be a sight closer than before by the time I must leave you."

"Yes, northeast. I think so, anyway."

"Look. It appears the cursed lands are falling behind us, now. So I'd better make my turn."

Ullin tightened his grip, though Swyncraff had him firmly. Ayreltide banked sharply and headed over the mountains and away from the Crack Between Worlds. Below were snow-capped mountains, and to his relief, he saw in the valleys and canyons between the peaks forests of fir and pine. Putting his head back down in Ayreltide's mane, he closed his eyes and stifled a sob. Too exhausted to even weep, he slept.

• • •

He dreamed that he was standing atop a low mountain with fir trees drooping under heavy layers of snow. Beside him was Micerea, who seemed impervious to the cold. Ullin did not feel the cold, either, and he knew that it was because of her. He was happy that she was with him, whether or not she dispelled his chills. He turned to her and was about to speak when she held up her hand.

"Wait," she said, "and watch."

At his questioning expression, she pointed to the left at a high ridge not far off, its icy slopes glaring in the afternoon sun. There, coming out from behind the ridge, was Ayreltide, his broad red wings gracefully stroking the air, and he carried a rider on his back.

"There you go!" said Micerea, grinning and taking Ullin's hand. "And soon you'll be away from the coldest parts of this region."

Ullin watched, amazed, until the creature and his passenger passed out of sight to the northeast.

"Do I have you to thank for this miracle?" he asked, taking her other hand and facing her.

"You have Islindia to thank," she said. "Robby introduced me to her yesterday. It was very mysterious. I didn't know why he wanted us to meet. I've learned not to question him, for he has little time, these days, for explanations. But when he introduced me to Islindia, she greeted me most cordially. I was nervous—even though we met in her dream and I could have left at any moment I wished. I was taken by her beauty and her grace. She seemed sad. Or maybe weary. I do not know which. Robby left us together, to talk in our own way, about our own things. I was anxious, and she asked if it was because she was one of the Faerekind. I was, but I told her that it was because I feared for your safety, which was also true. She told me about meeting you, and that she had explained to you about Esildre's curse. How it was not Esildre, but Secundur that was to blame. Then Islindia suddenly asked me if I loved you very much. She asked what I might give up for you, if I loved you enough to give up my own people for you, if I was willing to forsake my land, my father, and my duty for your sake."

Ullin looked at her searchingly.

"I told her that I would forsake all those things, and my own life, too, for you," Micerea continued. "Even if it was only for a chance to have a life with you. I told her that I would rather gamble on your love and our happiness, and lose that wager, than to live another day without any hope of such a dream. 'Your dreams are more powerful than mine,' she said, 'for mine have been only about what is passed and what has been lost.' Then she asked me if I would tell her where you were, and I gladly took her with me to show her your struggle. Together, we looked upon you yesterday, just as the blizzard bore down upon you. She saw me grieve for you, and I begged her to tell me what I should do. 'Do only that which you know is right by the light of your heart,' she said to me. 'And since I may have one day of each month to bring the dreams of my past into life, I shall do so tomorrow. And I shall send help to Ullin Saheed.' "

Ullin put his arm around Micerea and drew her close and kissed her and thanked her.

"I owe you more than my life," he said to her. "I owe you my heart. Not because you have asked for it, but because I wish for you to have it. My heart, my love, and my life. I say to you now that which I long to do, and that which I intend to do. It is this: As soon as I am free of my duty to Robby, and have fulfilled the promises I have made, I shall return to the south to find you. I care not where we go, as long as it is a place where you will be safe and happy, and where we may be together for the rest of our lives."

"Oh, Ullin, my love! Where might that place be? For those places where I may be safe, you would be in danger."

"You know that I am not afraid of danger. And I would rather be happy with you, than safe and alone."

"But are we not together now? Perhaps it is best that we meet this way, safe from the world."

Ullin frowned. "But I cannot come to you as you can come to me. I cannot watch over you, as I would wish to do, as you watch over me. What if I learned that, because I was not with you, something had happened to you? What if you fell sick and needed me to wait upon you? And are we really safe from the world while we are within this dreamland? It is a mystery to me, that it can be so real. Yet, when I awake, you will be gone. I long for the day that, when I awake, you will be by my side. Just as you were those mornings in the desert."

"Oh, I wish and long for that, too!"

Now Micerea transported Ullin to her own bedchamber, far off in the warm desert lands, where a breeze rustled the sheer curtains around her bed and flickered the low-burning lamp on the stand nearby.

"You are right," she said to him. "We cannot always live in dreams, no matter how real they are. It taxes the body to do so. And I blame myself, in part, for your fatigue. I should know better! To be with each other in this manner is to steal sleep from you."

"Oh. Does it also take away from your own good sleep?"

"Yes, my love. But I have a comfortable bed to laze in all the long day. You, on the other hand, have all manner of duties that require your wakeful attention, your clarity of mind, and the strength of your body."

"Surely my exertions are to blame for my weariness," Ullin countered. "And the awful cold!"

"They are bad enough, and would have been mortal had not Islindia sent her marvelous horse to your rescue. But each night I have drained you of needed strength. I am sorry, my love!"

"But, wait." Ullin thought a moment longer, then continued. "You have watched over me for how long, now? You shrug, but I know that it is for longer than you would say. Oh, my precious lady! If what you say is true, then you yourself must be worn out!"

"Oh, I do not suffer overmuch."

"I can tell that you make little of it. But it is true, is it not? That you, too, are weakened by lack of real sleep, by continually going out into the world through dreaming?"

"It is called dreamwalking. And, yes, it is true."

"Then we must find a way of being together in body, as well as in spirit! This is a thing to figure out, and we must do it! Oh, what is happening?"

Ullin suddenly shivered as a wave of cold air touched his body. And Micerea faded for a moment.

"You begin to wake up."

Before they could say their goodbyes, Ullin opened his eyes and saw that Ayreltide was circling a wood nestled in a little valley. Seeing a clearing, Ayreltide descended and came to a soft landing. Swyncraff released its grip on Ullin's wrists, and he slid off the horse onto his feet. After a moment, he was able to stand on his own and let go of Ayreltide's mane.

"I wish I could take you farther," Ayreltide said. "But it is late in the day, and if I am to return to Islindia, I must fly like the wind, and faster."

"I don't know how to thank you, Ayreltide," Ullin told him. "Or how to thank your lady, Islindia."

"The honor of serving Islindia is reward enough for me. And your gratitude is plenty enough for her."

"Still, I wish there was something I could do for you."

"Hm. Well, I want for nothing. Can't think of a thing. But should something occur to me, I shall endeavor to let you know what it may be. I hope the rest of your journey is somewhat easier. Farewell!"

"Farewell!"

Ullin watched Ayreltide rise up and disappear over the trees and away. Then, looking about, noting that the day was coming to an end, he decided that he would enjoy a nice warm fire, and he immediately set to work gathering firewood. Hearing the trickle of water, he found a nearby stream and drank his fill. As he wiped his mouth, a fish splashed the surface of the pool a few yards away.

"Hm. I may have jawrock soup tonight," he said, gathering up his firewood, "and sleep on a pine-bough bed, too. But tomorrow I may do a bit of fishing!"

Chapter 26

Miller's Pond

Tallinvale was safe for the time being, although many of the wounded seemed to be succumbing to fevers and festering. Some of the attending physicians began to think the Redvests used poisons on their arrows and blades. The uninjured set to work tending the wounded, putting out fires, and rounding up Redvests who had surrendered. Lord Tallin put aside his grief long enough to direct much of this work, making time to meet and thank as many of the Kingsmen that he could, along with the fighters that had come from Nowhere. He was treated with great respect and deference by all that he met, most of them having heard of Mirabella's death. But the press of work was too great and too urgent, at the moment, for anyone to mourn their recent dead.

Ullin, too, was out of immediate danger. As long as he could forage for food, find or make shelter, keep warm, and keep moving, he could be in Duinnor in a month's time. Micerea kept watch over him, dreamwalking from her father's house in the desert lands to the snowy forests of the north each night. They made their dream visits short to conserve their strength, but the time they did spend together bolstered their spirits.

Robigor Ribbon was traveling, too, on the road with Prince Danoss going south from Glareth by the Sea. They were making their way to Formouth on the north shore of Lake Halgaeth where the Prince's army and his Lakemen gathered. They rode as quickly as was safe along the icy roads, and with each mile, Mr. Ribbon's anxiety grew. It was often he, and not Prince Danoss, who urged their party to go more swiftly.

Queen Serith Ellyn, who was still in Glareth, was troubled about events in Vanara, and she was anxious to be on her way home. But, Thurdun, her brother, convinced her to put off until Prince Carbane completed his plan of action. So she spent her days and nights fretting, often pacing the castle walls that overlooked the sea. She spent as many hours gazing at the sea as she did at the fire in her hearth, and almost as many staring at the pages of writing that she made using her True Ink.

Robby continued to study, and to explore the world, finding time now and again to look in on his friends in Duinnor. He saw that Ashlord instructed Billy, often while Ibin escorted Sheila out to see the city. As for Sheila, she was truly transformed. Her clothes, certainly, made her appear lovelier than ever, but her manner was changing, too, it seemed to Robby. She looked the part of a young lady of the west, and she acted it, allowing others to open doors for her, accepting bows and curtseys, and giving them in return. And though she did not receive guests or company, many young men and women came to Number 3 Crescent Avenue to call, leaving their cards and regards in the foyer with Miss Tarrier. At first Robby was somewhat amused by all this. But after a few trips to Duinnor, giving in to the temptation to see her, he saw that there was more going on than play-acting. To him, she truly appeared regal, in an almost exotic way, and he imagined that if ever they met again, she would treat him correctly, with the finest manners, and with every courtesy.

He knew that she would be shocked at the change in him. He was now thirty years her senior, his appearance altered by time and by his ordeals. There was a painful wound in his back that he received in a tavern fight some fifteen years ago that never healed properly, making his movements somewhat more rigid than they ought to be. His right knee, dislocated in a fall from a horse nearly eleven years ago, was now constantly stiff and changed his gait. There was the back of his right hand and wrist, badly burned during a battle at sea, and they were still scarred and discolored, though the injury was over twenty years old. And his black hair was not curly as it used to be, nor as thick, his temples were silver, and streaks of gray ran through his beard. He was a man made old before his time, in more ways than one. But Sheila was still a vibrant young lady.

Sitting unabashedly in her room while Reysa brushed Sheila's hair before the mirror, Robby watched and sighed as he listened to their conversation. Sheila told Reysa about the marvelous gallery she had visited that day, full of paintings and sculptures. Robby was familiar with the place, having been there himself some days before just to look around. Sheila's reflection in the mirror occasionally looked his way in such an uncanny manner that he almost thought she could see him sitting comfortably by the fireplace. But it was only the way she had of looking off in consideration before settling on some conclusion, and she turned her eyes back to Reysa who stood behind her.

This would not do, Robby concluded. He floated out of the house and over the rooftops toward the western part of the city. It was just too painful to see her. Their time was done, and whatever she felt for him she would be sure to deal with. She would stop thinking about him, if she ever did anymore, and would eventually turn her attentions to someone worthier, someone closer at hand, someone who would love her truly, someone that she could love, too. This was the hardest part, Robby knew. To leave her alone, to do the business with her that he must do, but to give her the room she needed. Being near to her, even if it was only while dreamwalking, only caused Robby to love and miss her all the more. Some things, he concluded, did not change over time, nor with age.

So, Robby went to Sheila less frequently, giving his attention instead to the activities of others in that city. He paid special attention to Esildre's father, Lord Banis. And he spent many hours, too, watching the King himself. He listened to the King's conversations with his servant, and with those who were summoned to the High Chamber. Robby was continually attracted to the room that held the King's collection of Bloodcoins, and he contemplated the objects that were not really coins at all, pondering their history and their power.

• • •

Sheila, in the guise and persona of the Lady Shevalia, continued to explore the city, going about in the carriage that Ashlord put at her disposal. It was all new and fascinating to her, and she found it more varied and exciting than she could have ever imagined. She saw fine palaces and houses, and explored wonderful parks and markets. She saw, too, the terrible slums and those poverty-stricken people who eked out a living doing menial work, begging for food or coin, or who were engaged in less honorable pursuits. Once, when she ordered her driver to take another way home, he protested, saying that the way she wished to go was not fit for a proper lady to look upon. But she insisted, saying she wished to see all that she could. Reluctantly, he nodded and obeyed, and within a few moments they were passing through a narrow street lined with taverns and pawn shops, the way jammed with drunks and others being offered the services of countless prostitutes. Although the horses pulled as quickly as the driver dared to go, Sheila still heard the coarse language of the women, some who were girls not even Sheila's age, describing pleasures that could be enjoyed for only a coin or two. And she saw through the window of the carriage a most shocking scene of violence, a man beating a woman to death with a mallet while, only a yard or so away, a girl was scratching the eyes of an old hag who stabbed at her with a knife. Everyone around only laughed at the squabble as Kingsmen pushed through to quell the violence. At least that was what Sheila hoped the soldiers would do. Before her carriage made it away from that street, a bevy of urchins leapt up on its side and reached in with clutching hands. Surprised, Sheila recoiled from the window as Ibin yelled at them to get down, and the driver cracked his whip upon them.

Once they had passed out from the place, and were again in a safer quarter, Ibin and the driver halted the carriage and got down to see to Sheila's condition.

"We ought not go through such places, me lady," said the driver, "an' Halfton Way's the worst of them. I hope it wasn't too shocking for ye. Did them urchins get a hold of ye? There's a flask of brandy in the pocket under the armrest, if ye care for a sip."

"She, She, er, LadyShevalia, areyoualright?"

"I'm fine. Thank you both. And Mr. Yarman, please accept my apology for asking you to drive through there. It was foolish of me not to heed your advice, but I assure you that I am perfectly fine."

"No harm, ma'am. An' no apology needed. I'm just glad yer alright. Shall I drive on?"

"Yes, thank you."

Once underway, Sheila did find the flask and took more than a sip. There was something about the children that was shocking to her, in spite of having witnessed and experienced far worse. Perhaps their condition struck too close to home, she mused.

• • •

That night, she confessed the mistake to Reysa.

"Oh, ma'am, I know of the place. Halfton Way's notorious for its violence and seediness. I once had the misfortune to pass through it whilst running an errand for Lady Dassath. I took a wrong turn, and, oh my! I thought I'd never get away fast enough."

"Well, from now on, I'll heed Mr. Yarman's advice!"

"Oh, he's a fine old man," Reysa said as she put out Sheila's night gown. "I reckon he's been a driver for all my life and knows this city like no other does."

"Tell me, what do you do when you have a free day to do as you wish?"

Reysa looked at Sheila with surprise.

"Oh, pardon me, Reysa! It is none of my business, and I should not have asked."

"Oh, it ain't that, ma'am. Only I was taken by surprise, sort of, since no one I have ever served ever asked me such a thing. But I don't mind telling you. This time of year, I like best to go to Miller's Pond. It is so pleasant to watch all the people there, walking about the pond, or skating upon it. And, if I have a coin or two for pleasure, I enjoy having a cup of hot cider from the woman there. Or, if I have a coin or three or four, I might even rent a pair of skates."

"Rent a pair of skates?"

"Oh, yes, my lady. Anyone is allowed to skate there, and if you don't have your own, you may rent them."

"I don't know what that is. What a skate is."

Reysa stared at Sheila for a moment.

"Truly? You do not know?"

"Truly. What is skate?"

"Well. When it is cold enough, the pond freezes solid. And skates are special shoes that have blades on them. You put them on and you can glide across the ice most gracefully, if you know how to. Or if you don't, you can have a grand time falling down on your arse! Oh, pardon me, ma'am."

Sheila was laughing, and shaking her head, "It's quite alright. You say the shoes have blades on them? Don't they cut through the ice?"

"Oh, no. Not if the ice is thick enough. Do you really not know about skating on ice?"

"Until just now, I had never before heard of such a thing!"

"Oh, then you must go to Miller's Pond and see for yourself. It is up on the northmost of the city. Mr. Yarman will know it, I'm sure."

"Then I shall go. In fact, I shall do so tomorrow!"

• • •

The following morning, breakfast was brought up as usual to the parlor for Lady Shevalia and Ashlord. Ibin and Billy had their meal downstairs in the dining room as was more befitting her servants. Ashlord nibbled some toast and read a large bundle of sheets printed with the happenings of the town. Sheila devoured a plate of eggs and bacon, and a hotcake slathered with butter and syrup.

"Ashlord, may I ask you something?"

"Anything you wish."

"It is customary for ladies to visit shops and such, is it not? And to look at dresses and gowns and other things? And to buy what appeals to them?"

"Why, yes," he said, turning the paper over to continue reading. "It is a great and joyous activity with many ladies."

"And how do they pay for the things that they purchase?"

"Many do not pay, but put it on their accounts, a bill for payment sent to their house."

"Oh."

Ashlord picked up his tea and sipped, turning his eyes to look past the edge of the paper at Sheila, who was herself studying her napkin.

"And do all merchants send bills of payments? Even those who sell wares on the streets, or beverages like, say, hot cider and such?"

"No, most of them accept coin, my dear. Often from their escort or driver, or from the lady's own purse should she be without an escort."

"I see."

Ashlord put down his cup and put the paper in his lap.

"What is it that you wish to purchase?"

"Oh, nothing in particular," Sheila shrugged. "It's just that I left my money in Robby's house when I went to the festival. Mirabella said that the festival was all her treat to me. Then the Redvests came, and I never had a chance to fetch my purse."

"I see. Well, you need not fret. Should you wish to go shopping, just have the bill sent here, and I will see to it."

"Oh. Well, thank you, but—"

"But you wish to have some ready coin, as it were."

"Yes. But I have no means to repay any of this to you, or any hope of having any means to do so."

"It is not necessary that you repay anything to me," Ashlord said. "I have much, and I need little. I will give you a note to take to my financier.

Mr. Yarman will know the address. Tell me, what activities do you plan for today?"

"Well, Reysa told me about a place called Miller's Pond. I'd like to go see it."

"Yes, I know the place. And I remember the mill that used to be there, long before the stream was redirected elsewhere. It is a social gathering place. In the summer, people carry baskets and blankets and eat and drink on the grassy banks surrounding the pond, watching the ducks and swans and each other. And in the winter, people go there to skate."

"Yes, skating. Reysa was telling me about that last night. I'd like to see it."

• • •

Later, Billy hurried Lady Shevalia past a young man sitting in the foyer, who stood abruptly at her appearance on the stairs, but had hardly a word out of his mouth before Billy more or less pushed him aside.

"Lady Shevalia!"

Rolling his eyes, Billy tried to block him at the door, and when Ibin put his hand on the young fellow's shoulder, he looked up at Ibin quizzically.

"I will have you know that is a very delicate coat you have your hand upon," the young man said, "and an even more delicate occupant within. I only wish to have a word with Lady Shevalia."

Outside, Billy held the carriage door open for Sheila.

"Billy, who is that person?"

"Aw, why he's the feller what's been leavin' all them notes for ye."

"What notes?"

"I don't know, since I ain't looked at 'em, have I? Miss Tarrier gives 'em to Ashlord."

"Really!"

Sheila turned and went back up the steps, and the young man's face lit up with joy at her approach. He backed up from the doorway into the foyer, pushing against Ibin and bowing low as she entered.

"My dear lady," he was saying as he bowed. But she swept past him and up the stairs, much to his confusion.

"Ashlord!" Sheila said as she came back into the parlor where Ashlord was still pondering the newspaper.

"Yes?"

"I think you have something of mine."

"Oh? And what may that be?"

"Notes. Written to me. Left with Miss Tarrier."

"Oh, those! I have been meaning to chat with you about them. They are on the bureau."

Sheila went to the little desk and saw a tray filled with cards, slips of paper, and folded notes.

"I think you should have told me that I have had notes written to me. Really, Ashlord!"

"Word gets out concerning you," Ashlord said, unperturbed by her tone. "And I felt it best to let the calling cards gather some dust before bothering you with them or responding to them."

"Why?"

Sheila sat at the desk and began sorting the cards. She recognized no names, but most bore elegant writing, some with gold-gilded edges, with various greetings. One said, "It will be my pleasure to await you at your earliest convenience. Cordially yours, Miss Threestocking." "The honor of your company would be the honor of our house, Mr. and Mrs. Darbasher," said another. "Orlus Massington, Esquire," was all that was written upon one card. These were typical of most that she read, then she came upon a folded note, sealed with a bit of wax. Opening it, she read, "Lady Shevalia, Today I beheld you for the first time within the galleries of Hanton Hall. I was so taken by your beauty and elegance, by your thoughtful attitude as you observed the paintings, and by your grace, that I followed you to your carriage. When you pulled away, I felt my heart sputter at your departure. However, I was fated to see you once more, this evening, as your carriage pulled into the apartments from where I had just departed, having been told that a bookseller who lives there was not at home. After you went in, I endeavored to ask after you, and I discovered your identity. I would be honored to call upon you and to introduce myself. Your servant, Grant Farby, Esquire."

Sheila shook her head, and picked up the next card in the stack.

"Oh, good grief! Here's another note, from the same gentleman."

"I call again," she read, "should the convenience present itself to receive me, Your admirer, Grant Farby, Esq." And she found another, too, from the same fellow, "Alas, I am told that you are out. I shall endeavor to make myself more convenient to your hours by attending your door earlier each day. Your devotee, Grant Farby."

"My goodness! Unless I mistake my numbers, there are seven, no wait, here's another. Eight notes from the same person!"

"It seems that you have smitten someone with your charms," said Ashlord calmly.

"And he is downstairs this very moment!"

"Oh my! What shall we do?" said Ashlord, folding the paper back to look at a different page.

"You make light of all this! Who are all these people, and this one, especially, who leaves such notes?"

"It is the thing to do, Lady Shevalia," said Ashlord. "And it is in keeping with the customs of Duinnor, and many other societies. When people hear of a beautiful and mysterious lady, they are naturally curious. They wish to visit, to see for themselves whether all of the rumors and tales are true."

"What rumors? What tales?"

"The rumors and tales spread and told by those who think they know something of Lady Shevalia."

"Ashlord, what have you been up to?"

"I? Nothing but the business that we are here to conduct."

"I think you have been up to more besides that!"

"If I might mention to our landlady something of the ancient lands from which you have traveled, that is one thing. And if I might say on some other occasion how a great estate was bestowed upon you by the very highest of that country from which you hail, that is another thing. And if she, or someone else, might mistake country for realm, and may conclude that the highest must be some prince or queen or even king, rather than the Mayor of Passdale, that is entirely another thing. And if Miss Tarrier, or someone she may chat with, might then tell someone else, forgetting some part or adding some new part, then what can I do about that?"

"Why? Why would you say such things?"

"Because it is good that we fit our parts." Ashlord shrugged. "And if others may help us do so, all the better. Soon, Billy will be as ready as I can make him to see the people who hold power here. But you may be the one to open those doors for him. Those we need to see are watched and mistrusted by the King. It will be easier to see them on a social pretense rather than to barge in all a-flutter with dire news."

"I don't understand," Sheila said, standing and pulling on the bellrope. "How can I help? What social pretense?"

"One will arise. There is always some party or other in the works. And people mingle at such gatherings who might not otherwise see each other, or who might not dare see each other on different occasions."

"I still don't understand."

There was a knock, and Reysa entered.

"Yes, my lady?"

"Reysa, who is that young man in the foyer downstairs?"

"He gives his name as Grantham Farby, ma'am."

"What do you know about him?"

"Nothing, ma'am. Only that he has come to the house every day for the past week or more."

"I see. Very well. Will you have Mr. Yarman come up, please?"

"Yes, my lady. Will there be anything else, ma'am?"

"No, thank you."

Ashlord cocked a brow, but said nothing more as Sheila took a seat. In a few moments, Reysa knocked and led the carriage driver into the room.

"Mr. Yarman, my lady."

"Thank you, Reysa. That will be all," Sheila said, rising.

"Me lady, Mr. Sootking," Mr. Yarman said as he bowed, his hat in his hand, looking somewhat uncomfortable in this setting.

"Mr. Yarman," Sheila said, "I am told that you know this city like no other."

"Well, I don't know 'bout that, ma'am. But I do know it well."

"If I wanted to know about a person—if I wanted to find out about who a person is, and I wanted it to be private—who would I ask, since I know no one here? I ask you this, because of your knowledge of the city, and because I believe you to be trustworthy."

"I thank ye, Lady Shevalia. I hope I am trustworthy. Might I ask the nature of yer inquiries? Only so that I may know the best way to figure it out a bit, ma'am."

"I wish to know about a young gentleman named Grant Farby. He who waits downstairs."

"Oh, ma'am, he's gone. I saw him go, an' overheard him tell Miss Tarrier that he only waits for a certain while, it being improper to wait longer without bein' asked to do so."

"Well, that is the person I wish to know about."

"If he's been a pest, me lady, I can certainly see to that!"

"No, Mr. Yarman. My escorts are up to that if it comes to it."

"In that case, me lady, I shall make discreet inquiries on yer behalf, if ye wish. Else, should it be more to yer likin', I may give ye the names of some gentlemen who may make those inquiries."

"If you are up for the task, then I would prefer that you take it on," Sheila said. "And it will be made worth your effort."

"That is very kind of ye, ma'am. Let's just consider it part an' parcel of me job in lookin' after ye. Mr. Sootking, here, has already hired me exclusive-like, to wait upon yer ladyship, ma'am."

"Very well, then. I shall be down momentarily. Thank you."

"Not at all, ma'am."

• • •

When Mr. Yarman, with Ibin beside him, snapped his whip, and Lady Shevalia's carriage rolled away along the ice-crusted street, Billy shook his head and went up to his lessons with Ashlord.

"They always get to go off somewhars er other," he muttered. "But not ol' Billy. No, no. Seems I've a mighty lot of schoolin' to make up for, an' it's a heavy burden it is, too!"

• • •

Mr. Yarman directed his carriage first to a row of counting houses in the center of town. Ibin opened the door for Sheila and held his hand to her.

"Thank you, Mr. Brinnin."

"Not, not, notatall, myla, myla, mylady! I'llwait, I'llwaitforyou."

"Please do."

Sheila looked at the sign, "Poranger and Sarb," and a porter held the door for her, bowing as she entered. Inside were various high desks, with clerks scratching away at ledger books, and one, seeing her, stood and approached.

"My lady," he bowed. "How might I be of assistance?"

"Are you Mr. Poranger, or Mr. Sarb?"

"I am Mr. Sarb, at your service, my lady."

"I am Shevalia, ward to Mr. Sootking. I have a note from him, here," Sheila said, handing the paper from Ashlord to the gentleman.

"Mr. Sootking? Sootking, Sootking," Mr. Sarb said, obviously trying to recall the name as he read the note in his hand. He saw a symbol near the bottom of the note, and his face lit up.

"Ah, yes, of course! Mr. Sootking! I have not seen him in years," the man said, shifting his spectacles. "I do hope he is well, as he is one of our oldest and most loyal clients."

"He is well."

"I am glad to hear it. Let's see here, Mr. Sootking would like to draw upon his account. Only a small sum, I see. I believe this will be no problem at all. I'll just need to verify his writing and accounts. It won't be a moment, if you will excuse me."

"Certainly."

"Won't you have a seat, just there?"

"I prefer to remain standing, if you don't mind."

"Not at all, my lady." Mr. Sarb bowed again before retreating to a back room.

Sheila looked around, noticing that the other clerks glanced her way, and one of them upset an inkpot while doing so. As she turned away, she saw Ibin peering through the window rather than watching the street as he should be doing, but she missed seeing the face that abruptly pulled away from the glass only to reappear a moment later, half hidden by an upside down newspaper.

"Lady Shevalia," said Mr. Sarb, "would you be so kind as to step this way?"

He directed her to a table where he counted out twenty-five coins, ten of silver, two of gold, five that he called half-weights of silver, and several copper coins.

"That's fifty-weight, altogether, my lady. If you would just sign here, on this line beside the amount?"

He placed a ledger before her, and dipped a quill. Suddenly nervous, she took it and, with a careful hand, wrote out her new name, just as Ashlord had taught her to do, making her practice and practice. Mr. Sarb then took the quill, examined the elegant signature, and nodded. He then placed the coins into a purse, and held it out, bowing again.

"Thank you," she said, taking the purse and putting it into her muff.

"My pleasure, my lady. And, if I may be so bold, that is but a small sum, and may not suffice for the needs of a lady such as yourself. Mr. Sootking directs that you may come at any time to draw upon his accounts. You need only sign, as you just did, for the amount that you may require."

"That is very generous of my guardian," she said. "And quite thoughtful. Thank you, Mr. Sarb."

"Not at all, Lady Shevalia. Not at all," he said. He came around the table and escorted her to the door. "I look forward to our next meeting, my lady. And please give Mr. Sootking my best regards."

"I shall."

Ibin dutifully opened the door of the carriage for her, and she called up to Mr. Yarman, "Miller's Pond, please."

"Yes, me lady!"

Soon they were on their way, and not far behind them came another conveyance, a modest dogcart in which sat the driver and beside him none other than Grant Farby. Sheila was busy placing the coins into her lady's purse, somewhat in awe of the amount. Then, deciding that it seemed too heavy, she returned some of the coins back to the purse Mr. Sarb had provided, and looked about for a place to secrete it. Remembering the brandy flask, she looked into the pocket beside her seat and decided that under the flask was as good as any other place, and once that was done, she sat back and grinned.

As usual, the streets were busy, but it was not too long before they entered a wide open space and came to a halt. Looking out one side of the carriage, she saw they were in a line with many other carts, carriages, and horses, tied or parked together. Through the window on the other side, she saw the pond. It was not very big—no bigger than the pond where she had learned to fish back in County Barley. It was nearly circular in shape and completely iced over. And, amazingly, people floated across its surface with what seemed effortless ease. Some, after only a few steps, did not move their legs at all, and kept going for many yards, as if they stood still. Others sped along, turning and spinning, and going back and forth. Sometimes one would come to an abrupt halt, and the air around their feet would glisten with a spray of sunlit ice-dust. Children, men, and women, many finely dressed, and others in work clothes, all skated together, laughing and calling to one another. Others struggled to stay on their feet, falling and sliding, and Sheila winced with concern that they might be hurt. But none seemed injured while she watched, and she laughed, too, at their merry antics.

Men with ladies on their arms walked around the edge of the pond where there was laid a brick walkway. They were as varied as those who skated, and many were elderly, finely dressed in their winter coats and fur-lined hats. She saw the vendor's wagon that Reysa had mentioned, across the pond where there were benches to sit upon. She could even see steam rising from the cups of hot punch that people took from the woman who served them.

"Ibin, er, Mr. Brinnin, I would like to stroll around the pond."

Ibin, as enthralled as Sheila with the sights, suddenly shook himself and tossed the blanket from across his knees and scrambled down. She already had the door open and was stepping out, so he closed the door and followed her.

"Oh!" she said, turning back. "Mr. Yarman, I will be here for a while, I think. Do you wish to conduct other business and come back for me?"

"I could do that, me lady. How long should I tarry before I return?"

"Could you be back in time to have me home for supper?"

"I most certainly can, an' I shall, ma'am!"

Mr. Yarman drove off, and Sheila and Ibin walked down to the pond and made their way slowly along the sidewalk and around to the other side. Along the way, people bowed and nodded as they passed, and she nodded in return, but her eyes were ever drawn to the skaters. She stopped to watch a particularly talented girl who moved with such grace that it was nearly like a dance, with long smooth turns, her head held up to the sky and her arms outstretched, turning suddenly to actually go backwards, repeating the gesture with arms and head. The skater suddenly turned again, and spun around in place, speeding up and slowing down as she drew her arms in and stretched them back out, stopping suddenly, then darting across the ice in a different direction.

"Oh, how marvelous!" Sheila cried out, clutching Ibin's arm in excitement. "Don't you think so?"

"Oh, yes, yes, yesIdo! Ihaveneverseenanythinglikeit, haveyou?"

"No, I haven't. Oh, how beautifully they go! Come, let's have some punch and sit and watch."

This they did, and soon she had her cup of punch, and Ibin, too.

"May we take the cups to that bench?" she asked the old woman who served them.

"Why of course, dearie! But here, ye ain't got nothing to sit upon. Take this little blanket, an' bring it back with yer cups when yer ready."

The woman draped the blanket over Ibin's arm, as Sheila thanked her, and they were soon seated on a bench near the edge of the pond, and they had an excellent view of all the activities. Across the pond, just up the hill, carts and carriages came and went, as did the skaters and those who walked around the pond alone or with their wives or lovers or companions. On all sides, the spires and tall buildings of Duinnor rose up, with roofs of red tile or green copper, some with smoke billowing from their chimneys, and with a myriad of windows glinting in the sun. It was a beautiful day, even if it was cold, and when Sheila and Ibin finished their punch, she sent him back to fetch more. The graceful girl she saw earlier departed, but other girls launched themselves out upon the pond, just as skillfully, and many of the gentlemen were just as graceful in their movements on the ice. Many brought their own skates, Sheila observed, while others went to a wagon near the punch seller to acquire theirs. When Ibin returned, she had already determined that she wanted to give it a try, but was reluctant to do so, not wishing to make a fool of herself before all these people.

"Someday," she said to Ibin who slurped noisily from his cup, "I would like to learn how to skate."

"Today is as good a day as any to begin," she heard someone say. Turning, she saw standing beside her Grant Farby himself. He bowed, and, standing, she curtseyed.

"Mr. Farby, I believe."

"In person, my lady," he bowed again. "Fancy meeting you here."

"I suspect it was not by chance, sir."

"I have no idea what you may mean, my lady," he grinned. "I often take to the pond on such beautiful days. But never on a day such as this, made all the more beautiful by your countenance."

"I am sure that I do not know what you mean."

"Hemeans, hemeansyou, youmake, hemeansyoumakethedaybeautifuller, Lady Shevalia," Ibin said.

"Mr. Brinnin, I think you should escort Mr. Farby away from me," she said.

"Oh." Ibin put down his punch cup, stood, and drew his cutlass.

"Oh, my gosh!" cried Farby, throwing up his hands and backing away.

"Ibin! Please put that away!" Sheila cried.

"Is there some trouble here, my lady?"

Suddenly there was a Kingsman approaching, hand on the hilt of his sword.

"No, sir," stammered Sheila. "I mean, no. Only a misunderstanding."

"Gentlemen," said the Kingsman, "I beg you take your dispute some place else, preferably outside the city walls. As I am quite sure you are aware, the King permits no duels within the city. And this place, being under my watch, will not be a place of quarreling."

"Duel?" said Farby. "I haven't even a toothpick upon me!"

"Sir," Sheila said to the Kingsman, "I am sorry for the trouble. Mr. Brinnin, here, is my escort and looks to guard me against unwanted advances. He took a word from me too seriously, I'm afraid. There is no quarrel here."

Ibin, who had put away his sword and was grinning at the Kingsman, picked up his cup of punch and slurped, with one finger jutting out daintily. The Kingsman eyed him, then glared at Farby.

"I hope you are not disturbing the lady."

"He is not, I assure you," Sheila said. "Please, Mr. Farby, accept my apology for my companion's zeal."

Farby smiled, nervously, and bowed. "It is not worth the mention. If you were in my charge, and I had but a toothpick, I, too, would defend you with as much zeal."

Sighing, and shaking his head, the Kingsman bowed and strode off.

"Mr. Farby, what is it that you want of me?"

"Only to be your skating tutor, my lady. And to assist you in any other way within my power."

"I prefer to watch. For now."

"I see. But it is such a fine day. And who knows when I may be available again to instruct you?"

"I have a feeling that, regardless of what day I might come here, you would appear."

"That, too, is possible, Lady Shevalia."

"I think you are too impertinent to refuse," she said, smiling at last. "But I have no skates, and neither do you."

"That is soon remedied," Farby said, gesturing toward the rental wagon.

"Oh, very well! Mr. Brinnin, please keep a sharp watch upon us. And should you see anything amiss, I trust you will know what to do."

"Yes, yes, yesmylady!"

• • •

Mr. Farby saw to fitting Sheila with skates, making a fuss over the poor quality of the available selection. Once he and she were outfitted and laced, he took her by the hand and helped her up from the bench and to the pond's edge. After much hesitation and awkwardness on her part, he coaxed her out onto the ice, where they both immediately fell down in a sliding tumble.

"Well, that's a good start!" Sheila cried, trying too soon to get back to her feet and having no luck at all, falling again and again, in spite of Farby's pleas for her to take his hands.

"Oh, I give up!" she said, sitting on the ice with her legs splayed out.

"Oh, no you don't! Take my hands and obey my instructions! I insist!"

It took almost an hour, and Farby had to help Sheila back onto her feet more than once. But at last he began to make progress with her, showing her how to control her movements so that she would be less apt to fall.

"Just be still," he said. "When you think you are losing your balance, just calm yourself. Now, toe in, like this, and bring your feet closer together. That's right. If you spread your feet too far, they'll just keep going out from under you. You'll get a sense for it soon enough!"

Some people have the oddest talents, and they are to be found in the strangest ways, it seems. Who could have imagined that, after only another hour, Sheila, a girl who had never seen an ice-covered pond until today, could be skating along beside Farby who, after such a short time, only held the very tips of her fingers? It was as much of a surprise to Sheila as anything could be, and it thrilled her to move across the ice so smoothly. After yet another hour, she no longer needed Farby's hand at all, much to his disappointment. And from his careful instruction, she was able to turn almost whenever she wished. With only a few collisions with other skaters who failed to get out of her way, and only two or three times when she skated right up onto the bank, and after only a few more spills, she felt as free as a bird. Laughing hysterically at each collision, at each fall, she quickly gained her feet again, and was off.

Mr. Farby was amazed, and skated along at a safe distance from her, saying that she had some natural talent that he had never seen before.

"I have been skating almost since I could walk," he told Sheila. "But you will soon surpass me at my best!"

"Oh, I doubt that very much!" she laughed. "Whoops!"

Narrowly missing a couple who came gliding by arm in arm, she turned and came around Farby, who spun around to face her, now skating backwards in front of her.

"It's true," he said. "I am sure that you will soon be the most talented skater in all of Duinnor, just as you are already the most beautiful one."

"Mr. Farby, I must tell you that you should put aside any hope of wooing me. It would be quite impossible for me to have any feelings for you."

"Any at all? And you hardly know me! Would you crush all hope entirely, Lady Shevalia?"

"It would be my duty to do so."

"Then you are betrothed to another? A great lord, I am sure."

"I am not. But I have given my heart, and that is quite enough. And, besides, even if I was not committed to another man, I know you not at all, and you do not know me one speck."

"If what I have beheld is a speck, it is a priceless one! As any with half a wit would confess. And, as for not knowing each other, you may have something there. I am sure that I am not worthy of your attention, though I crave it and have connived to receive it from you. I will tell you anything you wish to know about me. In return, you need not tell me a thing about yourself, oh mysterious beauty!"

"I would prefer," Sheila replied, "that you tell me nothing, unless I do ask. In fact, I think it is time for me to go. I see my carriage has just arrived. Please do not come to my house any more!"

Farby shrugged, looking at her with disappointment.

"I offer my sincerest apologies for offending you," he said, taking her hand to help her to the stand to return the skates.

"You have not offended me," she said, sitting and immediately unlacing her skates. "The truth is, I am touched by your attentions. But I think they are not proper."

"Perhaps not," he said. "And perhaps I have been too forward, too enthusiastic, or too hopeful. But if I did things properly, we would have never met, I think. You would have found someone else to teach you to skate, I am sure. But, for me, this day has been quite the best day I can ever remember."

When they had their own boots back on, and Sheila curtseyed to him, he bowed, saying, "I shall never bother you again. I shall not call unbidden, nor shall I endeavor to meet with you. But this place shall be a very special place," he gestured to the pond, "for as long as I am blessed with the memory of it. My lady, I bid you goodbye."

"Goodbye, Mr. Farby. I do thank you for your instruction."

Sheila then hurried away to her carriage with Ibin trotting after her. When they were on their way home, she did not look at all at the passing city. She sat, staring at the empty seat across from her, feeling sad, and a little angry. But she did not know what she had to be angry about. Things were the way they were, and there was nothing she could do about that. Even if she could explain everything to Mr. Farby, and even if he could understand with some sympathy, it would change nothing. Impossibility after impossibility!

"Oh, I ache!" she said aloud, moving her sore shoulders about and rubbing her thigh. "How I ache."

• • •

When they arrived back home, she rushed upstairs to her rooms without even a word to Ashlord or Billy, and she plopped into the chair beside the hearth. After a few moments, she stood, took off her coat, and threw it onto the other chair and sat back down. A knock came at the door. She sighed.

"Yes?"

Ashlord stuck his head in.

"How was your day?"

"Fine."

"Did you receive the sum you required from Mr. Sarb?"

"Yes. Thank you, Ashlord. It was generous of you."

"Not at all. Are you well?"

"Yes. Just tired."

"Supper is prepared and ready when you are."

"I think I'll just go to bed. I am really quite tired. There's no need to send Reysa in."

"Very well. Good-night, then."

"Good-night."

• • •

The next morning, after sleeping late, Sheila entered the parlor to find it empty. She was so accustomed to seeing Ashlord there that she was somewhat surprised by his absence. The table was set, as usual, but only for one. She walked down the hall to his room, found the door ajar, and knocked. Peeking in, she saw that it was empty. Ibin's room was empty, too, and Billy's as well. Going downstairs, she found Billy and Ibin at the downstairs table. Ibin was eating in his usual enthusiastic manner, but Billy, incongruously, nibbled with a fork in one hand while studying an open book beside his plate. Miss Tarrier was pouring another cup of coffee for Ibin, and when she saw Sheila, she curtseyed.

"Good morning, my lady."

Seeing her, and since Miss Tarrier was there, Ibin and Billy immediately stood.

"Lady Shevalia, good mornin'," said Billy. "How do ye do, today?"

"Good, goodmorningLadyShevalia," said Ibin, his mouth full.

"Good morning, Miss Tarrier. Good morning, gentlemen. Please do not let me interrupt. I was looking for Mr. Sootking. I thought he might be in here."

"Oh, he went out early this morning, ma'am," said Miss Tarrier. "Might you be ready for your breakfast?"

"Yes, I think so."

"We'd be happy to have ye eat with us, ma'am," said Billy.

"That is quite alright, thank you, though. I'll take my breakfast upstairs, as usual."

"I'll be right up, my lady," said Miss Tarrier.

• • •

Later, as Miss Tarrier served her breakfast, Sheila asked where her guardian had gone.

"He didn't say, ma'am."

"Did he take the carriage?"

"No, ma'am, he left on foot. Would you like for me to send for it?"

"Yes, please," Sheila said. "Tell me, do you know where I might purchase a pair of skates?"

"Hm. I think Sorrier's footwear shop down on Bargus Street sells such things. Did you go skating yesterday? Reysa mentioned you might."

"Yes, I did. And I must say, I think I skated all the night long in my dreams."

"It is a marvelous thing, skating. Isn't it, ma'am? I certainly spent many an afternoon skittering across Miller's Pond, back in my younger days, that is. So you've caught the bug, as it were?"

"I think so. Anyway, I'd like to try again today. I was thinking that I'd like to have my own pair of skates. My feet are awfully sore from those I used yesterday. Not to mention all the rest of me!"

"Well, I think Sorrier will be able to fix you up with some right nice skates, and they're bound to be a bit more elegant than those rented down at the pond. Will there be anything else, ma'am?"

"No, thank you, Miss Tarrier. As soon as Mr. Yarman comes, would you send him up to me, please?"

Although she dearly wanted to go skating again, Sheila dreaded seeing Farby at the pond, as she was sure she would. But such was the powerful desire to enjoy herself by practicing her new-found skill that she determined to make the best of it, and would dismiss Farby by means of Ibin, if necessary. She ate her breakfast, thinking about the young man, and wondering if the way he looked at her was genuine, or if his blue eyes and beaming smile were just a mask. Perhaps Mr. Yarman would provide some answers when he arrived. And, much sooner than expected, there was a knock on the door. It was Miss Tarrier once more.

"Sorry to disturb, ma'am," she said, "but there is a lady come to see Mr. Sootking. I told her that he was not in, but she asked instead for you, or rather, for Mr. Sootking's ward. I told her that you did not receive company, but she insisted. Here is her card, ma'am."

Sheila took the card and read it.

"Lady Highleaf? Do you know her, Miss Tarrier?"

"I only know of her, ma'am," Miss Tarrier said as she cleared away the breakfast things. "She's the daughter of the late Lord Highleaf, and she and her sister inherited his fortune and considerable business interests. She has no husband or children, and spends her fortunes making merry, it is said."

"Do you know what business she may have with us?"

"I'm sure I don't, my lady."

"Very well, please show her up."

Lady Highleaf was a tall, fine-looking woman, with graying black hair gathered up under her blue velvet hat. She wore a dress and jacket of the same velvet material, under a long black coat. Her cheeks were somewhat flushed from the walk up the stairs, and she smiled as she entered. Her blue eyes twinkled as Miss Tarrier helped her off with her coat and gloves.

"Lady Shevalia, I presume?"

"Lady Highleaf, it is an honor."

"Oh, the honor is all mine!"

"Please have a seat."

"Thank you. My! That is quite a climb. Just the thing to keep away frequent visitors. Although I saw that the tray downstairs was filled with calling cards."

"Yes. It seems a popular thing to do, to come by and implore for an audience."

"But, as your landlady suggests, I am the first you have received. I feel quite honored, indeed!"

"You are the first to ask for Mr. Sootking, and I thought I should see if I could help you in some way. May I?"

"Sootking!" Lady Highleaf laughed. "What a name! Why on earth doesn't he change it to something a bit more suitable, I wonder? Like, say, Ashlord?"

"Pardon me?" Sheila tried to hide the fact that her heart was now nervously pounding. "I'm sure I don't know what you mean, Lady Highleaf."

"Oh, come, dear. I jest. I know he must have a good reason for it."

"What may I do for you?"

"Oh, this is merely a social call. However, you might answer the question I was going to put to Ash—, that is to say, Mr. Sootking." She stifled a giggle, then proceeded. "How do you find your things, my dear? Are they to your liking at all?"

"Pardon me? My things?"

"The things that I was asked to prepare for you. Sent along on the day you arrived."

"Oh! Forgive me! I adore them, naturally. And I am indebted to you for providing them. Do you come to see after the bill?"

"Oh, my, good gracious girl! No, I do not. I only picked out the things, to go on Mr. Sootking's accounts. I am sorry! I'm having a difficult time keeping a straight face. No, no, I did not pay the bill. He did. Even if I had, I would ask for nothing. It is my great pleasure and honor to do any little thing for Ashlord that he asks. Yes, yes, I know who he really is! He was a great friend to my father, and has been to me, too, for many years. I am so very happy that he has returned to Duinnor, and I long to spend some time catching up with him. His note was detailed in every regard concerning you, but one. He said you were, let's see, 'quite handsome' I think is how he put it. But he was far from the mark, as I can now see. I'm afraid the poor things I picked out for you do not do justice to your beauty."

"You are too kind," Sheila said, blushing, "and it is especially kind coming from one so pretty as yourself."

"Oh, stop it! I was not fishing for compliments. I know I'm over the hill, and I don't care. Now, what can you tell me about yourself? I assume that if Ashlord is your guardian, then you must be someone of very great importance in the world."

"I can tell you little, since Mr. Soot—, oh, very well! Ashlord, then! He asked me not to reveal anything. But I will tell you that I am of hardly any importance at all. I never have been, and I never shall be. I am only here by happenstance. Ashlord does me a great favor by looking after me, and since his business was to come here, I came with him."

"Hm. Ashlord implied in his note that you lost all your fine things along the way. Were you beset by highwaymen?"

"I will let Ashlord tell of any adventures that we shared along the way to Duinnor."

"I see. That's even better! There's nothing like mystery to enhance the beauty and charm of a lady, as I've always said," Lady Highleaf stated. She continued to smile at Sheila, and Sheila back at her. "I suppose, since you keep yourself here and do not receive guests, that you have not met many people in the city?"

"I tour the city almost every day in my carriage, Lady Highleaf. I have seen many wonderful and interesting sights. As for meeting people, you are right. I have only met a few."

"Oh, then as soon as Ashlord will allow it, I should like to take you under my wing and show you about the town myself. And, if it is to your liking, I may introduce you to our society. In point of fact, I am having a get-together week after next, in honor of my nephew who is just back from school in Vanara, or Glareth, or wherever his latest escapade took him. I would have had it sooner, but other things intervened. All the better. As of yesterday, I have already had replies from at least a hundred people, so my secretary says. When word gets out that the mysterious Lady Shevalia will be in attendance, I'm sure six times that many will come!"

"Lady Highleaf, I am honored by your kind invitation," Sheila said, trying to hide her utter panic, "but I feel I must decline. I am not at all sure that I am ready to meet everyone, and I'm not sure Ashlord would permit it, anyway."

"Oh, I see. I would not presume to guess at Ashlord's doings. But, my dear, unless you get out and dip your toes a bit, as they say, you'll never succeed in passing yourself off as Ashlord would like for you to do," Lady Highleaf said sympathetically.

"I'm sure I don't know what you mean, Lady Highleaf."

Lady Highleaf shook her head.

"There are a thousand little things that will betray you to the astute eye," she said. "And I have the most astute eye, if I say so myself. I see that you are dressed to go out, but a lady would never have her hair done so as you have it. Do you not have a lady's maid?"

"Why, yes, but this is her day away."

"I see. How inconvenient. Then your hair may possibly be excused. But look at your hands. When was the last time you had a manicure?"

"I don't know what that is, much less when I may have had one."

"Oh, dear! Your maid should have helped you with that, too. Now, as for your boots, they are quite jaunty, but are far too scuffed. And, besides your appearance, you should never sit with your knees apart like that. It is as if you have not had a governess."

"I don't know what that is, either."

"Dear me! Tsk, tsk! Ashlord may know a thing or two about this and that, demons and witches and Faerekind and such. But when it comes to proper ladies, he is an ignoramus."

Red-faced, Sheila was truly embarrassed. For the past few days, she had almost convinced herself that she could, indeed, act like a lady. Now, it was all laid bare as the act it was in only a few moments.

"Oh, my, what a look on your face!" exclaimed Lady Highleaf. "You must forgive an old woman who speaks too frankly! I meant what I said before about your beauty. Indeed, you are probably the most beautiful girl I have ever seen. However, being a lady has nothing to do with being beautiful, in spite of what some may say. There are many beautiful women who are called ladies but are nothing of the sort. And many of the finest ladies are, well, not so pleasing to the eye. Why does Ashlord wish you to be one? A lady, that is."

"He, he said," Sheila stammered. "I cannot say. I fear his plans are all pointless, now."

"Not so! Whatever his plans are, he has good reasons for them, I assure you. So we must not let him down. Besides, plans or no plans, Ashlord or no Ashlord, you have a natural bearing about you that very few are lucky enough to possess. Tell me, do you wish to be a lady?"

"I suppose. I mean, that would be a fine thing, I think. But one may as well wish to be a rock or a river, or anything else that one is not."

"Pish posh! Leave it to me," said Lady Highleaf, standing. "There is not a moment to waste. I shall make all of the necessary arrangements. When all is ready, I shall come again. Meanwhile, do not fret. But, pray, before you go out, please put a brush through your hair! And see to your shoes!"

"Yes, ma'am," Sheila nodded, rising.

"Good day!"

"Good day, ma'am," Sheila said as Lady Highleaf floated from the room. Sheila was still staring at the door, not quite sure what to make of the lady, or what she intended to do, when another knock came on the door and Miss Tarrier showed in Mr. Yarman.

"Mr. Yarman. Good day, sir."

"Good day, Lady Shevalia."

"Have you learned anything about Mr. Farby?"

"Yes, ma'am. An' I should have known the name, ma'am. He's the son of the Farby's of Old Town. The Farby's are wealthy, havin' inherited some of their great fortune, but Mr. Farby, the boy's father, that is, made his own fortune in the metal trades, steel an' iron, an' the like. He married well, into a high family, apparently. As for the boy, he is expected to carry on his father's interests, but apparently has no likin' for mines an' smeltin' an' such. He is said to be rather more learned than most, but also quite precocious, the adventurous sort, an' somewhat disrespectful. He's run away from home several times, each time hunted, er, that is to say, brung back by his father's men. He was schooled at the Gentilly School, a boy's school, then went to the King's Academy, as did his father, an' received the highest marks, completin' his term a full two years earlier than most. But he got into a bit of trouble, it seems, and, still quite young, he was sent off to further his learnin' in Vanara, but he ran away once again, this time goin' all the way to Glareth. When he was returned, not too long ago, he declared to be determined to build ships an' roam the seas. He is now twenty-one years of age, an' is still unmarried, though it is expected that he'll wed a daughter of one of his father's associates whom he has courted off an' on. He's got no brothers, nor any sisters. Well, that's about it, me lady."

"My, that's quite a lot for one day! Tell me, did you find out anything at all about what he is like? I mean, as a person."

"Well, not really, ma'am. Except," Mr. Yarman hesitated.

"What?"

"He got himself into a fight a while back. When just almost out of the Academy. It was in the papers, widely known. I remember hearin' 'bout it."

"Well, boys will be boys."

"Er, yes, ma'am. Only, well, he skewered a feller in a duel. It was over a girl."

"He did? A fight over love!"

"No, ma'am. It warn't like that. And it warn't a proper duel, really. She was, well, she was a lady of the evenin', ma'am, pardon me for sayin'. Seems young Farby came across this feller beatin' a girl most cruelly, down along Halfton Way. I'm sure ye remember passin' through the place, ma'am?"

"Yes. I certainly do."

"Well, young Farby came on this feller beatin' this girl, like I said, an' he intervened. One thing led to another, rapiers were drawn an' used. Mr. Farby was wounded. The other chap was quite punctured all over an' died later that night. Mr. Farby was arrested an' would've been sentenced to prison but for his father's persuadin' before the judges, an' Mr. Farby being only a lad at the time. That an' the many witnesses what said that Mr. Farby drew only when forced to. Still, the feller he killed was the private secretary to Lord Banis, an' so all expected it to go the other way."

"Why?"

"Why, ma'am? Oh, me lady! All an' ever'one knows that Lord Banis is second only to the King in power! An' Lord Banis gets his will done, one way or the other."

"Oh. I see."

Sheila went to the window and looked out. She remembered who Lord Banis was, and it was a rude reminder not only of the danger she and her companions were in, but also of the injustice that Ashlord often spoke of.

"Still," she said, "it is good that at least for once justice seems to have been done."

"Yes, me lady. Young Farby was barred from continuing on at the Kingsman Academy, though, even though he was near to graduating. An' some think Lord Banis got some word in against him. Anyway, it was after all that when Mr. Farby went off to Glareth when he was supposed to go to Vanara. An', it being a few years back, things have settled down for him, I do believe. If Lord Banis truly had it in for Mr. Farby, something would've happened by now."

"I thank you, Mr. Yarman, and I hope it was not too much trouble."

"No trouble at all, me lady. Will that be all?"

"Yes, for now. I'll be down shortly. And then I would like for you to take me to Sorrier's footwear shop, and then back to Miller's Pond."

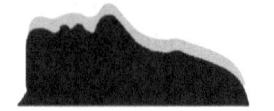

Chapter 27

Much to Do

In the following days, Sheila spent many hours going about town with Lady Highleaf, or visiting Lady Highleaf at her mansion. And Lady Highleaf filled almost every moment with Sheila with instruction concerning the ways in which a lady should act, dress, eat, and speak, how the ranks of society were ordered, and a myriad of other things. There was, of course, also time for Lady Highleaf to impart to Sheila whatever the current gossip about town was concerning various people. Sheila did not understand all of it, and it seemed that for the first day or so Lady Highleaf did nothing but correct this or that in Sheila's behavior or comportment. So it was a great relief to Sheila to go out on the ice at Miller's Pond whenever she could to practice her skating, to enjoy a bit of the joy and freedom that came with her new-found talent.

While Sheila did all this, Billy usually remained behind with Ashlord to receive his own instruction. Billy's great concern was to practice what he might say to those in power, should he get the chance to do so. He missed his homeland and his friends, and he constantly worried about those left behind in Janhaven. If he was impatient with Ashlord's constant instruction, it was only because he wanted to get on with things, to get on with the business of rallying support and aid for his people. But he had to admit that his lessons with Ashlord had opened his eyes to the broad scope of things, and to the many concerns with which those in power had to contend. And Ashlord reminded Billy that the invasion of the Eastlands by the Redvests was a great and important event, and so Billy's mission was also important. Billy agreed, and he redoubled his efforts to prepare himself to bear witness when the time came. Ashlord also reminded him that, should Robby succeed in his quest, Billy would have a powerful ally upon the throne of Duinnor.

Ullin, who was now safely camped, also thought on Robby's quest. He recovered his strength, eating plentiful fish that he caught in the nearby stream, and he kept warm under his pine-bough covering and beside his roaring campfire. He thought about Griferis, about how much Robby had changed, and about the Bloodcoins that he was carrying for Robby. And Ullin wondered how Robby intended to get from Griferis to Duinnor, and whether Robby really would become King of Duinnor. Perhaps, when the time came, Islindia would send Ayreltide to carry Robby to Duinnor. Ullin wondered, too, about the captain of Shatuum he had fought on the icy ledge and the power of the Bloodcoin to destroy such a mighty warrior. In the evenings, his visits with Micerea were brief for their mutual good, for peaceful sleep was what they both needed. They did not discuss any of the things that Ullin pondered. Indeed, she came to him only for short visits, only long enough for a few words of love, for a few sweet kisses, and for them to bid each other sweet dreams and good night.

For his part, Robby continued to forge his plans. They would be difficult to carry out. So many things had to come together, especially those having to do with Duinnor and its Throne. But there was more at stake than Duinnor, at least in Robby's view. During his many years in Griferis, he slowly came to the conclusion that he wanted more than to rule Duinnor, he wanted to do more than rescue his homeland and his people in the Eastlands. As far as he could tell, the previous Unknown Kings had squandered their opportunities to bring about meaningful change in the world. And the current king, who had ruled for so many centuries, had squandered the most. Robby thought it a travesty.

Robby also knew that he had advantages that no ruler ever had. He could dreamwalk. He had Griferis at his disposal. And he already had powerful allies in Vanara, in the Eastlands, and even in the Dragonlands. In only a short time, since obtaining Griferis as his own realm, Robby had learned much. But at every turn, it seemed, there were questions. And the answers eluded him.

He knew what method to use to destroy Secundur. But he could not figure a way to carry it out. He knew how to overthrow the Dragonkind King and put away the priesthood that served him. How to cure the Dragonkind of the desert ailment that made all of them dependent on darakal, the medicinal herb that was controlled by their king and his priests. But, again, the way to bring it about escaped him, though he felt certain the answer was right in front of him. And Robby puzzled over the Bloodcoins. He knew that he had to bring them together and open the Nimbus Illuminas so that he could offer the Elifaen a way out of their forlorn existence. He had a good notion of how it was to be done, but, even if Ullin managed to get those he carried to Duinnor, that still left Serith Ellyn's Seven. And, by now Robby knew that the Queen of Vanara would hardly give them up without a fight. But how hard would she fight? Robby searched himself. How much force—how much violence—would he be willing to use in order to fulfill his ambitions? As much as was necessary. In that he was resolved.

He fully realized that accomplishing his goals, though they would take time, would forever change the world. There was no helping it. Dark times were ahead, no matter what. Better that there be years of strife, with an end in sight, than for the world to be doomed to the darkness that Secundur planned. Robby saw that the longer Secundur held back his legions, the stronger they would become, the more dark powers they would acquire, and the greater their numbers would be. Secundur's destruction was necessary, and the sooner the better.

It was a lot of things to solve, a lot of things to accomplish. But they were all links to the great chain that Robby intended to forge and pull. If one link failed, none of the others would matter.

From his palace at Griferis, he delved the secret of the Crack in the World, and saw that it stretched all the way south to the far seas, emptying cold fresh water into the misty Craggy Sea, churning the coastal region there with incredible storms and wild currents and waves. No wonder the Dragonkind could never come by sea against Altoria; the seas were too violent and rocky for any ship to survive. Then, when Robby saw Lord Tallin release the trolls that held up his north fields, revealing his long secret to the world, he realized that there really was some hope of healing the Dragonlands of its sickness. When they put down their arms, letting drop the lintels that held up the ceiling to the secret reservoir they stood in, they were free. But they were aimless. Their one-time King, called Thunderfoot, was chained deep within the same troll cave where Bailorg had taken Billy. Robby understood that as long as Thunderfoot was chained, his people would remain aimless. They had to be led to the place where Robby needed them, and Thunderfoot was the one to do it, if only Robby could convince him to do so. Yet how on earth could Thunderfoot be freed of his chains, much less persuaded to become an ally? Robby felt he should know how to solve this problem, but the answer continued to elude him.

Robby went also to Nasakeeria, and to the old woman known as Traveshia, a witch, some said, a seer, others believed. Robby knew her to be like Certina, caught between worlds. She did not dream as other people did. She was awake when Robby came to her, in a trance-like state, just like the old Oracle at the Temple of Beras. To those who might be around her, she seemed to rant and rave, in a kind of delirium of madness. When Robby presented himself and spoke to her, she saw him as if through a mist. When she answered him, she spoke aloud, and those nearby could hear what she said. She and the Oracle of Beras were the only people that Robby had found who could do this, who could be awake and asleep at the same time. It went far to explain their odd behavior. And as soon as Robby understood this about them, he knew that they would be important to the plan that he was developing.

"Will you tell me again the lore of your people?" he asked Traveshia. "Of the fabulous city, flowing with water from its center to all its gardens and vineyards. Of how your ancestors stayed the water from its flow to spite Kalzar. And tell me how it came to be that you were protected here in this new land."

And she did. For hours, from beginning to end, she recited the tale handed down through her order from one generation to the next, taught word for word so that none was changed in the long ages since it was first told. Rocking back and forth as she squatted, her eyes often rolled up in her head as she spoke. At other times, she would jump up and dart around, waving her stick as she chanted and recited. During the telling, those around her were afraid, for it was not the time for the Telling of the Saga. Prince Nightar was called to watch, but he ordered that none should disturb her. Five times this occurred. And each time her people feared for her life, for she was frail, and to go without food or water for so long was not good for her. Robby knew this, and he hoped it was not too taxing for the old woman. But he needed to understand the tale of her people.

Robby looked in on many other people and places, too, including his father, who was traveling southward with Prince Danoss. He longed to speak to his father, but also dreaded it. There was no point, Robby thought, of vexing his father's sleep by giving him a dream filled with the terrible news about Mirabella. Let him have his rest. He would reach Passdale and find out soon enough, and then he would at least have his friends about him.

Robby found Lyrium and her daughters abiding their time near Glareth by the Sea. Lyrium was often in the guise of an old woman, with her two beautiful and mysterious daughters serving as her keepers. It was odd, he thought, that they remained in Glareth when, with their marvelous conveyance, they could be practically anywhere they chose to be. And it was a great surprise for Robby to learn that their seaside cottage was just down the path from the little house where Ullin's mother lived. Robby wondered whether or not it was an accident. He recalled what Lyrium's daughters once said to him:

"What one does accidentally..."
"...another calls fate."
"And what some call fate..."
"...others call destiny."

Robby also spent a great deal of his dreamwalking in Duinnor. By now, he purposely avoided the house on Crescent Avenue, trusting in Ashlord and Lady Highleaf to take care of Sheila. He missed her too terribly to look in on her, no matter how much he wanted to do so. Better to wait, he thought, until it was the right time, and done in the right way. Any sooner and he might never tear himself away from her. It would be too easy to waste away, ever gazing upon her, never to sleep real sleep until that which ends all sleep came, as it must to all mortals.

So he instead explored every inch of Duinnor's Royal Palace. It was there that he accidentally learned what to do about the trolls and how to get them to the place he needed them to be.

It was within the darkest, most foul depths of the King's Palace that Robby found the place where Raynor was kept. Along with many other prisoners, Raynor was chained by his wrists to the wall and forced to remain standing at all times. Yet the amiable old Melnari still managed to hold forth against the injustice of those chambers. He railed against the cruelty of those who wielded the tools of the place, and he decried those in power who permitted such devices. In spite of abuse and insult, Raynor spoke loud words against the King, foretelling dire reckonings to come.

When he saw the place, Robby was filled with anger, aghast at what he saw and heard, ashamed, embarrassed, and offended by the place. And it was there, filled with indignation and rage, that Robby accidentally made the discovery that would change so much.

Seeing the jailor come at Raynor with a red-hot iron, to add yet another scar upon the bared chest of the old man, Robby instinctively flew at the jailor and struck at his face with his open hand. His hand passed right through the torturer, but it also went through the iron cuff that bound Raynor's wrists above him. The pins flew out of the cuff, and it burst asunder, ringing across the grimy stone floor, and Raynor's chains fell away. In shock, the jailor backed away from the grinning Raynor. It was as much of a surprise to Robby as it was to the jailor. But Robby instantly understood, and, still enraged, he immediately took action.

Robby flew invisibly through the dungeon from prisoner to prisoner, and the irons they wore flew to pieces, and all of the locks on all of the cells broke apart. Terrified, the jailor shouted for help, waving his hot iron around to threaten the prisoners who were now free. Soon the jailor's associates arrived, and even some Kingsmen of the Palace rushed in at the alarm. With weapons drawn, they quelled any uprising that might be in the workings, and they put the prisoners back into the cells from which they had wandered. To Robby's surprise, Raynor had remained at his place the entire time, quietly watching the wondrous confusion and pandemonium with obvious delight. When it was over, and still grinning but saying nothing, Raynor willingly lifted up his arms so that his cuff and chains could be refastened.

"Oh, why did I not realize this before now?" Robby exclaimed, humiliated by his own stupidity. "This means that I can indeed do something real in the world while dreamwalking. Something worthy and needed. I am such an oaf for not understanding before!"

He was sorely tempted, upon visiting other horrible places of confinement, to set free prisoners wherever he found them. It was cruel, he thought, to make them wait for freedom. But if he acted foolishly, he might do them harm in spite of his intentions, for many he saw in Duinnor and elsewhere were too weak to make good an escape and avoid the inevitable wrath that would befall them when recaptured.

• • •

Instead, he immediately went to Thunderfoot, and in a dream he revealed to the King of the Trolls what he must do, if ever he was set free. But Thunderfoot doubted his dream. Night after night, again and again,

Robby went to him, his hulking mass like squarish-cut stones stacked upon each other in the form of a man, ever turning over in his sleep. During brief interludes of wakefulness, Thunderfoot gnawed away at the stones in his prison chamber, pulling on the chains that bound him, shaking the ridge with his power. But he was unable to break them. After a fit of anger and despair, he slept again, for that was all Thunderfoot could really do.

"I shall free you," said Robby to Thunderfoot.

"I shall eat ye," said Thunderfoot, unimpressed by the little fellow who brought light into his dreams and stood before him.

"No, you shan't, King Thunderfoot. For you cannot reach me. And you are not like your brethren, witless and without imagination. You were the first of your kind that Alonair created, and all others that followed were crude images of you, but with your form. It was Alonair who chained you, by trickery, for he has no love of you or your people. And it was Alonair who led your people away, to fulfill a promise that he made. I wonder, can you keep a promise?"

"Who are ye to ask such a thing?" roared Thunderfoot. In his dream, he scooped up a mountainside and devoured it in one gulp. "What promise has been given me, that I may know what one is?"

"If you were freed, what would you wish for?"

"For the destruction of he who chained me. For the annihilation of those who doomed my kind to their mean and low existence! And one thing more, I would wish, and that is to return to the earth from which I was taken, to wear away as all earthly things do. To be cut by water, and cracked by root, and worn by sandy winds until I am no more than a grain upon the seashore, or a speck upon the desert. Those are the things that I would wish for, since ye ask."

"Well said," Robby replied. "I will tell you, then, that your first wish will be granted, in time, for Alonair will go the way of all other things. And your second wish, too, will come to pass, for those who rejected you, who spurned Alonair's craft and sent you away from the far western mountains have themselves been forced into servitude. For they remained in the world when all of their brethren departed with Aperion's host, and, by remaining, they lost what they were. I, alone, of all upon the earth, have it in my power to grant your last wish, to let you go back into the stone wherefrom you were taken. I have discovered that place, and I have seen the marks left when you were carved out of it. If you heed me, you shall return to that place, and it will take you back."

"Thrice ye have told me this, and thrice I have doubted, for I know that I dream. What else is there for me to do? I know that ye take the strange form of my longings. I think ye are but another torture given me. The chains that bind me hold me tight. They are strong iron, they do not rust, and they are pinned to the rock above my reach. This is my fate. But what manner of dream can this be, other than a soft nightmare?"

"I come to you again, for I see what you wish for, and it is also the salvation of others who, like you, are shackled and enslaved. I do not make you this offer for your sake alone, but for the sake of right doing."

"What would ye have me do? How may I heed ye?"

"First, look to hope. The time soon comes when freedom will be yours. Rest easy, and do not wound yourself or worry the mountain by pulling against your chains. I make you this promise: You shall be freed of your chains. That will be the sign to you that I speak truthfully. Then, when that time comes and you are free, call your people. Take them west, into the setting sun, into the setting moon, stopping for no one and for nothing until you are at the place where the world ends. Sleep then, and I shall come to you and show you the way to your peace."

Thunderfoot looked at Robby suspiciously. He was, indeed, different from his brethren and sisters. He remembered being delved from the stone. He remembered the vain protests he made when he was assembled, block by block. He remembered the pain when he was made to take in air and breathe it out. All that came to pass since then was but a moment to a stone's life, a tremor in his long, steady history.

"I shall do it," Thunderfoot said. "Not because ye ask me to promise, but because what else is there to do?"

"Then we have a bargain," Robby said.

• • •

Suddenly, after so long, everything was coming together. And it was a relatively happy Robby that met with Finn one morning after breakfast. Celia was busy reading a book, holding it out so that Boxer could sit in her lap.

"When did Celia learn to read?" Robby asked Finn as they passed by the garden room where she sat.

"This morning, sir. She didn't so much learn. She remembered."

"Oh. Very interesting. Have you had any new recollections?"

"Why yes, my lord, I have. I remember when I was brought here, and why."

"You do?"

"Yes. But it is not a pleasant memory, my lord."

"I wish you would call me Robby. How many times must I ask? Or must I order you to do so?"

"No, sir. It is only that I must keep in practice for when we have others with us."

"If you say so. If you don't mind telling, I would like to hear about your recollection."

"Very well, sir. I shall be brief."

By now they were walking down the long hall to the library, and both enjoyed the bright sunlight that slanted through the windows after several days of gloomy snow.

"I was a criminal, after all, as I feared. Though not in the ordinary sense. My crime was murder, I am ashamed to say. I was an alchemist, and I lived near Glareth. I had discovered an admixture of sulphur and saltpeter, one that had peculiar and powerful properties of sudden fire. One day, whilst preparing a large batch of this new compound, I was called away from my shop, which was filled with great stores of my minerals and my prepared powders. I was some distance away, just going over a hill, when suddenly there was a tremendous flash of light behind me, accompanied by a powerful roar of thunder. I turned to see a great ball of fire and smoke rising up from my village. Entire cottages were thrown away as matchwood, along with all of their occupants. People and animals alike were flung high up into the sky to fall as smoking remains. Such was the blast and ensuing inferno that my entire village and several farms were utterly destroyed. A terrible catastrophe, my lord, for the few who were not killed outright were horribly maimed. None of my family survived the day. I knew immediately that I was the cause of the calamity. My mixtures had somehow ignited."

In the library, their usual meeting place, they took a seat across from each other at their usual table.

"Oh. That's terrible!"

"Yes. It was. After staggering through the remains of the place, I found what was left of my family. Then I ran, as fast as my legs would carry me, to the high rocky cliffs nearby, and there I threw myself into the sea. The next thing I knew, I was here, before the Judges of this place. They said that my life was forfeit, and from thenceforth I would belong to Griferis. They granted me a loss of memory, and said that I would not discover any secrets of this place, nor would my memory be restored, until after they, the Judges, were released to return to their own places. Since you took Griferis from them, my memories have been slowly returning to me."

"I am very sorry about what happened to you. A terrible accident. I am sorry about your family. I wish there was something I could do to change it."

"Me, too. But it was nearly a thousand years ago. In the meantime, I have been servant and helper to many people who have come here to be tried. But only one ever told me his name. That was you, my lord."

"And yet you rarely use it."

Finn shrugged and smiled.

"What news do you have of your activities?" Robby asked, getting to their business.

"My dreamwalking skill improves each night, my lord. The ledge that runs north and south is used by Shatuum, just as you suspected, to bring captives northward from Vanara and the Dragonlands," Finn said. "There is a low rampart, just south of us, where they have lowered a ladder so that they may climb up and down. They do not go north of that place.

There is something about our side of Algamori and the Gate of Griferis that repels them."

"And may we bring our people here along the same route?"

"It seems the best way, but they would have to avoid Secundur's wraiths and taskmasters."

"How do they bring their captives? Are they bound?"

"Yes, my lord. Many are bound with ropes, some with chains. It is done in such a way that only four or five guards are needed. And they walk the entire way, giving their prisoners very little to eat or drink."

"I see. I take it you have spotted a group approaching and have been watching them?"

"Yes, my lord. A group of ten prisoners. They are, I would guess, less than a fortnight's march away from here. The prisoners have a rough time, owing to the cold weather, and they are ill-dressed for it. They are five Dragonkind, two Men, and three Elifaen, my lord."

"Have you determined the nature of the Dragonkind? Are they soldiers?"

"No, they are not. That is, judging from their dreams. Five of the prisoners are women, my lord, including four of the Dragonkind."

"Women?"

"Yes, my lord. All were apparently taken from renegades who traded them for gold."

"Oh. Well, we must find a way to free them, and to bring them here. Do you think you can find suitable quarters for them?"

"Yes. There is more than enough room."

"I have discovered how to make the causeway appear," Robby told Finn. "We'll need to provide ladders or ropes for them to climb up from the ledge to the Gate. I'll work on that, if you will see to their quarters."

"Certainly, sir."

"I don't want them to know about me, though. Not until it is time. So continue to look upon their dreams, and report what you learn to me. Until we determine if they are trustworthy, they must be kept in the dark about things, and kept away from Celia. We'll give them shelter and safety, and permit any to leave should they wish to take their chances in that way. Do you think any of them might be convinced to stay on?"

"I don't know," Finn shrugged. "I can only say that, by their dreams, they all long to be home."

"I'm sure they do. While I am thinking of it, you mentioned that you located a store of clothes. Might there be anything befitting a lord?"

"Oh, why, yes," answered Finn enthusiastically. "Entire rooms of the most marvelous and splendid attire. For both men and women. Everything from slippers to boots, robes and capes, tunics and coats, and quite a collection of headgear, too."

"Wonderful. I hope we may find something that will fit us?"

"Us, sir?"

"Yes. My Chamberlain must dress befitting his station."

• • •

Yes, Robby thought, things were going well. After Finn departed to his duties, which included a promised game of cards with Celia, Robby put on his heavy coat and walked the walls. It was a clear, brisk afternoon, and the snow-capped mountains on either side of Griferis gleamed in the sunlight. Robby began his walk above the East Gate of Griferis, overlooking the expanse toward the landing where stood the marvelous arch, a tiny thing off in the distance. He then turned north to trace the circumference of the floating island, thinking on all that he had yet to do. It was much, but he now felt up to the task, bolstered by his new-found abilities. He must see to the safety of Sheila and his other friends as soon as possible; as his dreamwalking sojourns revealed, the spies of Lord Banis were close to discovering them. Having kept a watch on Raynor's apartment, they could not fail to note the comings and goings of Sheila and the others. Although Ashlord only went out occasionally, it was only a matter of time when they put the pieces together for Banis. Robby was somewhat appalled, at first, by Ashlord's audacity in locating the company there. He soon realized that the mystic conferred daily with Certina, who kept watch on Banis's men, and probably used some means of disorganizing their efforts. Still, Banis was dangerous, not only to his friends, but to others. And Robby was shocked to learn from Esildre's tortured dreams that it was Banis who had sent Bailorg to the Eastlands. This prompted Robby to make his own inquiries, in the dreamwalking way, and learned what Esildre must surely know: that Banis was responsible for her brother's murder. That was not the limit of Banis's treachery, either.

Robby walked on, wishing he could talk to Ashlord, and longing for the umpteenth time that he could spend just a little time with Sheila. He had known many girls and ladies, too, during his time in Griferis—or, rather, during his trials and forced sojourns from Griferis—but Sheila was always the measure he held against them. And now that the void of years between them was so great, he felt silly and somewhat ashamed for his continued thoughts of her, of his abiding feelings for her. It was one of the things the Elifaen had to their advantage, he felt. To them, time was not a thing that separated one from another. It might be their common enemy, but it was a moot thing to them. A man and a woman might court and be honorably united in wedlock in spite of a great difference in their years. Mirabella and her mother were examples, marrying Men much younger than they. But Sheila was young, as only a child of Men can be, and had many years ahead of her, to fall in love again, to have children and all the good things that growing up brings. Robby, on the other hand, felt as if nearly thirty years were taken from him, putting him all the closer to old age, dotage, and death. These were not new thoughts to him, and the sadness they brought upon him did not abate, so he tried to put them, and Sheila, from his mind.

Sighing, he tried turning his mind to other things just as he came to the northernmost side of Griferis overlooking the long and seemingly endless void, stretching out straight between the mountains all the way to the horizon. Suddenly, looking at the converging lines of the opposing walls of the mysterious rift, he felt its depth in a most peculiar way, almost as if he was standing in thin air over the chasm, between earth and sky. He was captivated by the notion of reaching in both directions, that the blue above held no limit to him, and that the misty depths of the chasm could not pull him down. It was a fearless thrill, unmitigated by the fragility of flesh. The surrounding mountains, mute to his ears, nonetheless sang their noble encouragement from above. A passing cloud lightly beckoned with soft, ever-changing gestures. And the air itself offered to freely hold him aloft. Enthralled, a sharp burning sensation ran across his shoulders and down his back, and he would have screamed in pain but for the hypnotic sensation he had of floating effortlessly skyward.

• • •

In the northwest green room, Finn put down a card and took one from the deck. Across from him, Celia pursed her lips, then put down two cards and took two.

"I think you try to fool me into thinking you have more than you do," Celia said.

"Never!" said Finn.

"Your turn. You must draw, or pick one up."

"I am thinking."

Looking up from his losing hand, he glanced out through the large windows and saw Robby walking along the northern wall as he liked to do on bright afternoons. He saw Robby stop and look out, the wind tugging at his half-buttoned long coat.

"Well," said Celia. "Boxer grows impatient."

"One moment, please," said Finn, fingering one card, then another, before finally drawing one and putting one down.

"Very well, then," Celia said, picking up his card, then laying all hers down. "I win!"

"Oh, drat."

"Really, Finn. That's three hands. I think you do not even try."

"I assure you, young lady—"

Finn glanced out the window and saw Robby climb up onto the parapet and stretch out his arms. Leaping up, upsetting the table as he did so, Finn ran from the room.

• • •

As Robby went for his walk upon the walls of faraway Griferis, and just as Finn determined that he would actually beat Celia at cards for once, Lady Shevalia arrived back at Miller's Pond for the fourth day in a row. She had spent most of the morning, as she had on the previous mornings for a week, going about with Lady Highleaf shopping, having her hair and nails done, seeing the sights, and receiving intense instruction from Highleaf on manners, speech, and conduct. They were exhausting days, but Sheila insisted that she was to have a few afternoons to herself.

She looked out of the carriage door to make certain that Farby was nowhere in sight, then stepped out, taking Ibin's hand to descend. He carried the basket containing her new skates, and followed behind as she marched straight to the nearest available bench close to the pond's edge. There, he threw a blanket over the seat, and Sheila sat, kicking off her boots as quickly as she could. Soon she had her skates on and laced, and, refusing Ibin's help, she clumsily made her way to the ice. Once she was upon the surface, though, and with only a momentary wobble, she pushed herself forward and smiled. After only a few yards, and several more strides, she was grinning. There were not nearly as many people out on the pond today, and she went in wide circles, close to the shore, faster and faster. She turned sharply and shot across the center of the ice, only to turn back the other way and again, in a long figure-eight. As she passed by the bench where Ibin sat, she saw him grinning back at her, and they waved to each other. He seemed nearly as thrilled as she was. She was flying, carefree, turning and going backwards, and then, to her own amazement, she managed a short low spin. Laughing, she kicked off and did it all again, and more.

All who saw her thought surely this was someone who had been born on the ice, so gracefully and skillfully she went. Ibin was not the only one mesmerized by her show. Many of those who strolled, and quite of few of those who skated, stopped what they were doing, sometimes in mid-sentence, and watched.

"Who is that lady?" they asked.

"That, I believe, is the incomparable Lady Shevalia," was the answer.

Carriages that otherwise would have passed on by were halted by their passengers, and soon the nearby street and carriage park were crammed with onlookers. Mr. Yarman, watching comfortably from atop his rig with a blanket over his knees, beamed at the other drivers.

Sheila passed around and back and forth, ever changing her rapturous course, and Ibin smiled cherubically. As she passed by, his forehead wrinkled over raised eyebrows and he swayed slightly, as if he heard music made by her motion, a vision of notes from her body's instrument played out upon the harmonious ice.

As for Sheila, she was like a bird. She had no thought or awareness of those who watched her. She knew only the air rushing past. All of the aches and pains of yesterday evaporated like mist. There was no Barley, no Steggan, no long-lost parents, and no blight upon her soul. She raised her eyes skyward, rapt, her neck back, needing not her eyes to see where she went, for her pace was perfect, her turns flawless, and her pirouettes a song. Above, the blue took her in, lifting her away and away. She felt the pain, but cared not; she turned it into loveliness. She took the fire running through her and made it into ice to skate upon. Without giving it a thought, she knew this feeling, this rapture, was how it once always was.

Ibin continued to watch her, and when she came to a halt in the center of the pond, and her spinning was gradually completed, her face remained uplifted to the sky. Her arms lowered to her sides, like two long feathers gracefully falling through air, and she stood quite still. Here and there, people clapped at the performance, but, sensing something wrong, Ibin slowly stood. Sheila suddenly fell hard upon her back, and remained motionless. Ibin tore down the bank and hit the ice only to fall immediately, sliding toward her on his belly. Trying to get up, he fell again.

"Sheila!" he cried, unaware of another figure who dashed down from the carriages with such speed that he shot straight across the pond on his shoes without falling, coming to her on his knees. He lifted her into his arms, and brushed her hair from her wide glazed eyes as she stared at the sky, her mouth open.

"Help me, Mr. Brinnin!" cried Farby. By now, Mr. Yarman and several onlookers were also coming out onto the ice. Together, they lifted Sheila and gently carried her up the hill and carefully placed her in the carriage. Ibin and Farby both got in, and Mr. Yarman did not spare the horses. Alerted by Certina, Ashlord was standing in the door with Billy when they arrived, and Miss Tarrier was there, too, with Reysa. Ibin took Sheila into his powerful arms, carried her the entire way up to the third floor without stopping, kicked open the door to her room, and tenderly placed her onto her bed. Ashlord immediately began his examination as Miss Tarrier and Reysa removed her coat. As they did so, pulling her up to free her from it, she moaned sadly, her eyes wide but blind to all that was happening, tears pouring out from them.

Farby, Ibin, and Billy watched helplessly. Suddenly, Billy took Farby by the collar and dragged him out into the hall, where he promptly struck him on the nose and then shoved him against the banister, ready to tumble him over the side.

"What have ye done to her, ye bastard!" cried Billy, cocking his fist for another blow.

"Nothing, ouch! I only—stop that! Why do you strike me, sir?"

"Billy, Billystopit!" Ibin cried out, pulling Billy away from Farby before the next punch could land. "He, heonly, heonlytriedtohelpSheila!"

Miss Tarrier and Reysa rushed out of the room and downstairs to fetch a pot of water and herbs as Ashlord had directed them to do. After a moment, Ashlord appeared wearing a terrible expression that froze all three gentlemen.

"What's the matter with her?" Billy stammered, on the verge of tears.

"Mr. Farby," Ashlord said, "I thank you for your assistance. But you are no longer required here."

"Are you a physician, sir?" Farby demanded, heedless of the blood dripping from his nose. "If not, I shall fetch one immediately. She burns up with fever!"

"There is no need for that. Her condition will pass, in time."

"What do you mean? What condition? I demand to know!"

Ashlord looked at him sternly, sizing him up.

"Ashlord," said Billy. "What is it? What's happened to her?"

"Sir, I go to fetch a physician right away!" Farby stated as he started off.

"No, sir. Do not!" commanded Ashlord.

"Then tell me why not."

"Only if you give me your word of honor," Ashlord said, "that you will not reveal any of this to any person outside of this house. I have already exacted such a promise from Miss Tarrier and Reysa."

"You have my word, sir. Now tell me, what is Lady Shevalia's ailment?"

"She is being Scathed, and will soon be Elifaen. Now, if you will excuse me, she is in need of my attention."

End of Volume Four

63 Days Remaining

Afterword

Afterword

Thank you for reading *The Dreamwalker*! I hope you are enjoying this tale. And I cordially invite you to share your thoughts, questions, and comments at

www.TheYearOfTheRedDoor.com

The Adventure concludes with
To Touch a Dream

Robby has taken Griferis to be his own domain, but his sights are set on the whole world. His conquest will be like none before. He will use his skills, his dreamwalking abilities, and his friends to bring about his goals. His education in power has been costly, and many have died for his sake, but he cannot stop now. Time is running out.

For there are powers that may be unstoppable, inexorably moving to remake the world as a place of ruin, a place of shadow, torture, and hopelessness. It is Secundur's goal to destroy all that is good and bright, not only Elifaen, but Men, too, as well as the Dragonkind. And his efforts are bearing fruit. The world has plunged into war, and Secundur awaits the chaos and strife. When the time is ripe, he will throw open the gates of Shatuum, and his legions will march. Leading Secundur's army of wraiths, witches, and goblins will be his mighty general, Throgallus, who is none other than the traitor of Tulith Attis.

All this is perfectly clear to Robby. But there is a kink in Robby's plan: Queen Serith Ellyn stands in his way. He needs her Bloodcoins, and she will not relinquish them. If he cannot convince her to give them over to him peaceably, he will have no choice but to take her Bloodcoins by force.

And the throne of Duinnor? Robby means for it to be his, and to become the Seventh King. He knows that the Seventh King will be the last King of Duinnor, whose reign will be brief. In fact, he intends for it to be so. For Robby's ambition is greater. Like Secundur, Robby's goal, too, is to remake not just a few realms, but the entire world.

I hope you will continue the adventure!

Thanks again!

William Timothy Murray

The Door is Open!

www.TheYearOfTheRedDoor.com

Maps, Stories, Chronologies,
and much more.

Leave a comment or ask a question.

The Author would love to hear from you!

Sign up for the newsletter.
*Get perks and exclusives
delivered right to your inbox!*

The Year of the Red Door

Volume 1
The Bellringer

Volume 2
The Nature of a Curse

Volume 3
A Distant Light

Volume 4
The Dreamwalker

Volume 5
To Touch a Dream

www.TheYearOfTheRedDoor.com

Made in United States
Troutdale, OR
10/11/2023

13628422R00246